Emma Madison

Master Meddler

A novel

In many crooked ways, God makes a straight line.

Portuguese proverb

WHAT READERS SAY —

A long book with lots of chapters, but don't let that stop you from reading this magnificent book! I absolutely loved this book. The best I have read in a long long time - I read it in three days only because I couldn't put the book down.

There is so much heart in this touching story. I found myself carried away by the small town of Medford, as well as the strength and determination of two strong women, who were determined to give Jasmine and her daughter a second chance. I didn't want to put this book down. There were so many 'behind the scenes' shenanigans that I found myself laughing out loud. But there was also sobering moments that gave the reader pause, and made them think.

Such a fantastic book! There are over one hundred chapters and each one adds immensely to the stories of several people in the gossipy small Canadian town of Medford. The stories are interlinked by those of Jasmine and her great aunt Emma. Sorrows, deep regrets, love, and rekindled love work through the pages. I thoroughly enjoyed this book so very much.

Great family drama! This review will not be a recap like a school book report. This is what you need to know: If you like reading about small-town, character-driven drama, this is your ticket. It's very well written and reading it was a pleasure. I kept telling myself, "Wow! I cannot believe how good this is!" Years ago [2014?] when I read Andy Weir's "The Martian", I thought it would make a great movie. Well, I'm having the same thoughts about Emma's book. I've already cast characters and can't wait until it shows up on Netflix, AppleTV, heck, even Paramount.

Terrific. I loved this book, very much. It's wonderful, each page is like a layer added to each character. I loved till the last page. I absolutely recommend it.

Compelling. I am an avid reader of mostly fiction. I found the characters to be fascinating and deeply interesting. Emma Madison, Master Meddler kept me guessing and involved right to the end. A must read for everyone.

Emma Madison, Master Meddler is one of the best books I have read. The writing is marvelous, and the story never disappoints. The chapters are short, so it is easy to sneak in a short "reading break", but it is difficult to stop at just one chapter! I was immediately drawn into the story, and I have enjoyed every page-turning-minute!

In my top five favorite novels. Right from the first page I was totally hooked, as cliché as that may sound. I loved the storyline of women's friendships being centered in the plot. There were so many charged topics, including loss, trauma, and forgiveness. But they were touched upon in a gentle, honest way that depicted real life experiences, with sensitivity to the reader.

COPYRIGHT

www.emmamadison.ca

Goodreads: bit.ly/emmamadison-gr

Facebook: bit.ly/emmamadison-fb

Instagram: instagram.com/pat.michener

PRINCIPAL CHARACTERS

Emma Madison, widow

Jasmine Holmes Carlisle, Emma's niece

Laura Carlisle, Jasmine's daughter

Thomas & Lianne Latham, Emma's next door neighbours

Margery MacClure, Emma's cousin/best friend

Jim MacClure, Margery's husband

Anna Parke, Jim and Margery's daughter

Royce Parke, Anna's husband

Mary, Christopher and Lily Parke, their children

Elizabeth & Max Stoddart, town leaders and movers

Arlena Stoddart, daughter

Mason Stoddart, son – Jasmine's former fiancé

Edna Matthews, Emma's friend

Simon Jenner, local funeral parlor owner

Martha Jenner, his wife

Alistair MacGregor, their nephew

Chris Byers, Alistair's friend

Sherry Byers, Chris's sister

Letty Lawson, Emma's neighbour

CHAPTER 1

It seemed for a long time her life had been blessedly peaceful and trouble-free. In view of her advanced age, though, Emma Madison slowly became suspicious of such good luck. Some sixth sense was warning her, telling her to prepare for a bump in the road. Nothing too serious, she hoped. She guessed it might be an illness, or an accident.

So, when Emma discovered the letter her sister had hidden in a book, she did not understand until much later that it was what she had feared – the bump. Now, whenever she was in the grip of the night terrors, she wished to heaven she had never opened the book. For the few hand-written pages it contained were not so much a letter as a Pandora's box spilling out worries, with only the dear Lord knowing what else was yet to come.

On this particular night, however, Emma was fretting over a more urgent problem.

In the distant living room, a clock struck a single, silvery chime. She listened to the note quivering in the still of the upstairs hall and the darkened bedroom. Then her legs twitched her out of her warm bed and into the chill passages of her house. A halting descent down steps crosshatched by shadows and the moonlight that slid between the rungs of the oak banister, and then she was at the door to the study.

In the icy light cast by the moon, rows of books gleamed dully on the shelves. Emma ran a finger over their spines. Somewhere – if she could only see – was a fusty old Victorian novel, which sometimes would do what a sleeping pill had not. In the darkness she fumbled for the desk lamp, reached for the chain. Then stopped. One hand in mid-air.

The neighbours. What if they saw a light? They might guess she was awake and sleepless in the small hours before the dawning of this singularly important day. And that would never do! No one must be given the slightest reason to think she had even a whiff of worry or a dab of doubt about today, and whatever it might bring.

Before leaving, Emma spied the metallic glint of a pen on the desk. She would bring it with her, for her purse, in case she had to take notes. It now seemed to her that she had made every possible preparation. All she needed was rest, a few hours at least, to prepare her for the long, fearsome day ahead. And courage, but not the foolhardy sort – unfortunately, the kind she needed could only come from being certain that what she was about to do was both necessary and right, which she was not.

As a measure of her desperation there was the short pause when she stopped in front of the liquor cabinet on her way to the kitchen. She remembered the insomnia remedy favoured by her deceased husband: a shot of rye in a glass of warm milk. At this moment it had an especially seductive appeal because more than sleep, she craved oblivion: an escape from the thoughts whirling in her head, all of them more or less disparate but still connected and leading her to the same frightening conclusion.

In a few short hours, Emma would undertake the single most selfless and generous act of her entire life. And she suspected – no, more than suspected, was by now mostly convinced – that she was making a dreadful mistake. For into her home, for an indefinite length of time, she would be bringing a woman whose exploits of the bedroom variety were the stuff of town legends. And a child she had never met but who, if she took after her mother at that early age, was sure to be a brat.

Since going to bed hours earlier, she had been turning the matter around and about in her mind. It was the last time she would have the opportunity to do so: the end stage of a pursuit that had occupied her for months. This time, however, the blazing stupidity of what she was about to do had revealed itself with a clarity that, up to this moment, had somehow evaded her.

She did not need light to find her way around in the kitchen. The shot of whiskey foregone, Emma took her mug of warm milk back to her bedroom, drank it and then, still cold and shivery despite the masses of quilts that covered her on this chill winter's night, lay watching the glowing radium arms of the clock on her night table edge slowly toward 2:00 a.m.

CHAPTER 2

Insomnia stalks Sunday nights. It follows after heavy dinners of roasts and rich desserts washed down by alcohol and mixed with anxious thoughts about the week ahead. It thrives in bad weather. And it feeds off guilty consciences. To a greater or lesser degree, all these conditions were present in the small town of Medford this evening. Rising winds and plunging temperatures signaled the approach of a winter storm. Of those lying wakeful in their beds, a good number were struggling with guilty consciences. Interestingly, some – less than a handful – engaged in this kind of agonized introspection were experiencing, along with the usual regret and remorse, a great deal of apprehension; all of which was focused on the imminent arrival in town of one of its former and more infamous residents, Jasmine Holmes.

Shortly after 2:00 a.m., this select group of insomniacs was joined by a latecomer. Normally a sound sleeper, Thomas Latham found himself jolted awake and swamped by worries remarkably similar to those of his next-door neighbour.

As he lay in the big four-poster bed beside his sleeping wife, Thomas was thinking about Emma and her journey. Generally, Thomas was fond of Emma. This once, however, he wouldn't mind if she veered off the road and into a tree. In fact, he secretly hoped she would. That was because of the cargo she was bringing back with her, and what they would bring with them: a passel of scandal he had hoped and prayed was long gone and buried, if not ever to be completely forgotten in this town of wagging tongues and lengthy memories. And, as he twisted in the bed sheets, as he thought about it and took in the reality, the immediacy of it – for now it was no longer just a topic of gossip, an eventuality, but was actually taking place tomorrow, no, in fact, it was already today – he felt his heart rate accelerate and beads of sweat break out on his brow despite the chill of the room.

When he first heard about Emma's plans, Thomas had been incredulous. Was she demented? Why do something that would only cause trouble for her and her family? For other folks too, not least him and Lianne, his wife! Absurd! There had to be other options!!

Lianne, who was close with Emma, agreed at first but then, even when he prodded, refused point-blank to talk to her about it. For weeks, the very thought of Emma's journey to fetch Jasmine and the catastrophe it was sure to precipitate sent him into a black funk. So he had simply avoided thinking about it until just recently, at a time when it was virtually staring him in the face.

Now he was still incredulous, but more at the unbelievably bad timing of it all. Yes, after years of being passed over, and just when he had learned he was finally in line for advancement, everything he had worked so hard for was being jeopardized by the one idiotic thing he had done in his life – which, thanks to Emma, was once again top of everyone's mind.

All of this was bad enough, or so he had thought. But then, recently – only a few days ago – Thomas had found out that in the grand scheme of things, it really wasn't that important. Just froth, in fact, floating on the top of something much darker, far worse.

Beside him, Lianne slowly turned. Languidly, one pale, thin arm stretched out, came to rest on the coverlet. Another half turn, and now she lay dreaming close beside him, warming herself against his body. He breathed in her scent: clean lavender with a tinge, faint but distinct, of medicine. It smelled different to him now, that scent – no longer so much familiar as clinical, perturbing. Minus the heavy odors of wet woolens and perspiring bodies, it was identical to the smell of the waiting room where he had sat, late last Friday, before he went in to see the doctor —

This was followed by a flood of raw memories dangerous to dwell on when in bed. Thomas concentrated on exorcising them. He was successful, mostly. But he could not so easily erase their residue: a sense of gathering doom, and a dull pain in his chest that he recognized as grief, its little teeth already nibbling at his heart.

Lianne's back was snug against his. Now she breathed a long, soft sigh, and the mattress dipped as she moved. Thomas angled his head to look at her. She was lying peacefully on her side. In the moon's beams her face was white as alabaster statuary. Her hands were folded under her cheek on the pillow, and she was smiling in her sleep.

CHAPTER 3

The moon finished its circuit. It thrust a last few bright fingers under the bedroom curtains before disappearing into a tangle of trees. Blackness descended. From the living room came the muted sound of chimes as the clock on the mantel struck three. Emma had given off waiting for sleep. She turned to find a more comfortable position and lay there, hoping at least to rest. She gave a loud yawn, nestled deeper into the mound of quilts and blankets. And then she got up, went downstairs, out the side door and down the hill to the lake.

There was a small red rowboat anchored near the shore. She climbed in. Too late, she found it had no oars, and she was at the mercy of the wind and waves.

Later she could clearly recall a moment of great fright when the lake became a river rushing toward a huge waterfall. And there was a jumble of other images; but most faded away in the dim circle of light from the bedside lamp she switched on after waking, damp and shaken, on the safe island of her bed. Only the sound of her dreams continued: low and menacing, the thunder of the falls.

While she slept, it seemed the wind had risen. Now it was a live thing, soughing through the trees, snapping branches against the roof and out on the lake nearby, churning the open water into towering waves that crashed down upon the ice shelf slowly encasing them. This was the sound that underlay her dream, Emma knew, and a sure indication of the weather she could expect for her journey to the city during the waking nightmare soon to come.

It was not yet six; behind the drawn curtains there was only night. The winter sun would not appear for hours, and in any case would stay hidden behind the masses of grey, heavy, snow-bearing clouds now arriving in flotillas from across the lake. But on this day of days she must rise early, as she did now, silencing the alarm clock before its clanging could further rattle her nerves, thrusting her feet into her old slippers and starting her preparations for the long, daunting hours ahead.

First, and especially important this morning, were her prayers. She knelt and recited them at bedside. Beneath the well-worn phrases, her thoughts skittered about to touch on matters less religious. Life was a vale of tears, a path riddled with traps and pitfalls. Emma gave thanks to God for her good fortune, since she had adroitly managed to sidestep most of them for over sixty years. This gratitude was tempered by the certainty that she had recently fallen into one of them. Not so much fallen, she thought, as been pushed. But only she and two others knew the truth of the matter, and one of them was dead, while the other, Margery, her cousin and former best friend, might as well be dead to her for all the trouble she had caused. Emma added a Hail Mary for uncharitable thoughts, crossed herself and stood up.

In the wardrobe hung the dress she had chosen for today. It was a good dress, a dark navy woolen she used for solemn occasions, but now she pushed it aside. On the window of her dressing room, a branch of the ancient maple tree tapped out an urgent weather alert. This would be a day for practical clothes: heavy skirts and sweaters and stout boots, and if this attire wasn't suitable for the occasion, then let them think what they want. "Let all of them think whatever they want," Emma muttered and this time, but for different, darker reasons, enlarged the sentiment to include friends and erstwhile friends, her circle of acquaintances and the town of Medford at large.

In this truculent mood, she banged pots and pans as she prepared breakfast, a hasty affair, for now she must allow extra driving time for the poor weather; she could not be late. Then she made a last circuit of the kitchen, to ensure that in her nervous, distracted state she had not forgotten to turn off the stove or leave on welcoming lights for the near-strangers who would soon call her house home.

This morning, for once, she did not pause to glance at the calendar that hung beside the stove. On it today's date, January 16, 1956, was circled in red -- a random but prescient choice from the pencil jar. Despite her advanced age, up to the time she made that red mark Emma had never truly experienced the inelastic, inexorable nature of time. Daily she had watched, first with consternation and finally with dread as that red circle burned ever more rapidly through the months, weeks and days that had led up to this hour and, much too soon, the moment of departure.

At the door she muffled herself up in her warmest coat, hat and gloves. Her hands shaking slightly, she took a key from her purse. When she inserted and turned it, she was fully aware that with this simple act she might be locking the door, perhaps for good, on her former solitary and peaceful life.

From the warm shelter of her house, Emma stepped out into a desolate, forbidding world. A fierce blast of arctic air struck her like a fist, almost toppling her off the stairs of the veranda as she descended. In the indistinct dawn of a deep winter's day, all was tinted violet blue: the lake below, now reduced to a patch of churning water surrounded by a vast, bleak expanse of snow and ice extending to the horizon; and the heavy, rolling clouds overhead, from which came driving snow as fine and sharp as ground glass. In its sweep, familiar shapes were blurred and distanced; the path to the garage she had walked so many times before had disappeared and she must pause to search it out.

Emma rounded the corner to the driveway. Then, suddenly, she stopped. Caught in a spell of winter, she stood motionless: a frozen figure in a frozen landscape. In the stillness her mind leapt back and forth like an animal in a trap. Through the driving snow she saw the kitchen window glowing warm and golden, a beacon of comfort and safety. How inviting it looked, and how easy it would be to turn around and go back in the house. She would phone. She would tell them she had changed her mind. None would blame her. In the town, talk would flare up briefly, then die down. A momentary embarrassment. Understandable, given her age and circumstances. The terrible weather.

Skeins of snow twisted around her ankles. The wind howled and keened over the lake. And yet Emma continued to stand stock-still, heedless of time or weather.

Once more she turned to look at the glowing window, took a half step. Then she paused. With a clarity chill as the wind and snow lashing her face, she saw herself standing there, a solitary figure peering out the window. Tomorrow. In a few months from now. Five, then ten years.

In her home with all its comforts she would grow old alone, untroubled by the mess and bother of life. She would swim through the empty days in that amber light, all the while it thickened and crystallized around her. Then old age and infirmity would conspire to keep her there, a solitary prisoner wondering what might have been, if only she had courage enough to find out.

Abruptly, she turned around. Now she would do what she set out to do. She struck out again along the snow-covered path. And it was at that moment – it was, in fact, only the space of an instant – the wind gave a mighty blast that parted the snow like a curtain. Suddenly she had a clear view of the road, and what she saw in that brief glance put an end to all indecision.

Sitting on a promontory overlooking the lake, Emma's large house was separated by a small waterfront park and a gravel road from a steep cliff that dropped abruptly down to the water. To either side of her property sat neighbouring homes. Further away, across the road, the land widened out to accommodate a single house. It was in one of its yellow-glowing windows that she glimpsed, out of a corner of her eye, the sudden flutter and drop of a curtain.

Emma's face flushed hot despite the icy chill. Now she could no longer dilly-dally with thoughts of turning back. That could only be Lorena Sykes at the window; no one else there was as likely to be up and awake and spying! And in a pinch, Lorena and her mother, whom she was probably phoning right now, would let the whole town know that Emma Madison had been standing stock-still, out in the cold, for the longest time ever before setting out on her journey to the city.

How the phone lines would have hummed if she had turned around and gone back into the house, Emma could only imagine. And now she was angry, furious, because this was the last in a very long line of decisions that, right from the very beginning of the matter, had been stolen from her by other people. Whenever did she have a choice? Here again, her very last chance to change her mind and perhaps escape with some scrap of her pride had been snatched away by a nosy neighbour!

The anger and resentment that bubbled up produced a rush of adrenalin that blew away the fog of fear in her mind. The muscles flexed in her jaw as she set her face in grim lines of determination. Then, without further ado, she marched through the snow to the garage where she started up the old black Plymouth on only her second try, backed out and drove away.

In the house next door to the Madison house, Thomas Latham lay in bed, waiting. His ears were pricked for the cough and whine of a cold engine turning over. He did not hear it; the sound was swallowed up by the wind. However, he did see the beams of light slide between the curtains, then glide across the ceiling, and he knew from whose car they came. She was on her way.

CHAPTER 4

Snow was falling heavily, in soft, thick flakes that muffled all sound. The solitary car proceeded slowly along the wind-raked main street that once past the east bridge became the highway to the distant city. Slowly the curtain of snow began to thin. Emma had been anxiously peering through the blankness. Now she relaxed her white-knuckle death grip on the wheel, and sat up straighter. A few ribbons of snow still streamed across the highway, but half an hour out of town she was clear of the heaviest weather and the driving was easy. She let the road take the car and allowed her thoughts to wander. She recalled her dream, so vivid that her stomach still dipped when she remembered falling, that momentary pause before she tipped over and into the boiling green water.

As the asphalt unfurled before her, she felt a little wave of fear. Her nightmare was becoming real. She was indeed approaching the brink; about to plunge into the unknown, a situation where it might well be a challenge to keep her head above water. But such thoughts would do no good. She cleared them with a shake of her head, and instead called up the slights and nasty comments, the fierce town gossip of the past months. This had the desired effect. Now, as the city came into sight, she was filled with an odd but energizing mixture of anger and exhilaration.

Her decision might prove to be the wrong one, but now no one could argue with it. For months, she had kept back one ace card. Then, when the time came right, she had played it brilliantly. In a stroke of luck, Elizabeth Stoddart had been the unwitting accomplice. And that was right and fitting. Because if it weren't for Mrs. Max Stoddart and her interference, she probably wouldn't be making this journey. Jasmine, her niece, might be a happily married woman. And her sister Sylvia might still be alive. There it was, and now Emma savoured it: the satisfying taste of revenge.

She had chosen her occasion carefully. It had to be at a time when as many of the local women as possible were in one place. The I.O.D.E. Christmas tea was the logical choice, and as former President she was required to put in an appearance in any event. The day was pleasant enough for late November, so Emma decided to walk. She passed by the stately homes set on sweeping lawns with century-old oaks and maples on her way to the Stoddarts' where the social was being held. It took longer than anticipated, and she was late.

The tea party was in full swing when she entered the large drawing room. She was amused at how the loud, staccato din of conversation sputtered as she made her appearance. By now, though, she had become more or less accustomed to sudden silences when she entered rooms and their occupants found it necessary to switch to other, safer conversational topics than Emma and her niece, Jasmine Holmes.

"Why hello, Emma," Marion Briggs, one of the younger members, said brightly. She was standing a little apart from the gathering with two friends. "Are you all ready for your new boarders?"

Emma looked at her sharply. In an earlier life, before her marriage, Emma did indeed have boarders. For only a few years, she took in young women teachers from the local private girls' school to help fill a few bedrooms in the large, rambling house she inherited on her parents' death. She had done it not so much for the money as for company during the long winter months.

It was a long-ago bit of her history that none had forgotten but few dared to refer to, at least within her hearing. Now Emma recognized this question for what it was: a slight. Marion, probably emboldened by all the disparaging talk that, like an undertow, was slowly pulling down Emma, her family, her reputation and judgment, had just given her a catty swipe of her claws.

You poor girl, Emma thought, rather pityingly. You're so very obviously a novice at this game. She ignored the question. "I have some news!" she said, just as brightly. "On my way here, I stopped in at the post office. We have a new postmaster and his name is Dennis O'Donahue. He's as Irish as Paddy's pig, and he has a brogue you could cut with a knife! His wife dropped by and I met her too. Her name is Nuala and she has marvellous long red hair. I think they'll be quite an addition to the town."

Excited by this juicy morsel of gossip, Marion's friends rushed in with questions: do they have any children? Do you know where they're living? Emma answered as best she could. Then, just as she was about to move on, she turned. "Oh, Marion, by the way, didn't I hear that you yourself had some boarders staying with you over Thanksgiving?" she asked.

"I don't know what you mean," Marion replied stiffly.

She at least had the intelligence to sense where this might be going and didn't like it. Emma pressed her: "Did you not have some company stay with you at Thanksgiving?"

"Ye-es," Marion said reluctantly, "my aunt and uncle."

"Not boarders then. Your relatives. Is that correct?"

"Yes," Marion replied sullenly, because now she knew she had been bested at her own game.

"Just so. In the event you weren't aware of the difference." Emma gave a light laugh of amusement as she turned away. One of Marion's friends concealed a smile; the other was openly snickering.

It was a minor humiliation, nothing more, still Emma was sorry for it. Although, seeing Marion's red face, she did hope it might also be a lesson.

The throng of onlookers parted before her while she made her way toward the serving table in search of a cup of tea. Emma was half a head taller than most, even without a hat, and Elizabeth Stoddart watched her approach. As the hostess and new incoming president Elizabeth was pouring, sitting resplendent at the table in a white hat and new navy and white suit. It was her mother-in-law's ornate Victorian silver tea service and Elizabeth was red in the face from the effort of hefting the heavy pot.

"So glad you could come, Emma," Elizabeth said graciously as she handed her a steaming cup. "Please don't rush away. I'd like to talk to you later if I could."

Emma quirked an inquiring eyebrow, briefly assented. As she walked toward the sweets table, she saw how the crowd slowly moved aside and away. What had happened here before she arrived? Her isolation was almost complete, save for greetings from a few friends. Feeling the chill, she herself made no overtures with the intention of leaving as soon as possible. To hurry matters along with Elizabeth, she went over to the tea table to say goodbye.

"Leaving so soon?" Elizabeth inquired; then, with a word to the side, left her daughter in charge of the table and the refilling of cups. "Now, perhaps for privacy we could speak in the hallway," she suggested in an undertone as she took Emma's arm and attempted to steer her away, out of the room.

But this did not fit in with Emma's plans. She held her ground. "There's nothing so private we can't say it here, Elizabeth," she replied pleasantly. "I expect this concerns Jasmine."

Elizabeth glanced around. She saw the faces turning in their direction, avid with interest, eyes glistening, carmined red lips no longer moving. It was plain she had no option but to square her shoulders and plough ahead.

"Indeed it does, Emma. I understand your niece has had some setbacks recently, and that your sister Sylvia asked you to bring her and her child to Medford. But Emma, we know that Sylvia was not completely sound in her mind during this last year. And this is quite an undertaking for you, at your stage in life."

Elizabeth paused, and looked around. "What we are all wondering is, wouldn't it make more sense for Jasmine to take what she receives from Sylvia's estate and make a fresh start somewhere else? You have to admit there would be difficulties in her returning to Medford, and not just for her – for some other family members, your neighbours – "

"And your son?" Emma interrupted.

"Oh that? That never was so serious, only a passing infatuation," Elizabeth answered dismissively. "But in the end, Emma, it's really about you, and as your good friends, we're genuinely concerned about all you're taking on."

Height has its advantages. Now Emma peered down at Elizabeth, and all could see the chilliness of her expression. "This is a private matter, a family matter and while your concern is appreciated, your interference is not," she said frostily. "As I understand, you feel you're entitled to talk about my sister's shortcomings, my advanced age, and why my family or neighbours might not want Jasmine around, but I am not permitted to bring up the subject of what might be your real concern here, your son Mason and Jasm– "

Elizabeth cut in smoothly: "What's truly puzzling to so many of us, Emma is: why would Jasmine want to return to a place where she's experienced and caused so much unhappiness?"

A good question. Elizabeth was too clever by half. While Emma did not dislike Elizabeth, she would like her better without her annoying habit of setting herself up as judge and jury, and persisting in viewing her as a rival.

As her mother used to say in one of her too-frequent aphorisms, "you can't sharpen steel on tin." Still, Emma was tired of being the whetstone for Mrs. Max Stoddart and her sharp mind and tongue. All the same, she did not take much pleasure in Elizabeth's discomfiture when she delivered what she knew would be the final, knockout blow.

"Unfortunately, there wasn't a great deal of choice in the matter, Elizabeth," Emma said, "because Jasmine is not well."

There was a surprised hum of whispers. Emma looked at the crowd pressing in to hear and raised her voice slightly. "Yes, in fact, unless matters improve more rapidly than expected, sometime after Christmas I'll be picking up Jasmine from the hospital in the city where she's a patient. The reason she's coming to my home is to recuperate."

A look of sudden comprehension and empathy swept across the faces of her listeners. This was something every one of these women could understand: a call to duty that could not be denied, the only expected response when a family member is ill and needs care. Emma had the sense the whole atmosphere in the room altered, grew lighter, brighter, once she spoke these words. A buzz of sympathetic murmurs filled the air, and where once there had been frowns of disapproval, kind smiles appeared.

Elizabeth Stoddart, on the other hand, looked as if Emma had delivered her a swift slap. "Well!" she said, "I guess that settles it! My apologies, and you can be sure I wish her a speedy recovery." Then, turning, she swiftly retreated behind the table where she busied herself with the pouring of tea.

Emma stayed only a little longer, accepting expressions of sympathy and politely brushing off questions about the nature of Jasmine's illness, with the excuse that such information must be private until Jasmine said it was something she wished to disclose. In the midst of this, Emma's cousin Margery rushed up to her.

"You never told me Jasmine was sick, Emma!" she blurted out. "In heaven's name, why didn't you say that?"

"There's quite a lot I haven't told you, Margery, and believe me, I'm glad I didn't; otherwise it would have been all over town, just like what I told you previously." Emma replied with some heat. "Now if you don't mind, I must be going."

"But Emma, why wouldn't you have wanted to share that information, because it changes everything!" Margery cried to her cousin's retreating back.

Strategy and timing, things you know nothing about. That is what she might have said. And even at the tea party it was risky. The earlier the news got out, the more likely it was that someone might start inquiring; or that there would be a leak, somehow, of what she had managed so far to conceal. Because the hospital Jasmine Holmes was in was not the normal, standard hospital for sick people, and she was not a typical patient.

Emma was driving through city streets unfamiliar to her. At the stoplight she checked her map: not much further to go. And now she had reached her destination. Once the guard admitted her, she drove her car through the gates of the high-walled enclosure and along the circular, tree lined drive until she arrived at the long, dark building known by all as the Hospital for the Insane, or, more colloquially, the nut house.

CHAPTER 5

It was 10:20. The social worker from Children's Aid had arrived at ten. The doctor and head nurse were there with her to observe the mother and daughter reunion. Afterward they absented themselves to the office to review last moment details before the discharge, or in cases involving a dependent child, what was commonly referred to as, "the hand over".

"What are your thoughts?" the doctor inquired. The head nurse was a 20-year veteran of the institution. He was her junior by ten years and had come to value her opinions.

"She hasn't been a model patient," the nurse said, in her first major understatement of the day. "However, she's as well as we can get her and she'll do better on the outside. As we discussed, so far as we know the manic episode was a one-time occurrence. There's a good chance it might never happen again."

The doctor fanned the sheaf of papers in the patient's file. "I see it's the aunt who's taking her and the child. I hope she's not too elderly. It says here she used to be a librarian."

"I hope she's got some physical strength," said the nurse, and then they exchanged looks that expressed doubt about the physical strength of librarians.

Had Emma known about this conversation, it would have explained why, when she walked into the reception room used for discharge purposes, with its sickly green walls and stick chairs, she noticed that the doctor and nurse seemed visibly relieved. Was it possible they thought she wouldn't come?

In fact, they were cheered to see that although her hair was iron-grey, the aunt seemed to be a strong physical specimen with no apparent handicaps, at least half a head taller than the patient. And as they spoke with her in private, before bringing in their patient and her daughter who were waiting in an anteroom, they found she had an equally strong, no-nonsense personality.

"Now tell me everything I need to know," she demanded authoritatively, then took notes and asked for explanations as needed. She requested a repeat of the medications. "I don't want to use our local pharmacy. Too many nosy people working there." The doctor willingly obliged.

She didn't cringe or complain when the final invoice was presented by the secretary but simply pulled out her chequebook and wrote a fat cheque. So, although the aunt was in her sixties, the doctor and nurse concluded that her vitality and seeming intelligence boded well for the continued recovery of their patient. And that was a relief because, unless medicated, the patient had wreaked havoc in the wards once she started to improve, and now they could discharge her into capable hands with a more or less clear conscience.

A door opened. Emma turned as soon as she heard the familiar sweet, melodious voice.

"Hello, Auntie."

Emma had carefully composed her face into a cheerful expression of greeting. Now she was glad she had. At the very instant she saw her niece she was overwhelmed by emotions: sorrow and pity and a sudden urge to cry. She stood up from her chair. She embraced Jasmine, feeling her skeletal thinness, and held her close for a minute while she swallowed the lump in her throat. Memories surged up, bringing tears she suppressed inside tightly closed eyes.

"Why Jasmine Holmes!" she exclaimed, as she held her out at arm's length. "Just look at you, so skinny! I'm going to take you right home and fatten you up!"

CHAPTER 6

If ever the collapse of hopes and dreams took the form of one person, for her aunt it was the woman who stood before her. This was not her fault but her fate. When Emma looked through the glass of years gone by, it was clear to her that the scene had been set for the tragedy of Jasmine Holmes well before her birth. The future of the young woman whom she had once loved like a daughter had been blighted by a past in which she had no part.

Now, as she gazed at her, she wondered: could I have done more? Her heart was bursting with sorrow, to which she added a large pinch of guilt. Because the warning signs had been there, long before, and she was perhaps the only one who saw them.

A few storm clouds appearing on the blue sky of her sister Sylvia's marriage. A husband increasingly distant, brusque, often absent. Then suddenly, beyond the end of all hopes and expectations, a miraculous pregnancy.

Emma was in the hospital room to see her sister's tears of joy when her baby daughter first was placed in her arms. Next to her at bedside, their mother, Sarah, was also crying copiously at the birth of her one and only grandchild, partly because it spelled a happy ending to her own long labour of years spent helping her daughter to bear the heavy burden of infertility.

Visitors crowded in; the doctor arrived. He faced the joyous gathering, delivered his little speech of congratulations. While speaking he had looked once, then again, more sharply, toward the back of the room. The second time, Emma followed his eyes. They were resting on the new father, Jason Holmes. The expression on Jason's handsome face was unreadable, his gaze focused on something far beyond them, there in that room.

At that moment of great joy where he was so obviously not a participant, she first began to watch and wonder.

The christening took place soon afterward. Emma, as godmother, was holding the baby's downy head over the baptismal font.

"Jasmine Marguerite." In response to the priest's question, Sylvia's bell-like voice spoke the name loudly and clearly. The sound reverberated in the soaring silence of the old church and the surprised silence of the congregation gathered there. And so, when she was a baby no more than a few weeks old, the troubles that would mark Jasmine's life began.

"Emma!" her cousin Margery hissed, grabbing her arm when she returned to their pew after the conclusion of the baptismal ceremony. "What kind of a name is that?! Jasmine! Is it some sort of foreign name? I thought you told me that her name was going to be Marguerite Elizabeth!"

And later, at the reception back at the house: "Jasmine," purred Ellen Riggs, wife of the Deputy Mayor and owner of the town brickworks. "What a lovely name. But I expect you'll want to call her Marguerite, after your grandmother."

"No," Sylvia said firmly, an edge to her voice, "we're calling her Jasmine, after no one in particular. It was a name we both liked."

"But that's not a Christian name!" burst out Margery, "how did you get the priest to agree to it? And why would you want a name that sounds so foreign? Nobody around here has that name!"

"Because," replied Sylvia, "she didn't look at all like the names we had chosen for her. We felt she should have a name that's distinctive. Something that suited her."

Later, Emma could only agree that Sylvia's intuition had been right. Those hardy, time-worn bible and pioneer names: Elizabeth, Martha,

Rebecca, or her own solid, practical name, Emma, would have been entirely unsuitable for the girl and woman that Jasmine would become. For where other girls in Medford were pretty, or attractive, perhaps handsome, Jasmine had the kind of beauty that set her above them all – like an orchid or some other exotic flower, strange and lovely, growing amidst the sturdy geraniums and pansies of the Medford summer gardens.

The problem was that "above" was also "apart", and therein lay all the difficulties experienced by Jasmine Holmes as she grew to womanhood in her small town. Emma had watched from the sidelines as her niece was isolated and barred from simple friendship by the envy, and later the desire her beauty excited. Then, for a short while, her star had burned brightly and it seemed as if happiness might be in her grasp.

But that time was long past.

Now the young woman Emma saw before her, under the sickly fluorescent light in the windowless green reception room of the Hospital for the Insane, was no longer beautiful. The only feature that remained the same, although dull and lifeless, was the great mass of coppery hair cascading down her back, which seemed pitifully incongruous with her emaciated form, her pale face and sunken eyes.

Why didn't they cut it? thought Emma, ever practical. I'll never get a brush through it.

Then she turned her attention to the child, who had just followed her mother in. She in turn was followed by the Children's Aid worker, who was introduced as Miss Grimes. Laura was standing to the back, a little behind her mother. Miss Grimes gave her a small push forward.

"Hello sweetheart," Emma said. "I'm your great aunt Emma. You can call me Auntie."

She took the two small hands in either of hers. The girl lifted her head and looked up. Emma saw first the eyes, deep blue shading to purple; and after that, the helmet of shining black hair, the perfect nose, rosebud mouth and the oval of her face. She suppressed her shock and the urge to draw in her breath sharply, for the child was lovely, and Emma had been unprepared for the possibility that history might repeat itself.

The doctor said something; then Emma returned to the moment. "I'm sorry, what did you say?"

"I have to leave shortly. Is there anything else you need to know before I go?"

"I think you've answered my questions. But how about you, Jasmine?" Emma turned to her niece, who had taken a seat. "Is there anything you'd like to ask the doctor?"

Jasmine gave no response. She was staring blankly ahead. Emma repeated herself to no avail. Then, worried, she turned toward the doctor and head nurse. "Are you sure she's alright? She doesn't even seem to have heard me."

Nurse and doctor glanced quickly at one another. "It's just that so much has happened today, so fast, that it's quite a lot for her to take in," the nurse said soothingly. "She'll be back to normal soon."

"Of course," the doctor added, "if you don't feel comfortable taking her on, we can wait awhile until she's at the point where she can leave here on her own."

"Or," said the head nurse quickly, "she can complete her recovery at Merrimore House, I think you've been told about this facility; they do good work with patients like Jasmine."

"Actually, that might be better for Laura," Miss Grimes interjected swiftly, as if she had been waiting for this opportunity. "Then she would be able to finish up her school year here. And her family situation is good. They said they'd be happy to have her back."

Emma surveyed the circle of expectant faces waiting for her answer. She stopped short at Laura. The child had her hands clasped in front of her tightly, almost prayerfully, and was looking at her with a strange, fixed intensity. Without thinking, automatically, as if hypnotized by that burning gaze, Emma responded.

"No," she said. "No, I'm not leaving here without my niece and her daughter."

She looked at her watch. "However, it's almost 11.45 and we should get an early lunch before we leave, if possible," she added briskly. "We still have to go to the apartment where they used to live and pick up their things before we can set out for home."

"Well, that's fine," said the head nurse. "But in that case, it might be best if I take Jasmine back to the ward for her lunch. You and Laura can go to the cafeteria, and we'll meet here again in half an hour. How does that sound?"

It sounded like a strange arrangement to Emma. But it might be a good cover up if, as she suspected, Jasmine wasn't able to handle a simple meal in a cafeteria. Emma now was almost certain her niece was not completely well. Nonetheless, clearly they were eager to get rid of her.

Just what on earth had she let herself in for?

If they wanted to discharge Jasmine early because she was difficult – a strong possibility – Emma felt she could deal with that. In the days following Jasmine's birth, Sylvia quickly discovered that her cherished dream of motherhood was quite different from the fussy, colicky, demanding baby she had produced. Since their mother was too elderly to be of much help, Emma had become a hands-on auntie – changing diapers, wiping bottoms, noses and tears, calming temper tantrums and later, providing Jasmine with a safe haven from troubles at home – almost to the day she upped and left Medford for good, taking Royce Parke with her and trailing clouds of scandal as she fled.

Jasmine deranged, however, was something Emma had no experience with.

The nurse opened the door. Beyond it stretched a long, dim corridor painted in the same bilious shade of green as the waiting room. "Come, Jasmine," she said.

Unusually docile, Jasmine rose to follow as Emma watched. A chill draft wandered into the reception room from the hallway. Over the heavy scent of disinfectants used for cleaning, it carried the faint but unmistakable smell of human excrement.

Now Emma heard sounds that previously she had only been vaguely aware of. They had been muffled by doors and distance and by their own voices echoing in the cavernous reception room. First were the normal sounds: people talking, the metallic jolting of carts clattering along, phones ringing. Then there were the others: moans, someone yelling, a low, continuous sobbing, and, arising from somewhere deep in the complex and slowly growing in volume, an unearthly wail she could barely identify as human.

It seemed to Emma that the nurse was holding the door open longer than was strictly necessary. And then, very suddenly, she understood. The kindly, care-worn face of the old nurse turned toward her in patient waiting. Emma met her eyes, which were glimmering at her from behind spectacles, and she gave the briefest of nods. The nurse smiled in return. Only then did she let the door fall closed behind her.

There had been an agreement of sorts. No words were necessary. It was more than she had bargained for, but at least all was now made clear. Emma would complete the work they could not finish, at least not here, in this place, the job of getting Jasmine well.

Turning, she saw the doctor as he departed through another door. In a few quick steps, she had hold of his arm. "Before you go, doctor, could you give me your direct number? Or an emergency number, please. Just in case I need it."

CHAPTER 7

The apartment building was an old, low-slung brick structure squatting amidst once-stately homes that were now reduced to dingy rooming houses. The superintendent was a short, heavyset man in his fifties, Emma estimated, but then noticed few other details about him, distracted as she was by the remarkable tufts of black hair that gave his nose the appearance of an inverted smokestack.

"That 'er in the car?" he questioned, his taciturnity turning into talkativeness following the handing over of the money, three months' back rent paid in cash. "She used ter be quite a looker," he said as he loaded the boxes and luggage into the trunk. Thankfully he had everything ready; Emma had been in a state of nerves about leaving Jasmine and Laura unattended in the car for even the few moments it took to ring him up from his basement flat.

"There were a friend, Bert by name, for awhile but then he left. When I saw the kiddie wearin' the same clothes and bringin' in the groceries, I checked and found 'er mom in a bad state."

Emma asked him what he had done then. "Police," he said tersely. "They know who to call for in these cases." He opened the door of the car on the driver's side for Emma. Shutting it after a long glance at the car's occupants, he gave the door panel a couple of thumps. "Good luck to yer," he said as she pulled away, "looks like yer goin' t'need it."

There was silence in the car. But oh! How different it was from the quiet of her earlier journey. This silence was heavy with the breathing of three passengers, with the burden of her new responsibilities, and filled with tension after that dispiriting farewell from the superintendent. Who would there be to help, if help were needed, she wondered? Well, she would have to leave that question to another time, at least until she recovered from the strain of this journey.

The dark was settling in early as always on these short winter days, but the sky had cleared and a full moon shed luminous light over the snow-covered fields as they sped down the two-lane highway. Emma was relieved to see familiar landmarks loom up. Soon enough they were turning off Medford's main street. Just two more turns and they were on their own street and pulling into the driveway. She turned to look at her passengers in the back seat.

"Welcome!" she said, "we're home." And she meant both of them, but the greeting was especially for Laura who wore a smile, the first one Emma had seen.

They stood for a moment, looking at the house and the bright circle of the moon, stretching their legs after the long drive. The wind had changed. In a strange quirk of winter weather, it was coming from the south. Although it was much too early for spring, Emma could hear melt water running. A breeze, warm as a caress, lifted her hair. It carried a whisper of scent from a place far away, the lightest trace of perfume from some exotic blossom. Emma saw Jasmine lift her head and sniff the air like an animal, and for some reason she was filled with unease.

"Come," she said, "let's all go inside."

She was bone tired and thankful that she had thought to have dinner already prepared, the table set. Plain but hearty food, a good stew and fresh bread and butter. She watched with satisfaction as Laura rapidly downed her meal leaving a clean plate, and drank two glasses of milk. Her table manners needed attention, but all in due time, Emma thought.

Jasmine, however, had not touched her food. "Come, Jasmine, won't you eat a mouthful or two?" Emma coaxed.

At the mention of her name, Jasmine lifted her head and smiled. "All right," she replied. But once she had spoken, she resumed staring fixedly at the bright moon, which was framed by the window in the kitchen door and the outstretched arms of trees.

"Well, I hope you'll at least take a cup of tea before bed," said Emma, and she went to the stove where the teapot was waiting, hot and ready under its frilly cosy. She set a mug on the counter. Just the way she used to like it, Emma thought, pouring in milk and adding a teaspoon of sugar. But when she turned around with the steaming cup, she very nearly dropped it.

Laura had taken the chair next to her mother. As Emma watched, the child gently but firmly placed a spoonful of food in Jasmine's mouth, patiently waiting while she chewed and swallowed. Silently, her small rosebud mouth puckered with concentration, Laura fed her mother until the stew was almost gone and Jasmine would eat no more.

CHAPTER 8

Thump! Once again Emma was in a boat. Only this time, instead of a rowboat it was a canoe. Someone sitting behind her – could it be Jasmine? – was hitting the side of the canoe with a paddle. Stop that, said Emma, stop it right now. But the noise continued, thump! Thump! A brief silence. Then there was another kind of sound, a gritty sort of sliding noise. At that, Emma's eyes flew open.

Earlier that evening once dinner and the washing up were finished, Emma had put everyone, herself included, to bed. She was beyond tired, what with the rigours of the day and the sleepless night before, and also far beyond caring what might happen if only she could lay her head on a pillow. So, at nine o'clock – late enough for a young girl and an invalid, she thought – she had shown them to their bedrooms.

Laura's bright face when she saw her small room, which Emma had equipped with books, a doll, a pretty pink quilt and other touches suitable for a young girl, had been reward enough for all she had done so far to make them welcome.

"Is this my room?" Laura had asked incredulously. "Is it really for me?" she asked, as she wandered about delightedly, looking and touching.

Emma had set out Jasmine's night dress. When she returned to her niece's bedroom, she found her already changed, in her bed and set for sleep, so that was that. Ignoring the heap of clothes dropped carelessly on the floor, she said goodnight and turned off the bedside light. She had given Jasmine the large bedroom down the hall, the one with the dormer windows facing the lake. It was only now, on waking, that she remembered.

The dormer windows. The only ones that didn't have storm windows. The dormer windows that opened out onto the roof. Onto the roof, which was just a few feet below the level of the windows and slanted down, in that place, at quite a gentle angle before it met the roof line and began its abrupt plunge to the gutter. The roof, the roof that angled off into empty space!

THUMP!

Oh my God! thought Emma, her hair standing on end, Jasmine is on the ROOF!!!

Running frantically down the hall, she heard Laura's panicked cry, "Auntie! Auntie Emma!"

The room was full of cold night air, the windows open wide and showing only night and stars. Emma rushed to climb the chair that had been moved under the windows and leaned out over the casement. There she beheld the vision that was to provide her with the stuff of nightmares for years to come. Well beyond arms' reach and a mere few inches from the steep portion of the roof, Jasmine danced under the silvery moon. Translucent in the light, her long nightgown floated about her as she spun. She let out a wild whoop.

"Jasmine, come in at once!" No answer, only a loud laugh that found echoes on nearby walls and roofs. "Jasmine, you're going to fall!" Emma screamed, hardly recognizing her own voice.

Then came a childish tremolo, full of terror: "Mom! Mom, don't fall!"

Jasmine paused for a moment in mid-twirl; then she slipped. Most of the ice and snow on the south-facing roof had melted, but a few icy patches still remained. Now her bare foot had found one. Losing her equilibrium, she began to fall. It was only with a violent twist of her body that she managed to save herself, landing heavily on the roof not far from the dormer windows where she lay, bruised and gasping, with one leg partially extended out over the roofline.

Emma always knew she was strong, but it seemed she had never really been put to the test. Later she could hardly believe what, in a wild burst of energy unleashed by fear and desperation, she had done. She leaned far out and grabbed Jasmine by one arm before she could tumble off the roof, roughly yanked her closer, hooked her under both arms, and then hauled her forcibly through the window. All this without any help on Jasmine's part – no, indeed, in fact she was trying to get away, she scratched her, but it was an uneven contest and soon they both fell in a heap on the floor. Most of the fight had gone out of Jasmine by now, sore and bruised as she was from the fall on the roof, but also from having landed beneath Emma's considerable bulk.

After she restrained and calmed her, Emma told Laura to fetch the pill containers that were on the kitchen counter near the stove, made Jasmine swallow twice the normal dose and then led her down the hall to Laura's room.

"Why are you taking her to my room, Auntie?' Laura had asked in alarm. "The bed is too small for mom and me!"

"Your mother will have to sleep here for now, Laura," Emma replied. "She can't get out the windows in this room, and we need to keep her safe. You can sleep in your mother's bedroom."

"But," cried the girl, her small face suddenly crumpling, "I'm scared of sleeping there! And I like my little room so much!" And she began to cry, the tears fairly spurting from her eyes, her shoulders shaking with great sobs.

Emma knew it was a release of the tension and emotion from the events of the day, especially the mad hour that had just passed. She put her one free arm around the child. She had just thought of something.

"Don't worry, sweetheart," she said comfortingly. "You can stay here tonight, in your very own bed. In fact, I think it would be better for both you and your mother if she stayed in my bedroom tonight. And for me."

The bed Emma normally slept in was a cherished antique handed down through generations of Madisons, a heavy, beautifully wrought iron bedstead. And Emma's last act before she went to sleep in the spare bedroom was to descend the stairs to the cellar and rummage around in Bill's dusty workroom, where she found a length of chain, some strong wire, pliers and one rusty but usable padlock with a key. With these she affixed one of Jasmine's ankles securely to the bedstead. Then she walked along the hall to the guestroom, climbed into the large, cosy bed with its invitingly clean, white starched sheets and tumbled down into a dark, dreamless hole of oblivion.

At around four in the morning, a small, timid ghost came to her room. It stood there without speaking, only a dark silhouette backlit by the moon. Emma, now attuned to all unusual noises, awoke at the small sounds of her breathing, the light whisper of her nightgown as she fidgeted, waiting.

"What is it, Laura?" she asked. She lifted the silent child up close beside her on the bed to warm her in the chill room.

"Auntie – " Laura said, hesitantly. "Auntie, will mother and I have to go back? Will I be sent back to the Stevensons?"

This was the family Laura had been placed with during her mother's illness. "No." said Emma decisively. "You and your mother are staying here. You won't be going back."

Emma had no idea how important this question was or her answer might be until she felt the rigid little body beside her on the bed suddenly relax. Now Laura was slack, drooping with relief and drowsiness. Emma took the child down the hall to her bedroom and tucked her in. Then she checked on Jasmine, who was snoring lightly. After traversing the dark passageway, she dove back into bed and plunged headlong into the deepest depths of sleep.

But not before she had spent a moment pondering the question: just what was it that had happened at the Stevensons?

CHAPTER 9

Snow started to fall early Tuesday morning. All was silent and empty of life under the swirling, snow-dimmed halos of the street lamps. Time passed, and the occasional shadow figure appeared, trudging through the dark and cold. Most townsfolk, though, were still lying snug in their beds. If they were awake they were waiting, listening for the one sound loud enough to pierce through the wind and the snow, the whistle from a passing freight train that signalled the start of another Medford day.

After waking to two unexpected early morning phone calls, Margery MacClure wrapped herself in her bath robe and went downstairs to make coffee. As she measured and poured, she checked the kitchen clock: 6:05. It would be another half hour before the town began to stir; longer still if snow blew to pile up on the tracks. Coffee made and set to perk, she went to the front door and peered anxiously through the snow-rimmed panes. Her daughter's call had been terse. "Something's come up, can you take Lily and Christopher?"

"Of course," she replied, her natural curiosity and talkativeness stifled by the knowledge that their party line was shared by three others, and that even despite the early hour at least two of them were certain to be listening in. This morning, she had actually thought she heard Walter Emery's snoring through the hand that Nina, his wife, would have cupped over the phone mouthpiece. Well, she wouldn't have found out much from her and Anna's conversation.

However, the few words she and Anna had exchanged left Margery with a roiling anxiety over what new misfortune might have befallen her daughter. Anna and her family lived nearby, so it was only a brief trip. Already she saw the little group of figures as they materialized out of the snow and darkness, then crossed the street and came up the walk.

"Come in, come in!" Margery drew the children through the door and brushed the snow from their hats and snowsuits, then off Anna's shoulders and the mass of hair on her hatless head. "You shouldn't carry Lily, Anna, she's three now and such a big girl!"

"Well, I'm in a hurry, mother, and she walks too slowly in the snow." Anna said, as they both bent down to unzip and unbutton snowsuits and remove small boots. The drowsy children, their snow-stung cheeks glowing red, stood there passively as the layers were peeled away to reveal pyjamas. As Anna worked, she talked.

"Now listen, Mom, because I'm out the door in a minute. Royce didn't come home again last night. He didn't show up for work yesterday afternoon and after all his absences likely he's lost his job. I told Mary to get herself to school; I made her lunch, so she won't be home 'til four."

Anna paused for breath. Her next words came out more slowly. "And it looks as if soon I'll not have a job too. The nurse I've been filling in for, Amy Schmidt, is coming back from sick leave next week, and right now the hospital doesn't have enough beds full to keep me there."

For Margery, there was no point in wasting time commiserating with Anna about Royce. Her daughter's husband had demonstrated his fecklessness so many times that she simply leapt over this fresh evidence of his failings to concentrate on the only item of news that was truly important. "Oh Anna, your job! What will you do?"

"Something will probably come up, it always does," Anna replied, with more conviction than she probably felt. "My babysitter will be along later. I'll phone her to come get the children so you can have your day."

As she stood and turned to leave, her mother laid a hand on her arm. "Wait, let me give you a hat, you'll need it in this snow." She rummaged briefly in the closet, then, as she handed her daughter a well-worn, woolly red toque, said, "Jasmine's back in town, you know. Yesterday your Aunt Emma was out the door just after six to fetch her, and they were home by five."

Anna looked sharply at her. "How would you know that? I thought the two of you weren't speaking."

"Well," Margery said evasively, "I had a call from Lorena." Silently, she gave thanks that she hadn't added that bit about how Emma had been standing out there in the snow before she left. In fact, evidently she had made a tactical mistake in telling Anna anything about Emma.

"So, she's been spying on Emma, then, has she," Anna said in tones of disgust. "Why don't the both of you just leave it alone, Mother?"

Margery yanked her chin up defensively. "You know very well why your sister and I are going on about this!" she answered hotly, "It's all the talk that'll be stirred up when Jasmine Holmes is back in town! If not for your own sake but that of your daughter, Mary, and what she might hear others say, I should think you'd be concerned!"

"Well, at some point Mary will have to find out what you're so very sure everyone else knows," Anna replied, her voice weary. "But right now that's the least of my worries." She donned the woolly red hat and opened the door to leave. "Anyhow, mom, it's old news, what went on with Jasmine and Royce. All of that happened a long time ago."

She set off down the sidewalk, skirting the larger snowdrifts piled up by the wind. Margery watched her, bemused. A long time ago? Nine years was not long! It was a mere eye blink in the collective memory of the town of Medford, where gossip could be either current or historic; where skeletons from times past, fifty years or even more, were regularly hauled out of closets, dusted off and set to dancing again. Nine years was not nearly enough of a barrier between past and present to afford any protection for Anna, thought Margery. The details of that scandal were, if not truly fresh meat, still tasty.

She looked at her daughter's retreating back, the red hat bobbing away into the snowy distance. It occurred to her that she had seldom, perhaps never, watched Anna in the act of walking away. She noted that Anna's figure seemed to have thickened of late. She no longer strode along in the free and easy manner Margery remembered. She also saw, with a pang, that Anna, once so lithe and upright, was beginning to hunch, the defeated set of her shoulders making her seem like an older woman.

"Granny, I'm cold!" little Christopher cried. The children were standing close to Margery, hanging onto her dressing gown. She came to herself with a start. She realized that she was still holding the door wide open to the wind and snow, and now she closed it. Sorrow clutched painfully at her heart. Anna was right, she thought. Nine years could be a long time. It has indeed been a long, a very long time for my sweet girl, my baby. Then she took one of Christopher's small cold hands and another of Lily's, and led the little ones up the stairs to the comfort of the warm bed, where they curled up like kittens next to their sleeping grandfather.

CHAPTER 10

Margery was now too fully awake to rest. Once dressed and downstairs, she poured herself a cup of coffee and took it to the kitchen table. She looked out the frosty window at the driving snow and thought of Emma and her journey. Then she thought of that fateful Monday morning in October when she and Emma had sat facing one another in this very same spot, their hands warming around cups of tea.

That was the last time her cousin, for many years also her closest friend and confidante, had visited. The next day a great rift had opened up between them, and soon after that the wheels were set in motion for the return of Jasmine Holmes to Medford. Both of these developments made Margery unhappy; but right now there was extra salt in the wound because she had admitted – only to herself and just recently and quite reluctantly – that she might be partly to blame. But of course, she consoled herself, anyone could see it really was Emma's stiff-necked pride that was at the root of all their troubles.

Margery fished out a cigarette from her secret stash beneath the kitchen sink. She lit up. Stale and slightly bitter as it was – she was down to just two a day now, and almost at the end of the pack – it went well with the coffee and her pensive and slightly bitter mood.

The problem was, the break between the cousins had thrown the family into turmoil. Jim, her husband, had never said anything much, but he radiated disapproval – Emma had ever been his friend and ally in his family of combative, outspoken women. Margery's daughters were more vocal, particularly at Christmas when the gap left by Emma in the celebrations was especially noticeable. It was at the Christmas table that little Christopher, more sensitive by half than any of her other grandchildren, had asked, "where's Auntie Emma? Doesn't she like us anymore?"

As time passed, the children stopped asking after her. But Margery still missed Emma, particularly at this dreary time of the year – her good humour, her quick laugh, and her common sense – although God know where that last went, Margery thought sourly, when Emma decided to bring Jasmine and her child back to Medford to live in her home.

In this little moment of peace and quiet before the start of her busy day, she sat with her cooling coffee and thought about what she might have done differently to change the course of events, or at least save her friendship with her cousin.

The problems started at the funeral of Emma's sister, Sylvia. As funerals go, it had been one of the most dismal Margery could remember, which was saying something. The rain had been relentless, turning what should have been a dignified procession up the long sidewalk to the church into a hasty dash for cover with a coffin in tow. The burial site was a welter of mud. Whoever had dug the hole for the coffin also seemed to have unearthed a spring, and for those attending at graveside, neither umbrellas nor galoshes succeeded in their mission.

While some were able to go home to change before the reception, Margery, Emma and the girls had to scramble back to the house and, in their damp and uncomfortable state, welcome the early birds and soon after that, the dozens of other mourners who came and stayed long past the expected hour. For on such a dull, rainy day, a funeral reception was not so much a last chance to offer condolences as a pleasant and welcome diversion, with the added bonus of Emma's and the MacClures' tea sandwiches and matchless lemon and butter tarts, cookies and squares. Later on, some of the die-hards had adjourned to the nearby tavern; and afterward she and Emma had had to deal with the wrath of wives who thought they were responsible for supplying the alcoholic beverages that accounted for the inebriated state of their husbands when they finally arrived home.

But then, right from the outset, everything had started badly. The day before, there had been that dreadful scene at the funeral parlour when Margery arrived to find Emma in an epic rage. Before she had the front door fully open, she had heard Emma's voice reverberating down the funeral parlour corridor and out through the foyer,

"You've made my sister look like a TART!"

Hurrying into the reception room, she had discovered Emma in a furious set-to with the funeral parlour owner, Simon Jenner. His assistant stood quivering nearby. Jenner was a short, thin man; Emma, with her considerable bulk and height, towered over him.

"We have done the best that could be expected," he said, standing his ground with admirable sang-froid.

"The best that WHO could expect!" Emma roared. "Let me tell you what I expect, and that is you will immediately remove that garish makeup from my sister's face before her friends and relatives arrive and think they're in the visiting room for a CLOWN!!"

Emma turned then and saw Margery, and she laid a commanding hand on her arm. "Come here, and tell me what you think of this. Look what they've done to her!" Tears of fury and sorrow sparkled in her eyes.

Margery dutifully looked. "I wouldn't recognize her," she said truthfully.

Her cousin Sylvia had been beautiful. Emaciation might have wracked her body, but once death smoothed away her habitual grimaces of confusion and pain, Emma and Margery had marvelled at the Madonna-like repose of her features. Now someone, Jenner's assistant perhaps, had smeared heavy pink makeup over her alabaster skin and made her mouth into a bright red gash. It appeared there had been an attempt to pencil in eyebrows. Spots of rouge glowed on her cheeks.

"I told you: very little makeup!" Emma was almost frothing at the mouth. "Now take her away and see what you can do; otherwise, we'll have to have a closed coffin and you can be sure that I'll let everyone know why!"

Still impassive, Jenner wisely said not a word. He and his assistant carefully disengaged the coffin from the flowers that surrounded it and rushed it away. Then Emma threw herself into one of the overstuffed parlour chairs and did something that Margery had never ever before seen and hoped never to see again: she cried. It shook Margery to the depths to see her strong, unflappable cousin in such a state. After all the months and weeks of nursing Sylvia without ever shedding a tear, now she wept copiously, the tears fairly spurting from her eyes. Finally, Margery laid a gentle hand on her back.

"Emma, do you think you can pull yourself together? It's less than twenty minutes to the visitation and we still have to find out what they've done to Sylvia."

In the end, they kept the coffin open. By drawing the blinds and lowering the lights, the bright pink makeup, which they had been less than successful in removing from Sylvia's face, had passed without comment.

But all these were small matters of little real importance. What had made the last passage of Sylvia Holmes truly depressing, Margery concluded, was the black shadow hovering over everything that took place. A shadow cast by someone who wasn't there.

Margery took a long drag to finish her cigarette and she ground it into the ashtray with unnecessary force.

If there had been talk, she hadn't heard it. But no one could have failed to notice the absence of the one person whom Sylvia had loved the most. Her only child, her daughter, had not been there for her during her last illness; and she had not come to the funeral. For those who remembered Sylvia in her better days, and how her daughter had been like the bright sun to which she always turned her face, it seemed a great sadness.

And now Emma has brought Jasmine back to Medford, Margery thought bitterly. At least she's come home to collect her inheritance.

She wondered whether things might have been different if she and Emma had been able to find a small, quiet moment alone during the proceedings.

"I need to talk to you after everyone leaves," Emma told her at the visitation, when there was a pause in the flow of visitors. "I want to tell you about Sylvia's last hours."

"Well, tell me now!" Margery had exclaimed, fairly bursting with curiosity.

"No, it's private, and it will take some time," Emma demurred, but by the end of the evening there had been no time, and there were still last-minute arrangements to be made.

"Perhaps we can talk after the reception," Emma suggested the next day before the funeral. But even with two of Margery's daughters staying on to help, they didn't finish the washing up until ten at night, when they all were exhausted beyond words and ready only for bed. Then, Sunday, the whole MacClure clan was still around and what with children and dogs underfoot and too many people to cook for, bed linen to change and the house to set to rights later in the day, she never had an opportunity to chat with Emma.

So there they were, that fateful Monday morning, sitting at the kitchen table with their steaming cups of coffee. It was blessedly quiet; no children, just Jim's old dog Shelby, sleeping on his mat beside the door. Outside, only a few tan-coloured leaves clung to the trees. The rain had washed the sky blue and clear. The low sun slanted through the windowpanes, spreading squares of pale lemon winter sunshine on the blue checked oilcloth and on the plate that contained the last of the funeral sweets.

"Well," said Emma, selecting a cookie. "It's quite a story. I have to pinch myself when I think of it."

There was no need to start at the beginning. Margery knew, from having seen it first-hand, the sad chronicle of Sylvia's life and more recently, her descent into illness, her cycles of recovery and relapse, hope and disappointment. She and Emma had been Sylvia's primary caregivers, aided by the hit-and-miss services of other paid and unpaid helpers. When Emma insisted on it, Margery herself had reluctantly but gratefully accepted payment, cash never being in great supply in the MacClure household.

"You know how Sylvia wasn't able to talk during the past four months?" Emma asked, as she got up to find a spoon to sugar her tea.

Well, yes, Margery certainly did. One morning she had arrived and found Sylvia sitting on her bed. On saying hello and asking Sylvia how she was, she said something unintelligible. From then on, nothing but gibberish. A small stroke, the doctor said, probably something temporary, likely she'll get over it. But as with all his other hopeful prognoses, she never did.

Sometimes Sylvia would stare at them with dreadful intensity and urgency, trying to say something. "Write it down!" Emma urged her at first. Then Sylvia would hold the pen over the paper, her hand shaking, and perhaps produce a scribble. But no words came forth, either from mouth or pen. As time wore on, Sylvia became less and less responsive to the goings-on around her. Finally, she was sleeping all the time, up until her death.

"Well, just before she passed away, Sylvia talked to me," said Emma, dipping a shortbread in her tea.

Emma's words cut through Margery's wool-gathering thoughts clean as a knife.

"What? What did you say?" she asked incredulously.

"Sylvia spoke to me, just as clearly as you and I are talking this minute," said Emma. "Clear as a bell. Now let me tell you how it happened."

And as Margery sat goggle-eyed, Emma related her tale with all the relish of a born story-teller, especially one now blessed with an audience hanging on every word.

CHAPTER 11

Sylvia Holmes departed this world on a Wednesday. It was one of those sun-shot, achingly beautiful days of autumn, the end of a late spell of glorious Indian summer. Margery and Emma had been taking turns staying with her around the clock once they sensed her time was near. On this particular afternoon, Emma had walked to her sister's home without a sweater, it was so warm. The wind blew languorously through the trees; a few golden leaves spun lazy arcs to the ground; the sky was a heavenly shade of blue. Emma reluctantly entered the darkened house and climbed the stairs.

It was oppressively warm and close in Sylvia's bedroom, the stale spent air smelling of medicine and something else indefinable and unpleasant, perhaps the scent of her advancing illness. Dust motes hung in the single beam of light that pierced the gloom created by the heavy curtains drawn against the sun. Sylvia was fast asleep, propped up on her pillows.

After Margery left, Emma took her usual chair at bedside but then, without too much thought about whether or not she was following doctor's orders, stood up and flung the drapes aside, and lifted the window sash to admit a little fresh air and a flood of golden sunshine. She sat down once more and began to go through Sylvia's mail, extracting the bills she needed to pay as Sylvia's guardian and the executor of her estate. All was peaceful and quiet.

Suddenly she sensed the fall of a shadow and looked up. The sun had been blotted out; the sky turned dark. Simultaneously, she felt a rush of wind and heard the sound of tens of thousands of beating wings. The glass in the window vibrated as the air outside filled with twirling, whirling masses of blackbirds on the wing. There were several large oaks and an elm near the house, and the birds settled in an inky cloud on every twig and branch of the bare-limbed trees. The noise was deafening: a loud, frenetic burst of sound and energy created by the rustle of wings and a cacophony of squawks, clicks, whistles and cackles.

Emma was standing at the window, awe-struck at this spectacle and the sheer numbers of birds in the migrating flock, when she heard a weak voice from behind.

"Emma?"

Turning, she found to her amazement that her sister was awake, and that along with regaining consciousness, she had recovered her voice. And in the scant half-hour left to Sylvia Holmes before she departed this world, she was able to tell Emma exactly what she had struggled and failed so many times to say.

When she was finished, she lay back on the pillows and, spent by her great effort, closed her eyes and died. At that exact moment, there came a sudden silence in the racket outside. Then, as if a signal had been communicated to one and all, the birds took flight. Wave after wave of blackbirds passed through the clear blue sky, heading out over Lake Ontario on their great migration south. And away with them on invisible wings, light as the air, flew the soul of Sylvia Holmes.

"And I hope wherever she is now, she'll find the happiness and love she never, ever had on this earth." When Emma concluded her tale, her eyes were full of unshed tears.

Margery, sitting on the edge of her chair, was completely unmoved by this display of emotion, and by now truly fit to burst with impatience. "Well, when exactly are you going to tell me what she said, Emma!" she demanded of her cousin. "For heaven's sake!! What was it she wanted us to do!"

There was a brief silence in which Emma mentally calculated whether it would do any good to sugar-coat her answer. "She asked me to bring Jasmine and her daughter back to Medford," she answered flatly. "She made me promise."

"What!" Margery exclaimed, aghast. Her face reflected her shock. "Bring Jasmine back here? Why, that's ridiculous! Jasmine hates this place, and for lots of good reasons! Besides that, where is she? We don't even have an address for her, down in Arizona or wherever it is she went! Sylvia hadn't heard from her in over two years!"

At that moment in their conversation, the phone rang. It was the MacClure's ring, two long and one short on the party line, but whereas ordinarily she would have dashed to pick it up, Margery ignored it.

Emma was reaching over. Now she pulled out an envelope from the handbag sitting beside her on a chair. "Well, evidently Sylvia had a letter from Jasmine last summer that she never told us about. She told me where to find it, in one of the books near her bed. It seems Jasmine is back here and living not far away, only somewhere in the city."

She opened the envelope and extracted two thin sheets of paper and a photograph. "It's her granddaughter Sylvia was most concerned about. She was worried about how well Laura is being cared for."

Margery took the letter and read it. It was unremarkable in its content, but the writing was spidery and a few of the sentences didn't seem to make sense. She picked up the photo. It showed mother and daughter, and although it had been taken from a distance, she could see that the daughter had regular features and appeared to be pretty.

"Who knows what that poor child has been through, dragged around the country the way she was," Margery said. Then she glanced up at Emma with a sudden flash of intuition. "She's not like your Hummel and Royal Doulton figurines, you know. You have no idea what you'd be taking on."

Stung by this reference both to her childlessness and her secret fondness for her large china collection, Emma replied tartly, "of course, I wouldn't know anything about children or small girls after helping you out with your five all these years, not to mention Sylvia's and now your daughters' children!"

Then Emma's dark eyebrows drew together and her long face became serious and intent. "Now listen to me," she said. "If Jasmine doesn't want to come back to Medford, I have no intention of forcing her. It's my hope there will be enough left in the estate to make her comfortable and give her other choices. But that remains to be seen."

"One more thing, Margery," Emma said, as she stood up to leave. "I know about you and your fondness for gossip. So before I go, I want you to promise me, God's word, you won't breathe a word of this to anyone else. Not your daughters, not Jim, no one! Not until everything's settled and I have a better idea of what needs to be done."

Now it was Margery's turn to be offended. "Well, of course not!" she said indignantly. "I won't tell a soul – only – "and she was wringing her hands with the strength of her emotions, "only, think hard about this, Emma! You know all the trouble it would cause. Really, I don't know why you would make such a promise!"

Emma had put on her coat and was buttoning it. She looked up. "My only sister. Her dying wish. Just what would you have done differently, Margery?"

Margery was quiet. She thought for a moment. Finally she said, "I would have shut the window."

Then they had both laughed, only this time it was a hollow, rueful sound, quite different from the merry peals of laughter they usually shared during their times together.

Before she left, Emma had turned at the door. "Remember!" she said, putting a finger to her lips.

But not ten minutes later Margery had broken her promise, the news was spreading through the town like wildfire, and soon her lifelong friendship with Emma was in tatters.

Margery was fuzzy on the details of just how this happened. She remembered that after Emma left, she had felt as if her brain were on fire with what she had heard. Through the window, she watched Emma walk away, her usual long-legged lope. She went to sit down. Then the phone rang. It was Lorena, wondering why she hadn't answered her call earlier.

Because Emma was here.

What did you talk about?

About Sylvia's last hours. That was safe enough, she thought.

What about her last hours, did anything happen?

She woke up and talked to Emma. Probably she shouldn't have told her that.

My goodness!! What did she say?

Oh, just some last minute instructions about Jasmine. She definitely shouldn't have said that!

Then, slowly but surely, like someone prying open a particularly hard nut or obstinate oyster, Lorena had picked and chipped and twisted away until, finally, out it popped:

"Sylvia asked Emma to bring Jasmine home."

Margery had reeled with horror to hear the words that were falling off her tongue, so then she had quickly added, "but she's not going to do it!"

But it didn't matter, because no one believed that last disclaimer she made, and soon the telephone lines were buzzing with the astounding news that Emma was bringing Jasmine Holmes and her daughter back to Medford.

That very afternoon, Emma was confronted on her way from the bank by friends who asked her if it were true. "And I was just struck speechless! I couldn't believe my ears!" Emma roared when she phoned in a fury, before banging down the phone and after she had declared that she was no longer telling Margery anything, in fact would no longer be talking to her, a promise she had kept, more or less, for the three long months of their separation.

What to do? Margery was still pondering over the problem of Emma when, forgetful of time passing, she jumped at the loud blast of sound that shook the house. Shortly afterward, she heard the high piping voices of children and Jim's low rumble as the sleepers upstairs awoke.

With a sigh, she dumped the ashtray and hid it under the kitchen sink, opened the window a notch to dispel any lingering smoke, and took out the big frying pan to prepare breakfast. Her busy day had begun, as it did for most folks in Medford, with the whistle of the 6:30 freight.

CHAPTER 12

Once past the trestle bridge, the train rushed past the Medford train station without stopping on its way to the city. The only crew aboard, the driver and the stoker, were preoccupied with keeping the train on the track and on schedule and shovelling coal into the fierce red maw of the furnace, and in any case would have had little idea that their fast-moving freight had become the de facto alarm clock for the small town located just over a mile away.

They might have been surprised to know that the sound of their locomotive's whistle reverberated so loudly through the streets that it could pierce through the deepest slumber to announce the start of the workday. They would have been even more surprised to learn that it was the fateful intersection of topography and a fatality that had led to this phenomenon.

Perched on high land overlooking the great lake, Medford was enclosed on three sides by water. Two sizable creeks marked either end of its long main street. Frozen now, in spring the Medso and Coshoni brimmed with deep, dangerous green water; then snaked lazily through their shallows lined with native marshlands during the heat of summer and into the crimson blaze of fall. During the course of their high water meanderings, these waterways had dug great, red-and-grey walled gorges that in some places soared several hundred feet into the air. When the railway was laid down, the trestle bridges were constructed in those locations where the gap between the cliffs on either side was narrowest. Unfortunately, this had left the town marooned a rather inconvenient mile away from its new railway station.

The land adjacent to the rail lines was largely undeveloped, and close by the Coshoni train bridge a small squatter colony had sprung up. These gypsy-like people, who earned a living in the summer picking fruit and vegetables for local farmers and selling fish from the still-pristine waters, found the trestle bridges an easy and convenient way to cross the creeks – although sometimes chased, infrequently caught, and given fines they generally never paid anyway, by railway police.

One such individual, Percy Tilly, lived with his wife and a brood of children in a house constructed of found materials close to the Coshoni trestle. It was on his way home from a session of heavy drinking at his cousin's house across the gorge that Tilly tried to outrun the 8:40 Sunday night freight on the trestle bridge, seemingly oblivious to the fact that right beside the track on which he was running was another track where he might safely stand while the train passed by.

"He ne'r was a sporting man, that I can recall," Clara Tilly said dourly when presented with her husband's body and the tale of his last, fatal race. But then the widow sued, successfully, for compensation from the railroad based on the fact that the driver of the train had failed to do more than feebly toot the train whistle before bearing down on the bridge, a charge to which her many relatives were eager to testify.

After paying out a rather large sum, the lack of a warning whistle was treated seriously by the railroad. The order went out that all drivers would be required to give two long and one short warning whistles on approaching a trestle bridge. Once the order was put into effect, it was then that the remarkable acoustic properties of the two long, deep gorges of the Coshoni and Medso were discovered by the townsfolk of Medford.

In the late evenings Sunday through Friday, it was though these tapering, winding walls that the long, sad wail of the 8:45 westbound freight and the rhythmic clatter of its wheels floated down to the town, muted by distance and trailing visions of distant places and echoes of infinite melancholy.

For those of a certain age, the mournful notes seemed to strike some inner chord that summoned up sad memories, bitter thoughts of futile endeavours, old regrets and lost chances. For the young, watching yet another lacklustre day in Medford draw to a dull close, the echoes were freighted with unhappiness at their lot, and the deeply felt sense that life was passing them by while at the same time someone, somewhere else, was enjoying the fun and living the life that rightfully should be theirs. And so, in the wake of the Sunday night train, to their parent's sorrow and the town's loss, many of its young folk followed their dreams down the track never to return.

However, now it was Tuesday morning when, at 6:30 am., the townspeople sat up in their beds as if jerked by invisible strings. Early each weekday the steam engine rolled in fast from the east, squealing around the bend and blowing its whistle loudly before it rattled across the bridge at top speed. Purely through some chance of their configuration, the cliffs lining the creek then functioned like the pipes of a huge organ to gather and channel the sound, so that during its long passage down the Medso it grew in strength and volume before breaking upon the town in a mighty blast.

Only shortly afterward, another whistle was emitted by the tannery at 7:00 a.m., the first of many used indiscriminately and at loudest pitch to announce shift changes, lunchtime and the beginning and end of the working day by the small factories that lined the banks of the rivers. Time and work in Medford were meted out by this method, for a wristwatch was as yet considered a luxury. As well, the broth of noise that bathed the town from morning to night included school bells, the tinny gong of the town hall clock, the deeper bass notes of the clock on the old commercial building, the bells of the horse-drawn wagons still in use to deliver ice and milk, church bells rung for daily services, and later in the day, bells or whistles blown shrilly from porches by mothers calling children in from play. In shipping season, there were also fog horns and the loud horn blasts of ships arriving or departing the harbour, and the toot of freighters signalling the solitary tug boat whose job it was to bring them safely into the berths near the factories.

This morning was different from others. It was winter, and a day of bitter cold. Ice had stilled the lake and muted the busy hum of the harborlands. Once it spread out a heavy blanket of clouds, the wind abated. The normal sounds of awakening were absent or muffled, as the town slowly filled up with the silence of snow.

CHAPTER 13

Tinkle tinkle. TINKLE TINKLE!

Arlena Stoddart was abruptly jerked out of the pleasant reverie she was enjoying as she made her daily trip through the looking glass.

Arlena sat at her usual place at the dining room table, a little apart from her mother and father. From this position she was able to project herself far, far, away, into the endless tunnel of reflections captured by the large, gold framed pier glass hanging on the opposite wall. This magical effect was created by a second, identical mirror behind her that multiplied her image to infinity. Her looking glass world at certain times, and this was one of them, often seemed more real and was definitely more appealing to Arlena than was the one that she currently occupied as the daughter of Max and Elizabeth Stoddart.

The dulcet tones of the dinner bell grated on Arlena's ears now, only because it was the newest and latest of her mother's affectations. Elizabeth rang the bell to summon their long-suffering housekeeper from out of the kitchen to play maid and butler at meals. When Bessie did not immediately respond, she rang it again, more loudly and imperiously. Bessie knew better than to complain. She came bustling out the swinging kitchen door armed with the coffee pot, which she would have done in any case so familiar was she with the family's routines, and she added an eye-roll over the heads of her employers for Arlena's benefit as she refilled their cups.

Elizabeth turned from her conversation with her husband. "There will be seven of us for dinner tonight, Bessie. Please use the good china and silver and include soup spoons in the settings."

Elizabeth was formerly Lizzie Dortmund, the daughter of the town baker. Over the years she had adroitly covered up these humble roots with a plethora of social activities and accomplishments. She had done well by her marriage, which had taken her several giant steps up the social ladder; but then so had her husband Max, who was now generally acknowledged to be the most influential and monied man in town. "She had the dough and he was well-bred:" was the tired old joke repeated about the upwardly mobile Stoddarts. In any case, it hadn't taken long for the baker's daughter, by any measure an intelligent, astute young woman, to acclimatize to such rarefied social heights as might exist in a small town like Medford.

Now thirty-nine years married with three grown children, a son, Mason, and daughters Althea and Arlena, Elizabeth sat at the head of the long, highly polished dinner table. Even at the early hour of 7:00 a.m. she was, as usual, highly polished herself and fully prepared for her day. She wore a tasteful black and white dress, a string of pearls and matching earrings. Her blonde hair was permed and in perfect order and she was fully made up with powder, rouge, lipstick and mascara. Arlena could not remember the last time she had seen her mother without makeup or nail polish. The perfect wife and matron, Elizabeth now was a little on the heavy side but still tall and imposing, with erect carriage and an undeniable air of command. Arlena found all of this, and her mother in general, vastly irksome.

"What are your plans today?" Max inquired pleasantly of his wife. He was a genial, somewhat stout fireplug of a man, with shrewd brown eyes and an air of barely repressed energy. It can be said that Max did not share his daughter's sentiments about her mother. Over the years, he and his wife had been tightly welded by reciprocal bonds of love, respect and burning ambition into a formidable team. Only a moment earlier they had been discussing the strategy for tonight's dinner, to which the mayor and a leading councillor and their wives had been invited. It was the day before a committee vote on rezoning. None of their guests would have any idea how important the outcome of this vote was for their hosts, or, during the course of the evening, how skilfully they would be manipulated to choose the option that favoured the Stoddart's business interests.

"I'm at the Women's Literary Society this afternoon," said Elizabeth. "With all this snow I'm not expecting much of a turnout."

Elizabeth was currently the President of the Literary Society. She had been president of every women's organization of any consequence in Medford. She was a success in whatever position she took on, every fund-raising venture she espoused, successful in every way. Except one. Her daughter, sitting to the right of her at the dinner table, never failed to imbue Elizabeth with a burning sense of frustration practically every time she looked at her, as she did now, venturing a quick glance over her coffee cup. Unlike their other children, Arlena was petite. She had Max's wiry dark hair, brown eyes, and was quite pretty, although with her pert nose and high coloring she bore an unfortunate resemblance to a mother-in-law Elizabeth had once detested. Despite all Elizabeth's subtle and less-than-subtle manoeuvres, at the age of twenty-five Arlena still was unmarried, with no fiancé and now, not even any prospective suitors in sight.

Usually Arlena spent her time at the dining room table silently ignoring her parents and their conversation and staring at the opposite wall. Perhaps because she felt her mother's eyes on her, Arlena appeared to have roused herself from her morning lethargy, and now she spoke.

"Well, for certain your President won't be attending," Arlena said. Her voice sounded strange and tinny to her ears; it was actually the first time she had used it since waking up. "Oh. I forgot. Emma isn't President anymore, is she? She resigned before the last election, and that's why you're President, isn't that right? Anyhow, I saw Bill Madison's big old black Buick coming along Main street around five o'clock yesterday, full of passengers."

Elizabeth turned the full force of her pale blue, slightly protruding eyes on her daughter in a cold stare and wiped the corners of her lips on her serviette, careful not to smear it with lipstick. She was also covering the natural downturn of her mouth on hearing these words, so well designed to irritate her. The elections had been held some months ago. Afterward, Elizabeth had heard there was talk, whispers that she would still be waiting in the wings as Vice President if Emma hadn't chosen to step down saying that she had been President too long and it was time for younger people to take over.

"Emma hasn't been at any of our recent meetings in any event," Elizabeth said dismissively.

"Yes, and I guess we both know why that is!"

Arlena couldn't help it, her mother had played right into her hands and she practically crowed the words. Her father looked at her in some astonishment, raising his heavy, salt-and-pepper eyebrows. Elizabeth watched his reaction. She knew Max was unaware that, for the past several months, she and Emma had been on less than friendly terms. He hadn't heard about their altercation at the I.O.D.E. Christmas tea party – Elizabeth had made sure of that. Now she intended that he continue on in that blissful state of ignorance.

It was too bad, she reflected, that she had asked Arlena to help out at the tea, because she was there to witness what happened. But swiftly, without a change of expression or a flicker of chagrin, Elizabeth changed the subject and went on the offensive.

She drew her chair back slightly. "Time to start moving. Arlena, shouldn't you be getting yourself dressed and ready for work?"

Her daughter was arrayed in her usual assortment of shapeless, unfashionable clothing that covered up her fine figure and astonishing bosom, a lucky inheritance from her mother. She wore not a speck of makeup.

"I am ready," Arlena said, not missing a beat. She was totally immune to this type of subtle slight by her mother, and she still had points to score. "Anyhow, since Emma won't be there, I can guess what the gossip will be at the meeting," she added. "It'll be all about Mason's old flame returning to Medford."

Her brother was a married man now, and Arlena was well aware that this chapter of his past was a closed and forbidden topic. However, Elizabeth did not rise to the bait but rigidly maintained her self-control. She gave a short bark of laughter. "Old flame," she said disparagingly. "There are so many old flames of Jasmine Holmes in Medford, I'm surprised that woman didn't burn the town down years ago!"

Max chuckled at this amusing sally as they all stood up. But on leaving the room, he wondered: why was Emma Madison no longer going to Society meetings? What, exactly, did Elizabeth have to do with it? And why, whenever he was with his wife and daughter, did he so often get the feeling that he was a spectator at some kind of bloodless but vicious knife-wielding battle?

Women! He gave the well-tailored shoulders of his new suit a shrug. Then he hurried off to his office for yet another pleasant and, by comparison, relatively uncomplicated day of empire-building.

CHAPTER 14

"Emma!" The voice, imperious, demanding, broke through her dreams. "Aunt Emma!"

Emma looked at her watch. Seven o'clock. She put her feet on the floor and made a worrisome discovery. She was bone tired, beyond tired. It seemed she had depleted her reserves of energy and overnight, like a child's balloon leaking air, gone all weak and flaccid. Just a few more hours of sleep, she yearned. Instead, she went down the hall to the bedroom and freed Jasmine so she could go to the bathroom, then picked her clothes off the floor and set them out for her to put on – the same ones as yesterday, until she could wash whatever might be found in the suitcases.

She hurried to get dressed. After cavorting on the roof in the moonlight, Jasmine appeared to be full of energy. It was now clear to Emma that she needed help to handle her. But rack her brain though she did, she could only think of one person to call on. No, she thought. No, I won't give her the satisfaction.

Just then, while doing up the buttons on her shirt, she heard a telltale sound: the squeak of the floorboards at the top of the stairs. Looking around the bedroom door, she saw Jasmine descending, and leaving off buttoning, Emma ran after her. When she finally caught up, Jasmine had shot the lock on the kitchen door and was about to exit the house. After marching her back into the kitchen, Emma looked down at Jasmine's feet. They were bare.

"Where did you think you were off to, in this snow and ice?" She inquired. Then, once Jasmine was seated at the table and picking at a plate of hot buttered toast, Emma found pen and paper and began to write.

CHAPTER 15

"Who could that be?"

The MacClures were sitting at the breakfast table with their coffee when they heard the loud thump from the knocker on the front door. Margery could reliably be depended upon to leap to her feet and rush to see who it was, so Jim, a big, greying bear of a man, stayed put. However, he was not immune to curiosity, and he raised one shaggy eyebrow in inquiry when she returned.

"That was Sammy Mitchell, the boy who lives a street over from Emma," Margery told him. "She asked his mother if he could drop this bag off to me on his way to school."

"I thought you two weren't talking!" Jim exclaimed, surprised.

"We aren't," said Margery. "And Emma is so proud and stiff-necked she wouldn't get in touch unless she was desperate, so this must be important."

She reached in the bag and took out a scarf she had left at Emma's house some time ago, then a cookie tin.

"Well, that certainly doesn't look important," Jim commented.

Margery said nothing. She took the lid off the cookie tin and took out a sealed envelope.

"What's that?" Jim asked.

"This is one of the ways Emma and I send messages back and forth when there's something we can't talk about over the phone," said Margery, opening the envelope and taking out a sheet of paper.

"What do you mean, 'can't talk on the phone'," Jim snorted. "Who's going to be listening in at this hour of the morning?"

"Everybody," Margery replied absently. She was reading. "Emma is asking me to come over and help her with Jasmine. She says she's too exhausted to get through the day and she'll explain more when I'm there."

"Will you go?" Jim asked. This was a rhetorical question. After 35 years of marriage, he knew that once she had read that puzzling, cryptic note, several truckloads of wild horses would not be sufficient to keep his wife from going to visit Emma.

Margery, however, took his inquiry quite seriously. "I guess I'll have to," she said with a good show of reluctance. "Though it's going to take every ounce of willpower I have not to slap the face of that Jasmine Holmes the first I see her."

Jim put down his coffee. "Margery," he said quietly, "we've discussed this before. So you might remember that Royce left town with Jasmine of his own free will. She did not tie him up and kidnap him. And he did come back and make Anna an honest woman."

"Oh sure he did, two months later, when she was already three months gone and starting to show, and the wedding plans were in ruins, and the whole town knew he had dumped her for a fling with Jasmine!" Margery exclaimed, her face red with fury.

Jim gazed off into space. "Maybe – perhaps it would have been better if he hadn't come back at all. Anna could have moved to another town, found a good man – a happier life."

"Well, then we'd have Mary, probably, but we wouldn't have Lily or Mark, would we?" Margery asked.

Jim's stricken face showed Margery that she had won this round. He doted on his grandchildren, especially Anna's three. "You have a point," he said.

Margery waited as Jim drained his cup and put on his coat and boots. Moments after he was safely out of sight and on his way to work, she had dashed out the door.

CHAPTER 16

Thomas Latham sat at the breakfast table marking the second last of his grade ten math tests. His concentration was seriously waning, the numbers swimming beneath his eyes. He put his pencil down when he heard the sound of the stairs as Lianne descended. This was a surprise. She was frail now, so lacking in energy that she generally did not get up until late in the morning, and then only with the help of Eleanor Mackie, their septuagenarian neighbour.

Thomas met her halfway up the stairs and escorted her down. She took her seat across from him at the table. He looked at her perhaps longer than he realized, taking in the sweetness of her expression, her beautiful limpid eyes, and all the while feeling tragedy stalking them, coming closer.

"You're thinking about what the doctor told you, my diagnosis," she said suddenly.

Thomas was taken aback. "How did you know that?"

"Because you were so nice all weekend and Monday. Because you haven't looked at me like that since I was 18 and we were just engaged," she said, dimpling. "No, it's because I can read your mind. And I knew weeks ago what Dr. Sheridan finally told me last Friday. I wasn't surprised."

So she did know. The doctor had made such a speedy exit that Thomas had no time to check. Then Lianne had said nothing about it, so neither did he. Nevertheless, Thomas was glad they hadn't talked about her illness so far. And he didn't want to discuss it now, for the simple, selfish reason that it would ruin his day.

"Well, since you're so good at reading minds, I'm going to take you around to see the board members who're deciding whether Mike Simms or I will be the next principal at Medford High," he said. They chuckled, both of them relieved at the change of subject.

"When will you know?" Lianne asked, serious again.

"Probably the end of next week," Thomas said. "If this business from nine years ago hadn't come up, I would have had it in the bag."

"Well, Mike has seniority going for him," Lianne spoke slowly, her eyes downcast at having to dampen his hopes. "What I'm saying is, you have to be prepared for any outcome."

"I'm tired of being prepared for bad outcomes," Thomas said, and when she looked up there was a suspicious redness around his eyes.

This time it was Lianne who changed the subject. "Last night – did you hear something that sounded like a laugh or a scream? It came from the direction of Emma's house. Sometime around one o'clock."

"I didn't hear anything," Thomas said, curious. "Did it sound like a child?"

"No." Two bright red spots had appeared on Lianne's cheeks. "A woman. It was the wind that carried the sound. It wasn't a child. Though – I would so like to see her, the child."

"Why?" Thomas asked, but he already knew the answer.

"Because I wonder what she looks like," Lianne said. "I can't keep from wondering if –perhaps – she looks like you."

CHAPTER 17

There was a feeling of deep comfort about the little room. The morning sun poured through the mullioned casement windows. The old pine floor boards and the wooden bedstead glowed goldenly in the light that reflected from their polished surfaces. There was a pretty quilted pink comforter with bows on it, a doll lying in a doll's bed, puzzles and books, and in the air, the clean scents of soap, wax and lemon oil. Laura absorbed all this and also, with a child's lens of acute perception, the aura of the old house itself, solid and sheltering, with its roots in an earlier century.

After breakfast she had retreated to her room, feeling the same thrill of pleasure as when she had first seen it: this clean, warm, safe place, the first room she had had to herself in a long while. Now she lay curled like a small cat on her bed in the sunshine, idly turning the pages of a picture book, when she heard a tap at the door.

"Laura, sweetheart, I'd like you to say hello to your Aunt Margery."

Another Aunt? She turned and saw a short, stout woman with glasses, her blond hair in tight curls around her face, her cheeks still pink from exertion.

"Hello," Laura said uncertainly, for the woman, who had been wearing a smile when the door first opened, was now staring at her open-mouthed. Laura was used to such scrutiny, but still it made her nervous. She ducked her head.

"Hello Laura," said the woman, "I have some granddaughters quite close to your age, I think. How old are you?"

"Eight, almost nine." Laura said shyly.

"Well. Well. Welcome to the family, Laura," said the new aunt. Although, from the way that she said it, somehow it seemed to Laura as if she didn't really mean it at all.

* * *

From afar, looking out of her vantage point high atop the house, Emma had watched Margery's ant-like progress as she navigated the snowy, sloping streets, her arms pumping vigorously. The old Madison house, built more than a century ago by one of her husband's seafaring ancestors, had once included a widow's walk. This structure had been removed, but a small cupola remained. It had one window and a door that, lacking the widow's walk, now opened directly out onto a steep, pitched roof. As she stood on the small round platform inside the cupola, Emma looked out the window and rejoiced inwardly at the prospect of salvation presented by the arrival of her cousin Margery. Meanwhile Jasmine, standing next to her, was still half-heartedly trying to open the door.

Since rising at seven, Jasmine had been full of frenetic energy. She wandered aimlessly through the rooms while Emma trailed after her, restraining her from touching some objects and occasionally trying to interest her in others, generally without much success. They were in a second floor bedroom when Emma turned her back for one instant and then suddenly, rigid with fear, heard the hollow thump of footsteps ascending the steep stairs to the cupola.

Was the door still locked from the inside or would Jasmine open it and tumble out before she could get there? Emma scrambled after her to discover that all was still secure, and she breathed a gusty sigh of relief as she peered out the window and waited for the pounding of her heart to subside. Then she gently guided Jasmine back downstairs to the kitchen.

"My goodness, Emma, you look awful!"

The very moment the door opened, those were the first words out of Margery's mouth after their separation of three months. Emma decided not to take offense. She guessed it was probably true, even if she hadn't a moment to look in the mirror since waking.

"Such flattery!" she said dryly. "Well Margery, I can see that all the time we've spent apart wasn't quite enough to tame your tongue."

And then they laughed. Not the usual merry sound, but rather the comfortable, amiable laughter of cousins used to trading barbed comments and mild insults; the relieved laughter of friends nearing the point of forgetting, letting go of the hurtful past and glad of it.

"Come," Emma said. "We'll go right upstairs and you can meet Laura. Jasmine seems to be staying in one spot for the moment, but we can't leave her for long."

The introductions were brief enough. After they left Laura with her books, there was an unaccustomed silence between them as they came down the stairs. Emma had not failed to notice Margery's restrained, slightly chilly welcome for her great niece on meeting her for the first time. She was not surprised, but she had an unpleasant presentiment of trouble ahead, with the awakening of old resentments and rivalries. For Mary, Anna's daughter, was the apple of her grandmother's eye. And with Laura's arrival, the blond, sweet-faced nine-year-old, whom Margery had more than once proclaimed to be "the prettiest little girl in Medford," was that no longer.

Jasmine was in the kitchen, for once sitting quietly in the banquette drinking a glass of milk. In the hall, where Jasmine was still visible but out of earshot, Emma quickly briefed Margery on her condition, her wanderings and the mad midnight dance on the roof, her own exhaustion and urgent need for rest. As she spoke in low undertones, Margery's face became a frozen mask of shock, while her eyebrows edged upward to perch practically on her hairline. She had uttered only a few hushed exclamations while Emma was talking, but now she burst forth.

"Emma, you must be a madwoman yourself, to take this on!" she exclaimed. "This is far too much for you to handle, and you know it! Once you saw her and her condition, then why would you ever bring her here?"

"Shhh!" Emma had expected this outburst and did not want it to reach Jasmine's ears. "Two reasons," she said. "I could tell that Laura – I'm not sure just why – was fearful of returning to her foster care family. And as for Jasmine, well, Margery, if only you had been there! It's a different world! If you had seen what I saw, you would know that to get better, she had to get away. She needs to be around normal people, to have normal routines and lots of talking to and conversation. She needs to be with family."

Margery looked at her skeptically. "So," she demanded, "what am I supposed to do with her while you sleep?" Then, in a lower voice she added, "you know, Emma, we've never been on particularly good terms, Jasmine and I."

"If you can get her to settle somehow, that would be good," said Emma, deliberately ignoring the last comment. "But otherwise just follow her around, let her exhaust herself. Make sure she doesn't break anything or hurt herself, and talk to her! Just talk! Bring her up to date on what's happened in Medford, the people she used to know and what they're doing now, that type of thing."

She could see Margery's face brighten. Margery did love to talk, and it so happened Emma had suggested her favorite topics.

"Now," Emma took Margery's arm, "let's go see Jasmine."

As they approached the bench where she sat, Jasmine turned to them a face devoid of expression or expectation, all flat, her eyes dull and lusterless. Her thinness had sharpened her nose and chin, and her collarbones stood out like knives against the sweater Emma had helped her into a great many hours ago, or at least so it seemed to Emma in her exhausted state.

"Hello Jasmine," Margery said; then, not quite enough under her breath she whispered to Emma, "dear me, but she's lost all her beauty."

"Margery!" Emma exclaimed, shocked, "she's not deaf, you know!"

While looking daggers at her cousin, it seemed to Emma that the expression on Margery's face was familiar. It was distinctive enough that Emma was not likely to forget it; she could recall seeing that same look not too long ago. Where? Now she remembered. It was in the kitchen during Sylvia's funeral reception, when Evie, Lorena's daughter, dropped and broke the last precious jar of Margery's quince jam.

And there was one earlier occasion. Etched sharp in her memory was Margery's sour face at the Matthison's bridge night back in September, when Betty Matthison, whom poor Margery had the bad luck to draw as her partner, completely overbid three consecutive hands.

That was the look Margery was training on Jasmine now, and finally Emma saw something move across the blankness of Jasmine's face: a small flicker of reciprocal dislike. Hurriedly she gave Margery her last instructions. "Well, I'll leave you two now," Emma said, then quickly ascended the stairs, went into the spare room that was now her temporary bedroom, and fell asleep before her head touched the pillow.

Jasmine watched her aunt disappear upstairs. She gathered herself to her feet and started to follow. Suddenly a firm hand reached out and grasped her forearm.

"No, my girl, you're staying with me," said Margery. "I've not had my coffee yet, so you sit tight, right here, until I figure out what to do with you."

And after a brief and unequal struggle, that is what Jasmine did.

CHAPTER 18

"Aunt Emma! Auntie Emma!"

The childish voice was sweet, but sharp enough to penetrate the hazy depths of Emma's dreamless slumber. She opened an eye. "Thank you, Laura," she said. "Tell Aunt Margery I'll be down in a minute."

Emma threw water on her face and, with a single glance in the mirror, confirmed the truth of Margery's observations when she first arrived. Descending the stairs, she followed the low murmur of her cousin's voice to the library and on entering was greatly relieved to find a calm and tranquil scene. The room was bathed in the glinty gold light thrown by a setting sun through the west-facing windows. By this, Emma guessed the time at well past four o'clock. Laura was sitting on the leather chair behind the big desk, contently drawing a picture with the new colored pencils Emma had bought for her. Jasmine and Margery were on the settee in front of the fireplace, poring over a photo album.

"And this would be your grandmother's sister, Maud, when she was about 75. She lived in Belfountain all her life and – well hello, Emma!"

Margery got to her feet. "You slept five hours, right through lunch. You must be famished! I put some chicken and potatoes in the oven, so dinner is half made for you."

Emma started to thank her, but Margery wasn't finished. "And do you know what else?" she crowed. "I pulled a few of these old photo albums off the shelf and Jasmine just loves looking through them! Don't you Jasmine? So, for a couple of hours now, she's been as good as gold, haven't you?"

Jasmine turned a baleful eye on Margery but then resumed turning the pages, looking intently at each and every photograph. Emma was surprised at Jasmine's sudden interest in a family she had, up to this point, alternately aggravated and insulted or ignored. But then the thought came to her: it's the past she's rediscovering. And it could be she'll find some of the bits and pieces of herself that she's missing in those pages.

"I wonder –" Emma said tentatively. "Just the other day I was looking at five big boxes of photographs up in the attic – you know what a lot of photos Dad took, and so did Bill. When you come tomorrow, do you think you two might start sorting them and putting them in albums?"

"That would be a good project, don't you think, Jasmine?" Margery asked. She stood waiting for an answer that never came while Jasmine studiously regarded the photo album. "Well, then, goodbye you two," Margery said and, before she left the room, gave Laura a brusque hug that was not returned.

In the foyer, as she donned her coat and boots, she complained to Emma. "Jasmine never said a thing to me, just a yes or no. I'm not even sure she knows who I am! And she's so restless, always wandering. I had to watch and follow her everywhere, and I'm quite exhausted! No wonder she's so painfully thin!"

Emma bit her tongue against the urge to remark that Margery, who was now more than pleasantly plump, might actually benefit from trailing after Jasmine in her wanderings. Instead, she asked, "Well, Margery, what are you going to say to Jim or your friends and family about Jasmine and her condition?"

Margery stopped buttoning and looked up with a face full of consternation. "Now that's a good question," she said. "I should think we want to keep this quiet, don't we?"

"For the sake of all the family," said Emma. "People mustn't find out what hospital she was in, and they must not be allowed to discover she isn't right in the head! You know as well as I do the problems that would cause!"

Margery looked suitably grave. "I do. I completely agree with you and I won't talk. But Emma, when people ask me what's the matter with her, what can I say? I have to say something!"

Emma had spent some time thinking about precisely this question and she had an answer ready. "It's simple. Just tell the rest of the family and anyone else who asks that it's woman problems. That should bring the questioning up short, especially if there are men around."

Margery looked unconvinced. "But Emma, that's not true!" she burst out. "And I can't tell a lie! When I try to, everyone knows I'm lying; then they go after me and after me until they find out the truth!"

"But it is true!" Emma replied hotly. "She's a woman, and she is certainly a problem! She's caused problems for herself, for her daughter, and for you and me. All kinds of them!"

"Woman problems," Margery said, musingly. "My goodness. Yes, yes, indeed she has!" She stood stock still for a moment. Then she pressed her lips tightly together. Her colour changed from pink to red. Her cheeks puffed up and then, suddenly, out spilled a great guffaw, and together she and Emma laughed and laughed until their eyes filled with tears.

"Women problems!" Margery gasped. "Oh Lord, how I've missed you, Emma! What a long, dreary winter it's been without you around to make me laugh!"

And after they had wiped their eyes and shared an embrace and Margery had stepped out into the frosty evening, Emma returned to the library. She was curious.

"Jasmine," she asked her niece, who was still poring over photographs, "I was wondering. Do you remember that woman who stayed with you today? Did you know who she was?"

Jasmine looked up at her with those remarkable eyes, dulled now but still uptilted and fringed with long black lashes. They were her one feature that hadn't completely changed, Emma thought, and she felt a sudden rush of sorrow and pity. She tried once again. "Do you remember her name?"

Jasmine's lips parted. She spoke. "Yes. It was Margery, the auld bitch."

CHAPTER 19

Stuck at home with small children and lacking other sources of entertainment, Marilyn Parsons took an avid interest in the doings of the family for whom she babysat. She and her mother were sitting enjoying the delicious apple squares she had brought for her visit when, from their vantage point sitting by the window, they saw Royce Parke walk up the street to his house.

"He's back," Marilyn said, and set down her cup.

"Will he be coming over to get the children?" her mother inquired.

"Never," answered Marilyn decidedly. "Only Mary or Anna ever does that. He doesn't want to be bothered with the care of them." She looked over at Christopher and Lily, playing happily with her two youngsters of similar age and busy with their cars and dolls. "Anna won't be along for a while; she usually gets home and starts dinner before she collects them."

"How long was he away this time, d'you know?" asked her mother.

"I've been picking up the children from Anna's mum for two days now," Marilyn replied. "But I might not have them much longer. Anna told me her job ends tomorrow and I don't think she has anything else lined up. It's too bad, because my two never know what to do with themselves without Christopher and Lily, so they fight. Plus, we need the money."

A movement out on the sidewalk distracted her. She stood up and peered through the falling snow. "There's Anna, she's early tonight. So she's home, and now watch out for the fireworks!"

* * *

She had briefly considered whether she should just tear into him and have it all out. But Anna was tired. She had neither the heart nor the energy for a spat. Besides, she asked herself, what difference would it make? They had covered this ground before, and time and again he had only left it littered with broken promises.

Anna had been looking forward to a few moments of peace and quiet before putting dinner on and picking up the children. However, trudging homeward along the snowy streets and looking into the distance, she saw that it was not to be. Inside her small house, lights she had not left turned on were burning brightly.

She came in the back door and after shedding her coat and heavy boots, she entered the kitchen. That was where she found Royce, sitting in a chair, a dark silhouette against the bright backdrop of the living room. Anna switched on the kitchen overhead light. At once it was apparent why he might want to stay in darkness. One of his eyes was blackened and almost closed, and below it a large purple bruise bloomed on his cheekbone.

"It looks as if you had a good time while you were away," she said in a flat voice. Then she got out the frying pan and opened the refrigerator.

Royce gave an unpleasant laugh and took a pull on his beer. "It was a celebration of sorts," he said.

"What have you got to celebrate, besides your black eye?" Anna asked as she opened a brown paper packet of ground beef and shook it into a pot.

"The black eye is beside the point," he said dismissively, as he fingered the bruise on his cheek. "What I was celebrating is a new job. And it's exactly the kind of work I want, a job that gets me out from under the thumb of the boss."

Now Anna looked at him directly. His rakish good looks had long ago lost their appeal for her. At that moment, though, his bruised and battered face was alight with enthusiasm, something she realized she hadn't seen there for a long time, perhaps years. In spite of everything she started to feel sorry for him; but then quickly reminded herself that he had made his own misery and hers as well, much more.

In response to her silent look of inquiry, Royce laughed, rather nervously, she thought. A long pause, and finally he said, "Yes, it's a good job and pays well. I'm to be the new caretaker at the Airdrie Estate."

"What?" Anna's mouth opened in a wide O of surprise. "Caretaker! But that means you'll have to live there, on the grounds!"

And she felt her pulse racing, her brain registering the first small explosions of indignation and anger.

"Yes, well, there is the wee house, but it's not quite big enough for the family," Royce said, and now he was openly nervous.

"Not big enough for the family! So then, what you're telling me is that you're planning to move out on us!" Suddenly she was furious, her pent up anger of the past few days spilling over with the shock of this new development, and she was gathering up her rage and about to hurl it at him when she heard the creak of the back door. A moment later, into the simmering silence walked Mary, newly home from school, her blonde hair glistening from the outside damp, her cheeks flushed bright pink. A few steps into the kitchen and she stopped short, her smile fading when she saw her mother's expression. Then she looked at her father.

"Dad!" she exclaimed, horrified, "what happened to your face?"

The light had faded from Royce's eyes. He took another swig of his beer. "Ask your mum," he said, sullenly, not meeting her gaze.

"Your Dad was celebrating and he ran into some trouble," said Anna, choosing her words carefully while she damped down her anger. "He has a new job on the Airdrie Estate. He's going to be the caretaker, so he'll be living in the house on the grounds."

"Does that mean we'll have to move?" Mary asked, suddenly apprehensive. The estate was in the town of Medford, but so far as Mary was concerned, still much too far from her friends.

"No, you'll not have to move," Royce answered her question. "It's only a wee house, just for one person or a married couple. But there is one small spare bedroom and one of you kids at a time can stay there. So how would you like to come visit your old Da, Mary?"

"No!!" Mary exclaimed, so loudly Royce jumped, but Anna barely noticed her daughter's reply. An important thought had just occurred to her.

"So explain to me," she addressed Royce, "just who is going to be around to watch over the house and children, and take Christopher and Lily over to Marilyn Parson's when I have to leave early for work?"

Royce laughed, his usual unpleasant, grating laugh, and suddenly Anna saw that beside his shiner, it appeared he had lost a tooth from whatever fracas he had run into within the past two days.

"So that's more what you're worried about, isn't it?" he asked jeeringly. "Well, Mary will do it. She's a big girl now, almost ten, time to be taking some responsibility in the family. Anyhow, you're not working anymore, you'll have time to figure it out."

"I am so working!" Anna retorted hotly. "I'm going to be taking over with Jasmine. Mom says she can't do it anymore, it's too tiring, and she wants me to have the work. I start Monday."

Royce gave a long, low whistle. "Well, who would have believed it!" he exclaimed. "You, playing nurse to your old arch-rival! So she's still sick, even after the stay in the hospital. What's her trouble, anyhow?"

"It's female problems, Mom says," Anna answered shortly.

"Huh. If I know Jasmine, it's more like man problems," Royce responded.

"Well in that case, then we'll have a lot in common to talk about, won't we?" asked Anna. She turned to stir the meat cooking on the stove. "Mary," she said, with her back turned, "once you've been upstairs, can you go over to the Parsons and get Christopher and Lily?"

There was no answer. Surprised, Anna turned to see her daughter, who was standing there silently, arms crossed. She was still a little girl, not nearly mature, but the sullen look on her face bore all the hallmarks of early adolescence.

"Mom," Mary said wearily, "you don't have to worry about me taking care of Lily and Christopher. I've been getting them up, dressing them and giving them their breakfast and taking them over to Parsons' most mornings anyhow. Dad said not to tell you but I guess it doesn't matter now." And then she turned on her heel and started up the stairs to her bedroom on the second floor.

Anna looked over at Royce. It was a look he recognized and had learned to dread. "Is that true?" she asked softly.

* * *

Rob Parsons had just come in from clearing the snow that fell overnight. He hurried to unbutton his overcoat. "Marilyn!" he hollered.

"I'm cooking breakfast, what is it?" Marilyn hollered back.

Rob put on his slippers and strode into the kitchen. Marilyn was at the stove turning the bacon. Their two children sat at table, busy with their bowls of oatmeal. "What?" Marilyn repeated, curious to see him smile at such an early hour of the morning. "What happened?"

Rob gave a great guffaw. He slapped his knee in merriment. "Remember how you said Royce Parke was gone for over two days and there was likely to be fireworks last night?" he asked. "Well, there he was this morning, out clearing snow across the street from me, and Holy Mither of God, did she ever deck him! A black eye and a bruise on his cheek as big as a plum! And she's half his size, she must pack a wallop like an elephant!"

Marilyn was holding her spatula erect like a baton. Now she thrust it roughly into his hand. Her eyes were as big as saucers as she exclaimed, "She never!! Oh, do finish this for me, won't you, Rob? I've got to use the phone; I just can't wait to tell Mum!"

CHAPTER 20

The weather was cold and blustery, but Emma had been housebound for four days, and except for brief forays outdoors to build a snowman and collect icicles, so had Laura. "We both need a good walk and some fresh air," Emma told her.

That Friday Emma skimped on her usual afternoon nap so that she and Laura could go out while it was still light. They planned to walk to the bakery and the butcher store for some essentials while Margery supervised Jasmine at home.

"We're going to make tea biscuits and have them nice and hot for when you return, aren't we, Jasmine?" Margery cooed at her charge as they watched Laura and Emma bundle up for their expedition. Emma took note of the expression on Jasmine's face, which was no longer dully blank but now actively registering degrees of boredom and distaste.

"I think she's getting better," she said to Margery in a whispered aside as she waited for Laura to finish buckling her boots.

"Yes," said Margery, "and she's also getting mouthier. Yesterday she said to me, 'talk, talk, talk!' So I told her, that's my job, to talk to you and bring you back to the real world. Then she made a sound, and it wasn't a nice one, I can tell you! Yes, it's the old Jasmine coming round, and it seems time hasn't done anything to sweeten her disposition. It'll be such a relief when Mary takes over after the weekend because, as I told you before, Jasmine and I never did make much of a pair."

Laura had finished dressing. Emma added a plaid scarf, tying it tightly around the neck of Laura's coat. "There. We're all ready."

She turned back to Margery. "While I think of it, could you ask Anna to keep a look out for someone who might be willing to stay here during the night? I'm fairly worn to a frazzle with putting Jasmine back in her bed. She was up three times last night! Also, the wee cot I'm sleeping on in her room isn't big enough that it's comfortable for a long string bean like me."

"Good heavens, Emma!" Margery exploded. "You have to have your sleep if you're to cope with this wild woman and her child! Do what you did the first night and chain her up to the bed!"

But Emma could not bring herself to do it, and said as much. Then she took Laura's hand and left, but not before she saw Jasmine slowly turn her head and glare at her caretaker with a look of baleful spite.

* * *

The child smelled the sweet tang of wood smoke on a wind sifted with silvery sparkles. She saw the gracious old homes nestled in rolling expanses of bright snow, the venerable trees with their limbs encased in crystal and glittering in rare winter sunshine. She heard the crunch of snow under her boots as she walked with her aunt, and felt the warm reassurance flowing from the gloved hand that held her mittened one tightly. For a moment, she felt a surge of soaring, miraculous joy tinged with disbelief. Her world had burst too suddenly out of its dark, cramped confines; and threaded through the brightness of this day was a ribbon of fear and a distrust of all that was too good to be true.

They had finished their errands and were on their way home laden with parcels. Laura carried a loaf of bread in one of Aunt Emma's shopping bags, and another small brown paper bag containing three sugar cookies, a present from the bakery owner. She had been petted and made much of during their afternoon walk. What she didn't know was that their outing was less to run errands than to advance her great Aunt's agenda. For Emma had every expectation that Laura's good manners, her sweet shyness, but most of all those great violet-blue eyes set in a perfect face would slowly win her mother a certain grudging acceptance she never would gain on her own merits.

As for Emma herself, it was a vindication of sorts. Now the friends and acquaintances to whom she had introduced Laura on their walk might better understand and sympathize with her decision to bring mother and daughter home to Medford – a decision, she would never forget, that none of them had supported.

The sun was hanging low in the sky on their return homeward. As they picked their way along the icy sidewalks banked with snow, an elderly lady came toward them, leaning on the arm of a younger woman.

"Hullo Emma!" she called out energetically. "Who's that youngster with you?"

They stopped for a moment to talk. The child liked the old lady immediately. Her bright blue eyes twinkled with good humour from under heavy, pink-lined eyelids. The hair escaping beneath her hat hung in fleecy white ringlets. With her sweet, kind, rather silly face, she reminded the child of a lamb, Mary's little lamb, in a nursery rhyme book she had once owned.

"Hello, Letty. This is Laura, Jasmine's daughter," Aunt Emma replied. "Laura, this is Mrs. Lawson, and her daughter Mrs. Byrd."

"Hello," Laura said.

Letty took Laura's mittened hand in hers. "Why, aren't you just the sweetest thing," she declared, with a nice smile. She stood for a moment looking at her. "Will you be going to school soon?" she asked.

"Auntie is taking me next Monday," the child answered shyly.

Letty turned to her daughter "She's probably just about the same age as your Noreen, don't you think? Noreen is Mrs. Byrd's daughter," she explained, looking at Laura once more.

"How old are you?" Mrs. Byrd asked.

Laura did not like Mrs. Byrd. She wore dark glasses and brownish lipstick that made her large, heavy lips look like earthworms when she spoke. "Eight, almost nine," Laura replied. She looked down then, because she didn't like to see the lips moving.

"And what's your name," the woman asked, in a loud voice.

Laura looked up, surprised. Hadn't Aunt Emma already told her? "Laura," she replied.

"No, no, not your first name, your last name," Letty's daughter said impatiently. "What's your last name?"

"It's Carlisle," Aunt Emma answered, somewhat shortly. She didn't like this line of questioning and wanted to be on her way; the sun was going down and it was almost time for Margery to leave for home.

"Carlisle!" Mrs. Byrd exclaimed, with a laugh that was almost a snort. "Why, then I suppose your mother must be Lady Carlisle! That's a name from Scots nobility, a good name to pick if you need one!"

There was a brief silence, and although the child did not understand anything that Mrs. Byrd had said, she shivered a little because the air around them suddenly seemed to have grown cold. Letty no longer looked so happy. She hurried to fill the silence. "And how is Jasmine? Better I hope?"

"Improving," Aunt Emma replied. "Yes. Well, we'll be on our way. Always a pleasure to see you Letty," she added, pointedly ignoring the younger woman.

And when they reached home, there were tea biscuits with raisins, and hot chocolate, and the child sat contentedly on the padded bench at the kitchen table and ate three tea biscuits with plenty of butter and drank two mugs of hot chocolate. A warm sense of well-being pervaded her. All in all, she had had a lovely day.

"Well!" Emma said. "That Cheryl Byrd never has been a favorite of mine, but after this afternoon, the less I see of her, the better!"

She and Margery were taking their tea in the dining room just off the kitchen, where they could keep an eye on Jasmine as she sat at the kitchen table with Laura.

"Tell me what happened," Margery demanded. She listened impassively to Emma's account of meeting Mrs. Lawson and her daughter. Then she shrugged. "Well, after all, Emma, what do you expect?" she asked. "At least Cheryl said it out in the open, right to your face. Don't think the whole town hasn't wondered about Jasmine's ex-husband, and whether he even exists! No one ever met him except Sylvia, and she's not here to tell. Who really knows if this Carlisle person is Laura's father, or whether it wasn't you-know-who?"

"Margery!" Emma said sharply.

"Well, you'd have to be blind not to see a resemblance," Margery replied. "Did you find a marriage license in Jasmine's things from the apartment? That would help."

"When would I have time to look for a marriage license?" Emma replied. "It was enough of a chore finding Laura's birth certificate for school. You're a better hand than me at keeping Jasmine busy; she's more trouble than a two-year-old. How was she today?"

They both glanced apprehensively in Jasmine's direction, but she was still seated at the kitchen table. "Every day is a little better," Margery answered. "Before she always wanted to get up and wander around, but now she knows that when she's with me, she has to stay put. We've pretty well finished putting your pictures in albums, so we're doing other things. We just shone up your silver and the tea service nicely. At least she's not getting into the garbage any more."

Among the peculiarities of her illness, Jasmine had a fascination with scraps of paper, especially if they had numbers on them. Magpie-like, she also took small objects and hid them whenever she thought she could avoid detection. And there were other strange behaviours, diminishing now in frequency, that made Emma wonder, more than once, what it would be like to live in Jasmine's strangely skewed reality. Was it painful and confusing, or magical and more enticing than the world she had left behind?

Now she was gratified to see Jasmine was improving, a testimony to her good care. The best medicine, Emma thought, with some complacency, was not the pills she administered morning and night, but hearty food, healthy routines and talk – a great or lesser amount of it depending on whether Margery or Emma was on duty. And now it had become a conversation, ever since Emma overheard one of Margery's monologues and then insisted that she ask Jasmine questions and wait for her to supply some kind of answer. Those answers, more often than not, were no longer monosyllables or random nonsense, but were showing a return to normalcy.

"Yes, soon she'll be back to her old self and able to get on her way," Margery said, in tones of satisfaction that suggested this was not an entirely disagreeable prospect. "Probably just after you hand over her inheritance. And speaking of that, are you almost done settling the estate? How much did it amount to?"

This was a subject Emma wanted to avoid, especially with Margery. "I'm just about finished," she answered cautiously.

"Well, for heaven's sake, by now you must have some idea of how much she'll wind up with! Can't you give me even a hint?" Margery prodded. Margery had helped with the cataloguing of Sylvia's jewelry and other possessions of any value, and rightly or not, she seemed to think she was entitled to know.

At that moment the telephone rang, saving Emma from a choice of being either evasive or rude. "It's probably Jim, wanting to know what I've left to put on for dinner," Margery said, leaping to her feet and running to answer it before a second set of rings brought more listeners onto the party line.

Shortly she returned. She had left the phone dangling over the kitchen counter. "It's for you, Emma, and let me warn you, it's Cheryl Byrd," Margery announced in a loud whisper. "She wanted to know if Laura could come over and play with Noreen Sunday afternoon. I said she'd have to ask you."

"Letty must have put her up to it," Emma said worriedly. "It's probably by way of an apology for Cheryl's behaviour today. I don't like the idea of Laura going there, but tell me, how do I say no?"

"Goodness!" Margery exclaimed. "It's only an invitation to play with another child! If she goes, Laura will know at least one of her classmates at school on Monday," she added. "Say no and it'll be all over town that you turned her down!"

"Alright," Emma said reluctantly. "But first, let me ask Laura."

And Laura, when told she had been invited by another little girl to come play at her house, shyly agreed to go. So, the matter was settled but, as Emma hung up the phone, the worried expression did not leave her face. "I'm not sure why," she said slowly, "but I have a very strong feeling I should have said no."

CHAPTER 21

When he arrived home, Jim MacClure did not bother to take off his heavy duffle coat or boots. Scattering clumps of snow on the linoleum floor, he strode into the kitchen, opened the refrigerator to look for the pot Margery told him would be there, found it, and after a quick sniff to determine that it contained fish stew, he put it on the kitchen stove on the lowest heat and then quickly exited out the back door. A brief tramp along a well-worn path through the snow and then he was in the old shed known to family members as Gramp's house. The pot-bellied stove was seldom cold; there were still a few glowing embers. He coaxed them into flame with shreds of bark and scraps of paper, then tossed on a few substantial logs for a blaze of warmth.

Jim's old dog, Selby, had followed him out of the kitchen. He curled up on a blanket near the stove while Jim doffed his coat and boots and sank into a moth-eaten armchair. It was the place where he did his best thinking, and in the scant half hour he estimated he had before Margery returned and all peace departed he had some serious thinking to do. His job and the wellbeing of his family, as well as that of the other 64 employees of the Stuttgart Leather Mills, might depend on it.

At three o'clock that day, Friday, he had been in the office of the tannery finishing the week's paperwork. Matt Laycock, the accountant who came in a few times a month to clean up the books, had taken the comfortable leather chair at the large desk usually presided over by the tannery owner, Nick Sergio, whenever he was there, something that had been occurring with less and less frequency. As they sat in the waning beams of sunlight that managed to penetrate the dusty windows, both were quietly engrossed in their work.

"Jim," Matt suddenly said in a low voice, "come take a look at this."

Silently, Jim left his desk and walked around to peer over Matt's shoulder. It was Matt's job to review all supplier invoices before the bookkeeper paid them and to deal with any other financial matters. He had just slit a large manila envelope that had arrived in the day's mail. Jim could see from the letterhead of the covering letter it was from the bank in Altona, some 60 miles distant.

"I probably shouldn't be showing you this," Matt said, still speaking in hushed tones, because by now the machinery had shut down and all sounds seemed amplified by the unusual quiet. He looked up. Employees were still passing back and forth as they finished the closedown procedures for the weekend, their faint, blurry silhouettes drifting across the frosted glass that enclosed the office area.

Jim took the sheaf of stationery and looked at the papers under the cover letter. They were documentation for another loan, a large one, written against the business and its property and equipment. "Whoa!" said Jim, drawing in his breath sharply; "it looks like, with what's already on the books, we're now mortgaged to the hilt."

The two men stared at the loan agreement, then Matt slowly entered the amount into the ledger. "How is business, anyhow?" he asked, in a more normal voice.

"As usual, maybe down a little," Jim said. "Product is coming in from different countries now, but with the exception of Italian leathers, the others can't compete with our quality."

Matt tucked away his pen and started to clear the desk. "Jim," he said, speaking in undertones once more, "we both know this business is on its way out. The town wants Sergio to deal with the effluent the tannery is dumping into the creek, the unions are trying to move in, all over the country the tannery business is dying and leaving for places where production is cheaper. And where is Sergio anyhow? When's the last time you saw him?"

Jim did not answer directly. "You probably heard his wife upped and left and took their three kids back to Italy in the fall," he said. "Their house has been sold. The last I heard, he was in an apartment near a friend of my sister's on Allen Street. She says no one ever sees him going in and out."

He paused and knitted his brow in thought. "He's not reviewing the payroll anymore. So, since he passed that job on to me, the last he came into the plant was – mid-January, the same week, and if I remember correctly, even the same day he signed up for that new loan. I think we can guess at why he wanted to use a bank that wasn't in town."

They exchanged worried looks. "I don't believe his wife has actually left him," Jim said slowly. "With what you've just shown me, it looks as though it could be part of a plan to scram."

"Bet on it," Matt said. "All the signs are there. But it would help if we could figure out what he plans to do next."

At Gramp's house twilight was over; night had closed in. Jim didn't bother to turn on a light. He just sat there in the dark, in his old, stained armchair. He was thinking about all the possible moves Nick Sergio might make next, and none of them were good.

CHAPTER 22

"You look upset," Margery said, her first comment when she opened the door to deliver Jasmine back home. "Oh, really?" Emma had replied, and then nothing more. Margery knew her too well. However, Emma had decided not to tell her about her day until later; perhaps not at all if she could get away with it. Right now the memory was too raw and searing.

It had been a day of extremes. Her Sundays were usually peaceful and rather boring. This one, however, had turned out to be a day of unrest where she had run the gamut of emotions from triumph to terror. Never before, and she devoutly hoped never again would she experience such dread, the paralyzing fear of learning that a child in her care was missing.

The morning started well. It had gone, in fact, better than she expected. Margery and Jim had driven over to pick up Jasmine at 9:00 a.m. "She needs a change of scenery, and Jim and I are on our own, no grandchildren this weekend, and no plans to go to church," Margery told her on Saturday. "Jasmine and I have fixed up your house nice and tidy; so now that she's making herself sort of useful she can help me out with mine."

Instead of having to tend to Jasmine, now Emma was free to fuss over Laura as much as she pleased. In preparation for the 10 a.m. service at St. Margaret's Church, she brushed the child's blue-black hair until it shone like watered silk. Dressed in the new houndstooth coat with the blue velvet collar Emma had bought for her before her arrival, and with her new hat and matching gloves, Laura was the perfect demure little miss. All eyes followed her when they entered the church, and after mass the women in the congregation had descended on her like moths to a flame.

Only Kitty Farraday, Emma's occasional bridge partner and long-time friend, stood back a little, watching. Before leaving she said, in a tone that conveyed some concern, "well, Emma, you've finally got your own little girl to spoil. I do hope she'll be with you for a while."

Just the reminder that Laura was only hers temporarily had taken the shine off the morning. Emma realized that in less than two weeks, Laura had lodged like a little cocklebur inside her heart. Perhaps that was one reason why, when the phone call came, she felt such pure panic.

* * *

With warmer weather, the snow had become heavier. It was packing snow, acres of it, whiter and much more enticing than the little grey bits that had been available to her in a city backyard, and the child longed to play in it as she walked docilely beside her Great Aunt to the small house of Noreen Byrd.

After they knocked at the door, Noreen had answered it. "Come in," she said in a bossy way to Laura, holding the door only partly ajar.

Aunt Emma would have none of it. She pulled the door fully open and strode into the foyer of the house. "Please fetch your mother," she said in tones of command to Noreen, who fled into the kitchen.

While the grownups made arrangements, the two girls eyed each other. Noreen had a pasty moon face, small eyes and the heavy lips of her mother. That would not have mattered so much except for her expression, which was not especially friendly. Seeing it, the child felt a sensation in her stomach, the tightening of the small knot of fear that was always there.

After Aunt Emma left, Noreen announced to her mother, "we're going downstairs."

Mrs. Byrd had not looked at nor spoken to Laura since her arrival. "Remember, you're taking care of your sister," she said to her daughter. "Take her downstairs with you."

Noreen took the arm of a small, grubby-faced toddler and the three of them clattered down some steep stairs into a half-finished basement. There was a concrete floor as a makeshift play space. A few toys were scattered about. The only illumination was provided by an overhead light bulb.

The child looked about the forlorn room and asked wistfully, "it's nice outside. Do you want to go out and make a snowman?"

"No, said Noreen. "I want to play school." She picked up a piece of chalk from the floor. "I'm the teacher. You sit at the desk there." She started to write on a large, ancient blackboard leaning against an upright wood beam while the child squeezed herself into a desk better suited to a four-year-old. Meanwhile the toddler wandered about, picking up toys, most of them broken, and throwing them.

"What is the world's biggest animal?" the teacher demanded.

"An elephant?" the child answered hopefully.

"No!" the teacher said loudly, and gave the child's hand where it rested on the desk a smart whack with a ruler. "It's a whale! Everybody knows that!" She turned back to the board and began to write. "Now we're going to have a test."

She asked a few more questions and luckily the child gave the right answers and all was well – for a while.

As she sat there, the child became aware that the damp, close air in the basement smelled vaguely of something, a nasty smell that she remembered only too well – pee. She tried to push away the other memories that smell had awakened. They kept on flooding in. Too vividly, they summoned up a similar place and, not too long ago, another time. Stuck in the sticky small chair in the Byrd's basement, she felt again the heavy weight of hour after hour of confinement with other children, wandering aimlessly, unkempt and untended. And then the too-familiar feelings welled up – the deep boredom, the fear. Suddenly she was suffocating. She could not stay here, in this place; she had to get out.

"Teacher!" She raised her hand. "I have to go to the bathroom."

"Really?" asked Noreen.

"Yes, really," the child nodded.

"It's upstairs. Go, but make it quick," Noreen said in her bossy way.

Once the child climbed up to the main floor she found her coat and boots beside the stairs where she was able to put them on silently and undetected by Mrs. Byrd, who was busy cooking Sunday dinner in the kitchen. The child quietly opened the front door and as quietly closed it, then ran rapidly down the street gulping in fresh air and trying to remember the way they had traveled on their walk to the Byrd's house. She was worried. Would Auntie be mad? Even worse, would she send her back?

It was four o'clock, approximately an hour after Laura had escaped from the basement of the Byrd's home. Emma hung up the phone. She was first hot with anger at Cheryl Byrd and how casually she had dealt with Laura's disappearance. And then she was cold with fear wondering if a little girl, a very pretty little girl who knew nothing of the town, would be able to retrace her steps, cross a main street, make several turns and reach home safely before the early winter dark.

Suddenly the phone shrilled again, and she rushed to answer it.

"I heard that," said a familiar voice. "And so did I – that Cheryl Byrd, honestly!" said another, highly indignant voice that Emma recognized from the party line. "I'm going out to look for your niece, and I'll phone my daughter and ask her to send her boys out too," the second voice promised.

"I can't go," said the first. "I have a pie in the oven, but I'll tell my husband, he'll help."

In no time at all there were many people searching. Emma herself hurried out the door without a glance toward the side yard where, if she took a moment, she would have seen Laura beginning to roll up the first ball for her snowman. When she returned, though, with every intention of phoning the police, Emma saw from afar a small, still figure sitting on the front steps in the descending darkness.

For the first time in many years – twenty at least – Emma picked up her feet and she ran, her arms outstretched, to catch up Laura in a hug so big and so tight that it squeezed all worries and fears clean away.

Now Margery and Jim were at the door. Emma thanked them for taking Jasmine for the day, and shepherded her back into the kitchen where dinner was waiting. Laura was setting the table and carefully putting the forks and knives in all the wrong places. Ordinarily Emma would have instructed her in the correct way to do it, but this evening, somehow, whatever Laura chose to do seemed just about right.

CHAPTER 23

It was Monday morning and recess had been called. Martha Lewin would have liked a coffee, but without the side order of aimless chit-chat, the recitals of what everyone had seen, done or eaten on the weekend, so she opted not to go to the staff room. Instead, she stood up from her desk and peered out the window. It was a gloomy, charcoal sketch of a day, all dull greys and blacks against the whiteness of the snow. The only thing she could see that broke with the perfect monotony was a daub of red against the fence of the schoolyard, a good distance away. Martha put on her glasses. The red daub materialized into the jacket worn by the new pupil who had joined her grades three and four class this morning.

Martha sighed. She had been a teacher at Saint Margaret's school for a good many years. For the most part she still enjoyed her work. But even now, nearing retirement, there was one thing she had never gotten used to: the casual cruelty of children. Earlier she had introduced Laura Carlisle to the class, with the express instruction they must help make her welcome. Evidently her words had had no effect. The child was all by her lonesome at the end of the yard.

A ripple of laughter drifted up to her. Martha looked down. Directly below the window, she saw that a knot of nine or ten girls from her class had gathered around Noreen Byrd, and she knew instinctively this had something to do with the isolation of the new student – Laura Carlisle, the great niece of Emma Madison, with whom she had become friends during visits to the library with her pupils.

Surreptitiously, Martha opened the window a crack wider and leaned closer to hear. Martha was of the opinion, based on her considerable experience, that beauty was a curse for young girls. Few had the maturity or confidence to handle the difficulties that accompanied it, one being the antagonism of other girls less attractive. She had already noticed that Laura's appearance had ruffled a few feathers. But Martha suspected there was more to it than that.

Another gleeful laugh floated up to her. "Runaway! That's a good name for her!" she heard.

Runaway? What sort of nonsense was this? Her lips pinched together before thinning into a grim line. She would get to the bottom of it, if she could, and nip it in the bud before it did the damage she knew was a very real possibility.

"...And then she just snuck out the door and ran away," Noreen Byrd had been telling her listeners. "So I've decided I'm going to call her Runaway, because that's what she is!"

The girls all laughed, though not very heartily. But Violet Stott, a large girl of nine who had an older sister and, more than her peers, was interested in the boys in her class, had seen the way they all eyed the new girl. She laughed again, loudly and boisterously.

"Runaway! That's a good name for her!" she chortled.

And unfortunately, despite all Martha Lewin's efforts to dislodge it, the name would stick.

CHAPTER 24

"Hello Jaz."

Silence. Jasmine did not lift her head but continued to look down. She had taken a little portion of her skirt in her hands and was intently folding it into small pleats.

Anna had been prepared, forewarned, but she was still shocked to see the change in her cousin. Especially since her Mother had told her that Jasmine was vastly improved over when she first arrived!

The silence wore on. Suddenly Jasmine looked up, and as quickly down. But Anna had caught the look. It was not as she expected, dull or unfocused, but knowing, intelligent. And there was something else she saw in that fleeting glance and was able to intuit from her cousin's demeanor: embarrassment, perhaps shame. Anna felt a quick surge of pity and empathy.

"Jaz," she said quietly, using the nickname that all except her mother's generation called Jasmine, "I know we didn't part on the best of terms." Anna sat down in the chair across from her. "The past nine years haven't been easy for either of us. And since you know how Royce is, I think you can guess what it might have been like for me."

Anna picked up Jasmine's limp, unresisting hand. "What happened between us doesn't matter anymore, Jaz. I'm far past being angry or even caring about what you did. We were good friends once, and I want to be your good friend again. Believe me, I'm glad to be here, to be with you, and nothing would make me happier than to help you get well."

Emma's knitting needles paused in their clacking. Discreetly out of sight but still within earshot, she listened in on this little speech, delivered with a complete lack of sentimentality and great sincerity. Of all her young relatives, she had always considered Anna to have the biggest, most generous heart. Here again was more proof.

Anna's words were followed by another silence. Emma couldn't resist peeking. She leaned to look around the corner and saw the cousins, their arms outstretched and encircling each other's shoulders to make a bridge between their two chairs, their foreheads pressed together. Emma leaned back out of sight.

In a minute or two she heard Anna say briskly, "now, about getting you well. We're going to do things a little differently —"

Later, Emma saw them in the living room, doing a few simple exercises on the wide expanse offered by the Persian carpet. As time passed, their hours appeared to be filled with activities: walks, reading, easy chores; and threading it all together, their ongoing conversation. At first, it was only Anna's low melodic voice, with the occasional monosyllable from Jasmine; soon, a more equal sharing and even occasional laughter. From the first day that Anna arrived, Jasmine improved rapidly.

But for now, sitting with her knitting needles stilled and deep in thought, Emma resolved to keep that sweet image of the cousins' embrace fresh in her memory, as an inspiration against those all-too-frequent occasions when she was tempted to fail in charity or harden her heart against forgiveness. However, she would allow herself one exemption. Sometimes, she thought, forgiveness was near impossible. Because his daughter was in her house, and her illness had played the strange trick of sharpening her features to accentuate her resemblance to him, every day Emma was far too strongly reminded of Jason Holmes.

This morning she had looked at today's date on the calendar and realized it was eleven years now since he had died – that strange, cardboard cutout of a man whom they had only ever seen the one side of, because he had so successfully hidden from them all the others.

There are events that stick in one's memory; so sharp and jagged they cause pain whenever the mind touches them. Even the passage of time fails to smooth their cutting edge. For Emma, one of these was walking into the study on a rainy spring evening to announce dinner and finding her husband Bill sitting lifeless in his favorite easy chair.

The night before, she had looked up from her newspaper to find him gazing at her with a fond and loving smile. "What are you smiling about?" she had asked, smiling back. "You," he said. "You've made me so very happy."

There was something about the way he said it. "Why Bill!" Emma exclaimed, alarmed.

But then he had reassured her that she had nothing to worry about; he only had much to be thankful for. And so in this way she had lost the great love of her life, and afterward she would forever wonder. If only she had probed more deeply, had asked more questions; if only the doctor, or Bill himself had told her about his heart condition –

The memory was a wound that throbbed from time to time, demanding her attention, but it didn't bear thinking about. She knew that she had to ignore it, navigate around it, if she were still to function and be useful.

There is another kind of memory that does not hurt or ache so much as harm; it is like a pustule buried in the mind. If prodded, it emits putrescence: toxins such as jealousy or anger, which poison the thoughts and actions of their host. Emma had one of these, and feared she would never rid herself of it. The great unfolding drama of Jason Holmes' death was too shocking and recent to erase from her memory, and besides its aftermath still continued. However, she did attempt to forget it because, each time she remembered, a seething eruption of disgust and fury threatened to sweep her back to a time and place of such darkness that it could easily spoil the sunniest day.

There had been good times, of course. In the years following Jasmine's birth, it seemed to Emma that all was happy and peaceful in the Holmes family. Sylvia appeared fulfilled and full of purpose. Jason's business prospered. Some years before, he had used Sylvia's inheritance to clear a mortgage on their other funeral home in Connemara, a farming community a little larger than Medford. Their life had settled into a routine. Jason bought one shiny new black Buick coupe after another and shuttled the 80 miles back and forth between the two towns, sometimes making as many as three trips a week.

Like all events so momentous they burn an indelible mark on your memory, Emma would always remember that time, date and place. It was 2:15 on a Wednesday afternoon, May 15, 1946. She was sitting at the main desk checking books in and out for the handful of patrons in the library that afternoon. The phone rang. Her assistant, Libby, answered it and handed it on. "Your husband," she said.

Emma took the receiver. "Bill?" she asked, surprised. He knew and respected her rule that no personal calls were permitted for library staff during working hours.

Bill was never one to waste words, especially when he knew others might be listening in. "Emma, I'm calling because there's been an accident. Marty at the funeral home phoned to tell me and now he wants to talk to us. Can you leave work?"

"Yes," Emma replied, burning with curiosity but not daring to ask questions. "I'll leave Libby in charge and you can pick me up right away."

The moment they opened the door of the funeral home and stepped into the cool dimness of the hallway, Marty Bourne was upon them. Jason's assistant manager was about sixty, a strong, short little man who was normally calm and imperturbable. Now his mop of grey hair was standing on end from running his hands through it, and he was brimming over with anxiety.

"Thank God you're here," he said. "Brace yourself. I have some terrible news. Jason has been in an auto accident and he's dead."

Not waiting for their reaction, he rushed on. "We have to get over there right away. I was called by the farmer who saw the collision and it seems there were some... well, irregularities. I asked him not to call the police until after we arrived."

"Where did it happen?" "How did the farmer know to phone you?" "What kind of irregularities?"

Marty held up a shaking hand to stop the questions. "The farmer, Oostrom is his name, was out plowing fairly close to the road where the accident took place at about one-thirty," he said, speaking rapidly. "No other vehicle was involved. Jason must have lost control, because it looked as if the car missed a curve, crossed the road, went over a ditch and struck a tree. He says he saw a woman in the car with Jason. By the time he drove his horses out of the field, tied them and got to the car, the woman was gone. He found an empty wallet with Jason's license and business cards on the car seat next to the body and figured out who it was. Then he called us, because this funeral home is closer than the other one."

"Tell me the location and I'll go there right away," Bill said. "I'll do what I can to keep the farmer from telling the police about the woman, so it's off the record, and in the meantime we'll invent some story about the woman for anyone else who might have been listening to your call."

"Well, no need to worry about that, at least," Morty said. "We pay for private phone lines here, always have, Jason didn't want anyone listening in on confidential matters. But if you can go ahead, Bill, then I'll follow right after you with the hearse."

They decided Emma would stay behind and call staff at the Connemara funeral home with the bad news: Jason had told Marty he would be presiding over a reception there that evening.

"Don't visit your sister yet," Bill warned. "Let's find out about this woman and see if we can erase her from the picture first."

Emma was in no rush to tell Sylvia the horrible news of her husband's death in any case. She nodded her vigorous assent. Little did she know that any worries they might have about the mystery woman in Jason's car would soon be dwarfed by the scandal about to erupt.

The sun slanted a few thin beams between the heavy velvet curtains that covered most windows. There were no funerals at the Holmes Funeral Home that day. The manse, for such it was, loomed empty and deserted and Emma, never quite at ease in this shadowy place of death and mourning, was anxious to depart. She sat down at the desk, enjoying the novelty of using a phone that wasn't attached to a wall. She made herself comfortable, and then gave the operator the number for what would be the most shocking, unforgettable phone call of her life.

"Connemara Funeral Home," a male voice answered at the other end.

"Hello," said Emma, "to whom am I speaking? This is Emma Madison, the sister-in-law of Jason Holmes."

There was a long silence. "I didn't know Jason had a sister-in-law. But alright, this is Edwin Byers, the assistant manager. How can I help you?"

Emma related the details of the accident, pausing for Edwin's exclamations of shock and dismay. "I know you were expecting him at the reception tonight, so I phoned you as soon as possible so that you could make other arrangements," she wound up.

Another silence. "There's no reception here tonight," said Edwin. Then, "have you phoned Lillian yet?"

"Who is Lillian?" Emma asked.

"Well, if you say you're Jason's sister-in-law, then you should know who your sister is!" Edwin replied sharply.

"My sister is Sylvia, Sylvia Holmes, the wife of Jason Holmes, who lives in Medford," Emma said with some frigidity.

Silence again. Finally, in a voice that was dismissive and full of distrust, "I think there must be some mistake on your part, lady. Jason's wife is Lillian Holmes, and they live in Connemara."

By the time Emma finished piecing together the facts with Edwin, who was at first surly and uncooperative and then, like her, horrified and disbelieving, she had discovered that Jason Holmes had two wives living in two towns 80 miles apart, and a son, Steven, two years older than his daughter Jasmine, who was working with him in the business. Jason had been married to Lillian for twenty-three years; Edwin remembered they had celebrated their 20th anniversary three years ago with a party, which he had attended.

There was a long sofa in Jason's office and when she finally hung up the phone, Emma staggered over and fell prone on it full-length, knowing she was close to doing something she never had done in her life before: fainting. The impact of all she had learned that hour was like a bomb exploding in her head. Half an hour passed before she was able to sit up, gather her feet under her and leave for home, a four-block walk during which it seemed the burden of knowledge she was carrying had doubled the weight of her body.

Automatically she made the dinner she knew Bill would need when he came home and then, herself unable to eat, sat in the gathering gloom to await his arrival.

Around 8:00 the door opened. Bill came into the dark kitchen. "Are you alright?" he asked anxiously, turning on a light; then, "we both need a drink." He poured two glasses with double shots of rye on ice and they sat facing each other at the kitchen table. "Well, it's been quite a day," he said, with his usual knack for understatement.

"Tell me what happened. How did an experienced driver like Jason go off the road in such good conditions?" Emma asked. She would not say what she had learned until she had a bigger picture, filled in more blanks.

Bill looked down, embarrassed, and swirled his drink around in its clinking ice cubes for a moment before he answered. "Emma, I'm going to give you all the details," he said. "Your sister doesn't need to know them, and the only reason I'm telling you is because I want you to stop Sylvia from ever making Jason into a saint."

"No danger of that, now," Emma had thought, and continued to listen.

"The farmer who was first at the accident, Jan Oostrom, had the good sense to throw a blanket over Jason to keep passing drivers from stopping and gawking," Bill said. "We had a heck of a time getting him out of the car, because he was more or less impaled by the steering wheel when the car hit the tree. But first we had to fix him up, because the police were on their way."

Bill looked down then, visibly upset.

"What do you mean – fix him up?" Emma prodded.

"His pants were open and he was exposed," Bill said, flatly, still staring at some indefinable spot on the table surface.

Somehow Emma was neither surprised nor shocked. "So the woman in the car – ?"

"Not sure how she escaped injury, but we think she must have gone through his jacket for the wallet, taken the money and cleared out; walked or perhaps hitched a ride at the crossroads. Marty said Jason would have had at least some of the monthly receipts for the Connemara home in his wallet."

"Did the farmer tell the police about the woman?" Emma asked.

"No –" Bill gave a brief and mirthless laugh. "I offered him $50 to forget about her when he gave them the details. I didn't know that his wife was listening in the next room, and then she came in and told me the price would be $100 for the two of them to keep their mouths shut. So I paid it."

Emma gazed at him fondly and put her big hand over his larger one. He was such a good man. "Thank you for that, dear Bill. Where do you think Jason was going?"

"Well, the car was headed in the direction of Tabens, a couple miles down the road," Bill answered, then stopped abruptly.

Tabens. Emma thought for a moment, then remembered it from their Sunday drives: a collection of tired old houses, most with peeling paint, and a general store. The tiny village was mainly notable for being less than a mile away from the only motel for miles, a place with lax management and, it was said, rooms that rented by the hour.

Emma found Bill gazing at her with a quizzical expression, one shaggy eyebrow lifted. "You're not at all surprised, are you, Emma?" he asked. "So, what have you found out?"

Emma found herself smiling. "How well you know me, Bill," she said. Her smile faded. "And how very little we knew about Jason Holmes."

Then she told him.

CHAPTER 25

After that day, or more accurately, the seven or eight hours in which everything changed, Emma's memories blurred and she could only retrieve them in bits and snatches. Perhaps it was because the cascade of bad, sad times that followed seemed so endless; or that she deliberately walled herself off from the great pain Jason Holmes had inflicted on his wife and daughter so that she would be strong enough to help them as they fell.

Medford had not had a good, meaty scandal for a long time. This one was prime: it was torn apart, feasted upon, every detail consumed with relish and only a side order of pity for its battered victims grieving the loss of the husband and father they once thought they knew. Lillian, her son and assorted relatives and friends from Connemara had made known their intention to come to the funeral reception as well as the church service. They could not be persuaded otherwise, and this created a veritable show of horrors for Sylvia, who was still in shock and barely speaking. The funeral home and the church were overflowing for both spectacles, at which not a word was exchanged between the wives and the two parties stayed as far away from each other as their surroundings would permit.

The visitation took place on just one evening, a time limitation that had been chosen in the forlorn hope that this would discourage attendance. From her considerable height, Emma looked over the crowd at the second wife, who was standing at one end of the closed casket. Lillian looked back, her eyes hard and glittering, her mouth set in an artificial half-smile, the whole of her radiating assurance and defiance. She was younger than Sylvia, not so lovely but still attractive, tall with fair hair – "bottle-ish blond", as Margery later described it – and well dressed, as befitted the wife of an important man in town. In addition, she had a bearing and self-possession that Sylvia, the cosseted and sheltered housewife, could never match.

From here and there, Emma and Margery garnered information. Lillian had worked for a short time at the funeral home, where she had been an assistant. Emma and Margery guessed she had become pregnant there, ("All those couches and settees! Imagine the temptation!" Margery exclaimed,) before she and Jason married. After a few years off work to raise their son, Steven, she became secretary to the town lawyer, William MacColm, a heavy-set, older man of considerable gravitas who, along with her son, was always at her side during the reception and funeral. There could be no doubt about the paternity of Steven. Dark-haired and tall, he resembled his father in every respect, right down to the way he stood, duck-toed, with a vague look of abstraction on his handsome face.

MacColm had achieved some fame in the court system. He would soon become a well-known and feared adversary for Sylvia and Archie Meddick, the young lawyer Sylvia had hastily hired for the initial talks to try to reach a settlement. A two-fisted, no-holds barred negotiator, MacColm waved away the fact that Jason Holmes' marriage to Lillian was bigamous and therefore invalid, while taking full advantage of Jason's failure to leave a will and dying intestate.

"How could Jason not do that!" Emma had fumed, "After seeing all the family dust-ups that happen when there's no will!"

"Pfft! Where there's a will there's a way," Margery replied. "But when there're two wives, there's no way for a will." Then she laughed at her own wit.

"Jason was saving himself trouble," said Bill evenly. "Even if there were some sort of a will, it would probably be contested because bigamy would cast all bequests to the second wife into doubt."

"What's so hard to believe is that the woman never knew he was married!" exclaimed Emma. And all three of them agreed that it was highly unlikely.

However, when every attempt at settlement failed and the case went to court, Lillian declared that she never knew Jason was married, and had no idea there was another wife in the picture. And since she had sworn to it, Emma concluded perhaps it was just another example of Jason's duplicity, to present himself as single and unattached in a new town.

"He phoned me every night and every morning when he was away in Medford," Lillian claimed. Which was exactly what Sylvia, her hot tears soaking Emma's blouse and shoulder several nights earlier, had told her Jason was in the habit of doing whenever he was in Connemara.

Emma clearly remembered the courtroom. If the proceedings had not been so serious, she would have been amused at how the judge, with his pouchy eyes and drooping jowls, looked just like a bloodhound; while William MacColm bore a marked resemblance to an old bulldog and Archie Meddick, with his nervous energy and snappy retorts, reminded her of nothing so much as the yappy terrier owned by neighbours a street away, which she had once seen leaping about tormenting a rat.

The judge was at the end of his circuit and plainly tired. He took exactly half an hour to dispose of a matter the two lawyers had argued about, at considerable expense, for almost a month. Solomon-like, he simply divided the estate in two, with the Connemara funeral home and the house adjacent to it awarded to Lillian and her son Steven, who was already working in the business alongside his father, while the Medford funeral home and the house in which she and her husband lived were handed over to Sylvia. He stipulated that Lillian would have to pay Sylvia a sum for the greater assessed value of the Connemara properties; but other than that, it seemed the judge made little allowance for the fact that Sylvia was Jason's legitimate wife and that an inheritance from her mother had helped to purchase the second funeral home.

"We have to think of Mr. Holmes' son Steven, who is already in the business. The children must be taken into consideration," the judge pronounced. Archie Meddick had previously pointed out that Jason's daughter also had worked in the Medford funeral home part- and later, full-time since she was 16. But once he learned she was engaged to be married, the judge's consideration did not appear to extend to Jasmine.

It was late afternoon when court adjourned; theirs had been the last hearing of the day. Emma and Bill sat in the car. Sylvia was in the back seat. No one was talking much. Disappointment hung, almost palpable, in the air.

"Wait. Just a minute," Emma said, laying her hand on Bill's arm as he was about to start the car. Silently, they watched as the judge came through a door. William MacColm had been loitering outside. He clapped an arm around the judge's shoulder. They crossed the street together and went in the bar entrance of Medford's only hotel.

"Cronies." Bill observed, "in a miscarriage of justice."

He turned around and looked at Sylvia, who was starting to sniffle again. "Cheer up," he said, not especially sympathetic. Bill was starting to tire of her endless tears. "I have something to show you when we get back to your house."

At Sylvia's he led them into the dining room, where he took the heavy satchel he had carried from the car and poured a mass of papers onto the shining rosewood tabletop.

"What is this?" Sylvia inquired.

"It's your living. Everything you need to live comfortably, once you sell the funeral home business."

Soon after Jason's body was delivered to the funeral home, Bill told them, he had gone through Jason's effects and found in one of his desk drawers a safety deposit key tagged with a number. At once he had Sylvia sign papers appointing him as her trustee for the estate. Then he went to the town bank and cleaned out the safety deposit box. It contained deeds for two commercial properties, one in Medford and the other in Connemara; the papers for a mortgage Jason held on another property and some savings bonds.

"Everything has been probated now and it's all yours, Sylvia," Bill said quietly. "Lillian can't touch it."

"Well, how could she?" Emma queried.

Bill had started to gather up the papers in some sort of order and he paused to answer. "At the bank, I found out who else could sign for the safety deposit box. It was Lillian, and she had the other key. When I went back the next day to do my own banking, they told me she came in just after me, and asked to open up the box."

He was grim as he told them that Lillian would have made sure all these assets were put into the estate that was up for settlement, so that she would get a share. There was also a strong possibility that, equipped with Jason's death certificate and her marriage certificate, she could get possession of everything without their even knowing it – "after all, she works in a law office."

There was a moment of quiet and then Sylvia said, venomously, "that whore!"

It was a shock to hear her sweet, prim sister use such a word, but oddly, it lifted Emma's spirits. It gave her hope that Sylvia's sorrow would run its course and change to anger – a more appropriate and energizing emotion to help her cope with the aftermath of Jason's betrayal and death.

But that brief spark of rage failed to kindle a flame. It was not in Sylvia's nature, and she quickly slipped into melancholia. Emma tried, over and over, to buoy her up, remind her of her responsibilities for her daughter, but in the end nothing worked. Sylvia's life had been too inextricably bound up in Jason's. She had not only lost him, but discovered that the upstanding, faithful husband she thought she was married to did not exist. The edifice of the man she had wrapped her self-regard around had crumbled. And now, so did she.

When Sylvia found that she had cancer, two years ago, it seemed to Emma as if she embraced it like a lover.

Someone was calling her. Emma's eyelids fluttered.

"Aunt Emma! Aunt Emma!"

Emma found Anna standing over her.

"Lunch is ready. I've made a sandwich for you, and since you said you're going out around one o'clock, I thought I'd better wake you up."

"I wasn't sleeping," Emma said, somewhat indignantly.

"Of course not," Anna smiled indulgently. "However, I know Jasmine got you up last night, she told me. I'm still looking for help for you nights. But come, join us."

From her chair, Emma could see the kitchen. Laura was already home from school for lunch. Jasmine was beside her at the kitchen table, a thin, wraith-like figure. Still caught up in her memories and the sadness seeping from them, Emma felt foolish tears spring to her eyes. There sits the real tragedy, she thought.

During lunch, she took pains to be cheerful, even amusing. Soon she would join her friends at their bi-weekly bridge party, always a pleasant event. But whatever she did, it made no difference; her enjoyment was spoiled. As she went out the door, the darkness was still upon her and it would colour the rest of her day.

CHAPTER 26

It was now two weeks after Matt Laycock showed him the books for the Stuttgart Leather Mills. Ever since then Jim had been waiting for the other shoe to drop.

He had grown increasingly anxious as the days passed with no word from the owner, his boss, who previously had been fairly hands-on and visited the tannery at least once a week. What was Sergio up to?

How he missed old man Stuttgart since he sold the business five years ago. Stuttgart had been tough and profit-driven, but he could be trusted to do the right thing. Jim had no such confidence in Sergio.

Now his worries had intruded on his sleep and he lay in bed fully awake while Margery snored lightly beside him. Jim did not find this noise annoying but reassuring. In fact, everything about Margery was reassuring for him: she was his rock. At every seeming catastrophe she rose to the occasion, feisty, full of energy, confident they could combat anything fate threw at them.

He had not known this about her when they married. He thought back to those too brief, golden years when they were barely out of high school and she had been the bubbly, cute, blond cheerleader every guy wanted to date. It was thought by all to be a good marriage. Jim was expected to step into his father's shoes as owner of the town's Ford dealership. A year later, his father's business went into receivership as a result of some foolish investments. Margery still married him. Soon after, about to be a father, Jim had been forced to take whatever employment he could get. The Stuttgart Leather Mills was to be a temporary job, but the old man kept promoting him, Margery kept having more babies, and time marched on –

She had never said a word of rebuke, never complained about their descent down the social ladder. She backed up every decision he made, encouraged him, loved him. She seldom even complained about the dreadful stinks he sometimes brought into the house from the tannery. Margery, at least, he could count on. Otherwise, it seemed that the world was slipping sideways, wobbling under his feet.

He sniffed. What was that? Suddenly, he sat bolt upright. The bedroom window was open a crack for fresh air. A slight draft came wafting in. On it, he smelled smoke, and something else unmistakable, the stink of the sulphuric compounds used to treat hides. The tannery was on fire.

Later, Jim realized that he instinctively knew what was going to happen; had been lying awake waiting for it. Now he felt not surprise but in a strange way, relief. His agony of suspense was over.

As he ran down the street, wearing his pajamas with a coat hastily thrown overtop and boots on his bare feet, he heard the pounding of other feet and soon was joined by more and more dim figures in the darkness as townsfolk roused from their beds by the smoke and now, the blare of fire sirens, raced toward the fire.

"That fucker has set fire to the factory!!" yelled a man Jim recognized as one of the workers engaged in working for a union at the plant, who rushed ahead to stand, stricken, a black silhouette against the great red and orange bloom of the inferno consuming theStuttgart Leather Mills along with the livelihood of sixty-four working men and their families.

Jim leaned against the wall of a building across the street from the plant. In the chill of the March night, the brick was warm on his back from the heat of the blaze. After a few minutes, a small shadow figure emerged from the crowd huddled a safe distance away from the smoke and blasts of heat and cinders carried by the wind. It was Margery. She sought his sheltering arms and he wrapped them around her and rested his chin on her head. Silently, they watched the wild flames and the valiant but futile efforts of the firemen to extinguish them.

"The plant is full of chemicals, most of them volatile," Jim murmured. "The fire has reached them now, and there's no way to put it out."

Margery turned her head and looked up at him searchingly. "One way or another, we always knew this day would come, didn't we, Jim?" she asked. Then she added, "don't worry, we'll get past it, and we'll do fine."

Jim only wished he had her confidence.

The factory was quickly burning down to embers and they prepared to leave. Suddenly, a small white ball of fur came streaking out of the darkness from across the road. It was the little white cat that lived in the plant to take care of mice and the occasional rat. She had been visibly pregnant a few weeks ago when Jim leaned down to pat her and now, as she darted toward him, he saw something in her mouth. At his feet she deposited a tiny orange kitten and then, quick as a flash, ran back toward the still-burning factory and disappeared.

"Wait," Margery said, picking up the kitten and cuddling it. "She's gone to get her other babies, and she'll be back."

A cold half-hour passed. The little cat never did return and Margery and Jim went home to bed, if not to sleep, at four in the morning.

* * *

On Sunday morning, before she set off with the children to the nine o'clock mass, Anna Parke noticed something odd. Looking out the back window she saw a pair of Royce's pants at the far end of the clothesline. They were near the cedar trees where ordinarily she would not have spied them, except that they were flapping in the wind. Royce was upstairs asleep in bed, recovering from a late night on the town. She had a few minutes to spare. Wondering if she had forgotten them when she collected the half-frozen laundry yesterday, she reeled them in. They were still more or less wet. Could he have washed them himself? But when she checked them for dryness, she caught a scent. She bent to sniff. Behind the perfume of the laundry detergent, faint but unmistakable, was the smell of gasoline.

For a moment she stood motionless, deep in thought. Then she pinned the pants up again and sent them down the line to their original position behind the cedars.

When she returned from church, Royce was dressed and downstairs. Later, she checked the clothesline. The pants were no longer there.

CHAPTER 27

"Will you be home for dinner after work?"

Why had her mother asked her that?

Arlena was almost always home for dinner. She was about to say so when she stopped, suddenly suspicious. She remembered that some months ago she had replied yes to a similar, harmless-seeming question. On returning home, she had found two strangers at their evening meal, and one of them was yet another "eligible bachelor" her mother had dug up – Alistair MacGregor, the red-haired nephew of Simon Jenner, the owner of the Holmes Funeral Home. Judging by the social standing of the bachelor, who might be in a position to inherit but was now only a lowly employee, Arlena concluded her mother must have decided her matrimonial prospects were dimming.

Earlier this morning at breakfast her father had been talking animatedly to her about the fire, then about business, when she caught a glimpse of her mother's face. It was closed and tight with jealousy. Elizabeth wanted her out of the house; that was plain enough. Arlena would have been happy to oblige, except that every time she floated the idea both her father and mother were vehemently opposed, for different reasons. Her father loved having her around; her mother hated having her around, but the only way she would let her leave was as a married woman – another project brought successfully to completion by Elizabeth Stoddart.

Now Arlena put on a look of abject apology. "Sorry, mother, I should have told you, I'm off to visit with Rose tonight. Albert is away on business and she's invited me over for dinner and to admire the baby."

Immediately her suspicions were confirmed. "Can't you visit Rose some other time?" Elizabeth asked. "Some very important guests are coming to dinner."

"No – perhaps I'll be able to meet them some other time," Arlena answered airily, and quickly made her escape.

Now she was walking toward her friend's house where Rose, pleased at the surprise visit, was waiting for her to arrive with a bottle of wine and some anecdotes from work to alleviate her long hours of baby boredom. On a whim, Arlena made a small detour to see the Stuttgart tannery. She stood on the sidewalk, looking. Two days later, the ruins were still smoking and all around the air hung heavy and acrid with the poisonous vapors of the harsh tanning chemicals. While she gazed at the aftermath of the great fire, Anna Parke came toward her along the sidewalk and she stopped to chat.

Arlena had always liked Anna. It cheered her to see her kind, sweet expression, after all the sour faces at her insurance firm today. "How is the family, Anna?" she inquired. "And how's your dad, after the fire?"

Anna's smile wavered a little. "Not bad, considering. But he's terribly worried about all the men who were working under him and how they're going to manage. The fire happened right before pay day, and many of those men and their families live from one pay cheque to another."

"Does he think it was arson?"

"He didn't say it in so many words, but he says the plant has been around for over 50 years and never had a major fire. Matt Laycock told him it was mortgaged up to the hilt, and all the money has disappeared. Dad expects the banks will fight over what's left, the property and any insurance payout. He's been trying to reach the owner, who's over in Italy, but nobody seems able to find him there."

Arlena studied Anna as she spoke. She was pretty in an old-fashioned sort of way, with her soft features and curly light brown hair, but her eyes were truly beautiful: large, clear, the whites very white and the irises a deep sky blue. There was something indefinable but rather sad about her that reminded Arlena of all the difficulties Anna and her family had weathered, and she felt a rush of sympathy.

"I'd be glad to help, if there's anything I can do," she said impulsively. "Whatever is needed. I mean it."

Anna looked at Arlena speculatively. She wondered if she could be trusted. "There is one thing," she said slowly. "But it doesn't have anything to do with the fire. You might have heard that I've been helping Jasmine Holmes recover from her illness."

Arlena nodded.

"Jasmine is improving, but she's still up and down at night fairly often," Anna continued. It's tiring for Aunt Emma, so we've been looking for someone to stay nights with her. If you know of anyone who might be interested and could ask them to get in touch, I'd be very grateful."

They exchanged a few more words before Anna set off toward home. Arlena watched her retreating back. Even before she had gone a few dozen paces, Arlena had come to a decision. Tomorrow she would tell Anna that she would stay with Jasmine. It was the perfect solution. It would get her out of the house at night, which was the very worst time, rattling around with her mother; and it would accustom her parents to her not being there, so that afterward she could move out. In a small way, it might also be some reparation for the great harm her family had done to Jasmine by sending Mason away.

And then there was the very best reason of all: it would drive her mother absolutely crazy.

CHAPTER 28

CRACK.

The ball sailed far into the outfield. Laura easily loped around the bases, accompanied by a ragged chorus of cheers from the other players. She had honed her batting skills in the dusty playgrounds of two Nevada primary schools, where everyone, boys and girls alike, played baseball incessantly and obsessively. Here, few of the girls played baseball. The one exception was Shawna Smith, a Métis girl a year older and a head taller than everyone else in her grade four class. Laura and Shawna had forged a firm friendship based on their outcast status, their love of baseball, and their mutual dislike of the other girls in their class.

Shawna had been absent when Laura first arrived at school. At the 8.55 am. bell on Wednesday, the girls were lined up in front of the school door waiting to go in when a tall, pretty, dark-skinned girl joined the queue. "Here's the squaw again," loudly announced Noreen Byrd, to the titters of most of the girls.

Laura hadn't really minded the name Noreen had given her. "Runaway" was better than some of the names she had previously been called. Besides, several years ago, her mother said something that had provided her with considerable consolation and immunity to slights. It was short but memorable.

"All girls are bitches, and most women too," her mother had told her. Then, after a moment's reconsideration, she said that the word was rude and that if Laura ever used it, she would wash her mouth out with soap. So Laura never said the word out loud. But she still liked the satisfying way her tongue curled around it, and now she muttered it under her breath: "bitches".

The dark girl, whose hair was centre-parted and defiantly styled in two heavy braids that proclaimed her Indian ancestry, was totally unperturbed. She came closer to Noreen and flipped her braids at her. "Yes, I'm a squaw," she said. "And I'd rather be a beautiful squaw than a fat white pig like you, Noreen Byrd."

Then, so fast the child could barely see it, the girl snaked out one hand to grab Noreen's ear and twisted it violently. Noreen screamed blue murder, and the teacher in charge of ushering the children into the school slowly walked over wearing a look of heavy resignation. "What is it now, Noreen?" she asked tiredly.

Noreen blubbered out her story, then the teacher turned to Shawna. "What have you to say for yourself?" she demanded.

"She called me a squaw," Shawna answered.

"Is that true?" Noreen was still crying. The teacher surveyed the blank-faced girls waiting in line. No one said anything.

Then Laura, well knowing that in doing so she was forever sealing her doom, spoke up. "She did."

"Well, Noreen," the teacher said. "Just maybe you deserved it. Shawna, you will still have to go to the principal's office with me."

"Sure," said Shawna. The bell rang, the girls slowly started to file in. With complete composure and an ease born of experience, Shawna stood waiting a short distance away from the teacher, where she was able to stick out her foot and trip Noreen on her way in the door without being seen.

The entire episode had left the child goggle-eyed with awe and admiration.

Now, as Laura rounded first base and headed for home, Shawna yelled out encouragement. "Wayda go, Runaway!" she hollered.

From her classroom on the second floor, Martha Lewin had seen the bat connect with the ball. She was watching as the child, her hair flowing behind her like a banner, ran the bases, her long legs in their navy lisle stockings only lightly touching the ground, like a colt born to motion.

There was a chorus of cheers as the child flew across home base. Then the teacher took off her glasses, turned and went to sit down at her desk, a bemused look on her face.

Runaway. The name wasn't a half-bad fit, after all.

CHAPTER 29

Jasmine was looking out the window of her bedroom when she saw something odd.

It was April and the buds were barely beginning to swell on the trees. Through the mesh of branches that usually obscured the view when in leaf, she could see someone in Letty Lawson's backyard.

Emma and Anna were busy making tea sandwiches when Jasmine came into the kitchen. "I just saw Cheryl Byrd going in the back door of her mother's house," she said.

"Mmm," Emma was cutting crusts off the egg sandwiches and not paying full attention. "Letty told me Cheryl was taking her to a doctor's appointment this morning. Maybe she forgot something. Anna, could you please hand me that jar of pickles?"

"She was in and out in a flash," Jasmine said.

It was strange, but Emma didn't have time to think about it right now. She put the pickles in a compote dish, wiped her hands on her apron and untied it. "It's almost one o'clock. She'll be here any moment now."

"Such a fuss," Anna commented, "for someone who's never even invited you to her home."

"Who told you that?" Emma looked sharply at Anna, who, uncharacteristically, returned her glare with something like defiance.

"Well, she may be Bill's daughter, but Mother says that Sandra takes something from the house every time she comes. And that she only visits to check and make sure you're taking good care of the house."

Emma turned away. She made no retort, because Anna's words rang true. Her step-daughter lived in the city. Her occasional visits were the source of some consternation on Emma's part, and that was all because of something Bill had agreed to, long ago, without consulting her. It had led to one of their rare arguments, and as she remembered it was a dilly.

The occasion was Easter. After the family dinner, Bill had asked his son and daughter to come with Emma to the study. There he explained to them the terms of his new will, drawn up shortly after they married. It was simple enough: Emma was to have the use of the house as long as she lived, the proceeds of his life insurance and a few other bequests to supplement her own income so that she would be comfortable; and the children would receive some immediate funds and later inherit the house on Emma's death.

Bill's son, Michael, quickly said he was fine with the new will; but Emma saw the look of dismay that crossed Sandra's face before she recovered her composure. There had been some limited discussion of the will's provisions. Then Sandra asked the question that led to the fracas with Bill, and later, the creeping anxiety that took hold of Emma every time Sandra phoned and inquired if she might visit.

"Dad – do you think it would be alright if I could have a few of mother's things from the house?" she asked hesitantly, in a deceptively soft voice.

"Why, I don't see why not – a few things, as long as your stepmother doesn't mind," Bill answered heartily. Then, belatedly, "what do you think, Emma?"

In the set-to that took place immediately after the families departed, Emma pointed out that if she had said no, she would be the ogre Sandra forever hated. And just how was she to distinguish her possessions from what was already in the house when they first married?

"I could help," Bill offered.

"You! You couldn't even tell my boots from yours, if yours weren't ten sizes larger!"

And then they both had laughed and made up; and Bill said he would talk to his daughter about it and have her take what she wanted just once, when they both were there to supervise. But he never got around to it. And so Emma had lost a cake plate she cherished, then a bone-handled carving set, and once Sandra had taken a picture right off the wall in a bedroom. But it was after Bill died that the real carnage began. Most recently, Sandra had asked for, and carried away a large silver serving tray Emma was certain – well, almost certain – had been her mother's. Not wanting to cause a rift and having no real proof, Emma stupidly had failed to object, and so the pattern was set.

Now she looked at Jasmine and Anna with some severity. "During Sandra's visit, whatever happens, she is Bill's daughter and the relationship is important to me. Neither of you is to say anything that will cause any problems. Is that understood?"

Anna didn't meet her eyes but only nodded her assent. "Jasmine?" Emma was particularly worried about Jasmine. Although normal much of the time, she still had strange outbursts and her behaviour was unpredictable. Right now, Emma wished she could wish the both of them away.

"I'll be as polite as I can," Jasmine promised. And at that moment, they heard the subdued chime of the front door bell.

Jasmine had disappeared while the greetings were taking place, reappearing when they were about to settle at the dining room table to start lunch. She had combed her hair and, for the first time since her arrival, put on lipstick. There was something daunting about her appearance. Emma stared at the transformation.

"Oh, hello. And who might this be?" Sandra asked, in the grand lady manner she had acquired as the family fortunes prospered.

"You remember Jasmine, my niece? She and her daughter are staying with us for a while," Emma replied.

"Now I remember!" Sandra exclaimed. "The last time I met you, you were engaged to Mason Stoddart. I wouldn't have recognized you; you've changed so."

There was a moment of dead silence. Then Jasmine coldly said, "yes, and you've certainly changed as well, Sandra." She was looking pointedly at Sandra's midriff, which had expanded considerably over the years. An angry flush rose up to mottle Sandra's neck.

Sensing the possibility that fur might fly, Emma hurriedly smoothed things over with a question about Sandra's daughter, Melanie, before sitting them all down to sandwiches and tea. Once primed, Sandra continued to talk at length. She talked about Melanie's successful marriage, her own husband's promotion to assistant deputy minister in the government, her beautiful house and garden and the trip to Europe she and her husband had recently taken. Then she moved on to the subject clearly of most importance: her recent appointment as President of the city Women's Garden Guild.

"I'll be doing a great deal of entertaining and fund-raising. It's quite a responsibility."

"I'm sure it is," Jasmine said as Sandra paused to take a bite of a sandwich. There was a definite tinge of sarcasm in her tone, and Emma immediately asked her if she could fetch the plate of squares and cookies from the kitchen, which she did.

"And what are you up to these days, Jasmine?" Sandra inquired when she returned, taking a brownie from the proffered plate. It was the first question she had asked of any of them since her arrival, and there was a knife-edge to her voice.

Jasmine was unruffled. "I've been in the casino business in Los Vegas," she said coolly. "I expect I'll return there after my visit with Aunt Emma."

Anna and Emma both stared at Jasmine. The lucidity of her answer had startled them. Sandra's hand, in the process of lifting the brownie to her mouth, stopped in mid-air. She turned to look at Jasmine in amazement, but quickly recovered. "How interesting. We'll have to talk about that some time."

She moved on to other topics, asking Emma and Anna a few desultory questions. Then she casually remarked, "what a lovely Crown Derby tea service you have, Emma."

Emma felt twinges of alarm. Was she going to take the tea things right off the table? But no, as it turned out, this was the lead up to quite a different request.

"Seeing as you have such good china for entertaining, I hope you won't mind if I take my mother's silver tea service today," Sandra said brightly. "You know I wouldn't take anything you really needed. Several fundraising events are coming up soon, and you can be sure it will be put to good use."

Heavy with ornate grape and vine figuring, the antique sterling silver tea service Margery and Jasmine had polished up shone resplendent on the sideboard. Emma had never thought to put it away. Now she sat aghast, wondering how to handle this latest raid on her prized possessions. "I'm sorry Sandra," she said eventually, "that tea set has been in our family for generations."

Gently but implacably, Sandra persisted. "There were so many at that time that looked identical; but I have the clearest memories of my mother at her tea parties using that service."

Emma had never noticed that Jasmine had left the table. Now, as she sat numbly staring at Sandra's set face, Jasmine slowly walked back in from the living room, leafing through one of the family albums she and Margery had put together. She found the page she wanted, then wordlessly placed the open album in front of Sandra. She pointed to the photograph, yellowed with age that showed her grandmother and great grandmother, barely out of the Victorian era with their heavy coiffures and long dresses, seated at a table. On it was the tea service Sandra was now claiming as hers.

"Great grandmother's 80th birthday," Jasmine said, sliding the photograph out of its black paper corners and turning it over to show the caption and date.

And now Sandra truly astounded them. She showed absolutely no trace of chagrin, no embarrassment at her mistake. She gave a merry trill of laughter. "My goodness, you're absolutely right! It has been in your family for a long time! I guess that my mother must have borrowed it, or something like it, because loaning out tea services was often done back then, wasn't it Emma?"

Emma nodded yes. It was true then, and in fact still was. Her silver tea service went to almost as many social events as she did.

"And I'd like to ask that same favour of you, dear Emma. Because I really do need it, and for a good cause," Sandra's voice was soft but there was steel in it. "Could you possibly lend it to me for my term as President of the Guild? Just for two years?"

Emma could easily see two years stretching into infinity. However, she was sideswiped by this new tactic Sandra had so cleverly devised. There was no way for her to politely say no. "Well, if it's just for two years – "

"I'm afraid not, Sandra." The words came from Jasmine. She had moved to stand towering over Sandra and spoke with decisive authority. "That tea service was inherited by my mother. Aunt Emma is keeping it for me, and even though she uses it herself, it's really not hers to lend. And I will not loan it to you. So, I'm afraid you're out of luck."

Sandra looked up at her. She was unable to conceal her dismay. Her mouth turned down bitterly. "Well, I'm sure you'll make good use of it at the casino," she said in a voice dripping with sarcasm.

Now Jasmine was smiling, a quite unpleasant smile. "Maybe I will, and maybe I won't. But one thing I know for sure: you should be ashamed of yourself, treating your stepmother's home like your personal warehouse. Emma gave your father some of the best years of his life, and she was no pauper when she married him; she had a job and a house of her own."

"A boarding house."

It just slipped out, Emma could tell, and it seemed that even Sandra herself was astonished at what she had said; her mouth now forming a round O of surprise.

But it was like a signal; as if Sandra had knocked over some final marker of what could and couldn't be tolerated. Emma watched in fascination as Anna rose from her place and came around the table. Jasmine was still standing behind Sandra's chair, and together they pulled it out.

"You've worn out your welcome and it's time for you to leave," Jasmine said.

"And don't come back until you've apologized to your stepmother," Anna added in a severe tone.

"You won't throw me out of my old house, my family home!" Sandra squeaked.

"It isn't your house right now. And it may never be," Jasmine said evenly. "If you keep packing on weight like that, Aunt Emma will probably outlive you."

Sandra stood up and left in silence. She cast one last baleful glance at Jasmine, who had begun to collect the plates and cups from the table and barely looked up to see her leave. There was a resounding slam as the front door closed. Jasmine went into the kitchen and began the wash-up. Anna came back and sat down with Emma, who was speechless. They listened as a car started up and drove away.

Anna leaned across the table toward Emma. Her face was pinched and white.

"Who," she asked in a voice barely above a whisper, "is—that—woman?"

* * *

Her bedroom was dim and cool. It was the refuge she needed, had waited for, in order to gather the scattered threads of her thoughts. Emma stared into the darkness and felt rather sorrowful. Sandra's visits, even if they were extractive, had allowed her to pretend she had a relationship with Bill's daughter. Dear Bill. Yet another tie to you that's come undone. The next time she and Sandra found themselves in the same room, Emma thought, I will probably be in a coffin.

Then there were other emotions not so familiar as sorrow. Astonishment. And an unpleasant and disconcerting prickle of fright at the Jekyll-and-Hyde suddenness of the change in Jasmine.

Lying in bed, Emma crossed her hands on her chest, an almost instinctive reaction. She remembered that the doctor had told her Jasmine's recovery could be slow or fast, a month, a year. "It's different for everyone," he said.

But how to explain the transformation, so startling, of Jasmine – who in the morning had been her usual vague and unfocused self, barely able to string her thoughts into a coherent sentence – into the strong, articulate woman of this afternoon? A clever woman, with a streak of ruthlessness and no scruples about telling a lie. Because Emma distinctly remembered that, after they had finished polishing it, she had told Jasmine and Margery her mother had given her the tea service. Sylvia got the French Aubusson carpets.

It was the look on Sandra's face as she left the dining room that truly summed it up. It was not exactly a look of defeat. Rather, it was a sullen awareness that she had been bested by an opponent who was more formidable than she.

Sleep that night came as swiftly as the flutter of an eyelid. When the morning sun shone through the open drapes, Emma awoke wondering whom she might meet at the breakfast table. As it turned out, however, Jasmine had no real memory of what she had said and done the previous day, or so she claimed, and Emma was inclined to believe her.

Without the stimulus of a worthy adversary, perhaps, she became again the non-communicative, docile individual Emma and Anna had known before. Once having seen a different Jasmine, though, both of them began waiting uneasily for that stranger to reappear.

CHAPTER 30

Ding-dong.

Emma was up to her elbows in greasy dishwater when she heard the doorbell chime. Jasmine ran to open the door.

"Who are you?"

"Hello Jasmine, I'm Arlena Stoddart. I think Anna told you I was coming. Can I come in?"

Jasmine had the door barely open and now she shut it in Arlena's face. Arlena heard the muffled exclamation: "Go away!"

Almost immediately the door swung open again. "Arlena, I'm sorry," said Emma, wiping her hands on her apron. "Do come in. We told Jasmine you would be here tonight, but it appears she's forgotten."

From the entrance, Arlena could see Jasmine's retreating back. They caught up to her in the living room, where she was sitting in an overstuffed chair next to a big floor radio and twisting her hands in her lap.

The phone rang, two longs and one short. "Oh dear," Emma said.

"Go ahead and answer it, we'll be alright," Arlena reassured her. Alone with Jasmine, she was silent for a moment. Jasmine was looking straight ahead, not paying her any attention. Despite the dark smudges around her eyes and although she was fragile-looking and too thin, Jasmine seemed to Arlena one of the most beautiful women she had ever seen. She had hair of a goldy-copper brown, and tip-tilted, tawny eyes a shade lighter. She was exotic, like a strange flower. Arlena felt they might be two of the same kind, both of them out of place in the dull grey world they found themselves in. Except that Arlena couldn't see herself as a flower – more as an unruly weed or shrub her mother longed to prune, clip and shape into something ornamental.

"Jaz, a while ago, Anna asked me if I could stay with you nights. I'll be in the little cot your Aunt Emma was sleeping in."

"I don't want you. Go home."

"Please don't make me go home. I don't want to go home."

Jasmine finally turned to look at her. "Why?"

"My mother and I don't get along. A lot of the time, I don't want to be in the same house as her."

Jasmine turned away again.

"Just for one night," she said.

* * *

As she lay in the small cot near the foot of Jasmine's bed, Arlena contemplated a sweet little slip of a moon shining through the bedroom window. Jasmine would not let her draw the curtains. She also insisted on a night-light. The result was Arlena was almost constantly awake and on alert, which was just as well because once again, here was Jasmine out of bed and poised for another midnight meander.

"Jaz, please get back in bed. It's one o'clock in the morning and everyone is sleeping."

It took no small measure of persuasion and the locking of the bedroom door to convince Jasmine that bed was her only alternative. Back in her cot with the key on a leather thong around her neck, Arlena once again asked herself: why she had been so stupid as to offer to help?

* * *

A bright half-moon illuminated Jasmine in her white nightgown, framed in the doorway.

"Jaz, are you up again? Do you have to go to the bathroom?" This time the creak of the bedroom door was the sound that lanced Arlena's dreams. "I'll come and wait for you." She scrambled out of her covers. "Your aunt told me the last time she let you go alone you lit out down the stairs and tried to get out the front door."

"I'm not doing that anymore! Why are you here anyway?" Jasmine turned to hiss at her. "I don't want your help!"

By now Arlena, sleep deprived and thoroughly fed up with her charge's self-absorption, was well primed for a rant. "Well, maybe you don't, but your aunt does! She has bags under her eyes from getting up with you all the time, taking care of you and your daughter all day and then always having to put you back in your bed at night! That's why I'm here!"

"Oh. Well. Alright." And for the first time, Arlena detected in Jasmine's voice a shade of apology, a hint of shame.

* * *

Her job at her father's insurance office was boring enough. However, with her nighttime duties it had become positively soporific and Arlena found that when she was at her desk, like cows and horses, she had mastered the art of sleeping upright. Then, finally, finally, it happened: one night, then another of deep, unbroken sleep, even with a full moon shining directly down on her closed eyes.

"You're sleeping better, aren't you, Jasmine? It's been weeks since I came here, and for some nights now you haven't gotten up at all," Arlena observed, during one of their increasingly rare times of wakefulness. "So – do you still want me to leave?"

"No. It's kind of comforting to have you here. Also, you don't snore like Aunt Emma does." There was a smile in the voice coming out of the darkness.

"Ha! Well – I do like being here," Arlena admitted. "Talking with you, it's like having a sister. Althea was married and gone when I was still a kid, so I've missed that. Mason and I are close, though. But speaking of Mason, you've never asked me anything about him. Aren't you curious?"

"No." Spoken with an emphasis that left no room for doubt. "I'm only curious about his wife. Catharine. The woman your mother chose for him. What's she like?"

There was a short, uncomfortable silence. Arlena didn't much care for her sister-in-law, and was finding it hard to be fair. "Catharine's attractive enough. To talk to, she's rather dull. She shops, golfs, and goes to her hairdresser. So far as I can see, she takes good care of herself and not much else. Mason spends more time with his boys than she does."

Now Arlena felt she might safely do what Mason had been pestering her about. "He's been asking after you," she said.

"I don't want anything to do with your brother. I hope you haven't told him anything about me."

"No. Like I told you, I promised Anna to keep my mouth shut." Arlena sat up to deliver the rest of this speech. "You know – what happened, back then, Jaz – it wasn't so much Mason's fault as my mother's, his going away."

"Don't make excuses for him. He was a grown man." Jasmine was clearly annoyed now, her tone frosty and dismissive.

"Sure. I'm sorry. But – he's asked if, sometime, he could talk to you. What should I tell him?" There. She had done it. Although Arlena had already guessed Jasmine's answer and that it would not make her brother happy.

"There's nothing he can say that I want to hear. If you must tell him something, you can tell him to go to hell."

"Ha! Well, I guess you think he deserves that. But I'll go you one better. How about I tell both him and my mother to go to hell? Let's include the two of them on that trip!"

Emma, who had trained her ears to listen for stealthy footsteps, and as a result now slept lightly, awoke just after midnight to hear the sound of faint laughter drifting down the hall.

Arlena saw her brother the following day. So that he would no longer ask her to be an intermediary, she had decided not to spare him Jasmine's harsh words. Mason showed no surprise. He only looked at Arlena with weary eyes and smiled a little sadly.

"Tell her for me," he said, "that I think I might already be close to it."

CHAPTER 31

The winter had worn away and with it, the time of ice was drawing to a close. Laura had learned the many kinds and had her favorites. Rubber ice, bouncy, excitingly treacherous and unstable, was a new addition. Before that there was the thin, brittle ice that tinkled like glass when shattered by kicking or jumping; plate glass ice, good for windows in snow forts, and icicles of various sizes, shapes and flavors from smoky to slightly sweet. What the child loved best was clear ice, frozen deep and thick, which, when struck with the edge of a sharp heel on a sunny day, would fracture into a magical prism of rainbow colors.

All these delights were melting away, along with the sparse snow that now lay in silver filigree patches beneath the pines and other shadowy places. Although there was less to do outside, after coming home from school Laura went out anyway because it seemed she could never get enough of freedom and open spaces.

She was happy in a way she had seldom been before. The fear she carried with her, like the alertness of a bird or a small animal, was slumbering temporarily. It occasionally quickened when the child saw her mother returning to be herself again and she wondered what might come next. For now, however, she warmed herself daily in the sun of her Aunt Emma's unstinting love and affection, which beamed down on her in innumerable different ways: the hot lunches, the cookies and cocoa at the end of the school day, the hand-knit mitts and sweaters, bubble baths, bedtime stories, hugs, embraces and above all her Aunt's enjoyment, so obvious, of the child herself and seemingly almost everything she said or did.

Emma was peeling potatoes over the kitchen sink and looking through the window at her great niece, sitting in the sunshine on the dry brown grass underneath the old chestnut tree at the side of the yard. She sighed. There was no one for the child to play with nearby, except for a pack of ruffianly looking little boys she occasionally spied up to some devilment in the lakeside park. The only little girl in whom the child had the slightest interest was Anna's daughter, Mary. They had got on together like a house on fire, right from the first time they met; but she lived too far away for after-school play.

Now, if the weather was good, the child mostly busied herself skipping, climbing, sitting with a book or whittling with her pocketknife under the chestnut tree until it was time to come in for dinner. When Emma asked her why she always chose that tree, the child had said, rather defensively, something strange: "Because it's a friendly tree and it likes me."

Emma had laughed at this charming whimsy. But she would remember it later when the old tree, never very fruitful, produced an extraordinary number of candle-like blooms in late spring and then, in the fall, for Laura's delight, an abundance of glossy chestnuts – more than Emma could ever recall.

Now, as she watched Laura bent over her carving, she saw a flash of color behind the hedge at the far end of the garden. A boy stepped out, appeared to hesitate and then walked up behind the tree where the child was seated. Emma recognized him immediately. With his dirty blond hair and oddly assorted clothes, he had to be one of the Fitzgerald boys. There were three of them and one girl, the children of Evan Fitzgerald, whose wife, May, had run off four years ago this spring.

It was the talk of the town when it happened; the more so because May had left with the town's window man, Jerry, who put up the storm windows in the fall and took them off for summer. As a result, many Medford residents were left to swelter in their overheated homes that summer and few had kind words for May. Still, Emma had no idea how May had managed to put up with her red-faced, choleric husband long enough to bear him so many children. She recently heard a rumour he had lost yet another housekeeper; that would make five so far.

All this went through her mind as she watched the boy jump out from behind the tree. Laura did not appear to be surprised to see him there. They talked for a short while, then both of them disappeared into the hedges and brush that served as informal fences for the large, sprawling properties in this old part of the town.

* * *

"Scared ja!"

"No you didn't. I heard you coming."

"Whadja doing?"

"Making a slingshot."

"Not bad."

The child looked at the boy as he examined her handiwork. She knew him from school. He was in the next class up and they had never spoken before. His hair was an uncombed tumble of dark blonde curls. He had a sprinkle of freckles across his nose and was missing one front tooth.

"Come with me. I wanna show you something," he said.

"What?"

"Can't tell you. Have t' show you."

The boy led her behind the tall, dense cedars to a rough pathway. There he took down his pants and showed her his penis.

"It isn't very big, is it?"

The boy's face clearly showed his disappointment. The child saw his cheeks blushing red as he tucked his equipment away, and was sorry for the bluntness of her words.

"Don't worry," she said kindly, "it will grow."

To cover up his embarrassment, the boy said something that he almost instantly regretted. "We're building a fort. Do you want ta' come help?"

"Sure!" she said. There was still an hour before dinner, and she was tired of whittling anyhow. She followed him as he loped off along the trail behind the cedars. He led the way in silence, because now he was trying to think of just how to explain her to the other guys.

The trail soon ended at a road that sloped down a hill to some derelict buildings. Between them was a small ravine, and it was here that two boys were busily engaged in interlacing brambles and branches over a skeleton of scrap lumber to make a good-sized hut. They all turned and stared at Laura with a look of something approaching horror.

"A girl!" one of them exclaimed unnecessarily.

The child ignored the unfriendly faces. The hut was the first she had seen so far that looked as if it might last for longer than a week, and she walked around it. "Good fort!" she said admiringly, and the hard faces around her softened. "But it needs a roof," she added, and their expressions changed once more.

One of the larger boys said scornfully, "so go find one then, if you know so much."

"I know where there's some straw," said the child helpfully. "It's not far away. It would make a good roof and we can use it to fill in some of the holes on the sides."

The straw was spread around the foundation of a brick house nearby, one of the oldest in the neighbourhood. The retired farmer who lived there told all who inquired about this practice that, once covered with snow in winter, it helped keep out the cold and drafts. But now it was spring, and to Laura's way of thinking the straw was no longer needed. Using a couple of burlap bags they found in the yard and an old sheet, the children had hauled away just about all the straw they needed to complete the hut when the farmer's wife ran squawking into the yard and chased them, hollering that they were stealing the straw she needed for her strawberry patch and vegetable garden.

To the little gang of three boys and one girl running, tripping, shouting to each other and whooping with laughter as they raced pell-mell down the hill, it seemed like a perfectly splendid end to a beautiful spring afternoon.

Suppertime. From 5:30 to six o'clock, all over the neighbourhood, whistles blew and dinner bells rang to summon children from their play. Emma surveyed her great niece, who had just arrived home with straw in her hair and down the front of her jacket and mud up to her knees. She asked very few questions as she helped her clean up for dinner. She only looked at the child's flushed and beaming small face. Then she gently wiped it free of the largest and dirtiest smudges while, smiling broadly, she drank in its gladness.

CHAPTER 32

Lianne Latham sat in the large, pillowy chair in the spare bedroom, at the window that overlooked the street. On her good days, of which this was not one, she would go downstairs with Thomas's help and sit in the sunroom after breakfast until Mrs. Mackie arrived. Today, sick and weak, she had left her half-eaten meal on a tray on the bed. Wrapped in her housecoat, Lianne was watching people in the land of living go about their business.

There was Lorena Sykes, on her way to work. Letty Lawson off shopping, her trundle cart rolling behind her. Mainly, though, Lianne was hoping to catch a glimpse of Laura Carlisle. And yes, there she was, on her way to school some six blocks away, walking along by herself. As Lianne watched, she saw the child take a few quick steps, then gather her feet under her and begin to run, fluidly and effortlessly, her long legs flashing as they carried her away into the distance. It was still early for school and from the look of her, Lianne guessed she must be running just for the sheer pleasure of it. For a moment, she enjoyed the remembered thrill of that feeling, of feet as light as air, and the air rushing by.

The child had the same blue-black hair as her husband, the same colouring. But perhaps she was just hoping for resemblances. Lianne thought of Thomas as he was this morning, so bereft of joy, his shoulders taking on an old man's hunch with the weight of his disappointment and discouragement. Yesterday they had found out: the principalship he had wanted and worked so hard for had been given to Mike Simms. The status quo would be maintained; Medford High would continue to plod along, indistinguishable from any other high school in the quality of its teaching and the engagement of its students. Thomas had taken so many courses, done so much reading and had so many good ideas; now, seemingly, it was all for naught.

And soon she would be gone too, Lianne thought. Then what would happen to the good man she loved with all her heart, as he had her, ever since they were young teenagers? They had ever been inseparable and sometimes, when he wasn't aware of being watched, she saw his face and could take the measure of what her loss would cost him.

Thomas was passionate: he loved deeply, felt deeply: that was his character and had more than once been his downfall. Should his heart follow her into the grave, Lianne suspected the rest of him would not be not far behind.

She rallied her energy. Reluctantly, she left the window to return to what she now thought of as the land of the almost dead – her bed. It was one effect of her prolonged illness that Lianne had become incredibly sick of thinking about herself and her condition. It had been so much a topic with the both of them, that, as she told Thomas, it was literally boring her to death.

Instead, for some time now, all her energy and concern had been for her husband. An idea was beginning to dawn, take shape, although it needed more work. In fact, she thought, she may just have found a way to trick fate, or whatever that malignant entity was that had laid them low so often. Yes, trick it into keeping him alive, in the land of the living; and not just as an empty shell, or one filled with bitterness, but vital, full of life – the man that even now she was losing.

As she settled into her pillows, Lianne wondered how much time she had, and thought about the days to come. Some of them were bound to be better; she would have more energy. And if she did nothing else with this particular morning, she decided, she would use her time to plan what might happen then.

* * *

Downstairs after finishing his morning housekeeping chores, Thomas sat at the kitchen table and gazed into the greening garden. He was not thinking of school, his loss of the principal's job or even, at that moment, of Lianne. He was remembering, in some detail, the dream that troubled his sleep last night following the one, fleeting glimpse he had caught of Jasmine Holmes as she and Anna went up the stairs of Emma's house yesterday.

He had awoken from it abruptly and too early; now he was edgy, jittery, unable to concentrate fully on the work before him. He must never, would never, have anything more to do with Jasmine Holmes. But although he was able to dispel his waking thoughts of her, still she must come in dreams to disturb his peace of mind and body.

Mrs. Mackie had arrived early and was bustling around the kitchen. She had put the ancient tin kettle on to boil to make tea for Lianne. Its bottom was uneven, and as it heated up it rocked and vibrated and made a light humming sound. It so exactly matched Thomas's state, full of unexpressed energy, that he half-smiled.

But all this disturbance was temporary. In the distance, drawing nearer with each passing day, was a vast, dark, cold lake of grief and loss. When he reached it, Thomas had learned from experience, it would effectively extinguish the sensations that now caused him such discomfort. For the present, however, he knew what he must do.

Put a lid on it.

He looked at the kitchen clock. It was getting late. He gathered up his papers and left for his first class.

CHAPTER 33

It was almost three months since Jasmine's return to Medford. To Emma, whose days were long and full of care, the time had seemed to pass with leaden slowness. Then, amazingly, suddenly, in a matter of a few weeks, Jasmine was well. Her caregivers had exchanged notes and they marveled at the rapid progress of her recovery once it took hold.

"Look at her eyes," Anna remarked to Emma. "The windows of the soul, they call them, and now I do have to believe it's true!"

Emma had noticed. Dulled to a muddy yellow by her illness, Jasmine's eyes had cleared to regain their unusual colour, a light-filled, golden amber. The dark circles beneath them disappeared. By virtue of Emma's good cooking, she had also put on some weight. Her features were filling out, her high colouring had returned and even now she was almost as beautiful as ever they could remember.

Emma felt it was like watching someone swim underwater for a long while, then rise rapidly from the depths and burst through the surface: a sudden and somewhat shocking transition to a different medium, which, in this case, was the everyday world. At the same time, Jasmine's docility and vagueness, rather desirable traits so far as Emma was concerned, were quickly disappearing.

In the kitchen: "this soup definitely needs more salt," she would say, then, without so much as a by-your-leave, put almost a half teaspoon of salt in a soup Emma had thought quite salty enough already. Or, "chicken again?" she would query, with a look of distaste at the tasty hot meal Emma had prepared, cooked and set before her.

"Don't you think this room could use a little freshening up?" was her tart comment on her bedroom, formerly Emma's. Emma's quick response was to move Jasmine into the spare room she currently was occupying, as "fresher and brighter". She never would change the décor of her old bedroom, which contained so many memories of happy days with Bill.

But it was in matters of childcare that Emma most missed the old Jasmine who, caught up as she once was in the whirling, churning merry-go-round of her unsettled mind, formerly took little interest in her daughter.

"Goodness, what's that outfit you're putting on the child!" Jasmine would exclaim. "She looks like a schoolgirl from 40 years ago!"

Then, muttering, she would find something more to her liking, make Laura undress and dress again before sending her out the door with only minutes to spare before the school bell.

"Too many baths! You'll dry out her skin!" Emma promptly pulled the plug and left Jasmine to try and clean with just a washcloth a child who looked as if she had rolled in mud. In fact, these days, as the only girl in a gang of small boys, the amount of fun Laura had seemed to be in direct proportion to how dirty she was when she arrived home.

For the most part, however, Emma maintained her good humour and equanimity – except for yesterday, when she flew into a rare temper after Jasmine answered the phone and loudly announced, "It's that old cow, Ida Maxwell."

Luckily Ida, who was a little deaf, seemed not to hear, even if those listening in on the line probably did. When reprimanded, however, Jasmine would not apologize. Instead she imitated Ida's voice, low and lugubrious, then made a mooing sound identical in tone and intonation. Emma was not amused.

With Jasmine's sharpening mind came an increased need for entertainment and diversion. The upside of this, for Emma, was that once the child was in bed most evenings were spent playing cards. After expertly shuffling the deck, Jasmine led them through the intricacies of Baccarat, Pinochle and many variations on the game of poker. There was one game at which she was practically unbeatable: Blackjack, where she amazed Emma and Arlena by her ability to remember cards.

"It's not really that surprising," Jasmine said, declining praise. "Mom taught me. By the age of ten I was playing bridge whenever she needed a fourth."

However, she would not talk about her past or tell them where or how she had come by her extensive knowledge of so many card games. And Emma, seeing her increasing alertness and ability to concentrate, knew that soon Jasmine would be preparing to leave and that almost any day now, she would ask her the important question she had so long dreaded answering.

CHAPTER 34

Medford had once been a tiny village. As it grew, it expanded to encompass the lands still held by one of its original settlers, the Airdrie family. Isolated in its privacy and seclusion from the town, their estate sat on forty acres overlooking the lake. A rolling expanse of manicured lawns, winding roads lined by flowerbeds, and dense woodland, the entire property was surrounded on three sides by a thick, eight-foot high stone wall. The last time the grounds had been open to the public, in a fundraiser for the local hospital six years ago, some visitors expressed surprise at how low, squat, and actually rather ugly the grey limestone manor house was. But then, it had not been constructed so much for appearances as to weather the violent gales that roared in from across the great lake. The lawn in back of the manse terminated in a wide breakwater constructed of huge, sun-bleached stones. Before the lake froze and during the storms of early winter, sometimes even this formidable barrier was not sufficient to keep the waves from tossing spume and spray to sheath the back of the house in ice.

The estate even had its own small harbour, and a stone warehouse beside a large dock. The family claimed to have made their first fortune in lumber before expanding into various other business enterprises. But as Anna and Jasmine peered through the large, wrought iron gates that afforded the best view, they agreed it was easier to believe the rumour that prohibition-era liquor smuggling had been the early foundation for the Airdrie empire.

They were on their afternoon walk, which usually included a stop at St. Margaret's School to pick up Laura after school ended. Today, however, was unusually fine, with plenty of glorious sunshine and fat little white clouds being shepherded across a brilliant sky by a warm wind, and Jasmine wanted to see the early daffodils in bloom in the Airdrie gardens. Waves of light perfume reached them as they stood at the gate and watched the fields of daffodils, a yellow ocean billowing in the wind against the deep blue lake rolling with whitecaps beyond.

"How often does the family come?" Jasmine inquired as they turned away.

"Almost never, a weekend or two a month, depending on the weather," Anna answered. The gate at which they had stood was at one end of the property. Next to it was the little gatehouse, nestled into a corner of the wall. Anna was secretly glad there was no sign of life. Royce was probably busy elsewhere on the estate. She had no desire to see him, and especially did not want him to see her and Jasmine together.

Just then a small girl with short flaxen hair, no older than five or six, came from across the street with her younger brother of perhaps three. She paid no attention to them. With practiced ease, she lifted the latch to open the rounded wood door in the stone wall next to the gate house. Then, leaving the door open, she ushered her brother through and along a narrow cobble path that led to the garden behind the gatehouse, and disappeared.

To Jasmine's raised eyebrows and questioning glance, Anna said, "Royce has baby chicks and bunnies in his back garden, and I guess they're a bit of a magnet for the local children. He also has a new rabbit hutch he made himself. He told me that in the old days the gardeners used to supply the great house with eggs and chickens, and since there was quite a large hen house not being used, he restored it. And now the Airdries are letting him sell the eggs, so long as he supplies their kitchen when they come."

"It's a little extra income – not that I'm seeing any of it," she added sourly.

Jasmine was still staring after the vanished children. "Somehow," she said slowly, "I never saw Royce as being all that interested in spending time with children. But I guess you'd know better than me."

She was curious. "How is he with his own children, anyhow? Is he a good father?"

"Not particularly," Anna said, "especially when I compare him with my dad. However, he more or less does what's expected of him when he's home, though he has always tended to favour Mark. But recently, now that Mary is getting older and has more to say for herself, he's gotten more interested in her."

She shrugged her shoulders dismissively. She wanted to leave. "He says lots of kids come to pick up eggs for the family and see the chicks and bunnies, so I guess he's grown fond of them."

In the short time they lived together after they left Medford, Jasmine had come to know Royce quite well enough. Her opinion was that there was only one thing he was truly fond of, with some of its more distasteful variations. That had been one of the compelling reasons she had literally shoved him out the door and off to Anna, with the hope that the responsibilities of parenthood might help settle him down.

"Just a minute, Anna. I want to see something."

Jasmine walked through the weathered wood door the little girl had left open. The cobblestone path soon ended at another gate in a tall fence that enclosed the garden belonging to the gatehouse. The child had left this gate open, too, and from this vantage point Jasmine could view the wide expanse of the caretaker's garden. She saw the two youngsters at the hutch, watching the rabbits hop about. Beside that was the henhouse. As well, there was a vegetable garden, and in one corner a plum tree, now in early flower and buzzing with bees. Near the house was a little stone patio and a large, comfortable looking wood bench partially shaded from the sun by the trees outside the wall.

"Well?" asked Anna.

Jasmine had rejoined her on the sidewalk. "That's a very pretty little garden," she said.

"Yes," responded Anna, rather bitterly. "He's made himself quite a nice nest."

Or web, Jasmine thought, with the image of the children disappearing into that enclosed space still vivid in her mind.

Anna was fidgety, anxious not to be seen should Royce approach. "Let's go sit in Airdrie park for a moment," she suggested.

Next to the estate was some land that had been donated to Medford by the Airdrie family. The town had wisely left the small park mostly in a state of nature. At the shoreline, the stones had been cleared away to create a small beach. A young mother was resting on the fine sand, watching her little boy throw stones into the water. Jasmine and Anna sat a short distance away, on a bench surrounded by fine, high grass near a massive willow. Its tent of long, trailing branches, newly in leaf, gave them some protection from the cool breeze off the lake.

"Jaz," Anna said, "Now that you're so much better, I've been looking for another job. And just a few days ago I was offered one. So, I wanted to tell you that next week will be my last with you and Emma. I hope you won't mind."

"No, of course not, Anna, though I'll miss you," Jasmine replied. "I've more or less been expecting it. What will you be doing?"

"I'm going to be an office nurse for awhile, replacing Doctor Miller's regular nurse who's having a baby soon," Anna replied. "It's closer to home. I'll miss you too, but I sure won't miss that mile-and-a-half back and forth to Emma's every day!"

So much for practical matters. Anna let the silence between them grow for a few moments, as they listened to the waves crashing on the breakfront nearby. Then, as casually as she could manage, she said, "Jasmine – would you mind if I ask you a few questions about Royce? About what happened back then?"

Jasmine did not look at her, but nodded. "It's alright. Yes. Go ahead."

"Can you tell me why Royce left you and came back to me?"

"I made him do it," Jasmine said without hesitation. "Once I found out from my mother that you were expecting, I told him I didn't want him around, that he had to leave and face up to his responsibilities. Then we had a scene, and I threw him out and he didn't have anywhere else to go, so he went back."

Anna gave a short, mirthless laugh. "That's what I suspected. But it's not what he told me, of course. He said he had second thoughts, and that he loved me, and he wanted to do right by me."

There was a brief moment of silence while they took stock of times past and possibly best forgotten. Then Anna asked, "Was there a reason you took Royce with you when you left town? From what I saw, I didn't think you were all that interested in him."

"Well, he had a car."

Anna looked sharply at her cousin, and then they both laughed.

"The reason," Jasmine said, fully serious now, "is that I knew, probably better than you did, that he was a skunk, a low-life, and I didn't want you to marry him. If you remember, it was in my crazy time after Dad died and Mason broke off with me. By then, I had burnt all my bridges in Medford and I was leaving anyhow, so I thought I'd do you a large favour and take him along with me."

"That's it?" Anna asked, but she already knew the explanation was that simple; it had the ring of truth.

"I did it because I figured that you would be angry at me, and probably upset for a while, but that eventually you would find someone else," Jasmine continued. "Someone better, a man who would be good to you."

"But then, of course, I found out you were pregnant."

Anna put her hand over Jasmine's. Her eyes were full of tears.

"What really puzzles me," Jasmine continued, "was why you ever wanted anything to do with him in the first place!"

"Well," Anna said, half-smiling, "he was good looking. Very good looking. And is, or was, until he got that front tooth knocked out. Now, it's almost funny, how women stare at him, right up until he opens his mouth, and then almost immediately, they all look away – but back then he was glamorous, or seemed that way to me. He was a couple of years older and had a good job at the cannery, and of course he had that car – that souped up red Ford convertible – and he was sort of a bad boy. I was a bit rebellious then, too. My parents didn't like him, of course. So we snuck around, and he kept at me, and at me, and then it happened – "

"But it wasn't like that," Jasmine said, her mouth tight. "It didn't just happen. Did it? He forced you into it, didn't he?"

"Yes," said Anna, her tears freely rolling now, "I didn't want to, but he made me do it, it was my very first time and then I found out I was pregnant, and oh! The pain and trouble I caused my Mom and Dad!"

There was another quiet moment, while the wind blew and the sun shone and the lake sparkled sapphire and silver. "Another thing I don't understand," Jasmine said, "is why, knowing what you did about him, how he goes after other women, cheats and lies – you still went on to have more children with him – your son and daughter."

Anna had dried her tears and was sitting up straight, recovered and back to normal. "Divorce isn't a choice for me. And by that time I had my nursing papers and could work part-time. He was making decent wages and he was better, then – well, not so bad, or nothing that I knew about, anyhow! I wasn't getting any younger, and I wanted my children. No regrets about that, at least."

By the slant of the sun's rays, they could tell the bell would soon ring to signal the end of the school day. Together, without need for a word, they stood up and left the park.

As they walked along the tree-lined street past the grand old homes that lined the way to the lakefront, Anna said gently, "I hope this hasn't stirred up too many bad memories for you – all this talk of the past."

Jasmine gave a short laugh. "It's not memories of Medford that caused my latest troubles, Anna. But thanks for being considerate. And also, I wanted to thank you for everything you've done for me. Oh, I know Emma has given you something, but you've really gone far and beyond to help me get well! One day, perhaps, I hope I can pay you back."

Anna turned to look at her out of her great blue eyes. Jasmine saw they had changed. A shadow had fallen over them, and now they were no longer soft and mild but hard and cold.

"You'll be leaving town soon, won't you?" she asked.

"Yes," Jasmine answered.

"I know you can't, but how I wish you could," said Anna, and she grasped Jasmine's hand. "Do it again. Take him with you when you go."

CHAPTER 35

The lawyer's office this Wednesday morning was busy as a doctor's waiting room, full of clients young and old displaying, instead of signs of illness, various symptoms of nervous anxiety. Across from Emma was an elderly man with a sun-beaten face and calloused hands. His wife sat beside him, looking gimlet-grim and determined. Probably here to sign papers for the sale of the farm, Emma guessed. Awkward and uncomfortable in his Sunday-best clothes, the farmer turned his hat round and around in his hands without stopping, so that finally Emma started to feel quite dizzy and had to look away.

Beside her, Jasmine shuffled her feet impatiently. "I really don't see the need for any of this," she said sulkily. "It's a waste of time. You're the executor, why can't you just give me the information?"

And the money, Emma silently added, but then said gently, "it's a little more complicated than you might think. There were various – entanglements with the estate. So I brought in Mr. Chappell to help. He's better versed than I to explain it to you."

At this, Jasmine began to look apprehensive. As well she should, Emma thought. "Oh," she said, and that was the end of her complaints.

After a small eternity they were called into one of the offices. "Sorry for the wait, but it's a madhouse here today," said George, somewhat flustered, running his hands through his sparse blond hair. He was a plump man in his late fifties, with a baby-smooth face that made him look considerably younger. But once he put on his glasses and bent over the file in front of him, a proper set of jowls appeared and Emma thought he had the right air of authority to deliver the news she knew would spell the end to Jasmine's hopes.

However, she certainly had expected he would cushion the blow a little better than to just silently hand Jasmine a cheque.

"That's it?!!" Jasmine exploded when she saw the amount. "It can't be! What about the insurance – the house? The money from the sale of the funeral home business!"

"That's what we thought, too," said George, giving her a sheaf of papers that contained details of how the estate was settled. "Here's my quick explanation of what you'll find in that report. The insurance money – it ended when your mother died. After the funeral home business was sold, your Uncle Bill invested the money for your mother. It did very well for her, but after he passed away, well, not to put too fine a point on it, she made some poor investments handling it on her own. The house – it still had a mortgage, dating from the time your father bought the funeral home in the 'thirties.'

"At the end, your mother was barely keeping her head above water financially. But still, just like you, we wondered where it could have all gone. Luckily, your mother kept good records. We went through her chequebook and, if you look at the last page, you'll see what we found."

At this, George paused while Jasmine found the page. "There it is," he said. "The dates and amounts of money she's sent you. Thousands of dollars in the past two years. You've already had your inheritance, young woman, I'm afraid."

There were a few other details to be covered. Jasmine sat in stunned silence as George explained the small trust fund set aside for her daughter, Laura, which she would receive when she was twenty-one, and set different papers in front of her for a signature. Jasmine did not read these but just carelessly signed them away, impatient, plainly wanting only to leave.

Finally, when it seemed the ordeal might be over. George stood up, but then waved them down when they made to rise as well. "There's just one more thing," he said, and went to a large safe that stood in the corner of the room. After opening it, he took out a square box covered in dark blue velvet and handed it to Jasmine. "Your mother's jewelry. Your Aunt gave it to me for safekeeping."

Jasmine opened the box. It was full, and inside were numerous rings, pins, bracelets and necklaces, many of them familiar to Emma as coming from her mother's things passed down to Sylvia.

"Of course you may want to keep them, but there's some good value there if you prefer the money – at least equal to what you received in that cheque. You could handle it on your own, but you'll do better if you use an agent to sell it; and I know someone in the city who's trustworthy and would do a good job."

George wrote out a name, phone number and address; then, murmuring his goodbyes and with a last, more-or-less sympathetic look at Jasmine, left them alone in the office.

"Did you see that letter?" Emma had spied a sealed envelope folded to fit inside the lid of the box. Now Jasmine opened the box again, and took out the envelope, which contained just one sheet of paper. She unfolded it. "Dearest daughter," she read aloud. "These jewels are not nearly as beautiful as you, but wear them in good health. I love you with all my heart and soul and always will. Mother."

She folded the paper up again and tucked it away. Now her tears began, the ones Emma had been waiting for, for so long. At last, Emma thought, she's crying for her mother. For losing the one parent who loved her so dearly; the one who gave her everything for her.

But, no.

"Oh, I'm so disappointed," Jasmine sobbed. "I've been counting on that money to get out of this hick town, and now there's barely enough to last a few months, let alone rent a decent apartment and set myself up someplace where I can find a good job."

Emma's compassion immediately evaporated. She stood up. "Well," she said briskly, "You can stay with me until you figure out what you're going to do. You should stay until Laura finishes her school year in any case. In the meantime, perhaps you can find some work."

Jasmine looked up. She was smiling through her tears. "I don't think there's much work for me here, Aunt Emma. There's just one thing I know how to do really well. And there's probably not much call in Medford for a croupier."

CHAPTER 36

As they walked the few long blocks from the law office to main street, Emma thanked her lucky stars she had the foresight to employ a lawyer. From the expression on Jasmine's face, it was clear that had she a gun, she would have willingly shot Emma if, instead, she had not arranged for George Chappell Esquire, LLB to be the bearer of bad news. But knowing her niece, Emma doubted she had given up all hope of improving her situation. When would she make her next move?

She didn't have long to wait.

"Aunt Emma," Jasmine said, in a voice she somehow managed to make both wheedling and hesitant, "is there any chance – you could perhaps loan me the money, a small loan, so that Laura and I can return to the States, where I can find work?"

Emma was prepared and had her answer ready. "No," she replied, in a tone that left no room for doubt. "I can't do that. My money is all invested. What there is gives me a comfortable income, but there's not much left over at the end of the month. In fact, having you and Laura stay with me is about as much as my budget can manage."

This would be a good time for a thank-you, Emma thought. But it was not to be. Jasmine had sunk once more into sullen silence.

* * *

Their route home took them down the town's main street, busy with cars and pedestrians now that lunch hour was approaching. Emma soon became acutely aware of all the eyes turned in their direction. This was a novelty for an elderly lady who usually felt cloaked in invisibility, except for greetings from the occasional acquaintance. Jasmine, naturally, was the object of attention. Emma soon detected there were different kinds. The women, depending on their ages, gave her measured looks tinged with varying shades of disapproval, dislike, or envy. The men, from youths to elderly gents, stared frankly or cast stealthy glances, their eyes first on her face, then traveling down her body. None failed to notice her.

Emma, who thought Jasmine had thrown herself together rather untidily for the lawyer's office, turned to look. With a stranger's eyes, she attempted to see what it was they saw. A tall woman, with masses of glossy, coppery brown hair. Lovely features: a rather sensual mouth and of course those unforgettable eyes. She wore no makeup except for a cursory dab of lipstick. Her dress, nothing special, could not conceal the lushness of her body: her full figure, small waist, long legs. Emma now saw her niece in a new light and, rather than being envious, felt rather sorry for her. Every time she went out, she would run a gauntlet of glances. She herself would not like that kind of attention, laced with lust and hostility; it was much more comfortable being invisible.

Though once, a good while ago, she too had turned heads. And now that she remembered, she had rather gloried in it. But it was attention of a different sort. Other women generally bloomed in their teens and twenties. For Emma, it had been her forties. Then her face, always a little too round and full, became thinner and her good bone structure emerged to give her a look of some distinction. Along with it was a wonderful head of hair that she knew how to dress well, her commanding height, good posture and something else quite rare in Medford – style. She had always dressed well and with care; and then, when it seemed like it almost didn't matter any more, she began to attract admiring glances from men. One day she looked in the mirror and realized that although she was not beautiful, cute, or lovely, she could now claim that word reserved for large, rather regal women – handsome.

And that was what Bill thought, too. He came often to the library to get books for Eleanor, his sick wife, for himself as well – he especially liked history and detective novels. When Eleanor passed on, and after a decent mourning period during which a number of eligible widows and divorcees shamelessly threw themselves at him, he asked Emma out. She was amused to think that, for him, she was a younger woman. And she was also amused at the barely concealed indignation of the rejected widows and divorcees, who could not believe, "that dried up, almost-spinster librarian" as she once heard herself described, had snagged the grand prize of a widower with a thriving insurance business and a house by the lake.

But she was not "dried up". No, not at all. Together they had lived a wonderful, comfortable, joyous life. As Bill joked, he had always wanted a hot librari—

Emma broke off her pleasant reminiscences. Who was that? A familiar face came into her line of vision as she and Jasmine crossed the street. This one, on seeing them, reacted with a quick flash of recognition, and then, shock. It was Mason Stoddart, his handsome face contorting into some sort of anguish with his first glimpse, in almost ten years, of his lost love.

Emma turned; she saw that Mason had stopped and now stood looking back at them from the sidewalk. They kept walking, and Jasmine was seemingly as oblivious to him as she might have been to any other stranger who stared at her as she passed him by on the street. Was it possible she might not have seen him?

"That was Mason Stoddart," Emma pointed out.

"Yes," said Jasmine, and a small tremor in her voice told Emma that perhaps she was not quite as unaffected as she appeared. "How strange, to see him just as we were crossing the street."

A rather cruel coincidence, Emma thought. Because she knew very well the story of how they met after the war. Sylvia had told it to her several times. She had also told it to Margery, and then to anyone else who might care to know how her daughter had captured the town's most eligible bachelor.

"He was just home and only a week out of uniform," she would say. "They were crossing the street at the same time, Mason going one way,

Jasmine the other. When he saw her, he turned right around in the middle of the street. She was waiting for him on the sidewalk, and they were engaged two months later."

"Why is he limping?" Jasmine asked.

"He was in a car accident," Emma answered shortly. She had bit her tongue to stop herself from almost adding, "in Germany". Jasmine did not need to know the history of that accident, with good reason, and she would keep it from her if she could.

The post office, one of Medford's few imposing buildings, was cool and dim after the glare of the street. The sound of their footsteps on the marble floor echoed off the high ceilings as they approached the one open wicket. The usual clerk, Elwood Maddow, with his frizzy hair and spectacles, was not there. From somewhere in the cavernous rooms beyond, the young new postmaster himself emerged to attend to them. He straightened up smartly when he saw Jasmine, and stared at her in something like disbelief. A smile spread across his face.

"Top o' the mornin' to ye, ladies," he said, rolling the words out and off his tongue in his best Irish brogue.

"More like the bottom, from where I stand," Jasmine responded sourly. The postmaster looked again, sharply, at her downcast face.

Emma put the stamps she had purchased in her purse. As they turned to leave, he spoke again to Jasmine.

"Aye, lassie, I hope your luck improves," he said. "A smile and not a frown t'would better suit yer loverly face." And he gave her a look of such compassion and kindness it melted even Emma's tough old heart.

"Sweet," commented Jasmine, as they went down the stairs.

"Married, with two children and a wife with red hair," Emma responded.

Jasmine gave a half-laugh. "You needn't worry, Auntie. I'm not in the market for postmen. Or for married men either, for that matter."

To which Emma might have tartly added, "anymore". Instead, she took a subtler tack. "I meant to tell you. I thought you should know that Thomas Latham's wife is dying. When I saw Lianne yesterday, she told me herself that the doctors have given her only a few months, more or less. She's asked me to look around for another caregiver, because Mrs. Mackie has told her that her legs are giving out and she can't handle the stairs anymore."

"Well, there's one job I won't be doing for sure!" Jasmine remarked with a sardonic laugh.

Emma herself wasn't so certain. Because, when she had visited Lianne several days ago to drop off some lovely, nourishing chicken soup she had just made, they had discussed a scheme so outlandish that she immediately discarded it out of hand. But now that she had had time to think it over, to weigh the pros and cons, it was beginning to make more and more sense.

She glanced at her watch. "My goodness! We have to hurry. I don't want the child to come home for lunch and find us not there!"

Jasmine shrugged. "You fuss too much. As I've said, I've taught her to be independent. The door is open and if we're not there, she'll just come in and make herself a sandwich."

Yes, Laura was self-reliant. However, Emma reveled in taking care of her. The result of her labours warmed her soul: she could see Laura soaking up her loving attention, relaxing, becoming a child once more. She thought Jasmine's relationship with Laura rather strange. There was no lack of love, but often they seemed more sisters than mother-and-daughter, with the child occasionally in the role of older sister.

In general, however, Emma felt that Jasmine was altogether too lax about her daughter and her safety. Lately she had been taking the child to the park. They ran foot races and then, down by the lake, Laura told her delightedly, they had jumped rocks. When Emma remonstrated with her, worried that Laura would fall and injure herself leaping from one great boulder to another along the breakfront, Jasmine just laughed. "She's a lake child, and she has to learn to jump rocks. Didn't you, Emma?"

Well, yes. Yes, she had. But there was a difference. "I did, but my mother certainly never would have encouraged it. And she would have whaled my backside if she ever found out!"

They had turned a corner and were on the final block toward the lake and home. Emma wasn't wearing her spectacles. Through dim eyes she saw blurry figures and some movement on the street ahead. There was an exclamation from Jasmine.

"Goodness! It looks as if Letty Lawson might be moving out! That's her daughter carrying a box out of the house, and the trunk of the car is packed with suitcases and boxes!"

"Oh! I certainly hope not! That would be a real loss to our little neighbourhood," Emma cried. They hurried toward Letty, who was standing listlessly on the sidewalk beside the car. Her daughter Cheryl had stopped beside her, with an empty cardboard box in her arms. She looked not at all pleased to see them.

"What's happening here, Letty? Are you clearing out some of your things? I do hope you're not moving!" Emma exclaimed.

"Well, yes, I'm sorry to say that I am," Letty answered. Her lower lip trembled and Emma almost thought she might cry. "I had hoped to stay here until my dying day, but it seems I'm getting absent-minded and forgetful; and the family thinks it would be best if I moved into the Fournier Home for the Elderly. So Cheryl and her husband and family will be your new neighbours."

She laughed a little, a sad, small sound. "They were going to get the house, anyhow, when I die. So I guess it's just a little early."

Emma was truly upset, not just at the prospect of losing Letty, who was beloved by all who knew her and a fine bridge player to boot, but at having her daughter as a neighbour.

Jasmine spoke up. "What happened, Letty? To make Cheryl think you shouldn't live here anymore?"

And she stared at Cheryl with a look that Emma saw was coldly accusing.

"Oh, dear Jasmine, I'm sorry not to have said hello to you; I'm glad to see you looking so well!" Letty said warmly, forgetting her distress for a moment in order to give her a proper greeting. Then she shook her wooly white head in puzzlement. "It seems that lately I'm forgetting things. Not long ago, Cheryl and I came back from the doctor's and I found out I had left two burners on high on the stove, just blazing away! The house could have burned down! That was the worst, but there were other things – my keys, they went missing and I couldn't find them anywhere, but then I discovered them in the icebox – and then I left the iron on, and Cheryl and I found it after she took me shopping for groceries –"

"I can't believe this." Emma was incredulous. "You've always been so independent, so sharp at your cards. I haven't seen any change in you, Letty – are you sure?"

"The strange thing is," said Letty, "I have absolutely no memory of doing these things. I really do feel like I could be losing my mind."

There was a small silence, in which Emma chanced to look at Jasmine and saw that she seemed to be gathering force, like a thundercloud about to shoot bolts of lightning.

"I think I know how it might have happened," she said in a dangerous voice. Cheryl Byrd heard the menace in it and she slowly put down her box, as if to free her arms for combat.

"What do you mean?" asked Letty, her watery red eyes open wide in bewilderment.

"Let's see –" said Jasmine. "You were at the doctor's on the morning of March the 21st. Is that right?"

"Yes," said Letty. "How did you know?"

"It's a date Emma and I won't soon forget," Jasmine answered. "We had a visit that day from Emma's step-daughter. And just before she arrived, Emma said you told her you had a doctor's appointment that morning."

"So – I still don't understand –" Letty looked even more bewildered.

"Was that the day you found that you'd left the burners on?" Jasmine asked.

"Mother, you don't have to put up with this nonsense," Cheryl said, nervously. She put her hand on her mother's arm. "Come in the house and help me sort out those kitchen linens."

Letty shook her arm off. "Yes, that was the day. Why?"

"Because I was looking out the upstairs window," Jasmine said. "And I saw Cheryl go in the back door of your house and then come out again, looking all around, a second or two later. Just long enough to turn on a couple of stove burners."

"Is that right?" Letty turned to her daughter who said, very quickly, "she's lying."

Emma spoke up. "No, she's not. When Jasmine came downstairs, she told Anna and me that she had seen Cheryl at your back door. It seemed odd to me, too, and so I remembered it. She's not making this up."

Letty stood there for a moment in silence. "Yes," she said quietly. "That would explain quite a lot. The iron. I had put it on the board, but I hadn't really started ironing before I went to play cards, and Cheryl knew I would be out. The keys – well, I would never do such a thing. And the stove – she drove me to that appointment and left me, then came back later to get me – and – there were other things."

Letty straightened up. Without looking at her daughter, she said, "Emma and Jasmine, could you please each take a box and, for just a few minutes, help me put some of my things back in the house? They're not heavy, and I would surely appreciate your help."

Emma immediately put down her purchases and her handbag, and for the next fifteen minutes she and Jasmine helped Letty bring her belongings back in the house. As they passed back and forth, they saw mother and daughter talking furiously, and heard Cheryl cry out, "but you have such a big house! And ours is so little, and so cramped for our family!"

And they heard her mother's retort, "at your age I had a little house too! And it's my big house, and I intend to stay in it! For a good long time!"

Skipping toward them along the sidewalk came Laura, on her lunch hour. Emma was glad to excuse herself from unpacking the car and take her home, while Jasmine stayed to help. The sweet child was like fresh air and sunshine after the dreary drama of greed and betrayal Emma had just witnessed. And, without Jasmine standing looking over her shoulder, she was free to give Laura a second slice of the bakery chocolate cake she had bought on their walk.

Emma could not know that there had been other witnesses beside her to the little drama on the sidewalk. Neighbours, hanging out of windows or standing unobserved behind porch latticework, had watched and listened. And, as Emma cut and fed her great niece chocolate cake, phones were ringing, and among those who loved Letty or disliked her daughter – both of whom there were a good many – Jasmine was even now becoming a heroine and a champion of the old and aged.

The first step in her rehabilitation had begun. The next had been planned, and would proceed from a most unlikely quarter, the sickroom of Lianne Latham. Tomorrow afternoon Emma would visit her, and together they would plan their strategy.

But for now, she cut herself an ample slice of cake, and she and the child beamed across the table at one another as they enjoyed the simple pleasure of a shared delight.

CHAPTER 37

Anna was disinfecting the forceps and needle Dr. Miller had just used to stitch up the latest scrape on one of the Fitzgerald boys, Alex, ten years old. He was a tough little number. He did not cry. He shut his eyes, then squeezed them, his mouth and cheeks, into a tight little knot in the centre of his face. They finished the entire procedure without hearing a peep from him, although Anna did detect a tiny tear trickling from the corner of one eye.

Dr. Miller was puttering about the examination room as they worked together in companionable silence. "Anna," he said. It was the end of the workday, and he used first names whenever they were alone. "I hope you won't mind a personal question. I've heard that Royce has moved out. Is that so?"

Did she detect a certain hopeful note in his voice? "More or less," she answered. "He's the groundskeeper at the Airdrie Estates and he has to live there, in the little gatehouse. So we don't see much of him." And could stand to see even less of him, she thought.

"How are your girls doing, these days?" Anna asked.

Keith Miller had lost his wife two years ago. She died leaving him with two daughters, Cora and Jane, who were about the same age as Lily and Mark.

By now Anna had put away the needle holder and forceps, and she turned to face him. He was a pleasant-looking man, a little older and taller than she was. There was nothing exceptional about him, except for the keen intelligence in his eyes and the kindliness of his expression.

"They're alright. I spend as much time with them as I can. I have a housekeeper, Tina Ambrose – you know her? She's good with them, doing a fine job, but they really need a mother's care."

Anna smiled. "Well, I suppose one of these days you might find one for them. There seem to be lots of willing candidates, from what I've seen." A horde of them, she could have added, as well as dozens of mothers looking for a nice doctor for their daughter.

"Yes, I might remarry someday," Keith said, as he made his last notes in the Fitzgerald boy's file. Then he closed it and looked at her directly. "But it won't be anyone like Eva."

Anna had known her. His deceased wife had been a somewhat difficult, demanding person.

"The next woman I marry would have to understand how important my work is to me," he said. "Eva never did. And kind, loving, unselfish – well, you would know." And he smiled, a little shyly, then abruptly turned away from her and left the room.

Just so. They would maintain a respectful professional distance. They would continue to be friends, not lovers. Anna was aware, though, that she had received as close to a marriage proposal as she was likely to get in her situation. She wondered how long he would wait. No matter: it was hopeless. Eventually, he would find someone else. Not for the first time, she rued her Catholic religion, and the iron bonds of obligation and family that kept her tied to a man like Royce Parke.

CHAPTER 38

"Arlena, can I talk to you?"

Oh no, thought Arlena, here it comes. Although she had prepared herself for it, knew it must eventually happen, her heart took a lurch and immediately descended into the bottom of her stomach, where it tied itself into a knot of misery.

She was in her bedroom, the small spare bedroom near Jasmine's, which she had moved into once Jasmine ceased her nightly wanderings. That was a good while ago. Arlena was certain that Emma and Jasmine were letting her stay on out of her need, rather than theirs. And now the thought of returning home was so distasteful she had been out looking for apartments, rather than spend one more night with her mother and her gloomy clouds of disappointment over her daughter's unmarried state.

Jasmine walked into the bedroom. Arlena could see from her face, which she had come to know so well, that Jasmine had read her thoughts.

"Well, you know," she said, gently, "Our arrangement here couldn't go on forever. It's no good for you."

"Why isn't it any good for me?" Arlena cried.

In response, Jasmine slowly shut the bedroom door. Then she turned, gathered Arlena into her arms and kissed her full upon her mouth.

It was so much the summation of all her wishes and desires that, after a moment's shock, Arlena melted into the embrace, almost swooning, her eyes shut in bliss. But soon, too soon, she felt Jasmine pull away. She opened her eyes. Then she began to cry. Because there was no hint of passion in Jasmine's face, no reciprocal desire, and even worse, there was pity.

Arlena cried out of sadness, out of misery and her disgust with herself, and from her great sense of betrayal by someone whom she would otherwise have loved in secret.

"Don't cry, little friend," said Jasmine soothingly, taking one of Arlena's hands in hers, and with her other hand gently wiping away the tears flowing down Arlena's cheeks. "I only want to help, and I just wanted to show you who you are."

"Who am I?" sobbed Arlena, in bewilderment. "I don't even know who or what I am!"

"You are a woman who wants to be with women, not men," Jasmine said. "And it's perfectly normal, but not for Medford. You will never be happy here. You have to leave. You will need to go elsewhere to find your own kind."

"Oh," gasped Arlena, "I'm so sorry. So ashamed."

"About what?" queried Jasmine, a little impatiently. "There's nothing wrong with you, Arlena, only with other people who are stupid and ignorant. Being attracted to women, not men, is something you can't help, just something to accept. There's no need for shame or apologies for what you truly are, a wonderful, kind person. Now listen. I'm going to the city next week to try to sell my Mother's jewelry. Aunt Emma is lending me her car. I want you to come with me, and we'll meet some women I know from the time I was living there. Wonderful women who are like you, who will take you under their wing. Say you'll come."

They sat on Arlena's bed. Jasmine eventually dispelled any of her lingering convictions that she was a hopeless freak. They talked for over an hour, long enough for her tears to dry, and for the prospect of a new life to take root and start to blossom in her mind. Outside the window now, birds were singing their evening song. The sun sank lower in the sky; the room grew dim.

Finally, Jasmine rose to leave. But before she reached the door, she heard from behind her a little, small voice full of hesitation. Arlena said, "please, Jasmine. I know you told me you didn't ever want to hear another word from Mason, but he's begged me to ask you – if you ever got any of his letters. A yes or a no. That's all he needs."

It was now fully dark; the long spring day had come to an end. She stood in shadow at the door, but her eyes glowed gold, almost tiger-like, reflecting the light of the lamp at Arlena's bedside.

"I told you," she said, and her words seemed to be coming from some distant, remote place. "That I want nothing to do with your brother. So, knowing that, if he's looking for an answer to his question, then he is looking for someone to blame. I won't answer it."

"Tell him," she added, " that it was hard, but I've made my peace with the way things are. Only that it's like a wound that's healed over with a scar, and even such little questions could start to crack it open. That's why I want him to leave me alone."

She left and only a moment later returned again, looking in from around the doorframe. "Your family does owe me something," she said. "For what they did to me. Please ask Mason if he can find Anna's father a job. A good job." Then she shut the door.

Arlena fell back on the bed. She knew that a chapter of her life had closed. It was one she would never forget. Another would start soon, in another place, and this one, she vowed, she would write all herself.

Through the window came a sound, at first muted, then growing into a long, lonely wail. The evening train, as it passed by the town, was calling her away. She went to the closet and took out her suitcase. Opening a drawer of the dresser, she began to pack.

CHAPTER 39

It had not been the greatest success, so far as Sunday night family dinners go. The boys, Terry and Ted, were lively enough, but Catharine was more lumpish than usual and Mason much quieter. They had brought two cars and now, as the evening settled in, Catharine was taking the boys home to bed. Mason was to stay behind. Once he saw his family off, he would be joining his father in the study.

They had an hour or so of work ahead of them. Tomorrow they were meeting with the developer of a new industrial park they were underwriting, and the draft contract sat before Max on the desk. This was the kind of work Max enjoyed: drawing up the terms and conditions, giving a little here, taking more there, all involving considerable business acumen, and he was looking forward to it.

Elizabeth had asked him if he wanted brandy, and now she brought it into the study on a silver tray with two snifters. Max rose. "Thanks for a wonderful dinner, dear," he said. After she put it down in front of him he pulled her close, and they embraced for a long, loving moment.

With his arms around his wife, Max looked over her shoulder to see his son standing in the doorway. It seemed to Max he looked rather sad. Elizabeth gave a little laugh, kissed Max on the cheek, then pushed him playfully away and went off to supervise the after-dinner cleanup.

"Brandy?" Max sloshed a golden half-measure into one snifter.

"No thanks, Dad," Mason answered.

"Why so glum, chum?" Max was trying to lighten his son's mood. But once he asked the question he was sorry. Because it looked as if he might actually get a real answer.

"Oh this and that. Just the usual."

Max relaxed. Good. It wasn't going to get serious. Now they could get down to business. He picked up his pen.

"Actually, it was seeing you and Mom together – you don't know how lucky you are, Dad. I'll never have what you have."

Max put down his pen. "I'm sorry to hear that, son." He looked down at the contract. It winked at him. It beckoned.

"In fact, I've been thinking about getting a divorce. Catharine and I are just going through the motions. Although I don't know that I would be any happier by myself. And there are the boys to think about."

Now Mason had his full attention. A divorce? This definitely was serious. He and Catharine's father, Allen Ballard, did a considerable amount of business together. Not good.

He looked at Mason, his tall, handsome son. He noticed, perhaps for the first time, how Mason's face, once so frank and open, seemed to have closed in on itself; the new, stern lines around his mouth, on his forehead. Slowly the heaviness of his son's mood started to infect him. It certainly was dampening his after-dinner glow of wellbeing. Suddenly he had a flash of intuition. "This wouldn't have anything to do with Jasmine Holmes, would it?" He had heard that she was recovered from whatever the female problems were that she had, and was out and about town.

Mason sighed. "Well, I did see her, on the street recently. But no, that's just more or less incidental. Although it did get me thinking. The fact is, I haven't been that happy for a long time. Anyhow, c'mon, Dad, let's get this done. Where's my copy?"

Max slid it silently across the desk.

His son was unhappy. He had known it; Elizabeth and he had spoken about it. Now, here it was finally out in the open. Perhaps because he had seen Jasmine Holmes. He stared at Mason and waited for him to finish reading the contract. Jasmine Holmes, lovely as a spring morning. No denying it, a beautiful girl. A sweet girl. Memories came flooding back, some pleasant, most not. Their engagement. Not what they had wanted for their son, but when he saw how in love they were, the joy in their faces, he couldn't help but be glad for them.

But then, less than a month later, here was her father, sitting in their living room, telling them how he had found Mason and Jasmine together. Furious, mostly with his daughter, insisting that the marriage date be moved up. Max knew who was probably at fault, his randy son just home from the war. Of course, the libertine, the bigamist they later found out he was, would always be the one most concerned about his daughter's chastity! Who cared? They were going to be married soon anyway! Ridiculous!

Then Elizabeth left the room. She came back with the letter from Tilde, her father's baby sister. Her husband was dead, and Tilde had written she was desperate for help to resettle her children and the grandparents after fleeing Berlin. A cooling off period, Elizabeth suggested. Two months, at the most.

Well, just what every young couple madly in love needs: a cooling off period! It was a bad idea from the start, but so was moving up the marriage date, an embarrassment for all concerned. Elizabeth was hoping, he suspected, that Mason himself would cool off the whole idea of marriage to Jasmine.

It was incredible to think of it now: they had sent their son, their dutiful son who had just miraculously survived five bloody years of war, off to the madness that was post-war Germany. How stupid, how naïve and incredibly stupid they were!

Finally, here was Mason. Coming home five months later, in the month he should have been married. Discovering her gone, hearing the scandal, the vicious gossip. Broken-hearted.

"Dad? Dad?"

Max blinked. He was sitting at his desk. Mason was looking at him worriedly. "Did you hear what I just said?"

"No," said Max. "I was thinking about something. Someone. Jasmine Holmes. How does she look?"

Mason had not been expecting this question; it took him off-guard. "She – she's so beautif--" He could not continue, and looked away. In a husky voice, he said, "she thinks I'm a monster, Dad. That I used her and left her. She won't see me, won't talk to me. I had Arlena ask if she got any of my letters, yes or no, and she wouldn't even give me an answer. I'm almost certain she didn't. But I guess I'll never know if they were intercepted or lost. Mom got a few of my letters, didn't she? So, what happened?"

Yes indeed. Just what had happened to those lost letters of love and longing? Elizabeth, standing and secretly listening just outside the heavy mahogany door of the study, could not be sure. One thing she was certain of: they should never have sent their son to Germany. Much of the country was destroyed, its cities and systems in ruins. Such letters as she had received from Mason and Tilde all were mailed from Belgium, with its functioning post. Later, she learned they had been given to friends or paid agents to mail. Were they to blame?

Or, more likely, did Tilde, on reading the letter Elizabeth had sent with Mason that explained the reason for his "cooling off" period and expressed her disappointment in his choice of a bride, choose not to mail them? Tilde, so strict a Calvinist, would have been shocked at the girl's lack of morals. Then, soon after, her letter that told of Jason Holmes' bigamy – no, she had spared her aunt no details. Perhaps Tilde thought she was doing them all a favor. But she was dead now, as were so many of that family, and Elizabeth would never know.

However, there was more than letters, lost or destroyed, to explain the mystery of what had happened to Jasmine Holmes. For Elizabeth had a secret: a dreadful secret. It was deep, like a hole or a pit, and filled with shame and remorse. For years she had tried, more or less successfully, not to think about it. She had covered it over and kept it safely buried, until she heard that Jasmine was returning to town.

Now she lived in daily terror that Arlena, her troubled, troublesome daughter would learn of its existence and push her in. Then the people she loved most in the world, her husband and son, would see her as she really was; and she would be fully immersed in the horror of what she had done.

Elizabeth stood beside the doorway in her pearls and Sunday dress, tears rolling down to trace pink pathways through her face powder as she listened to the misery in her son's voice. She knew that she would die, in her pit of shame, if he or Max were ever to hear the cruel words she had spoken to the distraught girl who came to their door, years ago.

She did not invite her in. She only spoke to her as she stood there, waiting on the steps of the house. She had said, no, there are no letters for you here. If you haven't heard from Mason, probably it's because he knows about your father, and what he's done, and he doesn't want anything more to do with you, or your family.

She heard the girl's sharp intake of breath. Her eyes had opened wide. She went white, just as if Elizabeth had lifted a hand and slapped her, hard. Then her face crumpled and she turned away to hide her tears. As Elizabeth was about to shut the door, she came running back, madly twisting and pulling at her finger as if she wanted to rip it off. She pushed the door open wide.

TING! TING! Ting!

Elizabeth heard the ring bounce across the marble floor. Then, calmly, coldly composed, she had stood at the door, listening to the sobbing, wrenching, sounds of heartbreak fading away into the distance as she ran.

The ring was under the small table in the foyer. Elizabeth found it and put it away for Mason, for when he returned.

In the study, inside the golden circle of light cast by the desk lamp, Mason had picked up the contract again. He was attempting to concentrate on it, but with no real interest, only in order to please his father. Max looked at his son. He had noticed the white patchiness that had appeared around his eyes when he spoke of Jasmine. More than if he had, it pierced Max's heart: a grown man trying hard not to cry.

Max had a great love for his son. He loved him almost as much as Elizabeth, truly the light of his life. He wondered. If he hadn't ignored the glowering disapproval of his lawyer father and his snob of a mother, and instead of Lizzie Dortman, daughter of an immigrant German baker, married someone like Catharine, what his life would be like?

He looked down at the paper on his desk, the same one his son was reading, and he saw what Mason saw.

Dust. All dust.

They spent half an hour, made a few trifling changes. Then rain began to patter against the window. Max, looking up, suggested that Mason should go. He and Catherine had recently moved into a new house a little ways outside of Medford. It was a bit of a drive, and Max patted him on the back and told him he wanted him fresh and rested for tomorrow.

After Mason left, Max immediately set about the real work. With a sharp pen, he added or cut and slashed until the contract was more or less the way he wanted. However, it was no longer fun but work, because his heart wasn't in it.

It was in a car, on a lonely country road, driving slowly though the rain toward a dark house.

CHAPTER 40

"No. Absolutely not!"

"It's a ridiculous idea! It would never work."

"I refuse to cooperate!"

Thomas had tried every argument possible to stop her, to derail her absurd, crazy scheme, but she was determined to go ahead. She even had allies! Emma was going to help!

Now he tried another tactic: "I forbid you to do this!"

Lianne laughed, quite heartily for someone so ill. "You can't keep me from doing anything I want. How are you going to stop me? I'm dying and I'll do as I please. If you don't want to cooperate and you ruin it, well, that's your choice, but there's more than you who'll be the loser!"

Thomas had dealt successfully with recalcitrant students, with teenagers who were openly disrespectful or disruptive, with almost every possible type of misbehaviour. This was new. He frankly didn't know how to deal with a wife who used her imminent death as a passport to do whatever she wanted, like some kind of get-out-of-jail-free card.

Now he tried logic. "Let's go through it again and I'll tell you why it won't work."

"It will work," she said, "because it's so simple. Emma will start it. She will tell the story of how you stopped Jasmine from committing suicide. Then how you helped her to recover and move on after what happened to her. It will keep the gossip mills grinding for days to come. Nobody knows that story now except the four of us: you, me, Emma and Jasmine. And Jasmine will come and help me, now that Mrs. Mackie is leaving. She needs the money anyhow, Emma says."

"I don't want Jasmine here," Thomas retorted. He was remembering his dream and the other sensations the sight of her had awakened in him.

"She won't be around while you're at work. Her daughter will come here too, after school, and keep me company. It will be lovely to have a child visit."

At this Thomas looked at her suspiciously. But then he continued, "nobody is going to believe it. That there wasn't something between us."

"Did you ever kiss her in public?"

"No."

"Did anyone ever see you in a car, a restaurant, or any other place together?"

"No. Except for that time in the library, in between the shelves, where I was holding her hands and talking to her."

"So what else did they see?"

"They saw me coming in and out of the Madison's house."

"So it could all be rumours. And you could have been just helping her, counseling her, after her suicide attempt."

"And pigs could fly. I would have had to be a saint to be around her that long and do only that, and I wasn't."

"But nobody knows for sure. So, basically, it was all just rumors."

"A woman that looks like Jasmine and a man, me, in a house for two hours? You're going to have a hard time convincing anyone."

"I don't need to convince them. I just need to confuse them."

"Well, you'll certainly do that!"

"To confuse them enough that they're less than sure the two of you were having an affair. So they're less likely to tell others that you were having an affair. So they're less inclined to say anything that would ruin your chances of getting a promotion, or a job you want in the future. Also, the story should make you something of a hero. And, once they hear what happened there should be some sympathy for Jasmine after the awful way this town has treated her. Jasmine's taking care of me will help make the story credible. Then, after I'm gone, she can find work, make some money and get out of here, like she wants."

Thomas walked agitatedly around the narrow confines of the sunroom where Lianne was cosied up in a blanket on the sofa, despite the warmth of the day.

"What about Jasmine? Does she know about this crazy idea of yours?"

"Emma has told her and she's agreed in principle. She's to start when Mrs. Mackie leaves and we'll see how it goes."

"I can't believe you want a woman I've had an affair with to take care of you!"

"She took care of you."

"Yes – oh, what are you talking about! Do you even know what you're saying?"

Lianne looked at him levelly. "She brought you back from the edge, Thomas. I was too much a part of everything that made you sad to be able to help you. You know it, and we've talked about it in the past, so why are you so surprised? Now, will you go along with my plan?"

In a crazy way, her plan did make sense. In fact, he had helped Jasmine. They had shared their heartbreak, consoled one another. And convinced one another that although the world seemed an unutterably sad and cruel place, they should go on living in it for the sake of the good they might do. That they did all this naked, in bed, was perhaps beside the point.

"I'll think about it," Thomas said. "Give me a week to decide."

"Two days," said Lianne. "I can't wait any longer."

Thomas looked alarmed. "Why such a short time? Is there something happening with you that I ought to know about?"

Lianne laughed, the merry, silvery peal of laughter he loved. Despite her thinness, she still had her dimples. "It's the phones. We have to do this now, before they're changed. They're taking out the party lines."

CHAPTER 41

It was only two and a half blocks from St. Margaret's grade school to the Airdrie Estate. How many children walked that way each school day? Jasmine had been wondering, and so it came to exert a pull on her, an attraction threaded with suspicion and curiosity. Now, without any conscious plan, she had sidetracked from her route to the school and her feet were finding their way there.

On this spring afternoon she left an hour early in order to walk and think before picking up Laura. Mostly, the child made her way back to the house at lunch hour and after school by herself or accompanied by a few of the neighbourhood boys. It was only occasionally that Jasmine or Emma met her to walk the six blocks home. Today, though, Jasmine felt she needed some fresh air, open spaces and solitude as an antidote – or was it a preventative? – against the confinement she would soon feel as a sickroom nurse. Next week she was to start at the Lathams and, although the work would not take up all her time, Jasmine was not looking forward to the duties of taking care of an invalid.

Last week she agreed to the wild scheme proposed by Emma and Lianne because she needed the money. As well, she could see its logic and it amused her: the idea of sowing confusion to bring about some kind of redemption, especially for Thomas. She planned to leave Medford soon with Laura anyhow, so did it really matter if people found out about that sad chapter in her youth? However, the practical aspect of the plan was that she would be caring for her lover's wife. And that was so strange and uncomfortable a prospect that she had not yet nearly sorted out in her mind.

The lake was smiling today. It was the first thing she saw, shimmering silver and blue, through the black iron rungs of the entrance gate. After its surly mood of the past week, where it reared and roared and crashed on the breakfront under grey skies, it was a welcome sight. She peered between the rungs at the rolling green expanse of lawn and the sunlit gardens and saw a flash of white, a bent figure. Today someone was there. It was Royce, and he had seen her.

Well beforehand, Jasmine had thought out what to say, what to do, if this opportunity arose. She waved. Royce stood in the midst of a flowerbed, where he had been cutting spent flower heads off daffodils. Now he downed his tools and left off working to come toward her. "Jasmine!" he exclaimed, a note of surprise in his voice.

The face that looked through the gate, however, was not especially friendly. "Jasmine Holmes," he said. "I never expected to see you again. The last time I saw you, you pushed me out the apartment door."

Jasmine laughed, a light, lilting sound. "Almost ten years is a long time to hold a grudge, Royce. How about we let old times be bygones? I've been wanting to see you and catch up. The real reason I'm here, though, is because I heard you have eggs for sale, and if you have any, I'd like a dozen."

His expression changed. She had disarmed him, and Jasmine guessed he was curious, too. He slid back the bolts on the wooden door to let her in. She noticed that there was not one but two sets of bolts, at the top and bottom of the door. Once she was inside, they stood and stared at each other.

"You look marvelous, Royce," she said, and he did: tall, muscular and tanned from outside work, more fit than she remembered. More handsome, even, except for the gap in his teeth.

"And you," he replied. "Beautiful as ever. I heard you were sick, but looks like you're recovered and better than new."

Royce had always been quick with a compliment, she remembered. And so was she. "You're doing a wonderful job here," she said, looking around. "But what a lot of work! How do you ever manage it?"

"Can't take all the credit." Finally a real smile slowly spread over his face. "There are two of us, Bernie Listowel and me, and between us we get it done."

They walked slowly along the road toward the gatehouse backyard. "You're lucky," he said, "you'll get my last full dozen."

Hesitantly, Jasmine said, "truthfully, Royce, there's another reason I'm here -- is there any chance you could show me the big house?" she asked. "I've never seen it before and I'm dying to."

He thought for a moment. "Sure," he answered, "I'll take you through before we get the eggs. It'll give us a chance to catch up. In fact, I've wondered what happened to you, after you kicked me out."

There was an edge to his voice. Jasmine felt the tiniest tremor of fear, and was not so sure she wanted to be alone with him, there, in that deserted house. Keep it light, she told herself.

"I only did what I thought was best for you and Anna," she smiled. "You have some beautiful children now, a family any man would envy."

"Yes, there's that." Royce's expression softened a bit. "But a wife and kids; maybe it's not the life I would have chosen for myself. If ever I'd had a choice." He turned toward the house. "Come, let me give you a look around."

The large porticoed entrance to the house was on its north side and already in shadow. Ornate and massive, the wooden front door was carved with the Airdrie family crest. Royce used one of a number of keys on a ring attached to his belt and opened it to reveal a spacious foyer paneled in dark walnut. An enormous brass chandelier hung suspended from the ceiling two floors above.

"Very impressive, but it's rather gloomy, isn't it?" Jasmine remarked. "Does the family come here often? How many of them are there?"

"There's a gathering of the clan at Christmas and Easter," Royce answered. "With children and grandchildren, about twenty-four altogether. Otherwise, it's just Ken and Wilma Airdrie, driving up from the city for the occasional weekend. Even then they only come if the weather is good, otherwise they always call and cancel. Guess when the weather is bad they find it gloomy too."

He opened a door to the living room, which was also fully paneled in wood and faced the lake. Unlike the entrance, though, it was filled with golden afternoon sunlight that spilled through the leaded glass windows and onto intricately patterned Persian rugs that glowed the colours of precious jewels. With its large brown leather chairs and sofas, inset bookcases and fine paintings, it was a room of great charm, warmth and comfort, the obvious gathering place of the Airdrie clan.

"So tell me what happened after I left," Royce asked as they walked the length of the room. "Did you stay at that job in the bar? And who was it you married? There were a number in the running, as I recall."

Jasmine had walked over to look at a large framed photograph of the Airdrie clan, taken against the backdrop of the lake. With their sharp features, bright eyes and hair in varying shades of red or snowy for the family patriarchs, they looked like sleek, self-assured foxes.

"I wasn't at the Dubliner for very long after you left," she replied. "Do you remember Sam Carlisle? About six feet tall, blond hair, with an American accent? He sat and had a beer with you once or twice when you were waiting for me at closing time."

"I do," said Royce. "Yes. The Yank. The construction super at that building going up across the street, is that right? And so you went with him to the States?"

Jasmine nodded. "That's right. But after what happened to me before, I made sure he gave me a ring. We had a city hall wedding, and then we visited Mom before we went to Vegas. There was plenty of construction going on then, and Sam had a job lined up before we left."

They were in the dining room now, and Jasmine laughed, amused. Royce looked at her questioningly. "All this wood," she exclaimed, waving an arm at the heavily paneled walls, the coffered ceiling, and the dining room table, which had no visible joins and appeared to have been hewn from one enormous walnut tree. "Most folks around here say that the Airdries were rum runners to the States. But after seeing this house, I'm finding it much easier to believe they made their fortune in lumber."

"It was a bit of both, if you want my opinion," commented Royce. "But no one knows for sure, or is likely to find out. They're a very private couple, the Airdries. Mr. Airdrie might want a word with me on Friday nights when they arrive, but that's it. Then I have to clear out. When they're here on the weekend, they don't want anyone else around."

He beckoned her toward the spiral staircase that led to the second floor. "Come, take a look from the top and then we'll leave. So fill in the rest for me. What did you do in Las Vegas?"

A little reluctant to go into this private part of the house with Royce, Jasmine slowly ascended the wide staircase. "Well, as you know, I've always been good at cards," she said. "Once we arrived and I got the house settled, I went to the casinos and played Blackjack. The first few times I won quite a lot of money; but then one of the regulars gave me some good advice. After that, whenever I made the rounds of the blackjack tables I always stopped after I made a certain amount that was quite a bit smaller. In a few weeks though, needless to say, they spotted me as a pro anyhow and it became harder to win."

They had reached the broad second floor landing, and now Royce led her toward a huge bay window composed of clear leaded glass with a spectacular lake view.

"Just as my luck was running out, I got an offer of a job dealing Blackjack," Jasmine continued. "The money and tips were good, and it was fun and far less nerve-wracking than being a player. Then I took almost a year off when I had my daughter. After a while, though, I went back to working nights, and Sam took care of the baby."

Silently they stood at the bay window and looked out at the panorama of blue sky, bluer lake, magnificent old oak trees almost in leaf, velvet green lawns and broad brushstrokes of tulips and daffodils outlining every path in red and yellow. "What a magnificent place this is," Jasmine said quietly, almost reverently. "It does you credit, Royce. You must love working here, judging by the job you're doing."

"Yes," Royce said with real sincerity, "it's the best job I've ever had, and I mean to keep it as long as I can."

He led her down a hall toward a second staircase. "So you have a daughter. Laura is her name, isn't it? A little younger than my Mary, what, nine, eight? I haven't seen her; does she look like you?"

The question was casual, but Jasmine detected an undertone of interest that unsettled her. "No, she looks more like her father," she was quick to say.

"And what happened to the father? Where is he?"

Jasmine took a moment to answer because, as they walked on their way to the other staircase, Royce had suddenly thrown open a set of double doors to reveal a large bedroom. It was decorated in tones of blue and white that echoed the lake shining beyond its windows. Just the viewing of such an intimate space with Royce Parke immediately doubled the sense of repulsion she had suppressed up until now.

"We grew apart," she answered shortly. "We're no longer together now."

He was looking intently at her as he stood by the open door. "How about it, Jasmine?" he asked. "A roll in the hay, for old times' sake?"

Working in the casino, Jasmine learned that there is no such thing as a poker face. A twitch of the lips, a slight frown, subtle hand movements or a change in the pattern of eye movements; all spoke volumes to someone as experienced as she. But her skills were not needed here. It was evident to her that Royce was cold, devoid of passion. Was he propositioning her just for form, only because it was expected of him? Because, beyond his coarse words, she could detect no real interest.

She laughed, as lightly as she could manage. "Now Royce, I came here for eggs, not to get laid! You know Anna is my best, probably my only real friend in Medford, and you're married to her. So, although you'll always attract the ladies, you must be my friend too, nothing more."

He slowly closed the doors to the bedroom, and Jasmine could sense that, on the whole, he was relieved at her reply. Then, however, he looked at her with suspicion once more. "I guess you and Anna have talked about me plenty behind my back."

"No," Jasmine responded, in her first bold-faced lie of the day. "She's been quite private about her personal life. But that doesn't mean I don't hear what other people say about you, Royce, and all your doings."

"Well, that might be, but it's all in the past now," Royce replied over his shoulder, as he descended the stairs before her. "I've changed my ways and I'm living clean. I'm a changed man."

He did seem a changed man in some indefinable way, Jasmine thought, as Royce led her through the side entrance of the house and into the garden. Yet he wasn't much older than she, perhaps four years, which would make him thirty-four. A man in his prime. And a man like Royce had one need, she knew, which essentially would remain unchanged and strong for many years.

They exchanged a few words of farewell at the small wooden door. She had only just left when, luckily, she recalled the reason she had given him for her visit. Turning, she saw he was still watching her as he stood at the open door, and once again his face was dark with suspicion. "Royce!" she called, "The eggs! I almost forgot what I came here for!"

Immediately his expression lightened. Together they walked to the gatehouse garden, and she waited for him there while he went into the house. She surveyed the garden, with its high wooden fence and gate. She noted that this gate bolted on the inside as well, with a new, large, heavy bolting mechanism positioned too high for a child to undo. And she also noticed that Royce did not bolt it after she had paid him for the eggs and they left the garden. Once he saw her out the small wooden door to the street, he immediately went back to work in his bed of daffodils. The small door to the street, which had been double bolted when she arrived, was now open. All the doors were open. It was almost 3:30. In just a few minutes, school would be out, the children on their way home.

Jasmine did not rush: she had told her daughter she might be late and to wait. As she walked toward the school, a small parade of youngsters flowed past her. Once more she saw the little flaxen-haired girl who had taken her baby brother inside the Airdrie gatehouse garden. Her sweet angel face was bright and animated as she chattered away to her older sister, who was holding her hand to lead her home. The sister was perhaps nine or ten years old, a little plump, with dark blonde hair. Her head was bent, her face a study in absorption. Then her little sister said something that caught her attention, and she turned and smiled at her, a smile full of love and affection.

Jasmine noted her purple-shaded eyelids. What ailed the child? Her smile, which had burned so brightly a moment ago, was as quickly extinguished. She lowered her head again and now the two of them passed Jasmine, walking demurely, hand in hand, toward their home just across the street from the Airdrie Estate.

CHAPTER 42

After three gentle "reminders", Thomas had run out of excuses and so here he was. Now he turned up the collar of his jacket and wished himself back home in his lazy boy chair with his coffee and papers.

Thomas had arrived at the cemetery equipped with pen and paper, a Brownie camera and a measuring tape. He laid these at the foot of a towering pine tree while he surveyed the Latham family plot. It was a chilly day, and the wind coming off the lake had set the flag overlooking the gravesites to snapping briskly.

Lianne was an inveterate decorator. She had turned every room in their house into a work of art. This talent was perhaps less appreciated by Thomas than the neighbourhood ladies, who breathed their admiration with oohs and aahs on their visits to the Latham home. While generally supportive, Thomas refused to let her touch his study and over the years had developed a deeply ingrained hatred of throw pillows, a decorating staple for Lianne, and threw them whenever possible into inconspicuous corners.

Now he had been deputized by Lianne to go to the cemetery for what he privately had concluded was a final and rather macabre decorating project. He picked up the camera and snapped the gravesite from several angles. Then he took pictures of nearby tombstones, including his father's, which had a space reserved on it for his mother, and he wrote down dimensions and measurements so that Lianne could make the best choice of colour, shape, size and location for her own monument.

Afterward he knelt down and brushed away the pinecones and needles from a small white plaque set in the ground. It was engraved with the name, "Michael James Latham" and bore only a single date: April 3, 1946. Beneath that little white stone lay a small white coffin, the bitter end to all his and Lianne's dreams for a family of their own.

The sight of it upset him, as he knew it would. He wondered if Lianne had forgotten how it might affect him when she asked him to go to the cemetery and take pictures. Get over it, he told himself. And he made to rise to his feet; but then he just stayed there, caught up in the web of memories the little white stone had cast over him.

Eons ago, or so it seemed, the future had glowed with the promise of happiness and it was impossible to believe it could be otherwise. Thomas remembered what joy he and Lianne had when they found each other. They were very young, but they knew immediately there could be no other so perfect. They would have a large family and share their love. Five babies at least, difficult on a teacher's salary, because a teacher was all that Thomas had ever wanted to be. But doable, because his parents would give him the family's lake house, large enough for many children.

After they married, Lianne quickly became pregnant. She lost that one early, at three months. Thomas was finishing Teacher's College after university when she lost the next one, at five months. Then the war years, the army, and it seemed every time he had leave, he left her expecting a happy event. A happy event that never transpired, and now it was weighing heavily on them, her sorrow, his loss, the silent grieving when two more babies were conceived but never born, miscarried at four and then six months.

Finally he was home for good after the bloody, brutal denouement of a war where he had won high rank but lost many good men and cherished friends. He was back teaching high school and now they were cautiously happy, because this baby was carrying to term, even if Lianne had been confined to bed for much of the pregnancy.

At the hospital, Dr. Soames, gowned and masked, took him aside before he went into the operating room. Smiling nervously, he said, "she's delicate, Thomas. In the future, you might want to think twice about any more children."

Then he disappeared, while Thomas paced, frantic with worry. Not long after that, he heard the joyful outcry from the doctor and nurses in the operating room – amongst the hospital staff Lianne was a favourite, beloved by all.

The sound of joy was short-lived. What followed was a deep and lasting silence. That silence, compounded of death and despair, was resounding in his head so loudly it muffled any of the meaningless words of consolation from the Doctor afterward, when he came to see Thomas in the waiting room. But even then, he might have made it through this awful ordeal, if it had not been for one thing.

They never should have given him the baby.

He had not seen the other dead babies, of course. Still, he had felt their loss keenly. This was different. He was still wandering in that dark place of silence following the stillbirth when the two young nurses came in. The one carrying a small blue bundle said, "I expect you'll probably want to see your son before they take him away."

Automatically he held out his arms, and the nurse gave him the dead child.

How could this be? Michael, his son, was perfect in every respect. Except that the tiny mouth did not move or cry. The pinched little nose did not breathe. The eyes peered unseeing, the little hands, limp and still, would never hold a rattle, a baseball bat, the shell-like ears would never hear his father's voice, that tiny little wisp of hair on his head would never grow any longer –

The dead child lay like a stone in his arms and on his heart; a forlorn little bundle of lost hopes. Then suddenly, something that was already taut, stretched to the limit inside him broke, snapped. He was having trouble breathing, standing. Now he saw the young nurses looking at each other with frightened deer eyes. One of them quickly took the baby and the other laid her hand on one of his arms, both of them still outstretched to hold the motionless bundle they had given him.

"Are you alright, Mr. Latham?" she asked, anxiously.

"Yes," he answered; but by then he knew he was anything but alright. He remembered nothing of what followed then, in the waiting room, except that shortly afterward he found himself outside sitting in his car.

When Thomas was quite small, four perhaps, he and his father and older sister went to the playground. His mother, much younger than his father, was at home with his baby sister making Sunday dinner. The weather was sunny and dry, a little windy. Dust hung suspended in the air. His sister was on the swings while father sat on a bench nearby, smoking his pipe and reading a book. Thomas was in the sandbox. The sand was new and clean and he was lifting it up and watching it sparkle as it sifted through his fingers.

Through the dull beams of sunlight that pierced the tall trees around the park, Thomas saw an animal approaching, a scruffy-looking dog. Little Thomas loved dogs. He stood up to go pat it. Just as he started to walk toward it, though, his father grabbed his shoulder and pulled him roughly back. Then Thomas could see that there was something wrong with the dog. There was a heavy rim of white slaver round about its mouth. It was leaning to one side, shambling, almost falling over. But it was still coming toward them, with intent and without stopping.

His father ran at it and gave it a mighty kick; it toppled over. As it lay there on the bare ground, the dog gave a piteous, demented and haunting howl. Then his father took a big stone he found in the bushes nearby, and dropped it on the dog's head to put it out of its misery. It was a mad dog, his father told him when he cried.

Thomas would never forget the sound of that mad howl. It haunted his nightmares for years afterward. Now, to his amazement, sitting in his car, he heard something very like it coming up from his own throat. It was a loud, wild keening that filled his ears and entered into all the spaces in his mind. It was the sound, like a signal, that marked the beginning of his descent.

When he awoke from a broken sleep the next morning, the reality in which he once existed more or less comfortably had shifted. An army began marching in his mind, relentlessly, round and around. The dead child, his stillborn son, had opened the gate. Now he was the standard bearer for the wounded and dying men who, as they passed, turned their leaden eyes on him in sorrowful reproach for the blood that still coursed in his veins, for his heart that still beat.

The tumult in his brain was unending. Now days of sunshine were dark, dark days were darker. Food had no taste, nights had no rest. And there was pain in his mind, in his body, worse than anything he had ever experienced and struggle as he might, he could not rid himself of it. He couldn't think, he couldn't teach. He was given compassionate leave, but the solitude was not healing; if anything it made things worse.

Lianne, always so much stronger than he despite her own sorrow and her delicate health and physique, tried her best to help him. And there were others: the Anglican minister, some friends, their doctor. But mere words or touches no longer could reach him. They only slid off the strange hard shell that had formed to hold him captive in his unending hell. And so he began to think of death. It seemed no longer fearsome but nothing more than a way out, when all other ways were closed to him. And he was pondering the hows and wheres of it, as he walked in the lakeside park that cool day in June, when he saw Jasmine Holmes, her copper-coloured hair blowing in the wind, stride purposefully along the pier that led to the lighthouse and without pausing, dive off the end of the pier and into the lake.

Thomas knew about Jasmine Holmes, of course. She had moved in next door last week with her Aunt Emma and Uncle Bill after her father's death, her mother Sylvia's nervous breakdown and the end of her engagement to Mason Stoddart. If he had been at Medford High during her final year three years ago, he would have been her teacher; but as it happened, he was away fighting a war. However, he had heard the other teachers speaking about her and her wild ways after her broken engagement. Most of them were sad and shocked, because they were so out of character with the shy, studious girl they once had taught.

Now Thomas knew immediately what she was up to, as he watched her strike out with a practiced stroke toward the middle of the lake. By Jove! he thought with real admiration, that's the way to do it! No messes at the bottom of cliffs, no bodies with purple faces hanging from nooses! No disgusting poisons or pills! Just let the lake chill and tire you; then disappear, perhaps forever. And if she keeps swimming in that direction, soon she'll hit the current from the Coshoni and then it'll help to carry her out –

Suddenly Thomas realized he had very little time, minutes really, to do something to save her, and that she must be saved. He might be permitted to die, but she was not! She was what? Twenty? She had her whole life ahead of her, and it would be ridiculous for her to die! At that time Thomas himself was only twenty-nine, but for the moment the irony of this escaped him. As he ran furiously down the slope that led to the lake, he weighed the alternatives: swim, or something else, and right away discarded the idea of swimming. With his big frame, he was a sinker, not a swimmer, and most certainly would drown before he ever rescued Jasmine Holmes.

But there were two things he was highly skilled at, after all his years on the lake, and they were boating and rowing. What with the wind and only him to man a sailboat, he knew his chances of plucking her out of the water would be much better in a dinghy or rowboat; and by a strange coincidence, there, bobbing up and down in the slip beside the dock next to the rowing club boathouse, he could see a little red rowboat.

The gravel spit up from under his shoes as he raced toward the dock. Damn!! There were no oars and the rowing club boathouse was locked! What to do? Thomas looked around wildly and then, on the boathouse wall, he saw the two crossed oars he and Al Schneider had nailed up for decoration some years ago when he was active in the club. They were weathered but still usable. With one mighty pull, he got the first one off; the second came more easily. A button popped off his shirt. Quickly he took the shirt off and put a rock on it so it wouldn't blow away, and now he was wearing only a pair of thin pants and ready for action.

The waves slapped against the boat as he wielded the oars with mighty strokes. As yet, the waves had not started to crest and he could still see her in the water, far away, because she was wearing a red shirt. He blessed that choice as he rowed quickly, much more quickly than she could swim, toward her. As he closed in, he could see that she was tiring, letting the current carry her as the cold water numbed her mind and her limbs. Then, after a couple more huge pulls, he was beside her, grabbing her arm before she could see him and react, which she did now, struggling wildly and trying to get away and almost tipping him and the boat in the process. Finally, he did what he really didn't want to do: gave her a good smack across the head and the side of her face as she cried and screamed at him to leave her alone. Then he quickly turned her, grabbed her under both arms and hauled her kicking and yelling into the boat. He held her close, for a minute, while she struggled, and he told her that she was not going to drown herself while he was in charge, and that was that; and that she had better behave herself and sit quietly or else he would knock her out cold and bring her back to shore that way, if he had to.

So she sat facing him, her head down, for most of the way back except when they got near the lighthouse, when she tried to jump over the side and he grabbed her and yanked her back into the boat and thumped her down, swearing at her loudly and telling her to behave or she was going to tip the boat and dump them both.

It was cold and getting colder. The wind was up now, the waves were building, and to add to the misery a chill rain had started to stream down.

But Thomas was feeling not miserable but elated! Somehow, in the flush of adrenaline, in the urgent rush to rescue the suicidal girl, the grey mist and dreadful black miasma that had covered him for so long seemed to have lifted. He got Jasmine out of the boat and she stood there meekly enough as he made a quick knot to tie the painter; then he grabbed her arm before she could even think about running away and began to march her toward her Aunt's home.

As they went up the hill, Thomas took stock: the blackness that had covered him had receded, even if he could sense it hovering nearby. He was feeling, hearing, even seeing much more clearly; he was alive again!

Unfortunately, some parts of him seemed to have come alive that he would much rather have stayed dormant. Because, as he looked down at the young woman he was forcing to march in quick step beside him, he saw her generous breasts bobbing under the clinging red shirt, the nipples tip-tilted and fiercely erect in the cold rain, and he felt a surge of something he had felt so little of, for so long, it seemed almost alien: desire.

Had she seen him looking? How could she not! But there was nothing he could do about it now. He swallowed, hard. "Once we get to your Aunt's I'm going to phone my wife and get her to come over to help," he said and his voice sounded rough even to his own ears. He was getting nervous. The rescue had been comparatively easy. But how was he supposed to handle the rest of it?

The front door of the Madison's home was not locked. As they stood there, lake and rainwater flowed off them, puddling onto the polished marble of the foyer. Beyond the foyer was a wide expanse of beautiful hardwood floor, highly waxed and shiny and too precious to ruin with wet.

Still holding Jasmine's arm, Thomas pulled her into the little bathroom opposite the cloak closet. With his free hand he opened and checked the few drawers and shelves to make sure there were no razor blades or sharp implements she could do herself in with. He told her to stay in the bathroom. Then he rummaged in the cloak closet until he found one of Emma's capacious coats and pushed it into her arms. "Get those wet things off and cover yourself up. I'm calling my wife. She'll take you upstairs to dress and then we'll talk," he instructed her.

Thomas would have liked to change too. His thin, wet and cold pants were sticking uncomfortably to him. But now he had to hurry. He thrust his feet into a pair of Bill's slippers he found in the closet, and almost ran to the study, where he knew Bill had installed a phone for when he worked from home. Quickly he picked it up and asked the operator to connect him, which she did.

His and Lianne's phone was in the kitchen, from where it could be heard all over the house. Ring rang rang. Ring rang rang. In a lather of anxiety now, he listened to the distinctive party line call of their phone, as it shrilled over and over again.

No answer! Where in hell was Lianne? Then he remembered. She was at the doctor's. Always at the doctor's, it seemed, and now, when he really needed her, not there!

What in the world should he do next? Emma! Yes. He would call her at the library. Jasmine would have the number. He would ask her.

His back was turned to the door as he faced the desk, listening to a phone ring in an empty house. Just as he set it down, he heard a light sound. He turned around. Jasmine Holmes stood in the doorway of the study. She was wrapped in Emma's big, navy blue coat. And, as he looked at her, she removed the hand that clasped it closed and let it open.

He saw her lovely face, only slightly marked by tears and the imprint from the slap he had used to get her into the boat. He saw her perfect, coral-tipped breasts, her tiny waist and the swell of her hips; he saw her—

"No!" he said. "No! I don't want to do this! I can't!"

But the words that burst from his mouth were in such obvious contradiction with what the rest of his body was telling her that she only smiled, a little.

"Oh yes. Yes, you can," she murmured.

Then she came closer and reached out.

The pine tree in the cemetery would have been one of the few to have escaped the logger's axe when the settlers came to Medford. It was old, at least two hundred years old, and immense. Thomas could sense something soothing and beneficent about it as it stood there extending its great sheltering arms over the dead. He leaned against it and thought again about the strangeness of fate. And about how he, the rescuer, became the rescued.

If Lianne had been home, or if by chance Emma was off work; if one or another of them had come and taken the girl away, got her dressed, talked to her, it was possible she would have been alright. But he would not. He knew with certainty that. slowly or quickly. the waves of darkness that had temporarily receded from his mind would have ebbed back to swallow him once more. At that exact moment, however, as a happily married man immune to the advances of other women, he had no plausible excuse for what happened next on the long brown leather couch in the study of the Madison house.

He had set down the phone. On turning he saw her standing there, glorious in her nakedness. Then she came closer and reached out. And from that very first touch he was gone, lost, submerged in fire. A river of fire, swirling over him to tear him away from all sense and reason; and even if he knew he must stop he could not, swept away by the fire that rushed through his veins in a torrent whenever he felt her touch, heard her voice, inhaled her scent, even at the sight of her, the very thought of her, burning and burning. Fire consuming him, body and mind, ever so steady, so hot and bright that it burnt the darkness cleanly away, even as it plunged him into sweet oblivion. And during the short, the too short time in which they were lovers, the fire had not nearly burnt itself out before Jasmine Holmes packed her bags and left town.

CHAPTER 43

"Who is this?"

Emma was just settling herself on the comfortable padded bench at Margery's kitchen table when an orange cat strolled in from the living room. It paraded across the linoleum floor, its tail curled in a question mark as if to inquire whom this unknown visitor might be.

"That's the cat we got from the fire," Margery answered. She reached for one of Emma's date squares. "We called him Blaze."

The cat gave Emma a disdainful look and decided she was not worth his attention. It made a circle around the kitchen in order to walk insolently in front of Jim's old dog Selby, who was lying on his mat in a corner. Selby bared his teeth and growled, then lunged and snapped at the cat when it failed to remove itself quickly enough. Blaze adeptly leapt aside and leisurely made his way toward the doorway, a satisfied look on his cat face, his tail slowly waving.

"Well, I guess we know who's the master of the house now," Emma said, as the cat disappeared, sauntering back into the living room. "But where's Jim? Is he home? How's he doing?"

"Not well," Margery responded dispiritedly. "There isn't much work around town. His men keep coming to visit him and it's getting him down."

Outside, digging around the rose bushes under the kitchen window and eavesdropping unabashedly, Jim silently agreed with his wife. He often listened in when Margery and Emma visited, because otherwise he would only hear an abbreviated version of what had been said. He also did it because the two cousins and long-time friends had a way of setting the world to rights. And right now, the way things stood, his world needed it.

Whatever folks might say about Elizabeth Stoddart and her snooty ways, she was the only one who stepped up to the plate to raise funds for the tannery workers after the fire. And for a couple of months they had rent money and could buy food, but charity doesn't last forever and now they were starving on the slim welfare the town afforded. Jim heard there were going to be jobs out at the new car plant going up on the outskirts of the city. And good luck to that. Even if they applied, the tannery workers' applications likely would wind up at the bottom of the heap.

Only this morning, Buddy Watkins had come to visit him. Jim had seen him not long ago when it was still cold, walking the railway tracks with a sack looking for coal and finding mostly clinkers. His honest pie face, weathered and red with a slice in the nose from some other hard job, was full of worry and desperation when he came and sat down in the spare chair in Gramp's house. He left with not much more than a pat on the back and five dollars, all Jim could spare. The MacClures were already well into their savings.

His men had looked up to him and he had taken the best care of them he could. The work was dirty, nasty and sometimes backbreaking, but the pay was reasonable and the men, all of them, worked hard. Most had families and few had any education and Jim did not know what would become of them. Or him, for that matter. He was in his 50s now. Who would hire him?

"You know the old Grimley sisters who lived next door?" Margery's voice floated out the window. "The ones who moved in from the farm about ten years ago? Well, both of them died this winter, one right after the other. Jim did all kinds of things to help them out when they became feeble, digging their garden, clearing their snow, and after all that work, guess what they left him in their will? All of their preserves! He made the mistake of admiring them once when he was down in their cold cellar. Of course, it couldn't have been their grandfather clock, or some furniture, or anything useful, and who knows how old all those jams and jellies and tomatoes are? I'm going to throw them all out!"

"No you're not," said Jim, who now appeared in the kitchen, drawn by the smell of the newly baked cookies Margery had just taken out of the oven and set to cool. "They told me they ate everything they canned, every winter, and that's why they aren't labeled. And I love canned tomatoes."

"That might have been true some years ago," said Margery levelly. "But they didn't even plant a garden last summer and if there is something that will go bad, it's tomatoes and you can die from eating them."

Jim reached for a cookie. "Don't touch that!" Margery barked sharply, and Jim quickly yanked his hand back as if burnt, his blue eyes big with surprise and hurt, like a child's. "They're for the bazaar," she explained belatedly to his retreating back as he headed out the door.

Now she turned to Emma and her face was tired and weary. "That man!" she said. "I love him but it's driving me crazy having him around all day! And lately we're so tight for money I'm having to skimp on everything, but you'd better believe I always pay his life insurance, because that's about all I can count on now!"

Emma saw the top of a head outside the window. "Margery," she said quietly, "I think Jim might have heard you."

Margery quickly whirled around, but before she turned to look, the head had disappeared. "Don't worry," she said airily. "If he did hear, he knows I didn't mean anything by it, and that I love him to bits. Now tell me more about Letty."

"Oh, yes," Emma said, remembering what she had mentioned on the phone before coming to visit. "Well, you heard about the kerfuffle out in front of her house when her daughter tried to move her out? Just yesterday, when we bumped into each other on the street, she told me she hasn't heard a word from Cheryl since, and that she's writing her out of her will and leaving everything to her other daughter and her son."

"So?" Margery's attitude seemed to suggest she thought Letty's decision was just about right.

"So, I think it would be best for both of them if this matter were resolved and Letty forgave her daughter," Emma replied.

"Why in heaven's name should she do that?" Margery's penciled-on eyebrows rose almost up to her hairline. "What Cheryl did was unforgivable!"

"I agree, it was awful, but let's be practical." Emma decided to eat one of the date squares she had brought over, since the cookies, which smelled heavenly, were evidently off limits. "Letty's son and her other daughter aren't in town, they're miles away. Who's going to take care of Letty when she's sick or needs help? Cheryl has always been there for her."

"It'll be about the same for Letty as it is for the other widows and women living alone," said Marjorie. "The neighbours will help out as they always do, whenever they can."

Yes, the neighbours would help out. Emma had seen it many times and she had occasionally been one of those neighbours herself. It was, she thought, only a halfway satisfactory arrangement, and without close family of her own she knew that would likely be her fate too, once she became more elderly. It was a rather depressing prospect.

"But Cheryl's family will lose out too, and not just on their inheritance," Emma persisted. "You know what a good grandmother Letty is, and the influence she has on those children. They won't see her anymore and that would be sad. So, I thought, since you're only a couple of houses away, could you not ask Cheryl if she could apologize and make up with her mother? I'm sure, knowing Letty, she would be happy to forgive her if she were sincere."

Emma waited. She knew that Margery loved to do this kind of meddling, especially if it resulted in a positive outcome.

"We-e-e-el-l." Margery looked off in the distance, seemingly distracted, uninterested. Suddenly she swiveled her head around, her eyes twinkling, her face impish. "Of course I will. You just knew I would, didn't you?" And they both laughed heartily.

"Don't we love to stick our noses into other peoples' business!" Emma chortled. "Sometimes I'm so busy doing it, I can't even tend to my own!"

There was a loud buzzing noise. The kitchen timer had alerted Margery, who stood up and went to the stove.

"Butter tarts!" Emma exclaimed. "My favourite! What are you doing, trying to make me fat?"

"Why should I try, when you're managing so well yourself?" Margery retorted, and again they laughed.

"Speaking of noses," she said, as she put a plate of hot tarts on the table, "Linda McKinnon told me that on Monday your Laura had a fight in the school yard with her son Bernard and that she clobbered him and gave him a bloody nose."

"Yes, I heard about the fight," Emma replied. "But I'm pretty sure Linda didn't tell you the reason why, did she? It was at recess. Laura had just beat him at marbles and he pushed her over and took her bag of marbles and threw them all over the place. When the principal heard about it, he made Bernard go out and pick them up."

"Well, still, it's hardly ladylike, is it?" Margery asked. "And now you've let her get all her hair cut off and she looks just like one of those hooligan little boys she's running around with in your neighbourhood."

"That's right," said Emma, without further comment.

"I also hear she's best friends with Shawna Smith, that Métis girl."

"A lovely girl. She's been over to the house a few times. Charming parents. She's taught Laura how to stick up for herself," Emma said, with a complacency that irritated Margery.

"I can certainly believe that!" Margery retorted, with some heat. "And I don't suppose you care that Laura took the Fitzgerald boys' soap box car and rode it down the hill to the creek and crashed into John Smither's iris bed! Or that she and her little gang of ruffians tied ladyfinger firecrackers on a string to the tail of Selma Louis's cat! Selma said it had lost at least three lives leaping around by the time she was able to get her scissors and cut it off!"

Now Margery stopped because, to her very great annoyance, she saw that Emma was trying hard to suppress laughter and that she was shaking with the effort.

"Honestly, Emma!" she exploded. "I can't believe you, laughing! Is there anything that child does that you ever disapprove of? She's running wild and you just let her! You need to get her away from that gang of boys! Why don't you set her up with Marilyn Mosley's daughter? She's just a block away; now there's a lovely child."

Emma was wiping away a tear that had escaped her attempts to stop laughing. "Now there's a child who's living a life I wouldn't wish on a dog," she said, suddenly serious, her mouth twisted with distaste. "All trussed up like a chicken in those frilly little outfits and always has to hold her mother's hand, even to cross the street in front of their house. And she's forever in the house, never out in the fresh air playing with other children, unless she's in that dreary backyard, all shaded and mossy! No, Margery, I have no idea how long the child will be with me, and it will break my heart when she goes, but up 'til then, I'm going to do everything I can to make sure she has the most wonderful childhood ever. And don't task me with the pranks she's done, not after everything you've done, including putting those garter snakes through Mrs. Travis's mail slot, and setting fire to the McKenna's old outhouse!"

Margery sat quite still. "Well," she said, rather lamely, because now she was remembering that she had done those things, and more. "Well, then, there's the matter of her name. What kind of name is Runner? That's the name Mary was calling her when she came to Anna's last week to play, a ridiculous name!"

"A nickname," Emma said gently. "At first – I don't know why unless it's because she's so good at baseball – it was Runaway. But all the boys that she plays with have short nicknames, and so they called her Runner, and that seems to have stuck."

The more urgent matter of butter tarts that had cooled enough to eat preoccupied them now; so the subject of small girls and their mischief was dropped.

"Umm!" said Emma, "you do make such wonderful butter tarts, Margery! I hope you've made enough for Anna and her three. I've been missing her, by the way, she was always such a ray of sunshine. How does she like being an office nurse?"

Margery wiped away a trickle of caramel that had coursed down her chin. "She likes it well enough, but last week she was offered a full-time position at the hospital. That's what she's been hoping for all along. Royce hasn't been helping out much with expenses, and the pay will be a little better than what she's been making at Dr. Miller's."

"Dr. Miller will miss her," Emma said, and she and Margery exchanged meaningful glances.

"The matches were a little too close to the kindling there," Margery added, one eyebrow arched. "Eventually, though, he'll find someone else and that'll be the end of it," she sighed, and for solace, took another tart.

"Jasmine told me that she and Anna are getting together with Arlena this weekend, before she leaves for the city. And I shouldn't, but I'll also have another one of those tarts," Emma said, as Margery passed her the plate. "Did I tell you that Arlena has found a job there, and an apartment already? But Arlena says her mother still hasn't given up trying to marry her off. And so, on this weekend, her last weekend in town, she's going to have to sit down to dinner again with Simon Jenner's nephew, that red-haired, freckle-faced wild man who is so plainly unsuited to the funeral business, or to Arlena, for that matter."

"Well, I wouldn't be too sure about that," Margery demurred. "Alistair MacGregor stands to inherit from his parents as well as Simon, and they own a flour milling operation in Standish that should sell for a pretty penny. Besides that, he plays the bagpipes. He's in demand for funerals for our first world war vets as they start to pass on. He just played the last lament for Charlie Struther's funeral at the United Church. And, speaking of Arlena, and her family, I heard a rumour that her brother's marriage is in trouble. I don't know much more than that, and I couldn't say who or why."

Although Margery might not know who or why or more, she always knew so very much that Emma was continually impressed with the scope of her intelligence on Medfordians and their doings. Emma had a good idea of how she managed it. Margery's daughter Lorena lived on the lakeshore, while another daughter, Anita and her husband, had a house on the town's northern outskirts. Lorena worked part-time as a telephone operator. Amongst them, they had the town's party line telephone exchange more or less covered. And this fact happened to be one among several reasons Emma had for visiting today, and undoubtedly the most important.

Now, seemingly apropos of nothing, she said, "isn't it wonderful, Margery? Soon we'll be able to talk like this on the phone. In just a week or so now, they'll start the changeover and all our conversations will be private. No more party lines!"

"I suppose so," Margery replied, looking rather disgruntled. "But it's going to be hard on our shut-ins and elderly, especially in the winter months. I know they shouldn't listen in, but they do, and then they feel like they're still part of what's happening in town."

Emma wanted to laugh at the expression on Margery's face, full of undisguised chagrin at this undesirable advance in communications, but she didn't. Instead she said, "speaking of shut-ins, I guess you've heard that Lianne Latham is in a bad way. And that her husband lost out on the principal job at Medford High."

"Those poor dears," Margery commiserated. "More bad luck than you can shake a stick at. But that Thomas Latham is really too good-looking to be a principal. He needs a proper potbelly and a bald spot to get respect. How can you have someone for a principal that looks like a matinee idol?"

"Yes, Lianne told me he fights off advances from students and even some of the teachers," Emma said. "He's had to keep his car locked after he found one particular individual lying in the backseat waiting for him. But there's never been a rumor of any falderal going on with him at school, so I guess he's been true to her."

Margery snorted. "With one notable exception. And now she's living right next door, once again! Talk about the matches being too close to the kindling! Well, anyhow, I'm sorry to hear about Lianne and how poorly she's doing. And, you know, I was wondering – with money being so tight right now, I'm looking for homecare work again. I heard that Eleanor Mackie is leaving, and the Lathams will need someone else. Do you think there's any chance – ?"

"No, I'm afraid not, because the position has already been taken," Emma replied. "But I did want to talk to you about that. And also, I have something important to tell you. It concerns Thomas and Jasmine, and something that happened almost ten years ago. The two of them, and Lianne, have finally given me permission to tell the whole story."

Margery had her head down, about to take a bite out of her third butter tart, but now she looked up and slowly set it aside, uneaten, on the plate in front of her. "What," she asked, barely breathing, "story?"

Then Emma told Margery about Thomas Latham wandering in the lakeside park. She described how he had rescued Jasmine when she was suicidal and intent on drowning herself. She related the tale as it had been told to her, omitting no detail. Or rather, she told her everything, right up to the point where the two of them found themselves alone in the house. Then she concluded her narration by saying, "and Thomas spent a good deal of time counseling Jasmine. And she says it was thanks to him, and the help and encouragement he gave her, that she decided to go on living and went on to build a new life for herself elsewhere. She wouldn't be alive today if weren't for Thomas, and she's well aware of it."

Until now Margery had sat spellbound. At this point, however, she reacted exactly as Emma had expected: she gave a big guffaw and a loud snort of disbelief. "Counseling? Is that why he was sneaking in and out the back door, or the front door, every day before you and Bill came home from work? And I'm sure that Jasmine was doing her share of counseling too, teaching him what she'd learned from running around town with every Tom, Dick and Harry!"

Emma stiffened. "You don't have to be coarse, Margery. You're entitled to your views. I'm just telling you what I know."

"And did you and Bill approve of this 'counseling' that went on in your home?" Margery demanded.

"Yes, we did approve of the counseling help that Thomas gave Jasmine," Emma said.

Margery was nonplussed. "Well, it appears I may have been wrong in some of my ideas about Jasmine," she admitted. "Anna told me not long ago that Jasmine took Royce away because she didn't want her to marry him, and that she made him come back to Medford once she learned Anna was pregnant. Anna says it's true, and I have to believe her. But frankly, Emma, I'm finding it near impossible to believe that those two were not having an affair. And if this is the truth, then why hasn't it come out before?"

"Think about it," Emma said. "Silvia was a nervous wreck. Obviously, so was Jasmine, perhaps even more so. Spreading the story of her suicide attempt around would have been the last straw for both of them, wouldn't you say?"

Now came the moment Emma had been waiting for. She made the most of it. She yawned, a pretense of boredom. Then she lifted her shoulders and shrugged dismissively. "In any case, Margery, does it really matter what you or I think? I guess the people most concerned here, Jasmine, Lianne and Thomas, are the ones who really know the truth of the matter. If there's any doubt, I should tell you that Lianne has asked Jasmine to replace Mrs. Mackie. And since Jasmine needs the money, she'll be starting with the Lathams next week."

Emma was not familiar with the symptoms of stroke. If she had been, she might have been alarmed at how Margery's eyes bulged, her mouth fell open and she flushed bright red as she lurched forward in her chair. "Jasmine," she gasped, "is going to take care of Lianne?"

"That's right," Emma said, rising. "Now, it's late, and high time I was going. Thank you for those wonderful butter tarts; they completely ruined my appetite, but they were worth it!"

Over her shoulder as she left, she added, "Jasmine says she doesn't mind if the story gets out. It was almost ten years ago; and she'll be leaving town soon anyhow. She just wants to make sure people get a more accurate idea of what happened. For Thomas's sake."

From the slight rise on the road where she had parked her car, she could see through the kitchen window of the MacClure's house that Margery had recovered from her choking fit. She was over in the corner of the kitchen where the phone hung on the wall, and she was talking into it, her mouth moving rapidly.

CHAPTER 44

As she drove away, Emma congratulated herself. She had taken the truth and stretched like a rubber band, stretched it until it almost snapped; she had twisted it like a pretzel. But as she told Lianne when she first agreed to the scheme, she would never tell a lie. And she hadn't.

She thought back to the events of that long-ago autumn when Jasmine was living with them. After she told her husband that her friend and co-worker Miriam had warned her of rumors of "something going on" at her house between her niece and Thomas Latham, Bill, that wise man, counseled her not to react too quickly. He pointed out that Thomas had been struggling with depression, and that Jasmine had undergone experiences that would lay anyone low. Thomas's career, not to mention his marriage, could be gravely affected if they handled the situation poorly, he said. And so they devised a strategy, a "smoke screen" as Bill called it.

The next work day, airily, Emma told Miriam that Thomas had a key and was in and out of their house all the time, and that his being there was nothing unusual. The following day, a Tuesday, she begged off work for a dentist appointment. She was sitting in the living room when Thomas came downstairs. He appeared not too surprised to see her. He called Jasmine down and they clung together like survivors of a shipwreck, while Jasmine related the story of how Thomas had rescued her from drowning herself, and how one thing had led to another.

There was little shame and less embarrassment. This surprised and rather shocked Emma until she heard Jasmine's story and saw how events had unfolded and the good it seemed to have done them both. Thomas was no longer the hollow-eyed wreck she had seen shambling about the lakeside park. Jasmine had come alive again, standing straight and tall and unafraid. It was only Lianne who was the injured party, and at the mention of her name Thomas looked properly upset and remorseful. The anger Emma was nursing had turned to compassion quickly enough. Then she told them what it was she wanted them to do. Together, she and Jasmine went to the front door and standing where they were clearly visible, they bid Thomas goodbye.

On Wednesday Thomas waited for Emma to come home. Once she arrived and dropped her handbag and coat, she and Jasmine stood at the front door and talked to him as he was standing on the porch. After a few moments, he waved goodbye to them as he went down the stairs.

The next day, Thursday, Emma and Thomas went out the back door. Jasmine joined them and helped Thomas move the garden bench from one spot to another in the backyard. Friday was the last day Thomas was to come to the house. After a few minutes spent chatting at the door, Emma saw him off from the front porch.

What Jasmine and Thomas did during the times they were waiting for her to arrive home from work was of no concern to Emma.

Lorena Sykes and Emily Barrett, who had clear views of the front and back of the house respectively and who were principally responsible for spreading the news of Thomas's comings and goings, were taken aback and confused by these developments. They puzzled over them. But it was too late. By then the scandal had acquired a life of its own, and all that anyone would ever remember was that Thomas Latham had been carrying on with Jasmine Holmes, just weeks after his wife had delivered a stillborn child.

Time went by; interest in the affair cooled as it moved on to subjects more novel and new. Now, on a Tuesday evening many years later, a still-incredulous Margery was relating Emma's tale of rescue and redemption to her daughter. When at last she paused for breath, Lorena slowly said, "you know, Mom, I do remember seeing Emma there. She was at the door with Jasmine when Thomas left the house. At least a couple of times."

It seemed that Bill's "smoke screen", which had fizzled out at first, still had a few sparks left in it. And fanned by the winds of gossip, it kindled and grew until, finally, it helped produce the billowing clouds of confusion he had once envisaged almost ten years before.

CHAPTER 45

"If you're going to invite yourself to dinner, then you can at least make the salad," Jasmine said pertly. Arlena laughed. She found a knife and started dicing the cucumber and green onions Jasmine thrust at her. Laura was there too, sitting at the kitchen table with a pencil, intent on the connect-the-numbers book she had just received from Arlena.

"Well, soon I can phone you without all of Medford listening in, and when I drop by to chat you won't have to invite me to dinner," Arlena said.

"Who said you were invited? And now you've got me curious. What's so important you have to eat chicken-a-la-king to tell me about it?"

"It's something my mother said," Arlena replied, busy washing lettuce. "It's so strange for her to say something like this that I started wondering about it. She asked me if you ever talked about her or said anything about her."

Jasmine could easily guess why Elizabeth Stoddart might ask that question. "Well, if you would like to give her an answer, Arlena, you can tell her that I've said nothing about her and that I have nothing to say to her. I hope you had a better reason than that to come here, or I won't give you dessert."

"What happened between the two of you when you returned Mason's ring? I've always wondered."

Arlena was prodding uncomfortably close to the root of the matter, and Jasmine was well aware of it. "She was perfectly cordial. Next subject."

Arlena knew her mother. The question Elizabeth had asked showed she was plenty worried Jasmine might say something about her. But Jasmine maintained there was nothing to say – or, more likely, nothing she cared to share. What was it? Something significant, Arlena was sure. But now she would never know, and she accepted her disappointment with good grace.

Later that night, she drank a cup of tea with her mother before bed and told her Jasmine's response: that she had nothing to say about her, or to her. Elizabeth kept her poker face. Arlena sensed she was relieved that what took place between the two of them would remain a secret. A secret never to be known by her daughter, who in turn might tell it to her father. And her brother.

Then Elizabeth asked, "why is she still in town anyway? I thought she would have left by now."

It was a matter of money, Arlena told her. She had a very small inheritance and needed more to leave and get settled in Las Vegas again. "Her mother, Silvia, had some valuable jewelry and so Jasmine's selling it to raise the funds she needs."

Her mother then asked another question that aroused some suspicion in Arlena. She wanted to know where Jasmine was selling her jewelry. Why would she ask that? "At Gildean's, in the city," Arlena answered shortly. She was tired of talking and wanted to go to bed.

Before she left the room, however, Arlena couldn't resist the temptation to rub it all in. "Too bad Mason didn't marry Jasmine. She's kind and good-hearted, and she would have made a great sister- and daughter-in-law. Instead, he married that twit, and now there's going to be a divorce in the family."

Her mother said nothing.

Now Arlena set down her knife and put the finished salad on the kitchen table. "Next subject? Well, yes, I do have something else to tell you, Jasmine. It looks as if my brother is headed for a divorce. It's Catharine who wants it. She's found someone she likes better."

"Is that good news or bad?"

"Good news, from Mason's standpoint. I don't exactly know the details, but soon I will."

"Why ever did he marry her in the first place?" Jasmine asked. "It seems they had little in common."

"I guess when you can't marry the person you want, then you settle for second best. Or third. Something like that. And she comes from money and will inherit money."

Jasmine could sympathize with Mason, because that was almost exactly what she had done. Except, unfortunately, for the money part. "Dinner is ready," she said, "and here's Aunt Emma. Let's put it on the table."

Emma was pleased to see Arlena, and thrilled with the bear hug from the child, who had missed her usual tea-and-cookie time with her Auntie after school. How Emma enjoyed the activity, the hustle and bustle of her little household! And how she would miss it when they all left – a depressing thought, so she resolutely pushed it out of her mind. But her heart still sank when she sat down to eat. She picked up her fork. After one date square and three butter tarts, Jasmine's lovely dinner was not chicken-a-la-king, but dyspepsia staring her in the face.

It was at that exact moment, just as she was lifting the first forkful, she heard the ring sequence for their call. Ring-ting-ting-ring! Ring-ting-ting-ring! Jasmine got up and answered it, then, with a look of worry and concern said, "it's for you."

Emma heard the sobbing before she picked up the phone.

"Emma! Come quick, come quick!" Margery cried. "I went looking for Jim for supper, and I found him on the bench out behind his little house, and he'd eaten almost a whole quart of those awful canned tomatoes and they're bad!! We can't afford an ambulance, please come drive us to the hospital! Come right away!"

As she raced through town to the hospital, running one of Medford's two red lights and ignoring stop signs wherever she could, Emma gave Margery, sitting in the back seat of the car with Jim, a piece of her mind. "Margery," she said, "if ever there was a time to keep your mouth shut, this is it. I think we both know why Jim might have eaten those tomatoes, with him in his down state of mind and all your money worries. He was thinking of his life insurance, and he did it for you! So let's hope to heaven he'll be alright, but don't you dare go blabbing to the doctors or anyone else how you told him they were poisonous and not to eat them!"

In the back seat with Jim, Margery said, between sobs, "Jim, if you don't get better, I'll eat a jar of those darn tomatoes myself! But don't you worry, Jim, you're going to make it through this! And then we'll get through everything else together just fine, you wait and see!"

Emma held both of Margery's hands as they sat in the emergency waiting room while Jim's stomach was pumped. The remainder of the quart sealer of tomatoes was taken away for analysis, but Emma had already sniffed it and knew it was off. Once Lorena, Anna and Anita arrived, Margery brightened up, but she didn't stop crying, large tears rolling down her face, until the doctor came in and said he thought Jim was out of danger.

Jim was being kept in for observation overnight. A nurse came by and told the family they could go in to see him. Since Anita had her family car and could take them all home, Emma decided to leave and said her goodbyes; but not before she gave Margery yet another piece of her mind.

"Margery, that man is pure gold," she told her. "He reminds me of my Bill, and there isn't a day goes by that I don't miss Bill so much I'd give everything I have just to spend one hour with him. I only wish I had appreciated him as much when he was alive."

She could tell by the look on Margery's face her message had hit home.

In the kitchen at eleven o'clock, Emma found that Jasmine had put her chicken-a-la-king dinner in the plate warmer. She was hungry. It was a little bit dry, but absolutely delicious, and she ate every single bite.

CHAPTER 46

Max Stoddart had about as much use for golf as he did for ping-pong or croquet. Maybe less, because even nine holes took an excessive amount of time, far more than most games with little or big balls more suitable to kids than grown men with work to do. But golf did have its uses, he conceded, when you needed to finesse a deal or fly under the corporate radar or generally work things out minus the distance of a boardroom table between you and the other party.

So Max was a halfway decent golf player and had memberships in two local clubs. This morning, he was on his way out to the Coshoni Heights Club to meet Kevin O'Malley, one of his protégés, for a quick round of golf. He had spotted O'Malley as a talent four years ago when he was appointed CFO and then General Manager of Foremost Steel, a steel rolling and forming company in the town of Barreston. Plagued by family ownership, the firm was a mess. Despite the obstacles imposed by warring family members, O'Malley cleaned it up neatly and the firm was back in the black in only two years. Before that he had been an accountant in private practice with a specialty in audits and a deserved reputation for helping small companies stay solvent.

So, although he was a little light in the credentials, when the position of Comptroller came open for the new car plant on the outskirts of Medford, Max had given him a referral and a reference. Subsequently O'Malley had taken a big step up and successfully landed the job.

All this Max told Elizabeth at breakfast and at the door as he was getting ready to leave, with his clubs already in the car. He mentioned that, at Mason's request, he would be asking O'Malley for a job for Jim MacClure, the former general manager of the defunct Stuttgart Leather Mills. Elizabeth looked concerned. "That's grand, but I've heard that Jim MacClure was taken into hospital last night with food poisoning."

"How is he?" Max didn't want to bother asking for a job for a sick or dead guy.

"Luckily, he's recovered. If they had waited much longer he might have died, Arlena says. She was on the phone this morning with his daughter Anna. He should be fine in a day or so. But if you're asking about jobs, how about the tannery workers, too? There are fifty or so who haven't found work yet, I think, and heaven knows they could use some help."

"Good idea!" Max said. He looked at her with love and admiration. His wife was a wonderful woman, always thinking of others. Then he told her that after golf he would be meeting Mason for lunch, and that he expected to find out more about this divorce business.

Now he was out on the course, having teed off with O'Malley around nine a.m. After they cleared up a few other minor items, he brought up the matter of Jim MacClure and was gratified when O'Malley said, "sure, we're looking for good supervisory staff. There shouldn't be a problem. Have him send me his resume and we'll find a place for him."

The car plant was still thin on management staff and O'Malley had a say in many decisions, including hiring. In response to Max's inquiry, he told him the first line workers would be hired in two weeks. Then, when Max asked about jobs for the tannery workers, he said something that immediately raised Max's hackles.

"We're not running a charity here, Max," O'Malley commented, in a tone of voice that, whether he realized it or not, made him sound like a bit of a pompous ass.

"Nobody is asking you to do charity," Max replied smoothly, as he hit a decent drive to within a couple of feet from the green. "These are capable, hardworking men."

214 | Pat McDermott

"I've seen those guys coming out of the factory," said O'Malley. "They're a rough looking bunch."

"Tell me how pretty you have to be to work on the line in a car plant," Max replied. He doubted that O'Malley, with his Irish lantern jaw and horn-rimmed glasses, would win points in any beauty contest himself.

"And what kind of education do they have? Not much, I guess."

"Grade eight to ten maximum, but they have great work experience." Max replied.

"Well, they can put their applications in with the others but they'll be judged on their qualifications and there's a minimum requirement of grade ten education," O'Malley made a short putt to par the hole.

"Well, then, plain and simple, they won't make it, will they?" Max asked. "They require special consideration. Your company will be the hero if they're hired. The whole town donated money for their support and now they're on the dole. We all want them to find jobs."

O'Malley shook his head. "Most of them appear to be in their '40s, and don't meet the criteria, so probably it's not that likely, Max," he said.

What was the matter with this lunkhead? Could he not see that this was a win-win proposition for the company? Max tried once more.

"The tannery was a big operation, and it could run lean because every worker was trained to do every job in the factory and fill in as needed. There was no deadwood, there were no dummies. Everyone there worked hard, at top speed. Stuttgart had no patience for loafers, and Jim MacClure ran the place like a swiss watch."

O'Malley was making a big deal out of concentrating on setting the tee so he didn't have to say anything. Max could see that he was still unimpressed, and now Max was getting irritated. What was going on here? Then, suddenly, in a flash, it dawned on him.

Of course! The Irish mafia! This guy was in every Irish organization, he was a bigwig in the Knights of Columbus, all his pals were Irish. He wanted to seed the initial job queue with his buddies and their kids! Give them jobs in return for favours done and yet to be done! And him not in his new job much longer than a month! What bloody nerve!

O'Malley made a good clean drive and now he could pay attention. "Alright, Max," he said. "I don't know if it will count for much, but I'll put in a word for your tannery boys."

"You do that," said Max, his eyes like slits and his voice flat. He made a better drive than O'Malley and he landed on the green again. "And tomorrow I'll be seeing your boss, Eric Rutherford, at lunch, and I'll tell him about all the good will the company would rack up by hiring the tannery workers. And I'll also tell him that the town, and the local government, will be looking hard at the initial hires for line jobs at the plant. And that they will not be happy if kids with names like O'Hara and Flaherty, or O'Sullivan and Kerrigan come roaring in on their motorcycles and jalopies from places like Barreston and get jobs, when we have good, experienced workers, local men desperate for work, sitting around on the dole."

Max could tell he had hit the mark because O'Malley immediately stiffened up and flubbed his next shot. In a short while he recovered, and said, not even trying to disguise his resentment, "there's no bias in the hiring process, Max."

"Of course not," Max said. They finished the game, which was one of Max's best to date this season, three shots under course par to win the match, with O'Malley trailing badly. Max couldn't wait to get away from the guy.

The next day he did exactly as he had promised, at a luncheon where he managed to speak directly to Rutherford. And Rutherford immediately saw the value of hiring the tannery workers, and promised to consider it. Max also made sure to advise the Mayor of Medford of what he had done, and the following day the Mayor made the same pitch to Rutherford at the plant opening ceremony. The editor of the local paper just happened to approach Rutherford in time to hear what the mayor had suggested, and he promised that if the tannery workers were hired, he would make it the lead story on the front page of the weekend edition.

In the end, the tannery workers, all those who applied, got jobs and did just fine. After that golf date, however, although Max might wave to him or say hello, he didn't have the time of day for O'Malley. Because he didn't know how to play the game. He didn't know the rules and he was a sore loser. He would always be an amateur in the only game that really mattered to Max, and for sure it wasn't golf.

Right now, though, once their game finished Max quickly escaped to the locker room, where O'Malley couldn't follow him because he wasn't a club member. Previously they had agreed to have a beer together after the last hole. Needless to say, Max did not follow up on his offer. So, he was parched and looking forward to lunch with his son, although he doubted the topic they were to discuss, Mason's divorce, was likely to be much of an aid to digestion.

CHAPTER 47

After stowing his clubs in the car, Max went to the golf club dining room. His son was waiting for him at a table. Mason looked happy. It was mildly depressing to Max that it was taking a divorce to make his son look as though he might be happy. They gave each other a dad-and-son hug and sat down. After they were settled with their drinks and had cleared the decks of some immediate business matters, Max asked, "so, do you want to talk about Catharine and give your mother and me a heads up about what's going on?"

"In a minute," Mason said. "First of all, I wanted to talk about Arlena. You know we've always been close, but I have to tell you I was totally flummoxed when she told me she's finally discovered her sexuality. She said she spoke to you and that you didn't seem all that surprised. So, have you told Mom?"

"Not yet. In fact, I wasn't surprised." Max said. "I've kind of suspected it for a while. Remember your great-aunt Barb, the one out in California? Well, right into her fifties she was always bringing girlfriends around when she visited Mom and Dad. Had to figure that one out for myself, because I don't think your grandparents ever did. Anyhow, I told Arlena it makes no difference to me. And it doesn't. I'll always love her just the same, and like I said, she'll always be my favorite baby girl."

Mason never failed to be amazed at his father. In some ways, Max reminded him of the vessel he had served on for most of his war years in the navy: the MTB war torpedo boat. It was small, fast, indefatigable and hardy and it popped up like a cork even when swamped by the heaviest seas. Now he marveled again at how casually Max was able to deal with the curve balls life threw at him and wished, as always, that he had been gifted with the same ability.

"But telling your Mom about this, well, leave that to me," Max continued, downing his drink and summoning a waiter for a refill. "There's no rush. She seems a little worried, preoccupied these days. Arlena said she'd let me figure out the timing. Now, what about you?"

Mason was positively beaming, "well, Catharine's leaving me. The good news is, I'm keeping my boys! Her new man isn't that fond of kids and she gave me primary custody without a fight. They'll stay with me, in the house, and she's moving out."

"Who's the new man?"

Mason told him it was one of the golf pros at Catharine's club, which happened to be the other golf club Max belonged to, the Forest Glen. "Jack Steeves. Do you remember him?

Max sucked his teeth for a moment and thought. "Tall, about 6'3", blond, brown eyes?" he asked.

"That's him," Mason confirmed.

"Yeah, I remember the guy," Max said. "Dumb as a post. Should be about right."

But not so dumb that he wasn't smart enough to hitch onto a million-dollar baby, Max thought. Too bad to lose all that money in the family, but oh well.

"Yes, thanks to him, I'll soon be a free man," Mason smiled. His father looked at him. There was something going on in there. Little wheels turning in Mason's head, he could tell.

"What are you thinking of?' Max asked. Mason didn't reply.

"It's her, isn't it?" Max said, and his spirits plummeted. "I'm right, aren't I?"

It truly was depressing; the drag the past had on Mason and how it kept its claws so tightly fastened on all his forlorn hopes for the future.

"Why don't you leave it alone, Mason?" Max asked. "She's already told you she doesn't want anything to do with you. There's no percentage for you in chasing after her. What is it you want?"

Mason looked down at his big hands, resting on either side of his plate on the table. "Dad, I was thinking last night that I can't remember even one conversation I've had with Catharine. But I can remember almost everything Jasmine and I ever talked about. She challenged me; she kept me on my toes. Now I just want to talk to her. I want both of us to have some clarity about the past, to find out what went so wrong. I want her to know I'm not a bad person."

You just want to talk to her. Oh sure. It occurred to Max that it wasn't even one o'clock yet and he had already had to deal with two lunkheads, and one of them was his son.

Patiently, he said, "son, nine years have gone by and this is not the same young woman you knew before. She would not be happy living in Medford. With the bad experiences she's had here and the life she's probably lived in Vegas, it's not likely she's going to sit down to a Sunday night roast beef dinner with the family and be all nicey-nicey. And that, son, is the kind of wife you need and that would make you happy."

Mason was clearly annoyed. His hands were now balled into fists. He said, with some heat, "it's great that you and Mom are such authorities on what kind of wife I need, Dad! I've been down that path with you two before, telling me how perfect Catharine was, and I wasted seven years of my life with someone totally wrong for me! The only thing right that came out of that marriage is my two boys. So don't give me anymore of your half-assed lectures!"

Max had to concede Mason had a point and generously told him so. By mutual consent, they changed the subject to one that interested them both: the new industrial park around the auto plant. Max had owned the land the plant was on and two years ago he had sold it to the automotive company for peanuts. But now Mason and he were setting up for the real cash-in; they were developing the business park themselves and already had suppliers to the plant lined up and clamoring for sites.

But as Mason talked, Max was only half paying attention. Instead, he looked at his son and wondered: just how long does it take for a dream to die? And, more importantly, what will happen when it does?

CHAPTER 48

"Hello Lianne."

"Hello Jasmine."

Jasmine had seen Lianne from close at hand only a few times, when she was in high school and had been pressed into service to help with serving and cleanup at Bill and Emma's parties. Now, propped up with pillows and reclining on a sofa in the sunroom, Lianne reminded Jasmine of Colette, the ancient French porcelain doll dating from the Victorian era that used to adorn her grandmother's dressing table. There was the same plentiful dark brunette hair, a bluish tinge to her white skin, and she was gamine, with a sweet uptilted nose and large, lustrous brown eyes. She differed from the doll in her extreme thinness, her neck and arms almost as stick-like as those of a malnourished child.

"I remember meeting you before, Lianne, at Emma and Bill's house. I thought you were very pretty then, and you still are."

Was that all she could think of to say? Jasmine was mildly embarrassed at the words that had tumbled out of her mouth; but it seemed they were about right.

"Why thank you!" Lianne brightened, showing every evidence of being pleased with her compliment. "Well, you're certainly starting off on the right foot, because I just love flattery."

They both laughed, a relieved kind of laugh, now that the first few difficult minutes were over.

"I'm feeling a little off balance because, frankly, I have no idea of how to act in this kind of situation," Jasmine confided. She intended to play it straight and honest. Even riskier, she wanted to deal immediately with some of the more sensitive issues that otherwise could simmer, unresolved, beneath any relationship they might develop.

"Yes," Lianne agreed. "The wife and her husband's lover. A little awkward." She said it in an off-handed way, as if she were not one of the principal actors in that drama, and laughed again.

Jasmine only half-smiled. "You must have hated me. I more or less threw myself at Thomas."

"From what he told me, he was a pretty good catcher."

"I wondered why you put up with us – with what was going on."

"Well, at the start, once I found out, I did hate you," Lianne said, pensively. "But then, I was relieved, and I might even say grateful. I had watched Thomas going downhill; he was worse, every day. I couldn't help him, no one could. He was in a tailspin and then, when things were truly desperate, you were the one who pulled him out of it. Afterward, he told me about you, how it started when you dove off the pier into the lake, and I knew that it – your time with Thomas – had helped you too. So, after thinking about it, I decided not to interfere, to stop anything that finally seemed to be doing some good."

"I think you must be a saint," Jasmine said, and she couldn't help it, there was a little sarcastic edge to her words.

"Not really," Lianne said. "Believe me, if things had been different –" and here she raised one small white hand and curled her polished red nails into a claw, reminding Jasmine of nothing so much as a small kitten attempting ferocity. "If the situation hadn't been what it was then, I would have scratched your eyes out!"

She was impish, dimpled, irresistible. This time, Jasmine couldn't keep herself from smiling.

"The way I see it," Lianne said, "it was part of his illness. From depression to obsession. Then recovery."

It seemed a strange thing to say. Obsession. An illness. Jasmine did not want to openly disagree but did so silently. She knew that what Thomas had felt for her was not so superficial that it could be explained away as a product of illness. There had been passion, yes, but also another emotion so deep and true there was probably only one word for it.

But she had not yet grasped the subtlety of this woman. Later on, she would guess that Lianne was attempting to create a neutral space in which they could form a friendship –something that would have been difficult, perhaps impossible, with the awareness that along with his mind and body, for a while Jasmine had also possessed her husband's heart.

It was time for a new subject. Jasmine drew up a chair next to Lianne as she lay on her lounge, and asked: "I know that we've gone over a few of the reasons we're doing this – why I'm coming to work for you – but I wonder if you can explain a little better what you think might happen?"

"A good question," Lianne said. "And to tell the truth, it's a gamble. Before I became so ill, Thomas applied for principal and vice principal positions at several schools. The problem is character references. They're so very important for teachers and – even a hint of scandal – I don't need to tell you how that might ruin his chances."

"But what if the rumours and gossip weren't true?" Lianne lifted her eyebrows theatrically. "That's the question we want people to ask themselves before they decide to say anything that would spoil his hopes of advancing himself. So, if there's some doubt, then they will only be able to look at his record, and it is exceptional!" She clapped her hands excitedly, like a happy child.

Jasmine was dubious. If this were a gamble, she herself wouldn't have risked much on the odds. But she only said, "I'm sorry. If I weren't here, none of this would have been necessary. I've brought all the old gossip back to life, I'm afraid."

Lianne shook her head. "No, you didn't. It never died," she said with some bitterness. "Gossip has a long, a very long life in Medford. It lasts, at the least, two generations. Your being here is not a disaster; it's an opportunity."

For the first time, it dawned on Jasmine. How must it have been for Lianne, if what she said were true? Imagine living in Medford with that cloud perpetually over your head: forever known as the slighted wife of an unfaithful husband, who was Jasmine Holmes' last fling before she left town with her cousin's fiancé!

It was a thought she had never entertained before and it was both startling and upsetting. Suddenly Jasmine was struck with shame before this woman's magnanimity, her selfless desire to help her husband at the cost of having to endure someone who must have caused her so much pain.

"I was the lucky one, it seems," she said, her eyes downcast. "I got to run away from what I did, but you and Thomas –"

The hand that came to rest over hers was soft, but the voice she heard was stern. "Just one minute, Jasmine. Listen to me. You're being frank and open, and I'm glad. It will make everything easier between us. There aren't any rules for the situation we're in, no Emily Post book of etiquette, that's for sure! But since I'm in charge here, I'm going to make a few rules. The first one is that there will be no blame and no shame. I don't want your apologies. They're not expected and they won't be accepted. What I'm saying is, there's no need to be upset about the past or what happened back then, nine years ago. Let's just move on!"

Lianne stopped talking. She motioned toward a neighbouring house that was situated on a slight rise with its windows overlooking the backyard and when she turned to face Jasmine, her mouth had narrowed into a thin line. "Well," she said. "there's no need to name names, but I can't tell you how much I'm looking forward to pulling the wool over the eyes of all those folks who caused us such a lot of trouble, and who just love to slice and dice people like you and me and Thomas!"

A fraction of a second following this outburst, from a cage almost hidden in Lianne's collection of sunroom plants there came a trill of bird song that was almost as loud, long and emphatic as her final words. On hearing it, both of them burst into laughter.

"I talk a lot to Dickie and as you can see, he's gotten into the habit of talking back," Lianne said. "He's likely upset because he's been forgotten. We usually hang his cage on the front porch – do you think you could? That's where he stays during the warm weather."

Jasmine stood up. "Just one more question about your plan. I'll be going in and out of the house, so it's easy enough to see me, but how about you? Are you able to walk short distances?

"I hope to take a walk with you, sometime soon," Lianne replied tentatively. "But I don't think I can, today. However, we can sit outside for a while in the backyard, when your daughter comes here after school. Then a few of the neighbours, including that nasty tattletale Emily Barrett, can get a good look at us. But apart from that, I don't think we need worry – we've just given Medford folks the juiciest bit of gossip than they've had for years!"

Lianne's eyelids had turned a darker shade of mauve. Within the last few minutes she had become as pale as old linen. Jasmine checked the schedule Mrs. Mackie gave her, and saw it was time for her morning nap. She put up no argument when Jasmine pointed this out. Once settled, her eyes immediately closed, like those of the china doll she so closely resembled, and in seconds she was deep asleep.

Sadly, Lianne was never able to take her little walk along the sidewalk with Jasmine. The body that housed that bright, strong spirit was too frail. Beneath her many coverlets, Lianne was as light as thistledown; and as Jasmine later told Emma, she feared the first strong gust of wind off the lake might blow her away.

The day passed quickly enough in small chores while Lianne slept, and light chitchat when she awoke. She had professed an interest in learning new card games, and Jasmine led her through some simple rounds of two-handed whist. After they had played for a while, it was Lianne who suggested her afternoon nap. "I want to be rested and ready for Laura when she comes back from school," she said, her eyes bright with expectation.

Jasmine used this time to prepare a simple dinner for Thomas and Lianne and to survey the sorely depleted state of the food cupboards and the contents of the refrigerator. She wrote out a long shopping list for Thomas. This would be her only communication with him; she was to leave at precisely 5:00 pm. before he arrived home. Jasmine was glad of the arrangement. She would not have to see him; her thoughts and feelings were already in turmoil and even considering this possibility was stressful, for reasons she did not wish to explore.

CHAPTER 49

"Jasmine! What time is it?"

"It's three-thirty."

"Your daughter will be here anytime now! Please help me up?"

By four o'clock Lianne was sitting in a chair in the backyard, her hair combed and fresh lipstick applied. From her air of nervous expectation Jasmine could tell how important this first meeting was to her and felt a small tremor of anxiety. What did it all mean?

Then came the knock at the front door and exactly like Laura, it was nothing timid or shy: the big door knocker lifted up and banged hard, three times in succession, by a little girl who enjoyed making a big noise. Jasmine ushered her into the garden and introduced her to Lianne.

"Hello Laura, I've been looking forward to meeting you! I've seen you running to school in the morning from my window upstairs."

"Hello Mrs. Latham. Yes, I like to run!"

The child was all enormous purple-blue eyes with pink cheeks from the trip home and the buffeting of the wind off the lake. Her hair was cropped short and, if trousers had been substituted for the skirt that showed off her knees, both of which were adorned with scabs from the last fall or trip, she could easily have been mistaken for a beautiful little boy. They sat together at a small white wrought iron table in the sunny backyard and enjoyed cookies and tea, with Laura's cup watered down to make a child's "pink tea" with plenty of sugar; and Jasmine was pleased to see her mind her manners and not gobble down the jelly doughnut that Lianne had set aside especially for her.

"I can't stay too long," Laura said, from a mouth covered in powdered sugar. "Max and Simon and I are going to catch grasshoppers in Simon's Dad's vegetable garden and he's giving us a penny for every grasshopper!"

"What will you put them in?" Lianne asked.

"A glass jar, I think," Laura replied, and seeing her mother's finger pointing to her serviette, belatedly used it instead of the back of her hand to wipe her sugary mouth.

"If it's alright with your mother, Mr. Latham could help make a cage for your grasshoppers if you can come over after supper tonight," Lianne offered. "We have an old window screen that would be perfect for the sides of a cage."

If it's alright with your mother. What choice did she have, after that? Jasmine smiled fixedly as her daughter responded with enthusiasm, but she felt a flash of anger. Things over which she had no control were moving too fast.

"I'm saving up for a bike," Laura confided. "If I can save up twenty dollars, Auntie Emma is going to help me buy one."

"Why then, I have a job for you!" Lianne said delightedly. "I haven't been able to weed my garden. Do you know what dandelions and grass look like? Can you show me?"

Yes she did, Laura said, and promptly left her chair and came back with samples of both.

"Well, if you can spend the next fifteen minutes pulling grass and dandelions out of my flowerbeds, then I will give you fifteen cents," Lianne promised. "And please save any dandelion seeds."

What a lot of money for just fifteen minutes! An excited Laura immediately set to work amidst the flowerbeds yanking grass and dandelions and depositing them into a big garden basket. Jasmine remained silent, and Lianne was quick to guess why. "I'm sorry. I should have asked your permission before going ahead and volunteering Thomas to help Laura," she said. "And probably I should have asked him too! I just got carried away with the thrill of having a child visit after, oh, such a very long time."

Her voice was so wistful that Jasmine's anger quickly dissipated. She only said, "Laura is my everything, so I should warn you that I'm possessive. But I won't be surprised if I can't talk her out of coming over tonight."

"Why did you want the dandelion seeds, Mrs. Latham?" Laura inquired, puzzled, when she presented her basket at the end of her weeding time.

"They're for my canary, Dickie, and he likes to eat them. Do you want to feed him some?"

"You have a canary that eats dandelion seeds?!" Laura exclaimed incredulously. "I sure do!" After Jasmine retrieved the cage from the porch and set it on a table in the sunroom, Laura dropped some dandelion fluff through the wires. Then she laughed uproariously to see the bright-eyed bird vigorously attack it, tossing it up in the air and throwing it around his cage as he pecked at the seeds.

Lianne watched the child with obvious enjoyment, delighting in her laughter. Then she paid her the agreed-on fifteen cents and, after Laura gave her mother a hug, demanded one herself before she reluctantly let her leave through the picket gate that joined the Latham and Madison properties.

"She's such a beautiful little girl." Lianne watched Laura rush toward the back door of her aunt's house, unbuttoning her shirt as she ran in her hurry to get changed and out catching grasshoppers.

"You know – her colouring is just like Thomas's. And the shape of her hands, and even the way she tilts her head just a little to the side when she talks. Is she – could she be – is Thomas her father, Jasmine?"

"No!" Jasmine said, instantly, automatically, even before she felt the first explosive little shocks of surprise and indignation at being asked such an intrusive and personal question. But when she looked at Lianne, she was startled to see that her big brown eyes were filling up with tears that even now had started to spill over and run down her cheeks.

"Well – he might be," she conceded: astonished at how much emotion Lianne had invested in this question, and unwilling to be the cause of such sorrow. Now she witnessed another rapid transformation, as Lianne wiped away her tears and gave her a tremulous smile, her face shining like the sun after rain.

"Thank you for that," she said. "It's such a comfort for me even to think there might be a chance that Thomas has a living child. That there's something of him that will go on."

Jasmine's day ended shortly after five. She opened the back door to the homely smell of frying onions and the sight of an aproned Emma bustling around the kitchen. "My goodness, what a relief to be home!" she exclaimed.

"Well, after that remark, I'm almost afraid to ask you how your day went," Emma said drily. "But I will, because I'm dying to know. How was it?"

"She's a lovely person," Jasmine replied.

"Yes, everyone likes Lianne. How did you get along?"

"Quite well, for the most part. Considering the situation. But I don't know if I can do this job."

"What!?Why not?"

"I have the feeling that Lianne has more in mind than trying to shine up Thomas's reputation so that he can find another position. Which I doubt will be that successful, anyhow."

"Well, I don't see why it wouldn't be. Three of my friends have already phoned me to ask if the story is true. But what do you mean?"

"She asked me if Thomas was Laura's father."

"No! Really! What did you say?"

"Without asking me, she also arranged for Laura to go over tonight after supper so that Thomas can help her build her a cage for her insect collection."

Emma stopped stirring her pot and looked directly at Jasmine. "If I know Lianne, she's worried sick about her husband and how he's going to fare after she's gone. It's likely she's trying to give him something to live for."

Jasmine stood there open-mouthed. Of course, that was the reason; and trust Emma to see it and cut to the heart of the matter in just a few short words.

"I think you're right. But her plans seem to include my daughter and me in other ways known only to her and with more involvement than I want."

"Well, I certainly can sympathize with you," Emma said, turning back to her pot. "Because that's somewhat how I felt after I discovered how ill you were and I was trying to decide whether to bring you here, or leave you in the hospital and Laura in foster care."

For a moment, Jasmine didn't reply. Emma guessed that her remark had hit home.

"There is a difference," Jasmine said, quite stiffly. "I am intending to leave soon and take my daughter with me." She turned to go upstairs.

But Emma couldn't let her escape yet, because she was burning with curiosity and Jasmine had not answered her question. She just had to ask her once more: "Jasmine, what did you tell Lianne when she asked you if Thomas was Laura's father?"

Jasmine stopped and gave her a knowing smile. "At first I said no, but Lianne looked as if she were about to cry. So, then I said that he might be, and she cheered right up." She paused. "I don't know why people object so much to a lie. Just a little lie, occasionally, makes everything so much easier."

So possibly Thomas wasn't the child's father after all, Emma concluded. But as she stirred a pot and turned the onions to brown, she wondered: which was the lie? She had thought it was Jasmine's last statement, but was it her first instead? With Jasmine, one never could be sure; and Emma's mind got all muddled up even thinking about it. When Jasmine came back downstairs, Emma asked her.

But the time for truth, if indeed there had ever been one, seemed to be past. She only laughed and said, "that's for me to know and you to guess."

Would she ever disclose who Laura's father was, Emma wondered? Just then the child burst into the kitchen, summoned by the dinner bell.

"Liver and onions, eeeeuh!" she said, wrinkling her little nose.

Emma's more sober thoughts vanished and were replaced by a wave of amusement and affection. "Go wash those dirty hands!" she commanded.

She would wait until Laura sat down at the table to tell her she had cooked chicken for her instead. And chocolate custard for dessert.

CHAPTER 50

If there was one thing of which Simon Jenner was absolutely certain, it was that there was never anyone more ill-suited to the funeral business than his nephew, Alistair. He was holding the office door ajar for him and watching him as he rushed along the hallway of the Jenner Funeral Home, late, as usual, for their meeting. Jenner had observed that Alistair never only walked; he sprinted. To his uncle, even his hair, a wild red bush no amount of Brylcreem could tame, seemed an affront to the somber dignity of the Jenner Funeral Home.

At 24, Alistair was simply too violently alive to be much concerned with death, Jenner concluded. Once again he wondered: should he phone Helena, his sister, and plead with her to call him back home? Alistair's latest disaster, which was the reason for this meeting, had almost convinced him; but then he reminded himself of how much he owed Helena and her husband Jack, and changed his mind.

"Please Simon," Helena had implored him, "just take him off our hands for a few months before Jack has a nervous breakdown or murders him! And who knows? He could be perfect for the funeral business!"

Not a snowball's chance in hell of that, Jenner thought sourly as he shut the heavy office door behind his nephew. Allowing for his sister's penchant for exaggeration, before Alistair arrived in Medford, Jenner had wondered how Jack McGregor, a slow-moving, stolid accountant type, could have gotten so worked up as to be capable of murdering his only son. Now he knew. Jack was admirably suited to be the owner of a large milling operation. Alistair, his son was not. He made no secret of how boring he found it and devised various ways to get up to mischief; and thus he found himself at the Jenner Funeral Home where, Jenner ardently hoped, he would soon make a similar discovery.

Lewis Smythe, Jenner's assistant, was already seated in his chair at the meeting room table, waiting with a look of happy expectation for the fireworks to begin. Lewis had heavy horn-rimmed glasses and with his receding chin and dye-straight hair falling over a low brow bore a striking resemblance to a ferret. He had been the butt of several of Alistair's practical jokes and was looking forward to seeing him get his comeuppance.

Jenner cleared his throat. "Alistair, I listened to our radio announcements yesterday, after several of our former customers commented on them."

Alistair looked at him with blue-eyed innocence. The only indication of any emotion was a slight upturn at one corner of his mouth and a quirk of his left eyebrow. Jenner guessed that his nephew was enjoying himself and felt his blood pressure immediately rise.

"You know that just about everyone in Medford, and in the area all around, listens to them to find out if anyone they know has passed on, and the time for the visitation and funeral services?"

Alistair nodded. "Yes Uncle," he answered.

"I put you in charge of updating our announcements thinking that you would take this responsibility seriously," Jenner said, with deliberate emphasis. "So I was horrified to turn on the radio and find that, instead of our regular announcements, the Jenner Funeral Home is now advertising a lay-away plan. Do you have any explanation for this and why you would have done such a thing?"

Jenner was holding onto his temper with great difficulty now, because he saw that Alistair was trying hard not to smile.

"Well, Uncle, Chris Byers and I thought it might help drum up some additional business for the funeral home and that it was worth a try. You know, people paying in advance."

Chris Byers was about the same age as Alistair, the son of the local radio station owner and another goof-off so far as Jenner was concerned. He guessed the two of them had probably dreamed up the idea of the advertisement after a few rounds of beer at Medford's local watering hole, the Statler Tavern.

"Yes, we do encourage paying beforehand for funerals, where possible," Jenner said. "We do not, however, use terminology such as a 'lay-away plan'. This may surprise you, Alistair, but most people do not think that dying is all that amusing. You're making fun of something that should be treated seriously, with dignity!"

"Well then," Alistair said in rebuttal, "tell me why we've had four inquiries about our lay-away plan since the ad started running three days ago! I picked them up from the answering service!" He had pulled a few slips of paper with phone numbers out of his pocket and was waving them at his uncle.

"You can follow them up if you wish. However, I suspect they will be like the phone call I answered yesterday afternoon," Jenner replied. "It was from some joker who wanted to know how much we would charge to have his mother-in-law laid away. No, Alistair, as of today, you are no longer responsible for radio announcements and Lewis will be taking over that duty. Now. On another subject. We have a funeral coming up on the long weekend, as you know. It's the Victoria Day weekend and there's a parade too."

Now Jenner stopped, because Alistair had groaned loudly. "Not another bloody parade where I have to play the pipes dressed like an idiot in a kilt and the funeral home banner!" he moaned. Alistair had a strong suspicion that this foolish getup was probably the reason for his notable lack of success with the Medford girls.

"Yes," his uncle went on inexorably, "another parade and another funeral and if you please, the family wants you to play the Crags of Sterling."

"Crikey!" Alistair exclaimed. "That's a bugger to play, why can't they just go with Amazing Grace or almost anything else!"

"Your language, Alistair! That's the music the family wants and you will just have to practice, and outside the house if you please. Your Aunt's been having some problems with headaches recently."

Alistair was living with the Jenners for the time being, which had become a source of increasing aggravation for both parties. With

234 | Pat McDermott

Alistair's electric energy and quick mind and mouth, having his nephew constantly around made Jenner feel as if there was no peace to be found anywhere, either at work or at home.

"Well, anyhow, we're missing out on lots of opportunities to promote this business," Alistair said sulkily. "I was just trying to help."

"There is no other funeral home around here," Jenner replied, as patiently as he could. "When they die, they come to us. What we really need," and here he paused and looked pointedly at Lewis, "is someone who can do a good job on mortuary makeup."

"I'm doing the best I can!" Lewis expostulated, looking up aggrievedly through the thick lenses of his horn-rimmed glasses. "I even went and took that course you wanted me to!"

"Well, don't look at me," Alistair said, slumping further down in his chair and crossing his arms.

"You can be assured," said his uncle, surveying his nephew's wild hair and the disarray of his clothes, "that was the furthest thing from my mind."

And as he regarded his nephew, now sunk in gloom, he thought with some satisfaction: soon. Very soon, you will want to go home.

CHAPTER 51

The pattern of Jasmine's days quickly established itself. A day on which Lianne was awake, sharp of mind and energetic, was generally followed by one where, because she had overextended herself the day before, she was drowsy and sometimes in pain she bravely tried to disguise. There were pills of various sorts, and at times the drugged sleep they brought gave Lianne her only respite.

There was no respite for Jasmine, however, from the probing and very personal questions Lianne tended to ask whenever she was awake, and Jasmine soon gave up being indignant or offended. Right now, when Lianne asked her what her former husband had looked like, she just smiled because her motivation was so transparent.

"Did he have dark hair and blue eyes, like your daughter?"

"No, Mike was tall, over six feet, blond and brown-eyed. But you have to remember, Lianne, my father had similar colouring to Laura's."

"Oh. That's right." Lianne was disappointed, and didn't bother to disguise it.

"You know, Lianne, you're asking me rather a lot of very personal questions," Jasmine said gently. "Some people might take offense to being asked such questions."

"Well, I don't see why it matters," Lianne responded pertly. "I'm certainly not going to tell Thomas or anyone else what we say when we're together. So you can tell me anything. I'm going to die soon and I'll take your secrets to the grave!" Then she laughed.

Jasmine was shocked. "How can you joke about such a thing?"

"I've had time to get used to the idea. It doesn't bother me anymore," Lianne said dismissively. "Now tell me about your father. What a handsome man he was! Aside from him having two wives, was he a good father?

Here was another minefield into which Jasmine did not wish to venture. However, by now her conversations with Lianne had taken on such a confessional quality that she only sighed and replied. "He did everything that was expected of him as a father."

"But was he loving, kind, and generous?"

A long pause. "No. I suppose I would have to say he wasn't."

He had been, in fact, cool and distant. During her growing-up years, Jasmine had tried so hard to win his approval and affection. And she would have been content with only her memories of the meager portions of both he doled out, if only she had not spent a half hour talking to her half-brother before their father's funeral.

"What was he like with his other family, I wonder?"

It was uncanny how Lianne seemed able to get inside her head, knowing what she was thinking, anticipating what she might think next. There was only one other person who knew this story from her past.

"Did Thomas tell you about the talk I had with my half-brother?"

"No. What happened? Did you have a chance to speak to him at the funeral?" Lianne was now eager to know. And after all, Jasmine thought, what difference did it make? Although the hurt was still there, not completely healed over, like an old injury that throbs when touched.

Jasmine had been sweeping the floor of the sunroom as she conversed with Lianne and now she set the straw broom down and sat on the chair beside her. She could see the lake through the windows. It was strange how it always seemed to mirror her moods. Today it was dull grey under a grey sky, the colour of her memories.

"I found a moment to speak to Steven after the ceremony. I've never spoken to him since. I asked him what Jason Holmes was like in their family, and the same question that you asked me, whether he was a good father. Steven said he was a good husband to Lillian. And a great father. He spent lots of time with him when he was growing up. He was patient, loving and kind. The best father a son could ever have had, he said."

"Oh, my dear!" Lillian exclaimed, visibly upset. "How dreadful, to be treated so unequally!"

"Yes. Dad was proud enough of my good marks and my good looks. But as a father he was harsh and critical. He paid for Steven's university, but he made me work at the funeral home to earn enough for my tuition. Hoping, I suppose, that I would get married first." Jasmine laughed bitterly. "However, as it turned out, the money I saved was my escape fund. To get away from this place."

Lianne's eyes were filled with tears. How odd, Jasmine thought, to have to comfort someone else for sorrows that were yours alone. She took the hand that Lianne extended to her.

"It was very hurtful. But I learned that it wasn't my fault he didn't love me as much as his son," she said softly. "My mother told me that she and Dad went through a rough patch where he asked for a divorce, just before she became pregnant with me. I guess he blamed me for not being free to do as he pleased. However, I didn't understand this until Thomas pointed it out to me."

She drew her chair up closer, because it was time for the short speech she had prepared for Lianne. It was a thank you, of sorts.

"You know, Lianne, in that time Thomas and I were together, I learned more about what a man should be, and how he should treat a woman, than I did in all the twenty years I lived with my father. That was the second way Thomas saved my life. Because from then on, I judged other men by him, and it kept me from making dreadful mistakes."

Now Lianne was crying, tears running freely down her face; and Jasmine knew the reason. "I'm so glad you told me," Lianne said, wiping her eyes. "That's made it all worthwhile."

Although Lianne had said there was never a need for regret or remorse, at that moment Jasmine was experiencing pangs of both. It was clear to her now how much suffering Lianne's silence and forbearance had cost her, during those summer days when she and Thomas met almost daily for the potent brew of sex and sympathy that had helped them both heal.

"Did it take you very long to forgive him?" Jasmine asked.

Lianne dashed away her last tears. "No. Of course I knew right away something had happened, he had changed so. He told me only that you had tried to commit suicide and he had to help you. That he couldn't leave you and he needed to spend time with you. Then, later on, of course, the details came out. He never lied." She sighed heavily.

"After you left, we talked for the entire weekend. I knew from all he told me he wouldn't have gotten better without you. So, at the end, I was just as glad to let it go. Do you know the last thing I said to him about the whole affair?"

"What was it?" Jasmine was always amazed at how rapidly Lianne could switch from sadness to smiles, and here she was again, almost giggling.

"I said, 'well, at least I hope you learned something new.'"

Jasmine laughed, from shock as much as surprise. "And what did he say?"

"He said, 'I think I might have.'"

"And then what did you say?"

"Then I said, 'so show me.' And he did!"

Thomas was in his study. The baseball practice he usually coached that weekday had been cancelled because of rain. On arriving home early, he had stealthily climbed the stairs and was busily engaged in lesson plans when he heard laughter floating up from the sunroom. Soon he heard the back door close and saw an umbrella bobbing toward the Madison house. He went downstairs.

"I heard laughter. What were you laughing about?"

Lianne was evasive, smiling a rather secretive smile. "Oh, nothing much. Nothing you'd want to know about."

Thomas guessed they had been laughing about something concerning him. It bothered him. For some reason he felt rather affronted. It was only later in the evening he admitted to himself that instead of laughing about him, he would have preferred them to fight.

CHAPTER 52

Mason Stoddart had caught wind of a rumour. It was a slow enough day that he decided to leave work early in order to follow it up. The weather was changing, with a restless wind roiling the water and bringing masses of low clouds to obscure the sun as he drove along Lake Street to visit Edna Matthews. Edna's old house had an unobstructed view of the lake and an expansive lawn that rolled right down to the rocky shoreline. These attributes alone made it one of the most desirable homes in Medford, and Mason wanted it.

Lake houses seldom changed hands. They remained in families for generations, customarily handed down to the eldest son. Where a family lacked sons, the house might be given to a daughter; but regardless of her marital status, the name of the original ancestor continued to prevail. On the rare occasions a lake house was sold off to people unrelated to the family, they found themselves dispossessed by the ghostly occupants of centuries past, whose surname the townspeople always used when referring to their home – no matter how many decades the current owners might have lived there.

All this Mason knew, but it did not discourage him in his pursuit of the Matthews' lake house. He wanted an old new home for himself and his boys. He had never really liked, and now actively disliked the modern new house his soon-to-be ex-wife had insisted on building on a two-acre lot in Wendell Lake Estates. Beside his suspicion that

Catharine had moved them there to escape the surveillance of nosy neighbours who might otherwise observe the comings and goings of Jack Steeves, Mason felt the new house was rather like the marriage he was leaving. It was flat, soulless, and lacking in character. Although he knew there was nothing structurally wrong with it, still it seemed to him as flimsy and insubstantial as a house of cards.

Not so the Matthews manse, sitting solidly foursquare and proud on a huge city lot. It would need work, a good deal of renovation, but Mason considered this a minor inconvenience when he looked back on his memories of its broad planked oak floors, glowing goldenly with their patina of polish, wax and wear; its high ceilings, beautiful hand-made moldings, and soaring windows that poured sunshine into generous rooms mellow with age.

The house in question had been occupied by its original owners, the Matthews and their descendants, for five generations. Edna, an elderly widow, lived there alone; and for several years it had been obvious to everyone except Edna that the upkeep of the house and property was getting beyond her. Her only son, Clem, was Mason's childhood friend and more recently, his investment broker. During their last conversation, Clem made it plain to Mason he had no plans to uproot his family and leave the city in order to become the sixth generation of Matthews to live in the Medford lake house.

So Mason had phoned Edna. She issued an invitation and now, on a Thursday afternoon, he was on his way to see her. It was merely a coincidence that his route happened to take him past the Madison house on Lake Street. And sheer luck that he was driving very slowly, because when he glanced at the house next door, which belonged to the Lathams, he saw something that so shocked and surprised him he missed a curve, went off the road and almost hit a tree.

CHAPTER 53

Along with an inquisitive and capricious patient, Jasmine had also acquired a spoiled and rather tyrannical pet bird. Dickie had been squawking – until recently Jasmine had never known it was possible for a canary to squawk – for someone to come rescue him from the front porch. The wind was blowing his cage about and occasionally showering him with rain, and he muttered angrily and indignantly as she took down the cage and brought him indoors. She never noticed the black car driving by, or saw how it suddenly swerved, left the road and barely avoided crashing into a large maple in the park opposite the house.

As Jasmine carried the cage into the sunroom, she braced herself for yet another round of questions, most of which, so far, had been uncomfortably probing and highly personal. Since Lianne awoke from her nap a quarter of an hour ago, she had asked Jasmine why she and her husband had parted (Jasmine was not completely truthful answering this question), about their divorce (uncontested and mostly amicable), and then, if she had had other relationships afterward. (Yes, but only a few and very discreet).

"Why was that?" Lianne inquired. A blast of wind and rain rattled the windows; Jasmine, hearing Dickie's noisy protests, made her escape and jumped up to rescue him. With Lianne one question only led to another, and each seemed to dig deeper and deeper into sensitive places. However, because Jasmine couldn't think of a good reason to deny a dying woman who had sworn herself to secrecy, most of the time she answered them.

Last week, Lianne had wanted to know all about life in desert city. That was more fun and less personal and Jasmine was happy enough to oblige. She had, in fact, actually enjoyed telling her Vegas tales of big wins and losses, describing the denizens of the casinos and gaming tables and then, with some further prodding, her own work. But now she wondered if Lianne hadn't just been priming the pump for the full-scale interrogation she seemed to be conducting this week.

"How much were you paid?" Lianne had asked.

"In my first job, just one silver dollar an hour."

Her eyebrows rose high in astonishment. "Goodness! However did you survive?"

"I more than survived. Often I had to call Mike to pick me up or take a cab home. Can you guess the reason? It was because I couldn't carry all the tips I was given. The casino only dealt in silver dollars and sometimes I made as much as four hundred dollars a night!"

Lianne had sighed, wistfully. "Oh, but you've had such an exciting life compared to me! It's just worlds away from anything I've ever known!"

With this and similar comments it was soon obvious to Jasmine that as well as the services provided by her predecessor, Mrs. Mackie, Lianne was relying on her for diversion, entertainment and lately, distraction from the pain and discomfort she seldom mentioned but that Jasmine could sense was almost always present. There seemed no other motive behind her endless questions – although Jasmine was discovering that, even if she appeared artless and naive, Lianne was just as devious in her own way as was she herself.

So perhaps, she conjectured, Lianne only wanted variety, a change of subject. Perhaps she had tired of last week's travelogue and instead preferred a soap opera, which was what Jasmine sometimes thought her own life resembled.

Now, setting the bird in his cage down on the table next to Lianne and seeing that she was about to resume her questioning, she quickly asked one of her own.

"Lianne, do you mind if I ask why you and Thomas stayed in Medford? Surely he would have had better opportunities someplace else."

Lianne lifted the canary out of the cage on a forefinger and gently stroked its feathers. It cosied up to her cheek and nibbled fondly at her ear. "We did think about moving, especially with all the gossip about Thomas," she said. "But the chances of being promoted were always being dangled in front of him, and he did love the school and the students and teaching there. Of course, now that he's been passed over for the principal's job, he's starting to look around. But I guess the main reason for staying was probably the house. The Latham house."

Of course. The house. Its roots were strong, and it would have threaded them in and around its owners, so as to hold them fast to this place.

The Latham house was a splendid edifice, inside and out. Like all the lake houses, it had been designed by Samuel Charters, an English architect. In 1830 Charters sailed into Medford with a commission to oversee the construction of his design for a government building. Shortly after his arrival, the choice of Medford as the province's capital was cancelled, thus dooming it indefinitely to its small town status, and all construction stopped. Charters returned to England. But not before leaving, as his legacy, a string of houses along the lakeshore. True pearls of Georgian architecture; they were the pride and joy of their original owners. For their descendants, however, the houses sometimes became an anchor, a drag on ambition that kept them stagnating in their small town; or, more often, a ball and chain making endless demands on their time and money.

Seduced by the grandeur of their historic homes, though, few of their owners understood this as clearly as Jasmine. She had lived in housing that sprang up out of the desert plain and practical, and although it might be lacking in both beauty and character, she had come to appreciate its simple utility.

Still, as Lianne lay sleeping and she walked through the quiet rooms, Jasmine could see how such a house might sink into your bones. When this happened over successive generations, she thought, the distinction between the owner and what was owned would fade. Soon the house might possess you, its needs fashion yours, and to a greater or lesser extent, it could devour you.

In all there were five bedrooms with great high windows, beautifully decorated by Lianne in the pastel colours she favoured and furnished with period antiques. Except for the Latham's bed suite they were like pages from a decorating magazine, filled with silent sunshine, empty of life. To Jasmine, the rooms seemed a little sad. They seemed to be constantly waiting: for guests that never came, for missing children. They would be an enduring reminder and reproach to Lianne for her infertility. How had she managed to remain so brave and cheerful all these years, and even now, while illness was eating her up? Such a small, fragile person, but still so alive, so tough and resilient: Jasmine's admiration for her was growing daily.

Until now, Jasmine's days as a nurse-housekeeper had passed peacefully and uneventfully for the most part. That afternoon, however, she was feeling unsettled. Earlier in the day, she had seen an unmade bed in one of the spare bedrooms as she collected the laundry for the wash. A shirt lay crumpled on a chair. Without thinking too much about what she was doing, she had picked it up and held it to her face before depositing it in the basket. She inhaled. First, a tinge of sweat. Then another scent: something dark, alluringly musky and unmistakably male. It was him, Thomas, as real to her as if she were lying in that bed, there, in the crook of his arm, her arm flung across his broad chest. Then she had chased the vision and all the sensations it evoked away as if it were a demon, but now, hours later, it troubled her still.

"What did you say?"

Jasmine was drawn out of her thoughts and once again back to the sunroom, where Lianne, lying on the sofa with Dickie perched on top of her head, seemed to have resumed her questioning.

"I said – I hope you won't mind me asking again – but before you left the room, you mentioned that after Mike, you had only a few relationships. And that they were very discreet. Why was that? I imagine you could have had anyone you wanted."

Jasmine laughed a little, trying to disguise her irritation. Lianne reminded her of a fox terrier, so tenacious once she sank her teeth into something she was set on that she never let go. But then, she asked herself once more: after all, what harm was there in giving her an answer?

"I guess I can explain. After Mike left, I didn't tell anyone except one or two close friends that we were getting a divorce. And certainly no one at work. The reason was that having a husband, especially someone as big and strong as Mike, and a young child, protected me against – let's say, unwanted attention. From some of the bosses and the owners, who were used to getting whatever they wanted. So I continued on as if I were still married. Does that answer your question?"

"I suppose so," Lianne said slowly. "Part of it, anyhow."

Jasmine looked at her sharply. "What do you mean?"

Lianne gently took Dickie off her head and put him, struggling and squawking, back into his cage. She hesitated, and for the first time that Jasmine could recall, she seemed embarrassed. Her eyes were directed toward the floor, her face averted.

"Well, according to town gossip, once you left, I heard that you liked men. A lot of men. In fact, if rumours can be believed, you – well, anyhow, it seemed like at least half the male population of Medford."

For a long moment, Jasmine looked at her in disbelief. She gave a short bark of a laugh. Then she burst into peals of laughter, a response so unexpected that Lianne's eyes grew wide in surprise.

"Was my question so funny?" She handed Jasmine a tissue. Although she might have expected tears of a different sort, at least she was prepared for these.

"Still, there had to be a reason for all the talk," she persisted stubbornly. But then she began to giggle too, until, carried away by Jasmine's gales of laughter, soon she was laughing so hard she started gasping and Jasmine became alarmed and they both stopped.

"Oh, but it feels so good to laugh!" Lianne said, holding a hand to her chest as she alternately coughed and gasped for breath. "So good, and I wasn't just laughing because you were, but because I don't think I've ever had such a bizarre conversation!"

Jasmine blew her nose and wiped her eyes. "It's purely comical, how my fame has grown in the years since I left, and how my little molehill of sin has become such a great big mountain! Oh, my goodness, this place! And the people who live in it, and the way they talk, and how glad I am that soon I'll be gone from here and far, far away!"

She stopped smiling. She turned the full spotlight of her gaze on Lianne, her amber eyes glinting with a hint of ferocity. "But Lianne, why? What's the reason for all these questions? You can't tell me it's just curiosity. What is it you're trying to find out?"

"It is curiosity," Lianne said defiantly. "I just wanted to hear your side of the story, what really happened. Because, since I've gotten to know you, I don't believe what people were saying about you."

"No," said Jasmine. "That's not the reason. This is really about Thomas, isn't it? You want to know whether he was sleeping with the town slut."

"That's a very ugly way to put it."

It was remarkable: Jasmine never would have thought so much blood was left in that poor little shrunken and diminished body. But there it was, and all of it in her flaming red face. Jasmine immediately felt contrite for her rough words, which had hit their mark and drawn that blood. It was Lianne, after all, who had suffered from the rumours that plagued her marriage, and was now making a last, super-human act of charity to neutralize them. She deserved some kind of atonement, an accounting at least. Jasmine decided she would tell her the truth that, up until now, she had shared with only one other person, her husband.

"I can tell," said Lianne, with some of her previous stubbornness, "that at heart you're not a bad person and that you couldn't have done what they say."

"Well, I don't know what they're saying, but what I'm going to tell you isn't likely to improve your opinion of me much." Jasmine moved to sit closer in the chair across from her.

"It was after I broke my engagement to Mason. He'd been away in Germany for months. In all that time, I'd had just two letters from him, both coming right after he left. Soon afterward, my father died, and you will remember the circumstances of that death. Then there were no more letters. I found out that because of my father, that is, because of Dad's other marriage, Mason wanted nothing more to do with me or our family. Well, I was already in quite a state, but once I heard this, I was wild with grief, heartbroken. And also furious, so angry, because I knew that all his talk of everlasting love, all his promises, were just so he could do whatever he wanted with me, and now he was tossing me aside –"

"Anyhow, I slept with his two best friends."

"What?!" Lianne started, her eyes wide with shock. "You did what?"

Jasmine was silent for a moment. Then said, "just once. Each."

A smile seemed to be tugging at Lianne's lips. She looked away. "Well, it's too bad you decided to do it with Gary Patterson. He's got such a big mouth I wouldn't be surprised if he fell into it and then came out with his nether end on his face to match his personality."

"I suppose so," Jasmine said. "Oh, but it was all crazy, stupid, I was out of my mind when I did it! And they disgusted me; I disgusted myself. It was all part of why I wanted to do away with myself, to die."

"Dear me," said Lianne, rather helplessly. Then she added, "but I guess there weren't really that many other ways to get back at him, were there?"

Jasmine looked at her in astonishment. She would never have thought Lianne capable of almost instantaneously guessing why she would have done such a stupid thing.

A heavy silence stretched out between them. Neither looked at the other, each submerged in her own thoughts. Jasmine was laying her memories of that time to rest again, covering them up. There had been some comfort in talking about them. Eventually, she hoped, they might throb painfully only occasionally, the same as any old wound slow to heal.

In the kitchen close by, the clock ticked the passing seconds loud as drumbeats. Dickie fussed in his cage, sensing the somber mood and emitting a querulous mixture of clicks and whistles.

Finally, timidly, Lianne ventured, "but then –"And was quiet.

Jasmine looked up. "But then, what?"

"But then," she exclaimed in a rush, "you ran off with that awful Royce Parke!"

Jasmine laughed; she shook her head in a sort of exasperated amusement. "You never give up, do you, Lianne? Well, I've told you so much that I suppose you might as well have the whole story. I wasn't ever that attracted to Royce. He was engaged to marry my cousin Anna, as you know. She was – is – my very best friend. Truly my only real girlfriend all the while I was growing up. I learned he was already two-timing her – and I say 'two-timing' because I had heard of only two other women he was seeing beside Anna. Not just that, he had been fired from his job."

"Alright, enough, let me guess," Lianne interjected. "You decided to take him away."

"I did. But then, later, I found out there was just one little problem."

"Yes. Baby on the way."

"There you have it."

Another short silence, in which Jasmine could only wonder what Lianne was thinking. Practiced as she was in this type of speculation, she was discovering that her patient was wildly unpredictable. She watched in some fascination as Lianne's face became sadder, her eyes suspiciously moist. But never could she have guessed what was to come out of her mouth next.

"It's not fair!" Lianne suddenly burst forth.

"What? What do you mean, it's not fair?"

"You! You've had so much of life, you've had a child and been so many places and had so many lovers and I've spent my entire life here, practically, with only one man and just had a lot of dead babies, five of them! What kind of life is that, and now it's almost over!" Tears were glittering in her eyes and even now starting to fall.

Jasmine felt a rush of sympathy, mixed with astonishment.

"I'm so sorry, Lianne. And to tell the truth, I'm amazed. That anyone should envy me. Because, so far, my life hasn't actually been that much fun."

"Maybe not. But at least you've lived; you've had so many experiences I've never had! And it would have been fun, having all those men. Anyone you wanted!"

Jasmine laughed incredulously. Then she looked at Lianne to see if she was joking, but she seemed genuinely aggrieved and upset.

"Well, I've not had so very many, but do you really mean it? Would you have wanted to have more men, more lovers?"

"Of course I would! I was married at eighteen! Don't think I wouldn't have liked some variety, just to see what it's like with other men, and I never, ever got the chance!" Lianne's voice was filled with something very like indignation and her eyes gleamed with tears.

"It's really not all it's made out to be," Jasmine said, rather gloomily. "I might as well tell you that since Mike, it's been hard to find someone. It would be easy, except that I want a good man. They're scarce everywhere, but there're almost none in Las Vegas."

Unbidden, the memories began to rise in her mind of that time, almost ten years ago. She was remembering her brief, passionate interlude with Thomas. His magic touch. His instinctive knowledge of how to give pleasure, as much as he got. And she knew Lianne had no idea how lucky she was, and so far as men were concerned, that was truly all she was missing.

"Still, Thomas is a really good lover, isn't he?" Lianne asked.

Witch! Get out of my head! Startled, Jasmine glanced sharply at Lianne. She wore a look of perfect innocence for someone who had just asked such an uncomfortable question on such an intimate matter.

"Ye-es," Jasmine said slowly. "Among the best."

For a long moment they sat there, smiling away at each other in a strange sort of complicity. Later, Jasmine reflected that it was for all the world like two women in a harem discussing the Pasha. It amused her a little, to think of how much it would have pleased Thomas, had he known about it.

Bang! Bang! Bang! The doorknocker sounded loudly at the far end of the house. In came Laura, smelling of fresh lake air and spring blossoms. She looked like a little otter, her hair unencumbered by the hood of her waterproof jacket and slick with rain. The conversation currently being carried on by Laura and Lianne was on nice, simple matters such as which were best: the chocolate or the butterscotch squares.

Sitting quietly nearby, Jasmine breathed a sigh of relief that this oddest of afternoons was over, and gave silent thanks with the hope that all questions had now been answered and might even be at an end.

CHAPTER 54

Margery left her umbrella open in the vestibule to dry. Emma led her into the kitchen, a haven of light and warmth on this chill spring afternoon. The stew simmering on the stove and the cookies baking in the oven added their bouquet to the atmosphere of homey comfort Emma was in the midst of creating for Jasmine and Laura, her little temporary family. It was a spell, a gossamer web she cast over them daily even if unaware that she did so, fashioned out of many little acts of love. Although it might not be strong enough to keep them here in Medford, she hoped a few of its strands might yet draw them back, someday, to see her while she still lived.

From the moment she opened the door, it could clearly be seen that Margery had no need of comfort. Her face was brighter than the sun hiding behind the heavy rain clouds outside the window.

"You must have something really important to tell me, Margery, or else you wouldn't have come so far on such an awful day," Emma said. "What is it?"

Margery, with her usual irritating sense of drama, would not disclose her news until she had settled her substantial girth on the cushion she always favored in the banquette. While she made herself comfortable, Emma set the kettle to boil for tea.

"I'm dying to tell you, but I won't while you're bustling around like that," Margery said imperiously. "Come sit down."

Rather resentfully and feeling like a well-trained dog, Emma sat. "So what is it?"

"The best, the most exciting news!" Margery burst forth. "Jim just was hired for a new job at the car plant, a wonderful job where he'll be a supervisor in the accounting department! Not only that, but they actually came after him for the position! They had heard about his work at the tannery!"

Emma clapped her hands with delight. "Why, isn't that absolutely marvelous! He must be over the moon! Doesn't Jim just deserve this good luck! When does he start?"

And they sat and talked and drank tea and ate fudge cookies with joy and gusto until this topic was fully exhausted.

"Now I have something to tell you," Emma said. Her tone betrayed that it was not nearly so joyful. "Mary is coming here for the weekend again."

"What?" Margery was surprised. "Again? Isn't this the third weekend in a row?"

"It is, and once again she phoned Laura and almost invited herself. Not that I don't love having the child, and Laura couldn't be happier, but it makes me wonder. What's going on at that house?"

"Anna tells me that the Airdries have been at the estate house every weekend since the weather became fine. If the sun shines, likely they'll be there this Victoria Day." Margery's face was grave and thoughtful.

"And when they're there," she added, "Royce comes home."

"So he'll be home for the long weekend. And Mary will be here."

The cousins stared at each other for a short space. Abruptly, Margery said, "I'll visit Anna the moment she's back from work. But what can we do, if the child won't talk, will never admit to anything being wrong? Her own father – really – how likely is it?"

Emma was about to answer that question rather bluntly when the back door gave its characteristic squeak and slam. Jasmine appeared at the top of the stairs leading up to the kitchen. Margery immediately leapt to her feet to give her a brief hug before quickly burbling out all her happy news of Jim and his new job.

"If anyone deserves it, Jim does," Jasmine said decidedly. "I'm so glad for him."

She didn't seem quite as surprised as Emma thought she might. It set her to wondering. Could Arlena Stoddart possibly be the one responsible for this happy turn of events?

There was something else Emma did not fail to notice. Jasmine had taken her usual walk along the lake, a brief spell of freedom after the daylong confinement of the Latham house. Her great masses of hair were tousled and windblown, her colour high. Even to Emma, who seldom paid much attention to her niece's appearance any more, Jasmine seemed especially attractive this evening: almost glittering, dangerously charged with some inner excitement.

"Excuse me, I'm going to change before dinner. And when Laura arrives, please don't give her any cookies, she's full of sweets from Lianne's. She said she was going over to Simon's for a while before coming home." Jasmine left them and went upstairs.

Rather sourly, her mouth pursed, Margery looked after her. When she was out of earshot, she said in a low voice, "you may or may not know this, Emma, but your story of how Thomas rescued Jasmine is all and everywhere the talk of the town. And some new details have come to light that more or less confirm everything you said. But right now, with the way she looks, it's going to be hard for anyone to believe he didn't lay a finger on her."

She leaned back in her seat. "Really, Emma, she ought to leave. This town is no place for her. She's like a swan in a hen house, and you know it."

"Ye-es," Emma agreed reluctantly, "and she will be leaving soon, probably after Lianne --"

"Dies," Margery supplied with her usual lack of finesse.

"Passes on," Emma continued, "but then, the child will go too, and I'll miss them both so, and her especially."

As if on cue, the back door slammed. Laura, pink-faced and bright-eyed, charged into the kitchen and the open arms of her great Aunt Emma. She was spilling over with news, the words tumbling one on another.

"Auntie, there are men in the Stoddart's back yard and they're building a little wood house! But it doesn't have any walls and it has a little green roof and stairs and I wonder is it a play house? Is it for kids? They don't have any little girls, do they?"

"I saw it too," Margery ventured. "It looks as if the Stoddarts are building themselves a gazebo."

"It's a nice high place where people can go and sit in the shade in the summer and drink cool drinks and read newspapers," Emma explained to the child's upturned face. She noticed Laura's pants were muddied, with a new tear in one knee, and her cheek was liberally smeared with dirt. "Now go wash those dirty hands and your face and then give your Aunt Margery a hug."

"I will, but first I want to show you something!" Laura said excitedly, then raced out the door once more.

"That Elizabeth Stoddart!" Margery sniffed when Laura had left the room. "What airs she gives herself! A gazebo, for heaven's sake! Well, I guess it's as near to a throne as she can manage!"

Another squeak and a slam, and Laura was back through the door and up the stairs again. She carried a large rectangular box with a wooden bottom and uprights, and window screen on the sides and top lid. She plopped it down next to the cookie plate on the table between Emma and Margery, then gave the latter a quick hug. But Margery paid no attention to the embrace. She was staring at the box.

"What," she asked with a sharp intake of breath, her eyes almost starting from her head, "is that!?"

"Thomas helped me make this box for grasshoppers but Simon's father says it's too soon for grasshoppers, so Simon and me got all kinds of other bugs from his dad's garden," Laura explained proudly. "We got crickets and spiders and that big black and orange beetle and there's another small green one under that leaf there!"

Through the thin screen that separated them from its creeping and crawling inhabitants, Emma also spied a couple of earthworms lying rather limply in the bottom of the box. Her horrified contemplation was interrupted by Margery getting to her feet so quickly she almost knocked the box and all its contents into Emma's lap. Emma stood up also, and gingerly picking up the box with her fingertips, she handed it to Laura.

"That's wonderful, darling, but it really belongs outside. Can you take it out please? NOW!!"

When Laura left they looked at one another, shaken and speechless. Then both exploded into laughter, forever their response to situations most other folks might greet with reactions ranging from anger to disgust.

"Oh my goodness gracious golly! " Margery exclaimed through their gales of hilarity, "I thought I was going to toss up all those lovely fudge cookies when I saw the spiders!"

She wiped her eyes. She slapped her broad waist with both hands. "And probably I should have! But thank you for them, and thanks to Laura for the laugh and for the great story I'll have for Jim when I get home. And on that note, I think I'll leave."

As she rose to retrieve her coat and umbrella from the front hall, they heard Jasmine's footsteps coming down the stairs. The phone rang. Jasmine was nearest to it on entering the kitchen, and she answered.

"Hello?"

She listened intently for a minute. "Alright. We'll expect you," she said, and hung up.

"Who are we expecting?" asked Emma. "Dinner's on in just half an hour."

"That was Edna Matthews," Jasmine replied. "She says it's important, and she's coming over right now. Whatever do you think it could be?"

"Your guess is as good as mine," Emma said as she turned down the burners under the pots on the stove. They exchanged puzzled glances. Then came an unexpected sound to break the silence: the clink of a spoon on a saucer. Both turned to look in the direction of the banquette.

Before the phone rang Margery had been just about to leave. She had squeezed past Jasmine on her way out to the front hall to put on her coat. Now, however, Jasmine and Emma saw that she had returned and resumed her seat in her usual spot at the table. She did not look at them; she was pretending that there was still something left to drink in the teacup she had lifted to her lips.

"Margery?" Emma asked in tones of surprise. "I thought you were going home."

"Oh, no. It's raining cats and dogs. So I'll just stay awhile until it lets up. There's really no rush. Jim is happy to have dinner anytime."

All the while she was speaking Margery batted her eyes rapidly. Her face wore a look of such innocence that both Jasmine and Emma burst out laughing.

"Margery, you are incorrigible!" Emma shook her head in amusement. "We know perfectly well you were on your way out the door before Edna called."

"She said it's a matter that concerns me," Jasmine added. Then: "you can stay. But only if you promise not to tell anyone what Edna says unless I say you can."

Emma cast her a warning glance. But it was too late.

"I promise, Scout's honour," Margery quickly replied, holding up one hand.

The back door squeaked and slammed. The child reappeared. "I put my bugs in the shed and I gave them some other bugs to eat in case they're hungry," she said breathlessly.

"Eeyuw! How in the world can you pick up a spider," Margery exclaimed, grimacing at the thought.

It was a rhetorical question but one that Laura took quite seriously. "You have to be fast because spiders run real fast," she explained. "You just put your hands 'round them like this, then real quick you run and throw them in the box. I use my foot to open the box."

Now she was balancing on one foot with her hands cupped, showing how she used her other foot to lift the lid of the box before throwing an invisible spider into it. The whole pantomime was so realistic that both Margery and Emma were cringing, their hands held to their faces in fright. Then, of course, they began to laugh, and Margery's infectious laugh sent Jasmine off too.

"Is it time for dinner now?" the child asked when she concluded her performance.

"Not yet," Emma replied. "In half an hour. You need to wash up first. And take off those muddy pants before you go upstairs. Then leave them in the laundry and put on some clean ones."

Laura immediately undid her pants and stepped out of them. "Good! Then I have time to read my new comic book." She raced down the hall in her underpants and they heard her thump rapidly up the stairs to her room.

"What's all this about spiders?" Jasmine asked as she picked up the mud-caked pants.

Emma put the kettle on to boil for more tea. Then she and Margery competed to regale Jasmine with the story of Laura's bug collection. And so the time passed in much merriment until the doorbell rang announcing Edna's arrival.

CHAPTER 55

This was the way it always began. They would stand facing each other, their fingertips loosely linked.

"First, I want to see your beautiful face," he told her the day after, when they met again.

And so, for a long moment, he would look at the lovely full mouth smiling up at him, and deep into the depths of those gold-flecked amber eyes. Then he would pull her toward him and wrap her arms around his back. He put his hands on either side of her face, and then they shared that first sweet, almost innocent kiss – before something far less innocent and much more passionate erupted, after the almost superhuman effort it cost him to keep it barely in check.

This evening, as he looked out the window at her retreating form while it faded from view on the misty path along the lake, his fingertips tingled.

"It's silly," Lianne had admonished him. "Can't you at least pop in and say hello, before you run upstairs and hide in your study?"

"I'm not ready for that," he replied flatly. And how could he be, when even time and distance were not enough to lessen this instinctive response?

As he peered from his window at Jasmine vanishing in the mist, he saw a car drive up. It screeched to a stop. The driver's door was suddenly flung open and Mason Stoddart leapt out. He looked as if he were about to set off in hot pursuit of the shadowy figure that, even now, Thomas could see, had been swallowed up in billows of fog.

Thomas watched as Stoddart slowly got back in his car. He drove it along the road until it was directly across from the Madison house. Then he turned the engine off. Obviously he was prepared to wait. He did not know, as Thomas did, that Jasmine would likely come home by way of the path through the cedars at the back of the lake houses.

What was he up to? Thomas wondered curiously. And felt a jab of active dislike, which later, reluctantly, he more accurately identified as jealousy.

CHAPTER 56

She was upstairs tidying the children's drawers and putting away their freshly laundered clothes when she heard the rusty creak of the back door. Her heart sank. It was one day too soon. Although, now that their home was so peaceful without him, most any day would be too soon.

"Hello Royce."

He sat at the kitchen table drinking a beer. In the dim of late afternoon his eyes and teeth flashed white in a face already burnt dark from hours outdoors in the sun. He ignored her greeting. "Where are the kids?" he asked.

"We had an early dinner. They're over at the Parsons and Mary is watching the children while Marilyn cooks for her family party this weekend. You're here tonight? It's only Thursday."

"The Airdries are making a four-day vacation of it. Family's coming for Victoria Day weekend," he said shortly. "Can you get me some supper?"

Anna heated up what was left of the stew and mashed potatoes. As she served him and he wolfed down the food, she kept up a constant patter, bringing him up to date on news of the neighbourhood, the children and all their doings. His head down and seemingly intent on his plate, he showed little interest. But he looked up when she mentioned that Mary was staying over the weekend with Laura and Aunt Emma.

"What, again?"

"Yes. It seems whenever you're here, she makes arrangements to be somewhere else."

Royce's expression darkened. "What're you saying? That she doesn't want to be around me?"

"So it appears. Can you think of any reason why?"

He shrugged his shoulders dismissively and took a swig of his beer before picking up his knife and fork again. "Beats me. Maybe just growing up. Getting funny, they way they do around their fathers, once they reach that age."

"I have no idea what you're talking about," Anna said stiffly. "I never felt 'funny' or anything of the kind around my father. And Mary's still a young girl, she's only just turned ten."

"Well, I guess you'll have to ask her, then, won't you?" He shoved his empty plate away so forcefully the cutlery on it rattled and clinked. Anna knew not to question him further; the subject was closed.

His jacket was on a chair nearby. With a bit of a flourish, he reached in a pocket, pulled out a wad of cash and dropped it on the kitchen table. "Here's some of the money I owe you."

She felt a warm wave of relief. Royce had given them so little since he started this job. The taxes on their small house came due soon. What with the water bill, the cost of heat and electricity, she had been worrying over having almost nothing left for food and other necessities. "Thanks," she said, although she did not think any thanks were actually due, and she went from where she was standing, near the stove, to pick up the stack of bills.

Suddenly his hand shot out. "Not so fast," he said in a low, dangerous voice, as he held her wrist in an iron grip. "First, you and me, upstairs. The kids aren't here and we have time before I leave. Let's go."

She felt her blood chill, and a kind of cold fury descend. "That money is for your children and their upkeep. Don't you dare hold it out on me, acting like I'm one of your cheap little chippies!"

He dropped her wrist then, gave his easy laugh. "That'll be the day, when I have to pay for it! But you! You're not doing your wifely duty, faking you're asleep every time I come to bed. Anyhow, now you're here and awake, so come on along."

Perhaps, she thought, if he ever came to bed sober and not at three in the morning. Perhaps if she had any idea of how he had spent the hours before, and with whom. Perhaps then she could do her duty, for by now that was all it was.

As he rose to his feet she took a long look at him. He was tall, fit, good looking. Women found him attractive; so had she, once. But now that she had discovered what was beyond that façade, she felt only repulsion. One more time, though, she would have to repress her feelings, deny them and play along. She was so tired of it. Sick and tired.

"Alright," she said, feigning passivity, and started toward the stairs. She knew that if she resisted in any way it would only excite him, make him more rough, even violent.

Halfway during their slow ascent she stopped, because she suddenly noticed that he had. She turned and looked down at him questioningly.

"What the hell." Royce stood on the second step. He gave a short laugh and she saw the black gap in his front teeth; it made him look quite sinister. "Why bother? You don't want to, and you know something? Neither do I. It's just going to be the same old jig-a-jig anyhow."

He backed down the few steps to the landing, and she knew that he had decided to go: go out the door and off to his usual haunts, to one or another of the taverns in and around town.

She was relieved, of that there was no question. But at the same time she was intensely curious. This was so very unlike him. "Really? You don't want to? So can you tell me what it is you've found to replace that old jig-a-jig?"

Standing silhouetted against the fast-failing light that came through the window of the front door, Royce presented only a dark figure, his expression undetectable. He gave a short bark of a laugh.

"You don't need me anymore, anyhow. Save it up for that doctor of yours," he retorted, his voice heavy with sarcasm.

Anna was immediately filled with rage. She could hardly restrain herself from slapping him; he was at precisely the right height for her to do so.

"Just because you're an alley cat, Royce Parke, don't think everyone else is as low as you are! Keith Miller is only a friend and our relationship is purely professional, nothing else! And how dare you accuse me!"

"Whoa! Look at that face!" he exclaimed in a light, lilting tone, backing away in mock fright. He was amused at her indignation, her rage; he was enjoying getting a rise out of her, and that infuriated her even more.

"I guess I'd better watch it!" he chuckled. "Or else pretty soon, instead of old stew, you're going to be feeding me poisoned tomatoes, just like your ma gave your dad!"

He saw her face change then, rapidly smooth out until it was flat and expressionless.

"Oh no, Royce," she said in a low voice that was devoid of anger, full of icy menace. She shook her head slowly from side to side.

"If and when I decide to do you in, it won't be any halfway measure. You'll be really and truly dead."

He took another step back. "Oooh," he exclaimed, mockingly, holding up his hands in a parody of fear. "I'm so scared! Oh, how you've frightened me!"

But in the last dull vestiges of daylight as he turned to go, she glimpsed the look on his face. And he knew that she meant it, and she could see that she had.

CHAPTER 57

Life was made up of too many irritating little details, too many small, trifling items, and lately they had been slipping through her fingers, falling out of her mind.

That was why, exactly when she was in a rush to go to Emma's house, Edna Matthews spent fifteen frantic minutes looking for her car keys, which she was sure she had put in her purse. Eventually she found them in her knitting basket, beneath the baby blue ball of wool she was using to make a sweater for her latest grandson.

One problem with living alone, she thought crossly as she put on her raincoat, was that there never was anyone else to blame for misplaced items and other things gone wrong. How she missed Sam, her husband, passed away four years ago last month.

The real reason for her absence of mind, she was sure, was that her day-to-day existence was as flat and flavourless as the three-day old chicken divan leftovers she had eaten for dinner last night. With her life being so dull and boring, no wonder she paid so little attention to the particulars of it.

By comparison, almost every day the past rose up in front of her displayed in glorious technicolour. Although it was like a screenplay she could only enjoy vicariously, it allowed her to leisurely poke around looking at things long ago that had happened too fast for her at the time.

So when Edna heard the story of Jasmine's attempted suicide, she was not especially surprised. Ever since she learned Jasmine was back in town, she had been revisiting one especially poignant memory. Now she wondered if it might contain a few seeds of that desperate act.

Before she dashed out the door, Edna stretched her mouth out wide and applied a good deal of lipstick, her favourite, Revlon Windsor Rose. Then she smiled at herself in the mirror, a small woman with glasses and a large mop of wispy blondish hair, not too wrinkly yet, wearing a yellow sweater to compensate for the dreariness of this spring afternoon.

The fact was, even before the fateful evening that marked a turning point in their relationship, Edna had never gotten along that well with Sheila, her second daughter. The second to last of her six children, Sheila had always been a bit of a handful. Edna loved her of course, mostly, but she was happy enough when Sheila married and moved away. Every week or so they still managed to argue on the phone, regardless of who was listening in. Even Sheila's letters, full of judgments, criticisms and opinions Edna usually disagreed with, were enough to get her hot under the collar.

But she had never played favorites with her children and so, just as she had for the others, when Sheila was sixteen Edna held an after-the-dance party for her and her classmates on the occasion of their first school prom.

'I don't see Jasmine Holmes' name," she said when she looked over the invitation list Sheila had made up.

"She doesn't fit in," Sheila replied shortly.

Edna made her add Jasmine's name. She told her she must invite her; otherwise she would cancel the party. Jasmine was Sheila's classmate and the daughter and niece of two of Edna's oldest friends: no excuses were acceptable.

Four days before the event, Edna was speaking with Sylvia Holmes and discovered that Jasmine was, as yet, still uninvited. That night, she had stood over Sheila as she sullenly put through a phone call and issued an invitation to Jasmine and her date.

"It's jealousy, pure and simple," she told Sam as he helped her with the preparations for the party. Dear Sam. He had so loved seeing all the young folk: the girls in their pretty dresses, the boys all slicked down and looking so grown up, almost as much as she did.

But as it turned out, it wasn't just jealousy. Nothing so pure and simple.

"What a beautiful girl!" Sam said to Edna, and it seemed to her that his voice held a note of awe. They were watching from the kitchen that evening as the young people filed into the house. Now Edna understood why Sheila might not have wanted to invite Jasmine to the party. She had come into bloom since the last time Edna really had a good look at her. Then she was Sheila's sometimes playmate, a gangly twelve-year-old, all legs and eyes. In the intervening years, a great transformation had taken place.

It was strange: there was nothing special about what Jasmine wore or how she had put herself together, but on that night she seemed to soak up all the light in the room. She was so lovely she was almost luminous. The boys snuck surreptitious looks or just gawked. Their dates, girls who had spent hours and a considerable sum of their parents' income on hair, makeup and dresses suddenly seemed plain in her presence. Nevertheless, she appeared unaware of her beauty, the spell it exerted; instead she was shy, self-effacing, and on the inside if not on the outside, seemingly not all that different from the sweet, sensitive girl Edna once knew.

Just then the young folk dove into the buffet. Edna became distracted and busy pouring drinks, giving directions, passing plates of cookies and squares and wiping up the inevitable spills, until once again there was a moment of quiet and she saw what she saw.

The strains of a Frank Sinatra song floated in from the living room where the rug had been rolled up and the furniture cleared for dancing. The crowd in the dining room had thinned. Jasmine stood alone. Her escort had wandered off to the backyard with some other boys, probably for a smoke. Edna watched as she approached another girl, smiled and made some comment that Edna could not hear. The girl seemed about to answer. Then Edna saw her look across the room. Edna followed her glance. She saw her daughter Sheila, her mouth set hard and thin, give the girl a slight nod. Immediately the girl moved away without responding or even looking at Jasmine. She walked around to the other side of the room, where she joined Sheila and her little gaggle of girlfriends, all laughing and talking and determinedly turning their backs on Jasmine as she stood alone at the dining room table.

The realization dawned on Edna that even if Jasmine had been invited to the party, Sheila had arranged it so that she still would be excluded.

She hurried over to where Jasmine stood by herself. Once her date returned Edna managed to strike up a lively conversation, drawing in another girl whom, it seemed, her daughter had somehow failed to conscript. But ultimately Sheila was successful: what she had done could not so easily be undone. Shortly afterward, Jasmine excused herself, pleading a headache. Her date took her home, but returned soon after to join in the party fun.

Yes: Edna had to concede that Sheila was right. Jasmine did not fit in. Certainly not in any place so full of spite and malice, where shyness was weakness and beauty only a liability.

As Jasmine stood at the dining room table, she turned away from the laughing girls. She had pretended not to notice. From the other side of the room, it was only Edna who could see the child-like quiver of her mouth, the hot flush creeping up her cheeks, the tears filling her eyes.

Afterward, Edna did not tell her husband. She was afraid that Sam might feel as she did, and that the contagion that had infected her might spread to him. For Sheila had incurred another sort of damage that night. Something happened to Edna's warm, unreserved, motherly love. It seemed to curdle in the bile that rose in her throat as she saw the scene play out. She felt she would never forget, nor could she completely forgive, the cruel gleam in her daughter's eye as she watched Jasmine standing there, isolated and ignored.

And what comfort was there for her at home? As she gazed at that lonely, only child, Edna wondered if she should speak to her mother or father. But lately both of them seemed so self-absorbed, so contained and aloof; perhaps not.

She had set down the tray of dirty dishes she was collecting. She hurried over to Jasmine and wrapped an arm around her, hoping that at least, into that aching void, she could drop a crumb of human kindness.

The Madison House! She had driven right by it. By the time she parked her car, Edna Matthews had just about finished revisiting her memories of Jasmine. There were few happy ones. She went up the stairs to the porch. The wonder, Edna thought, as she rang the doorbell, is that they let her survive at all.

CHAPTER 58

"Tell me about Edna Matthews," Jasmine asked Emma. "I've always liked her; she's a dear. Is there anything new?"

"Not much. Her children have all moved away to the city and other places, except for her oldest daughter, Sarah. She married Eric Peterson, who owns the appliance store, and they have three children and live on Lakefield Street. Edna lost her husband, Sam, a good while ago." Emma put down her cup in a final sort of way. It was her fifth cup of tea and she was heartily sick of the stuff.

"Yes, four years ago. And now Edna's canoodling widowers with casseroles, and on the hunt for another man!" Margery contributed.

"Margery!" Emma exclaimed, shocked.

"How can you canoodle a widower with a casserole?" asked Jasmine, who was plainly intrigued.

"Margery only means that Edna has brought one or two casseroles to men who've just lost their wives and are totally at sea when it comes to feeding themselves," Emma replied evenly. "It's a charitable thing to do, perfectly innocent."

"Oh really, Emma, don't be such a goody two-shoes!" Margery shook her head in mock exasperation. "You know perfectly well Edna almost threw herself at George Sawyer after Martha died, and Sheldon

LaCombe's daughter, Marcia, told Anna that Edna hung around Sheldon at the funeral parlour for so long during the visitation for her mother that some people were asking if she was family! She must spend all her spare time reading the obituaries checking for prospects."

"Well, I don't know why she bothers, when all she really needs is a good handyman," Emma said drily. "You can talk to them just about as much as you can a husband and you don't have to feed them. Anyhow, she needn't run after Sheldon anymore, I hear he's taken up with Cathy Reisler, the barmaid at the Statler tavern."

"What, that floozy?!" gasped Margery. "How could he?"

"Probably he was in the mood for something more spicy than a ham-and-potato casserole." Emma calmly stood up and went to the stove to make more tea.

Now it was Margery's turn to be shocked. "Emma, what a thing to say!"

Then they both turned and looked in surprise at Jasmine. She had been stifling her giggles and now was practically in hysterics. At that moment the doorbell rang.

"Margery, you had better answer it," Emma directed, quickly gauging that Jasmine was in no condition to do the job. "Jasmine, pull yourself together!"

"Yes, I'm going to freshen up and I'll be back in a minute. But it will be hard to keep a straight face when I look at Edna Matthews and imagine her canoodling widowers with casseroles!"

"Don't worry," Emma threw at her departing back while she finished filling the teapot, "I'm pretty sure she's here about something serious enough to wipe off that grin!"

There was a bustle and a commotion in the hall and then, "Oh, hello Emma," Edna said in her breathless way as she came into the kitchen, looking anxiously around her.

"Oh dear, isn't Jasmine here? This concerns her, mostly; I hope she hasn't gone out. Oh, I see from all the pots and pans on the stove you haven't had your dinner yet; well, well, don't worry, I won't take too much of your time."

Fussily as a hen arranging its feathers she settled onto the banquette, but then jumped up immediately to embrace Jasmine when she returned to the kitchen.

"Let's move to the living room, shall we?" Emma picked up the tea tray and led the way to the cool, high-ceiling room at the front of the house, bringing a note of formality to this impromptu meeting. They took their seats on the comfortable sofas and chairs and waited expectantly for Edna to begin.

"Dear Jasmine, I'm so glad to see you so well and all recovered from your female – from all your problems," Edna started off uncertainly.

"In fact," she said, peering at her near-sightedly, "I don't think I've ever seen you looking so – wonderful! The reason I'm here is that I thought you should know – Oh, I don't know how to say this! Well, I'm pretty sure that you're going to be hearing from Mason Stoddart very soon. And since it's more or less my fault, I thought I had better warn you. The last thing he said when left today is that he absolutely has to talk to you. He seems very upset."

"What happened?" Jasmine asked, rather nervously.

Margery suddenly stood up and moved from her comfortable seat on the sofa to an upright chair that was directly across from Edna. She leaned forward in eager anticipation.

"Well, Mason came to visit me today because I've decided to sell the house. Yes, the Matthews House. It's sad, because it's been in the family for generations, but you know, no one wants it, none of the children do, and it's getting too much for me to handle all by myself – I don't know how you do it, Emma, yours is just as big! Well, they've all been at me to move, the children that is, and speaking frankly, you know, I'm really more tired of all their nagging than I am of the house! So Clem, you've met Clem, my son, haven't you Jasmine? Well, he told Mason, the two of them have been friends for forever and now Clem is handling some of his investments – he told Mason that I was thinking of selling and so Mason came by yesterday to visit and see the house."

She paused. Pulling an old-fashioned white handkerchief with lace edging out of one sleeve, she blew her nose vigorously, producing an impressive honk for such a small woman.

"Sorry." She giggled in embarrassment, then neatly folded the handkerchief and tucked it back up her sleeve. "Just finishing up a cold, you know. Now where was I?"

"Mason came by to see the house," Margery quickly prompted.

"Oh yes. Well, we looked around and of course he wants to buy it, for himself and his boys. It turns out his wife, that is, his ex-wife, I suppose, since they're getting a divorce, is keeping the house out on the fourth line outside town, for now. We haven't discussed terms yet; I'm going to ask Clem to help me out with that. Anyhow, all the time we were talking and looking through the rooms, he seemed very nervous and distracted and I finally asked him, what was it, was there anything the matter? And he said he'd just seen something very strange; that he'd seen Jasmine taking down a birdcage and carrying it into the Latham's house. Well, I said, that's not so strange, if the weather is good they always put their canary outside for some fresh air and sunshine in the morning and then they bring him in, in the late afternoon."

"Yes," said Jasmine, "but today poor Dickie was being blown around a bit."

"Oh, yes, wasn't it so windy and rainy this afternoon? I had to run some errands and my umbrella turned inside out on the way home. And I had such a dreadful time dealing with it and all my parcels and –"

Edna paused for breath and immediately Margery leapt in, "so what did Mason say when you told him about the canary?"

"Oh, the canary. Yes. Well then, he asked, what was Jasmine doing there in the first place? And I told him you were there taking care of Lianne, helping out as a practical nurse. Then he asked me, well, how can she do that? I said, you know, that you had lots of experience taking care of sick people; first of all your grandmother, when she was sickly for such a long time before she passed on; bed-ridden for her last year, wasn't she? And then your mother too, when you had to stay home from school during the time she had pleurisy. Then later of course she had that bout of pneumonia, and I was explaining all this to him and for some reason Mason got quite agitated."

"Well, what did he say then?" asked Margery, who was starting to look quite agitated herself.

"He said no, no, what I want to know is, what is she doing at the Latham's house? Because you and Thomas were supposed to have been –"

"Lovers," Jasmine supplied, without any trace of the embarrassment with which Edna was now struggling.

"Having a – relationship," she finished up primly. "And then I asked Mason if he hadn't heard about how Thomas rescued you when you were trying to drown yourself. He said no, I haven't, what's all this? I said, well, you must be the only person left in Medford who doesn't know about it. I said I was surprised his mother hadn't told him, at least. Now he was getting really upset and he said, will you please, please just tell me what you're talking about? So I told him the whole story and at the end he sat there for a long while looking upset and angry."

Edna paused once more. "Are those chocolate cookies? Oh I do so love your cookies, Emma!" She took one, and then they had to wait, with Margery teetering dangerously on the edge of her chair, while Edna took several bites and a few sips of her tea.

"Mason looked angry, and then what happened?" Margery prodded when she finally set down her cup and finished the cookie.

Edna patted her mouth delicately with her serviette before continuing. "I said, Mason, you look so upset, can I get you something? I have some hot tea ready on the stove. And he said, I don't want any goddamn tea. I just want to know why she would have done that. She wasn't the kind of person to kill herself because she didn't get any of my letters, even if she was upset when she found out her father was married to another woman. He said none of it was enough; it didn't make any sense. That there had to be something more to it, to explain why she did what she did."

"Then he apologized for swearing, and for his behaviour. But he said that now he absolutely had to see and talk to you, and then he said goodbye and left right away."

Edna reached for her teacup again. When she looked up, Jasmine was standing poised for flight. She was unsmiling, her lips drawn in a thin line.

"Thank you, Edna, for coming; I really do appreciate your concern. However, if you see Mason again, perhaps you could tell him that the past is the past, and I have no desire to revisit it or to see him. He has no claim on me, and I refuse to be questioned about what was a very painful time for me. A time I'm trying to forget. And now, because I don't want to talk about it anymore, I hope you'll excuse me."

She was at the double doors to the room when Edna called out to her. "Jasmine, I just want to tell you that Clem met Mason on the day he came home from Germany, when he was barely able to walk after the car accident. He said Mason was heartbroken when he found you weren't here."

Jasmine stopped, her back stiffening as she listened. But she didn't turn around. A second more, and she was gone.

"In fact, I don't think he's ever recovered," Edna said to nobody in particular, once Jasmine left the room.

"If you'll excuse me, it's getting late and I think I had better leave too," Margery informed them and rising, she hurriedly departed.

Emma was disturbed by Edna's words. In her opinion, what Edna just said was exactly the last thing Jasmine needed to hear. That girl already had oceans of regret, enough for a lifetime. She did not need to know that had she waited, her life might have been very different.

But the message Jasmine had given Edna for Mason, because of the sharp finality of it, stuck in her mind. In fact, it came in handy that very evening, at around eight-thirty. She delivered it almost verbatim when Mason came to the front door asking to talk to Jasmine. He appeared to listen well enough, but from the set of his jaw when he turned to leave, Emma could tell he had already decided to ignore it.

After Margery's departure she and Edna had sat and finished up their tea. Once she regaled Emma with the latest doings of her children and grandchildren, Edna stood up to leave. Just then, however, a small face peeked around the doorframe.

"Why, who's this?" Edna asked delightedly.

Shy, but curious at the sound of an unfamiliar voice, Laura came into the living room. She had tidied up and changed her muddy pants. However, it seemed she had not troubled to look in the mirror. A big streak of dirt ran down one cheek.

But no matter: taking both of her hands, Edna sat her down beside her on the sofa, and in a few minutes they were fast friends.

Emma fondly watched Laura basking in the warm attention Edna was showering on her. Yes, she thought, Edna truly is a dear. Even if she does chase after widowers.

Only later in the evening did she realize that Margery had left without promising not to talk about what had been discussed at Edna's visit. Emma almost picked up the phone to call her. But knowing Margery, it was already too late. And after all, she thought, what harm could it possibly do?

* * *

Elizabeth Stoddart set the phone down quietly.

"That was a late call." Sitting in his easy chair reading the newspaper, Max looked at his wife over the top of his spectacles, one bristly eyebrow quirked inquiringly upward. "Anything the matter?"

"No. Just Amelia Hindson, with a few last-minute details about the hospital drive luncheon tomorrow."

She left the living room and went to her dressing room. She felt as if her legs might crumple beneath her before she reached that private sanctuary, so heavy was the burden of fear and worry she carried. Amelia had made some mention of the fundraising luncheon. However, the real reason for her late-night phone call was to tell Elizabeth about Mason's visit with Edna Matthews.

Once in her dressing room, Elizabeth relaxed her carefully composed features. Sitting at the table that held her perfumes, creams and other toiletries, she looked in the mirror. Now her face, pinched and white, revealed her strain. Taut lines ran deep on either side of her mouth.

What she had anticipated, feared from the first moment she heard of Jasmine's return to Medford was about to take place. She knew her son and his implacable, iron will. Mason would talk to Jasmine. He would soon make her repeat the words his mother had said to his fiancée years ago: those rash, ill-considered words that had sprung out of her disgust with Jasmine's father, her deep unhappiness at an alliance with such a disgraced family. He would learn how the mother he loved and respected had, if not lied, willfully concealed the truth from him; how she had blighted their young love. Their very lives! And after that, it was only inevitable that her husband and her daughters would find out too.

She took cream from a jar and began to remove her makeup. She felt the weight of consequence, so long delayed, beginning its inexorable descent. Fate would take its course. For now, all she could do was wait.

CHAPTER 59

It was around two-thirty in the morning. Even in sleep, her ears were attuned to every noise. There was the distant snick of a lock, the creak of a door opening. Anna heard the heavy footfalls coming up the stairs and she moved far over to one side of the bed. The hallway light flicked on. There followed a long silence.

She became curious. What could he be doing? She slipped out of bed and looked. The girls' bedroom was at the end of the hall. Royce was standing in the doorway. His back was to her and he was supporting himself with one arm draped around the doorframe as he peered into the dark bedroom. Anna got back in bed. After a few minutes he came in. He quickly shed his clothes on the floor and climbed under the sheets, bringing with him the heavy odours of beer and cigarettes.

Moments later he was snoring lightly, but Anna now was wide awake. She could not rest until she knew what he had been looking at. Silently she padded down the hall. In the dim light from the half-moon that shone through the bedroom window, she saw that Mary was no longer in her own bed. She was sleeping with Lily in her smaller bed, their heads on the same pillow, their arms entangled.

The next morning when Anna went in to wake them for school, Mary was back in her own bed. Lily had had a nightmare, she explained to her mother. But when Anna asked Lily about her nightmare, the child looked at her in confusion. Not me, she said. It was Mary who said she had a bad nightmare and got in my bed.

A deep, roiling sense of unease overtook Anna. It gnawed away at her all day. It was only relieved at five o'clock that Friday, when she had safely delivered Mary to her great aunt and cousin for the weekend.

CHAPTER 60

The day had dawned sunny and warm, and Jasmine was rediscovering the delights of spring in a northerly clime during a walk through the park before work. The air was full of perfume and birdsong, the trees misting green with newly opened leaves. Yesterday's lake, a cold grey sea, now unfurled whitecaps on water of a brilliant dark blue. The colour reminded her of Thomas's eyes, and he came in a rush to her mind. She had not seen him face to face; she had not spoken to him ever since returning to Medford.

How foolish he's being, Lianne had said. Ever practical, she had added: eventually he will have to see you anyway, and I've told him I don't want you getting reacquainted over my deathbed. But he won't cooperate.

Jasmine could guess why. Was the last time they met still as vivid in his mind as it was in hers? She had come early today; perhaps he would be there.

But when she walked through the front door, all was silent. The sunroom was empty, except for Dickie, chirping happily in the bright sunlight. Most every morning, Thomas helped Lianne downstairs, settling her amidst her mounds of colourful pillows on the long couch before he left for school. Jasmine saw that she was not in her usual place.

With a surge of anxiety, she realized that Lianne must be having a bad day. She bounded up the stairs. Although Lianne's death would spell her release, although she had seen the changes in her and was more or less resigned to that eventuality, she did not want her to die. It seemed to her she was already mourning her, the prospect of that bright light extinguished. How much more, she thought, must Thomas be dreading her loss.

In the bedroom, Lianne lay propped up on pillows, her face ashy pale. "Hello, Jasmine," she said weakly. "I think I'll stay here today. Can you help me sit a bit more upright?"

Gently, Jasmine lifted her to a half-sitting position, but still she grimaced and repressed a groan. "You're in pain!" Jasmine exclaimed sharply, alarmed. "This seems worse than the other times. I think I should call the doctor!"

"No!" Lianne said, and this time her voice had more strength. "What can he do? He'll just give me a needle or a pill and dope me up, and then I'll lose this day. I want to live it! Even if there's some pain, I can take it, I want to be awake!"

Jasmine was upset enough to be angry. "It makes no sense, your suffering. It would be better to at least take one of your pain pills; you'd still be awake, only more comfortable."

"It does make sense," Lianne said with conviction. "I'm not suffering just for me, but for someone else. To help them get to a better place. We're all connected, everyone is."

Lianne often said such things, arising from her great faith. Although Jasmine did not share it, she listened respectfully, if skeptically. Her sayings were thought provoking, however, and Jasmine pondered over them. Lately she had begun to wonder whether, poised as she was on the cusp between life and death, Lianne might have a better vantage point from which to glimpse the truth of a Grand Design.

Now she said, "well, that would certainly make suffering much easier to accept. Still, you won't get much out of this day in your condition. How about just one pill? Take it for me."

Lianne had a truculent expression on her face, but it vanished when Jasmine made this plea. She smiled her sweet, little-girl smile and obediently held out her hand. Once she swallowed the pill, she patted a spot on her bedspread.

"Come sit down. I have some good news to tell you, and a few other things."

Jasmine sat down. "What's the good news?" she asked, smiling. That Lianne was happy about something lifted her spirits.

"Oh, Jasmine, it's working!" Lianne burst out excitedly. "My plan is starting to work! Yesterday Thomas was offered the job of vice principal at Medford High!"

"Why, that's wonderful news!" Jasmine exclaimed, just as pleased as she. "He must be thrilled!"

"No, not really," Lianne responded, her enthusiasm quickly dampened. "He says he's been doing the job for a long time anyhow, and he'll only be doing the same things but with a title. And that Simms, the principal, knows he's looking around, and he's trying to keep him from leaving, because then he'll actually have to do some work himself. But anyhow, he got it. It will help him find a better position somewhere else, he says."

She drew a long breath, and Jasmine waited for her to gather the energy to continue.

"Thomas was upset when he saw how ill I was this morning. So he's taking the afternoon off to be with me, and you can leave today at twelve-thirty. But he has to go to the school Monday, on the holiday, to discuss the job and sign some papers. He wondered if you could come that day?"

Jasmine assented. She also agreed when Lianne told her that Thomas had found an old bike and fixed it up for Laura to use before she bought a new one. Would it be alright if he spent a few hours Monday morning teaching her how to ride it?

We'll be back in Vegas before Laura ever earns enough to buy her new bicycle in any case, Jasmine thought. She looked out the window at the sun shining, the wind blowing through the trees on its way to other faraway places, and felt the old, familiar restlessness setting in.

"You'll find your pay on the kitchen table," Lianne continued. "It seems so little for what you do."

"Every little bit counts," Jasmine responded cheerfully. "If I can sell my own and my mother's jewelry, it should be quite enough."

"It's so sad, having to sell those family things. Wasn't there anything you wanted to keep?"

"I did keep some gold chains and a few trinkets. The only piece I'm sorry to lose is a sapphire ring set with diamonds, but it was probably the most valuable."

Lianne was quiet for a few seconds. Then she turned her eyes on Jasmine with a look she had come to know only too well, the look that preceded a full-scale interrogation.

"Jasmine, you told me before that you made a lot of money. What happened to all of it? Why do you have so little now?"

Jasmine laughed, rather weakly. "Lianne, am I to have no secrets from you? You've extracted just about every detail of my life from me, and now this question! Don't you know enough already?"

Lianne opened her mouth. Jasmine knew what she was going to say. She spoke it simultaneously along with her, mimicking her word for word. "But your life is so interesting –"

Lianne, smiling, said, "well, you don't have to tell me if you don't want to. But I am so curious."

Jasmine sighed. "All right, I suppose so. But it's still painful to think about. So I'll be brief. Do you remember I told you that after Mike left, and our divorce, I tried to keep it quiet? So that no one knew?"

"Yes," Lianne replied. "It was so you wouldn't get pestered."

"That's right. And that's just about the perfect word for it. For almost three years I was successful; but eventually the news got out."

"And then it happened. You got pestered."

"Yes. An extremely unattractive man, unappealing in every way. But powerful, a gangster with an ownership stake in several casinos. I was worried; I knew he could fix it so I would lose my job and not be able to work anywhere else in Vegas, with the idea, perhaps, that then I would come crawling to him."

"So you decided to leave."

"Yes, but that wasn't the only reason. I wanted to start a business of my own."

She sketched in the details. There were two of them in on the plan. It could have, no, would have worked, and even now she agonized over the opportunity she had lost along with the money. He was a trusted friend: Frank Maitland – one of the first people she and Mike had met when they moved to Vegas. It would mean returning to Canada and with her mother ill, the chance to see her more often. Frank and his girlfriend Marlene would come with her.

"So I rented my little house, the one I bought after the divorce. I liquidated everything else and with Frank's matching funds, we had enough to set up a business."

"What was it?"

They had talked about it for days. They researched it thoroughly, drew up a business agreement. Although gambling was illegal in Ontario, it was permissible if done in a private club. Together they found a good location in the city, rented space and began to renovate. All the while they continued to work for the casinos in Vegas. They visited other social clubs, identified the big spenders and offered them free trips or hotel stays and other types of giveaways to visit the casinos. She also found a few places where she could join in card games. Mostly, she won.

"And so we were doing well enough, even while we waited for the club to be finished."

Jasmine paused. She had come to the difficult part.

"So then what happened?" Lianne prompted.

"Frank got greedy. He began to rent hotel rooms and run his own games, which put him in the way of the law. We argued. I think he might also have come up against some organizations that saw him as taking away their business. Maybe he got scared."

She had the duplicate key to Frank and Marlene's apartment. Jasmine felt once more the shock when, after her unanswered phone calls, she opened the door and found them gone; then the icy cold fear that followed that realization. She did not walk but ran to the bank, where she discovered that their joint business account had been emptied.

"Marlene used my identity papers and signed my name, and together she and Frank withdrew all the funds deposited for the club."

Not just her money, everything she had, but a considerable amount borrowed from her mother had vanished, along with the future she had envisaged for herself and her daughter. There were no funds to pay the contractors, honest folk who had done a good job, or for the rent of the space downtown, or the apartment she and Laura lived in. Her mother advanced her more money; she found a job. But the betrayal, the enormity of the loss, all her losses, gnawed at her. Very shortly afterward she had tumbled into that twisted black tunnel, the rabbit hole of despair from which Emma had extricated her.

Jasmine had been staring down at her hands; abruptly, she looked up at Lianne.

"And now you know everything," she concluded bitterly. "There's nothing more to tell. I'm going downstairs to get you something for breakfast." She stood up.

"Not everything," Lianne said under her breath.

"What?" Jasmine stopped at the door. "What did you say?"

"I'm sorry to have taken you back to such a sad, dark time." Lianne replied.

"It's all right. I've learned to deal with it. I won't be going there or doing that again."

"Older and wiser."

"Older anyhow." Jasmine turned to leave once more.

"Before you go, can you please help me into my chair?"

"Your chair? Lianne, you will do nothing of the kind! In your condition, you should stay in bed."

"Don't you tell me what to do! I only have weeks or days left, and I'll do whatever I want with them!"

Hand on hips, Jasmine turned and returned to stand beside the bed. "You are a very aggravating invalid!"

"It's the only pleasure I have," Lianne retorted. "Being aggravating."

Jasmine helped her out of bed. "Well, then you must be happy most of the time."

"Don't worry," Lianne said crossly. "I'm not planning to die today."

Jasmine slowly assisted her to her big armchair. "Good. Don't do it on my watch. Save it for Thomas."

And then they smiled at one another, as they always did at the end of their rounds of insults and repartee. Jasmine drew back the curtains so that Lianne could look down at the street. Then she went to the bed and tidied it, smoothing the sheets and rearranging the blankets.

"There's little Ralph Speyers, late with the newspaper again," Lianne observed. "Thomas won't be happy to have missed his morning paper."

Then, in quite a different tone of voice, she exclaimed, "Jasmine! There's a man on the porch!"

"How do you know?" Jasmine walked over and peered through the window. "I don't see anyone."

"Because he just came out and picked up the newspaper, and now he's back on the porch again, reading it!"

"Who was it?"

"I'm not sure. I could only see the back and top of his head. Brown hair. Tall, probably over six feet, wearing a navy-blue suit."

"Mason Stoddart."

"Yes, it might be. There's a black car over there, parked some distance away, see? It looks as if it might be his. Why is he here?"

Jasmine was visibly upset. "It's because he's decided he has to see me; he wants to talk to me. Edna Matthews came by yesterday to warn me. She said he visited her and she told him about Thomas rescuing me from drowning myself. Now he's set on finding out why I tried to do it; he even came to the door last night, and Emma sent him away! This has to stop! I don't want to see him or talk to him!"

"Well, why is he on the porch?"

"Maybe he thought I would come down to get the paper? No, now I remember: Edna told him that I put Dickie outside in his cage on the porch on sunny days. In fact I was going to do just that when I went downstairs. But for sure I won't now! How can I get rid of him?"

Back and forth and back again, Jasmine had paced the length of the room, almost wringing her hands.

Lianne was looking a little better. The pain pill was taking effect, and she had brightened up with the excitement. But her expression was puzzled.

"I don't understand. Why can't you just do what he wants and talk to him?"

"There are some details about what happened back then that I don't want to tell him. Or anyone," Jasmine said meaningfully, looking at Lianne.

Lianne lowered her brows and looked at her severely. "Jasmine," she said in a threatening voice, "what secrets are you trying to keep from me now?"

Even in her distress and agitation, she laughed. "Lianne, will you for once be serious! This concerns his whole family. His mother especially."

"Oh. It was something she said."

Jasmine stopped pacing and looked at her in dismay. "Thomas!" She was plainly angry. "Did he tell you? He's the only one who knows; he swore he would keep it secret!"

"Heavens no," Lianne replied mildly. "He's told me nothing! It was only a guess. Not even a very lucky one, just about anyone could have guessed it from what you said. But since I know this much, then you might as well tell me the rest. If I know the reason you don't want to speak to him, perhaps I can help."

And after a moment of hesitation, and only because by now it was almost a habit, Jasmine did. Slowly, haltingly, she laid bare the outlines of that story, which was sealed away in tear-stained tissues in a corner of her mind she never visited for reasons of self-preservation. Even years later, she feared that sadness like an infection lying dormant and waiting for a chance to engulf her once more.

But while she spoke to Lianne it seemed as if it were someone else, not her, who had spiraled into that dark void and felt such pain. When she finished she had a strange feeling, almost of relief. If it no longer hurt to remember, then she might now be healed.

They were quiet for a long moment. "Tell me again what Elizabeth Stoddart said to you at the door," Lianne asked, breaking the silence.

"She said, 'no, there are no letters for you here. And if you haven't heard from Mason, it's because he knows about your father, and what he's done, and he doesn't want anything more to do with you, or your family.'"

Lianne shook her head. Her lips were pressed tight. "That was purely evil." She struggled to stand. "She must have known about her son's accident by then. Help me back to my bed."

"We can't know that for certain. I'm not sure she meant to be heartless. It could have been one of those things that simply come out without much thought, that you say now and regret later," Jasmine lifted Lianne easily up onto her bed. She was light as a feather, only skin and bones.

"Well, you give her more credit than I do. She didn't ever follow up with you, did she?"

"No," Jasmine said. "But I went off the rails soon after that. Anyhow, it doesn't matter. None of it matters any more, except that right this moment there's a man downstairs on the porch. And the best thing I can do for him now is to keep my mouth shut."

"My goodness, yes." Lianne's expression was grave, and she looked up at her with eyes opened wide and serious. "If you spent any time with him at all, the truth would be sure to come out. Then the bitch would get what she deserves, but the family would fall apart."

"Exactly. And Mason and Arlena are so close; Lord only knows how she'd rip up her mother if she ever found out. But they all need her, even Arlena. Especially her grandsons, those two little boys whose mother gave them up to be with her lover."

"Well, let's think about this." Lianne bit her lower lip and furrowed her brow in concentration. "How can we make him go 'way?"

* * *

Downstairs on the porch, Mason had read his way through the business section, including the stock reports, then the front section of the newspaper, and was paging through to the comics when he heard a sharp tapping noise. After a moment he identified what it was and where it was coming from. It was the sound of something being tapped sharply against a glass pane, up on the second floor, directly overhead. It stopped, then started over again, insistently.

He realized the jig was up. Somehow, she knew that he was on the front porch. He left his comfortable seat on the porch swing and now, from the sidewalk that led to the house, he looked up.

She was standing at the window. When he saw her, more beautiful than ever, he couldn't help it. Everything he was feeling then: hope, love, was probably written there on his face for her to see.

But what was she doing? He saw her reach up and grasp a little ring dangling on a string above her. Then slowly, ever so slowly, she pulled down the heavy white blind, looking at him all the while, until it had covered the window and he could see her no more.

He stood there for a minute. The light left his face. Then desolation dropped over him like a blanket. His eyes filled, and he stumbled as he turned, his bad leg barely supporting him. He got in his car and drove away.

In the darkened bedroom, Lianne could see Jasmine's cheeks shining with tears as she turned from the window.

"I thought I was all finished crying over him. But oh! He looked so sad."

Sitting up in bed, Lianne opened her arms wide and Jasmine went to them. "He was my first love. And I did love him so very much once," she sobbed, "with all my heart and soul."

They held each other fast. "Dear Jasmine," Lianne said tenderly. "How I wish that life had turned out better for you."

"And I for you," Jasmine cried hot tears into the shoulder of Lianne's nightgown. "Fate gave us both such a poor hand."

"Yes – if we'd been dealt a good hand, then you would have married Mason. You would have held all the aces. And me? I would have had a full house."

Jasmine stiffened. She disengaged herself, wiping away her tears with a hand as she sat up. "Really, Lianne, that's most annoying," she said in a resentful tone. "Why do you do that? Whenever I say something that's sad or serious, you always manage to turn it into some kind of silly joke."

"Oh, do I? I suppose it's just one of my talents," Lianne replied in an irritatingly self-satisfied way. "Are you going to get me some breakfast?"

"I guess so. What would you like?"

"Something sweet, to make up for all the sour this morning. Cinnamon toast, with tea." She yawned.

"Cinnamon toast will make extra work for me, so don't you dare fall asleep before I come back upstairs."

"I'll especially enjoy it knowing that it made more work for you. And you're the one who wanted to give me the pain pill, so you'll just have to take what you get."

Jasmine, at the door, turned. They smiled at each other. Then she went downstairs. She took Dickie in his cage to the front porch, and as she opened the door, a business card fluttered down to the door mat. She picked it up, looked at it briefly and tucked it in a pocket.

When she came back with the toast and tea, Lianne was barely awake. She ate only a few bites before turning away, and within moments was fast asleep. She was still asleep when Jasmine left the house at 12.30.

Jasmine ate the rest of the cinnamon toast over the kitchen sink. She had loaded it with butter and brown sugar, then toasted it under the broiler, and it was delicious. While she ate she salted it with the tears rolling down her cheeks, as she cried for Mason, Lianne, for all things sweet that come to a bitter end.

CHAPTER 61

Young Alistair McGregor was in a foul mood, and Martha Jenner could guess why. She had heard from Eleanor Peters, who heard it from Muriel Farquarson, who had just left the drugstore at the time, what had happened to her nephew on Wednesday at the hands of the Tilly triplets and their brother.

Martha and Simon Jenner were childless and over the past three months Alistair had roundly confirmed the wisdom of that choice. Alistair, although twenty-four years old, was desperately untidy. He shed clothes, shoes, paper and various personal articles all over the house, and when his aunt gathered them and piled them in front of his door, he stepped over them on leaving, or else muttered a curse under his breath, then picked them up and threw them on the floor of his room. He had a voracious appetite and had doubled her grocery bill; and his constant chatter and wisecracks left them not a moment of the peace or silence they had hitherto enjoyed.

But be that as it may, somehow the fire-haired, freckled young fiend had driven a wedge in her heart. Now she felt for him in his humiliation as she passed by his room and heard the banging and sotto voce curses coming through and under his closed door. When he emerged into the kitchen a moment later, he was carrying his pipes and a sheaf of music. His wild red hair was wilder yet and his expression was thunderous.

Weiner, the Jenner's petted and overweight dachshund, was sitting on his pillow in the sunshine by the sliding door peacefully contemplating the birds outside as they flitted through the apple tree blossoms. Alistair had partially inflated the bag of his pipes. Now he put the blowstick in his mouth and from behind, gave Weiner a blast.

YELP! Although quite geriatric, the dog leapt an impressive foot or two into the air. On landing, he scrabbled away across the linoleum, knocking over a potted geranium Martha had ready to take outside and spilling dirt all over the clean floor.

"You can't play that in here!" Martha exclaimed, more concerned with the migraine she was certain to have if he did, than she was with the dog or the mess on the kitchen floor.

"Don't worry," he replied bitterly as he opened the door to leave. "I'm going outside, even if soon I'll be playing in the rain."

"It's not raining now, nor likely for a couple hours," Martha informed him. "Anyhow, if it does start to sprinkle you can practice under the covered porch."

"Oh sure. Last time I did that, your neighbour came over and told me I was giving her Scottie dogs a nervous breakdown. Why the hell am I playing this thing when no one really wants to hear it?"

"Don't swear. They want to hear it, alright," Martha said. "But mostly coming toward or going away from them. Not right there."

He gave her a ghost of a smile to acknowledge her witticism. Then he sniffed the air. "What's for dinner?"

"Irish stew with dumplings."

"Well, at least there'll be one good thing on this bloody awful day." He gave her another of his lopsided grins and went out the door to his usual practice place at the end of the yard.

His aunt had been kinder and more solicitous than usual since he came home. He suspected that, after his uncle related the basics, she must have heard all the details of what happened and now was feeling sorry for him. God! He fumed. If she knows, then everyone does, and I'm the laughing stock of the whole blasted town!

Alistair had a bountiful assortment of curses and cuss words, many of them acquired during his student summers with the armed forces Highlanders pipe corps. Now, as he traversed the lawn, he unleashed them on the town of Medford, his job, the Jenner funeral home, the Jenner's dog, the inhabitants of Medford – the Tilly triplets in particular – and on himself, for being such an idiot.

Because it wasn't as if he hadn't been warned.

"Stay away!" That was from Theo Van Stoep, one in a chorus of male voices that erupted when Alistair mentioned the names of Nan and Nell Tilly during the boys' regular Thursday beer night at the Statler Tavern. They had been discussing their usual topics, sports and women, with an emphasis on the latter.

"Don't waste your time," his good friend Chris Byers advised in an aside. Then he elaborated. "They're cute, sure, but their brothers have wised them up and they know that guys like you are only interested in getting into their pants. Plus, they're mean."

The triplets: Nell, Nan and Ned, were nineteen. All worked on Main Street, Nell at the drugstore, Nan at Woolworth's and Ned at the butcher shop. The girls had dark flashing eyes, bright smiles and amazing figures. Alistair was not so much smitten as desperate for female company. Back home, he would have had his choice of any of a half-dozen girls. In Medford, however, he was experiencing a dismaying lack of success with the fair sex. He was beginning, but only just beginning, to think that his previous popularity might not be due to his sparkling personality and good looks, but the fact that he stood to inherit a million-dollar flour milling and distribution operation.

The triplets came from a large family that lived in nothing much more than a large shack near the railway bridge. There were Tillys everywhere and all over town: clerking in stores, working on the roads, pumping gas, delivering parcels or newspapers, cutting grass. Including their mother, Clara, who babysat, cleaned houses and took in laundry, most of them seemed to have two or three jobs. With the exception of the second eldest son, Colton, who was said to be off at school or working somewhere, they all lived at home with their mother and her second husband.

Whispers that they were wealthy drifted down from the tellers working at the Medford bank. However, nobody knew that for sure, or, if it were true, just what if anything they did with their money. The mystery was solved only a few years later after Colton came back to Medford as a full-fledged pharmacist. Then, neatly upsetting the town's social order apple cart, the Tillys bought the main street drug store from its retiring owners, the Metcalfes; and not long after that, Clara purchased and moved into one of the large homes she formerly had cleaned.

But for now the Tillys were perceived as belonging to the lower strata of Medford society. There were also intriguing rumours that cast doubt on their paternity. The oldest Tilly child, Willard, looked nothing like the others. He was short and scrawny, with a misshapen face, watery blue eyes and sandy hair. He was unable to read or write and his brother Ned brought him each day to the butcher shop, where he swept floors and performed other menial, undemanding tasks. However, starting with Colton, the second-born, the Tilly children were all dark-haired and brown-eyed. They had an olive cast to their skin, and were tall, handsome and well-formed.

This mystery appeared to be solved when someone, perhaps a nurse or doctor in the maternity ward of the Medford hospital, noticed that all the fast-arriving Tilly babies were born in and around the month of April. Counting backwards, this seemed to point to the annual arrival in Medford of Mario Cartucci, the Fuller Brush salesman. In their small town where most were of Scottish, English, Irish or Dutch extractions, few failed to notice Mario, a strapping big man with a luxuriant head of black hair and an equally fulsome moustache. As the Tilly boys grew, especially once they started to sprout moustaches, their resemblance to the magnificent Mario became more pronounced. On a few occasions their mother had been seen in his company.

It seemed likely that Clara Tilly, after her unsuccessful initial experiment employing Percy Tilly, had wisely availed herself of different breed stock. Percy may or may not have known of the shadow cast over his paternity, but he was as proud of his brood of nine children as any man could ever be. In return he was much loved by them, right up to his desperate race with the Sunday night freight train on the Coshoni trestle bridge, after which he was greatly mourned.

Whether Mario moved on to another territory or was killed by a jealous husband, one August he was no longer there. Those who noticed and asked after him with his replacement were told he had passed on. Perhaps he had. But not before his last brush with Clara Tilly, where the three-for-one deal they transacted had the felicitous outcome, nine months later, of Medford's first recorded set of triplets, Nan, Nell and Ned.

Now, winsome and toothsome, Nell was sunning herself on a bench in front of the Metcalfe Pharmacy. It was five o'clock and Alistair was taking the hearse back to the funeral home after an oil change at the local garage. The only stop light in town had just turned red. Alistair, perhaps eight cars back, was directly across from Nell. He smiled at her.

"Hi Alistair," said Nell. "You shouldn't be driving that hearse."

"Oh? Why not?"

"With hair like yours, you ought to be driving a fire truck."

Alistair should have caught the scent of danger from this brief exchange. However, by now he was totally inured to wisecracks about his hair, as well as distracted by the tight sweater Nell was wearing. "I only drive my fire truck on weekends," he replied, smiling more broadly and revving the engine a couple of times for emphasis.

Then, like the dumbass he was, trying his luck, he asked, "how about a ride home?"

He was taking a risk. His uncle had been emphatic: "You must never, under any circumstance, allow anyone except customers in the hearse." But the side street after the light offered a direct route to the Tilly shack. Alistair gambled he could evade detection.

Nell smiled warmly. "Sure," she said. "But can you swing around the block first? I have to tell my brother I'm going home with you."

Alistair was having second thoughts even before he stopped at the pharmacy again. However, then he saw Nell, waving brightly. She was hurrying to get in before the light changed, so he just leaned over and swung the passenger door open. When he looked up, a flurry of Tillys had left their hiding places and leapt into the hearse. The triplets piled into the back seat, while Willard jumped in front. He was holding a large cardboard box.

"Let's go! What'cha waitin' for?" hollered Ned from the back seat. The light was still green. The cars behind them were starting to honk.

"Get out," Alistair ordered in a voice full of menace. "I'm not allowed to give rides in the hearse."

"Ha! S'too late for that, ain't it?" Ned hollered back. "Git movin', gonna miss the light!"

Alistair now saw that unless he floored it, he would be stuck at the stoplight with a hearse full of Tillys. He floored it; then, just as fast, hit the brakes. The light was red and the elderly man he had almost hit was shaking a cane and cursing him as he crossed the street.

In the back seat a loud argument had erupted. "Gimme that cab money, Ned!" Nell demanded. "No way; I'm usin' it t' buy beer!" chortled Ned. "Yes, you give it her, Ned, 'cause who was it got Red here to drive us home?" Nan asked heatedly.

And there was more, but now Alistair had tuned in to something else: the muted sounds of avian distress coming from the large cardboard box on Willard's lap.

"What's in the box?" he fatally inquired.

In response Willard, who was almost non-verbal and always more inclined to show than tell, lifted one of the flaps.

"Don't open the box!!" came the broken chorus from the backseat as hands lunged to stop him. But it was too late.

Suddenly the hearse was full of a whirling, screeching mass of half-grown chickens, four pullets with unclipped wings that Ned was taking home to fatten up, now interspersed with the thrashing arms and yells and screams of the triplets as they leapt to grab them. Soon one, then another chicken flapped out through the windows, and throwing open the back doors Ned, Nan and Nell dashed after them in hot pursuit.

The light had changed; horns were honking. From his vantage point frozen in horror behind the wheel, Alistair saw his aunt's friend Muriel Farquarson on the sidewalk. She was leaning on a lamppost in a state of semi-collapse, laughing, tears running down her cheeks. Worse, Sherry Byers, Chris's younger sister that he had lusted after, was standing on the steps of the drugstore holding her stomach, doubled over in paroxysms of hilarity. He looked across the street. Lewis Smythe was on the corner. When he saw Alistair glance his way he smiled. Then he took one index finger and very slowly drew it across his throat.

After that, it didn't take long. Not long at all. Just one hour later, Alistair was standing in front of his uncle, covered in flying spittle and calculating the odds of Simon Jenner having a stroke before he finished dressing him down. Two hours later, he heard the first cat call.

"Oh, Alistair! O awwk-puck-puck-puck-puck!" This was accompanied by a good simulation of flapping wings and gales of laughter. Then the three young women continued on toward the Statler Tavern, while Alistair, who had been walking in that general direction, turned around and headed back to his room. Since last night, he had emerged only for meals.

As she washed the dishes from lunch, Martha Jenner looked through the window over the sink. She felt her heart contract with sympathy as she watched her nephew slouch along in hangdog fashion toward the picnic table at the end of the lawn where he normally practiced.

Halfway there, in the middle of the lawn, he suddenly stopped in his tracks. He threw back his head and she heard a muffled roar.

"Y-A-AH!"

Alistair had been thinking about the unutterably awful timing of his encounter with the Tillys. At the parade tomorrow his humiliation would be complete. As he piped his way along Main Street, he would not only be subject to the usual dumb cracks about his hair, his kilt, what was under it or the lack of it, but like a highly infectious disease – the bubonic plague or the black death – the story of the Tillys would be passed from mouth to mouth. He would hear, over and over again, that chicken call in all its various incantations, while the speakers killed themselves laughing.

It was too much to bear. He felt as if the top of his head were about to blow off. Almost involuntarily, he gave out a huge, lung-emptying, therapeutic yell. Immediately afterward, he felt much better.

It was at that precise moment a strange and unexpected change came over Alistair McGregor. Into the vacuum so created, he felt the inflow of something he had always possessed, but to date had made very little use of – an iron determination. His resolve grew. Forged in the fiery crucible of his humiliation, it took on form and shape, pumping him up from top to bottom, straightening his back, squaring his shoulders, and lifting his head high and erect.

Still looking out the window, Martha saw Alistair set his bagpipe and his music down on the picnic bench. She saw him straighten up and raise a fist high to the sky. He hollered something, and she strained to hear, but the wubba-wubba rhythm of the wringer washer sloshing away in the next room drowned it out.

It would have astounded the Tillys, had they ever learned of their singular accomplishment. Because, in only a few minutes, they had succeeded in doing something that over the past ten years, Alistair's mother and father, his aunts and uncles, his sister, guidance counselors, student advisors, vocational consultants, family friends and even a few psychologists had all failed to do: instill in him a burning desire to make something of himself.

At the end of the Jenner's lawn just where the cedar bush began, Alistair raised his fist to the heavens. He pumped it as he roared:

"ONE DAY! ONE DAY, you'll kiss my ASS, Medford!

I'LL – SHOW – YOU!!"

CHAPTER 62

When Jasmine came into the kitchen for lunch, her face still showed the trace of tears. Emma saw this, but wisely held her peace. She only asked her if she wanted a bowl of homemade beef and barley soup.

"Yes please, but nothing else, thanks. I finished off the breakfast I made for Lianne and I'm not so hungry. Where's Laura?"

"She went to school early. She's teaching some of the girls who want to play baseball and she says they need to practice. How was Lianne today?"

"Not at all good. She was asleep most of the time."

They were both sitting at the kitchen table. Emma gently put her hand over Jasmine's. "Just as well. You helped take care of your grandmother and you saw how that happens, sleeping more and more. Nature is kindly that way."

"Ah, but she's so young. It's hard to watch."

"You've become attached to her."

"Yes. Yes, I have. It would be difficult not to."

Jasmine roused herself to change the subject. "What time can we expect Anna to bring Mary? I'd like to see Anna before she leaves."

"She'll be here shortly after Mary gets home from school, around four. The child will be here until Monday afternoon. For the whole long weekend."

"For the whole three days that her father is home," Jasmine said slowly. "For the third weekend in a row."

They looked at each other intently. "It's high time we found out why the child is avoiding her father," Emma said in her decisive way. "There must be a way to get to the bottom of this."

"Today." Jasmine stood up. "We'll ask Anna to stay for tea and figure out something together. She'll need our help, if it is what I think it might be."

After she washed her bowl and spoon under the tap, Jasmine turned and inquired, "is there anything you'd like me to do, preferably outside? I need some fresh air. I could sweep the walk or weed the front flowerbed, if that helps."

In fact, she would have preferred a walk, not chores, but felt she should at least make a token offer. So she was chagrined when Emma went to the pantry and came back with a box full of seed packets. Emma could tell from Jasmine's expression that it was more than she had bargained for, but she ignored it.

"I have to bake for the Victoria Day tea at the church tomorrow afternoon, and we'll be taking the children to the parade earlier, so it would be wonderful if you could plant my vegetable garden today. Just leave two rows at the end for Laura to plant peas, beans and carrots; she'll love watching them grow."

With a bemused look, Jasmine took the seeds. "I'll get out of these clothes first," she said, and disappeared upstairs.

Other folks had quickly given up their war gardens, but Emma had always had a vegetable garden and saw no reason to change her habits in peacetime. Thomas dug it for her each year, saying it was small recompense for all the soups, pies, casseroles and fresh vegetables that came their way from the Madison house.

From an upstairs window, Jasmine had seen him digging it after work last Tuesday. It was a warm day and he had removed his shirt and was bare-chested. She couldn't help wondering if he had done it for her benefit. He was a big man with a fine physique from working out with the high school students he helped train for football, baseball, basketball.... Bending and digging, the muscles rippled across his back while he worked, and she could easily see that he was in far better condition than when she had traced his ribs and the jutting sharp lines of his shoulders as they lay together, nine years ago.

Now, wearing a tee shirt and an old pair of jeans rather too tight for gardening, she stood beside the plot he had worked and prepared. The sun beamed warmly. Birds were singing and a light wind, silky and scented, ruffled her hair. She looked at the packets of seeds in her hands. The bright pictures of lettuce, radishes and other vegetables that created in Emma such pleasant anticipation were producing in Jasmine an entirely different reaction. Possibly because it was spring, the old restlessness she had staved off for so long had become more insistent. As she stared down at the garden plot and the seeds, a great wave of ennui rolled over her – boredom as intense as anything she had ever experienced in her teenage years.

It was the lack of change and challenge, she knew. There was the thrust and parry of her ripostes with Lianne, and an occasional foray with her aunt, but that was all. Her quick and nimble mind was like the buried scissors Thomas had unearthed during his digging and given to Emma: once bright and sharp, now rusting away.

These were her thoughts as she stood like a statue posed with a spade, holding the few packets of seeds she had taken out of the box. Bees buzzed around her. The sun beat down. Then she slowly lifted her head, the better to listen. Carried on the breeze, she heard several light sounds: a tentative few notes. Within moments, they had swelled into the rousing skirl of a bagpipe in full throat. The tune was being played, it seemed, with great gusto, like the wild battle cry it once used to be.

Something in Jasmine responded so strongly that she had little choice. It was an ancient instinct buried deep in her blood and bones. She had to follow it, to be a part of the great burst of vitality that informed that sound. And so, heedlessly, like a child spellbound by the call of a Pied Piper, she laid down her spade and her seeds and disappeared into the cedars at the end of the lawn.

* * *

For all his pretenses otherwise, Alistair loved playing the pipes. And he was talented beyond the norm; he knew it, although the bandmaster in the Highlanders Pipe Corps was always chiding him for switching up on the hallowed old tunes and adding his own turns and improvisations. Now he let loose with abandon on 'The Dark Island'. He sped up the melody, fashioning it into the musical equivalent of the great, life-changing vow he had sworn just minutes ago, full of fire and passion.

Back in the house, Martha Jenner hurriedly put on her jacket and grabbed her handbag. It seemed, over the past couple of months, she had developed a sensitivity – or was it an allergy? – to the sound of the bagpipes. Even though Alistair was practicing at the end of the yard, still she felt the throb of an incipient migraine. There were library books she needed to return, anyhow. She rushed out the front door and along the sidewalk, rapidly distancing herself from the wail of the pipes.

His eyes half-closed in enjoyment, Alistair saw a flash of red through the trees. He fully opened them. Someone was walking in the cedar bush and coming toward him. Then the branches parted. Stunned into silence, he dropped the blowpipe from his lips, even as the pipes continued to emit a few weak squeaks and squawks.

It was a girl, or rather a woman who emerged from the woods, but O Lord, what a woman! She was a mirage, a dream, the answer to his spoken and unspoken desires: Helen of Troy, the Mona Lisa and Aphrodite on the half-shell, all rolled into one. A beautiful face, long shining hair shades darker than his own, and a body set to test the limits of everything under his kilt. She smiled at him, a dazzling white smile, and took a seat near him on the picnic bench.

It was then she said the words that convinced Alistair that he had found the perfect woman for him. She didn't say much: just two small words. But they were the right words.

"Don't stop."

* * *

Emma had finished baking five dozen icebox pinwheel cookies and just put a spice cake in the oven. She peered out the kitchen window. No sign of Jasmine. However, the massive old maple tree was impeding her view of the vegetable garden. She took off her apron and went outside.

The yard was empty of all save sunshine. She saw the little box of seeds and the spade, set down on the grass next to the garden plot. Three of the packets of seeds were scattered about; whether by the wind or a careless hand, she could not tell. She gathered them up and looked at them: radishes, green onions and spinach, in enticing pictures that promised bounty.

A little riffle of wind lifted her hair. It was followed by a stronger gust that turned over the leaves of trees to show their silvery undersides. A few clouds were appearing, and the humming of the bees had diminished.

Then she caught just a whiff, but it was unmistakable: the sharp smell of ozone. Emma hesitated, looking at the sky, thinking of her cake baking. Was there time? No. Not really. But the spring garden lay waiting, the soil in its furrows, warm, fertile; and in their paper packets the seeds had sensed the coming of the rain and were clamoring to be born.

Dropping to her knees, she began to plant.

CHAPTER 63

They sat in semi-darkness, as befit the subject they were discussing. The living room curtains on the other side of the room were slightly parted, and the last dull light from an overcast sun as it sank beneath the horizon provided the only illumination.

"I just don't know what to do."

The children were outside on the porch with their books and games. Jasmine remembered as a child how delightful it was to sit on the porch swing with Anna, watching the rain stream down, drinking their children's pink tea and eating cookies. She was glad Laura could enjoy the same experience with Mary. Only, she desperately wished she were out there with them, and Christopher and little Lily, instead of sitting here, trying to solve an insoluble problem that might not even exist.

Through the wide bow window they could see Mary, the reason for this meeting. The two of them, Anna and Jasmine, had discussed their suspicions with Emma. Without proof, they concluded, there was little they could do. So far, the most they had accomplished was to dispose of a couple cups of tea each and a plate of pinwheel cookies.

"I can't keep trying to pump her about it," Anna said, her eyes large, her face pale with worry. "Either there's nothing, and I'm going to cause problems with her relationship with her father, or else something is happening, and for one reason or another she feels she just can't tell me. Heaven knows I've tried."

"Well, Mary is always welcome here on weekends. But your nursing schedule still leaves opportunities for him to be alone with her," Emma said. "Then you have Lily to think of – if he is doing what you suspect –" Her voice trailed off.

There was a short, tense silence. All that Anna had described, especially the image of Royce, his arm draped around the door frame, standing and looking at his sleeping daughters intertwined in Lily's tiny bed, had burned itself into their minds.

Jasmine said nothing. She was thinking of someone who reminded her of Lily. It was on the afternoon they had gone to see the daffodils that she and Anna first met the wee girl with the flaxen hair, looking like a little butterfly or a fairy in her pink dress. In her mind's eye, Jasmine saw again the child's sweet face as she took her baby brother over to look at the bunnies in their hutch behind the caretaker's house on the Airdrie estate.

The next time, the little girl had been accompanied by the family's housekeeper, and she walked along the sidewalk holding the hand of her older sister. Her protective, doting older sister, the one who was responsible for her care in that chaotic house with too many children and a sickly mother. Her sister with the purple eyelids and the downcast face, whom Jasmine had judged to be about the same age as Mary.

"Christopher has stayed over with Royce several times, in the small bedroom. They had quite a good time together. Royce has asked Mary, but of course she's said no. I've discouraged him from asking for Lily because she still needs to be watched, which he wouldn't do."

Anna offered this bit of information in a despairing sort of way, not as if it were of any use, only something to fill the silence. On hearing it, however, something clicked into place for Jasmine. She needed a few moments to sort it out.

Anna looked at her watch and sighed heavily. "We'd best be going home. Royce will be expecting us and I still have to prepare dinner. Anyhow, to change the subject, tell me how you're managing with Lianne, Jaz. Not an easy assignment, that one."

"Not as bad as you might think," Jasmine replied. "Except that it's difficult for me to watch her going downhill. I've become, perhaps, too fond of her, though it would be hard not to. Except for all the questions she asks me about myself – she's incredibly nosy. I have no idea why; I've never thought of myself as all that interesting."

Emma looked bemusedly at her niece. For such a clever woman, she was quite dense in some respects. Emma had long ago deduced what Lianne was up to, but if Jasmine couldn't figure it out for herself, then she had no intention of telling her.

Anna made to rise. "Now, Jaz, if you don't mind running us home – I wouldn't ask except that it's starting to rain, again, and it's gotten so late –"

She stopped, because Jasmine had laid a restraining hand on her arm, to keep her in her seat.

"Don't go yet, Anna. I think I might have an idea."

CHAPTER 64

Martha Jenner shut the door of the car and ran through the rain. Stupid to leave the house without an umbrella. But lucky that Angie Simms had left the library at the same time she did and offered to drive her home.

She let herself in the back door. There was a piece of paper on the kitchen counter with Alistair's distinctive scribble. She picked it up, read it and began to giggle. Then, still giggling, she put a generous amount of Irish stew and dumplings on a plate and inverted a soup bowl overtop.

The note was from Alistair, informing her that he was going to dinner with Chris Byers. He asked if she could save his dinner for him. Two dinners in one night! It was so typically Alistair. Wherever did he put it all? And how could he eat, after the disaster of the day before?

She was still smiling when, moments later, her husband came in by way of the back door. Both by profession and inclination, Simon Jenner was a man of few smiles. This Friday evening, however, his expression was thunderous.

She had barely mouthed hello before he launched into a bitter litany of complaints: the hearse full of feathers, its upholstery streaked with the calling cards of the chickens; the phone calls from acquaintances, some sympathetic but most barely repressing their hilarity, from whom he had learned that the funeral home hearse now was being widely being referred to as, "the chicken coupe" or "the Tilly taxi".

"Yes, I've heard," Martha replied. "Alistair told me."

Simon looked at her suspiciously. "I can't believe it," he said in an accusatory tone. "Are you actually feeling sorry for him?"

"Well, yes," she admitted. "With the parade tomorrow, and everything."

Simon rubbed his hands together briskly. "There's a silver lining to all this. Like I told you, he's hopeless at the funeral business and it's high time he went home. Now he's given me exactly the excuse I need to send him back to your brother."

She was silent. He looked at her sharply. "Why Martha! Don't tell me you'll be sad to see him go! Just a while ago you were complaining about all the messes he makes!"

She couldn't say what she was thinking, which was how boring it would be when it was just the two of them again, so she said, "well, he's kind of grown on me."

"Like a parasite." Simon was regaining his good humour. "So! It's Friday night, and this week I really need that drink before dinner. Will you join me?"

"No thanks." Martha went to the stove and set the pot of potatoes on to boil. She picked up a spoon to stir the stew.

There was a moment of quiet. Then, from the dining room where Simon had gone with his glass to get a drink, Martha heard a great roar.

With a clatter, she dropped the spoon she was holding. "Simon!" she exclaimed in alarm, "whatever is the matter?"

In the doorway to the dining room, his neck and face mottled purple with fury, Simon Jenner held up his prized bottle of Glenfiddich. He shook it. Only a few golden ounces were left, sloshing around in the bottom. So loudly his voice rattled the plates on the counter, he yelled:

"WHO'S - BEEN - DRINKING - MY - SCOTCH!!!"

CHAPTER 65

For the upwardly mobile Stoddarts, business and pleasure generally went hand in velvet-gloved hand on the occasions they entertained. However, after his brief conversation with Mason that afternoon, Max had little expectation of pleasure from this evening's social engagement. He had arrived home from work early seeking the solace of Elizabeth's company. Now he sat on the little Chippendale chair in her dressing room while she put the final touches on her toilette. Three children and thirty-eight years later, she was still a beautiful woman, Max thought. His spirits lifted a bit as he looked in the mirror, watching her put on the diamond and pearl earrings he had given her on their thirtieth anniversary.

They had spent a few moments in idle chitchat when he asked, "where's Bessie?"

"I gave her the weekend off. Why?"

"Oh, I thought we might have need of her. Anyhow, it doesn't matter. Mason has sent his regrets for tonight. And he won't be coming to lunch here tomorrow, after the parade."

"Why? Something the matter?" Now Elizabeth looked more closely at her husband's face in the mirror and saw the heaviness of his expression, his general lassitude. She turned around and looked directly at him.

He sighed. "Mason went over to the Latham's house this morning to meet with Jasmine. Now he's in a bad way. He doesn't want to see anyone, talk to anyone."

He would never know the effect his words had: how her heart slowed almost to a standstill while a chill wave of dread engulfed her from head to toe.

"What happened?" She could scarcely get the words out; her mouth felt almost as if it were frozen.

Max sighed again, more deeply. "It's what didn't happen. She wouldn't see him, and she let him know it's useless to try. He says that now he'll never find out what sent her off the deep end. He says it feels like he's losing her all over again, except that this time, it's final."

Elizabeth couldn't help the warm flood of relief that coursed through her veins, even if she saw that her husband was visibly distraught, caught up in his son's misery and pain.

"I'd be happy to cancel this dinner myself tonight, if it wasn't so late," Max said, his voice full of emotion. They were taking the president of a large auto parts manufacturer and his wife out to the country club, as a prelude to sealing the deal for a prime location in Max and Mason's new industrial park.

One way or another, Elizabeth had to conceal her relief. Otherwise she knew it would show in her face, her voice. She chose to show annoyance. "I'm amazed he's still mooning over Jasmine after all these years, and after she tramped all over town! Whatever can he be thinking?"

Max took the pearl and diamond necklace she handed him, and without the need for a word from her, fastened it around her neck. "Well, they're both divorced, or nearly so, in Mason's case. It's conceivable they could have made a fresh start. And, if you'll remember, Mason wasn't exactly a saint after he came back and found her gone."

In fact, Mason had gone rather wild. There had been many women before he settled for Catharine.

"That's different," Elizabeth said indignantly. "He's a man!"

"Is it?" Max smiled indulgently. "Perhaps. But nothing she's done seems to make a difference. He told me he was her first lover, and she was his first love. I guess he's like me. The first time I met you, I knew you were the one. It was that simple, and there wasn't anything or anyone that could change my mind. I feel just the same today."

Max's words sank like balm into Elizabeth's soul, even as she felt her heart pinch with sorrow thinking of her son. "What's Mason doing tonight?"

"He's with his boys. I think we can be glad he has them as a distraction. Also that he's never been much of a drinker, and not likely to drown his sorrows. But he says he needs some time alone; and he's asked if we could take them to the parade tomorrow morning and keep them overnight."

The thought of having two lively little boys for that span of time filled Elizabeth with apprehension. "Of course," she said, with seeming enthusiasm. But now she was sorry she had given Bessie the day off. She wondered if she could call her to come back. Then she squared her shoulders. She would just have to get used to it. The children needed her now, more than ever.

Max was about to leave. He stopped when Elizabeth held up a hand.

"How did Jasmine ever manage to convince Mason that she was never going to speak to him, unless she actually spoke to him?" This was the question that had been puzzling her almost since the beginning of their conversation.

Leaning on the wall behind her dressing table and looking at his wife's reflection as she daubed perfume behind her ears, Max told her how Jasmine had summoned Mason as he waited on the porch. He described how she had reached for the dangling cord, and then slowly, ever so slowly, pulled down the blind in the upstairs window until he could see her no more.

Max was a good storyteller. As he spoke, Elizabeth paused her toilette. Her hand was suspended, floating motionless as she held the silver hair comb she was using in mid-air. After he finished there was a short silence. Her mouth still fixed in a smile, Elizabeth stared at herself in the mirror.

They didn't have much time. In five minutes, she and Max should get in the car. In half an hour, she would have to greet their guests at the country club. She must be witty, charming and cheerful; nothing else would do. She could not allow herself to think about it, his story; she must save it for later when, God knows, it would take its toll of her.

A blind! So light and flimsy, but heavy enough, it seemed, to crush her son's hopes. And what of her, Jasmine, who had chosen to draw a shade over the past, and any future she and Mason might have together; how much had she lost?

No, there was just one winner from the events of this day, and little question of whom it might be. It was she, Elizabeth, safe once more in her web of deceit. She had been awarded a selfless gift of silence, for which she could pay only with regret and remorse.

The evening that she had anticipated now stretched out before her like a form of purgatory. She thought of the country club: the luxurious, dimly lit cocktail lounge, the bejeweled, expensively dressed women with their sleek, prosperous husbands, the meeting and greeting and endless chatter, the whole of it culminating in a dinner that all would consume with enjoyment. Except for her, who now had no appetite for it; not for any of it.

She glanced at Max, and found him looking fondly at her.

"What an original way of ending things, to show him that it's all over. She's very clever." She laughed lightly, a brittle sound to her own ears.

Max kissed the top of her head. "Yes. Clever and beautiful. Like you, my love."

He had meant it as a compliment. Why then, he wondered, did her eyes suddenly fill with tears?

CHAPTER 66

Martha Jenner had heard tell of the resilience of youth. Now here was the incontestable proof of it, sitting at her breakfast table after consuming three glasses of juice, four soft-boiled eggs and five pieces of toast with jam. Alistair was dressed in full regalia, handsome in his sash, kilt and sporran. When he stood up she said to him, "you're looking very bonnie!"

"I think the word is braw, Auntie M, but thanks, I'll take it as a compliment," he said with a big, lop-sided grin, and he grabbed her, pulled her next to him and gave her a loud smack on the cheek.

She watched him walk jauntily down the sidewalk with his pipes, head held high, while she thought about what awaited him on parade: the hoots, cat calls and laughter over his ill-fated ride on Main Street with the Tillys in tow. Despite that debacle, the dressing-down he had received, and his uncle declaring that he was deducting the price of a bottle of Glenfiddich from his next pay cheque, which would leave him with virtually nothing since his father was emphatic that he had to live on what he made, Alistair seemed ebullient and full of high spirits. What had wrought this transformation?

In fact, during the past twenty-four hours Alistair had entered into a state of detachment that would be the envy of many a yogi. Buoyed by his recent, life-changing vow and thrilling new love interest, he had transcended to heights where mere wisecracks and insults could barely touch him.

However, he hadn't totally thrown caution to the winds.

On reaching the grounds of the high school where the floats were lining up, Alistair quickly searched out the parade organizer. After relentless badgering, she changed his position in the parade. Now he would be marching in front of one of Medford's two new police cars.

The cars had sirens that produced a new range of sounds, from yelp to wail. After only a little persuasion, officers Padraic O'Flaherty and Mike Sloane agreed that this might be the ideal occasion to show them off. Between piper and police, the racket they created as they traveled the parade route effectively drowned out most other sounds, including the jeers, clucks and occasional cries of "chicken man!" that arose from here and there in the crowd.

But that was only the half of it. Because Alistair had heard a rumour, a whisper of warning, and now he was safe.

"Here comes Alistair!" The skirl of the pipes had reached the crowd of young people gathered at the side of the road and waiting for him like a pack of hungry wolves. There was a ripple of excited laughter. Once he came into view, however, a groan of disappointment went up from several who had been counting the hours to this moment.

His hair like a flare in the sunlight and piping his loudest, Alistair waggled his red eyebrows and winked at the young women in the crowd as he strode by. He appeared not to see the three young men standing at the edge of the sidewalk, their hands hanging limply and full of eggs – some rotten – that they dared not throw.

Alistair might not have noticed them, but officers O'Flaherty and Sloane had. In the police car, both sat up a little straighter and the corners of their mouths turned down. They had made their acquaintance on other, far less pleasant occasions.

* * *

From the back yard, Martha Jenner heard the door of the house slam. Alistair must be home from the parade! She was anxious about what might have happened to him. However, by the time she took off her gardening gloves and muddy shoes and went inside, he was gone. Upstairs, she found his sporran on the floor in the hall. On opening the door to his room, she saw his kilt, hose, and other piper paraphernalia tossed madly about to join the debris on his unmade bed and the floor. Good heavens, wherever was he going in such a hurry! This question would occupy her mind all the while she pruned the rose bushes.

Alistair loped through an alleyway, taking a short cut. He was suffused with a wonderful sense of invulnerability. Before it vanished, he meant to take full advantage of it. Having laid most of his personal demons to rest, now he was going to face up to his public ones. And he knew exactly where to find them.

* * *

Once the parade ended, most of the young people who had gathered to watch it adjourned to their usual watering hole. After trooping the few blocks to the Statler Hotel, they abandoned the sunshine and fresh air outside for the smoky twilight of the bar.

Chris Byers was there with his latest girlfriend. So were his sister Sherry and her steady boyfriend Howard, who was in town for the weekend from the university where he was studying to be an accountant. Tables had been put together and chairs pulled up to accommodate the large crowd. They had been there half an hour and the beer and conversation were flowing freely.

Howard had his arm around the back of Sherry's chair. He looked down at her possessively. She was a real catch: blond, blue-eyed and beautiful, the former head of the high school cheerleading squad, and smart too, already office manager of the town's largest law firm. He would soon join his father's practice, and his expectations also included making Sherry his wife. With true accountant logic, he planned to give her a ring for her twenty-second birthday this fall, with the only half-realized idea that then he wouldn't have to buy her a birthday present.

They were idly talking when a sudden hush fell. All heads turned toward the hall. With no appreciable sign of embarrassment, Alistair had walked in to join the party. He smiled, said a few words of greeting, and started to draw up a chair.

"Hey, chicken man!" Buzz Smith was the big, burly son of a local contractor. He was still stinging from his failure to egg Alistair at the parade. "Hey chicken man! I have to leave soon. How's about a ride in the Tilly taxi?"

314 | Pat McDermott

There were a few laughs around the table. Linda, Buzz's girlfriend, wasn't laughing. She had guessed he was spoiling for a fight.

"Only if you're in a box in the back." Alistair was standing while the waitress took his order.

An angry flush appeared on Buzz's face. "Nope, when we ride in the chicken coupe we're goin' first class, sittin' right up front just like Willy Tilly, right, Linda? So how about it, chicken man?"

Now Alistair turned his full attention to his tormentor. "She can come," he said, pointing to Linda, "but you can't. I've already given four dumb clucks a ride, and now I'm only taking hot chicks."

There was a loud outburst of laughter. Buzz leapt from his chair and came barreling around the table, head down, fists up. Now Alistair found a use for the miniscule amount of hand-to-hand combat he had learned during his summers with the Highlanders Pipe Corps. Stepping rapidly aside and lunging forward, he grabbed an arm and the back of Buzz's shirt and heaved him to land spread-eagled on the floor.

All eyes then turned to the doorway where Marty, the Statler's bouncer, had quietly appeared. Marty was normally stationed by the front entrance in order to check IDs. It was unusual to see him in the bar, but perhaps he had been alerted by the noise. He watched Buzz get up and rear back, ready for another round.

"Who started this," he asked coldly. A few fingers pointed.

"So it's you, Smith," Marty intoned. "You've been warned. The manager said next time there's a fight, you're outta here. So now get out, before I throw you out."

A fleeting look passed between Alistair and Marty as Buzz was escorted from the bar. None saw it, except for Chris Byers and his sister. "Had to be a setup!" Chris whispered admiringly.

Howard was still enjoying Alistair's joke on Buzz. "Haw, haw, haw" he chuckled. "Good comeback!"

He looked down at Sherry, who wasn't laughing so much. Instead, she was staring at the end of the room where Alistair was folding his long, lanky frame into a chair at the table. She had a thoughtful look on her face, and something else. Howard couldn't quite identify what it was. But he didn't like it.

The waitress came with his beer. Smiling broadly, Alistair lifted the frosty mug.

"Cheers!" he said.

CHAPTER 67

A raft had been towed out in the water near the town pier. The small lighthouse at the end of the pier also had a makeshift platform erected on top, and both of these surfaces were to be used for the fireworks in celebration of Victoria Day. Lianne loved fireworks. She also wanted to see all the people gathered in the lakeside park. There was a perfect viewing spot for both of these spectacles in one of the spare bedrooms upstairs. Now Thomas picked her up, carried her to the large wing chair he had placed in front of the window and sat down with her in his lap.

She was as light as a seven-year-old child, his beloved wife. Of all that had changed about her, perhaps the most upsetting for Thomas was how her voice, only recently so clear and bell-like, had become thin and weak. Even so, he observed, she hadn't lost her knack for ordering him around.

"Thomas!" she commanded in her new, whispery voice. "I want you to stop that!"

She had been looking at him to share her enjoyment of a pink-and-white, three-tiered starburst, the best of the fireworks so far. In the failing light she had seen that he was not watching but abstracted, his mind elsewhere. More alarming, she had caught him wearing that look of heavy grief, of deep sadness, that she remembered only too well from the dark times after the birth of their stillborn son.

"Stop what?"

"You know perfectly well. You're thinking about me dying and you're spoiling it! The fireworks, everything!"

"I can't help it. You're so light. You keep getting lighter and lighter, disappearing in little bits. I just don't know what I'll do when you're gone." Now his own voice had become thin and cracked, reedy with his anguish.

Lianne shifted in a rather irritated way in his lap. "Thomas, please! You have to be strong, so you can help me get through this. Strong for yourself too, because you can't afford to get sick, like before! You're too fine; too talented and good, you have too much to give. It's sad that this happened, but love, we'll only be apart for a little while."

She paused. "And, speaking of being apart, I want you to move into the bedroom across the hall. It's time for us to begin to separate, and this can be a start. Besides that, you're beginning to snore."

"Me snoring? I am not! And I don't want to move out! What if you need me during the night?"

"You are too! You woke me up twice last night. Remember that little silver bell with the handle in the pantry? Please get it for me when you go downstairs; then I can use it if I need you."

They were quiet for a while, watching the fireworks. With the thought of his solitary bed and solitary life shortly to follow, Thomas still couldn't help but feel the creeping onset of desolation. But now Lianne, with her uncanny ability to read his mind, lifted a gentle hand to his face.

"Thomas, I don't need your grief. What I really need, what would truly give me peace, is to know that you're going to live your life after I'm gone. That you'll find a good woman to love you, and be happy!"

"There's no one who can replace you, Lianne," he said quietly, with conviction. "I've loved you forever. Since I was fourteen."

"Fiddlesticks! I know of at least one, and there must be others. And I hope you'll get out of this house and out of this town! One of them is too big for you, the other too small. I've come around to thinking they're both unlucky."

The fireworks were almost over. Lianne turned her face back to the window. Thomas was feeling rather aggrieved at her lack of empathy, at having his deepest feelings slapped down in such a back-of-the-hand fashion. But he knew why she was doing it, and thought about what she had said. Leave Medford? Yes, although it would be hard to part with the family home, he had already made a start on that. And her veiled message when she talked about other women? Something to ponder. He had to get on with the business of living: deep down, he knew she was right.

Right in all except one thing. Truly she was irreplaceable, she had lit up his life. No matter how much she scolded him, when she winged away to brighten some corner of paradise, she would take a big piece of his heart. He wasn't sure how he could live without it, or whether he even wanted to.

A starburst, the last in the display, arced up into the sky and scattered sparkles of gold over the water. It faded away slowly, leaving them in darkness. Thomas lifted up his wife and carried her back to her bed.

CHAPTER 68

Laura was beyond excitement, hopping about, her eyes bright, cheeks flushed. "Isn't it time to go? Do I have to come with you, Mom? Gee, I've been waiting for so long!"

"Oh, for heaven's sake, why not let the child go on ahead," Emma encouraged with an indulgent smile, and in five minutes, when she estimated Thomas might have finished his breakfast, Jasmine did.

Thomas was already in the garage getting the bicycle when Laura racketed in through the side garage door. Thomas, so familiar with children and teenagers of all sorts, had taken his measure of this child. They had worked side-by-side building her insect box, and then he helped her identify the critters she collected, using a book from the library. After that there were a few trips to the soda fountain at the drugstore for an ice cream cone when he was headed there to get Lianne's medicine. And now that she was comfortable with him, there was talk, lots of talk, mostly about the happenings in her simple child's world of school and friends and play.

She was wonderful fun, a ray of sunshine breaking through the dark mood that usually settled on him when he came home. She wasn't at all shy, although not bold. She just met the world on its own terms, in a level headed way that was mature beyond her tender years. He loved her laugh, which bubbled right up from her belly full of joy and good humour, a tonic for his soul. From this, and also from her cheery outlook, he could tell she was a well-loved child. There was a hardiness, a resilience about her that boded well for her future.

As he adjusted the seat for her height, he told her his latest knock-knock joke in order to hear that delightful laugh. Then he put bicycle cuffs around her pant legs so they wouldn't catch in the chain, and together they wheeled the old bike out to the front of the house.

Upstairs, Lianne was already in her chair overlooking the window and Jasmine stood beside her, watching as Thomas and Laura appeared. She was still pensively thinking about all the extra pillows she had to tuck around Lianne to prop her up in her chair today, and how very little had been touched on the tray she brought downstairs.

"What fun!" Lianne exclaimed, with an amused giggle, as they watched Thomas holding Laura while she wobbled along the sidewalk, amid laughter and her mingled shrieks of terror and delight. It didn't take long, only five or six tries, before she found her balance and pedaled away shakily, all by herself, down the street. When she came gliding back, looking as if she'd been on a bike for years, Jasmine and Lianne clapped and she beamed up at them, her face shining. Then, with Thomas walking and Laura on her bike, they set out on a trip around the block.

What did they see, looking down from that open window one storey above the sidewalk? Only a young girl, learning to ride a bicycle. But from that vantage point there was more to be seen for the very observant as Jasmine, watching, slowly realized. Some obvious things: a similarity in build between the man and the girl; the same sort of easy, athletic movements. Standing side by side, the same high foreheads, straight noses. Two heads with the same blue-black hair.

And something else that Jasmine had noticed a few moments ago, which filled her with trepidation. A week before, Laura had her hair cut boyishly short, the way she liked it, even if her mother and her aunt did not. Now, one could plainly see how it grew. It radiated from a spot on her scalp, a whorl that was off centre and over to the left side of her head. At the beauty shop, the fiftyish owner of the salon had paused her scissors for a moment to say how unusual it was, that hair pattern, she doubted she had ever seen it before.

Just a few minutes ago, however, looking down from the window, Jasmine had seen it again, only in duplicate.

She was suddenly trembly and nervous, thinking of Lianne's sharp eyes that missed nothing worth seeing. To her relief, however, soon after Thomas and Laura disappeared around the corner, Lianne only wanted the help of her strong arms to assist her from her chair back to the bed.

Once there she asked for her bedpan. Trips to the bathroom were now too taxing. It was a new stage in her illness, to which both of them had adapted with ease and a total lack of embarrassment. After complaining about how cold the metal receptacle was, and why hadn't she warmed it up for her first, Lianne giggled a little and said, "Soon you're going to have to put me in diapers!"

"I'll try not to poke you too much with the pins, but it's going to be tempting." Jasmine helped her to a more comfortable half-sitting, half-reclining position after taking away the bedpan. "There! Now I'm off to clean up the kitchen."

Her back was turned, and she was almost out the door when she heard a quiet small voice.

"Jasmine, wait."

Lianne was looking at her with unusual intensity out of her strange, huge eyes with the pupils enlarged to twice their size by the drugs she was taking.

"She's his, isn't she? His child. Thomas's."

She had half-expected it before but not now, when she had thought she was safe. The question sent an electric jolt through her, or was it more like her first rollercoaster ride: a sudden surge of fright, a sickening drop to the stomach and her hair standing on end.

"What, are you on that subject again?" She donned her best poker face; she knew how to bluff. She looked at Lianne with an easy smile and laughed dismissively, sounding only mildly amused. "As I told you, my father –"

Lianne cut her off. "I think I told you, in fact I'm sure I did, that I used to work in the office at Medford Public School. I saw lots of little heads, and I saw the way their hair grew, the patterns, all different. And my husband, I married him at eighteen and I know every inch of his body, probably better than my own, and your daughter and he have the very same, unusual hai–"

She got no more out, because she was interrupted in turn by Jasmine who was standing over her bed, fierce with anger. "Laura is mine! My own child!"

She was shouting, but she didn't care.

"And now you're trying to claim her! Why are you doing this, always pushing and pushing for more! What do you hope to gain; what is it that you want?" She was flushed with emotion and unconsciously her hands had balled into fists.

"I want to tell Thomas."

"No!!"

After the small explosion made by that word, there was a long silence in which they glared at each other, enemies now, not friends.

It was Lianne who broke off the staring match first. She turned her head aside. Then she ventured, in a weak, whispery voice, "what if I said – what if I promised you that there would be no claims, no obligations of any kind, for Laura or for you, if I told him? Would that be alright?"

"I don't know." Jasmine thought for a moment. "Because what's the point, then? Why would you even bother? It could just cause him more pain."

Suddenly Lianne reached out and grabbed for her hand. Real urgency showed in her face. "Jasmine, you have some idea of what I've gone through with this man; you saw what he was like nine years ago, just teetering on the edge! So when I go, what is there to keep him here? No one to love, no child of his own, no family anywhere close, and all alone in this big house! Don't you see? He's always wanted to be a father, and if he at least knew he had a child, Laura, well, it could tie him to this world, give him a reason to carry on. Please, Jasmine, please!"

Jasmine had freed herself of Lianne's grasp. Even though she knew the effort and energy it took Lianne to speak loudly enough for her to hear, during this speech she was pacing back and forth along the carpeted bedroom floor.

"I'll think about it," she said, eventually. "But my feeling is, it would just make things more difficult and complicated."

Lianne was not about to give up. "He rescued you, once, Jasmine. Help him now, when he needs it!"

"That's blackmail," Jasmine said flatly. She stopped her pacing. "Purely blackmail, Lianne, bringing that up to hold it against me!"

"Yes, it is." Lianne admitted. "But I'll use anything I can. You should know that by now."

Jasmine looked at her. Then a corner of her mouth pulled upward. They both laughed a little, the tension broken; but she was still wary.

"Well," she said. "Maybe. But it will only work if you let him know he can't tell Laura he's her father. We'll be leaving Medford soon. He won't be allowed to contact us without first writing and getting my permission. No ties, that's the way it has to be. Those would be the conditions."

Once home in Los Vegas, Laura would have no need for another father – especially one who lived thousands of miles away. Mike, Jasmine's ex, doted on Laura. He still played that role, whenever he could.

"Then I can tell him?"Lianne's eyes were wide and pleading; she appeared to be holding her breath.

"I have to think about it."

But by the time she left, around one o'clock when Thomas was about to come home, she had said yes.

CHAPTER 69

By the parents of teenaged children at Medford High and students he taught and coached, Thomas Latham was widely recognized as a gifted and dedicated teacher. He enjoyed the respect and liking of all, even if no tomfoolery was ever tolerated in his math and physics classes; and since he had resumed teaching nine years ago, it was generally acknowledged that his influence on pupils at the school, their outlook and ambitions, had been immense.

Driving home after his Victoria day holiday Monday session with Mike Simms, a man he respected little and liked less, Thomas felt his enthusiasm for his work flagging. He had decided yesterday just to let the man talk himself out before saying much. It was abundantly clear after less than half an hour that Simms considered his new job of principal a sinecure, where he would only hold the ship steady until he could retire – four long years away.

Thomas was largely fed up with the school's methods, or lack of them, for handling student drop-outs, motivation, discipline – the list was a reasonably lengthy one, and so were his ideas on how to fix them. But he had selected only a few that he considered the most urgent to bring forward today. The common quotient was that all would require some work and reorganization, and so they had been relentlessly slapped down. To add insult to injury, Simms had tried to offload on Thomas some of the functions performed by the former principal.

Thomas had flatly refused; let him stumble along as best he could. His workload would still be double Simms'.

At home after two and a half hours of butting heads with this donkey and going through a raft of dreary paperwork, Thomas made himself a grilled cheese sandwich and found he had little appetite for it. On the stove, he discovered the potato-leek soup that Jasmine had brought over from the Madison house. She and Emma were supplying Lianne with their most delicious, digestible and nourishing soups and he was a lucky side beneficiary. He had a taste, then a large bowlful, and felt much better.

Lianne had been asleep when he first looked in on her but now, as he went up the stairs and the last two creaked under his weight, he heard her call his name. He went in. The room was full of sunlight and fresh air from an open window. Except for her dark eyes with their purple shadows and her dark hair, Lianne seemed to be vanishing, fading away into her pillows, her skin as grey-white as old bleached linen. This afternoon, however, Thomas saw two hectic spots of pink on her cheeks. Her eyes, still beautiful despite her illness, seemed even larger than usual.

"What is it?" he asked, because she had a curious, contained air of excitement about her.

"Come give me a kiss and sit down," she said, patting the bed beside her. Was he imagining it, or did her voice sound somewhat stronger?

"I have something to tell you," she said with the trace of a smile.

"Well, I hope it's something good after the morning I've put in with that dunce Mike Simms," Thomas said, settling himself on the spot she indicated.

She took his hand. "I think you will find it so."

Then he knew it must be something special, because she was building suspense, letting him dangle in silence until he finally had to ask, "what is it?"

"You know how everyone is always saying that you must be Laura's father because you two look so much alike?"

"Yes." Where was this leading? There was a little irritation in his voice when he said, "she probably looks like her father."

Lianne shook her head. "If you mean Mike Carlisle, no, he has blond hair and brown eyes."

"Is that right? I didn't know that. Then her grandfather, Jason Holmes. He had the same colour of hair."

Lianne shook her head again. "No. The reason Laura looks like you is because she is your daughter. Jasmine told me so today."

"What are you saying? She's my daughter? That's ridiculous!"

"No, it's true. There's no doubt about it. She's yours."

Thomas got to his feet. His face showed his shock. "No, I can't believe it. How could that possibly be?"

"The usual way, I suspect," Lianne smiled, a little wryly. Then she continued. "You know the funny way your hair grows, starting way off to the side? I've pointed it out to you before. Well, Laura's is the same, and this morning when I told Jasmine that after seeing it, I was absolutely sure you were her father, she finally gave in and said that yes, you are."

"She's mine? Are you sure?"

"Yes. Your child. Jasmine said so, and she should know. You're to meet with her tomorrow and she'll confirm it."

Thomas started walking back and forth. "I have a daughter? That beautiful child is my daughter?"

"She is." Now Lianne was beaming.

"I have a child," Thomas said wonderingly, walking back and forth. "I'm Laura's father." He stopped and looked at Lianne again. "Really? Is that really so?"

"That's right."

"Laura is mine? You're absolutely certain?"

"Yes, and yes again." Now Lianne was laughing with delight.

"This has to be some kind of a joke. You're laughing, it's just a joke." Now his face fully showed his disbelief and doubt.

"No, Thomas, Laura is really and truly your daughter."

"She is? She really is? Lianne, you're not putting me on, are you? Is it true? Because I can't believe it! That I have a child, that Laura – that she's my daughter, my little girl!"

Inside of him, a deep pool of grief had been growing, slowly threading its runnels into his heart and mind. Cold and bitter, it was intertwined with Lianne's illness and expanding at about the same rate. Now this news, so wonderful, so thrilling, amazing, had been added to it. Like oil and water, they did not mix. He didn't know how to handle this information, what to do with it.

He hid his face in his hands.

CHAPTER 70

Late Monday on the Victoria Day weekend, Chris Byers went to the family home with a large cardboard box. He spent only a moment in the kitchen with his mother, who was sitting at the table crying so hard she couldn't do much more than wave him away; then he went upstairs. He passed by the door of his sister's room, which was closed, although he knew she was in there because he heard her moving around, and went directly to his younger brother's room.

Two weeks earlier, Chris had moved into his own apartment. Since then, he had strategically timed his appearances at the family house at just around the dinner hour. Today he had had to work at the radio station and his schedule was much the same, except he left an hour earlier. The reason was that he wanted to be home ahead of his brother Jeremy, to get back all the stuff the kid had pilfered before and while he moved out.

First he found his Playboy magazines, all underneath Jeremy's bed except for two that he found later in the nightstand next to his father's side of the parental bed, possibly there for inspiration. After that, it was like mining, as with growing exasperation he located in various drawers and other hidden places his Brylcreem, several good shirts he had been missing, two sweaters, socks, a pack of condoms – dream on, little brother – a pair of shoes, records, and then! In a small wooden box on the top shelf of the bookcase, the prize he had vainly been searching for,

for days, and that Jeremy had steadfastly denied any knowledge of, his second set of car keys.

Chris had noticed a few times that his car seemed to have moved slightly from the position where he parked it while he was at work. In a fury, now he ripped a piece of paper from a notepad on Jeremy's desk and filled it with scatological descriptive comments before putting it back in the box that had contained the keys and replacing it on the bookcase for his brother to find.

Then he went down the hall with his box and stood at his sister's door. It was still closed. He knocked tentatively. "Go away," a voice said. The voice was neither as loud nor as hostile as he was accustomed to, so he took it as an invitation and went in.

Sherry did not look up at him but continued her task of sorting clothes. "Why is Mom −" he said, then stopped, looking around and down, in amazement. "Well, what do you know? This room has a blue carpet."

"Funny." This was said in a tone that indicated just how unfunny his sister considered this remark to be, although Chris had no intention of sarcasm. He honestly could not remember, from the time she was about thirteen, ever seeing enough of the floor of her room to know that the colour of the carpet was blue. Now it appeared that she was gathering the clothing and various items of debris strewn in stratified layers over the floor and tidying the room up. It made him both nervous and curious.

"Why are you doing this?"

"Oh − just part of growing up, being an adult," she replied, evasively.

"Really. Well, I'm in favour of that!" he said and now, yes, he was indeed being sarcastic.

"Then, Chris, why don't you do it?" she asked, sweetly.

Touché. Ever since she started work in a law office, it wasn't nearly as much fun trading barbs with Sherry. Chris set his box on a chair. "Why is Mom crying?"

Sherry picked another pile up from the floor and put it on her bed to sort. On the carpet under it there appeared a Little Lulu comic she might have enjoyed when she was eleven or twelve. "She's crying because I broke up with Howard. Or else because she's not getting rid of me as soon as she'd hoped. Probably more about Howard: she loves him, she's crazy about him. I told her, if she loves him so much she should marry him. Is she still crying?"

"She was when I came in. You broke up with Howard? Why? I thought you two were practically married!" Chris was genuinely shocked.

Sherry turned, holding up a pair of baggy shorts that could have been hers or Jeremy's but were his; he had lost track of them two years ago at least. "Here, are these yours? Whenever Mom doesn't know where things go, she's gotten into the habit of just opening the door and throwing them onto the pile," she explained, returning to her sorting after Chris took them and put them in his box.

She snorted. "Why did I break up with Howard? Because he's so dull and boring? Because he only wants to marry me so that when he starts his career he's got the whole package he needs to be super successful? No, actually, the real reason I broke up with him is because of his laugh. 'HAW, HAW, HAW!'" And she imitated him to perfection.

Then Chris knew that Sherry truly was finished with Howard. Because when you start noticing things like a laugh or occasionally picking your teeth, like he did with Mary Beth Foy, and finding them irritating, then it's definitely game over.

"How was your day?" she inquired casually. "Did you go to the radio station with Alistair?"

Immediately Chris's antennae straightened up and started quivering. For one thing, Sherry never asked him about his day, or about himself, for that matter. And how did she know that Alistair was going to the station with him? Now he remembered: he had casually mentioned it to his mother last night at the door as he was leaving after dinner; Sherry must have overheard.

"And why did he want to go with you?"

"He wants to learn the radio business," Chris answered. He was staring fixedly at his sister. "Why are you so interested?"

She stopped her sorting and just looked at him.

"No," said Chris, disbelievingly, "no! Not Alistair!"

"Yes," Sherry answered, with a shrug of her shoulders. "Why not? He's cute. And you know – there's just something about him. He's going places."

"Wow!" Chris was still in shock. "If you want to see Mom really cry, then go ahead and hook up with Alistair! You don't know the wild and crazy stuff he's done; he's been kicked out of almost every school he ever went to; he's a maniac! The only place he's ever going is the nuthouse!"

Sherry didn't look at all discouraged. "Just maybe I'll like wild and crazy better than dull and boring. Worth a try."

"Anyhow," Chris continued, "he's gone absolutely bonkers over Jasmine Holmes, or Carlisle, or whatever she calls herself, so you're going to have some stiff competition."

It was his sister's turn to be shocked. "But she's old!"

Sherry was incredulous. And perhaps a little apprehensive. She was remembering the time, about two weeks ago, she saw Jasmine at the post office. She had been standing in line to mail some legal documents. Two youngish men were leaning on the counter waiting for parcels or mail while the cute Irish postmaster took care of immediate business. All of them were directly or furtively glancing at her; the kind of attention she was used to.

Slowly one of the leaning men uncrossed his ankles and took his hands out of his pockets. The other one uncrossed his folded arms, and then both of them stopped leaning and stood up straight, while the postmaster seemed to freeze in place except for his mouth, which dropped open. Their eyes had slipped off her and were directed toward the door. Sherry turned to see who or what might have such an effect. It was Jasmine Holmes, or Carlisle. Whatever her name was, she had disliked her on sight.

"She's only thirty, six years older than Alistair, which doesn't much matter with a woman like that," Chris said.

Sherry held up a hand and used her fingers to count off: "She's old. Divorced. Has a child. A reputation! There's no way he should be interested in her!"

Chris sighed. "Well, sis, it seems you don't understand. I guess I'll have to explain it to you. You see, it's like cars."

"Cars! Women are like cars?"

"It's just a comparison," Chris said patiently. "To explain, someone like Jasmine Holmes is like a Rolls Royce, no, a Ferrari. When you get a car like that, at six years old it's almost a new car. You're so glad to have it, it doesn't matter much how many owners it's had, or the mileage; the only things that are important are the condition of the engine, the transmission and the chassis. Because you're getting a top of the line ride."

"Oh, that's so ridiculous! And you are absolutely disgusting!" Sherry wrinkled her nose in distaste. "You're a Volkswagen, an insect, a beetle, and you're totally bugging me!" She grabbed a towel off the bed and snapped him with it. "Get out of here!"

Chris picked up his box and prepared to leave. He only had a short time to stash the box in his car before Jeremy got home, anyhow. But as he went toward the door, Sherry had one last question.

"If she's a Ferrari – then – what kind of a car am I?"

Chris guessed she couldn't resist asking. He turned halfway around. "You? You're definitely a Cadillac, fully loaded. But you'll depreciate faster."

Then he hurried quickly toward the door; but before he could get there, he felt the full force of one of Sherry's tennis shoes thrown to hit him squarely in the middle of his back. "Get out!!" she yelled, enraged.

Once on the other side of the door, Chris stood there for a moment holding his box. He was thinking about how his eighteen-year old sister, fresh out of a commercial course, had walked into a messy, chaotic, four-lawyer legal firm and, within three years, had taken charge and reorganized both office and, to some extent, lawyers, so that everything ran like a top.

He opened the door again. Then he carefully poked his head around the corner. "You know sis," he said, while keeping an eye out for flying missiles. "I was thinking – if you could figure out a way to handle that crazy energy, then, actually, you and Alistair – well, you might just make a good team."

CHAPTER 71

On the last night of the holiday weekend, although the sun still shone and the voices of children at play rang through the streets, Laura's loud protests went ignored and she was put to bed early. "You've had two late nights, and now you'll have one early one," her mother said firmly but kindly. "However, you can read for a few minutes until Aunt Emma comes in to draw the blinds."

Earlier Lex, Sy and Mac, the terrible trio as Jasmine and Emma had dubbed them, came to the door asking for Laura to join them in playing knife toss. This was a game at which she excelled. It consisted of each player throwing his or her penknife at a circle drawn in the dirt, with the object of getting the knife blade sunk in the bullseye. The boys left without Laura but with some of Emma's freshly baked cookies, which, from the speedy way they were gobbled, appeared to be an adequate substitute.

Less than ten minutes after the protested bedtime, Emma entered the child's room to pull down the blinds and found her fast asleep. Her book was open in her hands. Emma looked down at the small face: the long eyelashes spread out like little black fans on the pink cheeks, the rosebud mouth slightly open to show the last top tooth that was still coming in. She spent a moment savoring the sweetness, storing it in her memory for the solitary times soon to come. Then taking Laura's Nancy Drew mystery book from her limp hands, she put it on the night table, lowered the blinds and went downstairs to join Jasmine on the front porch.

A week ago, Matthew, Emma's garrulous, elderly hired man, had set out the white wicker furniture. Once the blue and white chintz cushions were on the sofas and a gauzy white curtain had been hung from the pillars for protection from wind, rain or prying eyes, the porch was transformed into an outdoors living room. This evening, as the setting sun slanted its beams under the low eaves, Jasmine sat on the sofa in a golden pool of sunshine, busy with her pen and paper.

"Laura?" She looked up inquiringly when Emma came in with her customary cup of tea.

"Fast asleep minutes after you left the room," Emma replied, smiling.

"That monkey!" Jasmine laughed. "Although, if I hadn't put her to bed, she'd still be wide awake and playing without the least sign of being tired."

"Well, you certainly know your child," Emma observed.

"Well, you certainly wouldn't have said that a few months ago," Jasmine retorted rather acidly, remembering her battles with Emma over Laura's care and management.

Emma took no offense. "You were just recovering from being ill then, and I was getting used to not being in charge," she replied mildly. Then she asked the question that had been troubling her lately, whenever she thought about Jasmine's forthcoming departure.

"Do you think that – that illness you had might happen again?"

"No." Jasmine was emphatic. "I'll never again put myself in that kind of situation or let events affect me so. It was the loss of my savings – not so much the money as the future I'd planned out for Laura and myself – and being cheated by someone I thought was a good friend. No, I won't allow myself to fall into those depths, and never, ever again will my child have to go into care!"

"It doesn't seem to have done her any real harm." Emma said thoughtfully. She was remembering, however, the first time she saw Laura, and how eager the child appeared to come home with her.

"That reminds me." Jasmine put down her pen and paper. "Anna and I are moving along with our plans to find out what Royce is up to, with his new found interest in children. Can you spell me off by staying with

Lianne on Wednesday afternoon? I'll need to leave the Latham's about ten minutes before school is let out."

Emma hesitated. "Wednesday's my afternoon for bridge. How about Thursday?"

Jasmine assented; then there was a short pause in their conversation while Emma sipped her tea and Jasmine finished her letter. "Writing to Mike?" Emma asked. She had noted the regular flow of correspondence between Jasmine and her former husband.

"No, this one is for Arlena. I'm telling her as much as I care to, about what happened with Mason last Friday and letting her know that he needs her now. They've always been close, but with her new job and new life things have changed, she told me."

"That's thoughtful of you," Emma commented. "Also, it's nice that you seem to be on friendly terms with Mike, exchanging letters the way you do."

Jasmine looked at her smilingly, her eyes glowing amber gold in the failing light. Emma, whose perception was dulled by familiarity, seldom bothered to look at her niece much anymore. But now she did, and was struck anew by her unusual beauty. "What are you smiling about?" she inquired.

"You. I have to say that one of the things I truly appreciate about you is that you don't pry." Jasmine said. "By now Lianne would have asked me a dozen questions about my relationship with Mike, but you never have. Or questioned me about much anything else."

Emma set her cup down. "I always figured that if you wanted to tell me something, you would. But regarding Mike, to be honest and truthful, I don't have to pry."

Jasmine stopped smiling. Emma's tone was apologetic as she said, "well, you can blame your mother. She told me everything. She told me you and Mike were having trouble getting pregnant. Shortly after that, she read me your letter saying that he had been tested, and it seemed that Laura was going to be your only child. Then a year later, there was another letter with the news that you were getting a divorce. So, rightly or wrongly, I concluded your problems started when Mike found out he wasn't able to father a child."

"Look!" said Jasmine. It was obvious to Emma that her intention was to distract her, but she looked anyway. Jasmine was pointing a finger at the gravel road that ran in front of the house. Glinting in the last rays of the sun, great clouds of mayflies had gathered. They were beginning their stately courtship dance. Up and down, over and over again, they slowly elevated and then as gracefully descended, their filmy wings, as they caught the light, shining like silver filigree.

For a few moments, they watched this lovely spring ritual in silence. Then Emma became uncomfortably aware of other types of flying insects intent not on courtship but blood. "The mosquitoes are out," she said, "let's go in."

They gathered up the glasses and cups, the letters and newspapers. As soon as she had deposited her tray in the kitchen, Jasmine retrieved her letters and turned to go upstairs. But before she could disappear, Emma quickly said, "just to finish what I was saying – it would seem that Thomas is the father of your child, not Mike."

Jasmine stopped in her tracks. "I'm taking back my compliment," she said coldly. "Now you definitely are prying."

"It's not prying," Emma protested. "Only a simple deduction. Mike had what –? Mumps? A childhood infection, you told your mother. Unless you have other candidates for Laura's father, who else could it be? And she looks so much like Thomas."

Jasmine tossed her long mane of hair and continued to walk toward the stairs.

"Besides," Emma said to her retreating back, "Thomas told me today that he's Laura's father."

"WHAT!?" Jasmine stopped and spun around, radiating shock and anger.

"Yes," Emma went on, "this afternoon, while you were at the lake jumping rocks with Laura and the terrible trio, I took a big bowlful of that lovely egg custard we had for dessert over to the house for Lianne. Thomas answered the door and he looked happy for a change, instead of sad. It seemed so unusual that I asked him why he was looking so pleased with himself. He said, 'Well, I just found out that I'm Laura's father – that's what Jasmine told Lianne this morning. But of course, you knew that.'"

"Then he looked at me for a moment, and he asked, 'Didn't you?' When I didn't answer, he started to look upset and he said, 'Uh-oh, I don't think I should have said that.'"

Jasmine had thrown herself down on the seat of the banquette. She had her elbows on the table and was holding her head in her hands. Her long hair hid her face from view, and Emma had no idea what was going on behind that curtain. Her shoulders were shaking, whether from sobs or silent laughter, it was impossible to tell. However, after a moment she brought her head up and back, gasping for breath from her bout of laughter. Then Emma started in too, and together they laughed and laughed until Emma, wiping the tears from her eyes, said, "but I did tell Thomas that I already knew. Then he calmed down a bit. However, what I can't figure out is, how did Lianne get the truth out of you, when I never could?"

"Oh, it's hopeless trying to be a woman of mystery with you three around, especially Thomas!" Jasmine took a tissue and blew her nose. "And I would have told you eventually, I suppose, except that I hate the truth being teased out of me! Well, we were looking down from the window watching Thomas teach Laura how to ride a bike. Lianne started talking about the way Laura's hair grew, just like Thomas's, and that the hair pattern was so distinctive – why, Emma, whatever is the matter? Do you know something about this?"

She had stopped because Emma was laughing again, this time rather incredulously.

"Indeed I do!" she declared. "If this is about hair patterns being proof of paternity, Lianne discussed it with me after Laura's first visit. She noticed that the way Laura's hair grew was identical to Thomas's. I told her I didn't think it amounted to much, but that I would find out what I could. What I discovered, after checking library books and even talking to Doctor Sheridan, was that, so far, there's not a shred of proof hair patterns are hereditary. But my guess is, Lianne somehow managed to convince you they are."

Jasmine had been standing beside the kitchen table, but now she flopped down on the bench again. "I've been bamboozled!" she exclaimed in disbelief. "Outfoxed by a dying woman!"

Emma was putting a fresh kettle of water on for tea. She chuckled. "Don't be too hard on her," she said. "I went upstairs to see Lianne this afternoon, and she was awake and bright and cheerful enough because Thomas was happy. But I should tell you that now she has 'the look' on her."

"The look?" Jasmine's expression showed her puzzlement.

"There's a certain look sick people take on when they're about to die," Emma said gently. "I've seen it many times. She won't last more than a few weeks. I thought I should warn you," she added, watching Jasmine's eyes become moist. "Lianne knows it. She's asked if, after she dies, both of us could clear away her clothes and personal belongings so that Thomas doesn't have to do it. So can you stay on and help, Jasmine?"

There was a lump in Jasmine's throat, so she simply nodded yes.

"The last thing she said was that you and Thomas were supposed to meet tomorrow when he comes home from school."

Jasmine dabbed at her eyes with a tissue. "We're to discuss Laura. And the conditions I gave Lianne for permission to tell Thomas he's her father. She promised she would discuss them with him first. Frankly, Emma, I'm nervous. This will be the first time I've actually seen him face to face. He just writes notes instead of talking to me. As I told you, he's been avoiding me for months, and besides the occasional hi and goodbye, I've never really spoken to him."

"That's odd it's gone on so long." Emma pursed her lips. "But it's probably because there's still a spark there and he feels uncomfortable, given the circumstances. Anyhow, he won't be able to avoid you much longer. In Lianne's condition, she'll soon need care around the clock."

"Speaking of the clock." Emma looked up at the one that hung on the kitchen wall, "it's almost ten. I'm going to have another cup of tea before I go to bed. Care to join me?"

"Thanks, that would be lovely. And a cookie." Jasmine went over to the big yellow cookie jar shaped like a beehive that stood on the kitchen counter. She peered in. "What happened to all the cookies you baked this morning?"

"Oh! With all the goings on today, I forgot to tell you that your freckle-faced, red-haired boyfriend dropped by looking for you this afternoon." Emma was grinning broadly. "I gave him one cookie and he practically inhaled five more, talking non-stop all the time!"

"Alistair." Jasmine was smiling too, glad of the change of subject. "He's a force, isn't he? Brimming over with energy. Did you know he's asked me to marry him? For the sole reason that I'm the only woman he's ever met that enjoys hearing him play the bagpipes!"

"Dear me," Emma said disapprovingly. "He's just a lad. I hope you're not encouraging him too much."

"No, but Arlena told me a little about his father and mother, who're considered high society in their small town. They're also high Anglican, very prim and proper. It does give me sort of a wicked thrill to imagine Alistair coming home to them with me on his arm."

"Lordy, yes, wouldn't they just have a conniption!" Emma exclaimed, with a big hearty laugh. "Though anyone who gets you, Jasmine, will likely think himself a lucky man."

They exchanged a fond embrace; then Jasmine settled down at the kitchen table with her tea and the crossword puzzle from the daily newspaper. Emma paused at the door.

"Goodnight, dear. And thanks for all the laughs, they'll help me sleep soundly."

Jasmine's head was bent over her puzzle. "You're welcome. Although I do wish that they weren't all at my expense."

Emma, going toward the stairs, heard the wistful note in her voice.

CHAPTER 72

The air on that last night of the long spring weekend was as warm and soft as the breasts of doves. Under the starry, moonlit sky it pulsed with life, from the rhythmic thrum of insects to the calls of the nighthawks and the love songs of the spring peepers in the cedars lining the stream behind the lake houses. Thomas was too restless to sleep. He made a solitary silhouette against the moon-silvered water of the lake as he walked the pebble shoreline that lined the breakfront. He was hoping to be soothed by the gentle lapping of the water, a tranquil sound to calm the tumult of his thoughts. For tomorrow he would meet the mother of his child, and now he knew why she had been so often in his dreams and waking thoughts despite the passing years and the great distances that separated them.

Sometimes as he worked late at night in his study, he would lift his eyes from the page he was reading under the yellow circle cast by the lamp and feel, with a strange certainty, that she was thinking of him. Other times he would catch a few chords of a distant melody, or the scent of a certain perfume, and he would send his thoughts rushing toward her, evanescent as the trail of the moon on the water but as real, to ruffle her consciousness as the wind might her hair.

For, as he had just discovered, they shared the bond of blood together in that lively little tomboy they had created, that beautiful child with her purple pansy eyes and her laugh full of joy. But Thomas had no idea of what other bond he might be allowed to form with his newfound child or her mother.

Jasmine. When he rescued her from the lake and for a short while afterward, he had believed her to be just a silly, lovesick girl with a penchant for drama. He would help her become whole again, for he knew himself and that in helping her, he could heal as well. For a short while they would enjoy each other's bodies and the blessed oblivion of sex; soon they would part. Then he would return, restored to himself and penitent, to the wife he loved.

But when she started to emerge from the desperate state he had found her in, she was nothing like what he had conjectured. She had intelligence equal to his, a rapier-sharp mind and wit. She teased and taunted him, charmed and irritated, angered, enticed and captivated him and drove him mad with desire. He had become obsessed with her, as he had once told Lianne; but perhaps they both knew that it went deeper than that. Dangerously deeper, in fact, than that quasi-clinical term might suggest.

Sometimes it felt almost as if he had substituted one illness for another, depression for love-sickness: his fixation with this beautiful, elusive creature whom he had expected to dominate, but who so instinctively knew how to use all the wiles and ways to wrap him around her little finger.

He remembered the first time he made her laugh. He was talking, rather pedantically, he supposed, about how their getting better was a "process" in which they were engaged. Sitting on the bed half-naked, she gave a great whoop of laughter. "Oh! How Thomas-teacherish you are! A process! Should we write the formula for that process on the blackboard, Mr. Latham?"

Then she described, in some detail, what the formula might include, teasing him and tickling him mercilessly until he had not a shred of dignity left.

From then on, when they met, she would smilingly ask him what part of the process he wanted to start with, and he would answer in suitably unsuitable language, to make her laugh, and then – but this was not a train of thought he could afford to pursue; he could feel himself getting warm even at the memory. He would be seeing her tomorrow, and when they met he must be dignified, cool and calm.

Discovering that he had a living child had been a great gift, a present, although one that was yet to be opened. What might be inside? He pondered this question, and as he did, he was reminded of a similar gift. It was a memory from childhood, the last week before Christmas, years ago. He was a small boy of three or four then, and his mother had taken him shopping. They were in a large dry goods store, and in the centre aisle was a decorated tree with presents underneath, all wrapped in shiny, jewel-coloured foil.

While his mother was distracted at the cash register he had escaped and rushed back to the tree, where he quickly grabbed the biggest, heaviest present and set about ripping off the wrapping. To his immense disappointment, all that was inside the gift-wrapped box was a large stone. His mother brought him to the smiling manager and asked him to apologize, but Thomas had stubbornly refused because, in his child's mind, it was such a dirty trick.

Now, as he thought about his daughter, he wondered what kind of relationship they might be allowed to have. Because he knew exactly what he wanted. His years of caring for other people's children had not in the least diminished his yearning for one of his own. He wanted to see her every day. For her to call him Dad. He wanted to take her for walks and help her with her homework. He yearned to read her stories and hug and kiss her goodnight before bed, to watch her blow out the candles on her birthday cake, to go fishing with her, to twirl her around on a dance floor. To comb her hair and wipe her runny nose. All the little and big things, the intimacies that made up fatherhood, and she was eight, almost nine, and there really was no time to spare if he were truly to be her dad.

Yes, it was like a present. Eventually it must be unwrapped, and then he would find out what it contained. Would it be a stone lying heavy on his heart, with the knowledge that his daughter was growing up without him, so far away? Or might it be something else?

He would find out soon enough. In the meantime, however, he would be happy looking at his shiny new present, with its promise of joy, and try not to think too much about what might be inside.

On this lovely, starry night where the wind wound around him like warm perfumed silk, a star slipped down the sky. Thomas watched it fall into the silver path the moon made on the water. When he was a child, he had wished on falling stars. He did so now, although it was more like a prayer. Then he turned and began the long walk home to his solitary bed.

CHAPTER 73

Jasmine had found it difficult to sleep, restless with a curious mixture of dread and anticipation, and she awoke early. After they made their arrangements for the day, Laura set off for school. Jasmine was next to leave and had just opened the back door when Emma called out, "wait!"

She stood and waited without troubling to disguise her impatience. Emma noticed that this morning she had actually put some effort into her appearance, compared to her usual tumble-out-of-bed style of personal grooming. Of course: she would be seeing Thomas later, when he came home after school.

"I know you don't like surprises, Jasmine," she said. "So I thought I had best warn you that Lianne has something she wants to give you. I just hope you'll be properly appreciative."

Curious, Jasmine turned to fully face her. "What is it? And why wouldn't I be appreciative?"

"I'll leave the surprise to Lianne. However, some gifts are mixed blessings," Emma said enigmatically, and quickly left the kitchen before she could ask more questions.

It was in a heightened state of apprehension, then, that Jasmine ascended the winding, polished oak staircase that led to the second floor and Lianne's bedroom. Lianne was still awake. Propped up on her pillows, she smiled a welcome as Jasmine came into the room with her breakfast tray. Like any seasoned card player, when the need arose Jasmine knew how to wait. She stilled her curiosity and questions about the events of the weekend and prattled on about inconsequential matters until Lianne had taken her usual token sampling of the food before her and then declined the rest.

She also spent this time in a close observation. What was that "look" Emma had seen, which she said so clearly foretold death's approach? She noted Lianne's pallor, her lassitude and then, perhaps something new and rather strange about her eyes. Jasmine tried to find words to describe it but could not.

Other than a few short responses to her questions, Lianne only became animated just as Jasmine was about to take away her tray. "I told Thomas that Laura was his daughter last night," she said with a joyous smile. Her face became as bright as the sun outside the window with the memory of that moment.

"Did you? I hope you also told him about the conditions I set out." Jasmine put the breakfast tray down on a nearby table and stood beside her bed with folded arms.

Lianne's face immediately fell. Like a child caught in an act of disobedience, with downcast eyes she stuttered out in her whispery voice, "N-no. No, I'm sorry. I didn't. I just couldn't."

Jasmine did not trouble to hide her displeasure. Lianne hadn't kept her promise, a solemn commitment and the basis on which she finally had told her the truth. Coldly, she asked, "well, why not? What did Thomas say when you told him? How did he take it?"

There was a long pause. Finally, Lianne looked up at her. "He cried," she said simply.

Almost apologetically, by way of explanation she added, "you know how deeply he feels everything. Well, he's not much good at joy. He's not used to it; he's better dealing with things that are sad."

Jasmine turned and walked a few steps away from the bed. The thought of Thomas, that big, bluff man in tears on learning that he had a living child, moved her greatly. But it was Lianne who shook her soul, amazed and humbled her. She displayed none of the emotions Jasmine would have gladly allowed her: sadness, bitterness, knowing that another woman had borne the child she had five times tried and failed to give her husband. No, his joy was hers, sweet and pure and seemingly uncomplicated by any considerations of self.

But oh, what a heavy burden it laid on her, their joy! She had given it and soon she must take it away. Because Lianne had not kept her promise, the job of telling Thomas the conditions that would make him a father in name only would fall to her. She would be the spoiler at their meeting today, the first time in nine years she would see him face to face. More than ever she dreaded it, and regretted allowing Lianne to extract the truth. It had opened up a minefield of complications and she suspected this was just the first.

With these thoughts tumbling through her mind, she barely noticed Lianne stretching out a frail, thin hand out toward her night table. She was trying to retrieve a jewelry box covered in deep blue velvet that was easily within reach, but too heavy for her to pick up. "Jasmine," she asked hesitantly, "could you please get this for me?"

Silently, Jasmine handed her the box. This must be the surprise Emma had warned her of, for which she must show suitable appreciation. From its condition, she knew that whatever the box contained must be very old. Now Lianne opened it and looked at the contents for a moment before speaking. "Emma was visiting last night and I asked her to take this out of the armoire for me. I want to give it to you for Laura. For Thomas's child. It's family jewelry from the Latham's, and his mother gave it to me the day we married."

The old jewelry box was heavily worn by the passage of many years and hands. Jasmine guessed it to be Victorian-era jewelry: heavy chains, a locket perhaps, some small keepsakes of little real value. So she was totally unprepared for the exquisite necklace that Lianne now held up for her inspection. It consisted of an intricately woven gold rope in which small diamonds were enmeshed. Suspended from it was a gold locket in the shape of a rounded heart, encrusted with larger diamonds.

During her years in the casino, Jasmine had become a self-tutored expert in precious gems. Her work gave her numerous opportunities to see and assess jewelry that ran the gamut from flagrantly fake to fabulously expensive. It was at first a hobby, but became anything but casual once she realized its usefulness in helping to evaluate the relative wealth of casino clientele and their ability to pay their tab. Now she looked at the necklace Lianne was about to give her for Laura and was utterly dismayed.

"This is an extremely valuable piece," she said, taking the necklace from Lianne's outstretched hand. "Tell me something about it." In fact, it was the kind of jewelry that would confer instant status upon anyone who wore it. It might be very old, but the workmanship, the quality of the gold and gems and the simplicity of its design made it timeless and unique.

"It dates back to around 1800," Lianne said. "The provenance is on a slip of paper inside the lid of this box. It was made by Nitot, a famous jeweler who created the crown jewels for Empress Josephine. The story goes that it was brought back to England and the family seat in Lancashire by one of Thomas's ancestors who fought in the Napoleonic wars."

There was a tiny ornate clasp on the locket. Jasmine opened it. "Thomas's picture is inside!' she exclaimed.

"Yes," Lianne said, "and I do hope you will keep it there. So that Laura can remember her father."

As though it burnt her fingers, Jasmine quickly handed the necklace back to Lianne. This was a gift that aroused no gratitude but only suspicion and alarm; however, mindful of Emma's words, she tried to show some appreciation even as she refused it. "Your necklace is beautiful and obviously very costly, Lianne. But I can't accept it. It belongs to Thomas's family. One or another of his sisters should have it."

Lianne put it back in its worn velvet box. "No, Jasmine. The necklace belongs to me. It has always been given to the wife of the eldest son. And I am giving it to Laura, not Thomas's sisters, and to you for safekeeping. I do hope you will wear it sometimes, if you wish. I was worried that you might not want to take it. But if that's the case, Emma has agreed to keep it for Laura, and to give it to her when she's older."

"Does Thomas know about this?"

"Yes. He's fine with my decision. He wants his child to have it." There was a look on Lianne's face that Jasmine had not seen before: implacable, almost defiant.

Jasmine now understood the warning Emma had given her earlier this morning. She also knew that, once more, she had been tricked.

With a heart that held only Thomas and a gold rope studded with diamonds, Lianne had cleverly tied her into a web of obligations she vehemently did not want.

This priceless antique was no trinket she could hide away in a drawer and conveniently forget. How angry would her daughter be when she eventually received it, if she were denied the chance ever to meet or know her father, that handsome, kind-faced man whose picture was in the locket? And, in another brilliant stroke, Lianne had enlisted Emma to protect Laura's interests. Emma had years yet to live. She would take her responsibility seriously and ensure that Laura received her inheritance, and all the knowledge of family that came with it.

Jasmine looked around the bedroom. It was a lovely room decorated in muted shades of blue and green, full of morning sunlight and deceptively calm and peaceful. For her, however, it had become a theatre of war and she knew that she had lost this skirmish.

What choice did she have? She took the box. Even so, she was seething with anger.

"You planned all of this, didn't you, Lianne? You made me your friend; you got me to admit that Thomas was Laura's father; now you're using your necklace to make sure that Laura knows her father. You've trapped me!"

Lianne gave her a gentle smile. "I didn't plan it so much as I prayed it, Jasmine. All I know is that Thomas would be such a kind, loving father for your daughter. It can only be to the good for both of them."

"And what about me?" Jasmine breathed with repressed fury. "Does it matter at all what I want? What are your plans for me, Lianne?"

Her eyes had closed. She was escaping; slipping away and exhausted by their confrontation. "I have no plans for you, Jasmine. Only hopes. Just hopes," she whispered.

But what those hopes were became only too clear when Jasmine leaned over to take her tray from the bedside table. With a last surge of energy, Lianne suddenly reached out and gripped her wrist. She looked up at her with eyes that were pleading and full of a terrible anxiety.

"Jasmine, you are my friend. Truly my dear friend, I swear. And I know that you will, but still I have to ask – if you can't love him, then, oh dear God! Jasmine, please be kind!"

Jasmine said nothing; only turned and fled.

Once in the kitchen, she set down the tray and stared into space. This morning, she had seen "the look" Emma mentioned that foretold the coming of death. The planes of Leanne's skull were more sharply defined and in her eyes was the knowledge, an instinctive awareness, that her time was short. All this Emma had probably observed, but Jasmine, who had come to know her so well, saw something else. There was a hard, obdurate look, an obsidian quality to those large, dark-circled eyes. It might have always been there, only never so nakedly visible. What Jasmine concluded, based on the events of the past few days, is that Lianne had no need to conceal it anymore. With a mind like a steel trap and an iron resolve to bend fate to her will, she had accomplished most of what she wanted before taking her leave.

What was it she had said? That Jasmine and Laura being in Medford had presented an "opportunity". Now Jasmine truly understood what she meant by those words, and she smarted with resentment knowing that despite all Lianne's protestations of friendship, she and her daughter were the pawns in her plan.

She opened the worn blue box containing the necklace. The morning sun slanting through the windows set the diamonds ablaze with prisms of light. She estimated it could easily bring twenty thousand dollars at auction, probably more because of its provenance. But so far as she was concerned, the gold rope and locket might as well be a ball and chain. It had hobbled her, preventing her clean and speedy exit from Medford to Las Vegas and home.

She snapped the box shut and set about her work.

CHAPTER 74

"Grrr! Coming to get you, thistle!"

Weeding was almost fun and went faster, the child found, when she made pretend the weeds were her enemies. She, on the other hand, was the good guy armed with a garden fork and an old dinner fork, a giant defending the garden.

"Gotcha, dandelion!"

She knew all their names now, from plantain to pigweed, and only occasionally made a mistake and pulled out a good plant. When she came across a weed she didn't know, she put it aside hoping it wasn't a flower and later she and Thomas looked at his nature books and identified it. One thing puzzling her right now was, why are weeds so much stronger than flowers or good plants? She would ask him.

She dug her fork into some grass growing in a crevice among the rocks in the rock garden and watched in fascination as red ants exploded in every direction, frantically scurrying, transporting tiny white eggs away from the giant that had destroyed their home. To give them time to run away, she considerately moved to another spot and used the larger garden fork to attack a clump of crabgrass.

Today she was going to get thirty-five cents from Mrs. Matthews. Only eight dollars more! That's all she needed in order to get the shiny new CCM bicycle that cost sixty dollars and had been laid away for her in the Handy Hardware store. The bike Thomas gave her was good, but rusty and a bit too small, and before she got it Mom and Auntie Emma had already paid two-thirds the cost of the new bike – she had to pay the rest.

She took off the big floppy straw hat Mrs. Matthews had insisted she wear for the sun and wiped her sweaty brow, then put it back on and readjusted it before attacking the weeds with gusto. She wasn't hungry, still full of the lemonade and cookies Mrs. Matthews had given her. Soon her hour's work would be up and if she hurried home, there would be an hour left to play with Lex and Sy before dinner.

Right now, though, while she dug out the enemy invaders, she had to plan! Because Thursday Shawna was coming home with her after school, and she wanted to show her everything that was new. For sure she would take her to the new rope swing Lex's brother Duncan had hung on a branch of the big old elm that grew on the edge of the cliff near the creek. It was better to have two people anyway, because to make it to the bank on the other side of the tree you had to run real fast and push off hard with your feet before swinging out into space. When you didn't run fast enough, you just ended up dangling there, holding onto the knotted rope. Milt McCloskey, Lex's friend, tried it alone all by himself and he had to drop and broke his arm. But if there were other kids, they could hold out the long stick Duncan left beside the tree, and once you grabbed one end, they could haul you back to the edge of the cliff.

After the rope swing, she would take Shawna to see the chicken. On Monday she and Lex and Sy were down at the crick looking for turtles when they saw a dead chicken floating in the water. They fished it out with a stick and then Sy, because he's going to be a doctor, cut it open with his penknife so they could see what was inside. When they stretched them out, the intestines were at least six feet long! Shawna said she wanted to see them, but the child was a bit worried that by Thursday they would smell too bad or something might have eaten them. Anyhow, they could always climb the cliff close to the crick, or go pet the new kittens at the bakery, or check out Mick's new tree house, or climb trees.... Then, after dinner and before Shawna's mother came to pick her up, they were supposed to go over to Lex's. He had saved a cherry bomb firecracker from the Victoria Day fireworks and they were going to see if it was strong enough to blow the top off a garbage can.

But first off, right after school if mom said it was OK, they were going to stop by Grisham's store and get some penny candy. She'd spend ten cents of the money she made today, and make it up later by cashing in the pop bottles she'd collected. Blackballs were the cheapest: three for a penny. And then perhaps she would buy a couple of those red wax lips you can wear, then chew, that were two for five cents, or a pack of candy cigarettes they could pretend to smoke on their way home, or –

She had been humming as she worked away on the rock garden. Suddenly she stopped, because a dark shadow had fallen over her, blotting out the sun. From under the floppy straw hat she saw a pair of tan leather boots on the sidewalk before her, strange boots that had a big flap turned down, almost like a pirate boot. Peering up, she saw a tall, dark man looking down at her and smiling. Even in shadow with the sun behind him, she knew immediately who he was, because she had seen him in the framed pictures on the mantelpiece in the living room of Mary's house. It was Mary's dad.

"Hello," he said. "I've been watching you. You're doing a good job. A very good job. What's your name?"

He wasn't a stranger, so she could tell him. Without even thinking, automatically, she gave him the name they called her at school. "It's Runner," she answered.

"Rummer – that's a nice name." It was also the wrong name, but the child was too shy to correct him.

"Well, Rummer, I have a big garden to take care of, and I could use a good helper like you. How much are they paying you here?"

"Thirty-five cents an hour."

"I can pay you fifty cents an hour. How does that sound?"

Fifty cents! That was really good pay! "That sounds great!"

"Well then, if you can come tomorrow after school, I'll put you to work. I'm the gardener at the Airdrie Estate, not far from here, near the school and down by the lake. Do you know where that is?"

"Yes." She nodded her head vigorously.

"See you tomorrow then," Mary's dad said. "Come in through the little door beside the big gate. I'll be waiting for you."

He left, trailing his dark shadow behind him, and the child sat back on her heels in the sunlight and reveled in her luck. Here was a real gardener, who said what a good job she did, and he'd asked her to work and was going to pay her way more than anyone else!

CHAPTER 75

The hands of the kitchen clock had spun away her workday. In half an hour Thomas would be home and the dreaded meeting would take place. Jasmine had no clear idea, now, of how to manage any relationship he might have with Laura. However, she took some comfort knowing that once back in Vegas, the vast distances between them would be a natural barrier to prevent much familiarity.

She looked at the box containing the necklace, glowing bright blue in the sunshine on the dark kitchen countertop like some radioactive substance. She didn't want Thomas to ask questions about it, or see her taking it home after their interview. Lianne was deep asleep, and there was just enough time to take it back to the house before he came. Hopefully she could avoid Emma if she went in the front door and snuck up the stairs to her room.

But when she attempted to do just that, Emma was emerging from her bedroom at almost the exact moment as she reached the second floor landing. "Hullo?" she exclaimed in surprise, "you're home early!" Then she saw the box in Jasmine's hand. "Well, I see she gave it to you after all. I wasn't sure you would accept it."

"What choice did I have?" Jasmine took no trouble to conceal the bitterness in her voice. "If I didn't take it, then you would have! At least this way I have some control over the timing of when Laura finds out Thomas is her father – now that I've been trapped into telling her, that is!"

"Trapped," Emma repeated the word reprovingly. "'Trapped' is not what I would call it, Jasmine, and it certainly isn't the way Lianne sees it."

"Really? Well, it's not at all what I wanted, but that doesn't appear to matter in the least to either of you!"

Emma heard the rich note of sarcasm. She drew herself up and gave Jasmine a withering glance. "Why do you suspect people of the worst possible motives? Lianne has only done what she did out of love."

"Yes," Jasmine threw back hotly, "her love for Thomas, and all the rest of us are only the means to an end." Then she tried to get past, but Emma laid a restraining hand on her shoulder. "Let me go," Jasmine demanded angrily. "I have to get back to Lianne, and I've yet to see Thomas."

"I will," said Emma, and she dropped her hand. "But before you go, I'll tell you the words she said to me last evening. She said she had come to know and care deeply for you. And she knew that she could trust you to take good care of what was most precious to her. Whether you choose to see that as a burden or a blessing, Jasmine, is up to you."

There was still a sullen look on Jasmine's face as she turned and sped down the hall toward her bedroom. But Emma knew her niece, and guessed that the seeds for a different way of thinking had been planted in her mind. She hoped they might take root before Jasmine met with Thomas this afternoon.

* * *

Their meeting was off to a bad start and tumbled downhill from there.

Jasmine had been craving sunlight, flowers and greenery after being inside most of the day, so when she heard the car in the drive she went into the garden to meet him. The sky was a heavenly shade of blue, the old apple tree a mass of pink and white blossoms. But there was no place to sit. A storm had passed through during the night and the patio table and chairs were wet with rain. She hesitated, about to go back inside. Except that there he was already, on the path into the garden, coming toward her with a smile. He held out both his hands, reaching for hers.

It was the first of many mistakes.

How could he possibly have forgotten? Jasmine immediately tucked her hands behind her back, as if he had just offered her a couple of burning coals. Because this had been their greeting whenever they met, a prelude to passion, so much more than only fingers touching. He stopped, the realization of what he had just done bringing a look of consternation to his face, and he quickly dropped his hands to his side. When she saw his embarrassment, Jasmine knew it had been only a mistake. But she was still more than a little wary of him, the balance between them already unsettled.

In fact he had done it mindlessly and almost by instinct. Thomas had thought a great deal about this meeting, and what he might say. What he was totally unprepared for was what he would see: the physicality of her, Jasmine, standing in front of him, the sudden replacement of the memories he had called up so often, by flesh and blood. Then there was the great, unexpected surge of emotion he felt on seeing her lovely face, knowing that she had borne his child, a living bond between them.

Now he struggled to find the composure he had just lost, because much depended on this meeting.

"Hello Thomas."

"Hello Jasmine. You're looking wonderful!"

"And so are you. It seems we've both made a good recovery."

"How's Lianne? I should go up to her shortly."

"She's sleeping right now. Most of the day, as usual."

For her part, Jasmine, looking at Thomas and into his dark blue eyes, was feeling something she seldom did: shy. He was so male, his voice so deep. Cloistered for months in her little world of women, there were only two men she ever saw with any frequency: Alistair, who dropped by almost daily to visit, buzzing around her like a large red bumble bee intent on pollination; and Margery's husband Jim, in and out to check on Emma and always loudly present at Sunday family dinners.

The Thomas she had known years before was painfully thin. This Thomas was heavier, fleshed out into a model of good health. She noticed a new air of authority about him; part of it certainly had to do with his size. He was big, towering over her despite her being taller than most women, and broad, large enough to intimidate even the most recalcitrant and disrespectful pupil. He was also very handsome in a rough-hewn way, with his blue eyes, black hair and strong features. If he walked into the casino where she had worked, the signal, invisible to casino customers, would have gone out among the women and yes, a few of the men who worked the floor, that there, in the passing parade of humanity, was someone worth looking at.

Now she saw a few other changes: some new lines on his forehead and around his eyes. The indentations around his mouth, those little curlicues of good humour that she used to trace with her finger, had grown deeper. There was also an indefinable air of sadness about him, for which she could easily guess the cause. However, it disappeared, and he almost radiated joy when he said, "I understand I have a daughter."

"Yes. Laura is your child."

"She's such a beautiful little girl." He was beaming. "So bright and chirpy – she's a real delight whenever I get the chance to spend time with her."

"I'm glad you think so. We – I mean – I've done everything possible to make sure she has a happy childhood."

"I hope you don't mind my asking, Jasmine, but did Mike – did your ex-husband know?"

Thomas needed to get her talking, and that was because suddenly, he himself was finding it difficult. Something was happening to him. Too late, he was realizing the enormous mistake he had made in avoiding Jasmine, hiding out in his office whenever she was around and never making even a little casual conversation with her before or after her day with Lianne. Now all his senses were swimming with her being so close, standing facing him just a few feet away; he couldn't seem to concentrate. All he wanted to do was stop and look at her for a long, long while without having to say a word.

She was wearing that damnable perfume – or was it just her, her own scent? He never really had known. The unforgettable, sweet, silvery sound of her voice filled his ears; he saw the satiny sheen of her skin. And the sun had caught the gold flecks in her honey-amber eyes and the golden highlights in the dark red hair that tumbled down her back, those long, heavy tresses she often used to cover her breasts, once, when they were lovers....

"I was completely honest with Mike. I told him I was meeting you one last time. Then, after we were married and I found out I was pregnant, I told him there was a chance it could be your child. But Mike was such a good man, he only said that any child I had would be his as well as mine, he didn't care."

"So, if that wasn't the reason, then why – ?"

"Why we divorced? We both wanted another child – Laura had given us so much joy – but after two years of trying and several tests, then we found out he wasn't able to –. Well, I told him it didn't matter, it wasn't important, but I soon found that it did matter to him, a great deal. And – I guess I was disappointed too," she said, rather wistfully. "But it completely changed him."

"Eventually, we just agreed to go our separate ways."

She missed him, Thomas could see. Now she made it even clearer. "We'd still be together, if it weren't for that. I'll always care deeply for him, and Laura thinks he's her father."

It gave her a jab of sorrow just talking about that sweet, sad man who might always have felt a little less than her equal. On their last night together, she told him she couldn't stand to see him so miserable, and to go find someone who could make him happy. Which, to her surprise, in time he did: a pleasant, rather plain woman with two young sons.

Her eyes were downcast. Looking at her, in the little silence that followed these words, Thomas noticed how modestly she had dressed for this occasion, with a blouse buttoned almost to the neck and a loose skirt: a chaste, nun-like outfit. But just knowing that she had felt this type of garb necessary for their meeting seemed to be having the opposite effect on him to what was intended. She would have had to wear a sack anyhow, he thought, to disguise that figure – Without warning, she suddenly looked up, and there was a knowing look in her eyes and a smile on her lovely mouth. She had asked him something. Damn! What was it? He had completely missed it, and the reason was that he was caught up in a strange, overpowering new sensation.

As a physics teacher, Thomas had taught his students about force fields. But he had never actually experienced one until now. It was unmistakable: energy was flowing between them, strong as an electric current; he felt it almost like a warming fire on the front of his body.

When Jasmine glanced up at him, although not a muscle in his face had changed, she saw the look in his eyes. It was familiar and as easily recognizable to her as if he had spelled the word out loud: desire. It was not a welcome emotion. It would only complicate the discussion they should be having.

"I'm sorry, I missed that. What did you say?"

He hadn't even heard her question! Smiling, Jasmine repeated it again. "Did you never think that Laura might be your daughter?"

He laughed to cover his embarrassment. Then he said, "well, when I heard you were pregnant, it occurred to me, of course, but I knew that I'd taken every precaution. Otherwise, I did think that if we hadn't made a baby that weekend, then I didn't know how they were made."

It was meant to be jovial, humorous, but even as he said it, Thomas was horrified at the coarse sound of the words coming out of his mouth. He watched helplessly as Jasmine's eyes widened, and she blushed pink. That was not the answer she had been expecting, and at this delicate moment, a truly bad mistake. Instantly, it had carried them back to a place neither of them wanted to go, transporting them from the now to the then, from the green, wet garden where they were standing, to a darkened room in a downtown city hotel – the room they had left only once, for a quick meal, before rushing urgently back. Jasmine also remembered its aftermath when, on returning to her apartment, she had showered and washed her clothes, her hair, her body, once, then again, because everything was so overpoweringly full of the scent of sex, and the alluringly musky and male smell of him.

The memories flooding the air around them had drowned their conversation. Jasmine was first to break the silence. In a voice she tried to make light, but that somehow came out sounding silkily seductive, she said, "I think, Mr. Latham, it might be best if we forgot the past, for the present."

Then she couldn't resist adding, "However, that weekend is when it happened."

"But I was careful!" he blurted out.

"No," she retorted quickly. "Not at first."

He stared at her for a moment, his mouth half open. Then it all came back to him: the memory of how, maddened with love and longing, knowing that forever after she would be lost to him, he met her at the door at the very moment she came in. He seemed to recall that later, lying beside her and looking over her shoulder at the heap of clothes by the door and the trail of the few remaining articles of clothing leading up to the bed, he thought he might have forgotten something.

Jasmine saw the consternation dawning in his face. "Oh, Jasmine," he said with deep emotion, "I'm so sorry!"

"Don't be. There's no need to be sorry," she began, "you gave me the greatest joy of my life – " She stopped. "I mean, my daughter has been the greatest joy of my life, and I've never had a moment's regret – " Slowly she trailed off, and then they just looked at one another wide-eyed, wondering where next they might go with this blighted conversation.

The energy between them had become stronger, almost palpable. Also, Thomas could feel heat radiating from his own body, waves of it; he was fighting a losing battle with himself. Then, as he watched, she delicately put out her tongue and ran it over her top lip. It was only a nervous reaction, he guessed, but that tiny sexual gesture finally was too much; suddenly he was over the edge. Rational conversation now was no longer possible, and he knew he had to leave. Either leave, or close that gap of forbidden desire by grabbing and pulling her roughly against him.

"Jasmine, I think I've made a hash of things today," he said huskily. "I'm sorry, and I hope we can continue this later, when perhaps I'm not so tired or in better form. So please excuse me, but I'm going to leave now. I'll talk to you tomorrow."

Then he turned, and she watched his retreating back as he went into the house.

Lianne was deep asleep, or else she surely would have heard the loud thump as Thomas slammed his clenched fists against the wood wall in the basement. Then he leaned his head against the cool stone beside it, sick with embarrassment and chagrin, and disgusted with himself, his lack of self-control, his body and its primal sexual urges, even while his beloved wife lay on her deathbed upstairs.

But at the back of his mind, behind the flood of guilt and shame, a warming little light flickered: the thought that she must want him too. If a force field occurs when two objects exert a strong attraction on one another, why not human beings, Jasmine and him, and that strange energy he had sensed flowing so strongly between them? Thomas was a great believer in physics, and besides he could think of no other way to explain what he had felt this afternoon or exactly how it came to happen.

CHAPTER 76

Jasmine slowly descended the precarious path from the top of the cliff. She needed a walk along the lake before going home. As she picked her way down the steep slope, she laughed a little, thinking of the mess they made of their meeting. The same bug that bit Thomas seemed to have infected her too, so that toward the end she had been putting her foot in her mouth exactly like him. Some meeting! Nothing had been discussed about Laura, nothing decided!

Even so, much had been revealed, giving her plenty to think about while she walked the stony shore. Thomas was still mad for her. Unwittingly, he had made that as plain as the nose on his open, honest face. Jasmine was not particularly surprised. She was used to being desired; it had long ceased to be a novelty. More often than not it was a nuisance. Mostly, she ignored it and had devised strategies for whenever it became annoying or repellent. She knew her face and body were the attraction, whereas she, the actual individual inside, was just an adjunct to the uses her admirers wanted to make of her. And not an especially desirable one, since she was intelligent, did not hide it and occasionally flaunted it.

The result of such thinking was cynicism, which had given her valuable immunity against men, their charms and advances. But even if he had started off being more or less the same as all the rest, Thomas was different.

She changed her course to walk a little further up from the breakwater, away from the flying spume and spray. The wind was up, and once again the lake mirrored her mood, peaking in shades of blue from aqua to indigo, wind-tossed and turbulent. Years ago, Thomas had plucked her from that wild, rolling water. She had been saved, but only the shell of her. Inside, her spirit lay broken in jagged pieces. Neither of them would have survived or healed, she was certain, if not for those intense, emotion-filled hours they spent as lovers and confidantes. Thomas had opened his soul to her, and she had shared with him thoughts and feelings she had never told anyone else, before or since. They knew each other intimately, inside and out.

However, if it seemed that not much was different between them, in the past nine years everything had changed for her. She had her daughter and her independence now, caring friends, a house, and many chances for well-paid employment doing work she enjoyed. Her life and her home were elsewhere. But still –

The wind had a sharp, chill edge. She welcomed it, turned her face to it. It helped to cool her fever, the one she seemed to have caught from Thomas. This was the real surprise. Not until today when, naïf that he was, Thomas had fumbled and bumbled his way through their meeting, then left in a flush of embarrassment, had Jasmine ever had the sensation of being picked up and carried off by runaway emotions.

Unlike Thomas, however, she felt not a jot of guilt nor any sense of disloyalty to his wife, her friend, for what she felt. And that was because she knew that at her meeting with Thomas this afternoon, everything had turned out almost exactly as Lianne hoped.

* * *

"She's at the door right now," Emma said into the phone. "I have to go."

From the other end of the line, Margery ordered her: "don't forget to call me if there's any news!"

In a pig's ear, Emma thought as she hung up the earpiece. I might as well write up everything that happens at Lathams' and broadcast it all over town.

Margery had called, and after sharing a few items of news and gossip, said she had heard that Father Fitzgerald visited the Latham's house today, and that Lianne was reputed to be almost at death's door; was that true? She had also heard that Jasmine and Thomas were seen having a serious discussion in the back garden this afternoon. She said she hoped there wasn't any other problem, which Emma recognized as an obvious bid for more information.

Emma knew that one or another of the neighbours including that nosy Emily Barrett would have passed the gossip on to Margery's daughters, and from thence to her. It left her with the uncomfortable feeling she should draw the drapes and lower the blinds before she so much as scratched her bottom, the surveillance level in the neighbourhood was so high. But now here was Jasmine, coming up the stairs.

As soon as she said hello and before she could say anything more, Emma gave her the answer to the question she always asked when she walked in the door. "The child came home five minutes ago from her weeding job, and she was here for less than two minutes before she rushed out to play with the boys," she told her. Jasmine visibly relaxed then, and smiled.

"But I might as well remind you now that I have bridge tomorrow afternoon, and that Laura will be coming to you next door to check in," Emma added. "I won't be here to catch her, unless she's weeding for Edna again, in which case I should be in good time." She started to peel the potatoes for dinner. Jasmine took the hint and began to set the table.

"How was Lianne today?" Emma turned from the sink. "I thought I might go over after dinner to see if there's anything she needs, or if I can give Thomas a hand getting her ready for the night."

"She's very low," Jasmine replied. "Father Fitzgerald came to see her and gave her the last rites. It seemed to comfort her a lot, and then she slept most of the rest of the day. I managed to get her to eat a coddled egg, and some bits of toast, and some soup. She'll need a change before she's tucked in for the night, but more than that, Thomas could probably use the company."

Then there was silence, just the clink of silver and the sound of the peeler at work. Emma calculated they had conversed enough that she could safely ask Jasmine what she was dying to know without seeming too nosy. "How was your meeting with Thomas? Did you come to any agreement about Laura?"

"No, we didn't spend enough time on it," Jasmine said vaguely. "We're to talk some more tomorrow."

She was about to leave the kitchen and go upstairs. Emma knew that now she was definitely prying, but she just couldn't stop. It was not mere curiosity that finally drove her to ask, "When you met with him – were there any sparks?"

Jasmine looked at her, amused. "No, no sparks," she answered. Then, when she saw the poorly concealed look of disappointment on Emma's face, she added, "it was more like a conflagration."

As a former librarian, Emma was fairly certain she knew what that word meant, but still it sent her to the study to look it up in the Webster's dictionary. When she came out of the room, a smile was playing across her features.

CHAPTER 77

Auntie Emma had packed her a lunch, and Runner and some of the other kids who wanted more time to play baseball ate out under the trees in the schoolyard. Then they had the diamond to themselves for over half an hour before the big kids came to kick them off. Runner told Noreen Byrd she was turning into a really good pitcher, but she still needed to lean more into the pitch. The other girls were getting better too; they could hold their own with the boys now. The little team of eight and nine-year-olds was coming together, and sometimes, when she wasn't pitching or batting, Runner looked up and could see her teacher, Mrs. Lewin, at the window of the classroom, her glasses glinting and her face beaming approval.

Now school was over and she was running – walking was always too slow – toward the Airdrie Estate where she was going to work. When Mom and Auntie asked last night, she told them she was going to be weeding, but then Alistair came in and made silly faces at her and told jokes while he ate cake with them at the table and she laughed and they forgot to ask and she forgot to say where she was working. But it was alright, because it was Mary's father, and she would be getting home the same time anyhow.

Once she got there, the little wood gate beside the big gate was open and she went in and looked around. Mary's father was working over on the sunny side of the house trimming some bushes. When he saw her he waved; then he came walking to meet her. He had pulled up the flaps on the strange pirate boots he wore, and now Runner could see how they might protect his legs from the thorny bushes. His face was dark under his big hat. "Hello Rummer!" he said. "Are you all ready to work hard for me today?"

Runner nodded vigorously. "Yep," she replied.

"We're going to be good friends," he said, "so you can call me Roy." Then he reached down into his big blue gardener's vest that hung below his waist and took a garden fork and hand trowel out of a side pocket. He put one hand on her back and guided her over to a part of the garden that was in the sun, and showed her where to weed.

"Did you tell your Mom or Dad where you were going to work today?" he asked in a friendly voice.

"No, I forgot to," Runner said. She was going to add that it was OK because she knew he was Mary's dad, but then he quickly said, "that's alright. I won't tell if you don't. I guess you might get a spanking if you did, and we don't want you getting a spanking, do we?"

Now she had been weeding for a long time, in a part of the garden that didn't really seem to need much weeding, but trying to do a good job anyhow. He was wearing a hat, but she wasn't, and it was hot in the sun. A while ago, he had come around the side of the house and turned on a tap, and taken a cup out of his vest, and had a big drink of cold water. She was thirsty too, and as soon as he disappeared she went over to the tap to get some water. But there was some kind of lock on the tap, it seemed, and she couldn't get it to turn on.

The sun beat down. Working away on her hands and knees, Runner was hot and thirsty, tired and hungry: her stomach was rumbling. In all the other places she worked, the ladies at least gave her juice or lemonade, and she was starting not to like Roy, who hadn't even given her a drink of water when he was having one. From the sun's position in the sky, it seemed that it was time to go home. Then, just as she stood up to go find him, Roy came around the side of the house. "It's quitting time," he said, and put his hand on her shoulder. "Looks like you've done a good job. Let's go to my house and I'll give you your money."

* * *

Emma and her partner had easily won the last hand, but as they took one trick after another, a growing sense of unease had come over her. Her concentration was off, and she was relieved when the time finally rolled around to break for cake and tea.

"What's the matter, Emma?" worriedly inquired her partner, Norah Murray. Norah was also the hostess for today's bridge club. She and Emma played together frequently and when they did, they could read each other's faces almost as well as the cards they held in their hands.

"Probably nothing, but I have to check," Emma said evasively. "Would it be alright if I used the phone?"

The child was at Edna's – where else could she be? – but the thought niggling away at Emma's peace of mind was that she wasn't absolutely sure, because, when she looked at her watch and saw that school would be out by now, she recalled that neither she nor Jasmine had actually asked.

Emma took a little leather-bound directory out of her purse. She found the number, and dialed.

"Hello?" Thank goodness, she was home.

"Is Laura there, Edna?"

When she finally hung up, Emma was experiencing, in a cold wave that swept over her from head to toe, the same deathly chill of fear she had felt when the child went missing after going over to play at the Byrd's. Except this was worse, far worse, because the child was working for someone and she had absolutely no idea who it was, or where. And there was no place from which to start looking, except perhaps the school.

She had phoned her two other friends who had given the child weeding work; neither of them knew where she was. One of them immediately said she would walk with her dog and cover all the houses within the two blocks near her house. Edna was already out looking; she had shared Emma's concern and was even now checking with the neighbours.

Until she had to, Emma decided not to alarm Jasmine – she would be simply beside herself. She called Meg Smith, a neighbour from a street over, to ask if she could send her son to Latham's and their house to see if there was any sign of the child. Meg had not phoned back yet, but Emma did not entertain much hope of good news.

The cake and tea break was over. The ladies were all regrouping at the card tables, but Emma knew she could no more sit down and play cards now than she could sprout wings and fly to the moon.

"Norah," she said to her hostess, "I'm terribly sorry to break up our table, but I have to leave."

* * *

Runner was glad to be done with her weeding, and eager to go home. While Roy waited, she bent over to get her tools, the garden fork and trowel lying on the ground. When she stood up she saw him staring at her. She blushed a little, embarrassed. Had he seen her panties under her skirt when she leaned over? Because he had a funny kind of look on his face. Then he said, "you probably have to pee, don't you, Rummer? You can pee back at my house."

He put his hand on her shoulder again, to direct her steps toward his little house, which was behind a high fence around the corner from the big house from where she was working. As she walked, Runner was feeling rather shocked and somewhat wary of Mary's dad. He was a man, and not one she knew well. Her natural sense of modesty had been affronted by his casual reference to her bodily functions. And that word "pee" was not a nice word. She had been instructed never to use it, because it was rude. If she had to say something, she was supposed to say, "I have to go to the bathroom", or, as Aunt Emma had told her to say, "tinkle".

Besides, she did not have to pee. Like the guys in the gang, she seldom bothered with a bathroom when she was outdoors. She had already taken care of this need behind a bush.

Now, as they went toward Roy's house, the hand on her shoulder slowly slipped down her back, and then she felt it on her bottom. He patted it. "You must be thirsty. I've got a cold drink for you, and you can take a look at the chickens and see if there're any eggs. And I've got a baby bunny for you to hold," he said. That big hand was still on her bottom after he finished saying this, rubbing up and down, and Runner walked ahead a little faster to get away from the hand.

A sudden thrill of fear and revulsion passed through her. She was remembering, although she didn't want to, someone else who talked about pee and always was trying to put his hand on her bottom. Bruce. It was Bruce, the son of Mrs. Stevenson, the woman whose house she lived in before Aunt Emma came, when mom was sick and in the hospital.

Bruce, with his socks that smelled like cheese, and his breath and fingers stinky from cigarettes. In her mind, she saw his little eyes flickering behind his heavy glasses and his pimply face with a few black whiskers sticking out here and there. Her breathing came faster, and she started to slow down on the way to Roy's house.

"C'mon, we're almost there," he said, rather impatiently. And indeed they were. In another minute she would be inside that yard, with its high fence that looked so much like the one around the backyard at Mrs. Stevenson's house. Now she stopped walking altogether, and Roy seemed to realize something was wrong, because he dropped on one knee and gave her a big smile.

"What's the matter? There's nothing to worry about, sweetheart. And I can't pay you unless we go get the money."

This time, when he smiled, Runner saw a big hole where one of his teeth should be. All of a sudden, she was not so sure he was Mary's dad. In the pictures on the mantelpiece, there was no hole in his teeth, and he wasn't nearly so dark, almost black. Maybe this was the other gardener, the one Mary said helped her dad sometimes. Maybe this was a stranger! And she wasn't supposed to talk to, or go anywhere with strangers!

Runner became confused, looking at Roy-who-might-not-be-Roy or Mary's dad. He had stood up again and was waiting for her to make up her mind. The problem was, although she wanted to get away from him, what she really wanted was that fifty cents. She had worked hard for it. Why couldn't she just go in and get it, then leave? She took a step or two toward the gate. Roy went over and opened it wide for her to come in. Then, once again, she stopped.

A slight breeze, heavy with the scent of lilacs, ruffled her hair. The golden sunlight of late afternoon poured through the leaves of the trees interlaced overhead, casting shifting shadow patterns over the green grass and the worn yellow stone walkway beside the tall grey fence. Somewhere nearby, a robin sang its evening song. The child absorbed it all. She was acutely aware of everything around her, all her senses suddenly sharp, like a small animal taking stock of its surroundings and sensing a trap. But Roy was standing beside the open gate. He was waiting for her; he would be mad if she didn't come. Against her every instinct, she took one step, and then another, and another, along the path leading through the gate and into the garden.

* * *

As at a signal, three ladies in pearls, good afternoon dresses and shiny patent or leather pumps set out from the Murray home. Their hostess could not come, but the rest of Emma's bridge table, after various exclamations of dismay or reassuring remarks, put down their cards and followed her out the door to search for the child. They dispersed then, each walking along a different street toward the school. Harriet Sykes and Loretta Ackland had come on foot, and the route was on their way home in any case. It also gave them a good excuse to talk to neighbours they might otherwise not see from one month to the next. However, none of them underestimated the seriousness of the matter: of not knowing who it was that had asked the child to work for them, or where.

After they left, the remaining bridge players talked in muted voices, saying what they could not in Emma's presence. They spoke of the little girl from the shantytown beside the railway bridge who, two years earlier, after telling her mother she had a job delivering flyers, left and was never seen again.

"Edna!"

The voice came shrilling from somewhere nearby, just as she was about to go in the front door. She saw a head bobbing above the hedge that ran down the far side of her property to the street. It was Carrie Mitchum from three houses over, and now she appeared on the sidewalk, waving her hand to get Edna's attention before she disappeared inside.

"I just talked to Lorna," Carrie said breathlessly, "and she was looking out her window yesterday afternoon and saw a tall man in a leather hat talking to Laura when she was weeding your garden."

Lorna was Carrie's fifteen-year-old daughter. She had told her mother she thought it was Roy, the head gardener at the Airdrie Estate.

"In that case," Carrie reassured her, "there's nothing to worry about. There are kids going in and out of there all the time. And he's a married man with children of his own."

Edna knew Roy; she had bought eggs from him. She was greatly relieved, but first she wanted to make sure of Laura's whereabouts before she phoned Emma. It wasn't that far, so she quickly walked the two blocks to the Airdrie Estate. But when she got there, both the little and the big gates were locked. There was no one in sight. Edna paused thoughtfully for a moment. Then, as fast as she could, almost running, she dashed home and picked up the phone.

The smile had slipped from Roy's face as he stood by the gate, and when she looked up at him, the child could see something dark and unfriendly there. Once he noticed her eyes on him, his mouth flipped up at the corners again in the semblance of a smile. But it made no difference. Now she was wavering, reluctant to take the last few steps. He saw her hesitation and walking toward her, stretched out one arm to shepherd her inside.

Suddenly, from the vegetable garden inside the fence, a large bumblebee came sailing at top bee speed. The bee flew directly at Runner and collided with her forehead, bumbling and buzzing angrily before it disengaged itself and rushed busily away.

To the child it was a sign, the one she had been waiting for. The bumblebee had delivered a message, one that she understood perfectly. "Get away, run, run!" it had said. So she did. In a flash, she turned and ran toward the other gate, the little one that opened onto the street. Roy ran too. He caught up to her and grabbed her arm, and she stopped.

Now he was all big smiles again. "C'mon Rummer, there's nothing to be afraid of. That was just a bee, and it didn't bite you, did it? You don't want to leave without being paid, do you, honey? Listen, I've got something for you, right here. A chocolate bar, and you can eat it when I go in the house to get your money."

Then Roy started to rummage through the pockets of his big blue gardener's vest. Meanwhile, Laura stood stock still. Bruce was creeping back into her mind again.

"Laura, come here. I've got something for you." He was sitting on his bed as she walked by his bedroom.

"What is it?"

"A chocolate bar." Bruce held it up for her to see. Laura came in the door. She wanted the chocolate bar; there hadn't been much for dinner that night and she was hungry. She held out her hand for it.

But Bruce pulled it back, a little out of her reach. "You can have it," he said. "But first of all, you have to touch this."

He pushed aside his shirt that was hanging down, and there was his big dinky sticking out of his pants. Laura turned and ran toward the stairs going down to the kitchen. He came running right after her, grabbed her and spun her around.

"Don't you go telling my mother!" he hissed. "Or I'll come get you when you're asleep!"

Roy was finished with looking in his pockets. He had found the chocolate bar. "Here," he said, pulling it out and showing it to her.

It would always be a puzzle to him why, when he showed her the candy bar, her eyes suddenly went big and round, practically starting out of her head, while her mouth formed a perfect O of shock. Then she turned and ran, only this time as if her life depended on it, and when she reached the little gate and found it locked, she banged and kicked it and raged to get out.

Runner was beside herself with fright. Because the chocolate bar Roy pulled out of his pocket was the same, the very same as the one Bruce had offered her: it was a Crispy Crunch!

"Let me out!" she hollered at Roy as he approached, and she made her face ugly, the ugliest face she had, the one that Sy had told her made her look like Jimmy, his bulldog. "Let me out, I want to go home!" She jumped, seeing if she could push the latch up with her finger, but it was too high.

Roy laughed, an unworried, easy laugh. Everything she was doing seemed to amuse him hugely. "Well, have it your own way," he said, as he put a hand on her shoulder to draw her back from the gate and reached up as if to open it. "But your mom and dad don't know you're here, and if you come home without any money, you're sure to get a spanking."

She sensed his reluctance to let go of her. Then the child told a lie. "Mrs. Matthews knows. I told her yesterday I wasn't coming to her house today because I was weeding here." Now she was no longer so much afraid as angry, furious with this man who wasn't paying her and wouldn't let her out.

She felt his hand on her shoulder stiffen. "Well, then you come back tomorrow. I'll have your money ready for you," he said slowly.

Then, finally, he did undo the latch that was up so high, and as he swung the gate inward, he pulled her close to him to move her out of the way. She felt his hot body against her back, almost like an embrace. In a rage, she raked her nails across the arm holding her tight, and spun around to free herself.

"Why you little b– !" he exclaimed venomously. But now she was rid of him, out of his grasp, and charging through the gate.

As she whirled to dislodge his arm, she had knocked the Crispy Crunch out of the low vest pocket he had loosely thrust it into. It fell on the stone walkway and now, while she rushed through the gate, she gave it a mighty kick. It flew into the gutter, from whence she quickly scooped it up before running, running, running, until there was enough distance between her and him that she felt she could safely slow down to a fast walk. Then she ripped the wrapper off the Crispy Crunch.

She had most of it wedged in her mouth sideways, she was so hungry, and there was chocolate running down her chin when she met Aunt Emma, who was puffing up the hill on Lake Street. Her face was all red and anxious-looking.

"Child, child, where have you been!" she cried, before scooping her into a huge embrace and holding her tight for a long minute. When she let go, she had tears at the corners of her eyes and chocolate on the front of her best navy blue afternoon dress.

The child saw it and said contritely, "Oh-oh! I'm sorry, Auntie!" but she waved it away.

"Now," she commanded, "tell me where you were, and with whom."

They were walking homeward while the child told her about Roy, and her job, and what had happened. As she did, Aunt Emma started to slow down. Her face, which had been so hot and red before, became very white, and then, when they came to a house where the steps ran up a little hill to the front door, she had to sit down on the steps.

A minute or two later, the door of the house opened. A blonde lady leaned out and called, "Emma? Emma Madison, is that you? Are you alright?"

"Oh, hello, Susan," Emma replied, rather faintly. "No, I think I'm having a little bit of a spell."

* * *

Jasmine was at home in the kitchen making her second dinner of the day when she heard the rattle of the front door. Floating down the hallway came the sound of Emma's voice: "Thank you ever so much, Irwin, for the ride, and for picking up my friends."

The child ran into the kitchen and hugged her mother, then excitedly announced, "Aunt Emma almost fainted and Johnny Chalmer's dad brought us home in his car! But first we went and got Mrs. Sykes and Mrs. Ackland who were looking for me too and we took them home!"

Jasmine put down the knife she was using. Wiping her hands on her apron, she went hurriedly toward the door. "What's happened Emma? Are you alright?"

At that moment the phone rang. Jasmine was closer, but Emma rushed around her and lunged for it in such an athletic fashion Jasmine felt reassured of her full recovery.

"Oh, hello Edna," Emma said into the mouthpiece. "Yes, thank goodness, we found her! She was doing her weeding over at the Airdrie Estate. Yes, she's perfectly fine. The gates were both locked when you went there? Well, that probably was done after she left, I'm sure."

For a moment Jasmine listened to Emma's conversation with Edna Matthews. Then, her hands at her mouth in shock and consternation, she turned to look at her daughter. "You were at the Airdrie Estate?" she asked disbelievingly.

"Yes," the child replied, her eyes large and frightened, "are you going to spank me?"

Emma heard. She put her hand over the phone. "No, no one is going to spank you, Laura. But you are to go right upstairs to your room, and don't come down again until I call you for dinner," she ordered her sternly. "I have to talk to your mother."

Which she did, in great detail, after she hung up the phone. And at the end of her description of the events of that afternoon, Jasmine, sitting at the table with a drawn white face and eyes filled with unshed tears of fright and fury, reluctantly agreed to what Emma had decided as she sat in Irwin Chalmer's car.

They would do nothing, and the reason was that nothing could be done. The grim reality was that harm or clear intent to harm was needed. It had to be witnessed or proven, and there was no proof. They could only continue on with the plan that Jasmine had devised, which was now their one and only hope of catching a child molester at work.

Both sat in silence for a moment, weak with relief and the fearsome thoughts of what could have befallen Laura if not for a bee and a boy named Bruce. Neither of them had ever heard tell of Bruce. It seemed his memory, repellent as it was and just as likely repressed in memory, had surfaced in the nick of time to save their child.

Before they called Laura down for a dinner neither of them were able to eat, Jasmine exclaimed, "thank goodness it was you, not me, who took that call from Edna Matthews! And she probably called earlier, because the phone rang off when I came in the back door, and I just missed answering it."

They stared at one another, thinking of the consequences of that simple act.

"I'm sure we could have trusted her to keep quiet," Emma said slowly. "But she's a motherly soul. We've spared her some dreadful pangs of conscience, watching children going in and out of that gate and not being able to say a word of warning to their parents."

"Yes. For the time being, we'll not even tell Anna. And no one else must know."

For in a town like Medford, the suspicion, even the whisper of one, that Royce Parke preyed on young girls would spread out to envelop his family like a cancer or a great black spreading stain. While it was well enough known that he was a womanizer, this was different. It was the theft of childhood and the defilement of innocence, disgusting to all right-minded people. And it would blight the lives of his wife and children, making them the subject of malign speculation, and their only recourse would be to move away.

"I forgot to mention that Edna told me about that young girl you spoke of, Gussie, the one who works at Airdrie Estates," Emma said. "I'm not up to it right now, but I'll tell you what she said later."

Jasmine looked at her. Her amber eyes were stony, her expression grim.

"Never fear. We'll get him."

Yes, Emma thought. We might. And what in heaven's name will we do with him then?

CHAPTER 78

By now Chris Byers knew Alistair wasn't hanging around the radio station for fun or the pleasure of his company. He came most evenings when Chris worked late shift, eager to learn and showing surprising powers of concentration and retention when it came to even the more boring aspects of station operations. However, Chris had no idea of the real scope of his ambitions until this evening, when he finally asked him and he answered.

"I want to buy a radio station."

"Get out! You're nuts!"

Chris had just taken a swig from a bottle of Orange Crush; the result was a coughing fit. With fizz up his nose and in total disbelief, he looked at Alistair and saw that he was dead serious.

"Do you think your dad would let me sell advertising time, in my spare time? I want to give it a try," Alistair asked.

To date they had covered mostly technical matters. In this session, seated side by side at the console in the sound studio, glancing occasionally at the DJ in the announcer booth as Chris twiddled knobs and flipped switches, they were discussing radio advertising, the cost of spots and how many could be wedged into prime listening times like seven to nine a.m., noon, drive time and so forth. Alistair had become excited over the prospect of such grand revenue, which to date had never actually materialized for radio station CHLE ever since Chris's father started it in the 'forties. Now he wanted to sell radio advertising spots to local merchants, most of whom had proven highly resistant to shelling out for anything other than the occasional print ad.

Chris ignored his question. "What makes you think you can buy and manage a radio station?"

"I came into an inheritance from grandpop when I was twenty-one. My father thinks I'm an idiot, so under the terms of the will he's able to keep me from getting my hands on it until I'm twenty-five. Soon I can buy something, but manage it? Probably not. So listen, Chris, how about coming in with me? Your old man will never let you do what you want at CHLE, and he's young! You're going to be an employee for another twenty years!"

Chris looked at Alistair with a mixture of skepticism and interest. "You're right about that. He won't listen to my ideas about even the music mix and so it's geezerville every day on the airwaves here."

For once Alistair was quiet as he looked at him intently, waiting. Although Alistair hadn't actually done anything, bought anything and it was far too early to really even think about it, Chris was pretty sure they could work together, although Alistair was a bit of a maniac. However, he reflected, being crazy could very well work to his advantage in the radio business.

"Sure you don't want to be a miller?"

"I'd own a funeral business before a milling operation. At least in funeral homes you're dealing with people even if they're dead or miserable, and embalming is kind of fun. But this business is far more my kind of thing."

"I'll ask my dad if you can sell some advertising on commission."

That would be a good acid test for Alistair, because if he could sell, Chris felt he could do most everything else. He himself had tried and knew himself to be hopeless at sales.

At that moment an event took place that was so singular and unexpected Chris could only sit there astounded with his mouth hanging agape. The door to the studio opened and his sister Sherry appeared with a foil-wrapped plate that contained his dinner.

When, as assistant station manager and general dogsbody, Chris worked the four to midnight shift, his kid brother frequently brought him a care package from his mother, the dinner he had missed that evening. Jeremy did it because Chris paid him to; also because it got Jeremy time off homework and an excuse to get out for a smoke.

Chris's sister had never, ever, to date, brought him his dinner. Chris correlated the uniqueness of this event to the presence of Alistair and quickly reached his own conclusions. At a moment when Alistair wasn't looking, Sherry confirmed his suspicions by giving him a warning look and kicking his foot under the console when he opened his mouth to make a comment.

"Alistair, I saw your car in the lot as I came in," she crooned. "You're becoming quite a fixture around here."

"Yes, your brother is being super patient and telling me all about running a radio station, Sherry. But what about you? Why aren't you here, in the family business, instead of working with those legal beagles?" Alistair had always wondered.

"Why?" Sherry repeated. "Because I've worked here, off and on, ever since I was thirteen, and I know most everything there is to know about it. I got bored. The only thing I do now is review their books every quarter."

Alistair looked suitably impressed. "Working in a legal office is more interesting?"

"She pretty well runs the place," Chris said proudly.

Sherry gave him a grateful look. "There's always something new to learn. I especially like real estate and corporate law."

A little light was going on in Alistair's brain, telling him that if ever there was a girl whose talents matched up to his ambitions, Sherry was probably the one. However, it wasn't Alistair's brain making these kinds of decisions. He had already found the one, and attractive as Sherry was, it wasn't her.

He glanced at his watch. "Wow! Look at the time! Sorry folks, but I have to go. Chris, can you ask your dad that question for me?"

"I came here walking, it's such a lovely night," said Sherry. "Any chance I can get a ride home with you, Alistair?"

"Sure, if you don't mind a stop on the way home."

And so it was that Sherry Byers found herself sitting in Alistair's car, a red convertible De Soto, watching him while he stood at the front door of the Madison house talking to Jasmine and wearing the expression of a moon-struck calf.

Although it was dark, light streamed from the windows and the open door. As she stood on the porch, Jasmine glimpsed someone sitting in the car. She recognized her immediately from her dour expression. It was the attractive girl she had seen in the post office a while ago, who had given her the stink eye for no particular reason. Now she decided to give her a reason.

"Who's the girlfriend?"

"She's not a girlfriend. Just Chris Byer's sister. She was visiting the station and I'm giving her a ride home."

She's not your girlfriend yet, Jasmine thought. But if she's sitting in your car looking as if she'd like to kill me, although you don't realize it, she wants to be.

She took Alistair's hand, pulled him a little closer and gave him a big, soft, kiss on his cheek.

"I like it, I love it, do it some more, only on my mouth, but what's it for?" Alistair asked, astonished and breathless, moving closer.

"To make her jealous," Jasmine replied, perhaps too honestly.

She had assessed this girl in a single glance at the post office. She had seen the official-looking papers and mail she was carrying, the determined set of her chin, her air of competence and authority. She instinctively knew she would be ideal for Alistair, whom Jasmine knew was impossible for her.

Occasionally she would glance at him, a good-looking lad brimming over with youthful fire and passion, and wonder idly if his hair was as red elsewhere as it was on his head, and how that might be. But even with the wealth he promised to shower on her from his inheritances alone, she was disinclined to encourage him. She felt older than him, not by years particularly, but by several lifetimes.

So those little gestures of affection and possession she had just made were not meant so much for Alistair as for her, the girl in the car. For whom they would be, Jasmine knew, the equivalent of a red flag to a bull.

"Now, what is it you wanted to talk to me about?" She tossed her long hair and moved a little away, though she still kept hold of his hand. 'It's almost nine and I have work to do."

"Well, I have a proposition for you."

"What is it? Is it the same as the others?" She had not kept track of the number of marriage proposals he had made in his determination to wear her down.

"No. This one is purely business," he said. And he smiled his charming, devilish grin that was punctuated by one sweet dimple in his left cheek.

She felt a rush of affection that was almost sisterly. Oh yes, she was fond of him. And although she could not love him, with the right encouragement and the spice of competition, it appeared there was someone who would.

Their conversation ended. She watched as he rounded the car, put one hand on the door and leapt lightly into the driver's seat. Then she waved prettily at the girl waiting in the car. She was rewarded with another dour look and the furious flash of her eyes before the engine sprang to life and the taillights vanished down the long, dark street.

CHAPTER 79

The mail arrived each day at one o'clock delivered by Mr. Steeves, an elderly postman so punctual Jasmine sometimes wondered whether, instead of flesh and blood, his innards didn't contain the workings of a clock. She met him at the door after saying goodbye to Dr. Sheridan. The doctor's visits now were perfunctory and swift.

"He's lost interest in me," Lianne had said without a hint of bitterness.

It saddened Jasmine because she knew Lianne was right. They both sensed his air of defeat. His concern was with the living, and barring a miracle Lianne would soon depart their number.

There was the hint of a smile under Mr. Steeves' droopy grey moustache as he handed Jasmine a fistful of mail. "Looks t' be somethin' important there," he commented.

As she sorted it on the way up the stairs, hoping to give it to Lianne before she could fall asleep, she found it: a stiff, square white linen envelope embossed with the crest of Royal Sutton Boys' School in navy and gold, and addressed to Mr. Thomas Latham, Esq.

"What is it?" Lianne asked Jasmine who held the envelope up with a flourish as she entered the bedroom.

"What do you think?" Jasmine handed it to her. Lianne was lying on the sheepskins Emma and Jasmine had brought her as a preventative against bed sores, with just a thin sheet over her on this warm day.

"It's that boy's college Thomas applied to!" Lianne exclaimed excitedly, in her loudest whisper voice. "He had two meetings with them a year ago, and then nothing! So far as I know, they never did fill the position, vice principal, I think it was. But here's some mail from them, again, and, oh! I just have to know what's in it! Open it!"

Jasmine was shocked. "But it's for Thomas. I can't do that; it's his mail! He should be the one to open it."

"Oh, for heaven's sake, don't be such a saint. He won't care. Just open it!" Lianne was clearly frustrated, so anxious was she to find out what the envelope contained.

"No," Jasmine said stubbornly, "I won't. Just let's wait until Thomas is here, it won't be long now. Oh, and I should remind you, I'm leaving early today. Emma will be here when he comes home."

There was a small silence. Then Lianne said, in a wheedling voice, "Jasmine – Jasmine – could you please go downstairs and steam that envelope open?"

Jasmine gave a merry peal of laughter. "Really, Lianne, now how does that make it any better? You're still opening his mail without his permission!"

Then she saw Lianne's face, her look of sharp disappointment, and she relented. "Alright," she said. "I'll do it. But you'll have to tell me where to find the glue to seal the envelope again."

Ten minutes later she returned, tendrils of damp hair curling around her red face. "Here it is. I haven't looked at it." And she gave her the opened envelope.

Lianne took the letter out and read it quickly. Her face brightened with excitement. "They're having final selection interviews with the board, and they've given him a date, next Monday!"

Then her excitement dimmed as she and Jasmine looked at one another. "He won't want to go," Jasmine said. "He'll be frightened that you – that something –"

"That I'll die," Lianne said flatly. "Well, I won't, that's all there is to it. It's only one day he'll be away, if he leaves very early in the morning. Perhaps you can stay overnight on Sunday."

"No, I'll just come very early in the morning."

Jasmine had heard that phrase, 'the matches too close to the firewood', used often enough by Emma and Margery that unsurprisingly, it came into her mind when Lianne suggested such an arrangement. Earlier, just before he left for work, she had spoken briefly with Thomas. He said he hoped they might discuss Laura later this week. He also thanked her for all her efforts, including the wonderful dinners she had prepared for him. Then there had been a moment of simmering silence between them when, whether he realized it or not, he had looked at her as if she were a mouth-watering dessert for one of those dinners.

She sighed. Things were not going to be free and easy between them, as they once were. They would continue as stilted and formal as this morning. But that was probably all for the best.

Jasmine had resealed the envelope and she put it on the bedside table. "I'll be a very good actress tonight, when Thomas opens it and I'm so surprised," Lianne whispered, her eyes slowly closing as she drifted away.

She was such an imp. Jasmine watched her fall asleep. She saw how shrunken she was, reduced to just a bump beneath the thin white sheet. Then she thought about all the people she would like to put in her place, who were only half so alive as she so close to death, and about fate and irony, until she began to feel the now familiar ache around her heart. She pushed it resolutely away. Sorrow was just another emotion to be repressed as unhelpful, and sure to make things worse.

There were chores to do before Emma came to relieve her, and she turned and went downstairs.

CHAPTER 80

The MacDonnell lake house was a large, imposing structure in the early stages of dilapidation. A few of the shutters hung crookedly, damaged by the strong winds off the lake. Patches on the stucco walls were denuded of paint, an eavestrough on the third storey over the entrance dangled half-detached, and one of the steps leading to the porch was broken. Jasmine had walked by it several times and wondered how the owners of adjacent properties felt about this downward drift in their elegant, expensive neighbourhood. However, after what she had heard from Emma, she was inclined to feel sympathetic toward its inhabitants, at least some of them.

Edna had given Emma an earful about the Whites. A year after the elderly MacDonnells passed on, their granddaughter Nancy had moved in with her husband Cleon White and their brood. Cleon, a large, burly blond man reputed to have a nasty temper, owned and operated a gravel pit on the outskirts of town. "Rough around the edges," was the tactful way Edna had described him.

Since its occupation by the White family, as observed by Edna and her neighbours, the house had quickly slipped from its former glory of manicured lawns, trimmed topiary and hedges and well-maintained rose and vegetable gardens, all of which were quickly trampled underfoot by hordes of children. The White family included five boys and four girls, presided over by a sickly mother who seemed to spend much of her time in bed recovering from childbirth and various illnesses. Their housekeeper, a harried, heavyset woman in her early 'fifties, had her hands full.

Was there a girl about Laura's age? Emma had inquired and Edna replied yes indeed. Augusta "Gussie" White was in grade five at St. Margaret's, one year ahead of Laura. Aged nine, she was squarely in the middle child position, for now at least. The last time Edna had seen Nancy, she thought she might be expecting again. Though of course, after so many children, appearances might be deceiving.

The household appeared chaotic and disorganized, she said. Children seemed to come and go at will, although each of the three older girls had been made responsible for some of the younger children. This system obviously had its flaws. The second youngest White child, Jimmy, aged two-and-a-half, disappeared but seemingly was not missed until he was brought home at three in the afternoon by Rick, the milkman, at the end of his route. Rick had taken him along on his rounds in his horse-drawn delivery wagon after discovering him two blocks away from his house at eight in the morning, wearing nothing but an undershirt and a soiled diaper.

"He were pretty smelly by th'time I got'im home awright!" he told Edna when he related the story.

There was more from Edna, poured out into Emma's attentive ear during several long telephone calls. Jasmine mentally reviewed it while she searched the little park on the lake next to the Airdrie Estate. She was looking for something she was sure she had seen there on her last visit. So far, she had covered the edge of the small forest that flanked one wall of the estate. Now she turned to the tangles of driftwood along the shore.

Edna Matthews retained her knack with children long after raising six of her own. With her Pied Piper ways and an always-full cookie jar, she knew many of the neighbourhood youngsters. She had met all the White girls. So far as she could determine, the two older ones served their parents as unpaid domestics, always engaged in childcare or working in the house. Then there was Ariadne, only four, that little fairy with the white-blond hair whom Jasmine had seen going into the garden of the Estate gatehouse with her baby brother. She was a sweet child, the pet of all the family. The next oldest sister was Gussie. Gussie did some gardening work in Airdrie Estates. Perhaps what she made came in handy, for it was rumoured that money was in short supply in the White household. Edna had met her only once when Gussie came around looking for Ariadne, who was her special charge in that busy home.

"She was shy and barely said boo," was her only comment about Gussie.

As Emma observed, this would have been quite a defeat for Edna, with her ability to charm even the shyest child into trustful confidences.

Time was passing and Jasmine turned her full attention to her search. Near the breakwater that began at the far end of the beach, she parted some bushes. There it was! Brambles had grown over it since she last came: a clean-cut section of tree trunk, tossed up by the waves into the scrub brush that marked the beginning of the forest. It looked too large and heavy for her to move, but finding that it was old and very dry she quite easily managed to free it. It was hardwood, not pine, untouched by rot and still strong and serviceable enough for her purposes.

She had come carrying one of Emma's capacious handbags. Now she set it down and pulled out a length of strong rope, which she slipknotted to catch the stubs of the limbs at the bottom of the trunk so that it could be dragged. Then, like a horse straining at a plough, she set off through the trees, pulling, tugging and sometimes swearing when one branch that had not been cleanly lopped off got caught up in the brush. Finally, sweating like that same plough horse, she reached a clear space next to the wall and was able to drag the tree trunk more easily to the spot she had chosen.

Hand over hand, she lifted the heavy trunk until it came to rest leaning against the wall. She braced it with a rock, making sure all was secure. What remained of the branches were stubs just long enough to function as a rough ladder. With some difficulty, she worked her way up until she was near the top of the ten-foot section of tree trunk and could peer over the wall. She had chosen her location well. Through the green screen created by the leaves of a large basswood tree nearby, she could see the whole of the gatehouse garden, and in particular the small, limestone-terraced courtyard with its large wooden bench.

On the ground again, she looked with satisfaction at her work. She had moved a few more rocks, some dirt, branches and leaf duff around the base of the trunk so that no one looking at it would guess it to be anything more than deadfall. Now that all was in readiness, she went back to retrieve the handbag. After stowing away the rope, she washed her hands and cooled her hot face in cold lake water before setting out toward the school.

Her task had taken more time than expected, and now she hurried. Little groups of children were already starting to come down the street that sloped down from the school to the lake. Perhaps she had missed them? But no: at that moment, visible about a block away, she could see the bulky figure of the housekeeper wheeling a pram. Beside her were three of the children, including Gussie, holding her little sister's hand.

Gussie or Augusta, either was equally appalling! What wealthy great aunt had she been named after, Jasmine wondered, because what other reason could there be for giving that poor child such a name? A burden to carry throughout her life, until she grew into it in her sixties and had blue-rinsed hair and steel spectacles!

Now she began to walk slowly up the hill; it should not appear as if she had been lying in wait. Since Jasmine first sighted them, the housekeeper's mouth had been ever in motion. She's a talker, Jasmine guessed, and her hopes of getting something out of this encounter rose. A large, mannish woman with a big strong body, orangey hair and a ruddy complexion, she was nattering away a mile a minute to the mostly silent children. They were quickly approaching one another. Jasmine slowed down even more, and smiled.

"Hello. Are you Mrs. White?"

"Naow. Who wants to know?" Suspicious, peering at her out of sharp little eyes.

"I'm Mrs. Carlisle. I live in one of the lake houses across from the lighthouse park. Mrs. Matthews told me about your family, the White family, isn't it? And she said there might be one of the children who could lend a hand with our garden, just some weeding and tidying up work."

Her suspicions now allayed, the housekeeper smiled and began to talk, oblivious to the whimpers of the baby and the fidgetiness of her young charges. "Mrs. White is at home, raight now. I'm the housekeeper, Mrs. Pagett. These'er some of the children, nine of 'em altogether. If yer lookin' for a gardener, though, our Gussie here is the only one does that. But she's busy enow already, aren'cha?"

Singled out in this fashion, Gussie bowed her head and looked down at the sidewalk.

"Cat got yer tongue?" Mrs. Pagett prompted her roughly. "Answer the lady, won'cha! Can yer help 'er or not?"

Then, after a moment she laughed and shrugged, giving the girl a look of casual disgust when she remained silent and unresponsive. "That's our Gussie! Gloomy Gus, we call 'er, never smilin' or laughin' an' hardly ever talkin'! But she's a help to us anyways, takin' care of her little sister when she's not away gardenin' at the Estate across the road."

Jasmine's heart was breaking for the friendless child, with her sickly mother, rough, intemperate father and this callous woman who showed her so little kindness. "Gloomy Gus", they called her! With the other burdens Jasmine suspected she was carrying, her life must be a living hell.

Now, however, she must do what she had set out to do, although it was even more distasteful to her after this conversation.

"You're gardening at the Airdrie Estate?" she asked Gussie.

"Yes," the child finally volunteered, although she continued to look down at the sidewalk.

"She's bin gardenin' there almost ever since Mr. Parke took over," supplied Mrs. Pagett. "Gettin' to be right good at it, he says."

"Do you like it?" Jasmine asked. And then, more loudly, "do you like what you do with Mr. Parke?"

Suddenly the girl looked up at her, and Jasmine knew. It all was there in her eyes and her face: shock, shame, fear. Her lower lip was trembling, her cheeks had flamed.

Jasmine had had enough; she felt a wave of nausea. Quickly she said, "I'm sure you're a very good gardener. I'm going to give my phone number to Mrs. Pagett, and if you have any free time, and your parents approve, you can call. Then I'll let you get on your way."

The baby was now wailing loudly. "Yiss." Mrs. Pagett had started to look a bit anxious. "Gussie and two of 'er older brothers are settin' out t'go to the dentist soon's I git home. Bad teeth 'an too much candy, all of 'em!"

After she handed the slip of paper with her telephone number to the woman, Jasmine turned to watch them go. "Too many chocolate bars," she said to herself, in an undertone. Because of that visit to the dentist, part of her plan would have to wait for another day.

* * *

Emma was already home and so was Laura, sitting sulking on the couch in the study and doing her homework. The visit of her friend Shawna had been put off to another date and she was not allowed to play outside as punishment for not telling them where she was weeding yesterday.

"It's a very minor punishment for a very near disaster," Jasmine had said curtly to Emma when she tried to intervene.

"Now I can't show Shawna the chicken!" Laura had wailed, tears in her eyes. "And I didn't even get any money for all the work I did!"

While Jasmine was busy elsewhere, Emma inquired how much she was supposed to be paid. Then, after a trip to her purse in the closet, she dropped two silver quarters in Laura's hand. "Here," she said gruffly. "But don't tell your mother!"

Now Emma looked at Jasmine's grim expression as she came into the kitchen. "Were you able to talk to the White child?" she asked.

"Yes. It was quite upsetting. I'll tell you about it later, when there are no little ears around."

She picked up her mail from the sideboard in the dining room, preparing to go upstairs. There was nothing else she wanted at this moment except a little solitude and the distraction of reading the few letters that had come for her today. Perhaps then she would have some respite from the image, sharp-cut in her mind, of that poor child's face when she asked her that dreadful question.

But she could not escape so easily, because Emma was bubbling over with news.

"Well, Jasmine, as sweet to your sour, I have something to tell you! Just after you left, Lianne woke up and asked me to call Thomas. Did you see the envelope that came in the mail from the Royal Sutton School? She wanted him home as soon as possible to open it.

So he came and opened it, and the letter said they're considering him for vice principal, and they've asked him for a final interview. Isn't that wonderful?"

"Why, that's marvelous! When is the interview?"

Jasmine smiled to herself as she went upstairs to her room. Tomorrow she would tell Lianne that when the need arose, she, too, could be a very good actress.

CHAPTER 81

It was Friday, a day of scudding grey clouds and scattered raindrops. Tomorrow the rain was expected to begin in earnest, with a spring storm rumbling from across the lake to bring much-needed moisture to lawns and gardens.

The Airdries, with their visits always attuned to the sun, would not be in their family home this weekend. Accordingly, it was time for Anna to play her part in Jasmine's plan, a role she was undertaking with a mixture of distaste and uneasy foreboding. As the wind tossed a rattle of rain against the bedroom window, she opened a closet door and took out a small grey suitcase.

There was still an hour until the children's bedtime. Lily was with her brother across the street, playing with the Chalmers' children. Mary was in the bedroom she shared with her little sister, sprawled across her bed reading a book. Beside her, the little battery-operated radio she had received for her birthday from her grandparents crackled out the strains of an Elvis Presley song.

Silently, Anna opened the suitcase on Lily's small bed. Then she went back and forth to the dresser, taking a nightgown, underwear and other items of clothing out of Lily's drawer, packing the suitcase for her departure.

"What are you doing?" Mary inquired, looking up from her book. Then she sat up. "Why are you putting Lily's clothes in that suitcase?"

"She's going to stay with your father this weekend," Anna replied. She continued her packing. "He's picking her up in half an hour."

"But she's too little!" Mary's eyes had grown round, and Anna could hear the incredulity in her voice.

"No. She's four now, and your father's insisting. He says he'd rather you come, but you never want to go, so he's asking for Lily."

"No!" Mary cried out, "Lily can't go! Don't let her go, Mom!" Now she was on her feet.

"Why not?" Anna was smiling, pretending unconcern, as she continued to pack. She closed the suitcase and latched it.

"You mustn't! You can't let Dad take her, Mom!"

Anna picked up the suitcase and went toward the bedroom door.

Mary reached out and grabbed her arm. The child was beside herself now, tears starting out of her wide, frightened eyes. "No! Don't send Lily, Mom, I'll go, I will! Tell Dad that I'm coming! But please keep Lily here! She's too small, Mom, let me go instead!" she babbled, almost incoherent in her urgency.

Very deliberately, Anna took the little suitcase and set it down in the hall just outside the door. Then she turned and removed her daughter's hands that were still clinging to her arm, and held them gently in her own.

"All right Mary. I won't send Lily. But now you and I are going to talk," she said sternly. "You will tell me why you don't want her to go, and you must tell me the truth."

* * *

When the phone rang, Jasmine and Laura were playing chess at the kitchen table. With mild astonishment, Jasmine was observing her daughter's skill at a game she had learned less than two months ago. The child had made several moves that would do credit to an older, more experienced player.

Forethought and a knack for strategy seemed to come to her naturally, and Jasmine wondered whether this might translate into choices leading to an easier, happier life than her own. She hoped it might be so; but then reflected that her own problems had stemmed more from a lack of luck than any need of planning. From her school days, she retrieved the fleeting memory of a poem and one line in particular: "the best laid schemes o'mice an' men gang aft a-gley". With a footnote to Robbie Burns, she concluded, that was her life.

Repressing a sigh, she stood up and answered the phone.

From the other end of the line there erupted loud sobbing and barely contained hysteria: Anna's voice, except hardly recognizable. It was so unlike her cool, contained cousin that Jasmine immediately guessed what she had done and discovered. "Anna, is that you?" she asked, and it was less a question than a prompt for her to control herself and speak without crying.

Sitting at the table poring over the chessboard, Laura overheard the sharp sounds of distress coming from the earpiece and looked up with frightened eyes. But Jasmine only smiled at her reassuringly and spoke into the phone in calm, measured tones.

"When are you going to work?Emma's not here now, she's at the funeral home for the visitation for Rita Harding. You can come at nine? Good. She'll be home by then."

The visitation had ended later than expected because of the volume of friends and relatives who came, then stayed until it became apparent the weather was not going to improve. Emma was angry with herself for leaving the car at home, but at least she had come prepared for showers. Through the wind-driven blasts of rain as she approached the house, she saw Anna ascending the stairs. They met each other in the vestibule at the front door, both glistening with wet, shaking their umbrellas, rainwater streaming off raincoats and onto the marble floor.

"Hello Anna!" Emma had said in her jolly way, before seeing that the water in Anna's eyes did not appear to be all from the downpour she had just walked through.

Later on she would think of how, without any prompting, the three of them instinctively left the kitchen, that too-brightly lit gathering place for the enjoyment of family, friends, food and merriment, and went to sit in the cool, dim living room. Although beautifully appointed, the formal, north-facing room with its fine old Aubusson carpets and polished mahogany tables had never been a favourite of Emma's. However, seated in the circle of low lamplight, around the sofa in the bay window overlooking the black windswept lake, it did seem like the right place to discuss dark and dreadful matters that should never see the light of day.

Jasmine had thoughtfully brought along some tissues. Anna clutched one, dabbing at her reddened eyes as she spoke.

"He was using the threat of harming Lily, that's how he got Mary to obey him. 'If you don't do it, and keep quiet about it, then I'll do it with your little sister,' is what he said to her! Oh, the poor child was so embarrassed and ashamed, but finally she told me what he did. He did things with her that no father should ever do with a daughter – looking, touching and the like! But so far as I can find out from talking to her, he hasn't ever – interfered with her. Not yet, anyhow!"

And then she broke down and cried in earnest.

"Now it's my turn. When you're ready to hear it, Anna, I have something to tell you," Jasmine said grimly.

By the time she finished giving her account of Laura's employment at Airdrie Estates, and what had happened there, Anna was over her tears. She was sitting dry-eyed, her mouth clamped in a thin line of fury. She started to speak, but Jasmine interrupted.

"Wait," she said. "There's more."

Then she proceeded to tell her about her encounter with Mrs. Pagett and Gussie.

"There's no question in my mind but that he's using the same tactics with that child he's used with Mary," she said. "Ariadne, Gussie's little sister, comes and goes whenever she wants, visiting the chickens and bunnies, and Gussie likely pays the price for it. But this is still speculation; we have no proof."

"Oh, he's despicable, a monster!" Anna finally burst out. "Disgusting, horrible – and what a dreadful position I'm in! When he comes home, I'll have to look at him, smile at him, make his lunch and dinner, and watch him with my children! Even sleep in the same bed!" Her tears started to flow once more.

"How can I do it? How in the world will I keep from killing him, until we do whatever it is we decide to do about him?" she cried.

Jasmine had an answer ready. "For a while," she said, "until we find out what we need to, you'll have to be a very good actress."

Emma had been silent. Now she asked, "who's with the children when you're on late shift?"

"Mom has been helping me out. But that arrangement can't go on much longer," Anna replied.

"You must talk to her about Royce this morning. She'll need to know soon enough in any case." Emma rose to her feet. "And tell her that we'll need her help."

"Is that wise, Emma?" Jasmine did not need to spell out the reason why. She was taken aback at this suggestion when the need for secrecy was so great.

"Margery might be of use. She used to play with Charlotte Airdrie when they were children; and she's good at coming up with ideas. Don't worry, she can keep her mouth shut when need be. Like us, she won't want this going any further than necessary and most definitely, she will not want Jim to know."

"Perish the thought," Anna said, and shuddered. "Father would have a heart attack or get a jail term for murder if he knew about Royce and Mary! Yes, I'm sure it's safe to tell her. As you know, she does so love to meddle in everyone's affairs."

Jasmine was pleased finally to see the ghost of a smile cross her cousin's face. With comforting words, she helped her on with her raincoat and then, despite her protests, took Emma's big black Buick out of the garage and drove her to the hospital for her late night graveyard shift.

"Let me out here," Anna commanded. Jasmine stopped at the long sidewalk leading to the old mansion that served the town as a hospital. While the car wipers clacked back and forth, she watched Anna's bobbing umbrella grow smaller as she hurried through the lashing rain toward the glowing front entrance.

Her little spate of self-pity earlier in the evening was making her feel ashamed. "There is always someone worse off than you," her mother used to say, irksomely, whenever Jasmine complained about the unfairness of life. She knew herself to be, if not lucky, then certainly less unfortunate than her cousin in her life choices. Still gazing after that lonely figure, she watched as Anna, far away now, became indistinct from the long, black shadow that followed her as she walked toward the lights of the hospital.

CHAPTER 82

Max was hungry. His hand hovered irresolutely over the tray of appetizers on the kitchen counter before he gave up and went to the fridge, unwilling to spoil such symmetry. Marching around the oval silver platter were alternating rows of oval crackers, each row with either a square of cheddar cheese or a daub of cream cheese topped with a slice of olive or a tiny shrimp. Beside that was another, square tray with rows of square crackers spread with liver paste or devilled ham, all displaying a slice of sweet pickle or pimento on top.

The author of such perfection, Bessie, came back to the kitchen in a rush while Max's hand was still in mid-air, and the evil eye she cast in his direction may have played some part in his decision to forego the appetizers for a couple of slices of ham and bread.

"Oh, hello, darling, you remembered!" Elizabeth remarked brightly, giving him a hug and a quick peck on the cheek when she came into the kitchen to inspect Bessie's work.

As if he could forget without penalty of death, Max thought. He headed for a quick shower while eating the fast fix for his pangs of hunger after the 18 holes of golf he hadn't wanted to play, with a business associate he had to see. When he slipped out at seven this morning, Elizabeth was still sleeping or pretending to, something that previously happened so rarely he normally would have asked her if she were feeling unwell, but that now was taking place with alarming frequency.

A creeping sadness seemed to have come over them all. It had infected Mason and Elizabeth, and by extension him too, worrying as he watched them sleepwalk joylessly though their waking hours. Apart from his eldest child, Althea, who was too far away to provide solace, the only cheerful family member now was Arlena, happy in her new life, her new job and love interest. Max found himself longing to talk to her. He needed to derive, by listening to her chirpy voice, some reassurance that life could still offer joy and promise. He would phone her as soon as this nuisance Saturday afternoon cocktail party Elizabeth had dreamt up was finally done.

Not that he wasn't happy to have her take an interest in something, he thought as he briskly toweled himself dry. Lately Elizabeth had professed herself bored with most of the activities for which she had previously had such zest. What had happened? Something was eating her, but she would not admit it, would not talk. Nothing, she said. But when, sometimes, he caught her wearing that abstracted, melancholy look, he knew it wasn't nothing.

So he was pleased when Elizabeth had suggested this little social gathering as a sort of christening of their new – what was that word? Gazebo! A foolish word for a foolish structure, but yes, once the curtains were hung up it would be a good place to sneak off with a beer and his briefcase full of urgent business that she banned him from even opening on Sundays.

What puzzled him though, is whom she had invited. Old friends, certainly, but people they had moved on from, not the movers and shakers who made up their social crowd these days. However, perhaps Elizabeth needed the comfort of those old familiar faces. And it was, after all, not a dinner but only a casual afternoon get together, where he could relax with that gin and tonic he had been looking forward to since the fourteenth hole.

Max had just passed by the mirror in the hall enroute to the bedroom when he saw the bluish shadow on his jaw. Damn! Immediately he turned around and retreated once more to the bathroom. There he picked up a razor and did what Elizabeth, in her diplomatic but very definite way, would certainly have suggested if he had shown that face to her when he came downstairs.

* * *

As forts go, it was one of the best yet. It wasn't so much a fort so much as a clubhouse; you could almost stand upright in it, and the diamond-patterned lattice all around except for the one small opening allowed you to look out, while no one outside could see much inside.

This warm Saturday afternoon Lex, Sy and Run were hanging out there, after getting some large cardboard boxes from behind the appliance store. They flattened them out and spread them over the bare ground. It was a cool, dry, airy place, still smelling like fresh wood, with only a few spiders so far. However, Run – her name used to be Runner, but it had been shortened up for a better nickname – had brought her bug box and caught most of them, including a handsome black and white spider none of them had ever seen before.

Each of them came with a pile of comic books to exchange, and Lex also had a brown paper bag full of blackballs. They were reading and sucking blackballs and occasionally taking them out of their mouths to compare how they turned different colours. The guys always spit out the little seed in the middle, but Run ate hers.

Sy was laughing loudly at something in his Donald Duck comic book when Lex suddenly turned to him and hissed, "Sshhh! Shut up!"

Through the latticework of the little house on the Stoddart's back lawn, they could see adults approaching, coming nearer. Clomp, clomp, clomp! Now they were going up the stairs. Then there were the sounds of banging and scraping as they settled their substantial bottoms on the padded benches and chairs right overhead.

Sy turned and looked with frightened staring eyes at the other kids. "We're trapped!" he exclaimed in a whisper.

And so they were. There was only one way out, through the little door, and someone was sure to see them if they made a run for it. Then the adults would know, and the little door with its little gate would be closed up, maybe padlocked, and that would be the end of their great new clubhouse. After a hushed discussion, they decided to stay. They had lots of comics and blackballs, and no one was in that much of a hurry to leave anyhow. Dinner was not for a couple hours at least.

Overhead, the adults were talking, but their words couldn't be heard clearly through the floor. They made a fuzzy soothing sound, rather like the buzzing of bees. After a minute or two, the children ignored them and returned to reading comic books and sucking blackballs; only now no one was speaking in anything except whispers.

It was a jolly group that first assembled in the Stoddart's house, and Max was enjoying himself more than he expected. These were the friends he and Elizabeth had had from their school days, and now he felt a sudden rush of affection for them as they all raised their glasses and clinked them together in a silly toast to the new gazebo.

"Gazebo – gesundheit! They might sound alike, but one's for a breeze and the other's for a sneeze, and this one is nothing to sneeze at! Here's to the new gazebo, pergola, summer house, by any name, it's a great place for a good drink!"proclaimed Al Dillon, while his wife Caroline, his best cheering section, laughed uproariously.

"Well, it's really been too long since we've seen all of you, and here I am lucky enough to see you twice in one day," Elizabeth said in her best gracious hostess manner.

"Yes, even if it wasn't the happiest occasion the first time," Lisa Stendall added. "But the funeral was well attended and the music was lovely. And didn't Rita look beautiful!"

"Better dead than alive," Gord Scott commented and Andrea, his wife, gave him a sharp warning look.

"They must have someone new at the Jenner funeral parlour," Caroline said. "My Mum says it's either closed coffin or ship her off to another funeral home before Lewis Smythe gets his hands on her and lays the makeup on with a trowel."

"Actually," Lisa said in a confidential tone, "I heard who did the work on Rita. It wasn't Lewis. It was Jasmine Holmes."

"What!?" exclaimed Andrea, amid a few gasps and surprised murmurs.

Max, who had been chatting with Neil Stendall about golf in an aimless sort of way, and who preferred, by a small margin, talking about golf to talking about funerals, suddenly started paying attention. Why was it that name kept coming up in every conversation whenever he met old friends?

What he did not understand, because he was only occasionally a part of their world, was the fascination that the odd situation over at the Latham house exerted on almost everyone else who had known the family since childhood.

"How can she do that?" he asked.

Two voices started up, but then Lisa's won out and she continued. "Jasmine used to do the mortuary makeup for her father when he owned the funeral home, and I heard that the nephew of the owner, Alistair MacGregor, who's working there, asked her to help with Rita. Evidently she didn't like any of the clothes or jewelry Stan Harding and his son brought over, so she made them take her back to the house. She was the one who picked out that lovely blue cocktail dress and draped a silk scarf around the neck. And her makeup for Rita was perfect; she looked like a queen!"

"Well," said Andrea, in a querulous, rather sour voice, "I just can't believe Jasmine Holmes is back working there! I for one wouldn't let them put her hands on me!"

"I wouldn't mind her putting her hands on me," Gord supplied after his wife's remark. "However, I'd like to be alive at the time. Though I think, even if I was a goner, I'd come back to life if she did. Parts of me, anyhow."

Down below, in the clubhouse, the kids heard a sudden rapid movement upstairs on the floorboards. It was the sound of feet being shuffled nervously by most of the women, and a few of the men, too. They were watching the expression on Andrea Scott's face, which glowered somewhat like a thundercloud loaded with incipient lightning bolts. Her husband saw it too, but ignored it. He just laughed his big, comfortable, fat man's laugh.

"A resurrection of sorts, you might say," he added, quirking his eyebrow mischievously at his wife, as he threw more fuel on a fire that would probably scorch him once they got home.

Then most of them laughed along with him, after which Caroline rushed in to fill a rather loud silence.

"I was talking to Martha Jenner, and she was saying that her husband was expecting Alistair to quit work weeks ago and head back home. But to use her words, now he's tearing his hair out because since he met Jasmine, Alistair's stopped all talk of quitting and he's driving Simon berserk! Martha was laughing when she told me about it; I think she finds it all rather amusing."

"Well, I expect he'll quit when she's gone, and that will probably be soon," Lisa contributed. "Emma told Edna Matthews that Lianne Latham is very poorly and not likely to last out the month. Jasmine's going back to Las Vegas afterward."

"Do you really believe – " Elizabeth asked hesitantly, "that story about Thomas Latham rescuing her when she tried to do herself in, to drown herself?"

Now Max sat up a little straighter. Elizabeth never did anything without a reason. If she had invited these people here, she must have some sort of an agenda, and if he paid attention, maybe he could figure out what it was. For example, why did she ask that question?

"Well –" Neil started off. "I don't think there's much doubt of it. The details check out, don't they Gord?" Gord rumbled his assent.

"You know we both used to be members of the rowing club, that is, when Gord could still get in a boat without swamping it," Neil said, and Gord, unembarrassed, chuckled right along with him.

"Well, the day after the rescue was supposed to have happened, I got word from Mitch McCrae that someone had damaged the clubhouse. So I went there to meet him, and he showed me how the old crossed oars we had put up as decoration on the side of the building had been ripped off. We found them easily enough, though; they were in the little red rowboat that belongs to the club, which was tied up to the dock at the end of the moorings. We just nailed them up again, no damage done."

"Don't forget about the shirt," Gord prompted.

"Oh yeah. When we went over to the boat to get the oars, there was a blue and white shirt on the shore near there, with a rock on it so it wouldn't blow away."

"Came the next day and got it," added Gord. "No use wasting a good shirt. Almost brand new and size large. Wouldn't fit me now."

"Wonder why he didn't come back for it?" Neil queried.

"Probably too busy," Gord said, grinning lecherously, "with his counseling and such."

"So," Elizabeth interjected, "do you know if there was actually any hanky-panky going on between them?"

When it was put that way, so baldly, without even a shadow of window-dressing, it took them all by surprise, Max especially. He thought it was an article of faith for Elizabeth that Jasmine and Thomas had a hot little affair going before she blew town.

Now all the faces around the gazebo, except for Max and Elizabeth's, looked rather sheepish.

Finally Lisa ventured, "it was Emily Barrett and Lorena Sykes who first spread the rumour, I guess. Both of them have a good view of the Madison house, and they said that Thomas was in and out of there on almost a daily basis while Emma and Bill were at work."

"Don't forget," Andrea broke in, "Suzanne McCrae happened across Jasmine and Thomas when they were between the shelves in the library. She said they were standing there with their fingertips touching, and from the expression on their faces they might as well have been in bed."

"Huh!" Caroline snorted. "I've seen the books she drops off at the library. Romance novels, every one of them! I'd be surprised if her imagination doesn't run wild after reading all those bodice-rippers!"

"Well," Elizabeth said, "isn't there anything else? Any real proof? It just seems so strange that Lianne would want her help when she's so sick."

There was an uncomfortable silence. Al Dillon cleared his throat.

"I can only speak for Thomas," he said. "You know I took early retirement a couple years ago. However, in all the time I was superintendent of schools, I never heard a thing said about him. Him with other women, that is. These opportunities come your way when you're a male teacher, especially when you're a good-looking bloke like Thomas, and on a pretty regular basis. But there's never been a hint or a whisper he's taken advantage of them, to my knowledge."

"So – you're saying that he was in and out of that house and just 'counseling' her after she tried to drown herself? He'd have to be a saint!" Gord's disbelief was obvious, and tinged with sarcasm.

All of a sudden Caroline Dillon set her glass down with a smack on the glass-topped table. Elizabeth was immediately glad she had thought to buy plastic glasses for use outside.

"I have a question. Why are we blackening the names of these people just because of what Emily and Lorena saw?" Caroline was indignant, looking around accusingly. "Some of us here – well, Lisa and I anyhow – have been in and out to see Lianne, and so have many of her other friends, up until lately, and it was obvious to anyone that she and Jasmine are on the best of terms. They were joking and laughing together – how likely would that be, if her husband and Jasmine –"

"And just lately, we've heard that Emily and Lorena remembered seeing Emma with Thomas and Jasmine outside. Thomas was helping them with some outdoors work!" Lisa broke in. "Here's another thing to think about: probably everyone here has heard that Emma said she approved of Thomas counseling Jasmine, after her suicide attempt. Do you honestly think someone like Emma Madison would put up with this kind of thing, an affair, going on in her house?" Lisa's round face had flushed bright pink.

Elizabeth held out her upturned hands. She spoke, as Max watched in fascination. "Thank you so much for filling me in on this. I've heard a little here, a little there, but there were still so many questions – I guess that everything had to be kept hush-hush, because Sylvia Holmes was in such a state that she wouldn't have been able to take the news that her daughter tried to commit suicide – and I understand that Thomas himself had been off work because of mental problems after his son was stillborn. And a suicide attempt; well, no one would ever want that noised around!"

Everyone was looking at her, spellbound. Where's she going with this, Max wondered.

"I am certainly feeling a great deal of sympathy for them, after what you've just told me," Elizabeth continued. "And considering what you said, about Lianne having such a good relationship with Jasmine, and Emma and her approval of the situation, well, I guess there's a strong possibility that the real story might be very different from the one everyone has been gossiping about for years."

"Hear, hear!" exclaimed Caroline. "That's what I've been telling Al, all along."

Everyone's head swiveled as they turned to look at Al. Why should he give a hoot, Max asked himself, and waited curiously for an answer.

Al made an impatient move with his shoulders; obviously he would have preferred not to be put on the spot. He sighed and shook his head, shooting his wife a testy look from under lowered brows.

"Well, as Caroline knows, I've had a letter on my desk for the past couple weeks from Royal Sutton Boys' School in Kellington. They're gathering references for Thomas Latham, because he's applied for the job of Vice Principal there."

"Oh dear," said Andrea, amid the murmurs of surprise, "our daughter won't be happy to hear that. Her twins are going to Medford High next year."

"Yes, yes," Al said dismissively, "he'll be a great loss to the school, but you can't hold a man back from advancing in his career unless there's good reason. And I have no qualms about recommending him on the basis of his work; he's a gifted teacher and an excellent administrator. He's been filling in the gaps at that school without the pay or recognition he deserves for years, but –"

"Mr. Bluestocking here didn't feel he could give a reference to someone who cheated on his wife," supplied Caroline. "Which means that a lot of men teachers would find their careers stalled, if that were ever made a qualification."

"Someone known to have cheated on his wife," Al corrected, and he gave Caroline another stern look. "See, it's not just a matter of propriety, it reflects on the individual's judgment. However, whether Thomas Latham was guilty of infidelity has certainly been called into question this afternoon. It appears there's a reasonable doubt. On that basis, I don't think I can hold back my recommendation."

At this moment Bessie appeared, lumbering cautiously across the lawn with the trays of appetizers. Lying underneath the gazebo, the children heard the stairs creak with the heft of her as she made her halting ascent. For a while the bee-buzzing sounds stopped as talking was replaced by eating.

Then Andrea Scott asked the question all of them, and especially Max, were probably thinking.

"What's your interest in this, Elizabeth? Is it because Jasmine was engaged to Mason, that you want to know?"

"Yes, Andrea, that is precisely the reason I'm interested."

Elizabeth drew herself up fully erect, looking for all the world, Max thought, like a queen on a throne with her subjects gathered around her.

"She was a lovely girl, and I'd hate to see her maligned. Max and I are sorry their marriage didn't take place, aren't we dear?'

Here Max nodded his head vigorously. They were in agreement on that. Mason, Elizabeth and he had all suffered varying degrees of misery because of that slip between cup and lip, although the reasons why, and the timing, were wildly different.

"And I'm sure she would have been a wonderful daughter-in-law."

Max looked around. Everyone's chin appeared to have dropped to the floor. The fact was, as all these people knew at the time, Elizabeth was horrified at Mason's choice of a bride. Oh, well, he thought, as she so often did, Elizabeth was re-writing history. He glanced at her. She had stood up, and what was that he saw in her eyes? Tears! She was on the verge of crying! Whatever had brought that on?

"I'm – I'm afraid it's getting a little chilly. I'm going in for a wrap. Perhaps, Max... you could take our guests to the side patio?"And Elizabeth abruptly departed.

As if on cue, a nasty cold little wind seemed to have sprung up, and all of a sudden, the summerhouse wasn't so summery, more wintry. The sun had found a cloud to hide behind, and the women, in their thin dresses, started to shiver.

Max organized the men to take the tubs of ice, liquor and mix to the side patio, and then shepherded them down the stairs and across the lawn. Caroline accompanied her husband with a tray of glasses. Lisa and Andrea stayed behind for a moment, collecting used plates and glasses on a tray for Bessie and capturing paper napkins before they took flight across the long green lawn.

Under the gazebo, the crisscrossed latticework was beginning to seem much like the bars of a prison for three children incarcerated for almost two hours. They had long since run out of blackballs, though not of reading material, but this diversion had lost its charm.

"Are they gone?" Run whispered to Lex, who was closest to the little door, the only exit. He leaned out. He couldn't see them, but he heard their voices.

"They're a couple of them still up there, and they're talking about your Mom!" he whispered excitedly to Run. Together, they both stuck their heads out to listen.

"Jasmine Holmes, Jasmine Holmes. I'm so sick of hearing that name," Caroline had just said, tiredly. "Isn't there something else we can talk about? But can you believe the change of heart for Elizabeth? Now she'd be happy to have her as a daughter-in-law! Wonders will never cease!"

"I don't care what they say about her, that woman is just a cheap hussy!" Andrea's voice was full of venom. "I'm glad she's leaving and going back to Sin City, because that's where she belongs! I wouldn't be surprised to learn she'd turned a trick or two!"

"Andrea!" Caroline exclaimed in shock, "so far as we know, she's a respectable woman with a child! And she may have worked in a casino, but she was also the assistant manager there. And she's done a good, very conscientious job taking care of Lianne Latham so why..."

Her voice trailed across the lawn, fainter and fainter as the two of them departed the gazebo for the sunny side patio of the Stoddart's house.

Like small animals emerging from a burrow, the children cautiously crawled out the little door. "What does that mean, turn a trick?" Lex asked Run.

"I don't know," she said. But she was pretty sure it was something mean, like the other things that lady had said. She was struggling to get her bug box through the little door. Sy gave her a hand. When Run stood up, she could see the woman, the mean one that had said bad things about her Mom, going across to her car. As she watched, the woman took a sweater out of the front seat, shut the car door, turned around and went back to the house.

Lex quickly ran for cover in the bushes. But he was still curious. When he got back home, he asked their housekeeper, Mrs. Vickers, what it meant.

Mrs. Vickers was soft and cushiony, inside and out. She was always smiling. This alone would have made her an oddity amongst their seven housekeepers, none of whom had lasted as long as she. Mrs. Vickers would stay. She had fallen in love with the Fitzgerald children and instinctively they knew it, turning to her for all they had been lacking like sunflowers toward a warm summer sun. When they grew up, they would visit her regularly, at least more often than their father and his shrewish new second wife, always assured of a warm welcome and bountiful food and affection.

But now, as she put her soft, warm arm around Alex and looked down at him, she wasn't smiling. "Who said that, dear, and who were they talking about?"

Jasmine Holmes, or Carlisle. Mrs. Vickers had heard her story and was more inclined to sympathy than judgment. And of course, the speaker of those words would have to be that homely little woman, Andrea Scott, whom nobody in town wanted to work for because she was so fussy and cheap. Well, beauty was ever a lightning rod for spite by those less favored by nature, she philosophized.

"It means," she said rather vaguely, "to do acrobatic things – handstands and cartwheels and the like."

"Wow!" Lex, impressed, had new respect for Run's Mom, whom he had liked well enough already.

Standing in the bushes near the Stoddart's gazebo, Run did not have to ask what that expression meant. She sensed from what the other lady said that it was something unpleasant and not nice. That made her mad. Her Mom was the best Mom ever. Now she tried the handle of the car door that the mean woman had opened just a few minutes ago to get her sweater. It was unlocked. She opened it, and dumped the assorted spiders, sow bugs, beetles and centipedes from her bug box onto the front passenger seat. She was going to get rid of them anyhow, to make way for the grasshoppers starting to show up in Simon's dad's garden. Then she closed the door quick, before they could run away.

Before that, though, she carefully wrapped up the extra special black and white spider in a tissue, and now she put it back in the empty box. That evening Thomas helped her identify it. It was a Zebra jumping spider. They let it go afterward, but to Laura's great disappointment, it didn't jump but only scuttled along on its spidery way.

In the study, in the dimming light of the sun as it sank down into the trees, Max Stoddart sat and pondered the gazebo cocktail party. He wondered: what that was all about? Though now he knew for sure: Elizabeth truly was upset about something. Whatever it was, it had to do with Mason and Jasmine, and she didn't want to discuss it with him. To see her almost on the verge of tears, in front of all those people – it was startling. Earth-shaking for him, watching her, the mistress of self-control, in such a state.

If only she would talk about what was bothering her, it might help. She did not know, he thought, how much he loved her. She could say anything to him. It didn't matter how bad it was, it made no difference; he still would love her just the same. He would tell her that.

And when he found her in her dressing room an hour later, he did. And she cried again, a little, and they held each other tight. But when he asked, she said yes, she would tell him sometime, but not right now. And he had to be content with that.

At five thirty that Saturday evening, Emma received a phone call from Caroline Dillon, who was overflowing with gossip from the gazebo cocktail party. Once Caroline told her what had happened at the Stoddarts, Emma knew immediately what Elizabeth was up to.

She did not share her thoughts with Caroline who, although a decade her junior, was a close friend and one of her preferred bridge partners. It would do their friendship no good if she were to tell Caroline that she had been used as an emissary, a messenger, because that is what she was. And so was Lisa Stendall, who dropped by the house around seven o'clock while walking her old golden retriever, Boney. She had said she didn't have time to come in, but then kept her standing on the front steps for half an hour while she talked to her about what happened at the party.

A cocktail party for old friends: what a clever pretext! Elizabeth, that subtle woman, never did anything without a reason and this was all about Mason. By trying to repair Jasmine's reputation that she once helped to destroy, and by expressing her regret, perhaps she hoped to re-open for her son the door that Jasmine now had closed. Caroline and Lisa were the unwitting accomplices bearing her message to Emma, and through her to its intended recipient, Jasmine.

Yes, that was how Emma saw it, and that was where it was going to end. She refused to be a messenger for Elizabeth Stoddart. She would not tell Jasmine about the conversation that took place in the gazebo on Saturday afternoon. If Elizabeth had something to say to Jasmine, then she could pluck up the courage to say it to her face.

There was only one thing that puzzled Emma: the tears. They were very un-Elizabeth. But perhaps they were just for effect. She wouldn't put it past her.

* * *

The luminous hands on the clock that sat on the bedside table in the Stoddarts' master suite read two a.m. Elizabeth Stoddart was watching the minutes ticking slowly away, after waking from a short, unsatisfactory sleep. The tears she shed as she lay beside her sleeping husband rolled quietly down her face to sink into the wet pillow.

She had hoped to feel better after the cocktail party. Now, however, she could see just how feeble an attempt it was. Although what she had said in their gathering was sure to be widely repeated. At least it was something, she thought, and doing something was better than nothing.

There was a message she hoped would reach Jasmine, if she heard about the party. The message was one that only she would understand. It was that she was sorry. She was trying to make some kind of reparation, however small. Although there would never be a way to make up for what she had done. To her. To him. Oh Lord, and there was no one she could ever talk to about it.

Elizabeth had fallen into her pit of shame, the one she had dreaded for so long. The only difference was that nobody knew she was in there, and no one could help her to get out.

CHAPTER 83

Freedom felt odd to Jasmine, whose life in Medford seemed always circumscribed by work, childcare and helping Emma around the house. Such freedom as she had enjoyed to date was limited to short, solitary walks. So it was only natural that when she had this luxurious span of time, five hours alone all to herself, she might set out for a long walk, especially as this had turned out to be such a fine day. The bad weather forecast for the weekend had considerately condensed into torrents of rain on Friday and Saturday night, then blown away each morning to leave the sky shiny clean with only a few cloud streamers.

When she told Emma about Thomas's request to take the child fishing on Sunday, Emma had insisted that she, not Jasmine, would stay with Lianne during his absence. "You're going to be there Monday morning when Thomas leaves at five-thirty," she said. "You need a break, and I'm happy to have the chance to visit with Lianne."

Nothing formal had been arranged between Thomas and her regarding Laura. Perhaps it was best just to let things evolve, as they had on Thursday, when he surprised her by asking if he could spend time with the child on Sunday. He had put the kitchen counter between them when he made his request. Whenever he spoke to her now it was never standing opposite one another; he always seemed to position himself behind a table, a counter, a sofa. She had sensed it, the energy, an erotic current, passing between them. It seemed more troublesome to him than her, but barriers were perhaps a prudent measure.

There must be no trips downtown for ice cream or public outings, she had warned him. Why, he had asked curiously, and then she told him what Emma said. It seemed that even the few times he had taken Laura for an after-dinner ice cream had resulted in gossip flaring up about their relationship and the child's paternity. Best not to fuel that kind of speculation, Emma warned her.

So they would go fishing, and when the child asked if her friend Sy could come along, Jasmine thought that was an excellent idea. Once church was over Thomas had picked up two very excited children in his car. Then Jasmine locked the house and set out on her walk, with only a half-formed purpose in mind.

One last part of Anna's and her plan remained, the most critical one. It all depended on happenstance, and in truth Jasmine had little hope of seeing it completed today. If the weather continued fair, Royce would close the gates of the estate and go home around two o'clock for an early dinner, Anna told her. But since it was only twelve and her path led her in that direction anyway, perhaps she would check. Now, as she walked past the fine old Georgian homes so beautifully maintained and landscaped, their windows glinting in the sun, she saw the White house looming up in the distance with its eavestrough still dangling precariously over the front door.

Anna was in a state – so much so that Jasmine feared for her safety and, in her cousin's murderous mood, even Royce's. Royce would be home for Sunday dinner, Anna told her, and she had writhed on the front seat of the car as Jasmine drove her to the hospital a few nights ago. How would she stop herself from throwing scalding soup on him? Poisoning his pie? She was not a good enough actress to pretend she didn't want to kill him, she declared, and underwrote that statement with hot tears of anger as she muttered about sharpening up the kitchen knives and pushing him down the basement stairs.

Unless it could be made to look like an accident, sudden death was not part of the plan, Jasmine counseled her. Now, though, she idly thought about what might befall Royce during his work, nursing scanty hopes for lightning strikes and falling trees.

As she approached the Whites' house she saw, sitting on the front porch steps with beers in hand and apparently not a care in the world whilst their home tumbled down around their ears, Mr. White Senior and what appeared to be his eldest child, a burly young man of about eighteen. Jasmine knew she was wearing nothing that could have inspired the unwanted, leering looks they gave her as she walked rapidly by. White Senior had a heavy, pugnacious face and was powerfully built, a threatening presence. Jasmine noted that the children were giving him and their brother a wide berth during their play. Including the son on the porch and a baby who was likely somewhere inside the house, Jasmine counted six. Where were the other three children?

She was walking along the sidewalk and almost past the little waterfront park near the Airdrie Estate when the answer to that question appeared. The small wooden door beside the large wrought-iron entry gates opened and Ariadne and her little brother abruptly popped out, both at the same time, rather as if they had been given a push to the backside. As they came walking toward her hand-in-hand, Jasmine slowed down to take a better look at them: two beautiful wee tots with flaxen hair, looking for all the world like Hansel and Gretel just stepped from a fairytale book. She smiled at them and was rewarded with shy dimpled smiles as they approached.

"Where's Gussie?" she asked Ariadne. The question slipped out unconsciously; she did not even think before asking it.

In a sweet, babyish voice, the little girl lisped an answer. "Theeth helping Royth."

Then they were past her, and Jasmine stood immobile, her heart racing and near breathless at this unexpected turn of events. For Anna had told her that even if he was on duty at the estate over the weekend, Royce never worked on Sundays. That was his day off, he had told her, and other than being there, he had the right to do whatever he wanted. Today, it seemed, his plans included Gussie.

Had he locked the door behind the children? Jasmine would pretend she had come to buy eggs. She walked boldly up to the small gate and turned the handle. It was locked. There was no point in trying the large gate; it was heavily padlocked. So now, since she could not do her pretend errand, it was logical for her to retrace her steps. All this was for the benefit of the two men on the front porch, whom she could see were still watching her. She did not want to go into the park while they were there. However, it seemed she had no alternative because she had to hurry.

A loud voice boomed out, and although the words were indistinct, from the tone it sounded like a command. She looked to see Mrs. Pagett filling the doorway in the front entrance, hands on hips. Slowly the two men rose from their perch on the steps, and the children stopped their play to file into the house after them.

Lunchtime! "Bless you Mrs. Pagett!" Jasmine panted, hurrying across the sandy beach to the outcrop of brush and loping into the little stand of trees. She spied her makeshift tree ladder still leaning undisturbed against the wall and scaled it rapidly, stopping when her head neared the top of the wall; then inching up cautiously until she could just peer over the edge. The enormous basswood tree behind her extended its limbs out over the wall to create a sunlight-dappled screen of leaves. Through them, Jasmine could see the sunny front portion of the garden nearest the house, with its stone patio and a large, cushioned wood bench that stood in partial shade.

They could be anywhere. In the Airdrie house, in one of the gardens. But Jasmine was betting on the added privacy afforded by the gatehouse garden, with its tall fence and latched gate. Now she was certain she had made a mistake. The minutes crawled by. Under the ivy that covered the old stone wall, so did its many insect inhabitants including, to Jasmine's discomfort, a colony of large black ants that had a nest somewhere in its fissures.

The sun shone, a small breeze struck up. Were they already in the gatehouse, a place she had toured once in her childhood, dark and dreary with too few windows to admit the light? She was about to abandon her post when she heard the metallic snick of the latch. The gate swung open. Gussie came into the garden, followed by Royce. They did not speak. The girl stood there, limp as a rag doll, her hands hanging by her side, head down, looking at the ground. He took her by the forearm and led her to the garden bench.

The old basswood tree was covered with small yellow flowers that gave off a delicious, honey-soaked scent. Bees, dozens of them, meandered through the large, dark green leaves, drunk on nectar, the air filled with the sound of their gentle humming.

Although the perfume wafting to her on the breeze was aromatic and sweet, Jasmine would forever more find it distasteful, disgusting even. It would bring to mind too vividly what she saw on that lovely sunny day in late spring when she peered over the old stone wall. She saw the theft of childhood, the defilement of innocence. She saw what the grown man did to the nine-year-old child on the bench and had to control the desire to gag, so great was her revulsion. It went on too long. Finally, he stood up. So did the girl, and she tried to turn away, back to the gate. He took hold of her shoulders and pushed her in front of him, toward the back door of the house. She gave a little, despairing sound, like the bleat of a lamb.

Suddenly, Royce stopped. He turned, then slowly surveyed the wall. Jasmine felt her hair prickle in fright. His feral instincts had alerted him; he had sensed her presence. But after a moment's hesitation, he seemed to decide that whatever he saw was only some trick of shade or shadow. The wind blew, leaves obscured her view. Once she could see again, they had disappeared inside.

She could have screamed; she so badly wanted to! She could call the police. But as Jasmine weighed the consequence of these acts she faltered. Either one would unleash a tidal wave of misery to engulf two families, and perhaps destroy the young victim herself. A decision must be made; but it was not hers to make.

Dots swam in front of her eyes and her legs shook as she descended. On the ground, Jasmine found that she was, in fact, shaking all over and cold, chilled through. Near where the beach began, she found a large stump that had washed up on the sand and sat there shivering, her back to it as a shield from the wind. The sun warmed her a little, but now the lake was starting to seethe, slapping itself into waves as the wind grew stronger. She was feeling faint; she needed to go home. When she got there, finally, a great cloud of tiredness descended on her; she could barely drag herself upstairs to bed. And that is where Emma found her, when she returned home with Laura late that Sunday afternoon.

CHAPTER 84

It was like a black stain on her mind, spreading to push aside other, more wholesome thoughts, and Jasmine had to constantly remind herself that she was only the observer and not the victim. Gussie, her mental state and how she could pass her hours at home and school carrying her dreadful secret could not be imagined. Now, however, with the knowledge she had gained, Jasmine was charged to act on behalf of that child, the sad little victim. It was an urgent, pressing burden that gathered weight from the thought that it could have been her own daughter, and questions of whom else he was preying on, and who might be next.

The problem, as they discovered over the next two hours, was that no one really had any idea of what to do.

Margery had joined their group. They sat there, the four of them, in the dim lamplight of the living room late that evening while the tea cooled in their cups and the cookies on the plate were left uneaten. One thing they were agreed on: Royce must lose his job. As Anna told them, he put great value on his job, declaring it was the best he had ever had: healthy outdoors work with lots of independence. The reasons must now include that it provided the perfect trap for unwary children.

Anna would immediately confront Royce with his abuse of their daughter and tell him he could no longer come to the house or be with the children alone. To afford some protection to Gussie, she would tell

Royce she knew that he was employing a young girl to help with gardening, and threaten to visit the child's parents to warn them unless he immediately dispensed with her help. She would pursue an annulment, or if that were not possible, a divorce. In either case, she would lose the house and likely have to rent. But as she said, no matter which direction affairs took, there were hard years ahead for her and her little family.

And all must be kept secret. If she wished to remain in the town where her employment was and all her family lived, if her children were to grow up untouched by scandal, no word of what Royce had done could be allowed to leak out.

However, their discussion about what they should do about Royce in the long term, and poor Gussie White and her blissfully ignorant family in the shorter term, produced no answers, only more questions.

"I'm going to get in touch with George Chappell and ask him to come and talk to us about how we might proceed," Emma said authoritatively.

"Oh no, you're not!" Margery burst forth. "No lawyers will be brought into this! Any solution George suggests will be a legal one; it'll be the Whites pressing charges, then a court trial, a jail sentence if we're lucky and then in a couple of years he'll be out and back in town again! How long do you think we can keep any of that quiet? And how likely is it the Whites would let their child be examined and testify? And who has the money for lawyers anyhow – you, Emma? No: no police, and no lawyers!"

"Well, what would you propose, then, Margery?" Emma asked stiffly. She was not used to being contradicted.

"Jasmine should tell Mr. White what she knows and let him deal with it!" Margery practically bounced on the sofa with impetuous enthusiasm for her own idea. "Maybe he'll take Royce out to his gravel pit and dig a spot for him!"

"That's a wild card you'd be playing, handing that information over to the Whites." Jasmine scowled and waved a hand in dismissal. "How do you know what they'll do? They could just call in the police and press charges; they won't care if Anna and her family are dragged through the mud with Royce. And White Senior doesn't look like the sort to think things through: he might beat up Royce, and then the truth would be sure to come out!"

The arguments raged back and forth until the clock on the mantel struck ten, when they finally agreed on one thing: they couldn't come to an agreement. The problem of what to do about Royce was so ringed around with concerns about keeping things quiet while, at the same time, stopping him from preying upon children – two seemingly incompatible goals – that when they finished, they had made just the one decision: he must lose his job as soon as possible.

"Margery, do you still have your connection with Charlotte Airdrie?" Emma asked.

"Heavens no! That was forty years ago. After we were at St. Margaret's together, she went to a private boarding school for high school, and she's been married and living in North Carolina for years!"

"How about writing a letter?" Jasmine suggested.

"Royce handles the mail for the family home." Anna looked at her watch as she answered. "They have other homes, and people who take care of the mail. I don't know the addresses, except for the office address. It might take some time for an answer."

"I will go and see the Airdries if they're there on the weekend," Emma pronounced.

Jasmine shook her head. "It's better that I should go, Emma. Thank you for offering, but I'm the one who has the details, and the daughter, and can tell them first-hand what their gardener is doing. Now I'm leaving to take Anna to the hospital; she's starting earlier tonight and I have a five o'clock wakeup tomorrow."

She was on her feet, but Anna still sat. "Wait." She was white and drawn, and intensely serious. "There's one more thing I must say. I need to warn you about Royce. Royce is big and strong, and he's good with his fists. Don't think, though, that he's stupid! He's violent and he's dangerous. Remember that!"

They watched Anna and Jasmine leave. Then Emma turned to Margery with a grim face. "You'll be there with Anna when she tells Royce he can't stay at the house anymore?"

"Yes, and I can tell you I'm not looking forward to it. Where's he going to go once he loses his job? She'll not have an easy time getting rid of him, that's for sure," Margery replied, and for once she sat there in uncharacteristic silence.

They were both lost in thought for a long moment. Then Margery stirred herself.

"Some say it's an illness," she ventured.

"Faugh! He's just had his fill of grown women and now he needs a child in order to get himself excited! Don't you dare dignify it by calling it an illness, it's a disgusting perversion!"

"That child – I wish I could, but I can't stop thinking about her. Only nine years old, a year younger than our Mary."

"Yes! He hasn't just broken man's law, he's broken God's law and ruined a life!" Emma spoke with all the brimstone fire and fury of a circuit preacher. "He's destroyed sacred innocence and childhood! And here we are, stuck with having to protect him for the sake of his family. He should go to jail!"

Margery looked at her, gimlet eyed. She spat out the words. "No. He should go straight to hell!"

A rather macabre cackle burst from Emma, and for the first and only time this evening she smiled. "That, Margery," she said, "would appear to be the only real solution."

Then, their venom spent and a sense of futility settling over them, they went to the kitchen and waited there more or less quietly until Jasmine returned with the car and Emma could drive Margery home.

CHAPTER 85

Jasmine was curled up on the little cot that had been placed close to Lianne's bed. She wondered how it could accommodate Thomas's large frame. His feet would certainly hang off the end. In spite of Lianne's protests, he said he couldn't sleep in the bedroom across the hall without lying awake worrying about whether she might need him during the night. Especially now that she was so weak that she could barely lift the little silver bell to ring for him if she did.

Since he was no longer avoiding her, Thomas and she were often in Lianne's room at the same time. Watching, she could see at first hand their love and devotion, which glowed all the more brightly for being set against the darkness that had overtaken them. It also became evident to Jasmine that Lianne's fears about Thomas were well grounded. Their attachment was so deep that their separation was bound to be in equal parts as painful.

It was six o'clock and the light in late spring came early. It had been dawn when Thomas had set off on the long drive to Kellington. She gave him the sandwich she made for him the night before, an apple and some of Emma's cookies in a brown paper bag. "You'll not want to have your stomach rumble during the interview," she said.

His mouth turned up at the ends in the way she knew so well, with the little curlicues at the edges. He looked at her for a long moment with his deep blue gaze. "Wish me luck," he said, and she did, and he left.

There was something still lingering in the air where he had stood. She thought it might be the good luck kiss they both had wanted, but feared to exchange.

Now she made her own breakfast. Lianne would not wake up until later and when she did, Jasmine had made something for her too. It was her mother's old recipe for rice pudding; delicious and so digestible a baby could eat it. Once she discovered Lianne awake and had changed her and made her comfortable, she warmed the rice pudding. Then she put it in a lovely pink-flowered porcelain bowl with a little cream, and taking a sterling silver spoon from the set that had belonged to Lianne's mother, placed it with the bowl on a starched white placemat on a tray. In the sideboard, she found a pink serviette. With Lianne, the inveterate decorator, Jasmine had found that presentation was half the battle in getting her to eat.

The aroma alone would have enticed Jasmine, if she had not already had her breakfast. Now, as she put it in front of her, on the little bed tray on legs, Lianne sniffed appreciatively. "It does smell good, doesn't it? I'll take a spoonful, I think."

"It's full of nourishment, so you can be all bright-eyed when Thomas comes back," Jasmine encouraged, as she filled the spoon and lifted it to her lips. Lianne was smiling as she swallowed. But after only a moment it came right back up again, that spoonful, and when it splashed down into the pink and white bowl there was a large, bright red blossom of blood in the centre.

They both stared at it. Lianne spoke first. "Doctor Sheridan said something like this might happen," she said calmly. Then, more cheerfully, "it won't be long now!"

Jasmine was aghast, both at the sight of the blood and at Lianne.

"You said that just exactly as if you're waiting for a bus! How can you say it like that!" She could feel tears pricking at her eyes, and she blinked furiously. "That's your blood!"

Slowly, Lianne turned her head on the pillow. "Jasmine, I'm so tired," she whispered, exhaling that last word and filling it with all the heaviness of her fatigue. "You've had a baby; well, this is like that. Except it's me that's coming out the other end. And it's been too long. I want it over."

"You're in pain, aren't you?" Jasmine was finding the red spot in the rice pudding too distressful. She took the tray away. Now she stood over her, glowering. "Why won't you take your pills? It's utter nonsense, this idea you have about suffering for other people!" She wiped away a furious tear with the back of her hand. "You're not Jesus! At least he knew who he was suffering for! I want you to take your medication!" She grabbed the pill case beside the bed and shook it so it rattled. "I checked, and between Emma and Thomas, you've managed to stay off your pills for a whole twenty-four hours!"

Lianne smiled faintly. This little flurry of temper, she knew, was from Jasmine's upset at the sight of her blood. "If I take the pills, I sleep," she said patiently. "You know that. As much as I can, I want to be awake. But about Jesus. Could you please call Father McLaughlin? Ask if he can come give me the last rites."

"Again? You had them just last week!"

"It gives me comfort. He said I could call him any time. He doesn't mind."

"I see. So. It's sort of like fire insurance. Double indemnity fire insurance,"

Now Lianne was smiling more broadly. "No. You're thinking of confession for that. But if you could, tell him I'd like to go to confession too."

"Confession! Lying in that bed there, what have you got to confess?"

"A few things. Well, I tricked you. Yes. Tricked you into telling me Thomas is Laura's father. Then I broke my promise. I promised you I would tell Tom your conditions and I never did."

"That's all?" Jasmine was incredulous. "I've forgiven you for both those things, so you don't need to go to confession. But if you do, then how about I give you some of my sins? Some walloping big ones, to make it worth his while coming here?"

Lianne giggled, her eyes brightening with mischief. "Oh, my goodness. Can you imagine if I told Father McLaughlin some really spicy sins! Wouldn't you just love to see his face?'

Then they both were laughing, picturing him, with his cherubic moon face and earnest expression, listening to the racy confession of someone he had previously pegged as close to a saint.

Jasmine had sat back down on the chair near the bed. Now Lianne reached for her hand. She enclosed it in both of hers. "Thank you, dear friend," she said. "You've made being sick almost fun."

Jasmine placed her other hand on top, and for a long moment they looked deep into each other's eyes, smiling. There was no need for words.

Into every life come times one remembers with perfect clarity, some full of grace and blessedness. For Jasmine, this was such a moment. Birds were singing outside the window of the room where she sat in the small blue chair, at the bedside of the woman who had become her friend. The spring sunlight streamed in pure and bright, a golden aura surrounding them.

She did not realize then that this was the last of their times together. If she had, she might have said more, she thought. But perhaps what they were saying without speaking, the love and affection they saw reflected in one another's eyes, was enough. In any case, that was all there was.

Jasmine unclasped their joined hands and stood up. She smoothed Lianne's hair and took away her tray and the bowl with the bright red blotch of blood. But not until she had made her take one of her pills.

That evening when Thomas came home, he was exuberant. The interview had gone extremely well; the selection committee was in agreement with much he had to say. They had kept him there over lunch and for several hours afterward, to tour the facilities and drop in on classes, and they had promised to provide him with answers to some of the questions he had asked for which they did not have information. Because they were not the only ones who were choosing, he added; he had been approached several weeks before by another large private school in the city.

All this he shared with Jasmine before dashing up the stairs to tell Lianne. When he came down, he seemed subdued.

"How was she today?" he asked, his usual question, except that now there was an undercurrent of apprehension in the way he said it.

"She can't keep food down anymore. She's not able to eat." Jasmine saw no point in telling him about the blood. She would come early and tell him tomorrow morning.

It made her sad to see the joy and exhilaration drain out of his face.

CHAPTER 86

On Tuesday morning, minutes after Laura left for school and well after Jasmine had gone to the Lathams', the phone rang shrilly. Emma was still not used to the noise, so loud and startling compared to the low-pitched tones of the old party line.

"What is it, Margery?" she asked rather impatiently, for her cousin was babbling the moment she picked up the phone and she hadn't caught the thread of what she was saying.

"I said that last night I had a dream, and when I woke up this morning, I remembered! Charlotte Airdrie and I were best friends one summer when we were nine or ten. It was very hot and we went swimming almost every day, sometimes more than twice a day!"

Emma was used to the intricacies of Margery's explanations. "Oh? So what happened?'

"Well, as I said, we went back and forth to the park to swim, but we didn't have to go out the front gate to get there."

"Did you pole-vault over the wall?'

"What? No, of course not, don't be silly. There was a gate. There is a gate, in the wall facing the park, the one that runs down to the lake."

"Really?" Now Emma paused her dishtowel and started to pay attention. "I don't remember seeing anything of the kind."

"It should still be there, unless they bricked it in. But if it is, there's ivy growing over it. The reason I'm phoning is, do you want to go take a look?"

Emma glanced out the window. It was a beautiful morning, promising a fine day. She wasn't adverse to a little expedition. It might be fun.

"Alright. Yes, it would be a good idea if we could find another way in and out. An escape hatch, if ever it's needed. And I wouldn't mind a trip to the beach. Are you free this afternoon?"

* * *

The back gardens were wet with dew as Jasmine hurried to work. She had expected to find Thomas home and, having spared him a sleepless night, to tell him about the blood in the rice pudding, and her suspicions, and the doctor's visit. But early as she was, he had already left. There was a note on the kitchen counter, scribbled in his dashing handwriting.

He said nothing in it that would imply judgment, but from Emma's many sources of gossip she was well aware of developments at Medford High. Simms had not found another physics teacher to take Thomas's place, so he still had half his teaching duties in addition to those of vice principal. In the meantime, Simms was taking full advantage of Thomas's seemingly boundless energy and treating him like a workhorse, for his own relief. There had been no consideration, it seemed, for his wife's illness.

"Too much work. Had to leave early. Lianne awake this a.m., seems OK."

He had left without the lunch she packed for him yesterday. Now, most of the time, he ate at his desk. With some angry satisfaction, she thought there was a good chance he would need to return before lunch, leaving all his afternoon duties to the school principal.

Dr. Sheridan had been called. Too busy to come yesterday, he was promised for this morning. Now Jasmine went rapidly up the stairs and found Lianne dozing, propped up on her pillows. She did not awake or react when Jasmine lifted up her wrist to check the pulse.

It was a thin, weak and irregular thread of a pulse, and Jasmine felt the skin around her temples prickle with the fright of it. What if she passed away while Thomas was at work? Jasmine had never been a ditherer, but now she dithered: should she call the school? Or should she wait for the doctor to confirm her suspicion that inside, Lianne was bleeding out?

She had just picked up the phone to call Thomas when the front doorbell rang. After a quick briefing, Dr. Sheridan hurried up the stairs. Busy with his stethoscope, feeling her pulse, he did not look at Lianne's face until he finished, when he saw her peering at him through half-closed eyes.

"Hello Lianne," he said. "Feeling any pain?"

She moved her head a little back and forth, no, and gave him her sweet, Madonna-like smile. He took both her hands in his and felt a weak pressure in return.

"Goodbye, dear," he said. "It's been a long journey. You've been very brave."

"Goodbye," she mouthed, the faintest of sounds emerging as she struggled to speak.

And then Jasmine knew, watching him, his downcast face and the way he bit his lip as he turned away, that he had never lost interest in Lianne as she thought. He was only protecting himself, as he must, from the worst of the aches and pains of his profession.

In the front hall downstairs, they looked unsmilingly at one another. As usual, the doctor did not waste words. "Internal bleeding, judging from all the signs," he said. "It's not a bad way to die. There's little pain, and her heart will just stop."

"So should I call her husband to come home?" Jasmine asked anxiously.

"Yes, yes, as soon as possible. It's hard to say how long it will be, but not long. However long it is, much too soon for one so young."

He picked up his bag and let himself out the front door, because Jasmine had excused herself to rush to the phone. An eternity later, or so it seemed, she heard Thomas taking the stairs two at a time, and then he burst into the bedroom.

"Angel!" he cried, and gathered his wife in his arms.

Lianne was beyond words now. Her attempts to talk were futile; only her eyes and face expressed what she felt. Jasmine made her excuses to leave them alone. But as she went toward the door, she saw the head on the pillow turn and those dark eyes follow her with a silent plea. So did Thomas, who beckoned her, and she returned to bedside for one last moment with Lianne.

She placed her warm hands around Lianne's cold face. With the perfect understanding between them, few words were needed.

"Oh, Lianne. Dearest friend," is all she said. She did not, would not, say goodbye; would not let herself cry, and that was all she could manage without crying.

They gazed at one another in a silence too full of love and feeling to allow room for speech. Then Jasmine kissed Lianne's forehead and left her to Thomas, for whatever time remained to her now belonged to him.

Sitting downstairs in the sunroom with all her thoughts in the room above, she felt a total suspension of being as she waited out the next hour, watching the sun move slowly through the verdant jungle of plants that lived in that space, and the shadows that waxed and waned in the garden beyond. She had some acquaintance with prayer and, for a short while, renewed it. Then she went up the stairs to the bedroom.

"She's unconscious now," Thomas said, and shook his head, no, when she asked if she could bring him anything to drink. He was lying on the bed, holding Lianne in his arms.

The time crawled by, inching toward noon. Dickie, in his cage, hopped restlessly about. He was missing his routine, which included a daily morning visit with Lianne, and he moped in a corner when she offered him a finger. Jasmine took the sandwich out of Thomas's lunch bag, thinking to give it to him, then stopped. If he felt the same as she, there was no need for it.

She wandered the rooms; so used to constant activity, she could no longer passively wait. Next she searched the drawers and found some sheets of ruled paper. Then she sat and began to write a list of all that must be done, once the inevitable took place. It was only what Lianne, so everlastingly practical, would have wanted her to do.

The first tear came. It fell on the paper, a circular blur on the straight blue lines.

CHAPTER 87

When Emma stopped the car in front of the MacClure's house, Margery came out twirling a Chinese parasol. How had she ever preserved it from the depredations of the grandchildren, Emma wondered? It was an old one that had belonged to her mother, fashioned of red flowered rice paper with a bamboo frame and handle.

"To preserve my lovely complexion," she simpered comically, as she collapsed it and maneuvered her sizeable bottom onto the seat of the car.

"What in the world have you got in there?" She prodded the large black handbag that sat on the seat in between them.

"Oh, a little of this and that," Emma replied enigmatically. She turned the car around and drove toward Lake Street and the park. "I just had a call from Jasmine. Lianne is on her way out."

"Oh, that's sad!"

"Yes, but it seems she's taking her time. Still breathing, and when I get back I'll go over and relieve Jasmine so she can be there when Laura comes home from school. Jasmine and I will be busy enough soon after that with the funeral preparations – the poor man has no family around. Can I count on you to help?"

"Of course I will. I loved that girl. But how about Thomas's sisters? His mother?"

"They're both out in British Columbia with their families. His mother is too frail to travel. We'll probably see the sisters, but likely they'll just come for the funeral and then go home."

"But not until they've gone through Lianne's things and taken their pick, I'll wager!"

"Oh Margery!" Emma exclaimed in a shocked voice, "you always think the worst of everyone! I doubt they'll do that!"

"Bet!" Margery replied. "Let's make a bet! I bet you five dollars they do!"

Emma agreed. The conversation then changed to other subjects, too many for a short car ride, and she nearly drove past the park, they were so busy catching up to all that had happened since they last saw each other, three whole days ago.

The lake was smiling, a calm and sunny blue. They walked along the little sand beach until Margery led the way into the trees. This space was densely populated by basswood and poplar, and interlaced with the narrow paths made by children and animals. A little further inland, large oak trees spread their branches overhead.

"The door was located just behind the dock." Margery began to trail her hand along the wall, lifting up the ivy. "We can probably start looking here."

In short order they located it, completely overgrown by ivy and immovable, held in place by the iron grip of the gnarled old vines.

"Well, I didn't hold out great hopes." Margery shrugged. She tugged at one of the vines half-heartedly. "Let's go."

In response, Emma went over to the handbag she had left at the foot of a poplar tree and took out a folding hand saw, a pair of pruning shears and a large knife. "I didn't come all this way just to give up just because of a few vines," she said, and handed the shears to Margery, whose expression clearly indicated her lack of enthusiasm for this sort of work.

"Oh Emma!" she sighed, in a tone halfway between exasperation and admiration. "Won't you ever forget you used to be a girl guide? This is just too hard a job for us old ladies!"

But in the end, it wasn't. Once they set to, the ivy, not overly strong after its winter combat with the elements so close to the lake, gave up the fight rather easily. Then Emma fitted the blade of the saw into the gap between the wall and door and laboriously cut through the vines holding the door on the other side, until she came across something hard and unyielding.

"I've probably found the latch," she said. "But I think it might be padlocked."

Margery, however, had gained steam as she went along and now was eager to try her hand. "Where's that knife?"

With considerable effort she pried and pushed from underneath the latch until, with a rusty squeak, it gave way. The door opened a good two inches. However, it was still held fast by the ivy across the top, too high for Emma to reach.

"Put your shoulder to it, Emma!" she instructed. Then, on the count of three, the two of them pushed as one, and the door yielded another few inches. On the next push, with a loud squawk from its rusted hinges, the door opened a good two feet. That was space enough. They declared success in hushed tones, for peering through the door and looking beyond, they could see the expansive lawns of the estate and on the far side, bent over working in one of the gardens, Royce Parke.

Once they set everything to rights again, a day that had seemed a little chilly when they first arrived had suddenly turned too hot. With flushed faces and brows covered in perspiration, they took a seat on the large log facing the lake that served park visitors as a bench.

"Ooh, but that breeze feels good!" Margery exclaimed, and amplified it by fanning herself with one hand before she remembered her parasol and opened it. Then she noticed that Emma was leaning over to take something out of her handbag. "What's that you have there?"

Emma sat up. In her hands were two cups and a silver thermos. She unscrewed the top. "It's just some lemonade." She poured it into the cups, then passed one to Margery.

"A toast," she said. "To the final solution of the problem of Royce Parke."

"Hear, hear! I'll drink to that!" And Margery clinked her cup against Emma's.

There was a moment's silence; then she swiveled around to look at Emma accusingly. She seemed a little breathless. "Emma, you devil, that's not lemonade, it's almost straight gin!" she exclaimed.

"Only a little gin. You don't like it?" Emma asked with a sly smile.

"It's not that I don't like it," Margery protested. "It's just that, well, I would have liked to have been warned. So that I didn't drink it so fast. Is there any more?"

The red parasol twirled languidly over their heads as they sat there, two elderly ladies on an outing to the beach, laughing, enjoying their refreshments, each other's company and the lovely sunny spring day, and, for a pleasant moment or two, completely oblivious to all the problems in their own small world and the larger one beyond.

But when they left the park, they saw the Whites' house with its dangling eavestrough. It was a reminder, too forceful, of the broken child inside and they began the trip back home in silence. The car had traveled only a short distance before they spied the familiar figure of a small woman with a large mop of light blonde hair. It was Edna Matthews, pruning a bush in the front yard of her home. Emma brought the car to a stop at the curb.

"Oh, hello Emma! Margery dear! How nice to see you both!" Edna warbled. She appeared genuinely delighted to have her work interrupted. Emma guessed she was needful of company. "Would you like to come in for a cup of tea?"

"That would be lovely, Edna, but we'll have to take a rain check," Margery answered. "Emma has to be home soon."

"I just stopped to say hello, and to thank you again for your help when Laura went missing," Emma added, ducking her head to look through the passenger window.

Edna stepped a little closer to the car. " I went to the estate to buy eggs yesterday," she said, "and I found out why the gates were locked. Royce says he always locks the gates when he's working where he can't see who's coming in or going out. He asked why I was trying to see him."

"Oh? And what did you say?" Emma asked, with the sinking feeling that she already knew the answer to her question.

"I told him I was looking for Laura Carlisle, Jasmine's daughter," Edna replied, heedless of the expression on Emma and Margery's faces. And then off she went, on a long ramble about the estate, Royce and other unrelated matters; but now Emma was barely listening.

"We must have a real visit soon, when we can all sit down together. I'll give you a call," she interjected, when Edna finally paused to draw breath.

As they drove away, Margery voiced her thoughts exactly. "Well, now Royce knows whose daughter he hired to work and tried to finagle into the gatehouse garden."

"Yes. It's very unfortunate he has that piece of information. Also, I was thinking we should have waited to open the door in the wall."

"Why?"

"The ivy that was cut on the other side of the wall will die and turn brown. Royce will be able to see the outline of the door."

"My goodness, you're right! We should have thought of that!" Margery's expression was full of chagrin. "Well, all we can do is pray for a sunny weekend, so that the fair-weather Airdries will come to Medford before he has time to get suspicious."

But all their prayers and wishes would go unanswered, for on the coming weekend, as on so many others this wet spring, it would rain.

CHAPTER 88

That evening, once Laura was fast asleep, Jasmine and Emma went next door. They managed to get Thomas to consume some soup and a couple of cups of coffee, the better to stay awake. For although unconscious, Lianne was still breathing, her heart, ever fainter, still beating.

At ten-thirty he insisted they leave and go home. Jasmine, worn out, obeyed him; Emma stayed a half hour longer but then left Thomas alone with his wife, knowing full well she would not last the night. Pangs of conscience troubled her. She and Jasmine had talked about Thomas, the depth of his emotions, and agreed that in the hours after Lianne's death he should not be left by himself, alone in his grief and despondency.

The result was that once in bed, Emma waged a long, fruitless battle against sleeplessness. Finally, just as she was beginning to doze off, she heard the sound of light footsteps in the hall outside her door. She turned on a light. The door opened a crack, and Jasmine looked in. She was fully clothed.

Emma sat fully upright and her jaw dropped almost to her chest. "Where in the world do you think you're going?" She looked at the clock. "At one fifteen in the morning?"

"I'm going over to the Latham's. Lianne has passed." Jasmine began to cry.

"What are you talking about? How would you know that?"

"I just know." She gave a great sob. Then she closed the door.

Emma lay in bed, mulling over Jasmine's words and growing more curious with every passing minute. She thought about the next few days and how exhausted she would be if she didn't rest. She wondered if she should take one of her sleeping pills. Then she gave up and got dressed and went over to the Latham's where, it seemed, every light in the house was on.

Her face wet with tears, Jasmine was in the bedroom with Lianne, who had indeed passed away. Thomas sat in his study, a mostly blank page before him. He was trying to make a start on her obituary, he said, but it was obvious to both Emma and Jasmine that this task was beyond him. He was too distraught and exhausted, beside himself with grief.

They sat at the kitchen table while Thomas drank a mug of the chicken noodle soup Emma had brought over the day before. "You must go to bed, if not to sleep," she told him sternly. "But first, Jasmine and I have discussed what needs to be done, and before we get in touch with the funeral home, do you mind if we make a few suggestions?"

And so the next morning Jasmine was the one who called the funeral home, instructing them that she had been requested by Thomas to prepare Lianne for burial. Emma and Margery began their planning for the funeral reception, to be held in the Latham's home.

Before they left, Jasmine and Emma wrapped Lianne's body in a clean sheet, covering her face from Thomas's sight. They made sure that he was on his way to bed. Then they turned off the lights and went home, walking silently through the dark and misty gardens.

"However did you know that Lianne had died?" Emma asked as they approached the house.

"You won't believe me. I scarcely believe it myself." Jasmine held the back door open for her. "I felt something on my face. A touch, a gentle hand on my cheek. Perhaps I was imagining it. But I think it was her. Stopping by on her way."

When she came over in the morning Emma asked Thomas, who said Lianne had died at ten minutes past one.

For a long time, this memory would cause a major suspension of Emma's natural skepticism. But when she told Margery about it, she had a different twist.

"Stranger things have happened," she observed solemnly, then pursed her mouth into a knot, as she considered. "The question is, was she saying goodbye, or did she mean for you to get out of bed and go over and tend to Thomas? I'll bet that's what she wanted."

As Emma later remarked to Jasmine, Margery always did think the worst of people, even if they were dead and next best thing to an angel, like Lianne.

*   *   *

Lex's father had given him a dime to go to the newsstand to get the paper and buy him a pack of Buckingham's unfiltered. Laura was going with him, because everyone in her house was crying and busy with the funeral. Besides, she had found three pop bottles in the bushes near the tennis court and that was six cents for penny candy. Her mother made her brush her teeth when she ate candy now, honour system, and she had to ask before she went anywhere. But soon, even though it was raining off and on, they were pumping along to the store on their bikes, and when Sy saw them he asked to come too. Once they got the paper and cigarettes and the candy they went back to Lex's porch and sat on the old brown sofa watching the rain.

"When are you getting your new bike?" Lex asked.

Laura had grown; now her knees were practically touching the handlebars when she pedaled.

"It was supposed to be after school today but Mom is too busy with the funeral. She's crying all the time."

"My Mom was crying too," Sy shifted the wad of Double Bubble he was chewing to one cheek so he could talk. "And she said now that Mrs. Latham has died, your Mom will be going home."

This thought had not occurred to the child. She hadn't been sad before, because Auntie Emma had said Mrs. Latham was an angel, and why would you cry if someone became an angel? But now she realized because Lianne died, she would have to leave Medford. And Aunt Emma, and Thomas! And all her friends. And the chestnut tree, the lake, the creek, all their forts and —Suddenly a lump formed in her throat. She took the licorice pipe out of her mouth and put it, mostly intact, back in the little brown paper bag with the other one. She didn't feel like eating it or even pretending to smoke it any more.

"I have to go home," she said, because she was too sad and she didn't want to cry in front of the boys.

Back in the house, she went into the bathroom and big tears rolled down her face while she brushed her teeth.

CHAPTER 89

It seemed as if all the tears Jasmine had denied herself in the months she cared for Lianne had simply been stored in a reservoir. Now they pressed for release, and powerless to stop them Jasmine could only let them flow. She had been more or less in control until she washed and prepared that poor forlorn little body, so savaged by disease. The pathos of Lianne's physical state let loose the floodgates behind her eyes, and since then she had been untypically and almost constantly in tears.

Thomas had asked whether they should have a closed coffin. Jasmine told him that Lianne, with her touching little remnants of vanity, had asked her if it was possible, to make her look as good as she could and leave the coffin open. With cotton, makeup and several other tricks of the trade, Jasmine accomplished something short of a miracle, and at the Friday night visitation everyone was murmuring how lovely Lianne looked; almost as well as she had before she got sick.

The sisters, Roberta and Gale, arrived on Thursday afternoon while she was in the bedroom closet choosing clothes for Lianne. Handsome women, one older and one younger than Thomas, they both were tall, dark-haired, rather heavyset and had the same intelligent, probing eyes as their brother, which they fastened immediately on her. Jasmine was inwardly amused at how they glanced at Thomas, then at her, and the looks that passed between them when they thought she wasn't looking. It was almost comical, she thought, how everyone who saw them together in close proximity came to the same conclusion: that there had to be something between them. However, few, she thought, had done it so quickly or were quite so obvious about it as the Latham sisters, who knew nothing of her and Thomas's past liaison.

Whatever their suspicions, the sisters probably had too little experience with grief to know that it was the perfect antidote to passion. Both Thomas and she were caught up in their mourning. Hers found an outlet in tears; his had turned him into a silent, absent shell of himself, his eyes vacant, mechanically doing whatever was demanded of him. Now, whenever Jasmine and Emma looked at Thomas, they wondered and worried.

"That man is going to make himself sick with grief again," Emma declared in her decided way, but they were too busy to talk more.

Then it was the Friday evening visitation, and when Jasmine came in with some flowers that had just been delivered, she found the funeral parlour full to overflowing. A large and noisy crowd of Thomas's students, most of his fellow teachers, townsfolk who had been taught by him, and Thomas and Lianne's many friends from their years in Medford were milling about, meeting and greeting one another or standing in little knots talking, since the chairs were all taken. Soon the gathering began to seem more social than funereal, and Jasmine thought how this would have pleased Lianne.

Thomas and his sisters stood in a reception line while the crowd surged around them. Amid the din of conversation, Jasmine led Simon Jenner, the funeral home owner, into a quiet corner to ask him the whereabouts of Alistair, whom she had not seen for several weeks. A sour expression came over his face.

"I discovered that while he was supposed to be here, working, he was out selling advertising for the local radio station!" Jenner exclaimed indignantly. "I told him he had to stop or leave, and he left, and I've not had a word from him since!"

Across the crowded room Jasmine saw Anna, wan and pale, her daughter Mary in tow. With difficulty, she made her way over to them.

"We're free of him this weekend because it's raining, but I have to talk to you," Anna said, while Jasmine directed Mary to the room in the basement where Laura was busy drawing with her pencils and paper until it was time to go home.

"Lily and Christopher are at the Chalmers, and Mary is staying with the grandparents; I'm dropping her off to them here. She would be alright on her own until I get off shift, but I keep worrying that he'll surprise us and come home while she's alone! He'll be home for Sunday dinner – with luck I won't see him for more than a couple of hours. But Jaz, this is near impossible! Even just the sight of him turns my stomach! I only came here to pay my respects before I leave for work, but we have to talk tomorrow, perhaps at the reception, and figure out what to do – I can't go on like this!"

Jasmine murmured a few words of consolation and they hugged briefly. As she watched Anna leave the room, she was not aware that other eyes were watching her.

"Look at that woman," Margery hissed at Emma. "She's been crying for hours and in another minute or two she'll probably start up again. How does she look like that, so good, when the both of us look like we've been through the wringer?"

Emma knew her eyes and her nose were red from the tears she had shed. She didn't much care. But now she looked at Jasmine as Margery had and saw how her pallor, her tear-stained face, did not detract from her appearance; had, in fact, added a rather ethereal quality to her beauty. Then she wondered who else was noticing and automatically turned to Thomas, standing with his sisters.

Thomas was staring across the room but not at Jasmine, his gaze intent and focused. She followed it to see Mason, Max and Elizabeth Stoddart as they came in the door and joined the reception line. It was clear they did not intend to stay long. Once they had shook hands with the Latham family and offered their condolences, they went toward the door.

Before they left, however, Mason stopped and turned. He was tall, standing above the crowd, and Emma could easily see the expression on his face. It was wistful, sad; and it touched her heart because she could see that he was gazing at Jasmine, and at that moment she was oblivious to him. She was looking anxiously at Thomas, who was grey with fatigue as he stood beside his sisters, attempting to do his best but plainly struggling with his role of bereaved husband.

In fact, Jasmine had seen Mason. But she knew it would be no kindness to look at him for more than a moment. A long time ago, she had concluded that like currents in a river, some force, fate perhaps, was carrying them in different directions with no choice but to be swept along in its flow. Today they were separated by the width of the room and the milling people; but there were other barriers, too many, and one of them was time. What they once had, the love, the joy, was now only the stuff of memories. It was too far in the past ever to be retrieved or made new.

All of this she conveyed to him with one simple gesture: the turn of her head away. Standing still by the door while the crowd ebbed and surged around him, he understood, and when she looked again he was gone. Then she went toward the casket and knelt on the kneeler placed in front for those with an inclination to pray. It was a place where tears were appropriate, although now she was crying for more than the loss of a beloved friend.

Emma saw only part of this small drama. A few others, however, had watched it all. Mason's mother and father, waiting for him at the door. And, seeing Jasmine's eyes turn from Mason to him, Thomas, who felt his broken heart give a little leap that even in the depths of his sorrow felt very much like joy.

CHAPTER 90

The child's small hand hovered over the tray of tarts, squares and cookies. "Quick!" Emma hissed, "your mother will come through the door in a minute. Take one, and go eat it somewhere in the kitchen!"

But then, because she couldn't make up her mind, Laura brought up her other hand and grabbed two, a brownie and a cherry tart, and ran into the kitchen a split second before her mother came into the dining room of the Lathams' house. Jasmine was carrying a tray of crustless finger sandwiches, the last of the dozens Emma, Margery and she, along with a few other friends of Lianne had made up, and now all was in readiness for the funeral reception. Cars full of guests waiting for the doors to open were already lining the street outside.

Jasmine felt that she was truly cried out now. She had cried at the funeral, making up for all the deficits of Thomas and his sisters, who appeared dry-eyed and composed. Emma, Laura, Margery and Jim were with her, favored guests for whom pews had been reserved as almost part of the family. They sat in comfort behind the Lathams while others in the crowded church jostled for room.

On this day of rain and mists, huddled beneath their black umbrellas, far fewer mourners than had attended the funeral trudged along the winding path through the cemetery, past the stone angel to the freshly dug hole in the ground. Jasmine also cried at the graveside when the coffin was lowered and Thomas dropped a handful of earth on top. Although grief was etched on his features, the only real emotion he showed was as they were turning away. The gravediggers, soaked through and eager to leave, began their work. He flinched as he heard the clods of earth hit the top of the coffin, and angrily asked them to have the decency to wait. Then, seeing their honest faces and how uncomfortably wet they were, he apologized.

"That's OK, gov," the shorter of the two said in a voice full of compassion. "I know it's your missus, and we're wet enow already, and we'll wait."

Then Thomas turned and Jasmine couldn't tell if there were tears or raindrops running down his face.

She placed the silver tray with its array of sandwiches on the pink linen tablecloth beside all the others, and looked around. This was a beautiful room, with its gold-rubbed moldings and antique Regency chandelier, its precious old Persian carpet and highly polished mahogany furniture. Today, Lianne's good taste would be on display for all to see. This would likely be the last, sad occasion, for the house was to be sold, passing out of the family after four generations.

This thought led to another worry: no letter had come informing Thomas of the selection committee's decision. They told him they would let him know by mail by the end of the week. Had they chosen someone else as vice principal? On top of all his other crosses, that would be a hard one to bear.

She went into the kitchen, where Emma looked up from her tea-making at the clock on the wall and announced, "It's two-thirty! Time to open the doors!"

Taking off her apron and giving herself a quick glance and pat to her hair in the hall mirror, she went to the front door and opened it wide. The mourners, all equipped with healthy appetites after the rigours of the funeral, poured in.

"Jasmine!" A familiar face, coming toward her through the crowded, noisy room.

"Arlena! It's so good to see you!" And they embraced warmly.

"I noticed you with your parents at church, are they here?"

"No, they sent their regrets; the usual, busy with other commitments, and Mason is with his boys, but my goodness, Jasmine, it's a marvel how well you look! My condolences on the loss of your dear friend; you said on the phone she was near the end, but that was weeks ago."

"Yes, well, she managed to wait until she had everything arranged just about the way she wanted," Jasmine said with a half-smile. "Now tell me about you, and the family. Your mother, I think, has lost weight?"

"She has, and it's both good and bad, because she needed to, but this seems to be the result of a minor bout of depression." Arlena's expression was worried: her mother, so much the rock all of them relied on, was crumbling.

"They're both of them a little down, I'm afraid. My father too, because Mason announced last week he wants to leave Medford. He's been talking with my sister Althea's husband, Rob. Rob's starting a new housing development near Fresno and wants him in on it."

"But he and your father have so much going on here!" Jasmine said, disbelievingly. "How can he just walk away from it?"

"When you're not happy," Arlena answered, with a shrug of her shoulders, "you tend to leave the place where you're unhappy. You did, and so did I! And look at me now, with someone I love, and doing work I love. But I did talk with him and ask him to hold off until he's tied up loose ends here and things are more stable with the parents; so he says probably not 'til January."

"Jasmine!" Margery's sharp voice came from directly behind, "if you're finished talking, we could use some help here!"

Then Margery managed to recruit them both, and they were only able to resume their conversation an hour later, after she and Arlena had poured tea and passed the sandwiches and sweets to all the old folks unable to compete with the crowds at the serving tables.

Around four, there finally came a lull. Thomas surreptitiously edged toward the kitchen door. He needed to get away from the crowd. The earnest faces, the words of condolence, the press of hands and bodies had started to take on an unending, nightmarish quality, resonating strangely in his overtired, grief-shocked mind. From the kitchen, he wandered into the sunroom. It was unoccupied, except for Dickie, chirping in his cage, and a small girl who was sobbing her heart out.

"What's the matter, sweetheart?" He quickly sat down and put his arm around Laura. "Did you hurt yourself?"

He said this because there was a red streak underneath her mouth, which he belatedly recognized as filling from one of the fruit tarts. Her lips bore a few chocolate crumbs. He took out his clean handkerchief and gently wiped her face, then held it while she blew her nose.

Emma saw them as she came into the kitchen. Yes, that was typical of Thomas, she thought. Always so much better with the sorrows of others than his own.

"I'm crying," Laura said with a last sob, wringing her small hands in her lap, her voice tremulous, "because Lianne is dead. And because that means we're going home, and I don't want to go!"

It was like a jab, a poke to his heart. Suddenly the fog cleared away from his mind.

"By Jove," he said, "you're right! Well, we'll have to do something about that!"

CHAPTER 91

With a marked lack of enthusiasm after their energy-sapping labours of the day before, Margery and Emma went over to the Latham house after Sunday church to finish the clean up from the funeral reception. Jasmine had promised to follow them shortly afterward and now, as she came in the front door, she saw Thomas's sisters descending the staircase. Emma trailed behind them. Her face wore a rather sour expression.

"Good morning Jasmine!" Gail said brightly, and the three of them exchanged a few pleasantries. Jasmine was surprised to find she rather liked the sisters Latham. While not overly imbued with natural warmth, at the funeral reception they were definitely less chilly than they had been on their arrival. She guessed their suspicions about her and Thomas might have been at least partially washed away by the oceans of tears she shed for their sister-in-law.

"We're off for a walk around the old neighbourhood," Roberta informed her as she held open the door for Gail, both eager to set off into a world sparkling with sunshine and fresh-washed by rain. Before they could depart, however, Margery came out of the kitchen to thank them for doing the rest of the tidying and cleaning up; as she said, a very welcome surprise for Emma and her.

"There's almost nothing left to do, so we'll be leaving shortly." Reaching in the pocket of her apron, she took out an envelope. "And we're giving this money back to you, that you left for us on the counter, because none of us expect payment for what we've done. We did it for Lianne as a dear friend, and for Christian charity." The expression on Margery's face was neutral, but Jasmine knew that she had been offended by the pay packet.

"Oh well," Jasmine said quickly, "this is all Thomas's fault, he probably would have told you that we volunteered to help if he hadn't been so distraught. But it was very thoughtful of you, Roberta and Gail, and it would be wonderful if, instead, you gave it to a charity in memory of Lianne."

Then the tension was defused, and newly rich again – for they had left a considerable sum for the funeral helpers – the sisters set out on their reconnaissance of their old neighbourhood.

Emma had her purse with her, sitting on the kitchen counter. Now she went to it, took out five dollars, and handed it to Margery in payment of their bet.

"Hah!" Margery exclaimed with a triumphant cackle. "Didn't I tell you?"

"What's all this about?" Jasmine asked, mystified.

"Never you mind," Emma snapped, with a sour look and tone of voice that clearly forbade more questions. "Now, if you're going upstairs to sort clothes, I've done a little of your work for you."

Since Laura was busy building a new fort with the terrible trio and there was an hour until she came back for lunch at noon, Jasmine had decided to make an early start on the job she had planned for Monday: sorting and packing up Lianne's clothing and personal effects. Once in the bedroom, she found that someone else had already gone through them rather thoroughly, selecting the best pieces. She guessed it was the sisters. They were too large, however, to fit into most of Lianne's things. Along with a few neat piles made by Emma, there was still plenty to go to the poor box.

Thomas wandered in for a moment, grey-faced and listless, mumbled a few words of greeting and left. Tomorrow, after he put his sisters on the airplane that would take them back to their homes and families, he would be all alone in an empty house full of memories. Just from looking at him, Jasmine found herself anticipating the worst.

In one drawer of Lianne's bureau she found a little date book. It had been inscribed neatly with all her January, February and March appointments. As she became increasingly bed-ridden, the entries were fewer. Other dates, though, had been marked in: Emma's birthday, and in the very same week as Laura's, Thomas's, on June 25, two days earlier. She had never known! How old would he be then? Thirty-nine, she calculated.

In a rather bemused state of mind, she went downstairs and into the sunroom, wondering what else needed her attention in the few minutes before she left for home. As she stood there, she noticed something peculiar: it was completely silent. Usually she could count on a few clicks or chirps of welcome from Dickie. But now, glancing in the direction of his cage, she realized she couldn't even see him.

When Thomas came down the stairs again, he heard sounds from the direction of the sunroom. Following them to their source, he found Jasmine, her back to him on the sofa, bent over and crying once more. He came around and sat down beside her, just as he had their daughter the day before. Then he saw what was in her lap.

"Lianne's canary!" he exclaimed.

"Yes," Jasmine said through her tears, "I found him lying in the bottom of the cage. He's left us, and flown away to be with her."

Thomas sat there for a minute. Then, like a pump long disused, but primed over and over again, as he had been by the tears of others and now Jasmine's seemingly endless flow, he began to cry. It was not neat, quiet crying, but great wrenching sobs torn from some broken place in his heart; the crying of someone so bereft that any words of comfort would only ring like empty platitudes before the depth of emotion it contained. Tears streamed down his face, and all Jasmine could do was put her arm around him, wordlessly supporting him against the terrible sorrow shaking his body. She added more tears to his. They were partly tears of fright at the fierceness of the storm of grief he was enduring, and of relief, that at last he had found his way to mourning the great tragedy that was the loss of his wife.

He sobbed on and on, and his crying had only partially abated when his sisters, Roberta and Gail, walked in and found them there. Their pale, china-blue eyes, so different from his, almost popped from their heads to see their brother and his overly attractive neighbour in such a brotherly-sisterly pose, shedding tears over a dead bird.

"Oh dear, Thomas! I'm so sorry you've lost your canary!" Gail exclaimed.

Thomas looked up sharply then, his eyes red and his face wet and swollen from crying. Angrily, he exclaimed, "I'm not crying about the goddamned bird!"

There was something about what he said, and the way that he said it, that struck Jasmine as funny. Before she could even think about stifling it, she let loose a giggle. A second later Gail joined in, and then Roberta started laughing, a surprisingly hearty, infectious laugh, and finally, even Thomas. They kept at it for quite a while, their tears blending with the almost hysterical laughter, reminding Jasmine again how close one was to the other.

Laura would soon be home. Jasmine prepared to leave. It was so refreshing, she thought, to laugh, really laugh, after the sorrow and heaviness of the past days. She felt quite light afterward. Outside, in the rain-polished, shining afternoon, she lifted her face to the sun. It was almost summer.

CHAPTER 92

Laura had finished her Sunday lunch and now she went over to the Latham house on an errand for Aunt Emma. She had wanted to leave and help the boys finish the fort but her mother said no, she never got to spend time with her anymore because she was always out playing, and she would take her to the lake. Then, when Lex and Sy came to get her they asked if they could come too, and Mom sighed and said yes. After that Aunt Anna visited for a while, and she left Mary and Christopher and Lily. So all of them were all going to the lake, as soon as she got back from bringing Auntie's message to Thomas.

She went right upstairs because Thomas was always in his study if he wasn't anywhere else. She found him sitting with his elbows on his desk. His eyes were wet; he was crying. Laura felt a great sadness sweep over her to see Thomas so sad. She went up to him and did what her mother always did to her when she cried. She put her arm over his big shoulder and kissed his cheek.

'I'm sorry you're so sad, Thomas."

Then he put his arm around her and gave her a squeeze, kissed her forehead and managed a sort-of smile.

"Aunt Emma asked me to ask you and your sisters to dinner. We're having roast of lamb and a pie."

"Tell her thank you, sweetheart, but I just don't feel – tell her my sisters are away this afternoon; they might not be back for a while. And I need some time to be alone."

After he finished speaking, she continued to stand there, twisting her hands and jiggling a bit as she always did when she had something she wanted to say.

"Is there anything else, Laura?"

"Yes. My bicycle chain fell off. Aunt Emma said maybe you could fix it when you come for dinner."

Thomas gave a short bark of a laugh. He smiled. This time it was a real smile.

"Alright. You can tell your Aunt, yes, thank you. If my sisters are home in time, we'll come to dinner. And I'll fix your bicycle chain, sweetheart."

From the window of his study, he watched her cross the patio. She skipped for a few steps, then walked more sedately through the gate.

Laura. His child. His and Jasmine's daughter. With that thought, a little of the sunshine she seemed to have brought with her stole into his heart.

* * *

Although the lake today was as turquoise blue as a robin's egg, calm, smiling and sparkling, it was perhaps not the best time for a visit. During yesterday's rainstorm, masses of dead alewives had washed up and deposited themselves in smelly, silvery mounds on the stone beach. The children held their noses and delightedly made sounds of disgust as they trooped along the stony shoreline to a space where there were no dead fish and a light onshore breeze cleared the air of odours. Then, through a gap in the breakfront that gave access to the lake, the first contest got underway.

Each of the six children gathered four stones for the throwing contest. Lex easily won this contest, though little Christopher came a surprising second. Next was the stone skipping contest; Mary was the winner with four skips. The boys, except for Christopher, declined to participate in the search for the most beautiful stone and Jasmine directed them, instead, to look for the roundest stone. Then they all, even Jasmine and little Lily with her sister's help, took part in the rock hopping contest, leaping nimbly as mountain goats from one breakwater boulder to another, often barely pausing to check for footing. The only casualty toward the end was Sy with a bloody scrape on one knee, a new addition to the large collection of scabs on his legs, ankles and elbows.

These were the standard pastimes of lake children, all the more tempting for usually being forbidden unless in the company of an adult. As had happened with Jasmine, though, most parents gave up the battle in the face of their child's growing independence and self-reliance. The lake was like a lodestone, drawing youngsters to play and search for the treasures washed up on its shores. Even at its stormiest, it drew children to the overhanging cliffs to stand and watch, mesmerized and delightfully terrified by the huge waves speeding in to crash with great force on the breakwater.

Today it provided a pleasant afternoon's entertainment for seven children, as well as a welcome diversion for Jasmine. For like nails across a blackboard, the thought of Gussie White and that child's dreadful dilemma raked her mind, more painful and intolerable with every passing hour. Living much longer with it was out of the question. Gussie had had a portion of all the tears she had cried in the past few days; hers was the face that rose up accusingly when she closed her eyes at night.

Although even a week was too long to wait, still Anna had managed to extract that promise from her. During her work at the hospital, Anna had learned that two of the White children had german measles. As a result, all were in quarantine at home. It was a respite, of sorts, so Jasmine had reluctantly agreed.

During Anna's visit before she set off to her shift at the hospital, they reached a compromise: if the Airdries did not come next weekend and Jasmine was unable to speak to them, then she and Anna would go to the Whites and tell them about Royce and their daughter.

"Of course it would be best if he were to go to jail," Anna said bitterly. "Best for everyone except us, his family. For us it'll be a lifetime of purgatory. I'll have to move far away. My children will grow up without their grandparents and aunts and uncles and cousins. We can't stay in this town once people hear about their father. And in a few years he'll be out of jail, and what then?"

But, as she reluctantly agreed, it was the only other way to handle the situation quickly. Their alternate plan was no less flawed. Once Royce was dismissed from his job, he would be confronted by family members and made to promise to change his ways under threat of being reported to the Whites and to police. Jasmine, knowing what she did, held out little hope for his rehabilitation. For her part, Anna was repelled at the thought of having him back in the house for however long it took to arrange a separation or divorce. From any angle, it seemed that no plan was equal to the problem that was Royce Parke.

On this bright day she tried to wipe these dark thoughts from her mind as she led her little gaggle of children across the wide lawn of the park on the way home. Most youngsters carried souvenirs of the lake: bits of driftwood, stones or other treasures. As he walked along, Lex was already using his jackknife to cut the shaft of one of the seagull feathers he had found so that he could use it as a quill pen. Jasmine was instructing him, and so busy in this task she almost collided with Chris Byers, out with the family dog for a stroll along the lake.

"Jasmine! Exactly who I wanted to see!" he exclaimed. "Do you have any idea where Alistair is?"

"No, Chris, I haven't seen or heard from him for weeks. But I'm surprised you're asking me that question, because wasn't he doing some work for you?"

Chris, clearly disappointed, sighed. "Yes, he was selling advertising time around town, and doing a super job of it – even with folks who never bought before. Then all of a sudden, he disappeared. We were supposed to do some business together; he was keen on it. So I phoned his folks, but even they don't know where he is."

Jasmine told him about her brief conversation with Simon Jenner. Then, noticing several of the children hopping from one foot to another in need of a bathroom and others starting to climb trees, she said a hasty goodbye.

"I'll check with you again," Chris called after her, as she neared the road. "Because as long as you're here, Jasmine, he'll be back!"

* * *

Dew was beginning to fall as Thomas and his sisters wound their way along the beaten earth path from the Madison house. Fireflies drifted through the still, humid air, their cool blue light pulsing in counterpoint to the stars that twinkled above. In the little pools made by the stream deep in the cedars, frog choruses sang love songs.

"That was a lovely dinner." Gail broke the silence as they padded along in single file. "You're lucky, Tom, to have such good neighbours."

"Yes," said Roberta, "but your loveliest neighbour is about to leave soon. She told me she's going back to Las Vegas with her daughter when school's finished."

"I noticed you could hardly take your eyes off her," Gail observed.

"She was sitting right across from me!" Thomas was indignant. "What was I supposed to do, look at my plate all the time?"

"It was more the look on your face when you looked at her," Gail said reflectively. "Well, anyhow, if you're going to do anything about her, you'd better do it soon."

"Carpe diem," added his sister Roberta, the former teacher of Latin.

Thomas was aghast. He had been leading the way through the darkness, and now he stopped mid-path and whirled around to face them.

"I can't believe you, the both of you!" he said angrily. "My wife is barely cold in her grave, and here you are pushing me to go out and find a replacement! I'm in mourning! Think about if I told your husbands to go find themselves another woman, right after you died!"

Roberta snorted. "Hah! Well, beside the fact I would be dead and therefore not likely to mind, Frank wouldn't last six months without someone to take care of him. No, make that three!"

"Matt would be checking out the talent in the funeral parlour crowd," Gail supplied.

"That's ridiculous!" Thomas was shocked. He turned around and headed for the bright lights of their house.

"Well, you'd be happier with someone than just by yourself, after being married half your life. You're still young," said Roberta, his older sister, from behind him.

"You're not so very old yet," said Gail, his younger sister.

They had reached the house and Thomas was prepared to leave them at the door and go upstairs when Roberta put a hand on his arm. "We all loved Lianne," she said gently.

"Yes," Gail chimed in, "she was a dear. A truly wonderful person."

Still nursing his exasperation, Thomas looked at his sisters. Their faces were serious and full of affection. Then Roberta spoke, and afterward Gail nodded in agreement.

"She loved you so much, Thomas. She wouldn't want you to be lonely."

CHAPTER 93

It was relatively easy to clear away Lianne's clothes and other possessions. She had, in her usual practical fashion, either left written instructions or told Jasmine how she wished to dispose of them. After filling and marking four cartons, Jasmine took a break from what she was doing. It had been a depressing chore. For what she thought might be the last time, she walked through the silent house.

Thomas had taken his sisters to the airport for their early morning flight back west. Roberta and Gail were very attached to their family home; last night they had reacted with shock and dismay when he mentioned selling it. However, it was the only sensible thing to do, Jasmine thought. Not only would he rattle around in such grand spaces, but alone in these rooms he could never escape the memory of Lianne. Far more than the assorted items packed away in the cardboard cartons, the Latham house bore her stamp, was filled, top to bottom, with echoes of her presence. She had created a beautiful home. Now there was something distinctly melancholy about its well-appointed rooms, emptied of the spirit that created them, full of the memories of the children that never were, of a life ended too soon.

She was glad to leave the gloom of her thoughts behind and go home for lunch. Laura's cheerful chatter was therapy, her sunny ways always lifted her spirits. After a pleasant hour with her daughter and Emma, Jasmine returned to finish her task. The car was back in the driveway. Upstairs, she discovered Thomas already hard at work in his study. Although he was on compassionate leave, as usual personal matters had to be set aside because of the sheer volume of teaching and administration he was handling. A smile, a few words of greeting, and she left him to his labours and returned to the master bedroom to sort through one more dresser.

From her vantage point near the window she saw the bobbing blue cap of the mailman as he walked toward the front door. She heard the click of the brass mail slot as it opened. Immediately she left the drawer she was emptying and went downstairs, because the mail, these days, had taken on new importance. And, as she came down the last few steps, she could see that there was indeed important mail: an envelope with a crest on it. Scooping it up, she delivered it to Thomas. Then she quickly left the room because if the letter contained a disappointment, she didn't want to see it.

Minutes passed. Thomas appeared at the door. His expression was serious, and then suddenly he smiled, a wide, unmistakably pleased and happy smile.

"Tomorrow," he said, "I am going to have the immense pleasure of handing in my resignation to Mike Simms."

"You got it!" Jasmine was almost jumping with jubilation. "Congratulations!" And she went to him and gave him a hug.

It was shocking and surprising to Thomas: the disconnection between propriety, what he expected of himself and how he ought to behave, and whenever Jasmine was in the picture, how his body simply ignored this or whatever else was in his mind and went its own way. He felt her pressing against him and it was so much what he wanted that he held her close for a beat too long. When he let her go, just as she started to push him away, he saw her eyes lowered, her long eyelashes like half-stars on her flushed cheeks.

Then they looked at each other and she attempted gamely to bring things back to normalcy, difficult when he was still coping with the sensations brought about by her body against his.

"So you're going to be moving!" she said.

"Yes," he replied, the best answer he was capable of in the flustered state he was in. But then he had an idea.

"And I'm going to need help," he said. "Can you give me a hand when you've finished what you're doing? I need to get this place organized so I can sell it. I'm done with this town!"

* * *

Margery was over for afternoon tea. She had just had her hair permed and it clung in tight blond curls to her head. When the child came in from school, after kissing her "aunt", she couldn't resist taking one and pulling it. It sprang back in place like a coiled spring. Margery batted her hand away.

"Shoo! Show your elders some respect!"

Then she and Emma shared a chuckle, while Laura nabbed a cookie from the plate and thumped up the stairs to change into her old pants. A moment later, they heard a loud banging from the back door. It creaked open a space and a small sun-bleached head poked in.

"Is Run home yet?"

Mick, one of the terrible trio, came up the stairs to the kitchen table after Emma waved him in for a cookie while he waited. Standing there, he gobbled three in the few seconds before the child thundered down from the second floor. They both said a hurried goodbye and rushed out the back door.

"My goodness!" Margery exclaimed. "You're certainly going to find it quiet around here when she and her mother are gone!"

"Yes, and I'm not at all looking forward to it," Emma said with a heavy sigh. "I'll miss them terribly."

"And you're going to lose your nice, helpful neighbour, too. When is Thomas moving?"

"He'll be back and forth over the summer, and plans to be settled in Kellington by August before school begins. He won't have need of a real estate agent to sell the house. The day after he handed in his resignation and the news spread around, he heard from two parties who wanted to buy it."

"Oh yes, these lake houses are just like gold."

Margery sighed a gusty sigh of envy. Then she looked around, as if noticing something missing for the first time since her arrival over an hour ago.

"Where's Jasmine?"

"At the Latham's. She finished packing away Lianne's things on Monday, and then Thomas asked her to stay on and box up as much of the house as she could for his move. So she's there right now. And you can take that look off your face, Margery. Because he's not home. There was trouble at the school and he's had to go back to work already, and besides that, he's no longer a married man."

At her first words, Margery's eyebrows had elevated until they were notching up to her hairline, and she was wearing a certain arch expression that Emma recognized and did not at all like. "The matches are very, very close to the firewood there," Margery observed. "And he's still in mourning."

"Life is for the living," Emma replied, clanking her teacup down on its saucer for emphasis. "I, for one, would be quite happy if something did develop between the two of them. Lianne never would have wanted him to live the rest of his life alone."

Then she quickly switched the subject to one she knew was sure to distract Margery: the weather. Ordinarily they had so much of interest to talk about they would give short shrift to such a mundane topic. But now it was a matter of grave concern whether this Saturday would be foul or fair, rainy or sunny. The fate and happiness of many people hung upon the balance of the weekend weather report, not least that of the entire tightly knit MacClure clan. It was Thursday, and so far the outlook was good.

"Royce will be home Friday night and Anna will be keeping an eye on his whereabouts on Saturday," Margery said. "They've all been invited to a barbeque picnic that afternoon by one of Anna's hospital friends, so he should be well out of the way for Jasmine's visit to the Airdries."

She glanced at the clock. "I really must go." Another gusty sigh, and then she struggled heavily to her feet. "This whole business is making me so nervous! I'll be glad when it's over, though there's really no end to it in sight, is there?"

Once standing, she helped herself to the last slice of buttered date bread.

"This is divine! Copy the recipe out for me, would you?"

When Emma came back from driving Margery home, she found Jasmine at the kitchen sink, washing lettuce she had picked from the garden.

"I thought we might enjoy the fruits of your labours," Jasmine said with a wry smile, for, as they had discovered, she was no gardener. Then, with a look of concern, "Emma, are you alright? You're so pale!"

She wiped her hands on her apron and hovered over Emma as she plopped herself down on the banquette. Emma waved dismissively.

"It's nothing, nothing, I'm recovered now, but I surely did have a fright. Do you remember I told you Jim bought a car? Well, Margery has decided she must drive – last week she got her learner's permit. When I was taking her home she asked to drive the last three blocks. We went up over the curb and if I hadn't grabbed the wheel, and if she hadn't finally remembered where the brake was, we would have hit a lamppost!"

After Jasmine laughed, it seemed to Emma that she might now be properly primed for a discussion of more serious matters.

"Is Thomas just about finished with those casseroles and soups everyone brought over before the funeral?"

"Yes, and I returned some of the dishes to their owners during my walk this afternoon, on my way to the beach. I finally found that door you and Emma opened in the wall. It's still open, although there's some ivy grown over it on the other side that needs to be pulled or cut. So I'm guessing Royce hasn't found it."

"That's good." Emma would not be distracted from her subject. "But the reason I asked about Thomas is, I want to ask him if he would like to come here for his dinners at night. He can help out with a donation for groceries, if he must, but it makes no sense for him to make his own meals, with all that fuss and bother, when we have to make dinner for three anyhow. What do you think?"

"Probably a good idea," Jasmine said, with less than genuine enthusiasm.

Emma looked at her sharply. "Do you have any objections?"

"No, of course not." In fact she did, but none she cared to share with Emma.

The problem was that since that hug, the light sisterly hug of congratulations she gave Thomas that he had converted into a very unbrotherly embrace, the tension between them had returned. Electrical or chemical, it was an undercurrent growing stronger every time they met. At the same time, he gave every sign of missing and mourning his wife. The half-eaten meals, the sadness in his face, his general air of abstraction and disinterest in his books, newspapers, and things that had normally given him pleasure all testified to the depth of his sorrow. But he had been a well-loved man, starved for a long time of regular sex and affection. Part of him was asserting that need, and from the mixture of discomfiture and desire she read in his expression when she pulled away, he had been almost as surprised by it as she was.

He had himself under tight control now. However, beneath the surface she sensed he was simmering, slowly coming to a boil. What would it be like when they saw each other every day? She comforted herself that at least Emma and Laura would be there to moderate whatever effect on him she seemed to have.

"And I would like to suggest that you leave Laura here, with me for the summer, while you get settled in Las Vegas."

"What?" Fully occupied with her thoughts, Jasmine was stunned by Emma's suggestion. She stopped her salad making and whirled about. "Absolutely not!"

"I'm not asking you to make a decision now." With a brisk wave of her hand, Emma dismissed Jasmine's rapid-fire response. "I should also tell you that I intend to ask Thomas to stay here once you're gone. His house is going to be half-empty, then sold, and he'll be miserable rattling around in it while he tidies up all his loose ends before moving in August. It'll be better for him and if you leave Laura here, then he'll legitimately be able to spend time with his daughter. How often will he have the chance?"

Jasmine cast a jaundiced eye on Emma. "Well. You certainly do have it all figured out, don't you, Emma?" There was a decided edge to her voice. "My life, my daughter's and Thomas's, all neatly arranged and now you only need me to say yes!"

"You can say no if you wish, Jasmine." Now Emma's tone was conciliatory. She had expected exactly this reaction from her niece and was not at all discouraged. Jasmine would always and evermore say no before she said yes.

"What I'm proposing is only out of love for all of you, and right now, I'm just asking you to think about it. You know what Las Vegas is like in the summer, so hot and dusty. You'll be busy getting settled and starting work, and meanwhile Laura will be moping around inside, when she could be having a summer of fun with her friends."

What Emma said was undeniable, but the thought of leaving her daughter behind made Jasmine heartsore. Thomas had, in fact, just asked her how he could spend more time with his child. She had had no ready answer for him.

She silently returned to her kitchen tasks, gazing out the window at the green and flowery world beyond, the lake sparkling in the distance. Then she thought of Vegas, with its hot, arid city streets, the insect-like hordes of tourists humming in and out of the grandiose, gaudy hotels and casinos, the constant noise and traffic and flashing signs slicing into the darkness of the desert night. It was her world, and full of the challenges her nimble mind craved, but just now it seemed somewhat claustrophobic, oppressive. She also remembered the summer torpor of the palm-fringed streets in her quiet Vegas neighbourhood, baking under a scorching sun. Not much of a place for a child.

Outside, the air was full of birdsong. A breeze wafted through the open window, carrying the smell of sun-warmed earth and fresh water. Most of all, she thought, she would miss the lake.

CHAPTER 94

Emma opened her eyes, instantly awake and anxious, to the sound of rain pattering on the roof. In the darkness the luminous hands of the clock showed two in the morning. But when she left her bed and peered out the window Emma could see the moon. The clouds, silver strands crisscrossing an indigo sky, were already clearing away in preparation for the beautiful day that had been forecast. But still she was restless. She wandered the darkened house for a short while. She looked in on Laura, the picture of childish innocence, lying on her side in deep, untroubled sleep. Once back in her bed, she said a silent prayer for her, then another for that poor child whose peace of mind and innocence had been stolen away.

Jasmine found her the next morning with her rosary wrapped in her hands, fast asleep, propped up on her pillows.

"I hope a few of those Hail Marys were for me."

"Are you nervous?'

"No. Should I be?"

Now it was one o'clock and on this sunny afternoon Jasmine had declined the use of the car and was walking to the Airdrie Estate, where the gates were unlocked and the Airdries should now be in residence. On leaving, she had been cool and confident. Meanwhile, Emma was unaccountably worried. The child was with the boys over at the ballpark. Anna was keeping an eye on Royce. They had had several altercations where he threatened violence before walking out the door. Things were falling apart; however he still was making a pretense of normality by accompanying her to the party. Everything should go as planned. Yet something was off-kilter. Her sixth sense had picked up some vibration, and now she tried to tune in on what it might be.

The intricate wrought iron gates were open. Jasmine walked through them and along the circular cobblestone driveway toward the front entrance of the house. She saw no sign of habitation, but that did not concern her. Anna had told her the two cars that brought the Airdries, their driver, the housekeeper and supplies for the weekend were always parked in the large garage to the side of the house.

* * *

At ten past one, Anna was in the kitchen taking the casserole she had made for the backyard barbeque party out of the oven when she heard the phone ring. Her hands were full. After three rings, it stopped. She guessed Royce must have answered it. Five minutes later he walked through the kitchen to the back door. He slipped on his gardener's boots, folding the stiff leather down from his knees several times, and plucked a bag with a few tools and the heavy keys for the Airdrie house and gates off a hook.

"What are you doing?" Anna inquired, stunned at this development. "We have to leave for the party in less than half an hour!"

"Airdries just called. They're not coming after all. I'm going to lock the place up and I won't be back, I have to stay on duty. You take the kids to the party." Then he went out the door, and she saw there was already a taxi at the curb, waiting for him.

In a panic, Anna ran for the phone. With trembling fingers, she dialed the five numbers for the Madison house. The phone rang and rang. "Dear God, Emma, answer! Answer the phone!" Anna's voice was high and hysterical. What could she do? She had no car! Christopher and Lily, who had just come in the kitchen, looked at their mother with wide, frightened eyes.

Out in the garden, Emma heard the phone and she ran for it, catching it on the last ring. When she hung up, she was pale but composed. Her intuition had been working overtime; and now, with the rightness of her unease confirmed, she was more than half prepared for this development. From the bench beside the front door, she grabbed her large black purse and hurried as fast as her old legs would carry her to the garage.

Walking under the heavy canopy spread by the ancient oaks lining the drive, Jasmine approached the imposing, overarching entrance to the Airdrie home. There was no bell for the ornate front door, only a large brass knocker in the shape of a lion's head. She lifted the heavy ring and knocked. The second time she knocked louder. The echoes resounded in the silence within. She stood, hesitating for a moment, but instinctively she knew no one was there: the Airdries were not at home.

As she began to turn away, in the near distance behind her she heard a metallic creak and then a click. She swung about. With a great surge of alarm, she saw that Royce was at the gate, and that he had seen her.

If her eyes had not been so keen, if she had not known Royce well enough to know that he never would change, she might have stayed there at the door and waited trustfully for him to come. But from afar, she could see the expression on his face, dark and menacing, and then suddenly, perhaps because he hoped to confuse her, a bright smile and a casual wave as he advanced toward her.

Then she ran. She ran for her life, sprinting away from the door, around the house and toward the lake. There was no time to look for a hidden door in the wall, because now he was coming after her, running fast and gaining ground. When she quickly glanced behind her, the false, friendly face was gone, replaced by an expression of true ferocity as he loped behind her on his long legs, much longer and faster than hers.

She knew where her escape route lay: it was the little harbour where she could run to the boardwalk and dive into open water. Royce was no swimmer; he would be helpless to stop her as she swam through the chill lake to the public beach, where there would be other people and she would be safe. But from a corner of her eye, she could see that he had guessed her intention and was heading her off. He had angled to the left and was almost parallel to her. Now he came toward her and she had no choice but to take to the rocks.

The breakwater had been rebuilt by the Airdries two years ago at considerable expense. The boulders were massive, standing at least four to five feet high near the shore, and higher in the middle section where they were partially submerged but still towered over the water. Further out was the old breakwater, which had been pushed deeper into the lake. It was all jagged points projecting from the water, impassible and impossible to navigate for any desperate soul attempting escape.

Her only hope, Jasmine knew, was in the skill she had acquired as a child and over the past few months practiced almost to perfection. Now she jumped onto the rocks and with perfect balance leapt from one to the other, plotting with great concentration the path that would take her to the open water of the harbour.

Royce saw that she had left him with no choice: in order to stop her, he must take to the rocks. He had never lived near the lake, never played the games the lake children played. But the end of the boardwalk had put him so close to her, there still was a good chance he could catch her before she reached the open water. And although he was slow, at first cautious and clumsy, soon it seemed he might close the gap.

Now Jasmine felt the thrill of real fear, because if he continued, slow as he was, he would cut off her path of escape.

Even in her advanced state of anxiety, Emma had time to think of what a sight she must be, as she rushed into the woods past two goggled-eyed mothers and one father with their children at the beach. She still had on her dirt-smeared green gardener's coverall and was brandishing – what?! She took a look at the knife she was carrying as she panted along the path leading to the door in the wall. She had picked up a bread knife! Oh well, it was serrated and, as it turned out, did an admirable job of cutting through the few strands of ivy holding the gate fast. Now she was opening the door and rushing out, on the other side.

There was only one chance for Jasmine and she would take it. When he got close, she would leap toward him and push him, and he would fall. She would have to trust to herself and her own balance not to do the same.

As he neared Jasmine, Royce had other ideas. He made a quick decision. There was only one great, large jump to make, and then he would be upon her. It was taking a chance, but with his long legs he was sure he could make it to the rock she was advancing toward. He gathered all his strength, and then he leapt.

"Royce!!"

The voice, loud and urgent, somewhat familiar, came from behind him, and for a split second his concentration flickered. His foot landed just on the edge of the peak of the rock he was aiming for, too close to the edge, slipped, and then he fell with great force, his forehead striking the jagged, unyielding outcrop before he plummeted downward. He fell sideways into the crevice between two huge rocks. One leg, the leg he had instinctively stretched out to brace his fall, disappeared into a narrow opening full of water and surrounded by smaller boulders. Then all was blackness; he saw no more.

She stood looking down at him, trembling, disbelieving, her heart in her mouth, while a panting Emma pounded noisily toward her along the slatted wood boardwalk. It extended only so far, ending at a large rock that marked the halfway point in the harbour. It was here that she gamely attempted to scale the rocks, to see what Jasmine was standing and gasping over.

"Jasmine, are you alright?" she cried out. "What's happened to him?"

"I'm alright, but he is not." Her voice was faint and shaky. "He's gashed his head open and there's all kinds of blood!"

Emma had now managed to haul herself up on a tall rock. When she stood she had a reasonably good view of Royce and his placement between the two boulders. "Those head injuries always bleed a lot," she said dismissively, in a voice loud enough to cover the distance between them. "Can you get him out of there? I can't help you, it's too far and too much jumping for an old lady."

"I'll try."

Jasmine was numb, trembling with shock to see him lying there motionless when only seconds ago she fully expected him to grab her and bash her head against one of these very rocks. But now she steadied herself, and after judging the best way to move him, she wedged her body between two boulders to leverage his weight. Taking hold of his forearms, she pulled with all her might.

"I can lift him a little, but he's much too heavy for me," she called out. "One of his legs is caught in the rocks, and no matter what I do, it's holding him fast!"

And now Jasmine, down below the level of the boulders, slowly became aware of the changing sound of the water as it moved through the crevices. She heard its oily slap and suck, its growing agitation as it began to seethe. Ominous and unmistakable, it was the watery warning of something coming. Suddenly she understood why the Airdries were not home today when she came knocking at their door.

From where she crouched, she looked up to see Emma towering high and erect on her rock, a prophet-like figure silhouetted against the dull sky. Her normally confined grey hair blew free, streaming in the wind, her green robe flapped around her. With great decisiveness she spoke, and as she did she pointed.

"Then," Emma said, "we have no choice. We shall have to leave him to God and the lake."

Jasmine clambered to her feet. She looked in the direction of Emma's outstretched finger toward the horizon.

With a darkening sky and a strong freshening wind signaling its advance, a great storm was coming across the water. It was sweeping directly toward them, the black and deep grey clouds spreading and doubling even as they watched. Inside the clouds were flashes of pitchfork lightning, a glowering Devil's inferno that now emitted ominous rumbles of thunder. With every second, the wind grew stronger, the waves higher, frothing into whitecaps that surged against the outer line of rocks in the breakwater.

"We have ten minutes!" Emma cried out through the whistling wind as she clambered down the rock and onto the boardwalk again.

"Less!" Jasmine called back, looking out at the storm with a practiced eye. She had not moved. "We can't just leave him here!" she cried out, in her great terror of what awaited him.

"We must go for help, and Jasmine, you must come. Come now!" Emma commanded.

Her words rang out with authority, and because she was unable to do anything for him, to save him, Jasmine came. As they rushed down the boardwalk Emma bent and picked up something, a knife. Then they hurried through the gate in the wall next to the boathouse, taking a few precious seconds to close it fast. Just as they leapt into the front seat, the first wave of rain hit, sounding a great drum roll across the roof of the car.

Emma dropped the knife on the seat and instantly started up the motor. They were both of them shaking with exertion and emotion, and struck with sudden anxiety about Laura and her whereabouts.

"What's this?" asked Jasmine picking it up. "A bread knife? What were you planning? To slice him?"

Emma ignored the remark. "Anna must call the police," she said, straining to see as she drove through the curtains of rain. "Our being here will only raise questions if they learn of it. She'll have to convince them to go find him."

As they sped homeward, the storm in its full fury descended upon the town of Medford. Both fell silent, knowing that out on the breakwater, a man was dying. A bad man, but a man nonetheless, and there was no time nor means to save him. The storm surge, even by now, would have covered the first course of rocks on the breakwater.

Emma had advised Anna to go to the party and, as far as possible, to act as if nothing were amiss. At the Ritsons', Anna left the noisy, overcrowded main level of the house to take the phone call in an upstairs bedroom. She sat there for a little while, her hands folded, her face emotionless. Then she dialed the number Emma had given her for the police, although, she thought, she should know it well enough by now.

"That was Royce Parke's wife," Constable Sloane said when he put down the phone.

The others looked up from the table where they were seated. There were four of them in total, three policemen and Sven Robinson, who had been locked up drunk but now was sober and had joined them in a few hands of poker using beer bottle and soft drink caps instead of poker chips until the storm diminished.

"What's the problem now?" There were always problems associated with Royce Parke and Constable Montgomery only said what they all were thinking.

"She says he was working on the breakwater at the Airdrie Estate and he hasn't called in, and she's sure he's in trouble out there."

They looked at one another with the natural disinclination of men in a dry, comfortable place to leave and head out into the teeth of a savage storm. But in the end three went, including Sven, who was as strong as any two of them from his farm work and had voiced some fondness for Royce as a drinking and fighting buddy.

"I'm not doing this for that bastard Parke," declared Montgomery, who was winning and loath to leave. "Only his wife, who deserves better."

After opening the gate with the key the Airdrie family had provided for such emergencies, they drove in, parked, and walked through the lashing rain across the lawn to the lake. They stood there, and not one of them spoke. Even if they had, none would have heard, for the roar of the wind and the thunderous crash of the massive waves cascading over the breakwater and rushing in tumbling torrents of froth right up to the grassy shoreline.

At the Fitzgerald's house, Laura sat warm and dry with five other children watching the Cisco Kid on television and eating popcorn.

"We tried to call, to let you know she was here," the housekeeper, Mrs. Vickers, said rather accusingly to her wet and distraught-looking mother, "but there was no one at home."

CHAPTER 95

The circumstances of Royce's death were widely circulated and his funeral well attended, not so much out of any liking for the man as from horror, pity and a rather morbid curiosity. Two questions in particular flew from mouth to mouth. Why was he out there on the breakwater, and how had he managed to entrap himself? For when they found him, he was still held fast in the rocks, and his body could only be freed with the use of a pickaxe and crowbar. As the story was told time and again, one of his legs had slipped into an opening and twisted. It was held fast by his strange leather boot with its long cuff, which caught on the surrounding stones and defeated all their more simple attempts to pull him free.

Anna had asked Jasmine to be with her when the body was brought to the funeral parlour. Although well accustomed to seeing bodies in less than perfect condition, Jasmine took one look at Royce, bloated with water and battered almost beyond recognition, and ran from the room. She quieted her heaving stomach in the hall outside, hoping beyond hope that Anna had not seen what she had. Thankfully, she did not; so at least she was spared that dreadful knowledge. For as Jasmine said to Emma later, she could see that Royce's fingernails were scraped to the quick and torn, his fingers abraded from his desperate attempts to free himself.

"So he wasn't even granted the blessing of unconsciousness." Emma had listened, quiet and grave. "We can only hope it goes against his sin, and wasn't instead a sample of what lies in store for him."

At the church the whole MacClure family was marshaled to support Anna, who cried a few tears, enough at least to satisfy the requirements of funeral decorum. But no one could believe that anyone would truly grieve a husband like Royce Parke.

"We did have some good times," she confided to Jasmine when they shared an affectionate embrace afterward. "He was the father of my children, and no one deserves such a dreadful death. But what really makes me sad, Jasmine, is that I'm mourning not him, but the man he might have been if only he tried."

They stood at graveside under a grey sky while the coffin was lowered into the ground. Father McLaughlin recited a few last words. As the clods of earth began to rain down on top, Emma turned white as a sheet. She staggered and with help from the strong arms that were quick to support her, had to be sat down. However, she soon shook off her fainting spell, and was sufficiently recovered to spend five hours on her feet helping out at the reception.

It was not until all was over and done and they were sitting in the kitchen at home that she told Jasmine what had happened.

"While we were burying him, I had a sudden vision of Royce standing in front of our Lord God with that dreadful sin on his soul. I swear, Jasmine, it was so real I thought I might just pass out from the fright of it."

And as Jasmine complained the next morning, she wished she hadn't told her, for she had taken that horrid image with her to her sleepless bed.

* * *

It was a dreary task they were engaged in, Anna and her father, the clear out of Royce's personal effects from the gatehouse. Jim had his car and a borrowed trailer at the ready to take away the few bits of furniture and bags of clothing, most of it destined for charity. There had been one bright spot. When they arrived early Saturday morning, they were met by Ken Airdrie Sr., who apologized for missing the funeral Thursday. He added that his wife was indisposed; otherwise she would have come to the gatehouse with him to offer her condolences. Then he handed Anna an envelope that contained a hand-written note of sympathy, Royce's last wages and a substantial cheque.

"We'll find it hard to replace him," Airdrie said with great sincerity. He was a sleek fox of a man, with his immaculately groomed mane of red-and-white hair, sharp-featured face and small, shrewd eyes. He smelt of bay rum aftershave and was dressed down for the weekend in his country tweeds.

"Royce was a hard worker and he seemed to really enjoy everything he was doing here."

The unintentional irony of this statement was not lost on Anna, who repeated it later to Jasmine.

Jim was grumbling away about the cheque – which, although a fortune by Anna's reckoning, he pronounced stingy and said it reflected the fact such people didn't get rich by giving it away – when, reaching to the very back of a drawer in the desk in Royce's bedroom, he made an unsettling discovery.

"What's this?"

After extricating his hand from the tight space, Jim showed Anna a small cloth sleeve that opened to reveal a bankbook. He handed it to her and she examined it. "It's a passbook for the bank in Shelton." She had named a town about sixteen miles distant. "His name is on it. Let's see how much he has in it."

Only a few minutes before, Anna had located Royce's passbook for the Medford bank and a stash of bills tucked away in the drawer of the night table. She was feeling even less tenderly toward her deceased husband after comparing the meager amounts he had given her for the support of their family with the rather impressive savings he had accumulated during his employment at the estate.

Now she flipped to the page in the second passbook, where the first, and as it turned out, the only deposit made by Royce Parke was recorded. She gasped. "He has two thousand dollars in this bank account! And it was all put in at one time, on February 23rd!"

She turned to Jim. "Why does that date sound familiar?"

Her father grimly said, "it should. That was the date the tannery burnt down. The fire started on the twenty-second and it only finished burning late the next day. But how would Royce get to Shelton?"

"He used to borrow Bernie Listowel's car occasionally," Anna replied automatically. She was still staring at the passbook, but not seeing it. Instead, she was remembering a pair of pants on a clothesline, flapping in the wind. It was the day after the fire started, February the twenty-third, that she spied them: the pants Royce had attempted to wash, still smelling so strongly of gasoline. He had run the clothesline out until they were mostly hidden among the cedars along the fence line in their backyard.

"Why would he want to use a bank out of town?" Jim asked wonderingly.

Anna smiled. The things her father didn't know, even after living all his life in a town like Medford, a hotbed of gossip, where even bank tellers couldn't be trusted not to talk! "Dad, for folks in Medford who want to keep their financial matters private, going to another town to do banking is standard practice."

Then Anna told him her suspicions, which were more like the missing pieces of a puzzle Jim had been trying to sort out in his mind ever since the tannery burned down.

As they were leaving carrying out the last of the suitcases and bags to the car and trailer parked on the street, a black car slowly nosed out of the Airdries' drive. Now it pulled up close to the curb, stopped, and they saw Dr. Miller at the wheel. He opened the car door and came over. Taking the two suitcases Anna was struggling with, he lifted them easily into the trailer. Jim watched, bemused, as they smiled shyly at one another.

"We didn't have much time to talk at the funeral parlour," Keith Miller said to her. "But I just wanted to tell you how sorry I am about the circumstances of your husband's death."

As Jim said later when relating the events of that morning to Margery, "he didn't say he was sorry that Royce had died, only for how it happened. In fact, after seeing the way he looked at Anna, I would have to say that he didn't seem sorry at all!"

CHAPTER 96

It was eight thirty when Jasmine came downstairs after putting Laura to bed. By now Emma was usually sitting in the study, listening to the radio and knitting or darning. Tonight, however, Jasmine discovered her still bustling about the kitchen, and since the three of them – Emma, Thomas and Jasmine – had long ago washed up the dinner dishes, she knew Emma had something she wanted to say to her without the presence of certain small ears or Thomas. From the way she was noisily clanking the few remaining utensils and pots she was putting away, Jasmine could also sense that their conversation might not be altogether pleasant.

So, what was the problem? Curious, Jasmine sat at the kitchen table and waited. As usual, Emma started off with an oblique approach, talking about other lesser things before she worked around to the real meat of the matter.

"I'd like to know when you and Anna intend to go and see the Whites about Gussie."

"We spoke about this before," Jasmine answered patiently. "Anna has a few things to sort out first. She's to call them next week. However, she's decided it's you, not me, she wants with her."

Emma turned and stared. This was a surprise. "Why would you want me there, when you're the mother of one of the children concerned?"

Would a little flattery sweeten her up? Jasmine said, "because you're well known and respected in town and strong enough to handle Cleon White. From all accounts, he's quite unpleasant to deal with."

"Well, I don't mind going," Emma sighed. "I'll talk to Edna Matthews to find out if she can tell me something more about them."

Jasmine concluded that her little attempt at flattery had had no appreciable effect.

"Now, I also wanted to ask you if you've made any decision about leaving Laura here for the summer."

"Well, don't you think that's a rather large responsibility for you to take on? What if something happened?"

"Both Thomas and I will be here to take care of her. And she won't be doing anything she isn't doing here already, except I'd like her to take swimming lessons at the lake, just as you did when you were a child. That's something she won't get in Vegas."

Emma could see by Jasmine's face she still hadn't made up her mind, that the thought of leaving her daughter behind was distressing for her, and that as Jasmine always did, she was about to say no. "Never mind, we'll leave that for a different time," she interjected quickly. "Perhaps we should ask the child herself what she'd prefer."

Jasmine brightened. "Yes, that might be a good idea." Then, more briskly, "is there anything else? I'd like to take a turn around the block before bed." She knew very well that Emma did have something else to discuss, and that it was probably the reason for all the clanging and banging of pots earlier. She wanted it over and done with.

"Yes. I'd like to know what you plan to do about that man."

Jasmine laughed, a little incredulously, at this intrusion into her private affairs. "What man?"

"That man sitting across the kitchen table from you, the one you're torturing."

"You're the one who insists on having him for dinner! And I'm not torturing him! Whatever are you talking about?"

"Those too-tight blouses you wear. And pants. He looked fit to faint dead away tonight when your shirt popped open and he got an eyeful while you were standing reaching across the table with the dish of peas! Just what do you think you're doing? You can't play games with him like you do your other boyfriends!"

Jasmine was flushed and furious. Her voice rose in a crescendo, loud and indignant. "My other boyfriends! You ought to know I was a married woman, a faithful, happily married woman! And after that, perhaps I did go out with a few men maybe once or twice, then found out they were really just desert rats in disguise! And if I wear clothes that are too tight, well, that's your fault!

"My fault!" Emma exclaimed derisively. "How could it possibly be my fault?"

"Because all that good home cooking you do is making me fat! I haven't anything to wear other than the clothes that came with me! Until I go home and earn some money, I can't afford anything new."

Emma regarded her rather fondly. Then she said, "Well, you're certainly not fat. You were skin and bones when you came here, and now you're just about right. But Jasmine, I'm worried about Thomas. That man is in love with you. It's as plain as the nose on his face. And he's such a good man. I wouldn't like to see him trifled with."

Jasmine was still angry. Emma's words did nothing to placate her. "I have to respect the fact that Lianne is only recently deceased, and he's in mourning," she said frostily. "And he's not really in love with me, is he? He's in lust for me, and there are plenty of other reasons not to take it seriously."

"So – is that what you think, truly?" Emma looked at her shrewdly and had the satisfaction of seeing her lower her eyes. "You know Thomas, Jasmine. Do you really think that man, who has always been faithful to one woman – with one notable exception – is the kind to change? No, he would have lost interest in you long ago if he didn't have deeper feelings; that's just the way he is. And whether you like it or not, right now you, with your daughter, have his happiness in your hands."

Finally it seemed she had struck a chord. Jasmine put her elbows on the tabletop. She lowered her head in her hands and was quiet for a long moment. When she spoke again, her voice was full of emotion. "You may be right, Emma. And I know what Lianne wanted, and that you would be happy if Thomas and I were to –"

She stopped. Then she looked at Emma directly. "But have you ever considered how it would look for Thomas, at this point in his career as the newly appointed vice principal of a prestigious, old and rather stuffy boy's school, to have a wife who was once a blackjack dealer in a Vegas casino? Oh yes, there was more to my job, staff training, the odd special event, but when it comes right down to it, that's what I did. No one is going to know or care that it took skill and intelligence to do it properly, or that, in my case, the pay was better than being a teacher, or a bank manager for that matter!"

"The other problem, Emma, is, I liked my job! I miss the way it made me think and use my mind, my brain! How about my happiness Emma? What about that?"

Emma would not give up so readily. She got to her feet. "Yes, there are obstacles, and I see what you're saying. But if you love each other, Jasmine, then love will find a way."

"That's a lovely fairy tale sentiment," Jasmine called out to her as she went toward the study. "But in my lifetime so far, Emma, fairy tales haven't ever come true!"

In the study, Emma did not immediately pick up her knitting or turn on the radio. She sat quietly for a moment, thinking. There was no getting around it. Until now, everything had gone relatively smoothly. But this was the final stumbling block, and it was a big one. As the new vice-principal of a large private boy's school, ambitious and intent on stepping up to the job of principal, what Thomas didn't need was a wife – and a bored, discontented wife at that – who was a former Vegas blackjack dealer with a sideline in mortuary makeup.

CHAPTER 97

He was playing hooky today and felt not a jot of conscience. It was early afternoon and he had absented himself from the office after putting back on Mike Simm's desk a report Simms was supposed to read and digest, then comment on, a task that he had attempted to palm off on him. With it he left a note saying that personal matters required his attention and he was leaving early.

Several days before, Emma had come over to the house with Laura, who was bubbling with delight over her new bicycle and wanted to show it off to him.

"I paid for half of it!" she announced proudly. "And I got the last dollar and a half from grasshoppers! They were all in Simon's dad's garden and I caught them! At first I grabbed them in my hands but they spit tobacco on your hands and make them yellow, so after the first ones I just put a jar over the top of them when they landed and trapped them with the lid."

She wheeled back and forth in front of him so that he could admire the new bike, blue and white with stripes on the fenders, and then she left them for a turn around the block. Emma took advantage of her absence to have a few private words.

"Jasmine is doing a good job for you?"

"Yes. When we meet after I get home, she generally has a lot of questions about what I want to keep. She's been ingenious at getting rid of the stuff I don't want."

"She says you'd just as readily throw everything out."

"Um, well, she's made me quite a lot of money selling things. More than I pay her, actually! But now she's into the attic and I had forgotten just how much there is in there, or even what was there in the first place."

Then Emma had asked him the question he was increasingly worrying over.

"What are you going to do about Jasmine? It's obvious to me that you care about her."

Yes, he cared for her. In fact, he was longing, aching for her. It was a deep, bodily ache that grew each time they met, every time he saw her. A sweet agony that made him feel like some love-sick teenager, that disturbed his days and nights.

"Is it that obvious? I guess it is. But I have to respect her wishes, and she hasn't given me much encouragement."

Emma snorted in a rather unladylike manner. "You're respecting her wishes; she says she's respecting the fact you're in mourning. It seems to me there's altogether too much respect going on with you two, and that soon you will have respected her all the way to Las Vegas!"

Then Laura came rolling back, flushed and excited, and after he promised her a bell for her bike and she had given him a hug, they went home. But Emma had made her point.

Now, after parking the car, he let himself in the back door, took off his suit coat and tie and went upstairs to talk to Jasmine.

The staging area for items brought down from the attic was in one of the second floor bedrooms, almost bare now that the bed and dresser had been sold. This was where he found her, by the window, caught in a stream of golden sunbeams full of flickering dust motes from the objects she had just retrieved. Her hair hung loose in coppery tresses and she was flushed from the warmth of the day.

"Oh! My goodness, you startled me!" she said, her hand to her mouth. He was about to speak, but then remained silent. She was so beautiful standing there, outlined in her aura of sunshine. She was wearing shorts and her long legs, all of her, glowed goldenly.

"I thought you were Emma; she said she might come over. You're home early. Is there a problem?" she asked anxiously.

Thomas smiled. He leaned against the doorway and shook his head. "No, no problem. I just wanted to talk to you, and when I come from work there's never enough time before dinner."

He had made her nervous, with his sudden unexpected presence and these words, and she laughed a little too quickly and said, "yes, and I wanted to talk to you! Did you know that your birthday and Laura's are only two days apart? Hers is June twenty-seventh."

"No, is that so?" Amazing! He was aware it was soon, but not that it was so near to his. She was close to being his birthday present, and he had never known. At the thought, he felt a twinge of sorrow at all of the years of her growing up he had lost.

"Yes, and we have a party planned for her, but Emma and I would like to do something for you as well. Would you like anything special for your birthday?"

"Would I like anything special for my birthday," he repeated, rather stupidly, because he knew exactly what he wanted for his birthday but suspected that if he voiced it, it would earn him a slap across the face. Then he had an inspiration, though a rather brazen one. Should he dare to say it? But before he could think much about whether or not he would, the words tumbled out.

"In fact, there is something," he said. "Just a kiss. But I'd like it now, here, instead of on my birthday."

She looked at him uncertainly. "Thomas, do you think that's a good idea?" she asked, with every show of hesitation. She knew very well where this might lead, no, in all probability would lead, to a fire that would consume them from their first touch. But perhaps, she thought, it was time. There was so little time.

"It's the best idea I've had for a long while."

He came slowly toward her from across the room, his eyes deep sapphire where the sun caught them. He held out his hands, the palms facing her, and almost automatically she extended hers in the old gesture of greeting they once used. Their fingers touched, and he pulled her arms around him. Then he held her face between his hands and they exchanged a sweet, almost innocent kiss. She felt him tremble.

"There," she said, moving away a little, breathless: "you've had your kiss."

"But that wasn't the kiss I wanted," he said. His voice was deeper now, almost a growl, his breathing shallow and rapid. He was still holding her, drawing her close.

"It was the next one."

And then he kissed her, and she felt his length against her, the flame-like heat of his body, his tongue against hers, his arousal. They kissed again and again, and he bent to kiss down her neck into that sweet space, the cleft between her breasts; and a little later, when she began to swoon against him, he picked her up and carried her across the hall to one of the bedrooms that still had a bed and locked the door.

CHAPTER 98

It had been a different kind of dinnertime.

Emma sat in the study, her knitting paused. She had to count her stitches at this point in the pattern, but there was too much going on in her mind to do a proper job of it. She was thinking about the expression on Thomas's face as he sat down to dinner. He had looked like a cat with cream. And was he holding Jasmine's hand under the table? Then there was Jasmine, all flushed and glowing, and the looks she saw passing between them when they thought she wasn't looking.

Yes, something had been settled between them. This was progress, another step in the plan. The plan that would soon come up against a brick wall: Jasmine's departure and the particular kind of job to which she was returning.

Emma picked up her knitting again. There was nothing further she could do. Either what they felt for each other would be stopped short by that obstacle, or somehow, she ardently prayed, they might just leap over it.

* * *

Thomas was on the stony beach of the lake, keeping stride with a moon so bright it cast a tall shadow figure to accompany him as he walked. His step was light; he was lifted up by the joy of this day, his love and new fullness of life in the beautiful month of June.

He stopped to look out over the quiet lake. When he was a boy, he used to envision himself walking up that silvery path on the water to sit on the moon. Today, he thought, he had reached and was over it, over the moon.

He would not let himself think about how Jasmine would leave, shortly after this month, or how transient and fleeting most of his times of true joy had been. But before he scaled the steep path up the cliff to walk the sidewalk leading home, he made a vow. No matter what it cost him personally, he would no longer settle only for memories. He would chase and capture joy and then stretch it, if he could, from mere moments into years.

* * *

You hardly know me anymore, she said. I've changed. No, he shook his head. You may be older, more mature, but you're still the same person. She used to tell me everything you talked about during your days together. Perhaps not everything – I know you had your secrets – but all your conversations. I fell in love with you all over again, just from what she told me.

Lying on her bed that night, still languorous from their lovemaking and close to sleep, Jasmine was not thinking of Thomas so much as Lianne. It was now clear that what Lianne had done for Thomas, she had done for her. She had talked about Thomas, his past and present. She told her what he was doing, thinking, described his concern and affection for his students, his tender and loving care of her in her illness. Jasmine soon felt as if she had become reacquainted with him, the good man that he was, well before he and she ever spoke. Now she realized that this, too, had been deliberate, another of Lianne's loving, generous gifts.

That afternoon, she had cried in his arms. Just think, she said, how much she gave up for us. She put aside all the normal, human feelings that as your wife, anyone might expect her to have – the bitterness and jealousy, the anger – so that she could give us joy. I miss her so, Thomas. She'll always be in my heart, she told him, and he had kissed away her tears and wiped away his own.

Now, gazing out her bedroom window at the starry night, she prayed. If ever there was a saint, dear friend, it's you. So now that you've found your way up there, please help. Together, perhaps we can figure this out.

CHAPTER 99

The wisteria vine that covered the porch was in late bloom. It was as old as the house, planted over one hundred years ago, and due to Emma's diligent pruning and fertilizing, this June it was flowering abundantly. Emma was standing on the front lawn admiring it and inhaling its perfume, so sweet it was almost dizzying, when a car pulled up to the curb. The door opened and Edna Matthews climbed out and joined her in contemplation of the splendiferous wisteria and its pendulous lilac blossoms.

"Mine died some years ago," Edna mourned. "The house is just that little bit too close to the lake, and the poor thing caught a chill."

"Perhaps when you move, it'll be to some place more suitable for fussy plants," Emma offered consolingly.

"That's what I dropped by to tell you. I'm not moving after all." Edna was smiling broadly. She did not appear at all distressed, but delighted by her news.

"Mason Stoddart says his circumstances have changed and he's thinking of going to California. You know, Emma, I didn't feel I was ready to leave the house anyhow, so it's actually a blessing in disguise. When we all got together for my birthday recently, I told the children that the only present I wanted was for them to stop bullying me! Let me be the one to decide when I need to move, I said!"

Emma looked thoughtfully after Edna as she drove off, on her way across town to babysit the grandchildren. She finished plucking the spent blooms on the potted pink geraniums on either side of the front steps. Then she hurried into the house, because she was leaving Jasmine, Thomas and Laura to their own dinner preparations and going to a very important meeting at the MacClures.

* * *

"We've reached a stalemate here, Emma," Margery said. They had just finished dinner. Because of a simmering disagreement between father and daughter, by common consent and in the interests of good digestion there had been no discussion about Royce's estate, or how they would handle their upcoming meeting with the Whites. Now the four of them were proceeding from the kitchen table to the dining room table, which was covered by more or less tidy heaps of paper and documents.

"There's really only one sticking point," Jim said. "It's the money that Royce ferreted away in the bank in Shelton. It's a good sum, and I think Anna should pay down the mortgage on her house with it."

Anna's chin was firmly set as she replied. "It's tainted money. I'm absolutely certain it's the money Royce was paid for setting the tannery on fire. I want nothing to do with it. I told Dad I want to give it to the Whites, so they can get their poor daughter some professional help and counseling after what Royce did to her."

"And I told her," Jim continued, "that considering all we've heard about Cleon White, he'll take the money and spend it however he wants. Unless we sit on him, there's no way to be certain it will be put to its proper use."

Emma nodded. "I'm inclined to agree with Jim," she said. "However," and she paused for emphasis, "I think there just might be another alternative."

Three days later, Emma, Anna and Edna Matthews stood together in front of the White's front door. The dangling drainpipe still dangled from the top of the house, and they were grateful for the protection of the porch roof overhead.

After several knocks, the door swung open to reveal the considerable bulk of Cleon White. "So you wanted to see us about Gussie. What's this all about?" he asked aggressively as he ushered them in. Mrs. Pagett, the housekeeper, hovered inquisitively nearby.

"It's confidential, a matter for you and your wife," Emma replied brusquely, with a meaningful glance at Mrs. Pagett, who gave her a decidedly unfriendly look and disappeared into the kitchen.

Nancy White awaited them on the sofa in the living room, which was comfortably if sparsely furnished, clean, and obviously kept off-limits to the hordes of White children. In contrast to her husband, she was a slim and pretty if rather faded brunette, with a look of perpetual exhaustion about her. Her husband took the seat next to her, and left them to find chairs wherever they could.

"I heard about your husband Royce," he said rather gruffly to Anna. "I'm sorry for your loss."

"You may not be," Anna replied, "after I tell you why I'm here."

As she spoke, the Whites sat up straighter and, as Emma remarked later to Margery, turned a shade that was truly in keeping with their surname. Even Cleon, so heavily weathered, turned pale under his tan. It was painful to see the sorrow of Gussie's mother. The three of them, Emma, Edna and Anna, were touched to see big, burly Cleon take his sobbing wife tenderly into his arms, while glaring protectively at the intruders who had caused her so much distress.

"Cleon and I spoke about her, didn't we dear?" Nancy sobbed through her tears. "We couldn't find out what was the matter with Gussie, why her grades at school kept going down, or why she wasn't talking and looked so gloomy; she wouldn't tell us!"

"But she kept on going back whenever he asked!" thundered Cleon. "What sort of young girl does that? She must have wanted to do it, to keep on with him!"

Emma spoke up. "Gussie was protecting her little sister from Royce. If you speak with Gussie, I'm certain you'll find out that Royce threatened to hurt Ariadne if she didn't do what he wanted. That was the strategy he used to make your child obey him, because, as Anna can tell you, he did the very same thing in his own family. Now, if you don't mind, I want to bring up another matter. Your daughter is going to need professional help to heal, in order to be a happy child once more. I have the names of a few doctors who do the kind of counseling she'll need."

The Whites looked at one another. "We don't have money for that kind of thing," Cleon said dismissively. He turned to face Anna. "And seeing as it was your husband did this, oughtn't you to pay for it?" he challenged her belligerently. "How about it?"

Emma was the spokesperson, and she answered. "Anna's financial situation is very tight. That's why your neighbour Edna Matthews is here. As a close friend of Anna's family, she has very kindly offered to supply the funds for professional help for your daughter."

"That's good news," Cleon said, and now there was a light in his eyes. "When do we get it, and how much is there?"

"In fact," Emma continued smoothly, "the funds will remain with Mrs. Matthews. She will pay for the counseling and has even offered to take Gussie to her counseling sessions. Both of you already have busy lives. Edna lives nearby and she has the time and wants to help Gussie."

"How much is it," Cleon repeated again, insistently. "I'd like to know just how much we're talking about here."

"Two thousand dollars," Emma said reluctantly.

"Two thousand dollars! That's a fortune! And we're her parents! We have the right to do what we think is best for her with that money!" Now Cleon's face was no longer pale but had taken on a red, rather apoplectic hue.

Unexpectedly, after remaining silent during this entire conversation, Edna spoke up. She was just as irate as he when she retorted, "well, Mr. White, those are the only terms on which I will give any money for Gussie's recovery. You and your wife will have the last say over the doctor or professional person chosen to help; I 'll take her there and back and pay for treatment. This is a generous offer, and I'm only making it once!"

They looked on in horrified fascination as Cleon White grew redder and redder. He seemed about to explode when his wife put a gentle hand on his arm.

"Darling," she said, a term of endearment that rang oddly in their ears to describe such a brute of a man, "this is about our daughter Gussie. We failed her once, by not taking the time to find out what was troubling her. Let's not fail her again. This is a very good, very kind offer Mrs. Matthews has made. Let's just graciously accept it."

The transformation that followed was amazing. Her husband turned to face her, and with that one movement his expression altered from billowing anger to love and adoration. Afterward, Anna said that she was instantly reminded of Selby, Jim's old dog, and the look in his eyes whenever Jim patted him on the head.

"If you think so, sweetheart," he said to her; then, turning to Edna, "well, I guess that'd be alright then, after all."

So it was settled, and as they left the White's home, Nancy White shakily stood up and came toward Edna. She took her hand into both of hers and said with great sincerity, "thank you so very much. If you're able to come back tomorrow, the two of us can work out the details, and you can talk to Gussie."

While she waited, Emma took advantage of the short pause at the door to speak to Mrs. Pagett as she came bustling past them toward the stairs. "The matter we were just discussing is highly confidential," she told the housekeeper pointedly. "You can imagine the problems it would cause for Gussie and her family, and for Mrs. Parke if news of it ever got out."

"I'm sure," sniffed Mrs. Pagett in high dudgeon, "I've no idea what you're talking about!"

"And I'm sure," replied Emma, speaking more loudly now, so Nancy White could overhear her reply, "that it could only have been you I saw holding the hall door open a crack to listen, and that if even a whisper of what was said today ever comes back to us, we will know whom to blame!"

Edna was waiting for them as they descended the stone stairs to the street. They exchanged a few words and said their goodbyes before she left them to walk along the sidewalk toward her house.

"There goes that poor girl's best hope of recovery," Emma remarked as they stood beside the car watching Edna depart.

Anna was puzzled. "Why? Because she'll make sure Gussie gets the help she needs?"

Midway along the street, Edna turned for a backward glance. Then she and Emma exchanged a wave. "There's that, of course," Emma said. "But I really meant Edna herself, with her chocolate milk and cookies and her wonderful way with children."

She was remembering the near-delight on Edna's face when she proposed their tentative plan to her.

"I just knew there was a reason for me to stay on in the house; that God had something more he needed me to do! And now here it is!" she had exclaimed joyfully.

She would need all her remarkable mothering skills to help heal that sad, broken child. But although Gussie was sure to be a challenge, as Emma knew she would, it was one that Edna quickly took to heart.

CHAPTER 100

The flow of letters with U.S. postmarks to the Madison home, always steady once Jasmine and Laura took up residence, now turned into a river. Beside the usual faithful letters from Mike, more letters for Jasmine were arriving from friends and a new stream from potential employers. Although Jasmine did not speak much about her job search, it was obvious she would have no difficulty finding work on her return to Vegas.

The day's mail had just fallen through the mail slot and one letter in particular for Jasmine, from a jewelry store in the city, intrigued Emma. After picking it up and bending it experimentally, she detected the crispness of what seemed to be a cheque. Her curiosity was satisfied when, after returning from another dusty morning spent in the Latham attic, Jasmine opened it and uttered a little exclamation of happiness and surprise.

"My jewelry finally sold!" She waved the letter at Emma. "Everything went except one pin and a few bracelets. Even with the percentage to the store, it's twice what I would have gotten from a pawnshop!" Jasmine exulted. "I never expected them to go at full list, but it seems that would be just about what the buyer paid."

Although not especially familiar with the ways of consignment jewelry vendors, it seemed rather improbably generous to Emma. She wondered if there was a reason the purchaser hadn't bartered down the price.

The mystery would continue to tantalize her. It would only be solved many years later, although not by Emma. Arlena had heard of the munificent sum paid for Jasmine's jewels and had long nursed her suspicions. When Elizabeth Stoddart passed away and her two daughters were going through her effects after her death, the sisters had one of their very few disagreements. Tucked far in the back of a bottom dresser drawer, Althea found an old, worn blue velvet box. When she opened it, a variety of rings, bracelets and necklaces tumbled out.

If memory served, neither Althea nor Arlena could recall their mother ever wearing any of the items in the box. They amicably shared most of the jewelry, but then had a rather pitched and lengthy battle over who would get the best piece, a sapphire ring surrounded by diamonds. Eventually, through sheer persistence and determination, Arlena won out.

She was certain she knew to whom it had once belonged. She did not have to guess at how it came to be in her mother's possession. The ring was beautiful; too beautiful to hide away in safekeeping. She wore it often, as a memento of someone she once loved, long ago.

The cheque Jasmine received for her jewels was the last key to her freedom. She finally had the funds she needed for her escape. But for the occupants of the Madison house this time of early summer, the most brilliant and beautiful of the year, would be remembered as tinged with sadness. There was the lingering grief over Lianne's death, and now, the bittersweet flavour of the days winding down to Jasmine's departure. To Emma, the news that Sylvia's jewelry had been sold was yet another melancholy note of finality, eliciting thoughts of her sister, sparkling with youth and beauty, then slowly dimming and fading away.

Seemingly it also struck a chord with Thomas, who had returned home to Medford this Sunday with another small blue velvet box. It was for Jasmine, as a token of his love and hopes for the future and some compensation, perhaps, for what she had lost in the past.

On most weekends over the last month, he had traveled to Kellington to scout for living accommodation and spend time with Arthur McIntyre, the principal of the Royal Sutton Boys School. As he told Jasmine, McIntyre, in his early sixties, was nearing the end of a successful career. An affable, clever and dedicated educator, he had quickly won Thomas's respect and liking. It seemed his regard was returned. During their last visit, MacIntyre made it clear he was grooming Thomas to take over the reins from him and admitted he was looking forward to the day, not far away, when he would retire.

It was almost dark when Thomas let himself in the back door, and after walking through the house he found Jasmine on the front porch with Emma. Emma did not require persuasion to leave. She made her excuses and diplomatically disappeared into the study. Alone, the lovers held hands and silently looked into each other's eyes, words being a rather unnecessary embellishment to the feelings that had grown up between them. What they both experienced when they first met, magnetism, electricity or simple desire, had changed into something stronger, deeper. But their bond was still new and as he made the long journey home, Thomas was fearful that, weakened by time and distance, it might slowly dissolve.

He stood up and pulled the porch curtain across, and in that darker dark they embraced, but only for a moment. After that first, blissful afternoon spent together, Jasmine had insisted on caution, unwilling to chance any damage to Thomas's reputation and not incidentally, her own. There was speculation enough about them, she knew. She felt a thrill of fear almost every time she traveled the path between the Latham and Madison houses, sensing, even if she couldn't see it, the eagle eye of Emily Barrett peering down from the eyrie of her kitchen window.

The result was that Thomas had become filled with frustration at the nature of their relationship, with the fleeting encounters that left him, as he said, ravenous for her. He was a man passionately in love, willing to risk everything to be with her; but she stubbornly refused to let him do it. That was the issue casting a shadow over their relationship, and now it was taking on thundercloud proportions.

As they sat side by side on the wicker sofa, he reached into a pocket. "I've brought you something from Kellington," he said, and produced a little blue box. Jasmine quailed: was it an engagement ring? If it was, she could not accept it. He sensed her hesitation. "You're a woman who should wear jewels, darling. I'm giving you some of your own, so that you won't miss the ones you've lost too much."

Reassured by these words, she opened the velvet-covered box. He heard the sharp intake of her breath. "They're beautiful! And what a size! You shouldn't have, Thomas, but I do so love them. How thoughtful of you!"

And she immediately took the diamond earrings out of the box and put them on. She knew that, until she left Medford, she would wear them only for him.

"They should really be in a ring," he said rather bitterly. "But of course, as you told me, you don't want one; it wouldn't be right. Though it's all right for us to have these torrid love affairs; it was all right for me to inseminate you so we could have this wonderful child. But when I offer you the honorable state of marriage, you turn me down. It's confusing, but I'm going along with it because I love you; so instead of a ring I'm giving you the kind of gift one gives a mistress."

"Yes," she said, as she finished attaching the second earring, "I am your mistress. But don't think this lovely present will excuse you from giving me a proper set of wedding rings, because I will be your wife, one day soon. Only, Thomas, have faith in me! Let me work things out so that you don't throw away your chances in your new position, and so that I can marry you without being a liability!"

Even in the dim light she could see the penetrating look he gave her. "I'm beginning to think," he said, "you have other reasons for what you're doing that you don't want to talk about."

How perceptive he was. And of course there was a reason, not that she would ever tell him. She respected, admired, deeply loved this man, she knew she would never again find his equal. But she hated the prospect of her life as his wife. Not the marriage part – that would be wonderful, perhaps with the addition of a baby to give him joy, and Laura a belated sister or brother – but the teas, the fundraisers, the tiresome expectations surrounding her behaviour, and the sheer insufficiency of the role of being just, "wife of".

Perhaps she could have fit the mold when she was younger, had she married someone like Mason. Even then she doubted it would have been enough. She craved challenge, change, a life of her own. Medford had been a good enough place for her recovery. For the work of reinvention, however, she must go elsewhere.

"I have a house to sell and arrangements to make," she said patiently. "Aside from all the history trailing us, there's a period between the death of one wife and marriage to another that should be respected by a man in your position. Please, Thomas; please wait."

"You leave me with little other choice," he said flatly.

My gracious, but he was in a mood. Jasmine sighed and tossed her head. "Good heavens, what a grumpy Gus you are! I don't know why I ever took up with you again!"

She could always depend on his sense of humour. "And I don't know why I ever got back together with you, you're such a hard-headed woman!" he retorted. "And a saucy wench to boot!"

She put her arms around him, drawing him close and stretching sensuously against him. "You did it because you're such a big Tomcat, and I know just how to pet you and make you purr," she said, her voice soft and silky, her lips against his cheek. But he reluctantly pulled away.

"Don't start anything you can't finish here and now, because I need to sleep tonight." He bit off the words.

Oh, but he was so sour! How to sweeten him up? She thought she knew the answer. A good helping of sugar would do it.

"I was thinking – perhaps this coming weekend you could meet me in the city?"

He sat up straighter. Then in his teacher-principal voice, he said, "you're only trying to get back on my good side, aren't you, making an offer like that?"

Jasmine waited. Now, even in the semi-darkness, she could see the smile she had been hoping for, the one with the little curlicues indented on either side, that was not just on the mouth she wanted to kiss but dancing in his eyes.

"The answer's yes, of course! I would love you in the city this weekend."

Oh, you beautiful, blue-eyed man. How dreadful, how heartrendingly hard it will be to leave you. But I must.

CHAPTER 101

There was a whisper of rain, then a rush, hurled violently against the kitchen windows by the wind like pebbles or gunshot. It had been an uncustomarily soggy start to the summer vacations, a joint trial for children who spent most of their waking hours outdoors and their harassed caretakers. The Madison house, with its nooks and crannies, offered more scope than most for the entertainment of children trapped indoors. But by the end of an afternoon that included three games of Snakes and Ladders, Laura and her school chum Shawna had wandered into the kitchen in search of diversion.

Emma looked at the kitchen clock. "Why don't you two listen to the Children's Hour on the radio?" she suggested.

Laura went over to the big Crossley radio that stood in the corner and started to twiddle the dial.

"Some people have televisions," Shawna said meaningfully.

"Well, some don't." Emma found paper and coloured pencils, and settled her at the kitchen table. In the corner, Laura continued turning the dial. Suddenly there was a blare of noise, and the sound of a familiar voice.

"It's Alistair!" Laura exclaimed excitedly! "He's on the radio!"

By the time Emma went over, the voice had disappeared into a crackle of static. She made note of the number on the dial, then tuned in the soothing sounds of a British announcer reading a children's tale. Laura sat down, picked up a pencil from the table and contentedly began to draw.

From her usual vantage point standing on a spot by the stove where the blue and white linoleum was fading away from wear, Emma regarded her great niece with deep fondness, somewhat coloured by guilt. The child was hers for the summer. Although she had won that round, she remembered Jasmine's words and tears too vividly.

"It was you who did this, Emma! You've seduced her with all your cookies and lemonade and stories and hugs!" Jasmine had railed at her as she cried.

Because, when asked if she would rather stay with her great aunt for the summer or return to Vegas with her mother, Laura thought for no more than a second or two before replying, "I want to stay here." Then she turned on one foot and ran out the door to join the Terrible Trio, who were waiting impatiently outside.

"She's only being a child, Jasmine!" Emma consoled. "She loves you dearly, and she'll miss you terribly; she doesn't quite understand this separation. But you know, it's really a gift you're giving me. I do love her so. The both of you. She'll be there with you soon enough, and by that time Thomas will have left here too."

Jasmine must have seen something in her face then, the sense of impending bereavement, for that is what it would seem like with all of them gone and her house filling up with loneliness once more. She stood up and came around the table to give Emma a great, warm hug.

"I love you too, Aunt Emma. You've been more than a mother to me. I only wish you could come with us. You're what I'll miss most about Medford. You and the lake."

"And Thomas of course."

"Yes, but he'll be in Kellington and hard at work. Did I tell you he's found a house? From the sound of it, it's far too large; however, he says he bought it for a family. I'm afraid he's going to rattle around in there. And when will he find the time to set it up? Lianne used to take care of all those details."

"I'm sure there will be plenty of women glad to volunteer to help him," Emma said rather acerbically.

"No doubt." Jasmine agreed. "Don't think that thought hasn't crossed my mind." She was serious, although smiling. Then she added, "Thomas and I have been talking about how much work he'll have. So I have a suggestion for you. You don't have to decide right away. Only think about it."

And now, for the very last time, Emma was thinking about it. She had made her decision. And she planned to tell Jasmine when she came in, which she did mere minutes later through the back door, bringing a great rush of cool, fresh air and a spatter of rain as she shook off her coat.

"How did the coaching go?" Emma inquired.

"Your friends Norah and Caroline are teachable, but Betty Matthison will take more work than I have time."

With Jasmine's return to semi-respectability – although only a grudging acceptance in some quarters – she had inevitably been drawn into the neighbourhood bridge circuit. Good players were always in demand, but Jasmine, who had played competitively, was a cut well above the average middling Medfordian. Now, with the Latham house organized for the move and time on her hands until departure, several of Emma's friends had enlisted her help to improve their game. It was work she found she enjoyed.

Emma cleared her throat. Jasmine was immediately alert at this signal she was about to say something of importance. "Do you remember the question you asked me about Thomas?" Emma asked. "Well, I've considered it and made my decision. I thought I'd best tell you before he came over for dinner. The answer is yes. I'll be glad to help."

And to everyone's satisfaction, just like that, the matter was settled. Once summer vacations were over and Laura returned to Las Vegas, Emma would close up her house. She would move to Kellington in order to set Thomas's new home to rights. All during his first, frantic school term, she would be there as much for company as for support.

The bright and pleased expression on Emma's face as she gave her answer was Jasmine's reward for all her scheming. Not incidentally, the arrangement was an ideal one for her as well as Emma and Thomas. Now she would have eyes, ears and an ally in Kellington.

But even if one problem was solved another was urgently looming. While Jasmine set the table, she pondered the small matter of an excuse. She needed a good, a very good one to travel to the city and stay there over the weekend, certainly one less flimsy than the need to collect a few items of unsold jewelry. The excuse had to be plausible enough that Emma could believe and repeat it to all who inquired, some of whom – Margery in particular – were all too likely to have suspicions.

"There was quite a lot of mail for you today," Emma said, indicating the pile on the kitchen counter.

Jasmine sat down to open a few letters before dinner went on the table. And it seemed heaven-sent, the way in which her salvation arrived that very afternoon in an envelope with an Arizona postmark. Emma was at the sink washing garden greens when she heard her utter an exclamation of surprise.

"What is it, Jasmine?" She wiped her hands on her apron and came over to the table.

Jasmine flourished the letter in her hand. "My friend Katy writes that Frank Maitland and his girlfriend Marlene have been arrested for fraud in Louisiana! They're going to trial at the end of July."

Emma was familiar with the names and the story behind them. "What will you do?"

"The prosecutors are looking for additional evidence. Katy says I should send them the bank and police records and a certified copy of the statement I gave them."

"Do you think you'll get any of your money back?"

"Not likely." Her excitement deflated, Jasmine sighed. She folded the letter and replaced it in its envelope. "Frankie liked the high life. They've probably spent or hidden everything they stole. But If I can help put them away for a good long time, that's reward enough."

Now she could ask the question she wanted to, and no one could doubt the reason behind it. "Do you think you might be able to mind Laura if I go to the city on the weekend to look after this? Then I can stay overnight with Arlena, and we can have a good visit before I leave."

Emma was quick to offer help, and their arrangements were neatly tidied away when they heard a brisk knock.

"Hallo!" Thomas came in at the side door. He walked to the stove, and in familiar fashion took the top off a pot and sniffed. "Chicken and dumplings! Emma, you do spoil us!"

After dinner was over Jasmine tried to tune in the radio station Laura had discovered, using the dial number Emma had written down. They did find it, distant and drifting in and out of a cloud of static until, suddenly, there was a loud burst of noise and a Chuck Berry record came on; then the radio station faded away in a thin crackle of sound. If ever Alistair had been there, now he was gone. He had disappeared mysteriously once more, drifting in the ether of the airwaves someplace far, far away.

CHAPTER 102

It was seven-thirty of a sunny Wednesday morning in July when Dennis O'Donahue set out to his job as postmaster of the Medford post office. The air was cool and fresh and his step was light, as befits a happy man with few cares in the world and much to be grateful for. In one hand there swung a brown paper bag, the lunch prepared for him by a loving wife.

Dennis left the sidewalk to cross the road. It was then he sensed movement in the sky above. Lifting his eyes from the quiet, tree-lined street, he looked up. A large black bird was slowly flying in wide, deliberate circles directly overhead. The raven, as he soon identified it, landed on a dead elm marked with a red X that was awaiting the axes of town employees. Dennis continued to watch it with some curiosity, because, as he strode along, it appeared to be watching him.

From its perch high atop the skeletal tree, the raven cocked its head at his approach. Then it idly flapped its wings and glided down to inspect him more closely. Its dark shadow came floating toward him along the sidewalk. It slowly drifted over him, momentarily blotting out the sun.

For a second Dennis stopped in mid-stride to watch the bird, its mission seemingly accomplished, wing leisurely away. Despite the warmth of the day, he felt a sudden chill. However, being a modern man with little belief in portents, he soon dismissed the incident.

Arriving at the post office promptly at eight, Dennis unlocked the door. His helper, Elwood Maddow, came in a few minutes later. After exchanging a few words of greeting they stood at the counter and began sorting the mail for the carriers.

Dennis was experiencing a bit of indigestion, unusual for him, but he put it down to a latish night and the beer and sausage he had put away during a child's birthday party at his Polish neighbours. As he and Elwood worked quietly side by side, his heartburn became more intense. Suddenly Dennis remembered his father, taken away at the age of 49 by a massive heart attack. But he was only 34!

Then he tried to lift his arm and found that he couldn't, and the pain, which had been tolerable so far, suddenly struck him in the chest like an anvil. A shadow dimmed his eyes. He felt a strange, fluttering sensation. Dark wings slowly enfolded him; then all went black.

"He just dropped like a stone," Elwood said when questioned. Elwood was white and shaken, clearly in shock at the suddenness of it all, and after Dennis's body was taken away, he closed the post office and went home.

It was sad, yes indeed, so very sad! The town was consumed with the sorrow and shame of Dennis O'Donahue's death. Such a young man, so handsome and charming! And him with a wife and two small boys, all of them just over from Ireland three years ago!

One hour after the postmaster's demise, the phone rang and Emma answered. It was Margery, who had heard from her daughter Lorena, who heard from her sister Roseanne that their young postmaster had been pronounced dead by Dr. Sheridan half an hour ago and his body was being taken to the Jenner Funeral Home.

Once she hung up the phone, Emma and Jasmine commiserated. "His poor wife," Emma said pityingly. "Just settled here, and so suddenly a widow. I met her when they first came, although I haven't seen her since. She's a redhead, very attractive."

She could not recall her features, now blurred in memory, but there was something more recent nagging at her and in a while she remembered. Her friend Caroline had seen the postmaster's wife at the school fair in June, and had said at first she thought it was Jasmine.

Later that day a call came from the funeral home for Jasmine. When she phoned back, Simon Jenner asked if she could prepare O'Donahue's body for a Friday evening visitation. Jasmine agreed to come by on Friday at around 12:30. No, sorry, Emma heard her apologize; she couldn't help out later that evening, she was going to the city.

As she told Emma once she hung up, Simon was looking for extra hands at the visitation. Although his time in Medford had been short, the young postmaster was well known and liked, and the manner of his death sufficiently shocking that a large crowd of the compassionate and curious was expected.

"I have to warn you," Simon had added at the end of their conversation, "his wife is very particular. She asked who would be preparing the body and I told her Lewis Smythe and she said absolutely not. She wanted me to use whoever did Sid Callon, their neighbour, and that's you."

What he did not tell her, but which Jasmine heard earlier by way of Margery, was that likely as a cost-saving measure Simon had asked Lewis to handle the full preparation of their last "guest". A major row had erupted when his children arrived for the visitation and took issue with the carroty orange complexion of their father's face at his last public appearance. Amongst the mourners, a few of the less sensitive were heard to say the deceased looked more like something pulled out of the ground than about to be planted in it. His was a large family whose members vociferously broadcast their displeasure far and wide. Jasmine had a suspicion the story might have reached the ears of the widow O'Donahue.

"I honestly think the two of them must be color-blind," Jasmine remarked to Emma. "There's no other explanation for the makeup Lewis chooses, or the ties Simon wears."

It was full summer now. The golden, sun-burnished days slipped by so rapidly, it seemed to Jasmine no sooner did she open her eyes than night fell and she closed them once more. In a little over a week, she herself would slip away, flying back to the hot, arid city she no longer could quite think of as home. Perhaps because of their looming separation, each moment she spent with her daughter or Thomas seemed particularly sweet, even poignant, and altogether too short.

On Friday afternoon as she walked toward the Jenner Funeral Home, heavy storm clouds were massing over the lake and rolling swiftly inland. Until it slid beneath their dark leading edge, the sun glittered with a strange and unusual brilliance. To Jasmine, it was like the heightened perception she had experienced these last few weeks, which cast a new light over the ordinariness of everyday. The present, even as she lived it, seemed dusted with the golden glow of the fond memories it was too rapidly becoming. In contrast, whenever she tried to envision it, the future that arose before her was dark and indistinct, filled with barriers she sensed she would need all her strength to leap.

Inky clouds now obscured the sun, and she shivered in her thin clothes as the funeral home came into view. She was remembering her recent trips here: for Royce, whose drowned face floated up from the subterranean depths of her memory where she confined such nightmares; then, in a contrast as sharp as white to black, Lianne.

How fragile life was. In this somber, reflective mood she approached the walkway and turned her thoughts to another who had died too young, the father and husband she was about to prepare for burial, and his tragedy-stricken little family.

The wind was no longer gusty but starting to blow in a concentrated, purposeful way. A few heavy raindrops fell, the prelude to a major storm for which there had been little warning. Jasmine knew though, less from instinct than her years of living beside the lake. She had heard its roar and caught a glimpse of steely grey water and whitecaps from the verandah as she left home. From the long drive of the wave train it was clear a considerable force was powering it, and she guessed it to be a gale perhaps as strong as the one that took Royce's life.

A car, its motor running, was waiting by the curb in front of the funeral home. Through the rain-splattered windshield, she saw Cheryl Byrd. By mutual inclination, they ignored one another. Jasmine proceeded up the stairs to the foyer, where she found Letty Lawson struggling with an umbrella that refused to open.

"Why Letty!" Jasmine exclaimed as she took it from her hands, "what brings you out on such a dreadful day?"

"Oh, thank you, dear!" Letty said as she accepted the opened umbrella. "Well, we were shopping and I asked Cheryl to drop by so I could make a payment on my layaway plan." Seeing Jasmine's raised eyebrow, she added, "didn't you hear about the layaway plan? It was advertised on the radio a while ago; everyone was laughing about it. Well, once I stopped laughing, then I thought, why that's actually quite a good idea! Something new in the funeral business! Only now they're calling it something else" – here she turned and hollered at Simon Jenner, who was at his desk in the office with the door open – "Simon, what d'you call that layaway plan now?"

"It's funeral pre-planning," Simon answered curtly. He did not look up from his work. Judging from the expression on his face, he seemed out of sorts.

Jasmine found Letty peering at her keenly. There was a honk from the car waiting at the curb, which she ignored. "I hear you're leaving us soon for Las Vegas, Jasmine. Going back to the casino?"

"No, I've taken a job at the hotel next door. Giving up the cards for something more respectable." Jasmine accompanied this with a little laugh that, whether she knew it or not, did not sound particularly joyful.

"Oh, that's sad!" Letty exclaimed.

Jasmine looked at her in shock. Most people to whom she had confided her plans, including Emma, were warmly approving.

"I mean – why, you have such a talent and you've spent that much time to be good at it," Letty said earnestly, her hand on Jasmine's arm. "Anyone can work in a hotel, Jasmine, but you – " She jumped as a loud blast of the horn from the waiting car set the window glass to rattling. "Well, it's never a good idea to keep Cheryl waiting. I'd best be on my way. Good luck, dear!" Then she was out the door.

Jasmine watched her leave. She was pondering the sentence Letty had cut short. The few words spoken by the elderly woman had rippled through her like an electric current. They crystallized some of her own nascent ideas. But as she turned to descend the stairs, she set these thoughts aside for later, in order to concentrate on the task ahead.

The embalming room was in a high, windowed basement below the public spaces. Before entering she donned a heavy sweater against the chill, then her white coveralls. Lewis had already embalmed and washed the body, which lay draped with a sheet on the embalming table under the stark fluorescent lights, ready for her ministrations.

The style of the suit that had been provided by O'Donahue's widow was old fashioned. However, it was a fine tweed that fit him perfectly, of better quality than Jasmine might have expected. Because of the heart attack, his colour was somewhat cyanotic, blue from oxygen deprivation, but this was easily remedied. After she combed his hair and applied makeup to his face and hands to duplicate, as far as she could remember, his coloring when she had last seen him at the post office, even dead he was a very fine figure of a man indeed.

Suddenly the terrible waste, the deep sadness of it all swept over her in a wave, and even inured as she was to death, she had to bite her lip to stop the tears that pricked at her eyes.

Her work was done. But before she left, instead of her usual silent prayer of blessing, she bent over the corpse. "Goodbye, Dennis O'Donahue," she whispered. "Until we meet again, may God hold you in the palm of His hand." Then, leaning lightly on his chest, she gave a feather kiss to the cold lips that had smiled at her so sweetly on her day of disappointment, after the reading of her mother's will.

As she did so, she sensed, rather than felt, a slight crackle somewhere near the hand she had resting on his chest. Something there! What was it? Lewis had written in his note that he had gone through the clothing. Was it possible he missed something in one of the pockets? She looked in the inside pocket of the suit coat. Nothing. Was there a pocket in the vest? She could not find one; but then, sliding her hand a little further down, she felt a slight bump. Inside the lining of the vest was a tiny pocket just below the breastbone. A watch pocket, perhaps. A small piece of stiff paper was tucked in it. With some effort, she extricated and unfolded it.

It was a ticket. A lottery ticket for the Irish Sweeps. She looked at the date. The running of it took place this weekend. Tomorrow. On Saturday, the same day as his burial!

For a long moment, she held the small piece of embossed paper in her hand. It felt as if it were emitting a slight heat. A furious battle was being waged in her mind: her conscience clashing with her betting instincts. Should she put the ticket in the large wooden cabinet upstairs? In the drawer where all items found in the clothing provided for the deceased were left? Or might she take it with her to the city?

She turned once more to look at the postmaster as he lay beside her on the embalming table. "Is this your payment for my kiss, Mr. O'Donahue?" she spoke into the icy silence. "If it is, why thank you, and I hope your luck dead is better than when you were alive."

Then she put the ticket in her pocket and after placing the body in the refrigerated storage unit and performing her ablutions, she went upstairs.

Simon Jenner was wheeling a cart creaking under a weight of floral arrangements into the visitation room assigned to the postmaster. Jasmine followed him there. She was curious to see if there were any truth to the rumours she had heard about her and Nuala, the postmaster's wife.

A large wedding portrait had been placed on a stand near the spot designated for the casket. She leaned in to see better. "Yes," Simon's voice came from behind, "there's certainly a resemblance. She looks like you."

It was the height, the hair colour, red, although Jasmine's was darker. And there was no doubt about it: Nuala was a beauty. Small wonder her husband stared at me so when I visited the post office, Jasmine thought. She could be my sister.

"Interesting," she said. "Can you tell me something about her?"

"Only the little I've heard," replied Simon, who then proceeded to ramble on for a good ten minutes. It was said that Nuala O'Donahue had married beneath her class for love of the charismatic postmaster. Her wealthy Dublin family cut all ties when they wed. Now she was alone with her two little sons. Money was tight. There wasn't much insurance or savings laid by; nevertheless she was giving her husband the best funeral she could afford.

"She'll be out looking for work soon. She used to be secretary to some bigwig back on the old sod in Dublin, but there's not much call for that sort of thing here," Simon finished up. Having exhausted his knowledge and the scanty reserves of pity he extended to his clients, he bustled away.

Jasmine examined a few other pictures showing Dennis with Nuala and their little sons. Her steps were slow as she returned to the office. Taking an envelope from one of the desks, in it, she put, with considerable reluctance, the Irish Sweepstake ticket. But not before taking note of the ticket number and horse Dennis had chosen, "Starlight Dancer".

From the tingle in her fingers the moment she touched it, Jasmine knew it was a winning ticket. So she felt no surprise when, two days later, she checked and found that although his horse did not win or even place, Dennis had won a hundred pounds in the draw following the race. In a strange twist of fate, he had given his struggling family a substantial bequest that, if not for her kiss, he would have taken with him to the grave.

Including the chance encounter with Letty, this afternoon seemed full of strange coincidences. Jasmine found it difficult to dismiss them as mere happenstance.

Now, about to close the envelope, she wondered if she might give fate another trick to play. She found her purse. From her wallet she extracted a business card, slightly dog-eared from the time it spent there. She took an office pen and wrote on the back, 'This company is growing and needs good people.' After a pause she added a name below it: 'Lewis Smythe'. Dropping the card in the envelope, she sealed it and left a note informing Simon of the item in the cabinet for Nuala.

Heavy waves of rain were sweeping the streets. Jasmine stood poised with her umbrella at the side door, immersed in her thoughts as she waited for a break in the weather.

CHAPTER 103

The gale that formed over the lake swept ashore on fierce winds that towed in their wake drenching cold rain and thunderheads crackling and booming with lightning. In the harbour, Sunday sailors who had left their boats poorly moored arrived running. The wind-whipped rigging shrieked out storm warnings as solitary figures in spray-slicked macintoshes rushed about with ropes and fenders, struggling to secure crafts that plunged and reared like wild horses in the boiling surf. The streets in the town above were filled with cars, the sidewalks with people urgently running or wetly stalking toward homes where laundry had been hung on lines and windows left open with every expectation – no thanks to the weatherman – of a bright, sunny day.

In the general pandemonium, few took notice of an old green '46 Plymouth as it crept slowly along main street. Halfway through town, it turned onto the crossroad that led to the funeral home. Had the weather been more conducive to the pastime of discussing the state of the world, the retired farmers who usually occupied the benches in front of the pharmacy and post office probably would have observed that as a means of keeping them attached, one of the Plymouth's side doors and a drooping back fender had been lashed on with that handy and durable farmer fix-all, baling wire.

"Say, Al – is there a leak in the roof? My head is getting wet!"

"Hey! Dammit! Now my ass is wet too!"

Without interrupting his monologue or taking his eyes off the road as he drove, Alistair MacGregor reached an arm out behind him and grabbed a sheaf of newspapers from the back seat. He handed it to Chris Byers, who shoved most under his posterior and draped one over his head.

On this red-letter day nothing, much less rain inside the car, could dampen the high spirits of the two young men, which had been fueled by beer and fired by their extravagant dreams of a golden future. After an early lunch meeting at the Statler tavern, Chris had agreed to partner with Alistair in a dynamic new venture, the establishment of the MBB – MacGregor, Byers Broadcasting – radio network.

No matter that the first station in the proposed radio network was no more than a shack beside a transmitter on a wind-swept hill across the lake from Detroit; it was merely the beginning! Once Alistair got his hands on his inheritance, which his father and his lawyers could no longer deny him when he turned twenty-five next month, they would purchase another radio station and then, with all the money they would be making, another and another, and later a few television stations during the second phase of their roughly sketched and limitlessly ambitious plan.

As the funeral home drew near, Alistair abruptly stopped talking. Chris turned to look. Silent now, Alistair's mind was clearly on other matters. The thought then occurred to Chris that perhaps their new partnership might not be the first, but the second reason for Alistair's return to Medford.

They pulled into the funeral parlor parking lot. Near the entrance was a large carport sheltering the funeral hearse and pickup van, and Alistair backed his ancient vehicle into a parking spot beneath it. The rain stopped dripping on Chris's head; he removed his newspaper hat.

"I'm coming in with you, it's too wet here. I'll stay out of the way," he promised. "Will this take long? I have to get back to the station – wish I'd driven my own car. I'll hand in my two weeks' notice this afternoon; Dad will freak!"

Alistair made no move to get out. For a long moment he sat, nervously cracking his knuckles. "I hope Jasmine's still here. Her aunt said she brought an umbrella; maybe she's already left, walking."

Chris had the car door partly open. Now he closed it. In a voice of quiet sympathy, he said, "I wish you luck, buddy, but do you honestly think you stand a chance?" When Alistair failed to respond, more loudly, less sympathetically, he added, "frankly, I'd lay better odds on a bat in hell."

"Thanks, jerk." Alistair's tone was amiable. "Maybe not. But I still have to try." And along with these words was a look on his face and a set to his jaw that Chris would come to know well in the years ahead.

"Let's go." Alistair flung open the driver's door; they made a dash for it. Both were drenched by the time they reached the side entrance of the home.

Through the window Jasmine had looked on with amusement as the decrepit car shuffled into the parking stall, which changed to amazement when it disgorged its passengers and Chris Byers came out running, closely followed by a long, lanky figure with an unmistakable thatch of red hair. Once inside, Alistair planted a loud, wet smack on her cheek.

"Alistair!" Jasmine's face was alight with warm affection; she had all but given up hope of ever seeing him again. "What a marvelous surprise! Where were you? It seemed to us you'd disappeared off the face of the earth! It's so good to see you – but – why are you driving that car? Where's your car?"

This was not the way Alistair wanted their reunion to start. "It's a long story," he mumbled.

"A short story, actually," Chris supplied. "Alistair bought a radio station and the guy who was selling it wanted his car and gave him his in exchange."

"The convertible helped cinch the deal," Alistair conceded, turning and giving Chris the evil eye for spoiling the news he himself had wanted to announce to Jasmine with far more fanfare. "But I didn't know how bad his car was 'til I got it. It's only temporary – just like I agreed at noon today to partner with Chris in a radio broadcasting venture, and that, too, might be temporary."

With a start, Chris remembered his promise. "If you'll excuse me, I'm going to the office to phone Sherry for a drive back to the station. She can take time off on Friday afternoons if she wants, and her car doesn't leak."

Before leaving he recalled his sister's previous declaration of interest in Alistair; might as well earn a few Brownie points there. "You're staying overnight at your aunt and uncle's, aren't you, Alistair?" he asked. "After she drops me at the radio station, Sherry could drive you there and you can leave your car here under the carport so it can dry out."

"Oh, and could I catch a ride too?" Jasmine asked. "My umbrella's useless in this wind and rain. Our house is near the Jenners', not far out of the way. Do you think your sister would mind?"

"I'm sure she wouldn't," Chris answered, although he was quite certain she would. He started down the hall toward the office. Once he left, Alistair immediately turned to Jasmine. He took both her hands in his big freckled ones.

"You're more beautiful than ever, Jasmine," he breathed. "Come out to dinner with me tonight?"

Jasmine knew she was looking well. She was in love, and it showed. She wondered how long the effect might last when the object of her affections was no longer close at hand but thousands of miles away.

"I'm sorry, Alistair. I'm going to the city this evening on the five o'clock bus."

His disappointment was evident. But then he smiled and asked, "Jasmine, how many times have I asked you to marry me?"

"On the day we first met, and then every time we saw one another after that. I lost track around fourteen." She laughed. "Sort of a Chinese water torture method of proposing."

"Don't laugh, Jasmine. I'm deadly serious about this. I love you. I want to marry you."

"And I'm just as serious when I tell you that I'm the wrong woman for you, Alistair. I'm speaking plainly because I don't want to lead you on."

"Why not? I want to be led on! I'd love you to lead me on! It sounds like a big improvement over what you've been doing so far!"

It was at that precise moment Simon Jenner chose to come bustling down the hall. "Alistair!" he crowed when he caught sight of his nephew. "It's good you came here first instead of going to the house; you're just the man I want to see!"

He took up a position between them. Alistair let go of Jasmine's hands.

"Mrs. O'Donahue has asked if we could have a piper at the mass for her husband tomorrow morning," Jenner announced importantly. "And since you're in town, I offered your services. Luckily, you left your bagpipes in your room."

"Bloody Hell!" Alistair's complexion quickly changed to beet red with the force of his indignation. "I can only stay 'til noon Sunday! That will blow away half my day tomorrow! And what the crap does an Irishwoman want with an Anglican Scots piper at a Catholic mass anyhow? Makes no sense!"

"Alistair! Your language!" Jenner exclaimed starchily. "The Irish play bagpipes too, you know! She says her husband was very fond of the pipes. Come with me to the office and I'll give you the music she chose." Jenner then took a firm hold of his arm and short of shaking him off, there was nothing Alistair could do but follow.

Minutes later Jasmine saw Chris walk down the hall from the office just as a two-tone, blue and white Oldsmobile pulled into the driveway. It stopped at the side door. Looking out the rain-washed window, she could see Sherry Byers peering at her balefully from behind the steering wheel.

"Sherry's here already? That was quick! You go ahead and get in the car," Chris instructed her. "I'll see if I can rescue Alistair from his uncle's clutches." And he turned around and headed back to the office.

When there was a break in the downpour, Jasmine opened her umbrella and ran. She tried the car's back door. It was locked. With no great haste, Sherry reached over and pulled up the lock button. Jasmine climbed in. Since there was no greeting from Sherry, it fell to her to break the silence, which she did.

"Hello Sherry, thanks for the drive. How are you? I haven't seen you for quite a while, at least since Lianne's funeral."

In ice-coated tones, Sherry replied, "Yes. I've been busy." Then, after a brief pause: "you must miss her."

"Oh, I do, every day. She was like the sister I always wish I'd had, a dear friend."

"Well, of course," Sherry said in a voice rich with sarcasm. "The two of you shared so much!"

If she had hoped to provoke an angry response, she was disappointed. In the rearview mirror she watched as Jasmine smiled, a little ruefully, shook her head. Then she heard her gentle, amused laugh.

"Sherry, Sherry. I'm your friend, not your enemy. I think you're perfect for Alistair. And I'm about to make sure he knows it too. If you play your cards right, he's yours."

Now Sherry swiveled all the way around. She stared at Jasmine in astonishment, her mouth agape. "Whatever makes you think I'm even interested in him?"

"Well, it's obvious, isn't it? There's no other reason for you to hate me so much."

At that moment the side door of the funeral home burst open and Alistair and Chris galloped through the rain and jumped into the car. Alistair sat in the back with Jasmine, Chris in front. Soon a more normal kind of conversation sprang up to fill the shocked silence that followed Jasmine's words.

Once Sherry dropped her brother at the radio station, she drove the short distance to the Madison house. Alistair leapt out to open the door for Jasmine. Then he followed her through the rain to the shelter of the overhanging porch.

"Can I come in?"

"No, Alistair, I'm sorry but I'm short on time. I have to pack and attend to my daughter."

"I need to talk to you," he said, taking her hand.

"And I with you," she replied. "What I wanted to tell you is that on Wednesday I'm leaving to return to Las Vegas. So this is our goodbye, Alistair, probably for some time."

Instantly his face fell; his eyes moistened and reddened. He dropped her hand. She had to repress an urge to comfort him, he looked so very forlorn, slumping as he stood on the verandah against the grey and gloomy backdrop of the rain swept lake. This was a moment she had long anticipated; now, however, she was finding it almost as painful as he did. But she had no choice. To be kind, she must cut quick and clean.

His words were a long time coming. Even then they were disjointed, as he struggled to find the right ones that might change her mind. "You were my dream, Jasmine," he said, in a voice heavy with emotion. "I suppose I knew this might happen, sometime, eventually, but still – we could have been so good together. This is too sudden. I can't help, oh, being sad, so disappointed. Couldn't we – ?"

Jasmine stood on tiptoe and gave him a gentle kiss on the cheek.

"Well, I guess that about wraps it up," Alistair muttered bitterly. "Even my sister would have put more passion into that goodbye kiss than you did."

Jasmine made a wry face, forced a laugh. "Yes, you're right. It could have been better, the kiss, but it wasn't so much for you. I did it for the girl in the car, to give her the sign for all clear."

"What?" he asked, with a quick glance toward the car. "Chris's sister, Sherry? What're you talking about?" Alistair's red eyebrows notched up in disbelief.

"You really don't have a clue, do you Alistair? That girl is crazy about you."

Alistair snorted loudly. "Are you kidding? That girl laughed her ass off when she saw the Tillys chase the chickens 'round the hearse! Whatever makes you think that?"

Jasmine's smile wavered a little. "Because Sherry hates me," she replied. "Hates me so much she can barely talk to me or even be civil. And in my experience, the reason for that is, she's crazy jealous because of all the attention you show me."

She opened the door. "Don't think you're rid of me, Alistair. I'll be watching as you become famous and successful, and maybe one of these years I'll come calling and ask you to repay the favor I'm doing you right now."

Another too-bright smile, and she closed the door behind her. Alistair stood motionless for a long moment. Then he went down the stairs and got into the front seat of the car with Sherry. The motor was running. She did not put the car in gear but only sat, waiting. She had seen the goodbye kiss Jasmine gave Alistair, noted his dejection. Now she was witnessing his humiliation.

"I think," Alistair mumbled, almost to himself, "I may have been an idiot."

"That's alright." Sherry said in a kind, almost sisterly fashion. "It does seem she has that effect on men."

They drove to the Jenners' house in silence. Sherry was locked in mortal combat with her pride, which had her in a stranglehold to ditch Alistair at his uncle's and hit the gas. Alistair was stealing side glances. He was observing, not for the first time, how attractive she was: the prettiest, smartest girl in Medford, as her brother shamelessly promoted her. Also, he was pondering what Jasmine had said, although with the sinking feeling that after viewing the scenario on the porch, she might very well and quite justifiably no longer be all that crazy about him.

The car came to a stop in front of the Jenners' house. They sat for a moment in a silence broken only by the sound of the rain sluicing down and the rhythmic swish of the windshield wipers. During this interval Alistair's thoughts raced furiously. Would she tell him to get lost? Probably. But, at the very least, he had to give it a try.

"I'm only here 'til noon on Sunday," he said slowly. "I don't suppose you would be free tonight—" He stopped in mid-sentence and blushed bright red. What a jerk she must think he was, trying to date her up after being so obviously dumped by Jasmine. He looked down and away, twisting his hands about in his lap in a fever of embarrassment.

Perhaps that is why he never noticed that she had moved out from behind the wheel and was edging closer to him on the bench seat of the car.

Later they talked about that moment: the knife-edge on which their future happiness teetered. If Alistair hadn't asked that question, or faltered when he did, if he had been cocksure instead of shy, why then, Sherry said, in all likelihood they would have gone their separate ways.

She would never disclose the true reason she changed her mind, nor repeat to him the gentle words she heard in the car that rainy day: "if you play your cards right –"

Yes, she might have a winning hand. But this was no time for games. In a matter of hours Alistair would leave Medford, the town that had been the setting for his humiliation and disappointment. He would have no reason ever to return – unless she gave him one.

With this thought Sherry took her pride and kicked it to the curb, from where it rolled to somewhere beneath the car.

Alistair slowly turned. To his surprise, he discovered her lovely face just inches from his. She was smiling: a warm, wide, generous smile. Then she spoke.

It was only two words, but they were perfect. Soon they would make him a happy man; then, somewhat later, a successful and powerful man, surrounded by an admiring throng of family, friends and sycophants.

Over the years Alistair would often relate the tale of his ride in the hearse with Willy Tilly and the triplets, and how she chose him when he was the laughing stock of the town. He usually told it, his wife observed, whenever he wanted to lull his listeners into thinking he was a chucklehead, the better to best them in his business dealings.

But that was far away and into the future. Right now, sitting next to him on the front seat of the car while the rain poured down, she spoke only two words:

"Kiss me."

Then no more words were needed.

CHAPTER 104

Stop looking at me.

That man was as transparent as glass. Did he not realize that he was following her with his eyes, or that his expression changed whenever he did? And now she could see something else in his face, and so would Margery, looking at him with her shrewd little eyes.

If ever Jasmine needed a reason to put distance between them, this was it. Thomas was completely lacking in guile, a man who wore his heart not just on his sleeve but on his face. It endangered his reputation, so hard-won and only recently restored; it filled her with anxiety.

Finally Emma noticed Jasmine's furrowed brow. With a look of instant comprehension she turned to Margery, sitting beside her at the dinner table, and attempted to distract her, although it was probably too late. Now Jasmine could communicate to Thomas, with a short nod in Margery's direction, the words she wanted to scream at him. After a moment he understood and turned to speak with Jim, who was busy consuming his third piece of lemon pie, one of the two delicious desserts Margery had brought to this farewell dinner.

Without much prodding, Jim spoke enthusiastically of his new position at the plant. He had been promoted from office work to line manager to assistant floor supervisor, a demanding job that seemed to sit easily on his broad shoulders. The MacClures had a new car, money in the bank, life was good!

Thomas tried to make the right noises, say the appropriate words, but his conversation was desultory. How could he not look at her? She was a magnet for anyone's eyes, as she moved with a ballerina's grace around the table collecting the plates, the great mass of her hair loosely tied beside her neck and swinging as she went. He would drink in all he could of her, burn it into his memory and try not to think of the reason this was necessary. Because when he thought about her departure tomorrow there came a pain in his heart that, during the course of a lifetime, had become far too familiar.

Earlier he had been trying to rid himself of another feeling, one he knew was probably stupid and irrational: a sense of rejection. She knew how much he loved her, body and soul. He had asked her to marry him. She had said yes, but not now. And tomorrow she was leaving. Leaving without giving him much idea of her plans, only proffering the "don't count your chickens before they're hatched" kind of excuses for keeping him in the dark.

There were other worries. She had promised to be true. However, Thomas feared possible suitors less than other kinds of seducers – her new job, old friends, familiar routines, and those perennial enemies of love, time and distance.

As well, rather annoyingly, she was proving to be quite right about the members of the College Board, those ten individuals who held his future in their hands. Marrying her now would definitely jeopardize his new position. They were a stuffy lot. Not stuffy and rigid when it came to the school and the innovations he had proposed, for which, thank heavens, they were allowing him plenty of latitude. Only when it came to anything that might have a whiff of impropriety or was even mildly unconventional.

Added to this, the board included two women. One, Penelope Farland, was a divorcee about the same age as him, not unattractive. Her son Miles was in the upper school. It hadn't taken very long, only a few meetings, before she started making sheep's eyes at him – another complication he definitely didn't need.

In sum, Thomas was longing for domesticity, that protective and pleasant if sometimes humdrum state where work can be done, children raised and life, including sex, assumes satisfying, predictable patterns – so much better than the feverish condition of desire he constantly found himself in, which disrupted his sleeping and waking hours. Even the weekend he just spent with Jasmine, it seemed, had not diminished but increased it.

There was a large question in his mind, however, about just how well domesticity would suit Jasmine. In her he recognized the same restless energy he had, the same desire to make her mark. Not for her the pursuits of home and garden that had given Lianne employment and considerable satisfaction. She would get a job, Jasmine declared, after she dismissed his suggestion of going to the nearby university for a degree in mathematics, a subject in which she had once excelled. It would only lead to becoming a teacher, she maintained, and likely she was right.

However, if the board members were stuffy and conventional, then so was the city of Kellington. It was many times larger than Medford. Nevertheless, Thomas was discovering that overall, it still had the closed mentality more typical of some small towns. There would be scant opportunities for someone like Jasmine, with her bright mind and unusual talents, to find challenging work.

What on earth, he asked himself, will she do?

After such distressing thoughts, Thomas felt he owed himself at least one pleasant one. And so, at the moment that Margery was watching him watch Jasmine, he was thinking about the weekend they had just spent together and remembering when, after a brief absence, he had returned to their hotel room to find her wearing what she had described as her "mistress costume" – the diamond earrings he had given her, and a pair of high heels.

Suddenly, he noticed that Jasmine had paused in her rounds of collecting dishes. With a nod toward Margery, she flashed him a warning glance. He looked away. Then he looked down at the table. In some surprise, he discovered three little plates. It seemed that in his abstraction, he too, like Jim, must have consumed three helpings of dessert. From what he could see, his appeared to have been strawberry shortcake.

The children, Anna's three and Laura, had been given permission to leave the table. There was a loud scraping of chairs and then a general scramble as they headed for the back door. But Laura, sweet Laura, stood waiting for him. His daughter. The word still held its magic for him. Until the end of August, she would be his little consolation prize, and with this thought Thomas's spirits lifted somewhat. After he excused himself from the table, she took his hand and led him outside to show him the beans and carrots she had grown in the garden.

Little escaped Margery's sharp eyes. "Thomas seems very fond of Laura," she observed.

"Yes, they spend quite a bit of time together. First he was helping her with her insect collection, and now they've moved on to identifying birds." Emma's tone was deliberately offhand. After her labours she was enjoying her cup of tea; otherwise she might have left the table to put an end to this line of inquiry.

"They could just as well be father and daughter. They're as alike as two peas in a pod, both in the way they look and the things they're interested in."

Following this comment, Emma was almost relieved when Margery asked the question she had been dreading. "How did she get that bandage on her hand?"

"She climbed up the cliffs down near the lake, and when she put her hand in a hole where a cliff swallow was nesting, she got quite a pecking."

"Good heavens!" Margery exclaimed. "Those nests are almost thirty feet up! Didn't you or Jasmine tell her not to climb there?"

"She's been forbidden now. Before, though, neither of us could ever have dreamed she would do such a thing."

"And is that how she got that big scab on her knee and the bruise on her face, beside her eye?"

"Oh, a little bicycle mishap," Emma said evasively. "By the way, have you heard the news about what happened to Nan Heffernan's brother?"

Luckily, Margery was easy to distract with small tidbits of gossip. Otherwise, Emma would have had to relate how Jimmy Parkinson had stuck a stick in the spokes of Laura's bike while she was cycling. She fell off, thus the scabby knee. The bruise near her eye was from the one punch Jimmy managed to land during the fight that followed, before she gave him a bloody nose.

"Let's get going on the dishes," Margery suggested, and at this point Emma was happy enough to leave the table.

Out in the garden, Mary was pushing her brother and little sister on the tire swing Thomas had hung from the old maple tree. Laura was basking in Jim and Thomas's admiration for the beans and carrots she had grown.

Are you going to miss your Mom, Uncle Jim asked her. Yes, she had answered. Although that was not strictly accurate. For she wouldn't so much miss her mother as be sad she had to leave. Leave her and Aunt Emma and go to a place where it got so hot you couldn't play outdoors most of the time. A place not nearly so fun, where there were no neighbours like Mr. and Mrs. Barry, who sat in their garage on their lawn chairs on hot days with their newspapers and a jug of lemonade for anyone who wanted to stop by and chat. Or old Mr. Peterkin, the one who gave their gang the nickname that everyone in the neighbourhood called them now, "the Fearsome Foursome", and who was teaching them and his grandson Charlie how to make guitars out of his old cigar boxes.

Sad that she had to leave this perfect paradise, where the dust on the baseball diamond feels like silk on your bare feet when you play ball, and the baby wild canaries in the nest outside the bedroom window are almost ready to fly, where huts need building, trees need climbing. Sad because now that Mom was going, leaving a big hole in the place where she ought to be, it meant that soon she, too, must leave.

But still, happy she had a whole month of summer left, here with Aunt Emma, the golden days unrolling seamlessly in minutes that passed like hours – a very long time in the magical kingdom of childhood.

"Look how big they've grown already!"

And for a second or two Laura dangled the carrot in front of Jim and Thomas, before wiping the dirt off on the grass and eating it.

By the time Margery and Emma left the dining room and came into the kitchen, Jasmine had the sink full of steaming hot water and dirty dishes. Beside her, Anna stood at the ready with a tea towel.

"Shoo! Shoo!"

In her bustling, domineering way, Margery flapped her apron at them before tying it around her considerable girth and ordering them out of the kitchen. "Away with you, both of you; off you go! It's your farewell party, Jasmine, and you and Anna can take your tea and go out to the front porch to finish your goodbyes. Your Aunt and I are doing the dishes, and we can't talk about you if you're here!"

Obediently and not at all reluctantly, Jasmine and Anna giggled as they went to the front porch to sit on the long wicker sofa in a scattering of beams from the low-hanging sun.

"Your news first!" Jasmine commanded her cousin. "You're simply bursting with it anyhow, and I can tell just by the way you look, so marvelous, that it has something to do with Doctor Miller."

Since Royce's death, Anna seemed to have undergone rejuvenation. The lines of tension on her face had disappeared, her expression had softened. More recently, happiness had wrought another transformation, casting a rosy pink glow over her complexion and brightening her eyes. She now looked more like the pretty girl Jasmine once knew a decade ago than the frightened woman of several months before.

Anna clasped her cousin's hands in hers as she said, "Keith has asked me to marry him, Jasmine. It was indecently soon considering all that's happened, but he says he feels as if he's waited years for me. And, of course I said yes, but the marriage won't be until the end of January, another six months – mostly to lay to rest any talk – although there will always be some!"

Jasmine had her own reasons for thinking this seemed like a good excuse to delay getting married. "That's wonderful news, Anna; now tell me all your plans!"

However, when it came turnaround time and Anna asked Jasmine what she expected to do once back in Vegas, she got to her feet. "There's still daylight left, and everyone's busy for a while. Can you come with me to the lake? I'll tell you as much as I can – because so much of it depends on luck – but this is my last chance to see the lake. And after you and Emma, it's what I'll miss most when I leave Medford."

It was a strange enough attachment, but one Anna understood well. Once she too had lived near the great body of water now shimmering a luminous light blue in the last rays of the sun. It was not just a backdrop to their lives but insinuated itself into their thoughts and dreams with its sounds and moods – sunny, angry, and shades of everything in between – so that when far away and landlocked, the lake children felt its absence not so much as loss, but lack; a part of oneself, missing.

Hand in hand, the cousins descended the short distance down the hill to the pebble beach. Occasionally skipping stones or jumping rocks on the breakwater, they talked as they walked along the shoreline while Jasmine took her final leave of the lake.

CHAPTER 105

Two members of the Fearsome Foursome had dropped over to find Laura. All the children, along with several dogs, then joined other neighbourhood youngsters in a far-ranging game of hide-and-seek. Jim was with Thomas inside his garage, checking whether he could use any of the tools Thomas was disposing of before moving. In the kitchen, Emma and Margery had already made a substantial dent in the mountain of dirty dishes. Now they slowed down, because once they finished it would be time for the MacClures to go home and there was still so very much to discuss.

"Then you'll be leaving after Laura goes, at the end of August, Emma? My, but I'll miss you! Can Jim and I give you a hand closing up the house?" Margery was anticipating a windfall of canned goods from Emma's larder as a reward.

"I was going to tell you, Margery: I won't be closing it after all. You've heard that the Irwins are renovating? A few days ago, Deedee asked me if they could have it until after Christmas; they want to rent it furnished. So it's all settled, and what a relief knowing they'll take care of it until I get back from helping Thomas! What did you think of the house he chose?"

Before dinner Thomas had handed around some photographs of the house he had purchased in Kellington. It was an impressive structure: perhaps thirty years old, rose-red brick with black shutters and white trim, well situated on a large, beautifully landscaped lot. The current owners were leaving at the end of August – poor timing for him, only a few days before the start of the fall term.

He also showed them pictures of the Principal's house. It was owned by the College and sat at the far end of the school's large acreage facing the St. Lawrence River. Whenever Thomas was there, Arthur McIntyre and his wife Shelly insisted he stay in their guesthouse, a short distance from their grand, white-pillared home. The photographs showed a charming little cottage, which Thomas said had been equipped with every convenience by Mrs. McIntyre.

"Thomas's new house in Kellington? It's not a lake house by any means," Margery sniffed. "Although it is large. Too large for one person," she added suspiciously, with a sharp look at Emma. "Whatever does he want with such a big house?"

"A good investment. Cost just half what he received for the Latham House and it's bound to appreciate," Emma answered smoothly.

"Well. I must say. I never thought I'd see the day."

"What day, Margery? The day the Latham house was sold out of the family?"

"No. The day Emma Madison became a housekeeper."

Emma turned from the sink to glare daggers. "I am not a housekeeper," she declared icily. "Only a family friend, helping someone who's been like a son to me. There will be other people to clean, to launder and garden. I am there to organize."

Margery was sharp enough to change the subject quickly. It seemed they had not quite exhausted the topic of Anna's forthcoming marriage to Keith Miller, because now she returned to it with gusto. "I hope you'll be back in time to help me with Anna's wedding. Too bad to have it in a gloomy month like January; but for appearance's sake I guess that was the soonest possible time after Royce's death."

Suddenly she gave a violent shake and a shiver.

"Someone walk on your grave?" Emma inquired.

"No, I was thinking of Royce. Me walking on his grave, perhaps." Margery set down her dishtowel and looked at Emma with haunted eyes. "Emma, don't you ever wonder whether it wasn't us, you and me, who brought the Furies down on him? Remember that afternoon drinking gin at the beach, and what we said? Did we stir up the forces of hell to send the storm that drowned him? When I wake up at night and think about it, it scares me."

Emma paused her clicking and clacking of the silverware under the soapy water. "It would be rather nice" she mused, "to have that kind of power. There are a few other people I might like to do in. But no, Margery, it was sheer coincidence, I'm sure. And it was a lucky ending for his family, perhaps even for Royce; he was bound for an early grave anyhow. He spared them all the shame of being killed by a furious father or an enraged husband."

"Or in a bar room brawl, or at the end of a noose," Margery added, brightening as she got into the spirit of the thing.

But in the lengthening shadows, the thought of that dark, lost soul was disquieting for them both. Emma turned on the kitchen lights; Margery returned to her favorite topic. "Anna says she'll be going back to work for Keith in his office, but only a few days a week. They're looking for a house big enough for five children before they marry. So there's plenty for them to do while they're waiting. And they are waiting; waiting for everything, Anna says. Not like Thomas and Jasmine."

Emma, who had been listening with only half an ear, nearly dropped the precious cut-glass cake plate that had held Margery's strawberry shortcake, just as she was lifting it out of the dishwater.

"What do you mean, 'not like Thomas and Jasmine?'" she asked threateningly, unable to stop the sharp uplift of her voice.

"They're lovers," Margery said flatly. There was not a hint of doubt, only the fullness of assurance in her declaration.

Emma stood motionless at the sink as she continued, "I watched him at the dinner table tonight. He barely glanced at anyone else. And after we brought him his third plate of strawberry shortcake, he looked at her as if he had an appetite for something far more sweet and tasty. But she was ignoring him. Not looking at him, not talking to him; that is, unless she thought I wasn't looking! That was the biggest giveaway of all!"

Then there was a loud silence in the kitchen, which lengthened between them until Emma said: "Do you have evidence they're doing what you accuse them of? Everything you said is just a guess. But what of it?" she asked, with a coolness she did not feel. "They're adults, both of them, and free to do as they please. So, are you the guardian of morals here? If you are, Margery, then you should have watched your own daughters more closely!"

Margery ignored this jibe, in which Emma referred to her two daughters who were in the family way when they married. Shrugging it off with a toss of her shoulders, Margery added, "well, all I can say is, I hope it's just a fling. He needed cheering up after Lianne's death anyhow. But Jasmine would be just throwing herself away if she lets it go any further than that."

Emma took her hands out of the dishwater and wiped them on her apron. In the thirty-odd years of their friendship, Margery never had lost her ability to surprise, shock and aggravate her. Now here was a prime example of that special talent.

"Throwing herself away?"

A dreamy look passed over Margery's face. "If I only had her looks and brains, no chance I'd settle for someone like Thomas. Vice principal of a boy's college? Really, what can he offer her! After that poor choice of a first husband, wouldn't I just find myself a rich man, someone with the wherewithal to support me in style? Hundreds of men pass through that casino every day – surely she can do better than Thomas!"

Margery set the glass she had dried with a clink on the countertop, to underline the strength of her convictions. "Yes, it's just as easy to fall in love with a rich man as a poor man!" she concluded sanctimoniously, echoing, word for word, her mother's advice that she and Emma had laughed over back in their younger days, and that Margery herself had totally ignored in her choice of a husband.

Emma half-smiled at the memory, though her mind was clouded with worry. "Margery! I'm sure I told you that Jasmine isn't going back to the casino. She's been offered a job at the casino hotel; don't you remember that conversation?"

But Margery was on a roll and did not answer her question. "And while we're on the subject, I can't think of a worse match for Thomas than Jasmine. Just how would that help his career, having a wife who was a blackjack dealer in Las Vegas? Tell me it won't make a difference! It doesn't matter what kind of a job she has when she's back there, it won't change history!"

Margery was like a runaway train gathering steam and rattling on, and Emma did not know how to derail her, that is, until she added: "A woman he supposedly had an affair with, right after his wife had a stillborn child. In fact, it looks to me like the two of them have just picked up right where they left off!"

"STOP!!"

The word was said so loudly that Margery, her mouth slack with shock, looked around to see if the children had paused in their play, or whether Jim and Thomas might be standing, thunderstruck, in the middle of the garden. Then she stared wide-eyed at Emma, who, having abandoned the dishes in the sink, grabbed her arm with a wet hand and taking her forcibly over to the bench nearby, pushed her to sit down.

Several months before, in June perhaps, Emma had tried to explain to Jasmine the irresistible allure that gossip held for Margery. "It's like one of the delicious pies she makes. Margery could never sit and eat a piece of freshly baked pie all by herself. It's a treat she can only savour and enjoy when she shares it with others."

But Jasmine shook her head. No, she replied, it's nowhere near that innocent. She's dangerous. She has no idea of the harm she does when the half-baked rumours she spreads are repeated by others as the truth.

Now Emma could see quite clearly the poison pie of gossip that Margery had concocted. Doubtless she would share it with her daughters, then the dear Lord only knows where it would go from there!

Ten minutes later, with the petulance of a child denied a much-anticipated treat, Margery had been sworn to silence on the subject of the relationship between Thomas and Jasmine.

"No one, not even Jim, not a word! And long after Thomas's six-month probationary period ends! You know as well as I do how gossip travels – on the wind sometimes, I think! They're in love: do you want to be the one to ruin their happiness? And his career? All the gossip mills are quiet now, so if there's even a hint of a rumour I'll know where it came from and I will never, ever forgive you!"

"There's no need to threaten me, Emma," Margery's tone was one of injured dignity. "You've explained yourself well enough. She's like your own daughter, I know, and Laura – well, anyone can see how attached to her you are."

"In fact," she added, and there was a sly look to her as she eyed Emma, "in fact, wouldn't it suit you just fine, Emma, if everything worked out? It wouldn't surprise me either, to find you'd had a hand in the planning! Right at the start, suggesting to Lianne she hire Jasmine to throw everyone off the scent of that rumoured affair with Thomas. And then, oh my, what a good way to get the two of them back together again!"

"Nonsense and fiddlesticks!" Emma said briskly, and turned toward the sink. "Your imagination is running away with you again, Margery. Come, let's finish off these dishes."

Like a bloodhound sniffing a scent on the breeze, Margery gauged Emma's reaction and had an inkling she was onto something. She was even more certain when, a moment later, Emma casually asked, "did I tell you that I had to call Michael and Sandra to let them know I was renting out the house? It was in Bill's will that his children had to be informed of any changes; so I spoke to Sandra yesterday."

There was nothing more Margery could expect to get out of Emma on the subject she had just dropped anyhow. So she amiably allowed herself to be distracted.

"Oh, really? And how did that go?"

"She ranted and raved! I pointed out that under the terms of the will, the house was mine to use as I pleased as long as I lived. But that didn't stop her! However, I had the last word."

"What did you say?"

"I told her she should be glad I hadn't turned it into a boarding house!"

Then they shared a hearty laugh, and once again all was right between them. In short order they polished off the rest of the dishes. Emma refused to let Margery touch the pots and pans, though, for evening had fallen and the children needed their beds. After many fond farewells with Jasmine, the MacClures and Parkes packed into Jim's new car, waving as they drove into the night.

When Jasmine came downstairs after tucking Laura in, Thomas was lending Emma a hand with the kitchen clean up. "Shoo!" Jasmine said, tying on her apron and flapping it Margery-fashion at Emma. "Away with you! Thomas and I will finish this up!"

Before she left the room, Emma turned on the radio near the sink. "A little washing-up music," she said, and smiled as she climbed the stairs, thinking, in all probability, that later the two of them would make beautiful music of another sort altogether.

The last pot had been washed and put away. As Jasmine hung up her dishtowel, from behind Thomas brushed her neck with a kiss while undoing her apron. He went to the windows and opened them wide and turned off the lights. The night poured in then, filling the room with its moon and stars, the songs of night birds and frog choruses near the brook, and the soft sigh of a breeze trailing the sweet perfume of the old wisteria vine.

He took her hand and they danced to the muted strains of an old Cole Porter song on the radio, their long shadows swaying across the moonlit floor. This was their last night together. She was to follow him across the garden later, after he had made a good show of leaving from the front door. But even that short separation seemed too long, now that she was in his arms.

"Shouldn't you go?" she asked when the music paused, before the next song began.

Still he held her close. "Not yet. I'm enjoying this too much," he replied. "It's the first time we've danced together, darling. And when will I dance with you again? When will the three of us be together, a family? That's the question you still haven't answered me."

"You'll know," she whispered. "You'll be able to tell when the time is right."

This was far too cryptic for Thomas. He was about to question her further when, as so often happened, she distracted him. Because it was warm, he had undone the top two buttons of his shirt. Now she put her hand into that space, for a caress.

She loved the feel of him, his broad chest, and unlike the hair on his head, which was die-straight, the sparse hair here was rough and curly. But she had not realized how flammable he was, or the degree to which her touch would affect him, like flame to tinder.

He took a sharp breath in and rapidly unbuttoned his shirt fully open. Then, in what seemed one motion, he reached around, undid her brassiere, and pushed it and her light blouse up over her breasts.

"How dare you make so free with me, sir!" she cried theatrically, only half-joking, shocked and not a little angry.

"That's only the start of the liberties I intend to take with you tonight, my dear," Thomas answered, lowering his voice half an octave, and he stopped her protests with a kiss.

Now they were dancing skin to skin, satin against rough wool, kissing deeply, his body aflame against hers, hard and insistent with need. The moonlit trip to his house yawned like an impassible chasm; they could no longer travel there, nor go upstairs.

So she took him by the hand and led him to a place where doors would lock, and the books in their rows, sentinels of silence, muffled all sound. Toward the end, with his last, urgent thrust, he gave a cry that sounded very like a sob. They held each other then, their bodies cooling. And the question that hung in the stillness, spoken in all but words, was whether their love might end where it first began, there on the old brown couch in her uncle's study.

CHAPTER 106

Emma looked at the bedside clock. Five-thirty: too early. She was still tired after the party but unable to sleep. She occupied her mind with various things, one of them being regret she was not taking Jasmine to the airport. She herself had several errands to do in the city and would have enjoyed the outing. Jasmine, however, was set on taking the train. She said arrangements had already been made for Arlena to pick her up and drive her to her plane.

The station was quiet at eleven in the morning. Only a few people were waiting for the next train. The young clerk looked up from his money-counting when the door opened. Peering through the bars of the wicket, he saw approaching the woman who had enlivened his daydreams since he sold her a ticket a week ago. He put on his broadest smile.

"Hello, miss! Going to the city again?" He caught a whiff of some exotic perfume as she leaned over the counter and took a money purse from her handbag.

"Not today," she said, looking up at him brightly. And then she bought a ticket for another place, in the opposite direction.

* * *

Lex gave her the wooden whistle he had whittled under his desk that Mrs. Lewin returned to him on the final day of school. Sy presented her with a cherry bomb. Mac had duplicate bottle tops in his collection, and he donated them to her on the condition she send him any from the States different from his.

The evening before Laura left, the boys stood at the back door with woebegone faces. "It won't be nearly so fun when you're gone," Sy called back dispiritedly as they trailed away toward their homes through the purpling dusk.

Aunt Emma gave Laura two Classics comics, a new pencil case full of sharpened colour pencils, a pad of paper and instructions to send her a picture from her trip on the plane. She waved brightly at her as the stewardess took her hand and they walked up the ramp; then she went back to her car and had a good cry.

A few weeks later while preparing to leave Medford for Kellington, Emma cried a few more tears. They were foolish ones with which she had little patience. She wiped them away with the back of a hand as she packed up the odds and ends Jasmine and Laura left behind. Earlier that morning she had gone out to the front yard. In the folds of the child's clothing, she now put a dozen or so big, prickly, green chestnuts, part of the great abundance produced that autumn by the old tree for the small girl who was no longer there.

CHAPTER 107

Dear Aunt Emma:

First, thank you for the wonderful care you took of Laura and me. "Thank you"– such a paltry, insignificant phrase in return for all you've done! I shall repay you one day. Your package of odds and ends arrived. I showed Laura how to make bolas and conkers with the chestnuts; the former was taken away from her once she discovered they could be used as a weapon. Sorry to be short when I phoned to say she arrived safely – long distance is so expensive that letters will be my way to stay in touch.

Laura has her own room in the house we share with my friend Rita and her daughter Nancy, 10. The girls get along famously and Rita and I spell each other off on nights out. As I wrote Thomas, I have taken up bridge again. Thomas can tell you more about my work, but in brief, besides training staff on a new copy machine called the Xerox and typewriters that run on electricity, I handle arrangements for groups staying at our two hotels. Management would prefer these folks spend all their spare hours in the casinos; however, I've convinced them that by adding tours and attractions to their agenda, our guests will have such a good time they'll want to come back.

You asked about Arlena. All is about the same: happy with her ad agency job and her partner. News of her parents is not so good. Arlena says her mother is quite low and no longer interested in community work, which explains why you haven't seen much of her. She keeps busy with her grandsons, her only joy, it seems. Arlena worries about what will happen when Mason and his boys go to California in January. With her mother so down and Mason leaving, she says even Max has lost his usual zip.

Anna writes her January wedding will be small and quiet. She wants me in the wedding party, but when the lease on my house ends Jan. 15 I'm putting it up for sale and must be close at hand. So you're really moving back to Medford after the wedding! Thomas says he failed to convince you to stay. That means he'll be on his own then, which is of some concern to me.

I will sign off now because Laura is pestering me to go swimming at the local pool –her favorite pastime since her lessons at the lake. Please write and tell me how you and Thomas are faring in Kellington.

Much love,

Jasmine.

Dear Margery:

Thanks again to you and Jim for driving me to the train. I'm now installed in 96 Glenholme and hard at work helping Thomas settle in. The house is not nearly so grand as his lake house, but being newer and smaller is much easier to manage. He was living out of packing boxes when I arrived and there is much to do.

You were curious as to why he went to and from Medford in August when he could stay in the McIntyre's guesthouse to be close to work. Now that I've met Shelly McIntyre, the principal's wife, I suspect the reason was he didn't want to be talked to death! A charmer, but TALK! Never a quiet moment, and all the while her husband just smiles indulgently. Nonetheless, they gave me a warm welcome when I came to dinner there with Thomas after arriving. Once she found out I play bridge, she lined me up with her Thursday group. She also showed me their home, a lovely white house, a mansion really, full of light, with a pillared porch enclosing a tiled patio along the front. It overlooks the St. Lawrence and the property is beautifully landscaped and maintained by the school. Perhaps someday Thomas will live there!

They have a housekeeper but even then, Shelly's time is not her own; she has many responsibilities as wife of the principal. She is a little bird-like thing. Arthur is large, stout, and if our Sunday dinner was any indication, overly fond of his food and drink.

As we both know, there's no better prospect for a husband than a nice, well-trained widower. So you won't be surprised that the arrival of Thomas had the same effect as a ball of catnip thrown into a pack of cats. Many are mooning over him, but none so bold as a certain member of the college board. If you haven't had your laugh today, here's how I met her and ensured that we will never be friends.

Two days after I came, the doorbell rang. It was a woman, attractive in that glossy way only possible with money. Her white Lincoln was out front. She seemed surprised, unpleasantly so, to see me and asked imperiously for Thomas. I asked who I should say was calling. Penelope Farland, she answered shortly.

When Thomas came down, she gave him the bag she was carrying. And can you guess what was in it? It was a casserole! Mind you, she hadn't made it herself: it came from a snooty vintner in town and was no shepherd's pie but a fancy pork, veal and beef "potage" – but a casserole nonetheless!

The instant I saw it I thought of the time you, Jasmine and I were discussing Edna Matthews and how you said she was canoodling widowers with casseroles. And I couldn't help it, I laughed! A guffaw, really, and quite rude! They both looked at me as if I had lost my mind. I said, please excuse me, Penny, I have work to do. I just managed to get to the kitchen before collapsing in laughter, but before I was out of earshot I heard her say loudly, it's Penelope, not Penny!

Later Thomas asked me what set me off. When I explained, he laughed too and said, good grief, keep that woman away from me. If she comes around again, tell her I'm out! She's asked Thomas and the McIntyres up to her cottage near Sharbot Lake for a fall weekend. He doesn't want to go but says he has no choice; as a member of the board she will decide his future and he has to stay on her good side.

Last week, Thomas bought a TV! He wants to keep up to date with his students, he says. We saw the Ed Sullivan show Sunday night and I must say I enjoyed it. Yesterday I watched that soap opera you like,

The Guiding Light, and it made me quite homesick.

Well, this is a long enough letter. I will only add that Jasmine writes she is truly enjoying the change of job. She's also playing bridge and taking part in competitions. So she's often out at night, but fortunately her friend Rita is there to stay with the girls.

Please give my love to the family and write me with plans for the wedding and any town gossip.

Love, Emma

Dear Emma:

Thank you for your letter, though not for the scolding you gave me in it! Yes, I am often out evenings because I play bridge and it is not a daytime pursuit except on weekends. And no, I am not neglecting my daughter; that still leaves three or four nights a week and most of the weekend to spend with her.

I don't know why you would say Thomas is upset and jealous when I am not there for his phone calls. I told him my bridge schedule. And as I've explained to him, and now again to you, my bridge partner Lou Styles is married, short, bald, fat and fiftyish, and hardly a candidate for my affections. He is, however, a wizard at bridge and it was a great stroke of luck he agreed to pair up with me. We are a formidable team and getting better all the time. All would be ideal if only he gave up the cigars he chain smokes while playing. However, that should end soon. As we go up the ladder in tournaments they won't let him smoke since the way he sets his cigar down on the ashtray could be a signal for me.

I also don't appreciate you saying, "it seems you just can't seem to stay away from the cards." This is something I want, I'm good at it, and I refuse to let you make me feel guilty!

There – that's it for now. I really don't want to fight with you by letter when it's so much more fun in person. All is about the same here. Your great niece is doing well in school and playing baseball, walking fences and collecting bottle caps. I am enjoying my job and seem to have a knack for my work with groups, most of them here for conventions.

Thomas's weekend away with that man-eater Penelope Farland is coming up. It sounds ominous. I can just see her appearing in his bedroom in a negligee, and what's he to do then, holler for help? Is there no way he can get out of this? Although he does seem to enjoy telling me about how she's always in his office on one pretext or another. Is he trying to make me jealous?

Take care of yourself and don't work too hard. As the one who packed everything up, you have all my sympathy for being the one on the unpacking end.

Much love,

Jasmine

Dear Jasmine,

I am including a page from Margery's letter. If I sent all of it, my letter would be too heavy for airmail. Hers was mostly about the wedding anyhow. However, you may be interested in the attached.

ecru lace on the bodice and satin shoes in the same deep cream. Keith's mother plans to wear a navy dress. I haven't decided on my outfit yet.

I saw Edna Matthews at William Carson's funeral last week. Gussie White is staying at her house now. She said the White's house is too chaotic and Gussie wasn't getting the attention she needed so she suggested Gussie live with her and the Whites agreed. The child is recovering slowly, coming out of her shell with the help of the psychiatrist, she says. Though how Edna would know I have no idea, the way she talks all the time it's a wonder that child ever gets a word in edgewise.

The other news is Mason Stoddart has a new secretary – the postmaster's widow, Nuala O'Donahue – and several of the secretarial staff have been let go. She's only been there two months but is shaking the place up and making changes. It's said she has a temper.

When I saw Edna, she told me Mason wants to buy her house after all. So it seems he won't be moving to California. I guess that will make his parents happy. Does it have anything to do with his new secretary, I wonder? Everyone thinks so. Edna says she might sell her house to him and find a smaller one.

I was talking to Anna about her guest list for the wedding and I don't know how we can keep from making it larger. She may say she wants it small and intimate but our family alone is 22 people. She wants to limit it to 50 but with Keith's that leaves only enough for the main guests...

Now the real reason for my letter: your "man eater". We've caged her for now anyhow! A week last Thursday I picked up Shelly McIntyre for bridge. It's my turn to host it next. Not looking forward to it – a big group and lots of work. On the way, I asked Shelly if she was ready for the trip to Penelope's lake lodge the next day. She was surprised. Didn't I know? On Tuesday she told Penelope they had to cancel. Arthur's brother and his wife were flying in from Calgary on the weekend, and they were meeting them in the city. Is Thomas still going, she asked. He hasn't told me he isn't, I said. Then I asked did Arthur tell Thomas they weren't going? Probably not, she said, you know how men are and things are so busy at the school.

We were early. After I parked the car, we just sat there, the longest I've seen her silent. She knows as well as I do Penelope has designs on Thomas. Now, Jasmine, you have to credit your old Aunt with a stroke of genius. Because then I said, you know, Shelly, it seems to me if a member of the board is too chummy with someone on probation like Thomas, then how can they be impartial when it's time to decide if he should stay or go?

Shelly, who's no fool, said, my goodness, you're right. What a perfect way to stop her in her tracks. I'll get Arthur to talk to the board chairman. And he did, and now there is a non-fraternization policy until the six-month probation period is over for all new hires. It was voted in last week by the whole board, Penelope included. I guess she didn't want to be the only no vote. Seems to me this might make her keen to have Thomas approved at the end of his probation, too!

Needless to say, Thomas made his excuses. Now, Jasmine, I should warn you that "Bad Penny" is not just attractive and wealthy, having married then divorced into money, but wily. Because when he told her he wasn't coming, she said it was too *bad because her other guests were influential in Kellington and it would have been good for him and Arthur to meet them.*

We shall never know if there were other guests – though when Shelly asked Arthur, he said Penelope never mentioned inviting anyone else. Otherwise, you need not worry yourself about Thomas. He works hard but keeps the same routines he had at Medford High, working out with the school teams, a run after work and walk before bed. Shelly says she wishes Arthur would take a page from Thomas; Arthur's idea of exercise is a stroll to the mailbox.

Congratulations on making it to the state bridge club championships. We always knew you were good; now you're proving it. I won't scold you anymore, though I must say I have no idea why you're doing this.

Much love, Aunt Emma

Dear Margery:

Please excuse this short and belated reply to your long newsy letter but we have had plenty of excitement here, not the good but bad kind. Two weeks ago, the school principal Arthur McIntyre had a stroke. A teacher found him on the floor of his office and called the ambulance. Since then I have been driving his wife Shelly to the hospital – she doesn't drive and the poor soul is sick with worry, as well she might be. The stroke is a bad one and he has a long journey back to recovery. In the meantime, Thomas has had to step in and do Arthur's job as well as his own. He is, as you might guess, not at all fazed by the huge responsibility he has to take on and rising to the occasion.

Thomas says now he is exactly where he wants to be, only two years ahead of schedule. It's up to the board whether they look for a new principal or keep him there. He would be their youngest principal yet if they do. Arthur will take early retirement. The stroke affected his left side and he can't speak properly. He indicated in writing he has every confidence in

Thomas as his replacement, but what happens next remains to be seen.

There's not much else to report. Through Shelly and the bridge club I have met many pleasant women but compared to Medford the skill level is not as high. I hosted the last club meeting, a lot of work and now I know why they were so eager to foist it off on me, a newcomer.

Regarding Christmas, Jasmine and Thomas have made no arrangements yet. I will stay here, then return in January for Anna's wedding and move back into my house. Jasmine is in the Nevada bridge club finals now, busy with that and work. She talks each week with Thomas, except last week. When he phoned she was out at a master class in bridge before her last tournament. After he hung up, he laughed and said of all the rivals for her affection he expected to have, he had never thought of a deck of cards.

Much love, Emma.

CHAPTER 108

Vegas Duo Are Bridge Champs

Winning hands in the Nevada contract bridge championships on Dec. 8 were held by Las Vegas residents Lou Styles and Jasmine Carlisle, who took top ranking in the pairs division. Styles is owner of the well-known Las Fortunes jewelry store on Sahara Avenue. Carlisle is employed by the Flamingo Hotel. Their final score set a new state bridge tournament record. They will compete in the U.S. bridge championships in May.

Dear Aunt Emma:

What a week! First, beating far more experienced players, the six-year Nevada title holders; next, seeing my name in print for the first time – though the credit here goes to my partner Lou, a regular advertiser in the Vegas Review-Journal. Now, onto the next hurdle, the U.S. championships this spring!

In answer to your question regarding Christmas, nothing is decided. There is no need to tell me again time is getting short. I have matters to settle here, and Thomas is busy at the school and might not be able to get away. I will update you on Laura in my next letter, so please forgive the brevity of this one.

Now to the real reason for writing: I need a favour. Lou has tickets for a Vegas Christmas Special with Frank Sinatra. He bought them a while ago, saying that after the tournament they would serve as either a celebration or consolation prize. Happily, it's the former, and so I will be at the Sands, sitting at a table stage-side with Lou, his wife and a few of their friends. The show will be televised live a week next Saturday. I've checked and you can see it at 9 pm. your time on Channel 2.

Can you coax Thomas to watch? He wasn't enthusiastic when I mentioned it; I hope you can change his mind. There's a good chance you'll see me when the camera is on the audience. As well, Thomas will see he has nothing to fear from Lou despite all the time we spend together. Also included in this envelope is something for him for Christmas. Please give it to him right after the show.

Glad you are well and enjoying your stay with Thomas. I love you a lot, enough to overlook the fact that you sometimes tend to nag me in your letters!

Jasmine

Dear Margery:

Thank you for your last letter. Goodness, what a hotbed of scandal and intrigue Medford is, rivaling Guiding Light. And how endless the matter of wedding arrangements! Your descriptions are so detailed – leave us at least a few surprises!

So Sherry Byers and Alistair McGregor will tie the knot in May. I hope that girl knows how to steer a comet, for that's what she's latched onto. I'm sad to hear Letty Lawson finally gave Cheryl her house – a poor trade for us both: her nice house for an apartment and Cheryl instead of Letty for a neighbour.

You will see from the enclosed news clipping that our Jasmine has shown herself a champion. Remember playing bridge with her when she was 10 and we needed another hand? She also writes that Frank Maitland, her partner who ran off with the funds for their project, was tried and sentenced along with his woman sidekick in late November. She is waiting to see what, if anything, she will receive in restitution.

It's almost Christmas and Thomas is staying here over the vacation. I've been reluctant to tell you how it stands with them. Things are not going well. Not because of Jasmine, but Thomas – although Shelly McIntyre is mostly to blame.

Arthur is home from the hospital now. Before that, Shelly came for Sunday dinner. While we were at table, she talked about the pension the school gave him and how it was reduced because, with his stroke, he hadn't served out his term. She was very bitter. Then she asked 'and where's my pension? How about mine?'

When Arthur became principal 14 years ago, she said, she never anticipated the demands that would be made on her: the entertaining, hosting visitors, the teas, galas, and fundraisers etc. she had to organize or attend with or without him, and so forth. On and on she went, angry at all she had to do with no pay or recognition. She couldn't even take a part-time job to bolster the family finances, because the board said it was unbecoming to the role of principal's wife.

Thomas was quiet all the time, listening. When she ran out of steam, he said I know it's been hard for you, Shelly. I've spent half a year watching you go about your work. After she left, he sat at the table with his head in his hands. I can't do this to Jasmine, he said. If it was no life for Shelly, it would be hell for Jasmine; she'd be a wild bird in a cage. I'll try to get the board to give Arthur his full pension. And I'll have to tell Jasmine it won't work. It might have before, but I can't walk away from this job now when so many are depending on me.

I said, don't you think whether she takes on the role of principal's wife should be her decision? He said no. She would do it because she loves me. But I couldn't stand seeing what it would do to her.

Now I can see his heart breaking. Every day he's sadder and quieter. I have to confess that having to watch him makes my heart break too, especially because I know he's right.

Love,

Emma

CHAPTER 109

just back from reform school with a greasy duck-tail and driving an old woody wagon that might as well be a traveling motel. The stupid girl is crazy about him and Marcia can't keep her from sneaking out to see him, well we all know where that will end.

Stella Byers says they still haven't found a replacement for Chris at the radio station. Probably not offering enough money. The other son, Jeremy says he won't go into the business and wants to be a lawyer. That boy never tells the truth where a lie will do, what do you bet he ends up a politician.

So Jasmine and Thomas are on the rocks. I'm not surprised, right from the start she was a bad choice for him especially now he's principal of a snooty boys' school. She's had too much of life to stick around a cow town like Kellington anyhow. He needs someone to handle their social affairs. You told me about that woman who's after him, Penelope. Seeing as she's his age and besides giving the school wads of cash hasn't been much but a wife and mother, my guess is she'd fit the job better than Jasmine. Well, those are my thoughts.

Wishing you and Thomas merry Christmas though from what you say it doesn't promise to be very merry and bright. It will be so good to have you home in January. We miss you at our family gatherings.

Love,

Margery

Emma had brought Margery's most recent letter downstairs. This was the last page. After re-reading it, she derived a pleasant sense of satisfaction from consigning it to the fire Thomas had lit. The fireplace was in the living room, the coziest room in the house. It was also the location of the television, which she had turned on ten minutes ago in preparation for the special Christmas program Jasmine had asked her, and Thomas in particular, to watch.

But where was he? The show was about to start! He had only grudgingly agreed to join her and now he was gone. Glancing at her watch, she hurried up the stairs to find him in his study.

"Thomas, won't you come? The TV show is starting in just two minutes."

He did not look up from his work. "Why? So I can watch Jasmine with all her fancy friends?"

Emma had to bite her tongue to cut off a sharp retort to this childishness, which was so very unlike him. Then belatedly, she considered the shadings of emotion she had heard in his voice. Perhaps, she thought, even the sight of Jasmine might cause him pain.

"If for no other reason, Thomas, then please do it for me. She wanted you to watch, and I'll feel badly if I can't persuade you and I have to tell her."

He followed her downstairs and took his place in the comfortable armchair near the set. Frank Sinatra was already onstage, singing. Emma quailed, tense with anxiety: had they missed her? But no, it was still only the beginning of the show. She leaned forward and noticed he had, too. After Sinatra finished his song and the announcer introduced the star-spangled program with grand flourishes to whip up applause, the camera swung around to the tables of patrons at the Sands resort. And very suddenly, there was Jasmine. She was sitting next to a heavyset, peroxide-blonde woman, whose hand lay proprietarily on the arm of a smiling, bald man with a Churchillian bulldog countenance and a cigar firmly clamped in his mouth.

She was a magnet for the camera. It zoomed in and lingered on her, a beautiful woman bejeweled with diamonds, dressed in a deeply low-cut gown. But it rapidly swung away once she held up the locket suspended around her neck and kissed it, with a look that was directed at only one of the million or more viewers who were watching the show.

In the chair beside her, Thomas suddenly sat upright. Then he got to his feet and, to Emma's surprise and dismay, left the room. After a second or two she followed him, expecting he had taken refuge once more in his study. But no, as she listened, there was the sound of footsteps on the stairs down to the cellar. She waited. Finally, she heard a bumping noise as he ascended. The door opened and there was Thomas, with a large suitcase and a face filled with something very like suppressed joy.

"I'm going to see her, Emma," he said. "If only this once, on Christmas the three of us will be a family. It's no good telling her what I've decided over the phone. Perhaps we can work things out so that I can see my daughter, from time to time."

He started toward the hall with his suitcase. "I hope you won't mind if I leave you alone here for Christmas?" he asked, and she was touched by his solicitousness. "Tomorrow I'll phone Jasmine and then head to the airport to see if I can get a seat to Vegas or someplace close by." He disappeared around the corner.

Heavens, she had almost forgotten! Emma dashed to the sideboard in the dining room. "Wait, Thomas!" she called out as he started up the stairs. "Come back! There's something here for you, from Jasmine, that she asked me to give you right after the show!"

When he came in, she handed him the thick, stiff white envelope bound around with clear tape that had defied all her efforts to guess what was inside. If she had been able to open it, would she? Certainly not! The fact that Jasmine felt she had to go to such lengths to keep it from prying eyes – her prying eyes, to be exact! – awoke in her a certain amount of resentment.

Now, however, she waited with unabashed curiosity to see it opened. Thomas took a penknife from his pocket. He cut the triple-layered paper and the stiff cardboard underneath cleanly, and took out the unmistakable red folder that would enclose an airline ticket. He opened it, and when he looked inside, something there made his face flush and his eyes suddenly fill. He dropped the folder on the table and abruptly left the room.

Emma's struggle with her sense of propriety lasted exactly two seconds. If he had left it there, then why wouldn't he expect her to look?

She picked up the folder, opened it. A faint trace of perfume arose from the little note attached to the airline ticket for Las Vegas.

Thomas – There are no words to tell how much I love you.

Come, dearest, so I can show you instead.

J.

Oh yes, it was private, meant for his eyes only. Nevertheless, Emma could not be sorry she had read it. Instantaneously that little note filled her with a happiness and optimism she hadn't felt for weeks. She quickly dropped the folder back on the table and repositioned it in its original spot – not that Thomas was likely to notice. Then she returned to the living room to watch the rest of the show, although the black and white images flickering across the screen barely registered against the warm glow of the thoughts crowding her mind.

Later as she lay in bed she wondered. When Jasmine kissed the locket, that family heirloom entrusted to her by Lianne, what made Thomas leap to his feet? Weeks later, he told her that when a minute button on the front was depressed, it opened and his photo was inside. She never had known. But knowing just what she did, that a warm and loving welcome awaited him in Las Vegas, was sufficient. Despite Margery's prediction, in the years to come Emma would always remember the Christmas she spent with Shelly and her recuperative husband as being rather merry, and quite bright enough.

CHAPTER 110

This city bus to McCarran airport was by far the slowest way to that destination. It followed a wandering route with many stops as it drove through a sleepy residential area. Once on the outskirts, the bus driver pulled over near the Pines Seniors' Residence and two of his regular passengers climbed on. It was around one o'clock, just after lunch at the residence, their usual time to board.

The bus driver was not especially curious, but he had noticed that the two elderly ladies made little use of the walker and cane they brought with them until it came time to disembark at the airport. Then they asked his assistance, and he helped them down and opened the walker. He watched and wondered as, suddenly enfeebled, one leaned on her cane and the other pushed her walker, and off they went.

They progressed slowly through the airport until they came to the arrivals area. To discourage loitering there was only one bench, intended solely for the disabled or those unable to stand for any length of time while waiting for disembarking passengers. It was to this bench that Min and Irma picked their way through the crowd, which was light just before Christmas when most travelers appeared to be leaving rather than arriving in Las Vegas.

The bench was fully occupied. Min and Irma simply stood looking down at those who seemed the most able-bodied. Soon enough they gave up their seats. Once they had made themselves comfortable, Min took a bag of potato chips out of her purse and Irma opened a box of Crackerjack.

Across the floor, a security guard regarded Min and Irma with a jaundiced eye. The duo was as irritatingly familiar to him as spots on his back he often needed to itch but was unable to reach. The elderly ladies were regular visitors who had ditched the afternoon soaps on TV at the retirement home for the real life dramas in the international arrivals area: the tearful reunions, joyous embraces, and occasionally even a glimpse of a glamorous star or starlet. They were there at least twice a week. One time, a while ago, the security guard had been instructed by his superior to move them on.

"This bench is reserved for people who are actually waiting for passengers, and who are finding it difficult to stand," he told them.

They both looked at him blankly. "That's us," the one whose name was Min had said.

His supervisor then attempted several times to clear them away but gave up. Both Min and Irma had a legalistic turn of mind and asked to see documents or procedures manuals that provided grounds for their eviction from the bench. Failing that, if he laid a finger on them, they asserted, they would not only resist and cry out but also make sure he was charged with assault.

Now Min and Irma settled back and prepared to enjoy themselves. Irma took a can of soda out of her handbag. "Look over there," she said to Min, with a nudge of her elbow and nod of her head to the left.

A little apart from the crowd, a tall, lovely looking woman with dark auburn hair was standing with a young girl of about eight or nine. Both had a look of pleasant anticipation about them. The girl was hopping about the highly polished, patterned floor on one foot. Her mother regarded her indulgently.

"Yes," Min said, "could be interesting." No one else in the remaining crowd looked very promising, but you never knew. That was one of the best things about this pastime, the element of unpredictability. Anything could happen.

The passengers of a plane from Canada were starting to come out after being processed by customs. Now Irma demonstrated one of the other uses for her cane. She gently prodded the leg of a man who was blocking her view. "I'm sorry," she said, "but I can't see."

The passengers came in a trickle, then a rush. "There he is," said Min.

Toward the end, towering a head over the crowd, was the man they felt sure must belong to the waiting woman. He was a large, broad-shouldered man and handsome, with a good head of dark hair. On one arm he had a shopping bag, and the other carried a suitcase. Now he put it down, because the child had spied him and was running to meet him. He picked her up and gave her a big bear hug and a kiss, twirling her around before setting her on the floor again.

Now was the moment Irma and Min had been waiting for. Min was staring raptly as she reached into the bag for another potato chip. The man picked up the suitcase and went toward the waiting woman, who was wearing a smile bright as the sun. He set down the suitcase and they held out their hands to each other. He took hers and wrapped them around his waist; then he held her face between his hands and gave her a brief, quite chaste kiss.

"A friend?" Min queried.

"No, probably just married a long time," Irma said. It was disappointing. Having finished her Crackerjack, she helped herself to one of Min's potato chips.

However, it seemed there might be more. Now the man removed the shopping bag hanging from his arm. He showed it to the child and from his gestures, seemed to be encouraging her to look inside as he set it down a little ways from her mother. Then, while she was otherwise distracted by its contents – presents, probably – he turned his attention back to the lovely woman. He went toward her. They wrapped their arms around one another, and engaged in a kiss so steamy and passionate that, as the duo on the bench later related to their nightly euchre group, Min dropped her bag of potato chips on the floor and Irma almost put the one she was holding in her ear instead of her mouth.

"Hot damn!" Min exclaimed.

"Smokin'!" Irma concurred. "Better'n Rhett and Scarlett!"

"Shameful!" observed the dumpy little woman sitting beside them on the bench, adding a sniff of disapproval for this all too-public display of affection.

Min turned on her. "Shameful, is it? Or only a shame it's not you, and never will be?" she inquired in a hostile fashion. The woman got up and left.

When she looked back, Min could see that the man had lifted up the child again. Now they were embracing in a tight circle, laughing and talking all at once. Then he set her down so he could pick up his suitcase. The girl carried the bag of presents and slowly they walked away, their arms around each other and trailing clouds of joy.

"Five stars," Min pronounced.

"Agreed," Irma replied. She swiped at one eye. Movies and TV all were fine, but nothing beat real life.

She looked around. "Min," she said, nodding to her left.

Min turned to survey the ramp leading down from the arrivals platform. The last passenger to descend was a swarthy young man with a furtive look about him. His long hair was confined by a band around his forehead. Carrying a guitar case as well as his luggage and liberally adorned with male jewelry and tattoos, he seemed in a rush to leave.

"I'll bet he had fun at customs," Min said.

"I thought we didn't import, just export those from Vegas," Irma commented, and Min chuckled.

Over in the corner, the security guard was calling the cleaners on his walkie-talkie. There was a sour look on his face as he alerted them to come take care of a snack food spill in the arrivals area.

CHAPTER 111

The entry hall of the 'white house', as the domicile of the school principal had been dubbed by Thomas and Emma, was full of cardboard boxes when Emma arrived for a morning coffee klatch with Shelly.

"Whatever are you doing?" she asked with unconcealed surprise. Although it was obvious a move was in progress, it was only the second of January, too early.

"I started packing us up on Boxing Day," Shelly answered. "With that name, what better day for the job? Then the very next morning, I rented an apartment."

After his stroke, Arthur's temporary bedroom had been set up in the library; he was unable to climb stairs. As Shelly observed, it was an unsatisfactory arrangement.

"The apartment has just been renovated and it's empty. I'm going to move us in gradually." She ran a hand through her uncombed hair. Although usually perfectly coiffed and dressed, today she was bedraggled in a baggy sweater and old pair of pants. She waved Emma toward the kitchen.

"Come, let's sit down."

At the table, they faced each other over steaming cups of coffee.

"It's been harder than I thought," Shelly said. She was looking tired and strained. "But I can handle it, only not here. There's no point in delaying. We'll be gone by the fifteenth of the month, and then you and Thomas can move in."

"Except that I won't be here. I'm going to a wedding in Medford mid-month, and moving back into my own house shortly after that."

"Oh. I forgot you were leaving so soon, Emma. My goodness. That'll be hard for Thomas, rattling around all by himself in this big house. That man needs a wife!"

Emma laughed. "After what he's seen of your life, I'm not sure he wants to inflict that job on anyone!"

"So far as I know," Shelly said thoughtfully, "the principal has always had a wife. It seems she always took on a good deal of the entertaining and social events; back then, this house was perfect for it. But the job has grown by leaps and bounds in the past ten years, and so has the school – it was just under 400 students when we first came and now it's closer to 800."

She got up to refill their cups. "The board of governors asked me to come to their meeting next week. And I know the reason why. At the end of January, we always hold a reception for the graduating class and their parents. It's one of the school's most important events for fund-raising and endowments. Thomas isn't in any position to be of help yet."

"So, I bet you dimes to dollars they're going to ask me to handle the reception." she said. "As my last contribution to the school." She came toward the table with the coffee pot and smacked it down so hard that Emma jumped, fearing a splash.

Shelly's face twisted. Spitting out the words, she said, "and can you guess what I'll tell them? That they can go to hell!"

CHAPTER 112

On her way home, Emma spied a blue balloon. A remnant of the New Year festivities, it lay in the curve of a snow bank. It was a sad little object, flabby and wizened, slowly deflating. To Emma, it was like the bright happiness that had sustained her over the Christmas season. The hour she just spent with Shelly was depressing enough. As well, her pleasant thoughts about Thomas, Jasmine and Laura and their joyful reunion now had been replaced by worries about how they would fare if indeed he did what he planned and they were saying their final goodbyes. Her joy was leaking away, evaporating. All that was left was only a stubborn little residue of something different, hope or optimism perhaps, that refused to yield to such a harsh new reality.

Outside the front door, she stamped the snow from her feet before going into the house. He would be home around five o'clock, and at least she could give him a good dinner – although she knew from experience that food, that great comforter and cure-all for many ills, is at best a band-aid for a heavy heart.

Now she sat in the living room, her ears tuned for the sound of a car turning into the driveway. Still, she jumped when she heard the motor and its loud roar just before he turned it off. She hurried to meet him at the door; but while she was still in the hall he had already opened it wide. There he stood, and with one glance she could see that he was not at all what she had expected or feared.

He swept her into a big hug, the rough wool of his overcoat cold and a little damp from the falling snow against her face; then held her out at arms length. In the interval since she last saw him, he seemed to have shed ten years. He was tanned, radiating good health, and from the expression on his face, almost electrified with happiness.

He had said something. It seemed almost incomprehensible to her. He and Jasmine were married? Had she heard that correctly?

"Ww-what? How? I don't –" Her heart gave a disconcertingly little flutter, and she felt for the wall to steady herself.

Thomas was all apologies as he steered her into the living room and sat her down on the sofa. "I shouldn't have sprung it on you like that, Emma, but all the way back I've been looking forward to telling you! It was on New Year's eve; one of those quick, Vegas-style weddings. We'll have another, a formal one, later, but right now you're the first and only one to know, because it has to stay a secret."

Emma fanned herself with a newspaper. Ghostly pale before, now she was flushed with excitement. "Puzzles on puzzles!" she exclaimed. "Though, even if you almost gave me a heart attack with your 'surprise', at least I'd have died happy! Married! Well, pour us a couple fingers of whiskey, Thomas, this deserves a celebration! But first, tell me before I die of curiosity instead of surprise, whatever changed your mind?"

He had scooped up the snow his boots had left on the carpet and was depositing it in her dracaena plant as he spoke. "The moment I stepped off the plane and saw them waiting there, I knew I'd only been fooling myself, thinking I could live without them. But when I said as much, Jasmine sat me down and told me all she's done so we can be together."

Taking her hands in his cold, wet ones, he said, "we have a plan, Emma, or rather, Jasmine has a plan, to which I've added my two cents. And there's a role for you in it – in fact it won't work without you. Let me get us those drinks, then I'll explain it to you."

And, over the splendid dinner she prepared as a consolation that had become, instead, a celebration, Emma agreed to help. Several cocktails and a bottle of champagne later, the next morning she woke up with a rather vicious hangover. It was a small price to pay, she concluded, for the other sort of hangover she had acquired: a deep and lasting glow of satisfaction from all she had learned the evening before.

CHAPTER 113

The temperature was minus 20, eye-watering crisp, as she hurried to the white house. Maddie, the McIntyre's housekeeper, opened the door. It was brilliant outside; the sun on new snow so dazzling Emma's eyes took a long moment to adjust to the light in the foyer, which in itself was quite bright enough. They passed through the living room, where Arthur McIntyre in his wheelchair was basking in the swath of sunlight that fell from the bank of windows overlooking the St. Lawrence. He was a much lighter, slighter version of his old self but still as ruddy, having just completed ten circuits of the large room with his walker. Emma duly congratulated him on his progress. When she said she expected him up and around in no time, he emphatically mouthed something that sounded like, "damn right."

Maddie led her to the library, where she found Shelly on a ladder taking down books and stowing them in cartons. "Some, the ones higher up, have been here since the age of the dinosaurs. I'm leaving those, but there are a few of Arthur's scattered among them."

"Let me give you a hand." Emma took a carton and started in on the books lower down.

"Thomas is safely home?"

"Yes, in time for dinner. Hard at work now, of course. He had several calls to return to board members, and he said he'll make sure to speak to them about Arthur's pension."

"You can thank him for us, Emma, though I don't hold out great hopes of success. Since Arthur didn't finish out his contract, legally we don't have a leg to stand on. Ten percent may not seem like much to them, but for us it's the difference between having to pinch pennies or a comfortable retirement."

She moved the ladder over and reached for a new carton. They worked for a while in silence, an unusual state for Shelly, and then Emma ventured, "the board meeting they asked you to is this Friday, isn't it? Thomas thinks there might be a way to change their minds. And since you'll have their ear, it would be a big help to him if you could make a few other suggestions."

"I'd be glad to do anything I can to help Thomas," she replied. "Tell me what you'd like me to say."

Emma spoke for only a few minutes before Shelly held up a restraining hand. "Wait!" she said as she descended the ladder. "This is important. I need to give it my full attention and take notes. Let's go to the kitchen and discuss this over coffee."

CHAPTER 114

In winter the ivy on the circular building that stood somewhat isolated from other structures on the school grounds turned a mottled grayish-green. With his long grayish hair and mustaches, weather-beaten face and drab clothing, the old groundskeeper was almost invisible against this back-drop as he supervised two workers clearing the paths of snow. Perhaps that was why until he was almost on top of him, Malcolm Reynolds failed to acknowledge him and even then, when he was almost past, only said a curt, "hello Dusen," as he walked briskly toward the rotunda, as the circular building was called.

At the school he had worked for practically all his life, the head groundskeeper was known only as Dusen, and if once he had had a first name it was long forgotten. Now he watched curiously as Reynolds tried to peer through the dusty glass of the Rotunda's door, even rubbing it a bit with his fine leather gloves to remove some of the grime. Reynolds was a lawyer whose son, Martin, attended the school, and a member of the board of governors. Although he might be only a groundskeeper, by dint of long observation the elderly man had become a keen judge of boys and men. The son impressed Dusen as a good sort. However, over the course of the seven years the father had served on the board, Dusen had come to know him rather better than he preferred, and concluded that he was a bit of a pompous ass with an overweening sense of his own self-importance.

Nevertheless. Dusen pulled out his ring of keys as he went toward Reynolds, who was standing looking in the window. "Mr. Reynolds, would you like me to let you in?"

"Thanks, Dusen. I'm in a hurry, but I wouldn't mind a quick look. We were discussing the rotunda in our board meeting this morning. I've never actually been inside the building."

Dusen opened the door. Well, he hoped they weren't talking again about pulling it down. It was a piece of the school's history and a beautiful old structure, with a marvelous stained-glass dome protected from stray footballs and baseballs by the reinforced glass overtop. Along one end were curved windows with a fine view of the main school buildings. The floor was made of huge pine planks still smelling faintly of the beeswax with which they once were polished. But apart from that, it was a neglected, aging building, now used mostly for storage. Years ago, it had served the needs of a smaller school as a function space for writing exams or dances and graduations. But as the years passed and the school grew, it had fallen into disuse.

Reynolds walked between the dusty sheet- and tarpaulin-covered piles of chairs and tables to the centre of the rotunda and, looking up, turned around in the brilliant circle of light from the dome. Then he was out the door again with barely a thank you, bustling along the cleared walkway like the important man in a hurry he believed himself to be. Dusen could only hope that he had seen the fine lines of the building and sensed its almost sacred aura of antiquity. But he doubted it.

It was only the second time in months he had admitted anyone to the rotunda. It was a different kind of visitor last time, with an eye for all the beauty of the building and, as he clearly remembered, she quite the beauty herself.

Yes, Mr. Reynolds was only a blot on his memory, a face he would gladly erase. But he wasn't likely to forget her.

* * *

It had been a long day and a frustrating one with fewer billable hours than normal, and as he drove home Malcolm Reynolds was once again debating stepping down from the board of Royal Sutton School. An avalanche of pressing and urgent matters, with a new principal only just stepping up to relieve them of some of the decision-making, meant that the board had been meeting once or twice practically every week for months – all of it time, Malcolm fulminated, he could have spent making money. He would have quit long ago, probably, if it weren't for the steady legal work the school provided, the prestige of being a board member and the free lunch at meetings.

Now his heart sank as he opened the door to find his wife waiting for him with a too-bright smile and a before-dinner cocktail, a Manhattan, his favorite. He would have appreciated it more if he didn't know she was using it as a lubricant to get him talking about what happened at the board meeting.

Dianne's father and brother had graduated from Royal Sutton; many of her friends were old boys. She herself had served as head of the women's auxiliary and she had, so far as her husband was concerned, an excessive amount of interest in the doings of the board of governors. Now she sat him down in the most comfortable chair in the den and pumped him shamelessly for details of today's lunch meeting.

"What's the consensus on our handsome new principal?"

"Latham? There's general agreement he's grabbed hold of the helm and come up to speed fast. There's no doubt he's hardworking and capable. He already has the respect of the staff and students. If there's any handicap at the moment, it's that he doesn't have a wife."

"Oh? How so?" Dianne raised an inquiring eyebrow.

"Well, it has to do with the reception in January for the grad students and their parents. Actually, we're looking at a bit of an emergency. Arthur and Shelly always took care of it. It's on the school calendar, and unfortunately, no one thought to tell the office staff to hold back on the invites, and so they've already gone out."

"Whoops! I can see where that might be a problem. Did you find a solution?"

"Shelly came to the meeting. We asked her if she could handle the reception just this once, because we're in a bit of a bind with the timing. She gave us a flat no."

Dianne emitted a sharp bark of a laugh. "What'd you expect her to say? I don't blame her! What're you going to do?"

"Well, she did offer us an alternative. Latham is moving into the principal's residence at the end of January. His neighbour who's helping him settle in, Emma Madison, has offered to take it on, in a pinch. But Shelly says we can't expect her to handle the reception without being paid.

"We met Emma Madison," Dianne said. "It was at the reception for Thomas, remember? She's elderly, though with all her qualifications she would probably do a good job. But, frankly, Malcolm, it's a stopgap! Isn't it high time the board hired someone to handle these functions? What if Thomas Latham marries again, only some dimwit who couldn't organize her way out of a paper bag? Then you'd really be stuck!"

Malcolm gave a short laugh. "That's more or less what Shelly said. And that the principal's house is too small for school functions now. Fix up the old rotunda, she says – it would need a complete kitchen! Everything she suggested costs money!"

Malcolm noticed his wife staring at him with a hard and stony expression. "Malcolm, at this year's graduation at least 150 people will be crammed into that house. What's more important, yet another sports field? You and that board with too many men need more respect for what Shelly has to say, and for the job she's done for years for no payment but a thank you!"

"What's so difficult?" Malcolm asked, unwittingly sticking his foot in even deeper. "Just the occasional event, and we pay for a housekeeper and all the expenses –"

He trailed off, because Dianne had stood up, and with a face like thunder proceeded to tongue lash him for his ignorance after years on the board. Her words slid off him as effortlessly as water on a duck's back. He used this time to settle his mind on the trial he had next week. Then, suddenly, a phrase or two penetrated his consciousness and he realized that Dianne was repeating, almost word for word, exactly what Janet Mitchell had said.

The Manhattan had too much sweet vermouth and was seemingly devoid of alcohol. Once Dianne finished her rant and had left the room to attend to dinner, Malcolm got up and sloshed more rye in it. Flopping heavily back in his easy chair, he turned his thoughts to today's meeting.

One of the two women on the board, Janet Mitchell was a mother of five who took over her husband's metal forging company after his premature death ten years ago. At the time, it was verging on bankruptcy. Now it was a going concern, with a workforce of over 200. Janet was the CEO and president. She said little in board meetings, but when she did, all listened.

Once Shelly left the boardroom, Janet had said that hiring someone to handle social events who could also help with fundraising was long overdue. At this point, Penelope Farland piped up and said that she wouldn't mind doing the job. Malcolm chuckled aloud now, remembering the raised eyebrows and sly smiles around the table. Everyone knew Penelope was dead set on Latham, and that this would give her a perfect excuse to see him on a regular basis.

"But Penelope," Janet exclaimed, "it would mean you'd have to stay here for at least ten months of the year! What about your trips to Europe and your Florida home?"

As Penelope lapsed into silence, Janet also said that with the date only weeks away, they should immediately assign funds to pay Emma Madison to handle the graduating class reception. Then they should follow up on one of Shelly's other suggestions and have an outsider on any selection committee for the new hire, to prevent, as she said, "the nepotism that's so rampant here in the selection of non-teaching staff, with everybody's sister, brother, nephew or niece getting plum jobs for big pay and little work."

This caused quite a nervous ripple around the table, because many board members, including Malcolm whose nephew worked in accounts, had inveigled positions for friends or family at the school. That might no longer be possible with Latham in charge. He was reviewing hiring and retention practices, or the lack of them, and ominous signs of change were in the air.

Before he was called in to dinner, Malcolm had time to toss back another drink. At the table his wife was cordial, if cool, and had dropped the subject of the board meeting. That was good, because Malcolm did not want to give her the satisfaction of knowing that eventually the board had decided to hire a fund-raising slash events organizer, and get quotes for renovating the rotunda. She would find out soon enough.

However, when Dianne complained how unfair it was that Shelly never was allowed to add to the McIntyres' retirement fund by working outside the school as she had wanted, he did tell her that the board had agreed to not to reduce Arthur's pension, even though legally they were entitled to do so.

"Oh. Well. At least that's something," she said unenthusiastically. For some reason it seemed she was still mad at him, or them, he couldn't figure out which.

What he didn't tell her, and was glad she was never likely to find out, was that when the motion was passed, only he and one other board member had voted no.

Shelly McIntyre was quite a few years younger than her husband. She could still get a job and bring in a little extra money, if they needed it.

CHAPTER 115

She sat by the window of the train, gazing out at a world devoid of color. Monochromatic, muted in shades of white, charcoal and grey except for the occasional tuft of dun-colored grasses, the land scrolled by against the vast, windswept backdrop of the frozen lake. The view was not one to inspire delight, but after the hustle and bustle of Anna's wedding and her rounds of visiting in Medford, Emma found it soothing.

As she swayed in time to the clickety-clack of the wheels churning along the track, rocked to drowsiness, the events of the past days streamed through her mind. Soon she would have much to do and scant time to savor or commit them to memory.

Standing beside Margery and Jim in the church, Emma watched Anna walk down the aisle with her new husband and sent up a silent prayer of thanks to the good God who had ended the dark years for her and her family. Even if, albeit, it had been done in rather a grisly fashion, since it was Royce's demise by drowning that made it all possible. However, this was no time to think about that.

The small, intimate ceremony Anna originally wanted had swelled to 160. The reception venue had changed from the family home to the local golf club where, once Margery arrived, it soon became clear she was not accustomed to handing the reins over to hired help. In a trice, she had abandoned the sedate role of mother-of-the-bride that Anna had decreed for her. Beaming a thousand-kilowatt smile, she rushed to and fro, a whirlwind of activity in a pink frou-frou of a dress that made her look like a confectionary accompaniment to the wedding cake.

"Sit, mother, sit!" Anna implored her; then gave a helpless laugh as she watched her barrel through the swinging doors of the kitchen.

"It's because she wants everything perfect," her sister Lorena commented. "The problem is, only Ma knows what perfect is."

Finally the daughters joined forces to make their mother sit down, at least for the speeches and the cutting of the cake. A friend came by, pulled up a chair. Soon she and Margery were deep in conversation and Emma, seated nearby, couldn't help but hear.

"...my son-in-law, the Doctor –"

My, didn't Emma smile, then chuckle richly to think how well worn with use those words surely would become in the years ahead!

She half-expected to hear them again the next day, when she went for tea at Margery's. But as it happened, she did not. When she arrived at the MacClure's home at two o'clock on Sunday, other matters soon absorbed them. Even the wedding was set aside, although they both had been looking forward with relish to rehashing what had happened and who said what to whom.

Jim was at the door when she arrived. He said his hellos before clearing out for a walk with the dog. Then they took their accustomed places, as always, at the old kitchen table with its worn blue-checked oilcloth covering. On the wedding day there was snow, but that afternoon a wintry sun shone through the window to sprinkle them with weak sunlight.

"Well," Margery said, her face still wedding-shiny bright, "here we are once again, Emma. My, but it's good to have you back!"

Yes indeed, and wasn't it pleasant, recreating these small ceremonies of friendship: sitting in the sunshine drinking tea from Margery's good china cups, eating her buttery shortbread, with always an ample helping of gossip, talk and laughter on the side. Emma was only sorry that what she had to say was likely to spoil it all.

She complimented Margery on the perfection of the wedding, which Margery accepted as her due – with a gracious nod of her head, as befit someone who was now the wife of a supervisor at the car plant, and whose daughter was married to a doctor. But the smile she had worn for so many days it was almost a fixture faltered, then disappeared altogether when Emma told her she would not be staying in Medford.

"Oh, Emma!" she cried in dismay, "here I've been so looking forward to having you home, and now you're leaving? Why? What about your house? And for how long? Oh, how disappointing!"

Emma picked her way carefully through these questions, looking for safe answers. It had been a lucky break for her that the Irwins still needed her house; their renovations were not nearly complete. Another three months: by spring, they said. Good. That should give her time enough to decide.

Margery gazed at her with sad spaniel eyes as she gave her reasons for staying: her job organizing the reception for the graduate class at the school, and her appointment to a committee selecting a new school employee. Margery did not need to know that, fingers crossed, this last assignment was, for all intents and purposes, finished.

The week before she left for Medford, Emma had a phone call from Janet Mitchell. Janet had been tasked by Royal Sutton board members with finding candidates for the new job of coordinator of school events. Janet invited herself over to the house and, once they were comfortable with their coffee, she asked Emma if she could help with the selection process.

Emma didn't need to think twice. Could she? Of course she could!

A day after her meeting with Janet, the doorbell rang, When Emma answered it, Shelly McIntyre was on the doorstep. Their move from the white house was finished. Now that they were more or less settled, with her usual efficiency Shelly had arranged for professional help three days a week to assist Arthur in recovering from his stroke.

"But what am I going to do in that apartment?" she cried. "Arthur has his books and projects, but I need a part-time job, or I'll go crazy!"

It was the perfect opening. "What would you think," Emma asked tentatively, "about taking on the job of school events coordinator? The same job you used to do, except that you would be paid. For a year or so, just to give us more time to find a suitable replacement?"

Emma had already proposed this idea to Janet Mitchell. But the smile that slowly grew on Janet's face while she considered Emma's suggestion was nothing compared to the huge guffaw that Shelly let loose.

"Oh, I would take it, in a heartbeat! Even just for the delicious irony of having them pay me for it, after all those years of doing it for free! Rub their noses in it, wouldn't it, just? But don't expect me to do it for cheap!"

Yes, it was remarkable how it was all coming together, almost too easily, like the pieces in a child's puzzle – provided no board member put a spanner in the works to keep Shelly from being hired.

The renovation of the rotunda was set for spring. After it was complete, there would be no more social functions at the white house. It would return to its original use as the private domicile of the headmaster and his family.

So all was in place, or nearly so, except the most important piece by far. For all of their plotting and planning would come to naught if, instead of appointing Thomas, the board decided to find another candidate for the job of headmaster/principal of Royal Sutton School.

Someday Emma would explain all this to Margery, but not now. She poured herself another cup from the teapot. Then she looked at Margery and said, "Oh. And there's one other thing. I seem to have gotten myself appointed President of the local bridge club."

"But Emma, why? Why are you doing all this?" Margery exclaimed. "This is your home!"

Emma would not divulge the real reason. But she had a good enough one at hand. "You have your husband, your daughters and their children, Margery, a busy life. I don't! I've done my part for the community, then I stepped down so younger people could take the helm. In Kellington, though, I'm not a has-been but a could-be! Although I'm old, I'm still healthy and capable. As long as I can, I want to be useful; that's why!"

There was something of the psychic about Margery, or perhaps it was just that they knew each other so well. "I have the feeling," she said slowly, with a sharp look to gauge the effect of her words, "there's more to this than you're telling me. That there's a good chance you'll not be coming back."

But Emma maintained her poker face, and afterward they talked of this and that until it was time to leave. Their parting was bittersweet, filled with regrets and reassurances, and ended with a long, heartfelt embrace. Margery watched from the doorway as she went.

"I'm missing you already, Emma," she said. Then, with a sudden surmise, "this all has something to do with Jasmine, doesn't it?"

"Perhaps it does," she called back, striding quickly toward the road. She was glad Margery hadn't asked that question until she was through the door.

Outside the train window, twilight was tinting the bleak landscape blue. There was enough light for her to see that instead of the lake, it was the St. Lawrence, frozen wide along its banks but with rushing water still visible here and there in the centre. She looked at her watch. Thomas was meeting her at the station, and then she would tell him that she had decided to rent the last house they looked at together, and had phoned the rental agent to secure it.

"I have a perfectly good house that will be standing empty once I move to the white house and I have to rent it, so why don't the three of you just take this one?" he had inquired, puzzled and perhaps a little irritated.

She had looked at him fondly. Such an intelligent man, so smart, and in other ways so dumb and naive. "Thomas, you have absolutely no idea how gossip works!" she told him.

The train let out a final wheeze of steam and rolled to a stop. She saw Thomas standing under the lights, waiting patiently, and he waved when he caught sight of her through the window. Once he helped her down the stairs and they were together on the platform, she handed him the claim ticket.

"What's this for?" he asked.

"The bicycle," she replied.

Then a big smile spread across his face, and he went to get the carton containing the new bicycle his daughter had left behind in Medford when she flew to Las Vegas.

Jasmine was coming to town!

It was still hard to believe it was actually happening! He felt himself fill with the anticipation he had suppressed up to now. People turned around and smiled, wonderingly, and then he realized that he had laughed right out loud for sheer joy.

CHAPTER 116

The editor of the Kellington Evening Standard was the only employee with an office. Once Stan McKnight retreated behind the partitions with their frosted glass, except for dire emergencies only those impervious to verbal abuse or without need of a job came to bother him. He sat at his desk now in a mood that required no further inducement to be foul, looking over the copy for today's edition, which had been proofed and edited and was, in his opinion, dull as dishwater.

February was a poor news month. People stayed indoors and thefts, assaults, killings and other interesting criminal activities aside from wife beating had diminished. McKnight, at this moment, would have been happy with a car accident or dog bites man story. The newspaper was soggy with political blather, city council reports and bland and boring features that no one except those whose names were mentioned in them cared to read.

To add to his feeling of general disgruntlement, now to his dismay he saw above the frosted glass the gingery hair and horn-rimmed spectacles of the advertising manager. The two of them had worked together for almost twenty years and were friends except for at work, where they maintained an attitude of mutual antagonism. This was mostly due to the fact that Terry Lennox was frequently after McKnight to publish editorial favorable to their advertisers in the paper, and McKnight seldom complied.

At this moment he rapped on the glass, and without waiting for McKnight to tell him to piss off, as was his normal greeting once installed in his office, Lennox let himself in, closed the door and stood there with a smile.

Quickly, before the editor had time to unleash his usual stream of invective, he said, "You know the Wilson building over on Second Street that's being renovated, and no one knows what's going in? Well, I just sold ad space to someone who's setting up a business there, and I think it could make a story for you."

"Get lost." The editor was rising from his desk, his face a thunderous mask of disgust, clearly winding up for one of his famous diatribes. Lennox put up a restraining hand. He smiled even more broadly. There was a glint in his eye that made McKnight pause for a moment. "Wait. Just take a look before you cuss me out."

McKnight rose to his full height, where he could peer over the frosted glass into the newsroom. He saw a tall woman with long dark auburn hair. Her back was toward him and she was engaged in conversation with a staff reporter. Then she turned around.

"Oh."

Lennox watched the editor's scowling face in amusement. The deep crease between his eyes suddenly had vanished, as did the furrows in his brow. His eyes widened. In a second, his whole face had flattened out, opened up, and astonishingly, on his mouth there was the beginnings of a smile. He sat back in his chair.

Without a further word Lennox swung open the office door to admit the visitor.

New Bridge Club A First For City

Bridge players from novice to expert now have a place to meet and hone their skills at the Kellington Bridge Club, the city's first facility for devotees of the game.

Located in the former Wilson Office Supplies building on 2nd St., it is owned and operated by Jasmine Holmes, formerly of Las Vegas. She and her partner were pairs champions in state of Nevada bridge tournaments in 1956 and will compete in the USA bridge championships in late May.

The new club is equipped for bridge groups to use at nominal cost, with refreshments available onsite. Instruction in bridge at all levels will be provided, also in poker, blackjack and euchre.

Tours to Las Vegas at a discount to club members will be offered next fall, to include an inside look at casino operations and visits to local attractions. Holmes is an accredited bridge instructor and coach. She was a blackjack dealer before moving into administration at Flamingo Hotel and Casino, Las Vegas, where she was formerly Manager, Group Hospitality.

CHAPTER 117

He was abstractedly rolling a pencil back and forth with his fingertips and calculating how soon he could escape when he felt the eyes around the table on him and stopped.

It was the last meeting of the school year and Malcolm Reynolds suspected the other members of the Board of Governors were just as sick of meetings as he was, only putting a better face on it. Now he steepled his fingers together and tried to be patient while they waited for Thomas Latham.

For some months now it had never been in doubt that Latham would be confirmed in his appointment as Principal of Royal Sutton Boys School. He had done a stellar job under difficult conditions. Still, the vote had been somewhat of a cliffhanger because, unlike other matters that came before them, approval had to be unanimous. Especially worrisome were Roger Scheffler, an accountant who almost always voted no to everything, and Penelope Farland. But in the end, they all fell into line and there was an almost audible sigh of relief when the votes were counted, because no one ever wanted to go through the ordeal of finding a vice principal or principal again.

Malcolm had been particularly nervous about Penelope. He thought she might be a sour grapes no vote, due to rumors circulating about Latham. It was said he was sweet on the niece of Mrs. Madison. The niece had arrived in the city early in the year and opened a bridge club that was doing very well, by all accounts. Last month he read in the newspaper that she and her partner had taken second place in the U.S. bridge championships. So she was a bridge expert, which impressed him since he had never mastered the game. Although he had no doubt he could, if he wanted to.

Malcolm had seen her once, when he was in the same locale as the bridge club and dropped in out of curiosity. One of her staff went to fetch her when he asked for the owner. Her face, with those tip-tilted amber eyes, rose in his memory. It was the kind of face that sticks in a man's mind like a burr, although that might not be the best description for the effect she had on him.

There had only been rumors and, according to his wife Dianne and her spies, nobody she knew had seen Latham and her out and about together. However, because of what attractive specimens they both were, it was impossible not to think they might pair up. Plus, Latham was a frequent visitor, Malcolm had heard, again by way of Dianne, to the house that Jasmine – the name was as enticing as she was – shared with her Aunt, Mrs. Madison.

Emma Madison: now there was a formidable character, with her iron-grey hair, imposing height, and those sharp eyes peering down at him through iron-rimmed spectacles. Malcolm spent a few minutes chatting with her at the reception for the graduating class, and was left with the distinct impression that he had been sized up and found wanting. Dianne had insisted they attend. She needed to prove her point that the principal's house was too small for such an event. It was indeed crowded, and with all the sharp knees and elbows and loud voices of the gangly youths circulating around the room, particularly so.

Thinking of Emma Madison, Malcolm felt a rising bubble of irritation. She had been involved in that scheme to hire Shelly McIntyre to handle events, he knew. Malcolm had voted against it, but Janet Mitchell railroaded and browbeat most of them into a yes vote. He and the two other male board members who were overruled had commiserated afterward. Didn't anyone else see how humiliating it was? Like they had been cheating her, all those years she was doing the usual work of the principal's wife?

Sitting across from him at the board room table, Malcolm now saw Penelope Farland make a little involuntary movement, almost as if she had been administered a small electric shock. He turned to see that Thomas Latham had entered the room. Malcolm regarded him with his usual mixture of admiration and envy. He really was a handsome devil, and his eyes, as he faced the windows behind the boardroom table, were remarkably blue.

They gave him the news. That was one thing about Latham, he was an honest man with open feelings, and he didn't bother to disguise his pleasure when he was told that the board had confirmed his appointment. He made a nice, mercifully brief little speech of acceptance and left the room.

Malcolm started to rise but the Chairman, Cameron Scofield, pointed out that there was one final item on the agenda before they could leave, and he slumped unhappily into his chair once more. Then Scofield cleared his throat and asked the burning question: what should they do about the small guesthouse next to the principal's residence?

Who gives a flying fig about the goddamn bloody guesthouse, Malcolm silently asked himself, and from several muted groans and the faces of other members, surmised they shared the exact same sentiment. Then Roger Scheffler, an accountant and the one on top of school financials, stood up and droned on for quite a while about the costs of maintaining the little house, which were miniscule and nothing compared to the monthly outlay Malcolm's wife Dianne made on her clothes, hair, masseuse and facials.

Finally, Janet Mitchell broke into this dreary recital, and Malcolm could have kissed her when she uttered the words, "for the sake of brevity –" The obvious solution, she said, was to rent it. Then the guesthouse would no longer be an expense but a source of revenue. Great idea: approve it and let's get on with it! Malcolm thought, and they did.

However, Penelope Farland raised an objection. "It's very close to the principal's residence. With tenants so close, wouldn't it intrude on his privacy?"

"That's a good question," Janet replied, rather quickly, "and perhaps we should let the principal have a say on this. Why don't we let this matter rest until we've put it to him, and in the meantime, Roger here can come up with a reasonable figure for the rent."

There was a general rumble of assent from those eager to get out the door, which was everybody, followed by the adjournment and a scramble to leave. Only Malcolm remained at the table. He stayed there awhile. The courtroom lawyer in him scented something distinctly odd about the suggestion Janet just made. As well, why hadn't the guesthouse been discussed with the general housekeeping items at the beginning of the meeting – instead of being tacked on the end, at a time when the board collectively would have authorized the firing of a rocket to Mars from the roof of the school gymnasium, if only they could get out the door and back to work?

Also, the last time the subject came up, someone suggested they sell the house. It would be easy to move, having been built on a concrete pad. So why wasn't that option discussed?

Malcolm had a strong feeling of strings being pulled behind the scene. It stemmed from his sense that there appeared to be a triumvirate of conspiracy among Shelly, Emma Madison and Janet.

And he wondered, when Janet came up with that suggestion, just whose it really was.

CHAPTER 118

Jasmine was toweling down after her bath when she heard the springy rebound of the screen door in the small house she had rented with Emma. She glanced out the window. Then she quickly threw on Thomas's bathrobe since it was handiest, rushed downstairs and called her daughter back before she could disappear. She made Laura put on a sweater despite her protests, then watched as she was joined by the two boys next door, Jimmy, eight, and Billy, ten, and they ran off to the park.

"You know that she's just going to take it off, once they start playing," Emma said. She was smiling, even if she had been made to seem negligent, since she was the one who had allowed Laura to go out the door sweaterless.

"I'm just an overprotective Mom, and it's still cool for June," Jasmine smiled back. They were close now, having found their balance, and any little aggravations that cropped up between them were generally ignored or easily smoothed over."I do wish, though, she could find some girls to play with. Soon the boys will go their separate ways, and she'll need girlfriends growing up."

"It would be easier if the girls around here did anything interesting. They're house mice, most of them. Do you want coffee? I'm going to have another cup and then do some more packing and sorting before Thomas comes to collect me for the train."

They sat down at the table. "That was a wonderful dinner party last night," Jasmine said. "Such a good time, even with so few people." The four of them had celebrated Thomas's appointment with a stupendously expensive rib roast of beef, much wine and gaiety and calls to his sisters to share the news. Then, after Laura was in bed, they held a strategy session to discuss next steps.

"Did you pack my little gift for Alistair and Sherry's wedding?"

"Yes, and I'll remember you to him at the wedding and make sure he opens it. Sherry won't appreciate your sense of humour."

Jasmine had shown her the present: a gold-plated deck of cards on an exquisite enameled tray. Shortly after they met, Alistair had confided that when berating him for his escapades, his father was in the habit of telling him he hadn't been born with a full deck. Her note read, "Your father was wrong, but just in case."

For obvious reasons, Jasmine had not been invited to the wedding. However, as she once declared to Emma, she sincerely hoped never to return to Medford, even for Anna. "You're not really thinking of leaving us and returning to your house and that dreary little town once Thomas and I get married again, are you?" she asked her.

Emma went to the sink and rinsed her cup. "Jasmine, it doesn't matter how big the white house is; you and Thomas need your privacy and so do I. It's bad enough you have a housekeeper under foot, even if she has her own separate quarters. So yes, after your wedding I'll return to the lake house."

Jasmine sat at the table, silent, and as she left the room, Emma thought she seemed rather disconsolate. She went to her bedroom on the main floor, but in a moment was back.

"You look as if you could use a laugh. I thought I'd read you one of Margery's letters before I pack them away. Wouldn't she die if she knew! But it's too good not to share. She wrote it after I sent her the newspaper clipping about the opening of your bridge club in February. You were too busy then, anyhow, but when you hear it you'll understand why I didn't read it to you at the time." And she began:

Dear Emma:

Thank you for your letter and the clipping. What a surprise, who would expect this turn of events, Jasmine in Kellington where Thomas is and starting her own business! Isn't she a clever minx, the way she's whitewashed herself and managed to come out smelling like a rose. In that write-up, it sounds like she's even made a virtue out of being a blackjack dealer.

I guess it was part of her scheme to get that out in the open and make it sound like something anyone should be proud of. So she's sold her house in Las Vegas and pulled up stakes and is living with you. My bet is that she and Thomas are at it again hot and heavy. Let's hope for wedding bells soon to make it legal.

Jasmine threw back her head and laughed heartily. Margery's vitriol could no longer touch her, insulated as she was by happiness. "A whitewashed rose! Only Margery could mix up such a marvelous metaphor!"

"Was there anything else in that letter?" Jasmine might not miss Medford but she still enjoyed Margery's gossip, almost as much as Emma.

"Not really, it was mostly about Anna, and you keep up with her. But did I tell you what she said about Sherry and Alistair?She wrote what a scandal it was that they were shacked up together and living in sin, and that Sherry's mother was terrified that once he had the milk, he wouldn't want the cow."

"Oh my! Don't set me off again!" Jasmine exclaimed; then both of them were seized by a bout of laughter.

Before she folded it away, Emma scrutinized the letter once more. "There was one other thing," she said slowly. "She wrote she'd met Elizabeth Stoddart on the street and at first she didn't know her, she'd lost so much weight. Not a healthy loss, her clothes hanging on her. She was with her two grandsons."

"Oh? That's rather sad." Jasmine said, and she and Emma looked at one another, a world of memories in that glance. "It sounds as if she could have something a touch similar to what I had, when I was sick and you took care of me."

Standing by the door, Emma took a moment to ponder. She was remembering a piece of the past she had willfully buried. Now she wondered whether this might be the time to unearth it. Well, there was no reason not to, any more. She cleared her throat, hesitated. "A while ago, Jasmine, something happened that I never told you. About Elizabeth. It was last spring, over a year ago."

When Emma sat down again, Jasmine knew what she had to say was probably important.

"You know that silly gazebo the Stoddarts built? Well, my friend Caroline Dillon and her husband were invited to a little party Elizabeth and Max held to christen it, so to speak. It was just old friends from times gone by. And Caroline said you could've knocked her down with a feather when they began talking about you and Thomas and whether you'd had an affair, and Elizabeth came to your defense. Elizabeth said all the facts pointed to a different side to the story. It was because of the way she argued for you and Thomas, like a lawyer, Caroline said, that her husband Al finally wrote a good reference letter for Thomas when he was applying to Royal Sutton. Al's always been a bit of a blue-stocking, you know, and up until then, according to Caroline, he wasn't prepared to do it."

Emma had finished her story. Jasmine sat there, silent and deep in thought. "I won't ask why you didn't tell me," she said finally. She stood. "But I'm glad you did." Then she went upstairs to dress.

Not ten minutes later while she was tidying the kitchen, Emma heard the sharp rap of the brass knocker on the front door. When she opened it, Thomas came in. He gave her his usual bear hug. "Where's Jasmine?" he asked distractedly. It was apparent he was in a rush.

"Upstairs, getting dressed. But aren't you too early –?"

He had already bounded away and up the stairs, and she was left to guess why he was here now, two hours before he was due to take her to the train.

Jasmine was in the little hallway between the two bedrooms when Thomas found her, sorting through the fresh clothing in a laundry basket and arranging neat piles for herself and Laura. She was wearing his bathrobe and her hair appeared a little damp.

She stood and looked at him in surprise as he filled the hall, his head almost touching the low ceiling. "You're early!"

"I have some news, some very good news." He was smiling at the thought of how pleased she would be. "I had a phone call from Janet Mitchell early this morning. It seems that at the meeting yesterday, the board decided the guesthouse should be rented, as soon as they can figure out what to charge for it. But because it's so close to the white house, there was some concern about privacy. Janet wanted to give me a heads up that I'll have first choice of whoever gets to rent it."

"Why, that's wonderful!" Jasmine's eyes shone with excitement. "Now Emma won't have any excuse not to stay with us here in Kellington. Such a perfect little house, with that wonderful view of the river, even if it only has two small bedrooms! They can't charge that much for it, can they? Let's go down and tell her!"

"Yes, let's. But first – you know, we're not going to see one another all this week, while she's away in Medford."

From the moment he arrived, Jasmine had guessed why he was here, early, and now what he was hinting at. However, she wanted him just a little irritated, to toy with him, so as to put an edge on it. She looked at him innocently.

"Of course we are. This evening you and I and Laura are going to the restaurant for an early dinner. Tomorrow, the three of us will go for a walk. And on Tuesday night, you and I are meeting for a drink at the hotel – just as we planned last night."

"Yes, Jasmine, but, I'm going to be picking you up and dropping you off at the door. According to your plan, even if it's ridiculous, I can't come in the house. Because our chaperone is away," he said, and now she could see that he was indeed annoyed at having to make himself so plain.

"Oh." She tilted her head and looked at him from under long eyelashes, a smile playing on her lips. "So, when you said we're not going to see one another all week, you meant all of each other. Is that right?"

Now she could see the little curlicues at the side of his mouth tugging up, the beginnings of a smile: he had realized she was leading him on, teasing him.

"You're reading my mind."

"Well then, is this perhaps what you had in mind?"

She stepped back and opened up his big, roomy robe to display herself in all her naked glory.

The hall was cool, but Thomas suddenly felt lightheaded with the flush of heat, the burst of fire through his veins.

"Now it's your turn, darling," she said in her most silky, seductive tones.

"You've used that trick to get me to undress before." He began undoing the buttons on his shirt, his fingers fumbling in his haste.

She was coming toward him now, holding his big blue bathrobe open wide.

"That trick? Yes, and I remember you complaining loudly then. Now, not so much."

Gathering him inside the robe, drawing him close, she put her face up to be kissed.

CHAPTER 119

Laura was lying in bed and Auntie Emma was reading to her. It was a Nancy Drew book and exciting because it was getting near the end, when Nancy would find out who did the crime. However, Laura was only listening with half an ear because she had already read this chapter. She read it the night before with a flashlight under the bed sheets after her mother finished reading and forgot to take the book when she left.

Mom and Thomas were out tonight and Auntie was staying here, in the big house, until they got home and she went over to her own little house. Dad, not Thomas. It had been hard to call him Dad at first, but Laura was getting used to it. A while ago, Mom sat her down and said that now she was ten, she was old enough to keep a secret. Mom told her that Thomas was her real dad, not Mike, and that it would make him very happy if she called him Dad. And that her last name was going to change: now she would be Laura Latham instead of Carlisle.

"But I thought Mike was my dad!" Laura had cried, bewildered. "Why is Thomas my dad?"

"For now, that's all you need to know, that he's your father. I'll tell you why and all the rest when you're older," her mother answered.

Auntie Emma, who was knitting in her chair near them, had laughed a little and said, "that should be an interesting conversation."

Mom shot her a dirty look, but after that they smiled at one another, and ever since then Laura had tried to call Thomas Dad, especially because he looked so happy and pleased when she did, and she really did love him a lot.

Later, Mom had sat her down and taught her all the answers to give to the questions people were going to ask her about her, Mom, that is, and Dad. That had been smart, telling her what to say, because it wasn't just the kids at school. Their parents always were asking questions too.

Laura yawned, then sighed contentedly, settled into her pillows and closed her eyes. It had been a good day, but Saturdays were most always good because there was no school and you could play all day. After lunch, she had gone over to AJ's house. AJ was her best friend now. She met her two days after they all moved in with Thomas, Dad, that is, right after the wedding and Mom and Dad's honeymoon.

Laura was riding her bike around when she saw the wallet on the sidewalk. She looked, and sure enough, there was the black thread in the crack on the sidewalk. After she jumped off her bike she followed the thread underneath a bush and there was AJ lying on the ground.

For a while, she and AJ had fun. People would try to pick up the wallet and then she and AJ quickly pulled it into the bushes. Most of the people laughed, only a few were a little mad. But then a friend of AJ's oldest brother George came along and he grabbed the wallet and broke the thread and threw the wallet over the neighbour's fence. She and AJ went and got it from the neighbour's backyard. The neighbour lady, Mrs. Jansen, yelled they were mashing her flowers and chased them. Ever since then, she and AJ had been best friends, and in ten days they were going together trick and treating on Halloween.

The afternoon at AJ's house was fun. They had jumped in the big piles of leaves in the yard until AJ's dad and brother carted them to the curb and burned them. Next they shot arrows at the target on the tree using her second brother Wayne's bow and arrow set. It got boring after awhile so she shot the Grinell's dog, Mutt, who was lying nearby. He didn't even move.

"He's gotten used to the stuff we do to him," AJ explained. Then she said, "watch this!" and she shot Mrs. Jansen's cat that was sitting on the fence. The arrow hit the cat and the cat yowled and fell off. AJ didn't shoot that hard and it wasn't really hurt, but Mrs. Jansen was in her backyard and saw her cat being shot. Just then, though, Wayne came out of the house and grabbed the bow and arrows.

"You leave my stuff alone, you little jerks!" he yelled.

Mrs. Jansen had come running over and was in their backyard by then. When she saw Wayne with the bow and arrows, she started screaming at him and yelled she would call his mother. She went away before Wayne had a chance to tell her it was AJ's fault. So he was really mad and he grabbed AJ's arm and gave her an Indian burn.

"Nice going, dickhead!" he said, and then he went back in the house.

"He said a bad word. I'm going to get him." AJ's arm was really red and she was mad.

"Will you tell your Mom?" Laura had asked.

"No, she doesn't like tattle-tales," AJ answered.

They went in. AJ doesn't go into the house often because her Mom always asks her to take care of her little brother, Petey so that she can go and lie down. Petey was in the kitchen with his mom and when they came in, he was lying on the floor. AJ pretended to trip over him.

"Get out of the way, dickhead!"

"Amanda Jane!" her mother yelled at her, "I'm going to wash your mouth out with soap! How dare you say that word!"

"Dickhead?" Amanda asked, making her eyes all big and round. "That's what Wayne called me just now. Is that a bad word? What does it mean? Tell me, Mom, what is a dickhead, anyhow?"

Her mother didn't answer, only ran into the living room and smacked her brother Wayne. "Just you wait 'til your father gets home and hears how you shot Mrs. Jansen's cat with an arrow and then called your sister that bad name!" And they heard her yelling some more, only by then they were outside and rolling on the ground, they were laughing so hard.

"Amanda Jane!" Laura had been surprised. "I didn't know that was your name! Is that your real name?"

"It is," said AJ, "but I hate it, and don't you ever dare call me that!"

Aunt Emma had stopped reading. Laura opened her eyes. She said, "I'm not asleep." Aunt Emma started reading again.

The rest of the afternoon was fun too. They had gone to the kiddie matinee at the Hollywood Theatre. AJ's mom made her take Petey. He was so slow that by the time they walked the four blocks to the theatre they were almost late. That was good, though, because the ticket woman was in a rush to sell tickets to the kids waiting in line and she didn't ask Petey's age, and you had to be five to get in. The movie was The Blue Lagoon. Petey was so scared of the octopus he spent most of the time under his seat, and only came out for the Gene Autry movie.

Halfway through the last movie, they got kicked out of the theatre for throwing popcorn. It wasn't fair because they were only throwing popcorn at some boys who threw it at them. They were glad to be outside anyhow. They took Petey to the park and pushed him on the swing and the merry go round and ran races on the grass. They saw who could blow the biggest bubble with the Bazooka bubble gum Laura bought with the dime Aunt Emma gave her. Petey cried because AJ wouldn't give him any; she said he just swallows it and it would be wasted.

Then they went down to the river and threw rocks to practice for baseball. Petey was throwing and he was really good for four years old, but on the last throw he almost threw himself into the river along with the rock and got a soaker.

"My mom will kill me if she knows I took Petey to the river!" AJ said. "You have to keep her busy while I take him upstairs and get him dry socks and hide his shoes."

So Laura went into the kitchen. "Hello Mrs. Grinnell. AJ is taking Petey to the bathroom." Laura had never spent much time with AJ's mom before.

"Hello Laura," she said, and then after she had talked for only a little while she started right in asking questions, the ones the parents always did. "I hear your mom used to be a blackjack dealer in Las Vegas, is that right?"

"Yes, and she liked it. But she got bored when they started using machines instead of them doing the figuring in their heads, and so then she was a hotel manager and played bridge."

Mrs. Grinnell looked impressed with that, like most of the mothers. But now she asked a question none of the other mothers had. Luckily her mom had given Laura the answer. "Didn't your mother take care of Mr. Latham's wife when she was sick?"

"Yes, she took care of Auntie Lianne until she died. She says that was when she saw what a good man Thomas was, and so a while later she decided to chase him until he caught her."

Now Laura was getting sick of the questions, so she said what her mother had instructed her to. "Anyway, my mom told me when people ask questions about her and Thomas, they should just ask her and she's glad to tell them anything they want to know. She says her life is an open book."

There was a silence while Mrs. Grinnell was embarrassed. Then Laura saw AJ hiding behind the door and waving frantically at her to come. She went into the other room. "Laura!" AJ whispered loudly. "Do you have that last piece of Bazooka gum? This little jerk says he's going to rat on me to Mom about falling in the river unless he gets gum!"

So Laura gave Petey the last piece of gum she had been saving that she really wanted for herself and went home.

"Good night, darling." Auntie Emma had finished the chapter. Now she was bending over her for a goodnight hug and kiss. Laura loved the way Auntie smelled, like lilacs or some kind of flower. She smiled at her and Auntie smiled back, her eyes kind and crinkly behind her silver glasses, before she turned off the light and left the room.

Mom and Dad had gone out to dinner and dancing. Mom told her that she and Dad had something special to celebrate; she would tell her what later. Before they left, Laura and Aunt Emma had watched her come down the big staircase while Dad waited at the bottom. She was like a princess, in her blue dress and sparkly diamond earrings.

"My beautiful wife," Dad had said.

She smiled down at him. "My handsome husband," she said back.

Then they both just stood there awhile and looked at one another, and she and Aunt Emma looked at them. They seemed so happy that Laura could feel it, really, almost like sunshine on her face; it made her feel warm and happy too.

So, altogether, today had been a good day, a specially good day except for the gum. And tomorrow they all were going to the country to get pumpkins for Halloween.

She sat up. It was dim but not dark, and she could see that Aunt Emma had left the book on the nightstand. Laura leaned over the edge of the bed and felt under the mattress for her flashlight.

* * *

Once she was downstairs, Emma retrieved her bag with her book and knitting and went into the kitchen for a cup of tea. While she sipped, she enjoyed a moment of quiet introspection. It was during these solitary tea times she most often missed Margery. But not for long: she was coming for a visit the very next week, having discovered the delights of Emma's little house and its potential as a refuge from the demands of her large and growing family.

"It's just like a rest-cure, being here!" she had exclaimed the day after the wedding, sitting in the late August sun on the patio, watching the river flow by blue as the sky above. "You're in danger of having me a whole lot more than you want me!"

Perhaps, during her visit, Emma could weasel out of Margery what she and Jasmine had been discussing when she found them engaged in a secretive, guarded conversation, after dinner on the day before the wedding. It was a surprise to see them sitting together since, as Jasmine once remarked, she and Margery were as ill-suited to one another as chalk and cheese. When Emma walked into the living room, though, their heads were together like long-time conspirators.

But all she overheard was Margery saying, rather querulously, "well, I don't know exactly why you want me to do this, Jasmine, and I could probably do a better job if you gave me more information, but seeing as it's your wedding day tomorrow, I'll do my –"

They looked up when they saw her. Then Margery quickly said, "well, it's time for me to go help," and rose heavily to her feet, while Jasmine suddenly took an interest in the newspaper on the table in front of her.

The next day, Thomas and Jasmine had their church wedding, followed by a lovely reception in the school's rotunda; and every minute was so busy and shot through with joy that Emma temporarily forgot this little mystery. She only remembered it once the honeymooners had left on their trip to Maine, and just moments after Margery boarded the train home.

Her tea finished, Emma poured herself a second cup. She opened her knitting bag, sighing as she pulled out her book. It was Middlemarch by George Elliot. She had checked it out of the Royal Sutton school library the last time she was there. They were after her to help out with library matters, but for now, twice a week, she was helping the little duffers in grades two and three with their letters and reading, a pastime she truly enjoyed. Enjoyed much more than she did the book now in her hands, part of a self-improvement plan to catch up to some of the classics she had never read. This one, she concluded, had the stately progress of a funeral procession and was about as exciting. Still, she ploughed bravely on.

But what about Nancy Drew? Emma had been left wondering about the ending of the book, which was not at all apparent. There was just one more chapter, and as things stood, she might never get to find out whodunit. Thomas would be reading it to Laura tomorrow, Sunday night, He usually put Laura to bed, making up, Jasmine told her, for lost time, delighting in these last few years of her childhood.

The winding staircase in this house did not creak. She had to switch on a light when she reached the top step, however, and it was then she saw the dim glow shining from the crack under the door to Laura's bedroom. Suddenly it went black. Although Emma's eyesight was not of the best, there was nothing wrong with her hearing, and now she heard the distinct sound of hurried movements.

When she opened the door, though, all was still and peaceful, Laura was lying in bed, eyes closed and putting on an excellent show of being asleep. Emma picked up the book from the nightstand. She looked down at the child, her rosy cheeks, the dark stars of her eyelashes, the tousled mop of hair, and her heart swelled with love as she left the room.

Laura opened her eyes. Auntie Emma had taken her book. She wasn't that sorry. The words were starting to blur and jiggle on the page when she tried to read. Now she would really have to listen when Thomas read to her tomorrow night. Not Thomas, Dad. Her real Dad, who would never leave her.

The moon, a big round yellow harvest one, was shining through the bedroom window. She could hear the murmur of the river, and the wind rattling the dry leaves still on the trees. She lay quietly in her small bed, thinking about nothing and everything. Her mind wandered then, leading her along familiar paths. Once more she pondered the inexplicable miracle of being who she was, a most lucky child born into a world of wonders. And along with these thoughts came a lovely bubble of joy, so big she could barely contain it in her small body.

During her life she would experience much happiness, different kinds. But once grown she would still look back wistfully, sometimes, recalling those rare moments when a little, child-sized door in heaven opened and glories streamed through.

Now, as this one slowly faded into dreams, she turned to lie on one side. Her eyes closed. Her breathing slowed, and she slept.

CHAPTER 120

The fire was starting to die, and Max gave it a stir with the poker and dropped on another log. He pushed his reading glasses back on his nose from their perch on his forehead. Then he returned to his wing chair and newspaper. All his stocks save a few laggards seemed to be doing well.

From the sofa nearby came the sound of childish laughter. Peering over the top of the financial section, Max smiled at the charming domestic scene before him. Elizabeth sat with her arms around their two grandsons, reading a silly story they all were enjoying. The firelight beamed off her glasses and the bright faces of the boys, who were bathed, in their pajamas and ready for bed. She felt his eyes on her and glanced up, and they exchanged that special look that said what a very fine moment this was.

Elizabeth was so much better now. She had gained a little weight, and there were roses in her cheeks. Other things had improved, too. When he looked back at the months of their ordeal, he could see that in a way her illness – that sickness of low spirits – had done some good. It had been a wake-up call for all of them, a harsh lesson about how much they loved and depended on her. They had seen their eldest daughter Althea and her children more in the last six months than the past three years. Arlena especially had changed. A closeness had developed between her and her mother that had evaded them through most of her teen and early adult years.

Their grandsons had been a big part of the cure. Without them, Max was not sure she would have recovered. He had watched in admiration as Elizabeth, using every bit of that iron will of hers, hauled herself out of the dumps to give them the care and love they urgently needed. Their mother, busy with her new hubby and the Florida golf course he bought with her money, could barely remember their birthdays.

"Goodnight Gramps!"

The two boys snuggled close to him as he wrapped them in a big bear hug, gently rubbing his scratchy face against their soft little ones and making snorting noises to hear them giggle. It was Elizabeth's turn to take them up tonight. She said he made them too lively at bedtime with all his nonsense, but it was hard to resist.

Thank goodness Mason made the decision to stay in Medford! Without him and his children, Max thought, not just she but he would surely have foundered. And perhaps the children as well. For this, they might owe a thank-you to Nuala O'Donahue. She could well have been the catalyst for Mason's decision. Max had been struck by her resemblance to Mason's lost love when they first met at the office, the week after she was hired. But if anything interesting was developing there, it certainly wasn't obvious. Mason was mum on the subject and playing those cards very close to his chest, for which, considering past history, Max couldn't blame him.

The warmth from the fire was making him sleepy. He looked at his watch: 8.30. Dinner at six seemed eons ago. Elizabeth had put him on a diet two weeks before; he had already lost five pounds. Max debated whether there was time to make a run to the kitchen for bread and peanut butter. He had risen to his feet and was on his way when he heard her coming downstairs. With just one glance she guessed what he was up to.

"I'm going to make a cup of tea," she said, with a knowing smile. "Would you like one? And I'll give you a biscuit."

She gave him two, herself one, and as they sat contentedly watching the fire, drinking tea and reading their Saturday papers, he looked at her, thinking again how much he loved her and how glad he was of her improved health.

It seemed that strange little incident after church, in early September, might also have been responsible in some way for setting her on the road to recovery. Now he turned the memory of it around in his mind, as he had so many times since, puzzling over the message that had been delivered by that gossipy chatterbox, Margery MacClure.

Elizabeth and he were walking down the aisle after Sunday service at the Anglican church when she and her husband came alongside. MacClure, a big, personable man whom Max found easy to like, buttonholed him on the church steps. Meanwhile his wife started chatting up Elizabeth. It was odd to see them there in the first place, because they were only infrequent churchgoers. MacClure, however, did have a good reason to talk to him.

He had finally learned, he didn't say where, that it was Max's influence that helped him get his first position at the plant. Since then he had climbed up the ladder. Many of the men who worked under him at the tannery had also got well-paying line jobs due to Max's intercession, MacClure had discovered. He thanked him in a heartfelt, non-deferential way that didn't embarrass but pleased Max, who then asked him a few questions about the plant to get him talking.

Among his talents, Max had the ability to read upside down and also to listen to several conversations at the same time as he carried on a discussion with whoever was in front of him. Thus, while speaking with Jim MacClure, he was listening with half an ear to Margery's monologue to Elizabeth. Then she said something that pricked his ears wide open. As MacClure rambled on about developments in car manufacturing, Max concentrated on eavesdropping.

First Margery had asked Elizabeth whether she knew anyone who might be interested in renting the Madison lake house. This was a legitimate inquiry, because Mason and the boys were living with them, and Mason was starting in on the renovations the old Matthews house needed. He had offered to move out and rent; but Elizabeth told him not even to consider it.

Then it was a natural progression for Margery to tell Elizabeth that Emma Madison was now living in the guesthouse next to the principal's house at the Royal Sutton Boys' College. She had moved away to be with her niece and her family. Of course they had heard about Jasmine's marriage to Thomas Latham, the principal of the school, hadn't they? Out of the corner of his eye, Max saw Elizabeth nod her head.

Yes, they had. On hearing the news, Max had felt a surprisingly strong pang of regret. He never analyzed why he should feel this way, and none of them, including Mason, had ever spoken about the marriage.

Next Margery told Elizabeth how blissfully happy Jasmine and Thomas were. It was then it got strange.

"I'm quite amazed at the way things have turned out over time, aren't you?" Margery asked. It was a rhetorical question, because she immediately returned to her monologue. "I have to think it was all for the best, what happened with Jasmine and Mason. It was fate or providence, whatever you want to call it, and in the end, it seems to me that all of us are just the agents or the pawns who helped to carry it out."

It was these words that had burnt into his mind, and that he returned to now as he sat in his wing chair looking sightlessly at his newspaper.

After that, Margery started going on about her own daughter Anna, the twists and turns her life had taken, and how happy she was now, married to a doctor, Dr. Miller. Jim had good-humouredly interrupted the one-way conversation to rescue Elizabeth from Margery's rhapsodies over her son-in-law, the doctor, and then they went their separate ways.

One thing Max was sure of: Margery MacClure was a messenger. That woman didn't have a philosophical bone in her body, and it sounded as if she was parroting something memorized. Someone had put her up to it and told her what to say: those words about being an agent of fate, and everything ultimately being for the best. He knew it, and was sure Elizabeth knew it, and that they both had a good idea who had arranged for Margery to deliver it.

But what Elizabeth knew, which Max did not, was the reason she did it. And it was driving him nuts.

When he asked her what she and Margery had talked about, Elizabeth told him everything, except for those words about fate. Because she didn't want him questioning her about them. And now he couldn't ask her about them, because then she would know he'd been eavesdropping.

He wasn't dumb. Something happened between her and Jasmine, and Jasmine was telling her it was OK, it had all worked out for the best. But what, exactly, had happened? And why didn't she want to tell him?

Over the next few weeks, though, it seemed as if a burden had lifted from Elizabeth. Even her posture, which had become stooped, straightened and she regained her normally erect carriage. Her sad days began to diminish. Whether it was due to those few words on the steps of the church, or something else, Max was unable to guess.

The years would pass. There were times every so often he felt her trembling on the brink of a confession. She would hesitate, then draw back. It happened most frequently when they heard about Jasmine. Little bits of news, carried almost on the wind it seemed, found their way to them from acquaintances or sometimes people they hardly knew, from snatches of conversation overheard in a restaurant, at a social event. They told of Thomas and Jasmine's growing family, the success of her various businesses, the honors and accolades heaped on her husband for his work in education. Elizabeth and he would absorb this information silently. Afterward, they never discussed it.

With muted bongs, the clock on the living room mantel sonorously announced nine o'clock, their usual bedtime when they entertained grandchildren. Elizabeth and he finished up their tea. After she took their cups to the kitchen, she beckoned him over to the window and together they stood gazing at a harvest moon so big, round and yellow it looked like a child's balloon.

He put his arm around her; she leaned her head against his shoulder. They held hands as they went through the living room toward the hall, then he followed her up the stairs. They had never kept secrets from one another. He would just have to be patient. In time she would surely tell him.

But during all their long, happy life together, she never did.

CHAPTER 121

The last chapter was read, the book finished. Emma set it aside for Thomas, who would pick up the threads of the bedtime story with his daughter tomorrow evening. She yawned. It was past ten, too late for a proper job of knitting. However, the weather was lovely for October. It was one of the last temperate nights of the year and something, the part of her that never quite grew old, was calling her to go outside.

She walked through the darkened living room. As she did, a stray beam of light glanced off a silver object that somehow seemed familiar, and her heart gave a little leap. On a small side table, she discovered the beautiful, ornate solid silver frame from her mother and father's estate. It had been bequeathed to Sylvia and once held her and Jason's wedding picture. Emma had given Jasmine her mother's effects only recently, when she was clearing out the attic of the lake house prior to renting it again. Jasmine must have placed it there a day or two ago. She would not know its history.

The frame had been hidden away in a box with other mementos, and on seeing it the years fell away and the memories, sad ones, came rushing back. Emma had been present when, sobbing and distraught, her sister burnt her wedding day photograph in the fireplace after learning of Jason's great betrayal.

Now she lifted the heavy frame and studied the picture in it. She had no doubt that this photograph would never be consigned to the fire. The newly re-wedded couple in it, radiant with happiness, were linked with ties that went well beyond the simple romantic love that first bound Sylvia and Jason Holmes. Their love, she thought, was like the one she had shared with her Bill, and she would forever be grateful for that experience. Otherwise, she might envy them, as she knew some did.

But unlike Bill and she, the wedding pair in this picture was much younger. There was another aspect to their relationship, and she had felt it most keenly today. As Jasmine stood on the winding staircase looking down at her handsome husband before their evening out, Emma could feel some energy, almost electric, flowing between them. A current strong enough even to warm onlookers, and when she glanced at Laura, she could tell she felt it too.

Perhaps someday it would strike another bright spark like their daughter, the joy of her days and the apple of her eye ever since she had seen her pale, worried little face in the waiting room of the asylum.

She set the portrait back on the table and passed through the foyer. From the front door, she stepped into a night spangled with stars big as plums, wound round by a ribbon of wind with the tang of wood smoke and fallen leaves.

The sound of rushing water drew her, as always. Here the St. Lawrence was so broad only an inky smudge marked the land on the far shore. She crossed the lawn to stand beside the great river beating endlessly toward the sea. To Emma, it seemed as dark and mysterious as the fate that had carried them here – to which, she flattered herself, she had lent a hand, every now and then, by putting in her oar.

Although she wondered. Had she truly? Or was their course already charted, their destination sure, long before they flowed in the tide of humanity?

These were questions old as mankind, and too taxing for an elderly lady close to sleep. Still, for a long while Emma stood listening to the water whisper secrets to itself, before she turned and walked through the shadows toward the lights of the house.

* * * * *

Made in United States
Orlando, FL
08 July 2025

62749782R00331